D0581704

I MET A LADY

When he was a schoolboy George Ledra
watched the recruits of World War I
marching through the Manchester streets.
His account of his own life, which makes
this novel, concludes with the ending of
the second war. George Ledra was sent to
Cornwall for health's sake and to continue
his education as pupil of a retired professor
of Greek, Hector Chown. Two of Chown's
relatives, Sylvia Bascombe, an actress, and
her daughter Janet, are living in a half-
ruined mansion which it is the ambition of
Sylvia, a very rich woman, to reconstruct
as once it was. The rebuilding of the house
may be looked on as a symbol of the efforts
to pull the world together again after one
war, only to see it relapse again into ruin.
Ledra is half-way between the two women
in age. Both fascinate him, but it is the
older one he eventually marries. Throughout the story move men and women whose
destinies build up into a memorable novel.

By the same author

Novels
SHABBY TIGER
RACHEL ROSING
MY SON, MY SON!
FAME IS THE SPUR
HARD FACTS
DUNKERLEY'S
THERE IS NO ARMOUR
THE HOUSES IN BETWEEN
A SUNSET TOUCH
THESE LOVERS FLED AWAY
TIME AND THE HOUR
ALL THE DAY LONG

For Children
DARKIE & CO.
SAMPSON'S CIRCUS
TUMBLEDOWN DICK

Autobiography
HEAVEN LIES ABOUT US
IN THE MEANTIME
AND ANOTHER THING . . .

Plays
THREE PLAYS
(Jinny Morgan
The Gentle Assassin
St. George at the Dragon)

Criticism
BOOK PARADE

I MET A LADY

A Novel by

HOWARD SPRING

THE BOOK CLUB
121 CHARING CROSS ROAD
LONDON W.C.2.

THIS EDITION 1962

© Howard Spring, 1961
Printed in Great Britain
Collins Clear-Type Press
London and Glasgow

Whenever I called upon Father at his office, it seemed to me that Fred Byles and Ledra must have had an enormous opinion of themselves. The office was in a street running off Mosley Street in Manchester. It was where the two streets met, and the solid ashlar of the wall was rounded. The brass plate followed this curve, and upon it I read FRED BYLES & LEDRA in letters a foot high. The letters were done in squiggles and curlicues, most fanciful and self-important looking, and in their heyday they must have been a grand sight, shining in such light as Manchester provided. It wasn't difficult for me to imagine either Fred Byles or Ledra arriving in his carriage of a morning, going up the six steps to the right of the brass plate, and swinging through the big glass-paned mahogany doors, a silk hat upon his head. I could imagine it, I say, but I knew that Fred Byles had never done this. "He rode to the office," Father told me. "There were plenty of stables in Manchester then, and a groom from one of them was always waiting to take Fred's horse away. There was a closet opening off his room, and he would change out of his riding clothes and put 'em on again when he was ready to go home at night. The groom would be at the door with the horse. At home he would put on his evening clothes, and after dinner he would be driven to town in his Victoria. Sometimes it was cards at his club, but if there was a good concert or play he would go to that. He was mad on the theatre. In the long run, cards and actresses were the ruin of him."

"What did he look like?" I would ask, because, though I had often been told what he looked like, I could never hear enough about Fred Byles, who seemed to my boyish imagination a splendid and romantic figure to be flaunting among the utilitarian Manchester merchants.

"I don't remember much about him. I was only a youngster when he was put away. He was a bachelor, a big handsome chap, over six foot. He always wore a red carnation in the day-time and a white one at night. My father told me that all through his trial he wore a red one, brought in new for him each day."

"Why was he tried?"

"I've told you often enough. Don't let the chap fascinate you, George. He fascinated plenty in his time, and you've got nothing to thank him for."

But I *was* fascinated, and I would worm the story out of him time after time, though I understood little of it. Father said: "It was an odd thing; but Fred Byles and your grandfather came as near to loving one another as two men can. You never knew your grandfather. He was a tall, thin, grey man, rather like what I am myself now, and he was a strict Methodist. Once he got home from the office at night he wouldn't go out except on one day a week. That was to conduct his Methodist class meeting, and I had to go with him. I had caught a few whispers passing between him and Mother, and I knew that something odd was happening at the office. I know now that Fred Byles had confessed to Father that he had got into a financial mess and that to try and get out of it he had lifted thousands from the funds of Byles and Ledra. I went with Father to the class meeting that night, and I can see him now kneeling with his elbows on the cane seat of the class leader's chair, praying. He prayed for sinners, and 'especially,' he said, 'for those we love who have never walked in Thy ways.' Yes, there was a strange affection between those two, and the old man told me that Fred cried his eyes out as he made his confession, not because of his swindling but because he had robbed his friend in trying to cover it up. The old man paid out of his own pocket for the best lawyers to defend him. However, he went to Dartmoor. He died there within a year."

Fred Byles had been the brains of the firm. Even if he hadn't raided the funds, Byles and Ledra would have declined without him. Old George Ledra, whose Christian name had descended to me, was a steady unbrilliant slogger, and so was his son, my father. It was characteristic of George that, when Fred Byles was gone, he left the name-plate where it was, though the firm was now all Ledra and the name of Byles stank in the nostrils of righteous cotton merchants. "I sometimes thought," my father said, "that the old man dreamed of Fred Byles coming back, redeemed, from Dartmoor, and things going on much as they had done."

But that didn't happen, and when the business came to my father it was, as he used to say, "a shadow of its former self; and now, my dear boy, it is so thin that it hardly casts a shadow."

The greater part of the offices was let to other firms whose names were painted on a board inside the door; and outside the door the old plate of Fred Byles and Ledra still flaunted, but only as a ruin may flaunt, for it was never polished and the acids of the Manchester atmosphere were at it with the slow persistent industry of worms in a grave.

6

It was my father's wish that under me the glory should know a resurrection. I think he envisaged a brain as cute as Fred Byles's directed by a soul as pure as George Ledra's; or, for that matter, as pure as his own. We lived at Victoria Park, a quiet leafy place then, towards the western edge of the town, and I used to go in daily to the Grammar School, jammed in alongside the Victoria railway station, with the whooping of departing trains and the rattle of wheels and the ding-dong of the cathedral bells making a perpetual clamour of one sort and another in our ears. The cathedral and our school and Chetham's Hospital were all disreputable with grime but noble with memories. Every year our scholarship boys went on to Oxford and Cambridge, and as we droned away at our books there was hardly one of us, I imagine, who didn't, at first, see himself as a destined drop in that ever-rolling stream that bore its sons away to link the Irwell with Cam and Isis.

At first. But, with most of us, not for long. I was one of the most. It was soon clear to me that any mark I might make in the world would be made while Homer was nodding and Cicero, for once, had nothing to say. I wasn't very good even at English, not, that is, at estimating the relative importance of Pope's classicism and Keats's romanticism upon the course of English literature and things of that sort, though I lapped up Pope and Keats with an indiscriminate appetite and enthusiasm. "You eat too much and digest too little. That's what's the matter with you, George," one of my masters said. "You'll never be a scholar." I loathed German, was pretty good at French, and stood shivering before mathematics like a horse asked to jump a ten-foot hurdle. Certainly I would never be a scholar.

This didn't worry me so much as it worried my father. His parents had wanted to make him a Wesleyan parson. They sent him off to the training college at Headingley. He learned a good deal of Greek and Latin there, among other things, and he still, in my boyhood, read in those languages and loved them. But all the same, he never showed any enthusiasm for the ministry. I imagine it was the defection of Fred Byles that prevented his finding a way to a pulpit. He was only a boy when Fred was tried and sent to Dartmoor. Headingley came after that, but his father, with Fred gone, found life increasingly difficult, and when the youth more or less jibbed at taking up a parson's calling, the old man, with, perhaps, both relief and reluctance, agreed to his entering the business.

"I'm afraid I wasn't much help to him," my father said to me with his sad smile. " I failed him all ways—in not becoming a parson and in showing no particular enthusiasm for cotton. Certainly, the firm of Fred Byles and Ledra didn't find me a life-giving force."

Well, that's how things were when I was born on August 4th, 1901. I just escaped being a Victorian, even a very late one. The Queen had died at the beginning of the year ; and there I was with a brand-new century stretching before me and a brand-new king on the throne. All was new: my father's marriage, for one thing. It had lasted exactly a year when I gave my first cry in the Victoria Park house, and that was the end of it. My mother did not survive my birth.

I often find in novels men loathing the children whose birth robbed them of their wives. It wasn't like that between me and my father. He did not marry again. He loved the memory of my mother, but he loved me, too. It was not a demonstrative love, for he was not a demonstrative man. Mrs. Burnett, a widow who became his housekeeper, and he and I led a life that to some would seem grey and unvaried, but I remember those quiet early years as deeply satisfying. Little as my father had cared about the firm of Fred Byles and Ledra when he first entered it, he cared even less now that it was all his and he was a widower. I imagine that he did his work conscientiously, but not with enthusiasm. He did nothing with enthusiasm. It was not a word or an emotion that he liked.

I began attendance at the Manchester Grammar School in the autumn after the First World War was declared. " When you come out of school, call for me at the office," Father said. " We'll walk home." The walk to and from the office was his only exercise, and we made a habit of taking it together. I remember a broiling summer day of 1916. On our homeward way, we had reached All Saints. Coming towards us was a newly-enlisted body of recruits. Without arms or uniforms, with the city pallor still on the faces of most of them, wearing all sorts of clothes and all sorts of hats and all sorts of boots and shoes, they were a weary unimpressive bunch who yet tried to hold up their heads and put a good foot forward as they toiled behind a band and an officer mounted on a horse. The passers-by stopped, and some of them cheered, but not many, for in 1916 there wasn't much to cheer about.

Father stopped with the rest. He did not cheer, but he took off his hat as the men went by. He looked nearer to tears than to enthusiasm. I said: " If the war goes on for a few more years, I shall be old enough to join." I pictured myself marching, a little more smartly than these men marched, and my father, moved by pride and compassion, raising his hat as I strode along. " Would you *like* me to join, Father?"

8

He said: "Let's get home," as though wishing to escape from something that pained him.

What would have been the drawing-room in other houses was Father's study. He was a great believer in privacy. A french window opened from the study on to our bit of garden: not much as gardens go, just a few fine trees growing in grass. In winter nights the heavy curtains would be drawn and he would sit in his chair by the fire, reading. In the summer he would do his reading on the lawn, under a tree, with the evening light waning about him.

My own room was on the first floor. There was a bedroom with a box of a dressing-room opening off it. He reversed the purposes of the two rooms. The bedroom was my sitting-room and study; the dressing-room contained my small bed and washstand. "A man should be able to sleep anywhere," Father said. "Where he works is another matter."

I didn't do much work in my room, not, anyway, the sort of work that would, as they say, get me somewhere. I read, hugely, indiscriminately, just for the fun of it; and this reading included little Latin and less Greek. To this extent, I thought with a grin, I'm following in Shakespeare's footsteps.

On that evening when we had watched the soldiers marching by, I was standing at my window, looking down into the garden, and there was Father, a book on his knee. He wasn't reading. He had an air of abstraction. He got up and walked into the house, and presently I heard him coming upstairs. He knocked at my door. "May I come in, George?"

I opened the door, and he came in and walked across to the open window and looked down into the garden. "How beautiful that lime tree is," he said. It was in flower, and the evening air was heavy with the scent of it. "It's the sort of thing a man remembers," he said. "A quiet evening like this and the scent of the limes. Those men we watched marching into town. It's the sort of thing, I suppose, that some of them will be remembering in a year's time. Those of 'em who are left."

He sat down in my easychair, and I remained standing.

"You asked if I would like you to join the army," he said. "Well, I wouldn't. I hope the war'll be over before you have to decide. If it isn't, then I hope you'll decide to stay out of it."

I still had dreams of glory and did not answer.

"We've all got on to the wrong tack," he said. "We're all still after the beautiful to-morrow, and we play hell with to-day in order to reach it. If you learn nothing else, George, try to learn that that's an illusion. You'll find people always shoving down your throat their nostrums for a new Jerusalem. In the future. Never now. And the future recedes like a mirage. Come to that, isn't to-day yesterday's future? You're living in the future to that extent, and no one will live in it to any other. So

9

beware of big words and big promises coming out of big mouths. And in the present condition of the world, armed to the teeth with every power of destruction, the promise of the beautiful to-morrow to be reached through blowing to bits the present and the men in it is the stupidest of all."

It was a long speech for him. He got up and walked again to the window. "When you were on the way," he said, standing with his hands in his pockets and sniffing the fragrance of the lime, "your mother and I used to sit night after night under that tree. It was a beautiful summer, and we discussed the beautiful future that would dawn when you arrived. We were sure it was going to be a boy, and we were right up to that point. We were also sure that you would grow into a handsome and talented youth. And look at you!"

He turned to me with a smile of pure affection that left no hurt in the words. I was a schoolboy lout, and if I had any talent it had not yet astonished the world.

I gave him back his smile. "You'll have to take me as I am," I said.

"Yes. I find myself the perfect example of the radiant future promised to the world. There were all those dreams out there under the tree, and here is a grey widower with a so-so housekeeper and a so-so son. However, they were my own dreams and hurt nobody. Beware of the public dreamer, George, who wants to drive you to dreamland with whips. Now let's go out. I've got an appointment with Doctor Wetherby."

3

The heat was gone out of the day, and as we walked through Withington the swallows were circling and twittering against a greenish sky. Doctor Wetherby's house was just beyond the White Lion on the road that leads to Northenden. He was, so far as I knew, the only intimate friend my father had. Sometimes he would come to dinner and stay to play a game of chess, and once or twice he had shared the summer holiday that my father and I always spent in North Wales. He was a bachelor. Our relationships had always been of such friendliness that I was surprised that night to detect in him a professional air. It was the difference between meeting a master in the playing-field and in the class-room. He showed my father into the drawing-room, saying: "Make yourself comfortable in there, Bill. I can't offer you Plato, but you'll find yesterday's *Daily Mail*. Try to make it do."

To me he said: "Come along here, George."

We went down a short passage to a room at the back of the

10

house: his consulting-room. "Take off your coat and shirt," he said.

"What is all this, Doctor Wetherby?" I asked.

He said: "Nothing, I hope, but your father's got the wind up. Now let's have a look at you."

I wasn't much to look at: too tall for my age, too thin. The sight of my own ribs, as I looked into the bathroom mirror, always surprised and sometimes alarmed me.

I was prodded, poked, sounded. "Why don't you turn me inside out and have done with it?" I asked.

He said: "I wish I could. It would make my job easier. Well, put your togs on, and then stay where you are till you're sent for. If you want a read, there's *The Lancet*."

He went off whistling. I liked him. He was a good easy man to get on with. He had economically switched off the electric light on leaving. In the dusky room I didn't bother to read *The Lancet*. I stood by the window, looking out at the bit of untidy garden, feeling uneasy. What, as I had asked Doctor Wetherby, *was* all this? Was I at death's door? My father's voice and the doctor's reached me, muted and somehow fore-boding. What were they saying about me? Was the doctor bracing my father to face the fact that he would soon have no son?

"Come on now, George," Doctor Wetherby shouted. "Come and hear the worst."

I knew, as soon as I saw my father's face, that the worst wasn't going to be so bad. He was smiling. Doctor Wetherby was sitting at ease with a glass of whisky on a small table at his side. The only liquor ever seen in our house was a bottle of whisky kept against the doctor's visits. He would always press my father to join him, and my father always refused. "Ah, well," Doctor Wetherby would say, "perhaps you're right. I'm afraid I'm one of those men my father warned me against when I was young." He would take a swig. "Well, here's to tempta-tion. It keeps a man on his toes."

He took his swig now as I entered the room, then stuffed tobacco into his pipe and lit it. "This parent of yours, George," pointing the pipe-stem at my father, "has got to put up with you a bit longer. There's even a chance that you may outlive him. Not that you're any great shakes. If I were a mechanic I'd scrap you and start something fresh. You're a pretty disgraceful machine, but it's astonishing how the crocks keep rattling along."

My father listened, delighted, care wiped from his face. "You've been losing a bit of weight," Doctor Wetherby said, "and you're a damn' sight too good at catching colds and run-ning up temperatures. You must watch that, but don't let it

11

worry you. You're fundamentally—well, I wouldn't say sound, but you'll pass with a push at a donkey show."

I learned that there was a long history of tuberculosis in my mother's family. That's what had been worrying my father. " As a Manchester man born and bred," said Doctor Wetherby, squirting a little soda into a lot of whisky, " I'm ready to knock the block off anyone who runs the place down. All the same, if I had a son with rather wonky bellows, I'd think twice about letting him grow up in the damn-awful place. And what's more," he added with the war in mind, " before this lot's over there's not going to be too much good food to dish out. So there it is, Bill. It's up to you. Good air and country food are my prescription. Where they're to be found is your affair."

And this is why, when the term ended, I finished with the grimy old Grammar School alongside the Irwell and made the acquaintance of Hector Chown.

4

My father and the doctor got into one of their pow-wows, far over my head, and it was pretty late when we left the house. The moon had risen and the night was tender. " Just the night for a walk, George," my father said. " Let's go as far as Northenden."

We didn't cross the bridge over the Mersey, which divides Lancashire from Cheshire, but turned into the fields through which you can walk as far as Didsbury church. We dawdled along there in the cool moon-washed air, and my father said: " Well, George, that's that. I'd trust Wetherby's diagnosis as soon as any doctor's. It's hopeful so far as it goes, but I don't relish the idea of your going away."

" Neither do I, Father," I said, more to cheer him up than for any other reason, because if to the old every parting is a bit of death, to the young it can promise a bit of life.

" You haven't long to go to the end of term," he said, " and between now and then I'll have to think what to do with you when the summer holiday's over. Theoretically, you could come into the office. You're old enough for that, but that's not what I want for you. Not yet, anyway. One of these days, yes. But in the meantime . . ."

There are stiles in those fields, and he sat on one of them and began to tell me what he wanted in the meantime. I had heard it all before, and I half-listened to it again, my other half listening to the crunch of mist-vague cows pulling at the grass and to the owls that would never say *Too whit, too whoo,* which, according to the poets, is what they should say.

Father expounded his theories against specialisation for the
12

universal man. I was to go where I would become healthier and also become a better scholar than he was, and then I was to apply my mind to cotton and become also a better business man, a Solon on 'Change. I didn't see it, and I didn't want it. I let him run on, and presently gave a hypocritical cough and a shiver. He jumped down at once from the stile. " Good lord! " he exclaimed, " here am I meandering along, keeping you out in just the conditions you should avoid. This river mist is no good for man or beast. Let's go home."

He was up before I was the next morning, and when I came in to breakfast there was a letter, addressed in his hand, lying by my plate. He said: "I've written to Hector Chown about you."

I read the address: Hector Chown, Esq., Penruan Lodge, near Porthcrowan, Cornwall.

" Who is he? " I asked.

" A man I don't know, except through having written to him once or twice. He used to contribute to the *Classical Times,* and I took up a point he raised there. That's how we began to write to one another. I remembered when I got to bed last night that he mentioned having occasionally housed a boy for coaching to university standard. If he'll have you, I should think we couldn't find a better man. The air of the Cornish coast should blow up your lungs a bit, and you'll be in the hands of a sound scholar."

I didn't go down to Cornwall till the October of that year, 1916. In the meantime there was a good deal of correspondence between Mr. Chown and my father, and it all seemed to be satisfactory, for my father's enthusiasm grew and he was looking forward to himself making Mr. Chown's acquaintance. He postponed his summer holiday in order to accompany me on the journey, but, as things turned out, I went alone. That was because of the lime tree in the garden. It had become so dense that it darkened Father's study, and he decided to lop a couple of branches. I wasn't there when the accident took place. He had got no farther than resting the ladder against the tree and climbing it. One of the rungs broke and down he came. When I returned from a long walk that I had taken in order to say good-bye to some favourite places I was surprised to meet Dr. Wetherby leaving the house. He assured me that nothing serious had happened. " Just a wrenched foot," he said. "But I'm afraid he won't put it to the ground for at least a week."

It was a Monday morning when I set off, and very grown-up I felt at making my first long journey alone. Father had telegraphed to Mr. Chown, apologising for his accident as profusely as if he had contrived it in order to avoid a meeting; and in his precise hand he wrote instructions for me. I would reach

London in the afternoon and stay at a small hotel near Paddington station. In the morning I would board the Cornish Riviera Express, and it would be late afternoon when I reached a station called Gwinear Road. He had drawn a map which showed me Gwinear Road, up towards the north coast of the long Cornish peninsula. Below it, right down on the south coast, was Porthcrowan, and half-way between the two was Helston. "You will change at Gwinear Road," Father said, "and take a train down to Helston. The railway goes no farther. Mr. Chown has promised that a conveyance will be there to carry you on to Penruan."

5

I felt a long way from home when the branch-line train rolled into Helston station. A day of travelling, an evening of lurking in my small hotel because of my fear of mighty London, another day of travelling: I felt as far from Withington as though seas and continents lay between. It had been a lovely day, blessed with autumn's opalescent light; but now the light was gone. "Daylight saving" came the year after this; on that October evening the time was what my watch said it was.

A second suit, a change of linen, a brush and comb, and a few books made up my luggage, all squeezed into a small portmanteau. I took it up, surrendered my ticket—which felt like cutting off my line of retreat—and walked out of the little station. I was to be met by a "conveyance," but what conveyance I didn't know. Few people then owned motor cars, and, this being war-time, not many of those who did own them were able to use them. So I presumed that this which faced me was my conveyance: a trap, with a shaggy pony between the shafts, the lanterns lit, throwing a dim light ahead. A bearded old man wearing corduroy trousers and a tattered green tweed coat was lounging near the pony's head. "Are you from Mr. Chown?" I asked.

"Aye. You Mr. Ledra?"

"Yes."

"'Op up front then and chuck your bag in the back."

I obeyed his orders and joined him on the shelf of seating. "I'm Tiddy," he said when he had clicked the pony into sedate movement. "You sufferin' from this ole consumption?"

I said that I hoped not.

"So do I," said Mr. Tiddy. "Mr. Chown said you was comin' because you're not strong. I thought it might be this ole consumption. If it was, you might as well 'ave stayed upalong. Too soft down 'ere. Kills consumptives off like flies. Still, if you ain't got it, you ain't." He sounded a little disappointed.

14

I asked him if he worked for Mr. Chown.

"No," he said. "I works for Mrs. Bascombe, up to the 'ouse, if you can call it an 'ouse."

He didn't explain what he meant by this, and I didn't question him further. The long day in the train had tired me and the evening was turning chilly. The small unlighted town seemed dead, and when we had passed through it into the countryside, that seemed deader. I pulled on my overcoat, turned up the collar, and nodded. Now and then my eyes jerked open. Up hill and down dale. Hedges, an occasional furtive-looking slit of light that suggested a cottage. I had lost all sense of direction; we were in a maze, the hedges so tight about us that the roads we were on can have been nothing but lanes. The horse's unhurried clipperty-clop seemed to be bearing remorselessly into eternity. I nodded again.

Then there was suddenly a cold kiss of air on my cheek and a tang in my nostrils. I opened my eyes and could still see nothing except that the hedges were gone. There were a few stars in the sky and no other light anywhere, save for the feeble glimmer that the lanterns threw down to run ahead of us. Outside that, darkness was infinite. The wind blew again upon my cheeks, and the salty smell of the sea killed my lethargy. Then there was the sound that belonged to the smell: the slow rhythmic smash of waves upon a granite shore.

"Is there far still to go, Mr. Tiddy?"

"You'll be there soon enough," he said, as though promising me nothing good. "Keep your eyes open an' you'll see the light." We had driven for another fifteen minutes through the mesmeric darkness of what I took to be moorland country when he said: "There! Now you can see the light. They always forgets the curtains."

It might have been a glow-worm, or at most the glow of a cigarette, far off and low down on the earth. Then behind it two more lights appeared, higher up on the breast of the dark. "That'll be the 'ouse," said Mr. Tiddy. "They're lightin' up at the 'ouse."

He didn't explain what the house was, and the three lights didn't add up to a festal welcome. In another ten minutes the lamp-shine of Tiddy's trap picked out a white-painted gate. Beyond it, what had been the glow-worm light now showed itself to be an uncurtained window. "Well, that's it," Tiddy said, reaching behind him for my portmanteau and throwing it unceremoniously to the ground. "That be Mr. Chown's. Go an' bang on the door."

I climbed down stiffly; Tiddy drove his horse away; and I knew a moment of desolation, standing there half a kingdom away from home, with the sound of the waves beating on the shore and a few lonely stars in the sky.

15

I pushed on the white gate and it grated along gravelly ground.
I had to lift it to make it swing properly. This small event suggested all sorts of things to my mind. Father was precise in his
habits and almost fanatically tidy. On the first Monday in
every month he would go round the house oiling door hinges
and window catches. This gate wouldn't have suited *him*. So
my mind condemned the gate, and, by implication, Mr. Chown.
It was too dark to see whether there was a bell alongside the
door or a knocker upon it. I banged with my fist. No one came,
and I banged again. No one came. Behind me was the moor
we had crossed; before me, unseen, the turbulent water hammering the land. Tiddy and his feeble light had disappeared.
Suddenly the door opened. A girl stood there holding a cheap
enamelled candlestick with a stump of candle burning in it. The
light shone upward to a small dark oval face. Dark hair
streamed down her shoulders. She yawned, put a hand to her
mouth that the light reddened, and said: " Sorry. I was asleep.
Come in."

I went in and shut the door, and as I followed her I noticed
that she was bare-footed and that the dark hair fell to her
buttocks.

What we were in couldn't be called a hall or even a passage.
It was a small square entrance way, with rough coconut matting
on the floor, and three doors, one on either side and one at the
end. She opened the door on her left. An oil-lamp was hanging
from a hook in the ceiling. " Oh, heavens!" she said. " I forgot
all about the window. We're supposed to keep the place dark
because of the war."

She pulled the curtains across. Even to me, not much instructed in such matters, they were beautiful, a rich brocade
patterned with flowers and pomegranates and apes and peacocks.
I must have stared, for she said: " They *are* nice. Mother got
them at Liberty's." And then added: " Well, there it is. I fell
asleep while I was reading and forgot to draw them."

In the stronger light of the lamp, which had a crimson silk
shade, I could see her more clearly. The skin of her face and
bare legs had a rich glowing darkness. Her tumbling hair shone
like polished ebony. Her eyes were like sloes and had a mocking gleam.

When you are expecting to be met by an elderly learned
gentleman it is disconcerting to find instead a child. " What were
you reading?" I asked.

She pointed to a couch upholstered in what had once been a
lovely fabric, now threadbare, venerably disreputable with use

16

and time. A book was lying there, open and face-downwards.
I took it up and saw that it was Palgrave's *Golden Treasury*,
which I could almost have recited from cover to cover. It was
open at Keats's *La Belle Dame Sans Merci*. I read:

> *I met a Lady in the Meads*
> *Full beautiful—a faery's child,*
> *Her hair was long, her foot was light,*
> *And her eyes were wild.*

"I suppose," she said, as if only now remembering a duty,
"you *are* Mr. Ledra?"

"Yes," I said. "George Ledra."

"I'm Janet Bascombe. Uncle's up at the house with Mother.
He asked me to meet you and bring you along."

"Mr. Chown is your uncle?"

"Yes. We'd better go. Leave your bag here."

She put out the lamp, took up the lighted candle, and went into
the little hall. There she pulled long fleece-lined boots on to her
legs and flung a cape over her shoulders. She opened the door,
and when I was outside blew out the candle and joined me. She
banged the door behind us. "No need to lock it," she said. "No
one ever pinches anything down here."

Coming across the moor, we had seen lights which Tiddy said
belonged to "the 'ouse." They were no longer visible. Someone
had remembered to draw the curtains. I stumbled on the
rough unseen track we were following, and the girl said: "You'd
better take my arm or you'll be breaking your neck."

There was a slit in the side of the cloak. She put an arm
through and took mine. "Mother hopes," she said, "that one
of these days she'll have the money to get this road made up.
But that certainly won't be so long as this war's on. There! Do
you see? That's the house!"

I could see nothing but a deeper blackness on the blackness of
the sky ahead. We were nearer to the sound of the sea. Clouds
were breaking up, and now and then a new moon could be
seen, reeling about like a small yellow canoe on the surging sky-
billows.

Even in the all-but dark I could see, when we were close up to
it, that this house called Penruan was only half a house. Standing before the arched entrance, I was aware of a crumble of
ruins on my left and of solidity on the right. Drawing her arm
away from mine, Janet Bascombe lifted a heavy latch and I
followed her straight into a spacious room. The left-hand wall
was of undressed brick, new and glaring, shutting out the ruins.
The rest was of lovely golden stone, wainscotted in dark oak.
At the back an oaken staircase rose, swinging gracefully away
to the right, but cut off short at the left. A fire was burning in

a handsome stone fireplace and the chimney breast was carved with some emblems of nobility. Light came from twelve candles hanging in a wrought-iron chandelier. On a carpet before the fire was a small table at which two people sat, taking sherry. The man I guessed to be Mr. Hector Chown. His appearance dismayed me. He was small, dressed in abominable clothes, and his skin had the shrivelled look of a lizard's that has died and been left out in the sun to dry. His eyes were black and glittering, and his hair fitted upon his scalp with a precision which suggested that it was a wig. It was. His head was held to one side on his neck, and this increased my uneasiness as his dark eyes flickered over me.

Before he could speak, his companion rose and came across to Janet. It was a sight to see. She came like a queen, a long dress of shot silk, all fire and darkness, whispering as she walked. She embraced Janet and said: " Go to bed, darling. It's late for you to be up." Her voice was rich and caressing. Janet went across and kissed Mr. Chown on the forehead. He gave her a smack on the bottom and said: " Get away, you witch. Go to bed."

She went, skimming the stairs as lightly as a running lapwing.

Mr. Chown creaked up out of his creaking wicker chair and came towards me. " You're George Ledra, I suppose? " he said. His voice was at odds with everything else about him. It was low and melodious, reassuring.

" Yes, sir," I said. " My father sends his greetings and his apologies for having failed to come."

He shook my hand, and his skin was dry and scaly. " This is my niece," he said. " Sylvia Bascombe, that young witch's mother. You'll hear the witch call me uncle, but I'm not. I'm her great-uncle."

I gathered from his tone and manner that the witch was dear to him.

Mrs. Bascombe held out her hand and smiled. The hand was as warm as the smile. I had never known a mother or a sister. I was beset with sweet but troubling emotions, as I felt my hand lying cosily in hers. " We're just about to eat," she said. " I expect you're famished and worn out. Join us in a glass of sherry."

My father's teetotalism was strict. I knew I should say no. " Yes," I said. " That's very kind of you."

" Bring that chair over to the fire," Mr. Chown said as he and Mrs. Bascombe went back to their seats. The chair was standing against the raw brick wall. I took it up and found it unexpectedly heavy. It was upholstered in a fringed crimson velvet. I was not at home with such matters, but my very fingers could sense its antiquity, as my eye could not fail to see its beauty. It was one more of the strange contrasts in this strange room. The

18

chairs that Mr. Chown and his niece were sitting on were commonplace. The staircase, that looked as though it needed either the richest carpet or nothing at all, had strips of brown linoleum tacked to the treads. Mr. Chown's clothes seemed to me a disgrace. Mrs. Bascombe's had an elegance I was not accustomed to see on women. But then I knew nothing about women.

They sat on either side of the fireplace, I facing it. It was a fire of logs, with green, yellow and blue flame licking and flickering. Mr. Chown poured sherry, and said: " May I call you George? "

" Certainly, sir," I said, rather surprised at such punctilio.

" Well, George, I drink to welcome you and to wish you happiness."

" I, too," Mrs. Bascombe said.

I raised my glass, looked to one and then the other, and drank. My first dribble of alcohol warmed my stomach, and I drank again. The flames looked enchanted. The rumble of wind beyond the walls was reassuringly remote. The occasional *whoompf* of wave hammering rock was but an emphasis to serenity.

A tall thin woman suddenly appeared—whence I didn't notice. " You ready now? " she asked brusquely. " If so, I'll bring in."

Mrs. Bascombe said: " Yes, Mrs. Tiddy. Any time you like."

" That's the wife of the Jehu who hurtled you from Helston," Mr. Chown explained. He got up, his mouse-coloured wig a little to one side, and scuttled off in his wry-necked fashion through a door in the end wall of the room. Sylvia Bascombe and I were left alone, and I felt a disturbing shyness. I have never before, I thought, been sitting alone in front of a fire with a woman. And she was such a woman! She sat, not looking at me, not speaking to me, gazing at the flames. One knee was thrown over the other, and the one shoe of crimson silk that showed beneath the silken dress moved slowly up and down as if in measure with her thoughts. The dress was low-cut, revealing the swell of her breasts. The firelight laid a shadow between them. She was as dark as her daughter, but the dark of her eyes was a blue-dark, not black like Janet's, and her skin did not look weather-baked, but gleamed.

I was altogether bemused and confounded. It was impossible to believe that yesterday morning I was saying good-bye to my father in Manchester, expecting to find at my journey's end nothing but an old dusty scholar who was to drill ancient learning into me, and something called a lodge to live in. I suppose the sherry helped. I was ready for marvels, but all that happened was that Mrs. Tiddy came back, pushing a trolley, and behind her Hector Chown, lovingly nursing a dusty bottle.

Under the chandelier was an oaken table, its top three inches thick, and it was long enough to accommodate half a dozen people on either side. Mrs. Tiddy laid cutlery on to the oak, and beside each place set a tall glass with a gilt lip. The glass and the cutlery were beautiful. The plates which she now laid out could have been bought in the cheapest store. She wheeled the trolley away while Mr. Chown, operating a corkscrew, bent double over the bottle clutched between his knees. His wig slipped down over his eyes. "Blast the thing!" he said, and kicked it under the sideboard. The crown of his head was hard and grey, like a chunk of lava.

Mrs. Tiddy came back and left the trolley by the table. "I'll be on my way," she said. "The pie's in the oven. I'll give the dishes a lick in the morning."

Mr. Chown carved the golden roast of the fowl. Mrs. Bascombe served the vegetables. What the wine was I don't know; but Mr. Chown filled my glass, and said: "Enjoy it while you can. You won't eat and drink like this every day. Here's to your very good health. May you find your sojourn rewarding."

I raised my glass to him, and noticed that it was incised with the arms that were carved into the chimney breast. Beneath was the motto: *Rien sinon pour Dieu*. I looked up and saw him watching me with a smile. "A pretty piece of piety," he said. "It helped the Polzeaths to lay hands on some fairly extensive chunks of property hereabouts. Well, there's not much of it left now, and nothing of them. Only this mouldy relic that you've saddled yourself with, my dear," he said, turning his smile on Mrs. Bascombe, "and a dozen acres or so of land."

"Well," she said, "I wanted it and I've got it. I'll make something of it yet."

"Not with this war on."

"That won't last for ever. I'd better go and get the pie."

She went, and Mr. Chown said: "I thought I'd better warn you, George. You and I won't live here, but in the lodge. This is Mrs. Bascombe's place, and she comes and goes. She'll be gone to-morrow, taking the witch with her."

I was sorry to hear it. The wine had induced in me the mood called mellow. I hadn't known such a mood before, and enjoyed it. It was a mood in which it was easy to capture again the feeling of Janet's arm coming out through the cloak, taking mine, and leading me over the rutted path. Or the sensation of sitting in front of the fire, looking at Mrs. Bascombe's ripe beauty, withdrawn and aloof. I was about to say that I was sorry they were going, when Mrs. Bascombe came back, carrying the pie on an old tin tray which looked odd sitting there on that handsome table. But the pie was all right: a plum pie with plenty of cream. We were getting to the end of it when I looked up and there was Janet, standing at the head of the stairs, her hair streaming down over a long white nightdress. Her mother noticed her at the same time and said: " Janet! Whatever are you up to? Get back to bed."

" I can't sleep," the child said. " I can see the moon through my window."

" Janet, darling. Don't be difficult."

" But I *am* difficult," she declared. " And there's the wind as well as the moon, and Mrs. Tiddy said there was going to be plum pie."

" Well," said Mr. Chown, " that's what I call a *very* difficult situation. She'd better come down, Sylvia. There's still some pie left."

" Very well," Mrs. Bascombe said with resignation. " But go and put on a dressing-gown. And," she added, as Janet disappeared, " you'd better put on your wig. You look disgracefully naked."

" Oh, damn the wig," he said. " The thing's a perfect nuisance. I never know whether to glue it on or use a few tacks."

However, he groped under the sideboard, found the wig, and put it on rakishly.

Janet came down, wearing an old woollen dressing-gown. " There are no more chairs," Mr. Chown said. " You'd better sit on my knee."

She did so, and ate some plum pie, and asked: " May I have wine?"

" Certainly not," said her mother. " Whatever next?"

" Next?" Mr. Chown asked. " The next thing that suggests itself to my mind is coffee and brandy. Have we any?"

" George Ledra has been drinking wine," said Janet.

I blushed guiltily, and Mrs. Bascombe said: " It's bad manners, darling, to make personal remarks. Now I'll go and see if I can find coffee."

She went, and Mr. Chown poured a few thimblefuls of wine into a glass. " There you are," he said. " That can't hurt a witch."

She drank it, made a wry face, and said: " Horrid stuff! Why aren't you and George Ledra sitting over your port? I thought gentlemen always sat over their port when the ladies were gone."

Mr. Chown said: " For a child of seven, you read far too much nonsense. Now off to bed with you before your mother comes back."

She went, pausing at the top of the stairs to say: " I shall only lie awake, looking at the moon and listening to the wind and thinking of drowned sailors."

" She dramatises everything," said Mr. Chown. " I suppose it comes from having an actress for a mother."

" Is Mrs. Bascombe an actress?"

"For goodness' sake," he said, "don't let her know you've never heard of her. She'd die of injured vanity."

I asked: "*Should* I know of her? Is she famous?"

He considered this; then said frankly: "No. Not famous and not very good."

I found it hard to believe. I was prepared to hear that she was a goddess.

"She's efficient," he said. "Good enough to find plenty of work, but never on the top line."

Mrs. Bascombe came in at that moment with the coffee and a bottle of brandy. We went back to our seats by the fire and Mr. Chown threw on a few logs. "You'd better not take brandy, George," he said; and Mrs. Bascombe took none either. Conversation died, and I, at any rate, was well content to sit there, savouring the feeling of being thrust so suddenly into the heart of so strange a family, warm, well-fed, and dog-tired.

Half an hour later Mrs. Bascombe got up and said: "I must go to bed. There's a journey to-morrow, and that always wears me out."

She kissed Mr. Chown, and then, to my surprise, kissed me. It was only a peck on the cheek, but it disturbed me deeply. A scent she was wearing seemed to flood all my senses. "Good night, George," she said. "Be a good boy."

Mr. Chown stuffed his wig into his pocket, pulled on a wide-awake hat, and threw a cloak over his shoulders. We went out, and the big oak door gave a reverberating bang behind us. It was pitch dark, a little rain was falling, and the wind blew hard into our backs off the sea. In ten minutes we were at the lodge. Mr. Chown took me into the room where, a few hours before, I had found Janet. He walked to the big couch on which her book still lay, picked it up, and said: "Keats! Good God! What next? When I was seven I was reading Hans Andersen. Well, you'll have to sleep on the couch to-night, George."

I lay down with a cushion under my head, not expecting to find rest in so unlikely a place, but I slept like a log.

CHAPTER TWO

1

I awoke in early morning light, and was surprised for a moment to find myself clothed and lying on a strange couch. I was frowsty and dishevelled and needed a bath. There was a towel in my portmanteau. I pulled it round my neck like a muffler and stepped out into a world of dew and of mist so thick that I could not see more than twenty yards ahead.

I chose a path at random. The road along which Tiddy had vanished after setting me down last night was only a rough track, and the way I went, striking off from it to the left, put me on to little more than a rabbit-run. It went through heather that was full of upthrusting rocks. The heather, I could see, would flame purple when the sun came, and the rocks would be a glory: green, yellow, grey, orange and russet lichens were thick on them.

The wind of the night before was gone, and there was no sound of the sea. I hoped I was going towards it, for I wanted to swim.

Slowly the mist turned grey, then pink, and it began to thin and rise into the air. The sky, which had been invisible, was a veiled and tender blue. The dew upon the great boulders caught a sparkle here and there, so that rocks, where they were flat, looked like tables scattered with jewels. I began to see whortle-berries among the heather.

I stood still and listened to the awakening day. It had been silence until I listened, but listening raises its own murmurs, and now the little sounds were all about me as though the earth were stretching and yawning as the sun touched its eyes. Its deep quiet breathing reached me: the invisible sea. I made towards that sound, and as the track began to run downhill sloe-bushes closed upon it, head-high, thick with purple fruit. So narrow was the way that my movement brought a drench of water tumbling upon my face, down my neck, waking me from my musing. I stood still, looked up, and saw the first rays of the sun coming through clear. The sea stretched away before me in a surge of vapours, and down at my feet I saw that the formid-able granite walls were riven by a tongue of sand, golden and shining. Where it touched the sea's ripple it was about a hundred yards wide, and the wedge of it drove inward to lose its point in a cave. The cliffs were sheer. The full morning was now flood-ing that playing-floor with light.

23

It was so obviously the place for my swim that I began to move quickly down towards it. Then a movement out in the deep water arrested me. It was a white arm flashing. Then from farther out, emerging from the mist, came another, and a voice, clear in the silence, shouted: " That's enough now, darling. Better come in."

It was Mrs. Bascombe's voice, and I had no doubt she was talking to Janet.

I froze where I stood, hidden by the bushes, and watched them wade naked ashore, glistening in the sunshine. They were both beautiful, the one full-breasted, the other budding. They took up towels and dried themselves, and then pulled off their rubber caps, and their dark hair streamed about them. It was a moment that belonged to the beginning of the world.

" Now you must warm up," Mrs. Bascombe said, and they began to run like lovely unselfconscious animals upon the sand, tossing a ball high and catching it, throwing it to one another.

" Now, home," Mrs. Bascombe said at last. " Tiddy'll be calling before we've had time to eat."

They bundled their hair into the caps, pulled sandals upon their feet, and threw cloaks around their bodies.

I trembled, fearing they would come by this path and find me there. I was about to fly like a hare when they set off towards the other side of the cove. There, too, hidden from me, was a path. They began to climb, and soon were out of sight. I stood for a long time looking down at the maze of their footprints, foolishly wishing that the tide would never come in to wash them away.

Now birds were singing, and gulls were leaning on the air, letting it carry them where it would as though they were on invisible aerial surf-boards, and down on the tawny floor the gregarious sand-pipers were making their darting runs. I didn't know then that they were sand-pipers. There was so much I didn't know about this place, which lay beautiful as paradise had lain under the sun of its first morning. This baptism into its loveliness seemed to wash my eyes and make me see as I had never seen before, and I wanted to know and understand what I saw.

But Mrs. Bascombe's words were in my ears: " Tiddy'll be calling before we've had time to eat." The thought that she would be gone without my seeing her again plagued me, and I was in half a mind to race back at once along the way I had come. Last night was in my thoughts, when she and I sat alone in the candlelight, and the fire-flame streaked her silken clothes and threw a shadow into the valley of her breasts. And she had kissed me: the first woman's kiss I had known.

I wanted her to kiss me again before she went away.

It was an odd moment. Another voice came to me, Janet's,

saying: "George Ledra has been drinking wine." And that took me back to Manchester. I could not believe that it was only three days ago. My father, parentally dutiful and responsible, was giving me a talk on the perils of life, his face flushed, his words stammering. Women and wine. That was what it came to. Women and wine that had ruined Fred Byles. He tried to make it a half-joke. "Saying this hurts me more than it does you, George," he said: and added: "Well, you've got common sense. Just use it."

Common sense had little to do with the emotions that were troubling me now. The picture of the two goddesses at play upon the sands under the morning's virgin light remained, and I was compelling it to remain. But some residuum of my upbringing sent me down over the stones, between the thorns, on to the beach.

I threw off my clothes and stood for a moment looking at the sun-splashed water, so different from the grey water of the North Wales coast which was all I had known till now. The mist was quite gone, and the sea was a burnished silver-blue except close inshore, where it was emerald and amethyst and turquoise, and these colours, I saw, were thrown upwards to stain the under side of the gulls' wings when they drifted low, making them magical.

I ran quickly down and without parley took the shock of immersion, then lazed on my back. I swam for ten minutes and then came in and made for the centre of the maze of footsteps that Sylvia and Janet had left. Sylvia. I was thinking of her as Sylvia. I towelled myself on the very spot where they had stood, and I dallied, because now, perversely, I was determined that she should be gone when I got back. My foot felt something hard, and I looked down and saw a shine of gold. It was a bracelet, and I was sure it had fallen from Sylvia's arm. It was too big for Janet: a flat golden band with overlapping ends fashioned into serpents' heads. The eyes were emeralds.

I dressed and put it in my pocket, more than ever determined now that she should be gone, for I did not want to give it back to her. When I reached the lodge I found Janet and Mr. Chown, wigless and with the sun shining on his lava head, standing by the ramshackle gate. "How on earth can you overtake her now?" he was demanding.

"Oh, easily, easily," she assured him.

Mr. Chown turned to me. "Mrs. Bascombe is gone," he said. "This witch was to have gone with her, and——"

Janet interrupted. "Mother's lost a bracelet. She thinks on the sand, but I wanted to be sure it wasn't in her bedroom. I searched and searched, and then she went off without me in a pet. There's gratitude for you!"

"She's been gone for twenty minutes," Mr. Chown said, "and
25

this witch assures me that she can easily overtake her. How are you going to do it? On a broomstick?"

Janet ran behind the lodge and came back wheeling a bicycle. "On this," she said. "That old horse of Tiddy's can't do three miles an hour. I'll catch them up before they're half-way. Tiddy can bring the bicycle back."

She leapt upon the machine and was gone without so much as a nod. Mr. Chown turned to me. "Women!" he said. "Leave women alone, George. Stick to good wine."

I fingered the bracelet in my pocket and followed him in. It only now occurred to me how odd it was that I had not handed it to Janet.

2

The lodge had once been two rooms. The room in which I slept last night had been the bedroom, and in the other a lodge-keeper and his wife had cooked and lived. The old cooking-range was now gone, and the room was Mr. Chown's bedroom. I had noticed last night a third door opening off the pokey hall, and through this door Mr. Chown now led me. We entered a room as wide as the two bedrooms and hall put together, and a great deal longer. When his niece had bought Penruan just before the war, she had invited her uncle to make it his home. He had just retired from the Wardenship of an Oxford college. All his holidays had been spent in Cornwall, and he had for long been in mind to retire there. But he was a solitary who disliked the idea of sharing a house, and his living in the lodge was a compromise. It was too small for his library, and so this room had been built of concrete blocks, whitewashed on the outside, rendered over with grey cement within. It was thirty feet long and almost as wide. Not only every wall was loaded with books. Shelvesful jutted out here and there into the room, making small bays, to one of which, furnished with chair and table, he pointed, saying: "That's where you will work, George."

There were no pictures, no ornaments: nothing but books, an immense carpet, and a fireplace in the far wall. Near it was Mr. Chown's own writing-table.

"Did you sleep well, George?" he asked.

"Very well, thank you," I said. "I was up early and went for a swim." I described the lovely cove, with the path running down to it through the sloe bushes.

He took his wig from his pocket and put it on, smoothing it into a close fit with both hands. He looked at me, skew-necked and smiling. "Was anyone else there?" he asked.

"No," I lied. "That's what was so beautiful about it. Bar a few birds, I had it to myself."

"You must have missed 'em by a short moment," he said.

I looked at him with an air of innocent inquiry, and he said: "You might have met the witch and her mother. They have pagan habits."

He left it at that, went over to his big writing-table, arranged some papers there into three or four piles, put a rubber band round each, and said: "Order. Learn habits of order, George. Order, persistence and moderation. Well, let's go and find some breakfast."

We went out and followed the path along which Janet and I had stumbled through the wind last night. It was deeply rutted, and on either side stretched what once had been a tended field and was now nothing but an expanse of overgrown tussocks, from which sprang briars, burrs and ragwort. Even so, in that October light it was beautiful. The briars were sepia and amber, the ragwort was shining gold. There were agriculturally deplorable thistles, too, beautiful as the rest.

The house had been separated from this field by an iron railing, but only a bit of it, rusted and sagging, remained here and there. Inside the railing was a great stone pavement running the length of the house. And now I saw clearly what had been only dimly apparent last night: half the length was a ruin. To the right of the doorway through which Janet and I had entered, the place was fair enough, habitable at any rate. To the left I could see that all had once been symmetrical, that side repeating the right; but now the roofs were fallen, and some of the chimneys; the walls, where they remained, were cracked, with flowers and saplings growing from the ragged tops, and some were altogether gone. The companion of the splendid oriel window had lost all its glass; one of the granite mullions had disappeared, and another lay across the window as though it would soon go too. In this ruined half the story of the field we had walked through was being repeated. Vegetation had gone mad. Ferns sprouted in chinks of stone; ivy rioted; and old man's beard spread its grey froth over the standing bits of the oriel. Through cracks and crannies I could see that from the very floors of the rooms elder and sycamore were springing.

We went in through the splendid porch, over which, I now saw, were carved the arms of the Polzeaths, with their motto: *Rien sinon pour Dieu*. In the morning light the great room seemed gloomy. With the fire burning and the candles lit and the curtain drawn across the oriel, it had wrapped me in a sense of security and grace. Now the candles showed their greasy guttering; the fireplace was a desolate grey heap of ash; and dust, unapparent then, was now seen to be everywhere.

As if sensing my reaction, Mr. Chown asked: "Why does

27

she want it?" He stood looking about him as though seeking an answer to his own question, when Mrs. Tiddy opened the door at the back of the room and said: " Oh, you're 'ere at last! Thought you didn't want no breakfast to-day. Come an' get it while it's 'ot."

Mr. Chown murmured: " Grace abounding," and we followed her out. We went down a dark passage and turned into a small room on the left with windows looking upon the path we had followed from the lodge. It was cosier than the great hall, and it was complete.

" This is as far as her ladyship has got," said Mr. Chown, " in bringing one bit of her plans to fruition. She has a scheme for every room, including the ones that aren't there. Usually, we eat here, but last night she was in a mood of grandeur."

It was a lovely little room, and over the fireplace was an oil painting of a beautiful woman, standing on the brink of a stream, her hands full of flowers and her face distraught. My eyes turned to it again and again as we made our way through the coffee and bacon and eggs. Presently, watching these glances, Mr. Chown said: " Well?"

I said: " She looks as though she's going to jump in and end her misery."

" That is just what she is going to do," he said. " She is Ophelia, painted by John Collier, not a favourite artist of mine, but I think he's got something there."

He gave me his sideways grin. " Do you see the family likeness?" he asked.

" With whom?"

" With me. She is my sister. Well, perhaps you'd better *not* see it, if it's there at all. She wouldn't have liked it. I don't suppose you've heard of Margaret Napier?"

No. I hadn't.

" Now she *was* an actress," Mr. Chown said. He got up, put on an enormous pair of horn-rimmed spectacles, and peered closely at the canvas. " Yes," he said. " It's good. It's Maggie. But there again, she'd have bitten my head off, if I'd called her Maggie after she was about as old as our witch. Yes, she *was* an actress if you like. Not like poor Sylvia."

" She was Mrs. Bascombe's mother?"

" Yes, our witch's grandmother."

He folded his spectacles, sat down at the table again and said no more of the matter. He began to talk about the Polzeaths who had owned this place time out of mind. " Little more than farmers to begin with," he said. " But one of them was a lawyer who went up to London and got on the right side of Henry VIII when that gentleman dissolved the monasteries. He went about the country, taking inventories and keeping the thieving in good legal order, and some nice slices of ecclesiastical property were his reward. He became Sir Richard, and there was another Sir Richard at Elizabeth's court—one of those handsome chaps she couldn't resist. It was he who built this place on the site of the old Polzeath farm. Then they came out on the right side in the Civil War, suffered under Pontius Cromwell, and rose again after the Restoration. After that they quietly settled down into the customary nonentity. The last of 'em died a hundred years ago, and the place has been falling into ruin ever since. Sylvia bought it from lawyers representing some vague relatives with a vague claim. They were glad to let it go for a song."

He scraped back his chair and got up. " Now," he said, " no work to-day. Not for you, anyway. Have a look round. You won't find a room locked in the place. Be a ghost and haunt it till we find some more intelligent use for your time."

I stood at the window of the beautiful little dining-room and watched him going back towards the lodge with his curious sidling gait and sidelong glance. Mrs. Tiddy, who had carried the breakfast things away to the kitchen, poked her head through the doorway and announced: " I'm off." Then I turned to examine the room. The walls were wainscotted in pine that had been polished till it was a gleaming honey colour. Above that the plaster was painted off-white. The ceiling had some delightful scroll-work, leaves and flowers radiating from a big central rose. From the rose an elegant gilt chandelier, such as you often see in the paintings of Dutch masters, hung down. Twelve shades of crimson silk would make a rich glow at the touch of a switch, but there was no switch to be seen. There were beautiful electric fittings on either side of the portrait of Margaret Napier, little springing garlands of gilt leaves, each containing two lights, but these, too, were dead. The honey colour of the wainscotting was repeated in the carpet, but this was deeper: the brown wallflower colour that glows in honey gathered from heather-flowers. This same colour was in the heavy velvet curtains hanging before the single stone-mullioned window. The long table with rounded ends was as gleaming brown as a peaty trout-stream, and the leather seats of the chairs were again the clear shining honey of the wainscot. Except for the portrait of Margaret Napier, there was no picture, but on either side of the fireplace was a recess painted light willow-green, containing what seemed to me to be valuable and lovely little figures in porcelain. They had obviously been chosen with care. All were women. All were dancing.

One on either side of the fireplace were two chairs of dark shining wood. Their upholstery was fringed with leather, tooled in gold.

I found the room soothing but incredible. I was of utilitarian stock, and so were the few friends of my father whom we

29

visited. Solid comfort surrounded us, but there were no frills. And yet, I said, surprising myself, there are no frills here, either. I sat down in one of the chairs by the fireplace to think it over. The day had warmed up. Through the window I saw a sky of clear blue. Suddenly three swans flew across it, necks straight out like rods, wings beating down upon me, a sound I had never heard before, full of wild strength and freedom. It was the last touch. Swans gobbling bread thrown from perambulators upon a municipal lake. That was all I had known about swans. You'd better accept, I said to myself, that you're in a new world: the lovely women coming up from the sea, the wild swans beating out towards it.

A voice behind me said: "Do you think you ought to be sitting in that admiral's chair?"

I sprang up and turned to the door. "Please sit down," said the young man who stood there. He spoke as calmly as though he owned the place and I was a nervous visitor. I sat, and he strolled into the room and let himself down gently into the chair facing me, holding the arms as he stretched his leg out carefully full-length.

"It won't bend," he said.

"What won't?"

"This leg."

He was thin and dark, with eyes like a hawk's. He wore reddish tweeds and brown brogues.

"It was the damndest thing," he said, "to get shot like that. I suspected the chap was a German in Belgian uniform, and I was just going to grab him when he pulled out a revolver, shot twice, and ran. Got me through the calf and knee."

"You've been in the war?"

"Yes," he said casually. "Who are you?"

I told him, and he said: "My name's Gomm. It's a corruption of Gomez."

We seemed to be talking in circles. I left it to him. He said: "I suppose there's no coffee about? Let's go and see. I know my way round this place. Give us an arm."

I gave him an arm and he got to his feet. "It's getting up that's the devil," he said. "Once I'm up I'm all right. Only just given up crutches."

He hobbled to the kitchen, which I had not seen before, and we found a pot half full of coffee. Gomm lit a spirit stove, we warmed the coffee, and carried it back, with cups and a sugar bowl, to the dining-room. He lit a cigarette and turned the sugar bowl in his long fingers. It was of chased silver. "Nice," he said. "I wonder where she found that."

"Who?"

"Mrs. Bascombe. That chair—it really did belong to an

admiral. Both of 'em did. Pity the poor sailors who got wrecked hereabouts in those days! Well, and long after, if it comes to that. But this was when the Armada was snooping round. The *Absolución* went ashore here. She was cleaned up like a wheat-field by locusts. The very shirts off men's backs. A couple of Spanish matelots stayed, including a Gomez. He married a local girl. Hence the Gomms. Hence me, Jose Gomm. Those two chairs got shoved into the local beer-house. And not only them. There was so much *Absolución* stuff in that place that they began to call it the Absolution. The pub's still there, and it's called the Absolution to this day. My father runs it now."

I had never been in a pub, and I had no idea what pub-keepers looked like, or what their sons looked like. A mixed lot like anyone else, I told myself reasonably; but there was still a doubt. This didn't look like a pot-boy.

"The devil of it was," he said, "having to come down from Oxford before I took my degree. Though I don't suppose it would have been any good to me."

Oxford! That made him look less of a pot-boy than ever. I had noticed his delicate fingers when he was examining the sugar bowl.

"Well, that's me," he said. "Who are you?"

"George Ledra, of Manchester. I've only just arrived. I expect you know Mr. Chown? He's going to cram me with Greek and Latin."

Gomm looked at me with his disturbing black velvet eyes. "Oh no, he's not," he said. "To call old Chown a crammer makes him sound like a nasty little man driving into the skull of a nasty little boy just the minimum to make him jump through the hoop. Old Chown is a high priest of the mysteries, and that's another matter."

He refilled the coffee cups as though he were the host, and when we had emptied them he said: "Let's get out."

"I'd better wash the cups," I said.

"Let Ma Tiddy do it. Lazy old slut." He seemed more at home here than I liked him to be.

I gave him a hand up, and in the hall he took an ash stick from the stand. We went out into the strengthening sun of the morning. As we stood by the great front door he said: "You see the general lie of the thing. The house faces straight down this little valley. The sea's at the bottom, with a bit of beach. Well, what Mrs. Bascombe owns is old Chown's lodge and the field that leads up to it, the house, such as it is, and this valley. When the Polzeaths had it, they had a lot more: all the surrounding country, in fact. In their day the valley was what you'd expect a small Cornish valley to be: just scrub oaks and hazels and a general mess. It was one of the eighteenth-century Polzeaths who cleared it up. That was the great time, you
31

know, for taming the wilderness—then and during part of the nineteenth century. The place must have been a sight in its hey-day. The old stuff was rooted out and all sorts of gorgeous trees were planted on the slopes. Smaller things were put in as under-growth: rhododendrons, camellias, azaleas. It's all still there, but dreadfully overgrown. If you're here in the early spring you'll have an eye-opener. All that lovely show among the docks and nettles and wild convolvulus."

He leaned heavily on his stick, and my eyes followed his down over the treetops of the descending ravine to the blue of the sea beyond.

"Well, there it is," he said. "The house and the garden are all part of Sylvia's dream. Rebuild the house, reclaim the garden. I wonder . . ."

After a moment he said: "Oh, damn this leg! I'm asking too much of it to-day."

There was a pile of masonry fallen from the ruined part of the house. He sat down on it, and said: "In a way, it was old Chown who started it all. Before he retired he used to come down here for his holidays. He always stayed at the Absolution. The only guest we ever took in. He loved sitting in the bar at nights, knocking 'em back and talking to the locals. Well, one year Sylvia came down to keep him company. She stayed in Tiddy's cottage. When she saw this place she just went crazy about it. That's how it began."

I looked over my shoulder at the ruins. "But it'll take a fortune to do anything with a wreck like this," I said.

"She's rich," he said shortly.

"Do actresses make all that money?" I innocently asked.

"Oh, there's more to it than that," he said evasively. "Some day perhaps you'll hear the whole story."

He lit a cigarette, and for a time we watched the gulls, and smelled the sea and the heather and the hot granite, and were quiet.

"It was old Chown who started me off, too," he said after a while. "I used to go in to school at Helston on my bike, and my father was mad on my getting a scholarship to Oxford. My Latin was groggy. On the first day of Mr. Chown's holiday one year he found me sitting on a rock trying to hammer some sense out of a bit of Ovid. I told him about the scholarship and about my difficulty. 'It sounds so foreign. It doesn't look like a language at all,' I said. Then he took the book and said: 'How does this sound?' He read the passage, and damme, it did sound human. Indeed, it sounded gorgeous."

He sat quiet, savouring that moment of revelation. "None of our masters at school could read it like that," he said. "Well, let's cut it short. He took me in hand, really put me through

32

the hoop, all the time that holiday lasted, and university holidays last a long time, especially the summer one. We were at it again in the next holiday, and I got my scholarship."

"I suppose Mr. Chown was very pleased with you."

"Oh, no, he wasn't," Jose said. "He was fed up because I didn't much want to go to Oxford. He almost had to drive me there. I wanted to be a carpenter." He spread out his long hands. "Look at those hands," he said. "They know what wood is."

Jose had, from the time he was a child, played about in the workshop of the local carpenter, who was also the local builder and undertaker. "The old scoundrel never paid me a penny," he said, and added with a laugh: "I'll never forget my pride when I made my first coffin. I was fourteen, and it was a damned sound job. It was a coffin that Chippendale might have made. Not a nail in it. All oak pegs."

He didn't know, he said, how he'd got to hear of Chippendale. "But somehow, when you're crazy about a thing, you soak it up like a dry field soaking up dew. Chippendale, Sheraton, Hepplewhite—I got all the books I could on these chaps from the Helston library."

His new knowledge gave him new eyes, and he began to see a number of things at the Absolution in a new way. "By the time Sylvia began playing about with this house," he said, "I really did know something about furniture. I'd been up to London once or twice, and spent all my time in the Victoria and Albert and other museums." He had his own workshop now in a yard behind the inn, and he salved everything he could lay his hands on out of the stuff that the wreckers had put there. "Those chairs from the admiral's cabin were only part of it. I made 'em look something, and I sold 'em to Sylvia."

The superb refectory table at which Mr. Chown and I had dined with Sylvia last night was a Polzeath relic that had found its way to the inn when the house was falling into ruin. "It had been in the bar-parlour for donkey's years, looking like nothing on earth," Jose said. "Well, it looks all right now, though one of the legs is a fake. It was rotten with worm, so I carved a new one."

What it all came to was that he was Mrs. Bascombe's adviser on the furnishings of the house that she was trying to resurrect. "The war heaved me out of Oxford," he said, "and a damned good thing, too. I shan't go back. I'll make a living somehow by doing what I want to do, and that doesn't include what they were trying to drive into me there. However, in the chapels and halls I learned a lot about wood and pictures and fabrics. So my time wasn't wasted."

He got to his feet, and I caught him as he swayed and nearly fell. "Thank you," he said. "The damned thing's not doing so well as I hoped it would. If you've got nothing better to do, come and have a look at the Absolution."

We walked back past Mr. Chown's lodge and through the field and came to the track that ran westward. The day was at its autumn best, the heather rippling about us like a purple undulating sea. A pair of buzzards hung almost motionless in the air, and small birds, nameless to me, flirted about among the wind-wizened landward-streaming shrubs which were all that could get a hold on the sparse earth that clothed the bones of the land. To our left was the sea: the unpredictable monster, quiet now, blue and beautiful.

We walked for a mile, and that took us an hour, for Jose had often to sit down. "I think you ought still to be having a doctor for that leg," I told him, and he said: "Oh, I'll be back in the quacks' hands soon enough. It's only by luck that I'm here at all. I'm still a patient at a hospital in London. One of the doctors there is a Helston man—our own family doctor, in fact. He was due for a bit of leave, and how he wangled it I don't know, but he made the journey by motor car. As I was theoretically in his care I was allowed to come with him. We go back to-morrow."

"If I had to be in hospital, I'd hate it to be in London."

"It's pleasant enough," he assured me. "It's a temporary hospital, a big house at Highgate, overlooking the Heath. I expect Sylvia'll come out now and then to see me."

I thought of Sylvia, whom I had seen, only a few hours before, running like Atalanta on the golden sand.

That sight recalled sent a shiver through me, and I disliked the thought of Sylvia calling to see Jose Gomm.

"What about Janet?" I asked.

"Oh, she'll be back at school. She won't be in the way."

In the way. I liked it less and less and could say no more.

The path swerved a little southward and downward, and there was a village, cuddled into the embrace of rocky arms. The north winds would blow over it, straight out to sea, but southerlies and south-westers would roar into it as into a funnel. It was nothing but a handful of cottages, higgledy-piggledy wherever a shelf gave a level for foundations, with a thread of road running down to the sea, and the sea here was piled with rocks that stood in small sharp pinnacles and lay in broad reefs. They were tranquil as the water lapped and gurgled; but I could imagine what vehement sounding-boards they would be when winds and a running tide smashed rollers down upon them, what a welter of sea-fountains would arise and run in front of the wind to shatter upon the cottages that were dozing idly now in the autumn warmth. They were whitewashed, and fuchsias were abloom on them up to the roofs. Jose leaned on

34

his stick and looked down upon it. "Yes," he said. "That's where the Gomms crawled ashore from the sea."

We walked down into the village. Such few young men as had ever lived there were gone to the war. A few children played; a few women knitted in doorways; a few old men were mending nets, and there were boats pulled up on the one small patch of sand that burrowed a way into a rocky cleft on the western side of the cove.

"I shouldn't have thought," I said, "that anyone would want to take out a boat over that lot."

"Nobody wants to, I imagine," Jose said. "But needs must. It's not bad if you know the way and if God is good. Well, here's the Absolution."

It was the biggest building in the village. Most of the houses were cubes; the pub was an oblong, two-storied, whitewashed, with woodwork painted dark green and a sign, the work of some local amateur, swinging over the porch in which there were two benches of weather-bleached wood. "I've got a hunch," Jose said, "that those were knocked up out of the *Absolution's* timber, and when the poor old *Absolution* came ashore here she didn't look like what you see in the picture. Never did look like it, come to that."

I looked up at the painted ship. Certainly no ship of the line in Elizabeth's day had looked like that. I imagined the stern quarters with a railed walk and the bulging curve of the cabin window that opened upon it. But some local boy had made good with what might have been Sir Thomas Lipton's *Shamrock*. He had painted *Absolution* on the bows.

"The old man paid him a fiver, and is proud of it. I suppose the boy did his best, which only shows how often the best is not good enough. Some day I'll get the *Absolution* painted as she was."

We went into the stone-floored pub. On either side of the passage was a room with a window opening upon a view of the sea. The windows were of bottle-glass, so that the view was blurred. There were red curtains, old settles near the fireplaces, up-ended barrels for tables, oil-lamps hanging, photographs on the walls showing notable catches of pilchards and such matters.

"Just a typical pub of its time and place," Jose said. "And no one's got so far to go home that he has difficulty in getting there. Not that there's much to be had to cause difficulty in war-time. An occasional barrel of weak beer. Well, you'd better be hopping or old Chown will wonder what you're up to. I'll be off in the morning, but I expect I'll be seeing you again."

We shook hands and I trotted back to Penruan.

I saw Mr. Chown walking from his lodge towards the house

35

and met him at the front door. He was hatless and wigless. He never wore country clothes, but always a rusty old down-and-out town suit. " Let us see," he said, " what la Tiddy has prepared for our sustentation. And while you're at it, eat well. I sometimes dine up here when Sylvia's at home, but when I'm alone take only breakfast and luncheon. For the rest, I make do with biscuits and a glass of wine. I think you'd better opt for tea or cocoa."

We went into the little dining-room and Mrs. Tiddy brought in our food. " And what have you discovered this morning?" Mr. Chown asked.

" I met Jose Gomm, sir," I said.

" Then you have exhausted the scholastic resources of this province. I understand that he goes back to Hampstead tomorrow. Then you'll be cast upon my mercy."

" He told me that he expects Mrs. Bascombe will visit him in hospital."

" I have no doubt she will. They will talk about Penruan: what it was, what it is, and what it shall become. He prefers her dream to mine."

I looked at him in perplexity. " I've no doubt," he said, " that Jose has made his dream and her's clear enough. Mine was simply to turn a country oaf into a scholar."

" What you've taught him will do him no harm, sir."

" You must continue to delight me with your penetrating observations."

" Where does Janet go to school?"

" Nowhere in particular. Now and then she is sent to some new establishment, persuades her mother that it is horrible, and is then withdrawn from beneath that particular wing of learning. After a few months of loafing about she goes somewhere else. I believe that at the moment she is in the establishment of a lady named Popplecock, in Berkshire. Or perhaps that's the one she's just left. I'm not sure."

He wiped his lips with his napkin and pushed back his chair. " However," he said, " my concern is with your education, not hers. Women have a way of educating themselves for their own fell purposes, without benefit of curricula. We shall begin on you to-morrow. I suggest that you spend this afternoon in writing a long letter to your father. Give him my courtesies. I shan't disturb you. I walk in the afternoons."

Every morning, when we had returned from breakfasting at the house, we went into Mr. Chown's big room and read Greek and Latin. I don't think he found me too bad a scholar, but I was never a brilliant one. At any rate, I worked hard ; and, as for him, it was enough that he had a neophyte to be dipped in the only waters that seemed to him to provide a valid baptism. I had feared what I should find when first my father proposed this venture ; but I began to enjoy it. As autumn passed into winter, our mornings in front of the roaring log fire became deeply satisfying. Sometimes Mr. Chown was severely the preceptor, stern and, if need be, angry with me. At others he was the lover of his theme and I simply an audience. There was, as an example, a tearing morning in December. We staggered to his lodge after breakfast against a wind that knocked the breath out of us, and his first words as we sat down by the fire were: "Well, young George Ledra, I want you to imagine a day rather different from this in Epidaurus. Three hundred years before Christ. Someone was putting on a play by Sophocles, who had been dead for some time. You know something about his *Electra*. We've done it together. Well, that's the play they were doing. Let's go along and have a look at it."

Then for an hour he talked, and as he talked I saw the people streaming over the countryside towards the theatre, and felt the sunlight falling upon the rising tiers of seats, and heard the hush as the drama began to unfold. He took me through the play, making the actors come to life, and when he had finished I felt as excited as a Greek boy who had been taken, as a treat, to the theatre for the first time and had found it beyond expectation.

"Well," he said, after he had sat silent for a while stuffing tobacco into his pipe, "now you know, I hope, what it was like to be a Greek and to go to the theatre. Keep what I have told you in your mind when you are reading the plays. A play needs three people: a man to write it, a man to act it, and a man to listen to it. I've tried to show you the three working together in Greece."

"Sometimes a woman may play it," I reminded him, my mind still preoccupied with Sylvia, though now she had been gone for two months.

"Yes," he said, "that is so now, but for a long time all acting was done by men. That Ophelia whom John Collier has deposited in the dining-room was first played by some pretty boy. After the Restoration actresses began to appear."

He went on to talk about the Elizabethan stage—the buildings, the actors, the playwrights. He was like that. Divagation with him was a practised art. "Beware," he once said to me, "of a schoolmaster who sticks to the point. A point is merely a key, and a key should open up all sorts of wonders."

CHAPTER THREE

1

I wondered for a time whether Sylvia or Janet would write to me. Neither did, and I was disappointed. Their brief irruption into my life affected me disproportionately for several reasons. To begin with, there was my father's dislike of women's company which had caused me never to know a woman except as someone casually seen in the street or talked to in a shop. Then there was the chance that Sylvia was an actress with extrovert, even exhibitionist, manners, which made her, on so slight an acquaintance, show herself off to me and kiss me. Most of all, there was the pagan loveliness of the morning and of the women themselves as I watched them coming out of the sea, making a picture strikingly different from that in which Botticelli imagined a similar moment. These were no goddesses, unapproachable by man. They were manifestly and disturbingly and most beautifully women.

The weather had turned too sharp for bathing, but my daily walk often took me that way, and even when the south-westerly wind was driving the waves in, cold and bitter-green, shooing them up the sand like grey hissing ganders to the very mouth of the cave, and the December air was a drench of mist, this elemental present did not obliterate the thought of the recreated vision of that other moment, as elemental in its way, and to me, in that mood, far more satisfying.

But necessarily the conscious hugging of this sharp moment of experience lost its intensity. There was so much else to do, so much to discover, whether through my sessions with Mr. Chown or through my solitary walks. They had to be solitary because he insisted that his should be. Whatever the weather, he would set off alone when luncheon had been eaten, and, watching him go, I would choose a way not likely to cross his. Thus I got to know the sea in its moods, and the wide windy downs; and at night, with the fire roaring in Mr. Chown's great study, he would sit silently reading or writing, and in my book-lined alcove I would busy myself with whatever task he had set me. Sometimes it was so quiet that the crying of the night-birds could be heard: and sometimes there was the pounding of the sea and the thud of the wind buffeting the house, and always the sense of our small hermitage islanded in wide and uninhabited space. At ten o'clock I would go to bed, leaving him reading there; and always then, before passing into oblivion, I would wish that the morning might bring me a letter from Sylvia or Janet. It never did.

2

The play that Sylvia was appearing in was a frivolous thing called *More Fish in the Sea*. She was doing better in it than, I gathered, she had done in other plays. Soon after the opening Mr. Chown had shown me a batch of pieces from the newspapers that she had sent to him, and all of them spoke well of her. We were at breakfast in the dining-room, and Mr. Chown looked up at the portrait of his sister, Margaret Napier, and said: "I don't know what *she* would have thought of this." I gathered that Margaret Napier would have preferred to be found dead rather than to appear in such a play as *More Fish in the Sea*.

I knew nothing about plays, except that one read them as part of schooling. Theatre-going was not something that my father had time for, and perhaps the cautionary tale of Fred Byles that he had heard from *his* father had a lot to do with that. However, my own ignorance of such things, leaving me no standards of judgment, made it impossible for me to accept Mr. Chown's disparagement. It was easily outweighed by half a dozen clippings that praised Sylvia. I was in a callow state which permitted me to think that what appeared in a newspaper was necessarily to be taken seriously. Mr. Chown squeezed the cuttings into a ball and aimed them at the fire. They missed, and fell inside the fender. I gave him time to start off for the lodge before me, and then rescued them. That afternoon I put them in a box that already contained the bracelet I had picked up on the sand. It was an old cigar-box of Mr. Chown's. It had a cedar fragrance which seemed to me to fit its purpose as a reliquary. I could not inhale that fragrance without vividly recalling the moment when Sylvia bent down in her crackling silk and kissed me.

3

Throughout that winter and the following spring we existed almost in a vacuum. I wandered in the wildness of the little valley reaching from the house down to the sea, and witnessed the miracle that Jose Gomm had promised me. There was a tree of wintersweet, something I had never seen before, that flowered in December, filling the air with fragrance, and in December, too, the camellias began to bloom. The new year was hardly started when rhododendrons flowered, and on a February day I found to my astonishment a mimosa tree swaying its abundance of feathery gold in a light wind against the blue of the sky. The little valley reeked with beauty and decay, like the house to which it belonged. The rotting leaves of years filled every crack and crevice of the earth, and bursting through were sheets of daffodils and snowdrops all mixed with unfolding ferns and a riot and rampage of every imaginable moss and weed. The place tinkled with streams, and when April came it rang with birdsong. The green of the larches shone in the bottoms, and higher on the valley sides beech and copper beech shook out their emerald and ochre loveliness. Then the bluebells came, turquoise lakes, and everywhere the primroses lifted gentle and modest faces to the sky. Looking back on it now, it seems to me to have been like some tired and ancient and beautiful civilisation, existing in and on its own decay, changeless, and doomed.

Half-way down the valley, alongside what had once been a path and was now a tangle through which one stamped, booting down the briars and burdock, was a cut-back into the bank, a small platform, and upon this was the ruin of a summer-house. The sides sagged and the roof was falling in, but the place held together and the seat against the back wall was of teak, durable and still fit to be used. The afternoon sunlight fell in there and I often brought a book and settled down to read, confident that no one would disturb me. When April was almost ended I strolled down one afternoon and saw to my annoyance that someone had discovered my retreat. A girl, her back to me, was lying full length on the seat, so still that I judged her to be asleep. All I could see of her was a hat that looked like a beret —not a usual sort of headgear at that time—a soiled mackintosh, thick black woollen stockings and sturdy muddy shoes. I supposed it was some girl from the village who had been taking a walk, had sat down to rest, and been overtaken by sleep.

I stood still, looking at her so quiet amid the singing birds and the half-heard sound of water, wondering whether to wake her or to go on and find some other place to settle in for my reading, and I was overcome by a feeling that surprised me. A girl, alone. I wanted to touch her, to awaken her, to speak to her.

She said: " Why are you standing there, staring? It's George Ledra, I suppose. I heard you coming."

She sat up, swung herself round, and faced me. It was Janet. I looked at her, stupefied. "I thought you were at school," I said.

" So I was, but I ran away."

I remembered what Mr. Chown had told me about Janet's changes of school. "I usually get sent home after a term or two," she said. "This time I didn't wait to be sent." She unbuttoned her mackintosh and displayed a uniform of what, even to me, seemed horrid coarse blue serge, with a belt of some red plaited stuff. "Look at it," she said. "Isn't it ghastly? And this." She pulled off the beret, allowing her hair to fall about her shoulders. "Did you ever see the like?" she demanded. "No wonder the children used to laugh and shout at us as we promenaded through the village." She held out her legs and surveyed her stockings and shoes with disgust. "I hate girls, anyway," she summed up, "and school is all nonsense."

"Where was your school?"

"Hertfordshire."

"You've had a long journey."

"Oh, these things are easy enough," she said airily. "London was no distance at all, and I had enough money to pay the fare. I presented myself to Mama, and she was most annoyed."

Janet got up and began walking about, smiling at the thought of Sylvia's annoyance. "She said rations were difficult enough in wartime without having an extra mouth planted on one. An extra mouth! That's a nice thing for a mother to call her child, I must say!"

She pondered her mother's absurdity for a time, and then said: "Well, the long and the short of it is that she rang up old Miss Poppycock and had rather a stormy conversation. Have you seen Sylvia stormy?"

I said that I hadn't. "You will," Janet promised me. "I hoped when the storm had blown out to be allowed to stay with her in London. I like her flat. But yesterday morning she took me to Paddington and put me on the Riviera Express. She said she'd telegraph to Uncle Chown to have me met at Helston. But she was so mad I expect she forgot."

And, indeed, Sylvia had forgotten.

"So there I was," Janet said philosophically, "all alone last night in Helston."

"What on earth did you do?"

"Oh, I read somewhere that you can always ask the police for a night's lodgings. So I did. They were very nice. They gave me a cup of tea, and one of them played draughts with me till it was time for him to go off duty. Then he took me home with him and his wife gave me another cup of tea and put me to bed. Really," she said, "outside schools, people are quite decent."

"And have you walked to-day all the way from Helston?"

"No. One of the policemen who wasn't on duty brought me on his bike. I stood on the back step and held on round his

41

chest. There was no one in, so I came down here to ponder my next step," she ended.

The reasonable next step seemed to be to return to the lodge, which we did. Mr. Chown, back from his afternoon walk, arrived at the same moment as a boy with a telegram. Mr. Chown read it aloud: "Regret failed to inform you yesterday Janet's arrival Helston. Has she come? Am in a state of great anxiety, Sylvia."

"Don't you believe it," Janet said, grinning at my tutor. "Now come in and let me make you a cup of tea. Then I must change out of these odious clothes."

4

"You have been here for six months," Mr. Chown said, "and you have done reasonably well for a person not destined to do *very* well. I think it's time you took a holiday. I could bear your absence for a month."

We were eating breakfast, and Janet came in to join us. She overheard his remarks and said: "I'm surprised George has stuck it for so long. Why don't you run away?"

Mr. Chown said: "George is not made to be a rogue and vagabond like all the women of your family."

She looked at me mockingly. "You can see," she said, "that he's nothing but an old stick-in-the-mud."

Mrs. Tiddy laid before her a plate of fried eggs and fried bread. For so slender a creature, she was a hearty eater. She had been with us for a week and lived alone in the house. "'Ow did you sleep last night?" Mrs. Tiddy now asked her.

"Like a princess," she said, "in Mother's vast four-poster. Have you ever awakened, Mrs. Tiddy, to find yourself surrounded by a tapestry of apes and peacocks, unicorns and greyhounds?"

"No, I 'aven't, and neither 'ave any respectable woman."

"You are besmirching my mother's name," Janet said, looking severely over her coffee cup.

"Give me the creeps, you do, thinking of you alone in this place o'nights, an' all them old Polzeaths everywhere."

It was Mrs. Tiddy's belief that, once darkness was down, the Polzeath ghosts squeaked and gibbered about the rooms and corridors of Penruan. Sometimes, looking back towards the house from Mr. Chown's lodge when night was falling, I found it not too difficult to believe that she could be right, and the thought of Janet, alone, perhaps in the great hall, perhaps in the bedroom behind the oriel—one of the few rooms Sylvia had furnished—gave me the creeps, too.

But, in the day-time hours of that strengthening spring, no

42

shadow of these night thoughts hung about her. We walked together every afternoon, for, even now that Janet was there, Mr. Chown insisted on walking alone. Sometimes we went down the stuffy little valley to the sea; sometimes we wandered on the downs with the fat white clouds ambling across the blue above us, and against that whiteness you could see the larks ascending and the rooks ganging up to chase away some intruding buzzard. And Janet, in a passionate fit of Swinburne-worship, would chant that the hounds of spring were on winter's traces or that even the weariest river wound somewhere safe to sea.

"Can you imagine me," she cried one day, "walking with twenty female louts, all dressed in blue serge, dear Miss Hawkins in front and dear Miss Dawkins at the back, and all of us pausing at times to be instructed about some humble wayside herb? Miss Dawkins always called them humble wayside herbs, and Miss Hawkins would chime in with a word on the beauty of humility. It was Miss Dawkins," she added, as though that explained a lot, "who found Swinburne under my pillow."

"I have read somewhere," I said, "that he was a very small man. She might almost literally have found him there."

"Oh, if she only had!" Janet cried. "What a moment that would have been in the pedagogic history of England!"

Sylvia had written to Mr. Chown, deploring the necessity of planting Janet upon him, and promising to be on the look-out for another school. "The trouble is," she wrote, "that headmistresses want to know why a girl left her last school, and they are even impertinent enough to write to the school to find out, so that the Janet problem is becoming complicated. However, you may be sure that I am giving the matter all my attention."

Mr. Chown smiled grimly at this, as he read the letter to Janet at the breakfast table, and she said: "You do well to doubt her good intentions. I'm full of them myself, and I know what they're worth."

He looked severely at his witch, and then his dry old face crinkled into a smile, and I knew that between them Sylvia and Janet could do what they liked with him so long as they kept out of the way of his work.

"Well," he said, "we'll put up with you a bit longer and see how things turn out."

"When George is gone you could teach me yourself, if you promised not to be too tedious."

"I could teach you nothing," he said firmly.

I set out for Manchester on a day of late April, feeling immensely older than when I left home six months before. Seeing that during all my time in Cornwall I had talked to hardly more than half a dozen people, it was difficult to explain why this should be so, but I imagine that to be one amid hundreds of thousands can be more isolating and mentally stultifying than to be one among six, especially if the six include a man like Mr. Chown and a woman like Janet. For Janet was a woman, even though the chrysalis of the child was still upon her. Mr. Chown might chaff her at times as though she were a child, but he would rise when she came into a room, and I had learned to do this, too, and to observe the other small courtesies one accords to a woman. She accepted these with a curious inborn adultness. Yes, she was a woman, and a most wayward one. But I had ceased to think of her as only a woman. She was a comrade, too. Sometimes during our walks she would put her arm through mine, and this no longer excited me. But I could think sentimentally of Sylvia as I looked at the bracelet and press cuttings in my reliquary. Sylvia was still all woman.

Tiddy took me in his pony cart to Helston and inquired kindly how my consumption was getting on. He refused to be depressed when I told him that, so far as I knew, consumption and I were strangers. "It'll declare itself," he assured me cheerfully, " it'll declare itself in God's good time. The soft air down here will bring it out. Mountains. That's what you want—mountains. Kill or cure you, mountains will. Do you get this ole sweatin' at nights?"

No sweating, I told him.

" Don't build too much on that," he begged me. " I've known cases where the sweats 'eld off till the death-throes was on 'em. They come in the end."

Tiddy went in for death-throes in a big way. I had only once been in his cottage, which was half-way along the track from Penruan to the Absolution. It was built of mud held together by whitewash, and the rooms were so low that a six-foot man would have to crouch to dodge the beams. The small never-opened window of the sitting-room and the vigour of the fire on the hearth made the place stuffy, but it was cheerful enough. Indeed, I commented to Mr. Tiddy on its cheerfulness. He sat in an arm-chair near the fire, smoking his pipe, and said: " Aye, it's cheerful enough—too cheerful, Mr. Ledra. It's easy enough to forget that in the midst of life we are in death, and that the Lord cometh in what hour no man knoweth. So them's there to remind me."

He waved his pipe around the walls, and I looked at the steel engravings hanging there in immense smoke-blackened gilded frames. One showed John Wesley on his death-bed—"Ole John on the way to glory," Mr. Tiddy explained: and another was of Nelson laid low on the deck of the *Victory*. " An' where 'e's bound for I wouldn't like to say. 'Ad a mistress, 'e 'ad. Did you know that, Mr. Ledra?" At that time I didn't, and said so.

" Well, 'e 'ad. What I call a border-line case. I been a sailor myself in my time, and I admire 'im *as* a sailor. But I dunno, I dunno. I wouldn't like to swear to 'is destination."

The death of Chatterton also found a place, and the death-rattle of scores of Christians could be heard echoing from an enormous work by Doré, showing self-satisfied lions in a Roman arena making short work of man and maid.

" Well, there they are, Mr. Ledra," Tiddy said. " The beginning of life is one thing: the end is another. It's what you see when the death-rattle's in your throat that matters."

So when I got into the train on that late April day I was not surprised to find an immense woollen muffler thrust at me through the window. " Been workin' on that for you all the winter, Mrs. Tiddy 'ave. Just keep that throat well wrapped up now, an' watch that cough. A cough to-day is death-throes to-morrow."

It was a time of death-throes. There were plenty of soldiers travelling to remind one of that, if one were capable of being reminded. I was not. It may be a blessing—at any rate it is a matter of surprise—that the human mind can insulate itself from what does not personally concern it, however devastating. I had no relative engaged in the war. In the remote place where I had spent the winter the war's signs did not appear. I was young. It was a lovely day, and in my pocket was a letter from Sylvia. Mr. Chown had told her of my holiday and that I would be spending a night in London before going on to Manchester. She had written to me saying that owing to the war there was not a hotel room to be had for love or money and that I had better come and shake down in her flat. She drew a plan to show me how to get there. " It's hardly more than ten minutes' walk, and that's as well, for you won't be able to get a taxi."

What I thought would come from my brief visit to Sylvia I don't know, but I was in a state of excited expectation. And I didn't meet her after all. Her flat, I found, was on the top floor of a tall thin house. I was climbing the stairs when a door opened and a young woman asked: " Are you Mr. Ledra?"

I admitted it, and she said: " I'm afraid your luck's out. Mrs. Bascombe's had a breakdown. She's been overworking herself dreadfully—Red Cross in the day and the theatre at night. She just flopped when she got in yesterday. Luckily I

45

was about. I was able to get her to my father's nursing-home. That's where she is now."

She went back into her flat and brought a key. "She asked me to give you this and to say you were to make yourself at home. Drop it into my letter-box when you go in the morning, will you?"

I promised to do so, and climbed the last flight of stairs. I was fumbling with the key when the young woman, whose name I found later to be Jessie Lewis, appeared again and shouted up: "What are you going to do about eating? I don't suppose Sylvia's got anything laid in."

I didn't know what I was going to do. I had counted on being catered for, and I had no idea how to go about finding a meal in war-time London, even if I had the money to pay for it, which I hadn't. I must have looked flummoxed, for Miss Lewis laughed. "Come down here at about half past six," she said. "I'll see what I can rustle up."

Miss Lewis's laugh made me feel small. I could imagine Sylvia saying: "I'm expecting a Mr. Ledra," and the last thing the girl would look for would be a rather shabby, very gauche schoolboy of fifteen years. I almost slinked into the flat; so different an arrival from what I had expected. But, I asked myself, what had I expected? I didn't know, but I felt disoriented, fidgety, not knowing what to do with myself. My woman-shyness, which Janet had helped to break down, rushed back upon me. I was terrified by the thought of going to eat with the self-possessed young woman downstairs. I supposed she was about twenty.

It was most annoying that I had been wearing Mrs. Tiddy's muffler, a horrid mixture of vitriol-green and magenta. I could have strangled her with it. I flung it on to a hook behind the door in the hall, hung my overcoat there, and walked into the sitting-room. It was very quiet in that high-up room in a road off the traffic stream. I looked down upon a strip of turf in which a few trees were growing—trees at their spring-time best. Laburnum dangled golden chains and there were cherries of red and white. I hadn't Jose Gomm's talent to diagnose the furniture, but all seemed to be elegant, quiet, restful. On the writing-desk was a photograph. I saw that it was of Mr. Chown's sister, Sylvia's mother, whose painted image was over the fireplace in the Penruan dining-room.

I explored. A small kitchen, a bathroom, a box of a room with a divan-bed. That, I supposed would be where Janet slept: an austere cell. Then I entered another room, hushed, carpeted, luxurious. I saw at once that this was Sylvia's bedroom. The air held a faint perfume. A pair of furred mules stood by a chair across which was thrown a transparent nightdress. My throat was dry, and I wanted to touch the nightdress, but a sense of
46

profanity overwhelmed me, and I tip-toed back to the sitting-room. I was tired from my journey and a divan invited repose. But I was too restless to use it. I longed for Sylvia to be there, and I was glad that she wasn't. An hour must pass before I could go down to eat with the young woman on the floor below. How on earth was I to employ so vast a stretch of time? There were books, but I couldn't read. There was Sylvia's desk. I sat down at it, took a sheet of paper and a pen.

"Dear Mrs. Bascombe," I wrote. "Thank you so much for arranging as you did with the young woman on the floor below, whose name, I'm afraid, I don't know. She has kindly invited me to go down and eat with her to-night. It was a great shock to me to learn that you were unwell, and I was moved to find that at such a moment you thought of what was to be done about me. I do hope that this is nothing more than a passing illness and that you will be quite well again soon. I was looking forward to seeing you in your play, but I sha'n't go to see it with you not in it. Thank you for letting me stay here to-night. Janet is well. Yours sincerely, George Ledra."

This small task steadied me. Then I went to the bathroom and wallowed for half an hour in comforting hot water. I dried myself on a luxurious towel, standing on the downiest bath-mat I had ever had beneath my feet. I wished I had stylish clothes to put on, but there was nothing save the shabby lounge suit I had travelled in. I shrugged myself into it, took my letter so that the young woman might deliver it to Sylvia, went down and tapped timidly at the door.

6

"Oh, it's you," she said, as though it might have been someone more acceptable. At any rate that's how it seemed to my apprehensive nerves. I wasn't helped by seeing that she had put on an evening dress of sorts. She was a middling girl: middling in height, middling in girth, and she wasn't notably either fair or dark. But her eyes were dark. They were attractive, lively and amused.

"Come in," she said. "I'm not much of a cook, but by luck there is something to eat. I've just received a parcel from my aunt in Belfast. By the way, my name's Jessie. Jessie Lewis. You can call me Jessie."

The table was already laid. The room was well furnished, but it hadn't the luxurious feeling of Sylvia's flat. The pictures were prints. The carpet was over-worn, and even to me the curtains didn't seem very good. There were lots and lots of books, thrown about everywhere. It was not yet dark, but the room was rather dusky. She had lit two candles on the table, and between them was a pottery vase containing a few tulips. She was doing her best to make it a little " occasion." I remembered Mr. Chown's manners with women, pulled out her chair, and thanked her for inviting me. Having done that, I was at the end of my resources. I didn't know what to talk about, and my mind kept wandering to Sylvia's nightdress thrown over the chair alongside her bed.

It was a frugal meal. We ate cold ham and a little salad, and then cheese, and then chocolate. The cheese and chocolate had come from Belfast, " and so did some coffee, fortunately," Jessie said. " But I'm afraid I haven't any sugar. Do you mind?"

I said that I didn't, and she went to the kitchen and made some coffee. Then we sat side by side on a divan, with the coffee on a low table before us. She lit a cigarette. " Now tell me," she said, " how is that mad little daughter of Sylvia's?"

Poor Jessie! As I see it now, I don't suppose she cared tuppence about Sylvia's mad little daughter, but had to dredge up some topic or die of boredom in the presence of Sylvia's odd and inexplicable friend. I talked about Penruan and the moors and the little flowery gulch that ran down to the sea. Jessie leaned forward to tap her cigarette ash into a tray, and her hand touched mine, reaching for my coffee cup. I shivered.

She, aware of this, looked at me sideways, troubled. I noticed that her hair, arranged in a flat coil over each ear, was attractive, and I longed to finger it. She got up and, as though despairing of further conversation now that I had done with Penruan, asked: " Do you play draughts?"

I said that I did. She cleared away the coffee things, and our supper things from the table, switched on a light, blew out the candles and pulled the curtains across the window. The room seemed cosier, and we sat down at the table and began to play. I hadn't the *savoir faire* to know when I should get up and thank her and go, and she, I imagined, disliked the idea of saying to a friend of Sylvia's: " Oh, get out, you bore, for heaven's sake!" which was perhaps in her mind. She became as speechless as I was myself, and we went dully on and on, she slaughtering me ruthlessly in every game.

It must have been about nine o'clock when we were startled by a continuous imperative ringing of the door-bell. " Who on earth . . ." she said, moving quickly to open it.

And then the dead dreary atmosphere was suddenly convulsed with passion. A young man of Jessie's own age edged his way in, cluttered with the gear that private soldiers carried at that time: a pack, a mess-tin, a water-bottle, a gas-mask, a tin hat, an entrenching tool, and all the rest of it clattering about him. One arm was squeezing Jessie tight into this collection of iron-mongery, the other held a rifle. Neither seemed aware of me, and I was shocked by the naked hungry look on their faces as they stood before me, kissing. The coils over Jessie's ears became loosened, and her hair streamed down her shoulders. " Oh, darling! " she said, and buried her face in his shoulder. He bent over her, kissing the back of her neck. She was sobbing. " I didn't know you were coming," she said, and he said: " Well, here I am. Unexpected leave. I wanted to surprise you."

They pulled themselves away from one another, looked at one another in wonder, their faces shining. " Where are you staying?" she asked, and he: " Where d'you think?"

He looked all question till she slowly nodded her head, and then again wrapped themselves up in one another. At last I knew when I wasn't wanted, and slipped out of the room.

I hardly slept. I had understood the significance of the young soldier's question and Jessie's mute answer. I was tortured by imagination, and I was diminished by the sense of my insignificance that they had conveyed to me. Jessie hadn't thought my presence worth explaining, and the young man hadn't even bothered to look at me. I dozed towards morning and woke early on the cot I supposed to be Janet's. I dressed at once, and, putting my hand into my pocket, found the letter I had written to Sylvia. I had forgotten after all to give it to Jessie. I tore it up and threw it into the fireplace, then took up the bag that lightly held my few things and walked through the quiet wakening town to St. Pancras. I breakfasted on a sloppy cup of tea and a bun and loafed about till train-time came.

7

It was mid-afternoon when the electric tram stopped at Platt Fields, and I got off and turned into Victoria Park. I was glad to be back. Leaving Cornwall the day before, I had wondered how I should ever put up with Manchester. Now I knew that I should put up with it well enough. Victoria Park was all right at that time of year—plenty of trees and shrubs in flower, and the limes in our garden were a miracle of young green. I could, too, be a boy again, I thought. Sylvia, Janet and the chance-met Jessie with her soldier-lover seemed a long way off, and I could settle down for a time undisturbed by the titillations of my awakening manhood. Not that I consciously put it like that, but all this, I am sure, was implicit in my mood of freedom and relief. I stood watching a pair of swifts, the first I had seen that year, flying high in the blue, then walked up the path and rang the bell, thinking how surprised our housekeeper, Mrs. Burnett, would be to see me. I had written nothing about my holiday, hoping to give her and my father what I trusted would be a pleasant shock.

She opened the door and certainly looked surprised. "Oh, Mr. George!" she exclaimed. "How did you know?"

Her face, her manner, told me at once that something was wrong. "Know what?" I asked.

"About your father. I thought perhaps that nurse let you know, though I told her not to. Not till we saw how things went."

I walked through into my father's study and she followed me. The word *nurse* was ominous. The way Mrs. Burnett said *that* nurse suggested antipathy. "Mrs. Burnett," I said, "I know nothing. I came home because Mr. Chown thought I should take a holiday. What has happened?"

Three days ago my father returned from the office looking what Mrs. Burnett called his usual self. But, she said, when she took in his evening meal he looked queer. She noticed that when he tried to pick up his knife and fork his left hand was astray. He got hold of the knife all right but missed the fork and had to fumble for it. This and his general appearance caused her to linger in the room. He said: "It's all right, Mrs. Burnett, quite all right. You needn't stay," and he had no sooner said it than he slipped from his chair to the floor. She made him as comfortable there as she could, with a cushion under his head, and then rang up a doctor. "Your father's still there," she said, "in the dining-room."

The less heaving about the better, the doctor said. So a divan was carried into the dining-room and made up as a bed. Father was gently lifted on to it. "I keep an eye on him in the day-time," Mrs. Burnett said, "and that nurse comes in for night duty. The doctor says it's a matter of time. He's better, and he can talk a bit, but his left hand is cramped and his face twisted."

She was evidently trying to put the best construction on a bad situation. "You'd better go in and see him," she said. "He'll know you."

I said I'd wait till I'd seen the doctor and that she must say nothing to my father till then.

I washed away the tiredness of the journey and drank some tea in the kitchen. Mrs. Burnett was solicitous. She was obviously trying to make me understand that she was not to blame for this disaster. She lived in fear of blame. "It wasn't my fault," was a catchword with her. It rarely was, but she couldn't believe that other people would acknowledge this and that she would get through life without hanging.

"As sure as I'm sitting here," she said, "I gave him a good breakfast, and when he was gone to town I turned out his study, and when he got back he was as well as ever in this life. I'd managed to get a lamb chop for his supper, too, and that takes some doing these days. If that nurse looked after him as well at night as I do through the day I'd feel happier. Reads, that's what she does, just reads all the night through."

I said that that was a very quiet occupation, and that one could hardly expect the nurse to sit alongside my father's bed doing nothing whatever. But Mrs. Burnett was not to be deprived of her grievance. " It's *what* she reads," she grizzled. " I've seen the books lying open on her table. Always something funny."

It seemed to me that if I were condemned to a night session with an invalid I wouldn't want to spend it reading the Bible or Mill *On Liberty* ; but I said nothing to make Mrs. Burnett feel that she was creating for *that nurse* a favourable rather than disapproving reaction in my mind.

The doctor came, a stranger, for Dr. Wetherby was gone to France. Like the rest of them, he had not expected me. I was surprised to find him so old ; he seemed surprised to find me so young. His look was almost disapproving of the fewness of my years. He said he'd see how my father was, and decide whether the moment was appropriate for giving him the shock of knowing that his son was in the house.

When I was at last called into the dining-room, I found my father not at all the wreck I had expected. He was sitting up, propped with pillows. His face was indeed, as Mrs. Burnett had warned me, twisted, but not much. There was a slight but ugly contraction round the left side of the mouth and a drooping of the left eyelid. His left hand lay on the bedclothes, and, though nothing was visibly wrong with it, I noticed that he did not move it all the time I was in the room. He gave me his right hand and held it for a long time, and he smiled at me and said: " Good boy."

It was only when he smiled and spoke that I felt a shiver of fear. The smile was not quite right. There was something like contortion in it. And the words had the same quality. They were audible, but there was a blur along their edges.

Dr. Mickleham, who, I learned later, had been retired for ten years and had crawled out of his seclusion because so many doctors were with the armies, said: " I'll see you later." I took this for dismissal and, giving my father a smile, left the room.

When the doctor came out he told me that my brief visit to the patient was all that could be allowed for the day. " I'll be along again to-morrow," he said, " and then we'll see."

What on earth was I to do with myself? I wondered. Not merely to-day, which seemed to have still an endless length to run, though now it was five o'clock, but throughout all this ill-fated holiday. To go out and walk seemed heartless. To do nothing was unthinkable. I went up to the little room that had been set aside as my study and wrote a long letter explaining my situation to Mr. Chown. " Whether, in these circumstances,

I shall ever return to Cornwall I don't know." I looked at the words and hard-heartedly wished that I was in Cornwall now. Provided, of course, I added to get right with myself, that everything at home was as before.

Mrs. Burnett brought supper to my room and when I had eaten it I sat down to read, but could interest myself in nothing. She came back at half past nine and asked permission to go to bed. She said she was fair worn out and would have to be up at six in the morning. I told her to go. "You can let that nurse in," she said. "She comes about ten. Just let her in. There's nothing to tell her. She knows what she's supposed to do."

I took note of the word supposed and wished her good-night.

8

If the doctor had surprised me by the greatness of his years, that nurse surprised me by her youth. I had imagined I was to meet someone like Mrs. Gamp, who might conceivably spend the night tippling on gin at my father's bedside. A gentle ring at the front door-bell promptly at ten o'clock took me down to find a slight smiling creature on the doorstep. She said: "Hallo! Who are you?"

I explained myself as she stood under the dim hall light removing a cloak of dark blue serge and then standing revealed in a uniform of sorts: I remember a white collar and apron. She laid a book on the hall table. I saw it was Jerome's *Three Men in a Boat*. Its levity, I was sure, would annoy Mrs. Burnett. "I didn't know there was anybody except my patient and old sourface," she said. "My name's Halford—Elizabeth Halford."

I remembered Mrs. Burnett's words. "Just let her in. There's nothing to tell her." So I said, business-like: "Well, Miss Halford, I mustn't keep you. You'll be wanting to get in to your patient."

"Oh, there's no hurry about that," she assured me with a smile. "There's really nothing to do, you know, except just sit there. Dr. Mickleham never uses me for anything more than that. If there's real nursing to do he gets a real nurse. I'm not properly trained for anything more than a night-watchman's job."

I liked her frankness, and now that my eyes were getting used to the pin-point of light, I liked the look of the girl herself, and enjoyed the low conspiratorial pitch of our voices. She touched a white bow at her neck, and I admired the long flutter of her hands.

"Well . . ." I said.

52

She took up her book and turned to the dining-room door. "Well," she answered. "See you later."

Mr. Merriman, the chief clerk in my father's office, was one of those tiresome people who move remorselessly from Log Cabin to White House. The graph of Mr. Merriman's career had no staggers or fluctuations. It just went up. He began as a messenger-boy, became an office-boy, and now was at the top of the tree. It wasn't much of a tree. It was only in his imagination that his career had been spectacular, but with a man like Mr. Merriman imagination is enough. Messrs. Fred Byles and Ledra were not only cotton merchants but manufacturers, too. The mill was a small one, but busy enough in those war days, and now that my father was on his back Mr. Merriman saw himself as carrying with the ease of genius a burden that would have crushed a lesser man. I had often heard my father say that, so far as the mill went, he gave it little thought, for an excellent manager was in charge. But that was not how Mr. Merriman took the matter. With manufacturing added to marketing—which was how he insisted on seeing it—his stature became gigantic, and he looked upon me as a small pebble indeed on the wide beach of his concerns.

He came out to Victoria Park on the day after my return, having first rung up Dr. Mickleham so that their visits would coincide. He wanted to talk to my father about the business and hoped to gain the doctor's consent to an interview. Dr. Mickleham gave him a short answer: "No, sir, my patient is not fit to see you, much less to talk business with you." So Mr. Merriman seized upon me. "Well, young Ledra, if you've nothing better to do, let's take a turn in Platt Fields."

His manner suggested that I was unlikely indeed to have anything better to do than trot at his side and lose myself in wonder, love and praise. He was tall and dark and looked a bully. I took the first important decision of my life. "Well, you know," I said, "I have plenty to do," and without telling him what the plenty was (which would have been difficult) I turned towards the stairs.

I had noticed before, when calling on Father at the office, that if anything annoyed Mr. Merriman his already protuberant oily eyes, that looked like well greased ball-bearings, seemed to stand out on stalks. This happened now. I made up my mind not to be impressed. I told myself that he looked like an angry prawn; but I was rather shaken. "I wanted to discuss the affairs of the office," he said, as though these concerned my immortal soul and were to be neglected at my peril. Give him his due, he lived for the firm.

I said: "I know nothing of the affairs of the office, Mr. Merriman. As soon as my father is well enough to discuss them with you, I'll let you know and you can come and talk them over with him. In the meantime, I'm sure they're in better hands than mine."

It would have been surprising if they were not, but the absurd remark seemed to mollify though not placate him. I looked at him standing there hesitant: the protuberant eyes, the crimson silk handkerchief, the fawn-coloured spats. These three things had seemed to me to make up Mr. Merriman ever since I had known him. But I was to find that there was more to him than that.

10

Hypocritically I said to Mrs. Burnett: "I'm afraid my father's illness is putting a lot on your shoulders."

"It's all in the day's work, Mr. George," she said as though minting a new coin of wisdom.

"At all events, you should get to bed early now that I'm here. I can let the nurse in."

I had been thinking of that slight smiling creature. I may as well be honest with myself and admit that I had been thinking more of her than of my father. I had spent an hour in his room, but my thoughts were not in his room. There was nothing to keep them there; for, once he had mumbled a difficult greeting, his eyes closed, and whether he was in coma or sleep I did not know. The young are capable of sharp spontaneous outbursts of affection, but the long devotions of love are beyond them. My mind left him, left his room, and wandered: Penruan, Sylvia, Janet, that chance-met girl and her soldier-lover, that nurse. I could not conceal from myself that I was waiting for ten o'clock when I would see her again.

"Hallo!" she said. "You still here?"

I had been waiting on the stairs, and rushed to the door as soon as she gently touched the bell. "Couldn't be served quicker in a cook-shop," she said, and gave me a smile of feminine wisdom which confessed her knowledge that my quickness on the mark was due to my lying in ambush for her. I suppose she was about eighteen years old.

I said fatuously: "I'm so glad you've come," and more fatuously still, held out my hand as though greeting a visitor. She didn't take it. Instead, she put her arms round me, gave me a hug and a warm kiss on the mouth, and said: "That's what

54

you've been hanging round for, isn't it? Now get to bed. I've got my job to do."

I tried to detain her. She said: "Go on now. Don't be a fool," and lightly slapped my cheek. "You'll have old sourface down," she warned me. "That'd put the fat in the fire good and proper."

She dropped her cloak on to a chair, took her copy of *Three Men in a Boat*, and quietly stepped into Father's room.

That was the beginning of it. It happened again for three nights after that, and each night the hugging and kissing were more prolonged. On the third night she said: "Stop it now. Don't be a fool." She was always telling me not to be a fool. "Tell you what," she said. "See you to-morrow. Be outside the White Lion at half past two."

"Don't you need sleep in the day-time after being up all night?"

"Oh, lord!" she said. "You are the funniest boy. I can please myself, can't I, whether I wake or sleep?"

"Yes, of course," I agreed.

"Very well, then. Do you want it or don't you? If you do, meet me to-morrow."

I didn't know what she meant. We walked out into the Cheshire countryside and she taught me.

11

I wanted her to come out again the next day. She laughed and said: "Beginning to get the hang of things at last, are you? Well, I'm not coming. I've got to get a bit of sleep some time."

I pleaded with her. She said: "Don't be a fool," but added: "Tell you what. Three days from now."

It seemed to me an intolerable time to wait for the next trip to paradise; and when the third day came I couldn't go. It was heart-breaking, so lovely a spring day, warm, and the lime tree full of singing birds. Unfortunately, my father was feeling better. I trembled with self-contempt as the thought passed through my mind and I realised its implications. But it was there, try as I would to stifle it. That morning Dr. Mickleham called and found my father anxious to talk to Mr. Merriman. "I'll ring him up," Dr. Mickleham said, "and ask him to be here at half past two. I'll be here myself. I'll not have you overdoing things at this stage. I'll keep an eye on you, and when I say he's to go, he goes."

My father said, in his speech that was still slurred: "You'd better be here, George. I want to talk to Mr. Merriman about you."

I was overwhelmed. "But, Father," I said, "is that really necessary? Wouldn't it be better . . ."

Dr. Mickleham eyed me sternly. "That'll do, boy," he said. "I'll have no arguments at a moment like this. You'll do as your father tells you." He turned again to the bed and asked: "What sort of nights are you having?"

"Fair," my father said. "But if they were dreadful I'm afraid that nurse wouldn't be much good. I chanced to wake up last night and she was snoring in her chair."

"I'm sorry about that," the doctor said. "It's a difficult time for finding a good nurse. They're all in the hospitals. But by luck I've got an experienced woman at last. She can come in to-night, and I'll call on that other flighty young thing and switch her to a job that won't matter so much. I'd never have sent her here but for the sad times we're living in."

Oh, but they're not sad times: they're wonderful times, I thought. I imagined her arriving at our meeting-place and not finding me there. It seemed to me desperately important that I should see her, explain the situation. I said, as casually as I could: "I can nip round to her now, if you'll give me her address, sir. Save you the trouble."

"That won't do," he said. "I must give her a wigging, and there's this other case to be explained. No, you'd better stay where you are. Your father's a little better, and it won't hurt him to have you in the room awhile. Well, Mr. Ledra, I'll be back at two-thirty, and I'll bring Mr. Merriman."

12

I didn't know her address, but she knew mine. If she had wished to communicate with me, she could have done so. That she didn't do so seemed to me unbearably callous. There were moments when I believed that only some calamity was keeping her from me. It would not have surprised me to hear Dr. Mickleham say: "It's sad about that wee nurse. She's been killed by a tram." It was impossible to think that what had happened was, to her, casual, an afternoon's spree. I chanced to meet her years later getting off a tram in Cross Street. She was stouter and, I saw, wore a wedding ring. She said: "Hallo! You still about?" I blushed as a knight might do on meeting someone who knew that his scutcheon had not always been spotless. She laughed and said: "You are a funny one," and crossed the road, carrying a shopping-bag and looked irretrievably virtuous and domestic.

I went into a café and drank a cup of coffee, recalling the time when my father was ill and thinking what a lucky escape I had had. I had thought myself in love. For days I wore

56

myself out with longing, and Dr. Mickleham said: "You'd better take more exercise. Get yourself out into the air, boy. I'll have you on my hands next."

Yes. It had been a lucky escape. She could have got her claws into me. I was thankful that this first experience was with a flighty good-natured little fool. It was her good nature I preferred now to remember. She had taught me a lot, and especially she had taught me that I need not consider myself in love with every woman I met. In a week or two she was out of my system. I was able to think more calmly of Sylvia and Janet. The new nurse was no disturbance. She was middle-aged, spectacled and slightly bearded. A treasure, Dr. Mickleham assured my father. Mrs. Burnett shared this view.

13

That conference at which four of us were present—my father, Mr. Merriman, the doctor and I—was concerned with my future. Perhaps my father foresaw his end. Certainly he renounced his dreams. I was not to return to Cornwall. I was to go into the office at once and Mr. Merriman was to bring me up in the fear and admonition of the cotton trade.

"You will have the sense," my father said to me, "to put yourself entirely in Mr. Merriman's hands. Even after I am gone, though the business will then be yours."

"You're not gone yet," Dr. Mickleham said, more from a sense of duty, I imagine, than from conviction.

Be that as it may, my father had a second and fatal stroke a few days later. I found myself the sole heir of all he possessed. In his will he appointed trustees to administer the estate until I was twenty-one years old. That seemed to me a long way off, and it also seemed to me that there was no sense in remaining throughout those years in the Victoria Park house. I said so to my trustees at the first meeting we had after the funeral, and they approved this unexpected financial prudence. They found a tenant—a scientist who had come to Manchester University to work on some secret matter concerned with the war. He and his wife and children moved into the house, and we got a good rent for the place furnished. Mrs. Burnett went to live with a sister in Bootle, and I found lodgings—two rooms in a Withington back street.

Thus all was set for my entry into the cotton trade. On a Monday morning in June, 1917, I walked for the first time, as the boss of the whole concern, to the offices of Fred Byles and Ledra in Mosley Street.

CHAPTER FOUR

1

The cotton trade was to mean nothing to me, except that it gave me a financial competence. The years I spent in Mosley Street were dreary. The war had drained the young men from the staff, and the people I worked with were old, except Mr. Merriman's daughter Wendy. She was a girl of twenty, joint secretary to her father and me. Not that I found much work for her to do. I learned what I could from Mr. Merriman, and that was not much. For one thing, he obviously did not want me to learn. He enjoyed power, and now that my father was gone, all power was his. He was determined to keep it so. I must be just to Mr. Merriman. He worked hard, and he worked with understanding. "In these times of opportunity," he said, the dreadful opportunity that was unrolling itself at Passchendaele, "we must put our shoulders to the wheel," so that I could almost see his shoulders, which were broad enough, applied to the wheels of a gun-carriage stuck in the mud. I never liked him. There was a false friendship between us, and now and then he invited me to tea on a Sunday at his house in Altrincham. There he addressed his daughter fondly as Wendy. In the office he called her Miss Merriman. He had a great sense of propriety; and, I imagined, an idea that Miss Merriman, or Wendy, it hardly mattered which, might do worse than marry me some day. He spoke at one of these tea-parties of a young man of twenty, who had escaped conscription by being "indispensable" to the cotton trade, and who was just about to marry a girl of twenty-five. "What's a difference of five years?" he demanded. "No disparity, my dear George. No disparity at all." Miss Merriman was civilised enough to give me a wink behind his back. I rather liked her, but I had learned that liking need not cause sleepless nights.

I accepted a very small salary for my very small services, which were no more than a junior clerk's, and that, added to the rent I received from the Victoria Park house, kept me in reasonable comfort. I was glad when the day at the office was ended and I could dig in at my rooms at Withington, especially when winter came. The coal ration didn't see us through the week, but when there was enough for a fire I would invite my ancient widow-landlady to sit by it and get on with her knitting or reading while I read or wrote.

I wrote often to Mr. Chown, and in the winter of 1917-18 he sent me one of his infrequent answers.

" My dear George,—Hearing the other day that a consignment of beer had reached the Absolution, I went along there in the evening to listen to the wisdom of the ancients who like to think that their ancestors entertained the Phoenicians. I have never seen any evidence that they did, and, between you and me, the ancients, as usual, kept to themselves any wisdom they may chance to have. It is an illusion of romantic writers that the conversation in a local has a cut-and-thrust brilliance. Not in the Absolution, anyway. What I like about it is its somnolence. I like to drink from my can and listen to the same old tale being told for the hundredth time. It's almost as good as being in an Oxford senior common room. As for news, all I gathered was that young Joe Gomm has been discharged from the Army. That leg of his, it seems, can't be mended.

" I wandered home through a black and blustery night, the waves booming like guns on the Lizard, and I remembered that in your last letter you asked me to try and find that book by Trelawny which you left behind you. I am sending it on, though I advise you to treat with reserve many of the things the old ruffian says. However, what I want to tell you is this. While I was looking for the book I found in a drawer a cigar-box, and, hoping it might contain something fit to smoke, opened it. I needn't tell you what I found. You know very well, you thieving young rascal. The bracelet has a special significance for Sylvia, and I have sent it to her, with a specious lie about how I found it. The newspaper cuttings I have thrown into the fire. So, like a barbarian Jute or Saxon, I destroyed your shrine, or what I took to be some sort of shrine, and, finding a cigar elsewhere, spent a pleasant half-hour by my fireside, pondering the erotic or erratic emotions that caused you to set it up. I went to bed at 2 a.m. Altogether it was a perfect evening.

" Janet has joined her mother in London, where that absurd play continues to make its unheartening testimony to the taste of the British public. But don't let highbrows like me make too much of that. The British public which is fighting this war has a right to do almost any damned thing it likes in other directions.

" I take it we have not seen the last of you? That when the war-doubled ardours of the cotton trade can afford to let you go, we shall again see you for a time amongst us? Hector Chown."

I thanked Mr. Chown for the book, but said nothing about the shrine. What on earth was there to say that would not have seemed absurd?

Mr. Merriman was now using Father's room. And why not? He was doing Father's work as well as his own, and, so far as I could see, doing it splendidly. He observed protocol. If any member of the staff raised a point he would say: " I'll speak to you about it later. I must discuss it with Mr. Ledra."

This always made Mr. Ledra's ears burn, and Mr. Ledra was never quite sure whether the punctilio had a barb in it. He was sitting, this Mr. Ledra in whom I could never quite believe, at a small desk near Mr. Merriman's big one, and he hardly dared to raise his eyes lest he should intercept a wink passing between Mr. Merriman and the clerk. But it is unlikely that there was a wink. It would not have consorted with Mr. Merriman's dignity.

He introduced me to people on 'Change ; he showed me over our mill and explained what was going on there ; he took me to lunch and was careful to be always the one to say: " I must be back to the office. Can't dally in these days." I thought it strange that he never invited his daughter to join us at lunch, but he never did. Wendy at Altrincham was one thing ; Miss Merriman in the office was another.

It was in May of 1918, when I had been at work for a year, that he turned suddenly from his big desk to my small one and said: " Well, George, how are you liking it? How d'you reckon you're shaping?"

I said inconsequently: " I think that next month I'll take a fortnight's holiday."

" As you wish, lad. As you wish. It's only for you to say."

" When are you taking yours?"

" Me?" he said, surprised. " Good lord! I haven't taken a holiday since the war started and I sha'n't take one till it's over."

" Why not? I should think that Mr. Meagher could carry on for a fortnight?"

" Leave Ledra's to Meagher? Good lord, George, have a bit of sense."

Such sense as I had told me that Mr. Meagher was a competent person. It also told me that Mr. Merriman would not set aside his overlordship for even a fortnight. His resolution made me feel a feeble and worthless creature. " The fact is, Mr. Merriman," I said, " I'm not getting on at all, and, what's more, it doesn't seem to worry me. Should it?"

His prominent eyes looked at me in sadness and wonder. " You know," he said, " I began as a lad with the packers." I could read the unspoken implication. " And look at me now— the king, even though the uncrowned king, of this business. I can't understand a lad who doesn't want to forge ahead in the cotton trade."

That is what he was saying to me. I said: "Perhaps it would have been better if I'd begun at the bottom myself. That's how it always happens in the story books."

"Well," he conceded, "you have only to say the word."

I said the word. I was sick of paper work that I imperfectly understood and had no lively wish to understand. I wanted to move out of Mr. Merriman's orbit. The glance of his half-reproving, half-commiserating oily eyes was becoming more than I could bear. There was a growing tension between us, for, reasonably enough, he was boiling over with the wish to let fly at me. Indeed, one day the explosion all but came. I had gone out to lunch alone and dallied over my meal longer than I should have done but he been there to give the Quick March order back to the office. I knew that work that day was exceptionally heavy, and when I looked in he was up to the eyes. As I threw my hat on to a peg he stood up with a sudden violent gesture, his face red with anger. "Look here!" he shouted, "I should have thought that in times like these even you . . ."

He realised that he had gone too far. He stopped, and stood looking at me, fighting down his baffled rage. He wiped his forehead with his crimson handkerchief. The worst of it was that Miss Merriman was sitting at the little table she used when taking her shorthand notes. She paled and looked sorry for both of us.

I said: "Leave us for a moment, Miss Merriman," and she gladly scuttled away.

When the door was shut I said: "I'm sure that I deserve everything you were going to say to me, Mr. Merriman. But all the same, you mustn't say it. I'm sorry, but there it is. You mustn't."

He tucked his handkerchief neatly into his pocket and subsided rather than sat down. "I'm sorry, too, George," he mumbled.

I said: "I know that you're doing two men's work, and doing it well. I wish I could be more helpful. But I can't. There are people who take to this sort of work like ducks to water, and there are others who don't much fancy it but honestly do their best and make a good enough hand at it. I don't belong to either of those sorts of people. Why don't you ask Mr. Meagher to take over this desk of mine?"

He looked as though the suggestion would make him fly out again, and I said without too much malice: "Even Napoleon had to appoint marshals."

He mumbled: "I'll think it over." I don't suppose he did. Anyway, he carried on alone.

I touched the bell that called Miss Merriman into the room,

and when she was seated at her table I said: "Well, I'll leave you now. To-morrow I shall present myself in the packing department. Perhaps you'll give the necessary orders."

It was a lovely summer day. I took a train to Marple and walked on the hills.

That afternoon I lay in heather and listened to larks, and was deeply ashamed. I thought of the bloody business across the Channel. Words out of the last few years wrote themselves on the sky: Mons, Ypres, the Somme, Passchendaele. I tried to attach those flaming realities to the grey repellent reality of the cotton trade. I suppose economic thinking could have supplied the link, but I was incapable of economic thinking. I told myself angrily that I was incapable of any sort of thinking. But even without thinking one could accept what was plain to so many: that this job which Fred Byles and Ledra were doing had to be done. Well, then, like a soldier I would do it without understanding; but what was certain was that, in my present position of pretence and presumption, I was doing nothing.

So I went in a happy frame of mind to the packing department the next day, and I worked in other menial departments so long as the war lasted. Like Mr. Merriman, I even refused to take holidays. But I knew that this was not, and must not be, the old story of starting at the bottom in order to arrive at the top. One thing I had resolved on as I lay in the heather beyond Marple was that, when the war was over, my connection with the cotton trade would be over, too.

3

Shoved behind some crates in the packing-room I found the portrait of Fred Byles. It was a sizable thing painted in oils, unsigned. I never discovered who the artist was, but I had no doubt about the subject. My father had described Fred Byles to me often enough. However, I took it to Mr. Merriman and asked him if he knew who it was. "Fred Byles," he said shortly.

"How does it come to be knocking about in the packing-room?"

"God knows. It's always been knocking about ever since I can remember. It used to be in your father's room. I suppose he got sick of it, because then it appeared in the clerks' office. It's made the acquaintance of all the departments," he said, looking at me as if to suggest that I might with profit do the same. "No one seems to want the thing. Chuck it away."

I took it to my lodgings and hung it on the wall. The bold, even brazen, face pleased me. There was a carnation in the lapel of the jacket. I remembered my father saying that even during his trial Fred had worn a carnation. I smiled at his self-assured cockiness. He seemed to return the smile. I felt that I could easily have liked him.

4

I was seventeen years old when the war ended in late 1918. Captain Robert Meagher was twenty-five. He was demobilised in March of 1919, and when I first met him he was still in uniform: three stars on his shoulder-straps and the M.C. ribbon among the service ribbons on his chest. He was tall, dark and thin, with a close-clipped moustache. I met him in the office, where he had called to take his father out to lunch—quite an event in the life of the old man who was accustomed to stay at his desk and eat a few sandwiches of *ersatz* meat. All I had heard of Captain Meagher was a casual remark long ago by Mr. Merriman: "Meagher's got a boy at the front." I suppose the old man had mentioned my father's death and my presence in the office in letters to his son, for Captain Meagher seemed to know who I was. He said, with a faint ironic smile in his eyes: "Would the sleeping partner consent to join us?"

I was so tired of meeting nothing but boys and old men that I gladly did, and we got on well together. I asked him to join me in a walk on the following Sunday, and he said he would, as he had nothing better to do. "An odd situation for me to find myself in," he added.

It chanced to be an unusually good day for March, and we took a train into Derbyshire whose blessed accessible moors are one of the things that make it possible to live in Manchester. We lunched at a pub and walked all through the afternoon, and his tongue gradually loosened. I learned that he had joined the army as an infantryman and had transferred to tanks in time to be engaged when those grey iron monsters first wallowed into history at Fliers. "I wonder," he said, "what Douglas Haig thought of us? I believe that even the tanks didn't open his eyes. He probably thought of them as something that would at last smash an opening wide enough for his beloved cavalry to sweep through to victory. I saw him once or twice, riding about on his horse with his lancers behind him, their little pennons as pretty as paint. They'd have looked a treat in a Lord Mayor's show. No, I'm sure the old boy never saw the meaning of petrol."

"Look," he said some time later. "Drop this Captain Meagher business. My name is Bob."

He was not wearing uniform, but an old tattered tweed jacket and flannel trousers. He was Bob Meagher to me henceforth, and that afternoon for the first time I heard Bob Meagher on petrol, the theme-song of his life.

63

It is odd to think now that even then, in 1919, petrol was no worry to anyone. For example, during all our walking of that day we did not see a motor car, and though, soon afterwards, they began to appear in numbers that slowly increased, few people then guessed that this increase would swell with the fabulous speed that now makes us leap into a car in order to dash madly to some place where cars will not trouble us. Bob Meagher knew that this was coming. It is not only poets who have visions. As 1919 moved along we met almost every day. We took lunch together and we held long sessions in my room at Withington. One of these sessions lasted all night. I remember going out with him into the dawn. The trees were budding and a few birds singing. We waited at Fallowfield station for a tramcar which would take him into town. They ran about every hour through the night. As the vast contraption came lumbering and clanging towards us, the trolley-pole knocking blue sparks off the electrified overhead wire, he said: " George, these are prehistoric monsters, but they don't yet know it. In no time at all you will see big comfortable buses on all these services."

He shook my hand and said: " Well, wish me luck. I've taken a job in Coventry. I shall be off to-morrow."

I looked surprised, and he said with a grin: " That's not the end of the bad news. I'm engaged to be married. I give you three guesses."

I said: " The Queen of Sheba. Joan of Arc. Cleopatra."

" Wendy Merriman. But keep it dark. We haven't told the old man."

5

The old man wasn't looking on me with much favour. Now that the armies were being demobilised and men were drifting back to the office there seemed to me no sense in continuing my pretence of working. In two years' time I should be twenty-one, free from the shackles of trustees, of whom Mr. Merriman was the chief, and on the rare occasions when we met he brought this fact before me and urged the importance of my making a more serious effort to understand the business. He talked of the need for reorganisation, cutting out the old wood, as he called it, and bringing in younger men. " There's a heavy time ahead of us, George," he said. " The cotton trade's going to be busy with the switch-over to civilian consumption. We mustn't be hampered by old fogies like Meagher."

Mr. Meagher was no older than he was himself, and I rather liked him. I had found him willing to go out of his way to make things clear to me. He would say: " Well, Mr. Ledra, look at it this way," and go patiently on; while, in a similar moment, Mr. Merriman would be likely to say: "It's as plain as a pike-staff, isn't it? If you'd bothered to give the matter a bit of attention for the last few months . . ." and on and on, telling me nothing that I needed to know.

I said to him now: "Reorganise to your heart's content, but I refuse to allow you to reorganise Mr. Meagher out of the business."

His eyes bulged. "I have a duty towards you," he said, "and I should be failing your dear father if I did not discharge it. You are a minor and your affairs are in the hands of trustees. If we decided that it was in your interest that a more vigorous personality should replace Mr. Meagher, we should have no choice but to remove him."

I was getting very tired of Mr. Merriman. Moreover, in a recent letter to me Bob Meagher had written: "Wendy is on edge. She thinks the old man more than half guesses how things are. Anyway, he's very short with her." This sudden urgent need to remove Mr. Meagher could well be Mr. Merriman's riposte.

I said: "All the trustees have behaved very fairly to me, and I thank them. However, their services will end in two years' time. If one of them should use his authority to override what he knew to be a very dear wish of mine, it could be unfortunate for him."

Mr. Merriman was the only one of the trustees on whom I could, to put it vulgarly, get my own back. He knew this, and sensed a threat. He hated to give in, and sat at his desk, drumming his fingers on the blotting-pad. At last he said: "In your own interests I must keep a close eye on Meagher. I shall reconsider his case from time to time."

I accepted it as surrender. "Yes," I said, "do that. And, by the way, will you bring before the trustees the case of our house in Victoria Park. You know that Professor Williamson has just packed up and gone back to London. It's almost impossible in Manchester now to get a house for love or money. Put the place in the market. You'll get a good price."

He said surlily: "We have discussed it. We are aware of our responsibilities."

I didn't believe him; but the house was sold at a fantastic price to a couple of girls just down from Oxford who put themselves into the grip of a building society to find the money and opened a kindergarten school. I met the trustees in full conclave, pointed out that they had the right to advance money to me, and asked them to let me have the price of the house. I explained, truly, that I had been drawing next to nothing out of Fred Byles and Ledra and had lived through the war on scraping. If I could have a fair sum now I would draw on the firm no more and could still live comfortably till I came into my full inheritance. Three of them agreed. The fourth, Mr. Merriman, thought their business was to " nurse my capital," not squander it. I think it was my recent talk with him about Mr. Meagher that made it not too difficult for the others to persuade him to their view. The upshot was that for the first time in my life I had a fair sum of ready money. I bought myself a new suit and gave my landlady an electric kettle.

<h2 style="text-align:center">6</h2>

In that summer of 1919 I wrote to Mr. Chown and proposed myself as his guest for a week. It was presumptuous of me to do so, for I had not kept in touch with him since my father's death. A letter or two had passed between us since that time, and then I wrote no more. He now responded with a letter that was good-mannered rather than cordial. I travelled as usual by way of London, breaking the journey there; and I at last saw for myself what Mr. Merriman had been trying to drill into my head. "Don't you see," he used to say, " that we have entered into the Renaissance? War is behind us. There's no reason why it should ever come back."

"What's reason got to do with it?" I asked obstinately. "If war were a matter of reason, war wouldn't have come at all."

"George," he said sadly, "you *will* argue. It's a bad habit. Try to get out of it. I'm telling you that we are living in a time of renaissance. A renaissance of British trade. There's an immense opportunity before the firm. We must seize it with both hands."

I said: " If this firm provides opportunities, anyone can have them. As soon as the word is mine, I shall sell out."

He looked at me, startled. " You mean that?"

" I do."

He said no more, but I could see that something was stirring in his mind.

Travelling to London, I saw evidence of the Renaissance. I arrived at the station only a minute or two before the train started. I stood in the corridor all the way to London. Every seat was occupied, and every place for luncheon had been booked. England seemed to have turned into a nation of commercial travellers ; and I found it so the next day when I went on to Cornwall. I stood as far as Plymouth, and the corridors were as packed as the carriages. It was the same with the hotels. The station hotel at Paddington couldn't take me in, nor could half a dozen others. I was reduced to trying fusty and furtive-looking places in side streets, and at last found a fusty and furtive-looking bedroom in one of them. I was asked to pay in advance, and did so. A down-at-heel slattern in a cupboard labelled Office said: "You mustn't bring anyone in with you."

I gave her what I hoped was A Look, and got on to a bus which took me to Piccadilly Circus. I found the restaurants and cafés overflowing like the trains. I was not enjoying being a child of the Renaissance. I bought some fruit and took it into the Green Park. There, at last, I rested, with the roaring of Piccadilly at my back and the immortal view before me, closed by the outline of Whitehall upon the blue autumn sky. It was the first time I had sat in a London park. I ate my fruit, closed my eyes, and dozed.

I was awakened by a sudden clamour, and saw that I was not alone. Away from me at the far end of the seat was a young woman, so respectably dressed and modest-looking that I hesitated to speak to her. But I did. I said: "What on earth was that noise?"

"A police-car chasing someone," she said. "A smash-and-grab, I expect."

She smoothed creases out of her mauve cotton gloves, and said: "I don't know what London's coming to. All sorts of horrid people about. I suppose it's the war."

I said that I supposed it was.

"It was so peaceful," she said, "and then a thing like that breaks it up. You'd think that quiet people could be undisturbed in the parks." She looked distressed by the unseemliness of mortals. She came a little nearer to my end of the seat and sat down again, lifting one shapely leg over the other as she did so. She took a powder-puff out of her little mauve bag and delicately dabbed at her nose. "Still, the parks *are* quiet," she said, shutting her bag with a snap, "and if I could help to amuse you in any way? I know places . . ."

She looked like a curate's wife fresh from the altar. I felt pity for her, but no attraction. I shook my head.

"No hard feelings?" she said.

"Good lord, no."

She got up. "Perhaps some other time," she said. "I'm usually about in the afternoons."

I watched her go with a slow swaying walk and sit down on a bench a hundred yards away. An old gentleman had just settled there with a newspaper over his face. Five minutes later they walked away together.

The afternoon and evening were before me, and they must be got through somehow. Seeing that I was on the way to Mr. Chown I thought of Sylvia and Janet. In his letter of invitation he had not mentioned them, and I knew nothing of what they were doing. Since going back to Manchester, I had neglected them, as I had neglected Mr. Chown. I was able to think calmly of them both. The brief but complete escapade with that nurse had left me, I was pleased to think, knowledgeable about women, and I had decided in my wisdom that the pleasures of their company had been made too much of. Still, there was nothing else to do, so I went to a post office to look up Sylvia's telephone number. I found that she either wasn't on the telephone or was one of those people who keep their numbers out of the book. I decided to call on her. Feeling rich, with a bit of money in my pocket for the first time in my life, I made the journey in a taxi. There was no lift in that house, and there were a lot of stairs to climb to the top floor. It was this, I told myself, that made my heart beat rather rapidly, though this may have been accelerated by a sudden recollection of that first morning at Penruan when I watched the bathers come dripping out of the sea.

I pressed the bell-push timidly, and, as though he had been waiting for me as I had waited for that nurse on an evening which now seemed long ago, a stout, cross-looking man, dressed for the street, almost barged into me.

"What is it?" he demanded, as though he suspected me to be one of the commercial travellers of the Renaissance. There were soon to be plenty of them, with all sorts of trash to sell at the doors.

I asked him if Mrs. Bascombe still lived there, and he shouted back, already half-way down the first flight: "Never heard of her. Sorry. I must be off. Appointment."

I watched him disappear. No doubt a son of the Renaissance, rushing to seize some opportunity with both hands. I remembered the girl in the flat below, the girl with the soldier-lover. Perhaps she could tell me where to find Sylvia. I couldn't recall her name; but it certainly wasn't J. Washbourne-Wotherspoon, M.I.C.E., which was the name that confronted me pinned to the door.

Behind that house there is a bit of grass with a tree or two, and a seat or two, and there I sat, enjoying the autumnal calm and watching the sparrows hopping and chirping among a few yellow leaves, the first deserters from defeated summer.

It was so beautiful there. Not the beauty of Penruan, almost stifled in springtime with exotic flowers, almost deafened in winter with the clash of water warring with granite land. Not the austere beauty of Derbyshire moors. But the tall houses, and the homely urban birds, and the silken sky, even the susurration of traffic, muted and remote, combined to make a moment that was reassuring and caught at my heart as I contrasted it with my journey hither in the morning: a journey that had an unsettling urgency, feverish, and with a sense of a temperature rising to burst the thermometer.

It was a strange moment for me. I looked at it and asked myself what it was all about. Who was I to chuckle at Mr. Merriman's Renaissance and at its knights such as the one who had rushed out of Sylvia's old flat, wearing a black Homburg like a pit helmet and carrying a furled umbrella like a lance? I intended to sell out of Byles and Ledra, and that would make it possible for me to sit here and enjoy an oasis of metropolitan calm like this, keeping well clear of the yelping traffic, savouring only its faraway murmur. What right had I to do this, to perch myself above the battle, and to do it on the strength of victories which my father and grandfather and Fred Byles had won in the battle itself? Spenser's port after stormy seas was all very well; but was I entitled to the port without the hazards and endurances of the voyage?

I was startled by my own ruminations. Introspection had never troubled me before. I thought of the neat soft-spoken girl on the bench in the Green Park. Life can't be all honey, I said to myself. Everyone has to make a living somehow. She put me to shame.

And then, oddly, as though coming back from wandering, I was there again, on the seat, under the few autumn trees, enjoying the serenity. I thought of a phrase that had passed through my mind: " A few yellow leaves, the first deserters from defeated summer." I turned it over on my palate. I liked it, and took a small diary from my pocket and wrote it down. I didn't recognise the moment for what it was. I had decided on my career. I was to be a writer.

8

I telegraphed to Mr. Chown to say that I would travel the next day on the Cornish Riviera Express. To my surprise, Sylvia met me at Helston. Not, this time, Tiddy with his pony and cart, but Sylvia with a blue Buick. I had noticed from the newspapers that her play, which had survived the war, had died with the war's end. We shook hands, and she smiled and said: " You don't look a day older."

" Neither do you," I said. It was a deserved compliment; but

I was disappointed that, to her, I looked still a boy. I made some remark about the car, and she said: "It's only a second-hand old thing that I had to pay through the nose for. Even so, I can't use it much. No petrol. I hope that soon I'll be able to drive all the way down from London whenever I want to. As it is, I keep the thing here and use it very little. Get in."

I sat next to her, and as she took the driving wheel I noticed the bracelet on her wrist. I thought of the morning when I had found it on the beach. I thought of her wading like a goddess out of the sea. The car was small. My thigh was against hers. I trembled, and with a trembling joy I wished that the journey could last as long as the one I had taken with Tiddy. At least we should be alone together.

She said: "I promised to pick up Mr. Chipplewhite and take him home."

I was too disappointed to ask who Mr. Chipplewhite was. We were running down Coinage Hall Street, and she stopped outside a shop at the bottom. Jose Gomm was waiting on the pavement. On the fascia of the shop was painted: "Gomm: Antiques." So Chipplewhite was an absurd nickname. I felt resentful that Joe had earned the right to an intimate little joke. He was supporting himself with a walking-stick in each hand and managed to wave one of them in greeting. "I'll get into the back," he said. "More room to stretch 'em out." I remembered that during our only meeting he had said that Sylvia would visit him at the hospital at Hampstead, and I sensed an easy intimacy between them that made me feel a superfluous third party.

We were outside the town and Jose talked about the shop. It wasn't open yet. He was just pottering, getting it in order, trying to assemble a few things worth putting on show. There were lots of people, he said, under the weather after the war, finding it difficult to make ends meet. Soon they'd be selling up. No, he didn't expect to make a fortune out of it—just to keep the wolf from the door. There was a disability pension that would help. Sooner or later people who'd been mewed up by the war would begin to take holidays again. Plenty of customers.

I tried to get hold of the conversation. I apologised to Sylvia for having never thanked her for allowing me to use her flat when I passed through London a few years ago. I said that the girl in the flat below had taken pity on me. "Poor little thing," she said. "God knows what happened to her. She just disappeared. Her boy was killed at Passchendaele."

The thought of the hungry young lover kept me silent for a moment, then I asked: "How is Janet?"

"Quite incredible," she said. "Very beautiful. And she's stopped running away. She's a serious person."

"Is she at Penruan now?"

"Oh, no. At her own request," she said, underlining the words, "she's at school. The best school I could get for love or money."

I would have liked to hear more about Janet, but Jose Gomm leaned forward and spoke between our heads. "Sylvia," he said, "you ought not to wear that bracelet day in, day out. It's a thing for special occasions. D'you know who made it?"

"No. I know nothing about it except that it belonged to my mother. She'd never have it off her arm. Why? Who did make it, d'you think?"

Jose said: "Fabergé, I'd bet my boots. It's unsophisticated by his usual standards, but you can't mistake those snakes' heads. It's worth a pretty penny."

"All right, Mr. Chipplewhite," she said. "If you think you're going to put it in your shop window you're mistaken. I lost it once, and now I'm extra careful."

We were at the lodge gate. "You go in, George," she said to me. "I'll run Mr. Chipplewhite home, though that road is death on springs and tyres."

9

Mr. Chown received me with a cordial handshake. His skull was bare and meshed with deep wrinkles. He had given up trying to master the art of wearing a wig. He looked like a wise old lizard. He took me through to his big study where a log fire was burning, unnecessary but cheering. He had made some tea for me, and we sat down and drank it and ate dry biscuits. After a while he said with a smile: "Yes. It works."

I looked at him inquiringly, and he said: "I like to try it out with people. If you really like someone, there's no need for a lot of talk. You can sit happy and silent with them. So when I meet someone I haven't seen for years, I try out the atmosphere. Sometimes you're aware of a change. You've drifted in different directions. There's a chasm, and I'm getting rather old for jumping across chasms. I don't think I'll have to jump with you."

I said I was flattered to hear it. "You're the same idle young rascal as ever," he said, passing me the biscuit plate. "Your face hasn't formed into anything worth looking at. I suppose you're just loafing about, living on your father's money. Did he leave you much?"

"He left me four trustees, who give me a dole that keeps body and soul together. When I'm twenty-one I'll have the lot, such as it is."

"And then, I presume, your body will grow fat and your soul, whatever you mean by that vague word, will die."

71

I refused to be drawn. "Anyway," I said, "thank you for asking me down and for finding me as static as you had hoped."

"I didn't ask you down. You proposed yourself for a visit. And I haven't used the word static. That's your invention."

I said: "You're a cantankerous old devil, and I'm not your pupil any more."

"No," he said. "That's one burden God has lifted from my shoulders." He smiled and refilled my tea-cup. "All right, George," he said. "We shall get on together."

John Collier's portrait of Margaret Napier, which I remembered being in Sylvia's dining-room, was now facing me, hanging over the fireplace—the only picture in the room. Ophelia's long white arms were raised to her head, pressing her temples in a gesture of desperation and despair. I saw that one arm was encircled by a bracelet with serpents' heads. I dared make no comment on this to Mr. Chown, for with shame I remembered his finding the bracelet in the cigar-box. But he noticed the direction of my eyes and said: "That picture belongs to Sylvia, but she allows me to keep it here for memory's sake. Not that I need to be reminded of Margaret."

I was to wonder for a long time why he told me the story, but I knew at last. He and Margaret grew up in a poor and violent home. "I think," he said, "that it was our deep shared love for our mother that made us so close together. We suffered agonies in seeing her suffer, and we wept in one another's arms night after night."

Their father was a bailiff to a small Yorkshire landowner. They lived in a cottage on the estate, and both attended a village school. There was only a year between them in age. "We toddled to school together, and came home together, and worked at our books together, and cried our eyes out together when my father knocked my mother about."

This was the spectre that haunted their youth—violence. Their father was the son of a baronet of ancient vintage, and he was the shame and despair of his family. He was born cruel. He kicked the dogs and tormented the horses; he was sent home from school after school for knocking boys about unmercifully. He was packed off to Canada and came home again, tougher and more unruly than ever. His father and elder brothers were at their wits' end about him, and then he solved their problem by marrying a parlour-maid in his father's house. This was the mother of Mr. Chown and Margaret Napier. His father offered to stake him in a small farm. He told him to go to hell—he would manage his own life.

He became a bailiff, and the odd marriage was a success of a sort to begin with. Then one night when Mr. Chown was five years old his father kicked him. "Perhaps," he said to me," I

72

had inherited something from him. I don't know. But I kicked him back. I was wearing hob-nailed boots."

He seemed to recall the moment with satisfaction, but added: "It wasn't a wise thing to do. He flamed. He nearly killed me."

The mother intervened, and was knocked almost senseless.

It was as though this episode were the shifted stone that loosens the torrent. "For years after that," Mr. Chown said, "life was hellish. He never laid a hand on Margaret, but my mother and I seemed never to be unbruised. Of course, it got talked about. My school-master saw me coming to school black-and-blue day after day, and, though my mother was shy about showing herself in the village, she had to go there sometimes and people talked."

When it had gone on for a long time, the school-master and the parson called at the cottage and remonstrated with the father. It had no effect, and then they laid a complaint before Bailiff Chown's employer. He, too, remonstrated; "but he was a weak man," Mr. Chown said, "and my father was an excellent bailiff whom he didn't want to lose. Again and again he threatened to sack him if he didn't mend his ways, but he never did."

He looked up at the portrait. "Poor Margaret!" he said. "I was a tough little brute and could put up with it. She suffered more than any of us. How many times I've seen her as she is in that picture—her hands to her head, desperate but helpless.

"How on earth can you explain a man like that?" he asked me. "It wasn't drink. He never touched a drop. It was pure devil, and I don't suppose he wanted to be inhabited by the devil any more than I should. Sin is a mystery that I've never professed to understand. After one of his smashing attacks on us my father would sit smoking by the fireside, not speaking, brooding, obviously suffering as much as we were."

We saw Sylvia go past the window on her way down to the house. He lit his pipe and sat brooding as his father had done. At last he said: "He released us—and I am sure in my bones that he saw it like that and *released* us from his devil—by committing suicide. I was fourteen."

He paused again, puffing at his pipe like a stolid old Indian brave. "So I'm a cantankerous old devil, am I? Well, perhaps the ancestry explains it. However, at that moment I knew nothing about my ancestry beyond my father and mother. But there it was. One of my grandfathers was an aristocrat, the other was a pig-breeder. Fortunately, the pig-breeder was dead, and so it was the other who stepped in. The estate where my father was bailiff was in the West Riding of Yorkshire. My grandfather's estate was in the North Riding. I never met him, and I've never met my nephew who is the present baronet. The point is that York is a convenient meeting-place. My grandfather wrote to my mother and asked her to go there. She came back glowing like an angel. I don't think I've told you that she was a beautiful woman." He looked up again at the portrait. "No," he said, "Margaret was not a bit like her. She was beautiful, too, but it was a different sort of beauty. If ever you care to look at it, there's a portrait by Reynolds in the National Gallery of one of the eighteenth-century Chown girls. 'Mrs. William Handaside,' it's called. Now that's Margaret to a T when she was looking happy."

After a moment he said: "My mother was glowing because Sir Richard Chown had taken over the financial responsibility for us children. We went to live in Bradford to get some schooling. It was an extraordinary change. We'd been born in Wharfdale and had known nothing but fields and clean streams, and now we were in one of a row of tiny houses, with ten square yards of barren garden and town, town, town, town pressing us in. But, by God, old Keeling made up for all of it!"

He looked at me as though the name Keeling ought to sound a trump in my ear. "Who was he?" I asked.

"He was headmaster of the Bradford Grammar School, and out of that school went a boy named Delius, who was to be heard of as a musician, and a boy named Dyson who was to become Astronomer Royal, and half a dozen painters, to say nothing of novelists and poets. And a cantankerous old devil named Hector Chown. He leathered hell out of us and learning into us. He taught me to love Greece."

I could sense in his voice the lift of the heart that had come when the shadow over their lives was blown away. The Grammar School was a day school, and so was the Girls' High School in Manningham Lane that Margaret attended. And thus every night they were at home, and home now was without tears. "What with school and home," he said surprisingly, "I knew what men felt like who lived in the Renaissance. Energy and joy."

He got up. "We'd better go and see what Sylvia's up to. She expects us to eat with her to-night. And there's nothing much left to say. From there on it was more or less a straight line. I wasn't much of a burden on my dear baronet. I was a devourer of scholarships. I was up at Oxford, and Margaret was in her first play when our mother died. Have you brought a dinner jacket?"

"I haven't such a thing."

"All right. Let's go as we are. She'll have to put up with hoi polloi."

74

We didn't dine in the big hall as we had done on that faraway night when I was first at Penruan. But we drank sherry there, and I looked about me for signs of some forward march in Sylvia's enterprise. Perhaps some new bit had been added, but nothing struck me. Except Sylvia. She always had a taste, I was to find, for rich dark silks. Crimson at that first meeting. Blue now. A deep midnight blue, with touches here and there of starry silver.

Mr. Chown apologised for our appearance as though we had presented ourselves at a St. James's levee in plus fours and nailed brogues. "George has brought no dinner suit. I have a spare one, but I ask you to imagine what he would have looked like if I had lent it to him."

She smiled and said: "He's very welcome as he is. I think he's improved with the years."

"Yes," said Mr. Chown. "The years away from me."

We went through to the dining-room, and Mrs. Tiddy, who brought on the dishes, seemed surprised to see me. "Oh, you're back, are you?" she said. "'Ow are you feelin'?"

I said that I was feeling very well, and asked her to give my greetings to her husband.

"'E never expected to see *you* agen," she assured me. "'That's the last of 'im,' he said, when 'e came back from givin' you my muffler. Did you wear it?"

"Yes, Mrs. Tiddy. It probably saved my life."

"For the time bein'," she said darkly. The years with Tiddy had clearly not been in vain.

"Well, eat that," she said. "A bit of good food won't 'urt you meanwhile. Tiddy never liked the look of your neck. 'E says it's too thin."

When she was gone Mr. Chown asked: "Why do you bring that grisly spectre to our feasts, my dear?"

"Because she's all I can get," Sylvia said frankly. "It'll be different some day."

"What makes you think that? What makes you think you can induce trained servants to come and work for you here? The nearest town Helston, miles across a moor."

"You'll see," she said confidently.

"It's just a dream," he warned her. "Sell it all up while you can—if you can. Sell it all except the lodge. Leave me that to die in. Or sell that, too. I can end my days at the Absolution. One could do worse."

She smiled at him. "I want to *rescue* something," she said. "This place was very lovely. Why shouldn't it be lovely again?"

"You might as well try to rescue the Acropolis," he said, " or rebuild the theatre at Epidaurus and put on plays there. Remember your Belloc:

*A lost thing could I never find
Nor a broken thing mend.*

There are things that are lost, things that are broken, beyond hope. Better be like me and live in a dear world that once was lovely."

"You'll see," she said again.

"Look at that stinking motor car that you've just bought," he said. "What's that got to do with this? Can't you see what it's a symbol of? If you can't, you're blind. Don't try to live in two worlds at once."

"I could live in a dozen worlds," she assured him. "And why not?"

"Live in one like me," he said. "And best of all, let it be a dead one that can never disappoint you."

She let the matter drop, and I inquired about Janet.

"I hoped," she said, " that Janet would be with us for the holidays. She may even yet give us a little of her time. The trouble is that she believes her time to be valuable. As you know, George, she spent a lot of it running away from one school after another. Well, she's had a change of heart. At the school where she now is she has met a girl named Medea Hopkins. Medea's mother is like my uncle here—a learned old woman."

"I'm not a learned old woman," Mr. Chown protested. "And, what's more, Mrs. Hopkins is not a learned old woman. With pain and sorrow I read one of her books."

"These books," Sylvia explained, " are written for young people, and they are about life in ancient Greece."

Mr. Chown snorted. "They are about nothing of the sort. Judging from the sample I came across, they are about life in Golder's Green, with the Co-op shoppers wearing white robes finished off with a key pattern in gold."

"You scholars are always jealous of one another," Sylvia twitted him. "Anyway, I'm not competent to judge. All I can say is that I met Mrs. Hopkins at a half-term gathering of parents—than which there is no more grisly function known to man. She was paddling through the dew of the playing field, wearing sandals of goatskin. They were hair-side out, and if you had looked only at the feet you would have imagined an old Friesian cow."

Mr. Chown swigged his wine. "Cows have hoofs," he said. "You are incapable of exactitude."

76

"You know what I mean," Sylvia persisted. "Her big toes looked both comic and revolting. I could have excused even that. But fancy calling an innocent child Medea. I'd rather be called Mabel, and that's a pretty big concession."

"Your mind is a rag-bag," Mr. Chown said. "I've told you that cows have hoofs. They don't have toes, big, little, revolting or enchanting."

Mrs. Tiddy brought in the coffee, and announced: "I'm off. I'll clear up in the morning. I must get back and let Tiddy know that Mr. Ledra is still with us."

The room was dusking. Sylvia lit candles on the table and went on: "Well, this Medea is a bit older than Janet—not a bad-looking child apart from protruding teeth and spectacles. Her teeth are wired with gold and her eyes swim towards you like fish coming to the side of a bowl."

Mr. Chown said to me: "How well these actresses speak their lines. One can almost believe what Sylvia is saying."

"I had plenty of opportunity to observe," she went on. "Throughout that week-end I was not allowed five minutes alone with my own child."

"All that Sylvia is trying to tell you," Mr. Chown explained patiently, "is that she is jealous because her daughter has at last succeeded in making a friend at school. About time, too. The child has been scandalously brought up, doing nothing but peck at crumbs, with no understanding of the loaf. Rather like you, George. Well, the witch appears now to be bewitched, and probably by a quite charming and good-looking older girl. I don't think Janet would fall for anyone who resembled Sylvia's notion of Medea. Janet's notion, as I gather from her letters, is of a serious girl whom she wants to be like. But these infatuations pass, and there's plenty of time for Janet to return to her usual irresponsibility. Meantime, she's spending the holiday at Mrs. Hopkins's place in Norfolk."

"Well," Sylvia said, "now that the judge has summed up, let's go and sit on the terrace. There's a full moon."

"There's ague in my bones," Mr. Chown said. "I'm far beyond the years when sitting on a cold terrace in the light of a dead world could give me pleasure. If you insist on doing it, wrap yourselves up."

11

When he was gone I carried two wicker-chairs out to the terrace. Sylvia put on a warm coat over her silk dress and took rugs from an old chest in the hall. There was a duck-board to keep one's feet from contact with the stone with which the terrace was paved. We sat side by side watching the moon, which was not yet high enough to be bright. It was a huge copper gong. The sea, that could scream and rage like a fishwife, was all but dumb. Only the lightest lisp of the ebb stole up from the cove, through the wooded valley, and touched our senses with a whisper.

Sylvia said: "Let me be fair. That Medea child is quite good-looking. She doesn't even wear spectacles. But she's too earnest for me. I hope Janet doesn't become over-fond. It's a danger to all the women in our family. My mother did it, and I did it. But with us, it was men."

"Mr. Chown has been telling me something about your mother," I said. "About the tough time he and she had when they were young."

"So far as she goes, it was not only when she was young. When their mother died they were left stranded. But he had his Greeks. Did you hear his advice to me to-night? Live in a dead world that can never disappoint you. I can't do that, and my mother never could. Oh, you can't imagine what she was like—so alive and vital. She once told me that that was the first thing Arthur Craven ever said to her. He'd seen her acting. It was only some small bit, but he was fascinated and wanted to paint her. He wangled a meeting, and that's what he said: 'You're so alive!' I don't know what became of that painting. He painted her again and again."

I had heard of Craven, and I knew what he looked like. In memoirs of that time his portrait often appeared. He was a very famous painter, and sculptor, too. As she spoke I could recall that distinguished but weary-looking countenance, white-bearded. I said so, and added that I supposed he was much younger when he met Margaret Napier. And why Napier? Had she married so young?

"Oh, it was just a stage-name that she took," Sylvia said. "She disliked Chown on a play-bill. And Arthur Craven wasn't young. He was seventy when they met, and she was nineteen."

The moon had turned small and golden-bright, and I watched a coaster out there treading over the sequinned carpet that trembled on the water. I listened to the tale of how this all-but-child was flattered by the attentions of the famous old man, who had had much experience of that sort of flattery, and of how she found herself soon living in the house in St. John's Wood, going on with her own work, but being, in the eyes of the curious, Craven's mistress.

"But she wasn't, you know," Sylvia said. "She often talked to me about that time. She enjoyed it. She enjoyed the old man's courtly manners, and the company she met at his dinner parties, and the fame that was reflected from him upon her. But that's as far as it went. It was a strange affair, a spectral love. It was her beauty and youth that he adored and never tired of painting. I suppose that's one way of reaching back after one's own youth. It lasted about five years, and she was, by then, on the road to being as famous in her line as he was in his."

She lit a cigarette and was silent for a moment, and then said: " I don't know how long this could have gone on. They were both getting a good deal out of their association and neither was interested in what people thought. So there's no reason why it shouldn't have gone on and on. But then she fell in love. She left Arthur Craven when I was on the way."

I asked in my innocence: " Didn't he know that she had married? "

" She hadn't married."

" Who . . .? " I began, but that was a question I had no right to ask.

However, Sylvia said: " Who was he? If I knew that I'd be able to decide whether to tell you or not. But she never told me. She said there was every reason why I shouldn't know."

She got up and said: " You'd better be off to bed. Old Socrates loathes being disturbed once he's got to sleep. Good night, George."

I said: " Good night, Sylvia."

I got out the name—the first time I had used it—with such difficulty that she smiled in the moonlight. " You are a funny boy," she said.

I didn't disturb Socrates, for I found that the window of my room in the lodge was open. I heaved myself through, and as I was getting into bed I was puzzled by the thought that I had heard those words before. *You are a funny boy*. Of course? It was what *that nurse* had said to me.

12

I didn't see much of Socrates, as Sylvia and I called him thereafter between ourselves, for his routine was rigid. He worked in his study in the mornings, walked alone in the afternoons, and dined with me and Sylvia, except for an occasional evening when he enjoyed what he called the rude Doric of the customers' conversation at the Absolution. The only time we saw much of one another alone was at tea, which he prepared himself and ate in his study. On an afternoon when the weather had turned blustery, and the sea was booming, and in the little valley the leaves rained down, dithering in bewildered hosts, he put a match to his fire. It blazed like a beacon to warn us of invading winter. He squatted on the mat in front of it, toasting muffins. In that attitude, and with the firelight gleaming on the shrivelled skin of his head, he looked like an old toad. It was difficult to believe that he and the lovely woman pictured on the wall above him were brother and sister. There was a long table, not more than eighteen inches high, on the hearthrug, and we sat on the floor with our food on this, and ate with the welcome warmth playing upon us.

I said: " Sylvia was telling me something about her mother the other night."

He munched his greasily buttered muffin and cocked his head askew up at the picture. " A fat lot she knew about her," he said.

" You all deal in mysteries," I complained, and he said: " Every living being is dealing in mystery, but most of 'em are too dense to know it."

I wasn't in a mood to be put off by philosophic platitudes, and said: " I know next to nothing about Sylvia herself. She's an actress—not a very good one, you say—and she's Janet's mother. I've known the three of you off and on now for a few years, and that's all I know about her."

" What is there to know about *her*?" he demanded, still looking at his sister's image as though comparing Aphrodite with a witch on a blasted heath. After a moment he said: " All the women in my family are mad, you know. But there's a difference. In some, it's a glorious madness, in others—well, an intelligent being can't understand it. Sylvia, for example, married at seventeen. If she hadn't, I suppose we shouldn't have had this nonsense about restoring a ruin. Bascombe was twenty years older than she was, and he fortunately died when they'd been married for only three years. I had no use for him. A barbarian. Janet was two when he died."

The muffin he was toasting singed and smelled. He looked at it with satisfaction, as though it were the insufferable Bascombe getting his deserts. He flicked it off the fork with a knife and it went up in flames. He said: " All I can say about Bascombe is that he came from a long line of money-makers. He made none himself. He was incapable even of that. He was notoriously unfaithful to Sylvia. I suppose that when she married him she mistook the schoolgirl gush of her feelings for love. But she'd certainly got over that before he died. The only good thing to be said for him is that he died without making a will, and so she's very rich and can play about with things like the house that's round her neck."

He seemed glad to have got Mr. Bascombe off his chest, and I decided to let that sleeping dog lie.

It was soon after this that Janet turned up with Medea Hopkins. No one was expecting them. Miss Hopkins was a tall, grey-eyed, grave girl, with promise of beauty. But it was clear to me that, with her about the place, there was no room for me.

Janet was absorbed in Medea and Sylvia was absorbed in Janet, and Mr. Chown became absorbed in the Absolution's beer. I took occasion to bid them all good-bye and returned to Manchester.

CHAPTER FIVE

1

In 1922 I was twenty-one years old, no longer that legal non-entity, a minor.

I walked down to the office, and that was something I hadn't done often of late. When I entered the room that Mr. Merriman and I were again sharing, now that my adventures into " beginning at the bottom " were ended, he said: " Many happy returns of the day to you, sir."

Sir! I wouldn't have been more surprised if he had said Sir George. But there was no reason for surprise. I should have known that Mr. Merriman was a man who, as he would have said, kept his place, and that he would methodically know that this was the day when his long service as chairman of my trustees ended.

He had risen from the chair at the *smaller* of the two desks, and walked over to the larger one, pulling out the chair for me to sit down. It was an act, but he played his part well, looking heavily responsible, like an elder statesman inducting the younger Pitt to Prime Ministerial office.

I dropped into the chair that he had been warming and said: " Sit where you've been used to sitting, Mr. Merriman. I hope you'll go on sitting there. I was a minor yesterday and am not one this morning, but I didn't wake up on the stroke of midnight feeling an experienced cotton merchant."

Mr. Meagher knocked and entered, and he, too, wished me many happy returns of the day. I got up and shook his hand, which I had forgotten to do with Mr. Merriman, who looked at him sourly. " Yes, Mr. Meagher? " he asked.

He had always been afraid of Mr. Meagher's efficiency, and now, I knew, he was pretty near to hating him, for they were related by marriage. If you touched the bell for the secretary there was no Wendy to answer it. There was a girl who had been a sergeant in the W.A.A.C.s and had a forbidding air, as though she might at any moment bark you to attention. Wendy was Mrs. Bob Meagher, and Coventry was a long way off.

Bob Meagher was an insatiable correspondent. Every week there was at least one letter, and often enough there were three. Like so many hard-headed men, he had a touch of nauseating

81

sentimentality—the touch which had caused Mr. Merriman to call his daughter Wendy. Bob spared me nothing of Wendy's excellence, and with these epistles were enclosed letters to Wendy herself, which I privily conveyed to her. "It's not surprising," Bob wrote, "that she dare not have letters addressed to her at the house or the office. The old man would be down like a ton of bricks, and who can wonder at that? I know that if I had a daughter like Wendy I'd be pretty alert about anybody who tried to walk in and snatch her away." And so on, Wendying his weary way through page upon fatuous page.

I was glad when the thing came to a crisis just before my autumn visit to Mr. Chown. "Well, George, I've taken the bull by the horns and told old Merriman how it is between me and Wendy. I've been frank with him and made it clear that if we marry now we'll have a thin time! Good God! These post-war prices! I've been making a few inquiries. You wouldn't believe what it costs to buy a dust-pan and brush, and as for sheets and blankets! Well, anyway, I've told old Pop-eye that she'll live thin for a bit, but that she has prospects of living like a duchess in the long run. Or words to that effect. And I mean it. Even as it is, I'm earning enough to keep her in a decent little two-up and two-down, and with Wendy that were paradise enow . . ." And so on. Four pages of Wendy.

I decided to be regular in my attendances at the office after this reached me. It would be worth while to observe Mr. Merriman's reaction. There was some trifling thing I wished to dictate to the secretary, and I touched the bell. Mr. Merriman said: "Sorry, George. You'll have to wait till this afternoon. Miss Merriman hasn't been at all well of late. This morning she was quite exhausted and I packed her off straight away to my sister in St. Anne's. A bit of sea air should put her right. I've asked a secretarial agency to send us a temporary girl. She's due after lunch."

"What a nuisance to have two of them away," I said, for Mr. Meagher was at home with influenza.

"I don't think our Mr. Meagher's absence should stop the works," he said shortly.

"How is that son of his getting on?"

"What should I know about his son? He's a mechanic somewhere, isn't he?"

I let it drop. "Well," I said, "I hope Miss Merriman will soon be back. She knows her job inside out."

"She should, with the training she's had. Shall I send her a message from you?"

Still his hopeless dream, I thought; and said: "Yes, do."

But Wendy never got my message and never reached St. Anne's. She rightly interpreted the purpose of her exile and bought a ticket to Coventry.

"I couldn't believe it," Bob wrote. "She'd just arrived at the door of my lodgings when I got home from work. Oh, George! Do you know what it feels like to be snatched suddenly from misery to bliss? . . ." And again on and on.

Well, that put paid to Mr. Merriman, and it was not surprising that he and Mr. Meagher, who were now joint grandfathers to one Jocelyn Meagher, did not feel like jocund brothers-in-arms.

2

There was to be published soon a book called *Lancashire for Sale*. Cotton boomed. Financiers nipped in and bought up mills, and, as the boom continued, were able to sell them again at great profit almost overnight. Gentlemen from London, who owned race-horses and music-halls, and drank champagne, and did many other things that needed money, saw how easily it was to be picked up in Lancashire on this buy to-day and sell to-morrow system. And when the boom ended there was this hopelessly over-capitalised trade, tottering towards a bleak dawn which did not fail to appear.

The mill owned by Fred Byles and Ledra was not a major plum to tempt these greedy gobblers. But it was a plum of sorts. It was in 1924 that I heard of a bite. It was a warm June day, and even Mr. Merriman was in an expansive mood. He had invited me to join him at lunch in the Midland Hotel, a costly caravanserai that he did not often visit. He had recently confounded me and everyone else in the office by marrying again. "I'm a man that likes responsibility," he said. "I must have someone under my wing. There was my mother to begin with, when I was beginning to work up from the bottom, and then there was my wife, and there was Wendy. Did I ever tell you, George, she was named after a girl in a play by a man called Barrie? I forget what the play was, but it was homely. There was a man in it who lived in a dog-kennel.. I thought that a bit daft, but, yes, on the whole it was a sound English homely home. And there was this girl Wendy. And don't forget: after that I took you under my wing. I suppose it's something protective in my nature. I can't help helping other people. So now there's Paddy."

It was to this new burgeoning of Mr. Merriman's protective soul that his expansive mood was due, I thought. He was lashing out a bit. He had bought, for the installing of Paddy, a larger house than he had shared with Wendy. He had even been known to say "Good morning, Meagher," to his pet abomination; and now, in the Midland, he dallied and ordered coffee. "Let us then be up and doing" was, for the moment, forgotten. I tested his mood by inviting him to take a brandy with me over the coffee, but at that he shook his head. "And I advise you, too, George, to lay off it," he said, enfolding me in a protective wing. "Your father never touched it."

I ordered brandy.

Suddenly he said: "George, I've had an offer."

I had not been taking much notice of what was beginning to happen in the cotton trade, and, for all I knew, it might have been an offer to star in the Moss Empire music-hall circuit. I could only say: "Oh."

"Yes," he said, and leaned towards me confidentially. "See yon chap?"

I saw yon chap, and didn't like him. He looked slick enough to be able to split a five-pound note into two.

"He's not a principal," Mr. Merriman said. "He's only an agent, acting for chaps in London. Just seeing what there is to be picked up."

The chap got up, passed by our table and slapped Mr. Merriman lightly on the back. "Don't forget," he whispered. "The offer's open till the 25th. Consult your principals."

Mr. Merriman's bulbous eye gave me the only wink that ever passed between us. "Principals!" the wink said. "What a lark! He little thinks that you're the principal. And, indeed, looking at you, whoever *could* think such a thing?"

I was abashed.

"I've told him where he gets off," Mr. Merriman said, "and I've told him where all the likes of him can get off, too. I'm a cotton man: always have been, always will be. We don't want that sort. We can manage our own business, and if we don't, then sooner or later so much the worse for us."

Give him his due: he was an honest man. I had heard my father say that he couldn't imagine the place without Mr. Merriman; and on my behalf he had, through difficult years, been a watchful steward. To him, the Lancashire cotton trade stood up, monolithic, world-famous for honourable conduct and sound goods, with never a rascal or shady dealer in it; and I am sure he would rather have died than give an inch to the rats who now were gnawing away towards its undermining.

I said: "I'm not surprised, Mr. Merriman, that you smile at the idea of my being principal of the firm. It's you who should be that."

For the first time, I saw him moved. He was unable to answer for a moment; then he said: "Come, George, you're young, and perhaps a bit foolish. But you'll learn. I'll be there to keep an eye on you. After all, there's tradition behind you. Your father, your grandfather. Why, lad, cotton's in your blood."

If it literally had been, I could not have felt more uncomfortable. I knew that I was not interested in cotton and that I never would be; and I somehow felt, too, that, in this improbable setting of the Midland's glittering French Restaurant, we had reached a crisis.

I said: "How would you like to own Byles and Ledra? I mean for me to walk out altogether?"

He looked thunderstruck, then said: "Between you and me, George, it's been the dream of my life—to rise from the bottom right to the top."

I said: "Leave out the fancy stuff that I hear some people talking about. What would you say, as an experienced cotton man, the thing was worth—the whole thing: the mill, the marketing business, everything."

"Nay, George, you can't jump like that, even under the influence of brandy. It'd have to be thought about. It'd take some working out, you know."

I got up. "Well, work it out. And when you see where you are, let me know."

3

Mr. Merriman was what they call a warm man. He had never thrown his money about, and he had no expensive vices. In his capacity of trustee, he had often pointed out to me the divine arrangement by which capital produced interest. No man and no business, he said, should ever touch a penny of capital. Where a firm was concerned, the profits of the capital should be what he called ploughed back. As for the individual with capital, he could, I was instructed, spend every penny of the interest so far as Mr. Merriman was concerned, but the wise, of whom he hoped I was one, would spend only the necessary minimum and use the rest as an addition to profit-earning capital.

This is what he had done himself. He might, I sometimes thought, have given Wendy more than the compulsory minimum of education, for she was an intelligent girl who would have profited from it. As it was, she was the obvious example, long under my eye, of the way his system worked. A broad education was not strictly necessary, as he saw it. Cotton was the only subject in which he had educated himself. If you gave him half a chance, he could talk to you for hours about it, ranging from the depredations of the boll weevil to the African native taste for flamboyant designs in printed goods and the importance of Indians' loin-cloths. "Let the Indians take to trousers," he once said, "and Bradford will smile, but Manchester will weep."

It is not surprising that he had accumulated a bit of capital, but he hadn't enough to buy Byles and Ledra. His Paddy had money, too, and she was a woman who shared his outlook. But even with the addition of her money, there still was not enough. Mr. Merriman consulted the bank manager who had been one of my trustees and who therefore knew how Ledra's stood. He was satisfied that it was a sound firm, and cotton was booming, and it could well have been in his mind that Mr. Merriman wanted to buy in order to sell out again at the fancy prices that were agitating so many minds. In any case, the bank found the rest of the money; the legal formalities were gone through; and by the autumn of that year 1924 I was a man of means and Mr. Merriman had fulfilled his life's ambition. He was at the top.

I did not intend to stay in Manchester. I went to the office to say good-bye to one or two people, and ended up with Mr. Merriman himself. He sat now, with no twinges of conscience, at the big desk, like a king on a throne, or a striving mountaineer surveying from a summit the valley out of which he had climbed. He wished me luck in whatever I chose to do, and said: "Paddy and I thought of a little farewell dinner at the Midland—just the three of us; but we decided against it. You must take the will for the deed, George. It would have looked a bit ostentatious, and then, too, we've got to think of the pennies."

Paddy was with him heart and soul. They had sold the big house into which they had hardly moved. No ostentation. They were in just such another little suburban house as the one in which I had occasionally taken Sunday afternoon tea with Mr. Merriman and Wendy. Somehow I felt a twinge of shame, as though I had pushed them into it.

I went out into the mild autumn weather. It was strange to be walking the Manchester streets without even a pretence of having some commitment to the city. My aimless wandering brought me to the doors of the Technical College just as the students were coming out from the morning session. I had been over the place with Mr. Merriman, who had suggested that I might enrol as a student and learn something of the technical basis of making cotton goods. And now here were those who were learning that and so much else. I stood there watching them: among the many English a few Indians, a few negroes, a few Chinese. "What happens," I had asked Mr. Merriman, " when all these guests of ours learn how to do what we are now doing for them?"

"They never will," he said. "They haven't got it in 'em. They haven't got the tradition. They may learn to pick up a few of our crumbs, and they're welcome to that."

"Don't you think," I said, " that a nation, like an individual, may start at the bottom and get to the top?"

He gave me a sharp look and said: "There's only one top, and Lancashire is on it."

I was becoming unbearably depressed and restless. At Ledra's I had been like a dinghy tied up behind a ship, having nothing to do with where the ship was heading for, but, at least, attached. Now the painter was cut. I was adrift.

I went into a tea-shop, bought a roll and a cup of coffee, and then sat smoking a pipe. A man sitting opposite leaned suddenly across the marble table-top and said earnestly: "Now take Lombroso . . ."

I rose and fled, disturbed by the thought of the strange labyrinths in which some being, within an arm's reach, may be wandering.

Instead of Lombroso, I took a prosaic tram, moved to a sudden resolution. I put my few things into a handbag, paid my landlady a month's rent, bade her good-bye, and boarded the next train to London.

4

One half of me was determined to be the cautious citizen who would earn Mr. Merriman's approval. But I had another half. All through my life these two George Ledras have been at loggerheads within me. And no doubt there are a few more whom I haven't clearly recognised. Here is the George Ledra who will suddenly cut his smoking by an ounce a week, not because he is hard up but because a bit of pettifogging self-denial is the sort of thing that this George goes in for. The other George, without even asking the price, will enter a Bond Street picture-dealer's shop determined to have a picture that has taken his fancy. This is the George who despised Mr. Merriman, remembering an occasion when, improbably, pictures were being discussed, and Mr. Merriman said: "I'm not a picture-buying man. If I were, I'd never buy a picture unless I were sure that I could sell it at a profit any time."

I knew nothing about London hotels, and on that day of my sudden flight from Manchester the cautious George directed my steps to the dingy and disreputable-looking doss-house in which I had stayed once before. This was to be my base while I looked about for a flat.

I had kept in touch with Mr. Chown and he had given me Sylvia's address. She was now appearing in a play called *All Saved but Honour,* and the day after my arrival I booked a stalls seat at the theatre. The spendthrift George was nauseated by the threadbare and down-at-heel place he was staying in, and decided to eat out before going to the play. I hadn't much in the way of clothes and passed the afternoon in putting this right. I knew nothing of Savile Row and suchlike places, and apart from that I wanted a dinner-jacket outfit for the evening. I went mad in a ready-to-wear shop in Regent Street and bought this outfit as well as a new overcoat, two lounge suits, shirts, socks, ties, a white silk scarf, and handkerchiefs galore. My Merrimanian half stepped in and frowned forbiddingly at an opera hat. But I bought a black felt hat and three pairs of gloves. "Shoes, sir?" Certainly shoes. Thank you for reminding me. I had only brown ones, so a black pair for the evening was added to my riotous loot. I piled it all into a taxi-cab and went back to my dreary abode.

I caused no sensation when I walked into the Café Royal that night, but I was as self-conscious as if all heads were turning towards me. This was my first entrance into a fashionable eating-place, and for all my finery I was as nervous as a mouse strayed into a convocation of feline dieticians. I played safe and ordered roast beef and vegetables with a steamed pudding to follow. I frankly asked the waiter what I should drink, and he said: " A half bottle of Pommard, sir."

I calmed down when this was settled, and, even in that, to me, exotic setting, I was able to think about Sylvia. I was enormously elated by the role I was playing: the well-to-do young-man-about-town dining out before going to see an actress he knew in a play. The Pommard helped. I dreamed my way through the meal. I had seen so little of Sylvia. I was a boy of fifteen when first we met, and that was eight years ago. She had stayed then, I remembered, but for one evening. Since then all our few contacts had been meet-and-part in that same way. Or even, as when I stayed in her flat, not meet at all, despite an arrangement to do so. I had seen more of Janet, and that was perhaps why I thought less about her. And I should never forget the first meeting of all, when the world I had entered into was new and enchanting: the half-ruined house; the sound and smell of Cornwall; the woman who had kissed me; the morning, dropping misty veil after veil, to reveal at last Sylvia, as no woman before had been revealed to me, beautiful as the morning itself, shining like a pearl, on the saffron sand against the background of reeling and rolling vapour that might have been a new world coming to birth. Of course, there had been Janet, too; but it was of Sylvia I thought when the moment came back. Janet was only a child.

Going out after, I think now, heavily over-tipping the waiter, I caught sight of myself in a mirror. I wasn't displeased. My absences from the office had meant long wanderings on Derby-shire moors and by Cheshire fields and meres. I was feeling fit, and I looked fit: as tall as I was ever to be, which is to say just under six feet; thin, brown, and wearing a close-clipped

88

dark moustache that I had been cultivating for a year. Even Mr. Tiddy, I thought, would now give me a month or two to live, barring accidents. I told myself that evening clothes became me, and that I carried them well. I decided that I would at the first opportunity buy an ebony cane with a silver knob. I readjusted the white silk scarf at my neck and, warm with food and wine, strolled out into Regent Street.

Even to hand over hat, overcoat and scarf at the cloakroom seemed a handsome and metropolitan action. Had this been Manchester, I would have stuffed hat and coat under my seat. But this wasn't Manchester. This was London, and George Ledra, emerging from the haunt of Oscar Wilde and Aubrey Beardsley and all those chaps, was in a London theatre.

I walked down the ramp towards the stalls, hoping to hear the rustle and *brouhaha* of a great theatrical occasion. I was disappointed. At the very moment of entering I was aware of a listlessness and lassitude, a sort of drugged decorum, through which the orchestra was dragging a tired and commonplace air. There was only a sprinkling of audience, so that I felt isolated and conspicuous as I sat with empty seats to right and left. I was assisting at the obsequies of a flop.

A feeling almost of panic overcame me. I had never seen Sylvia act, and I had come to see her act rather than to see a play. And I had come in what I sensed at once would be a moment of humiliation and defeat. She would hate to know that I had been there. I decided to walk out of the theatre, and had risen when a roll of drums announced that the National Anthem was about to be played. So I stood where I was, and the few people stood about me, looking like monuments of mayors and of good but uninspiring women who had suffered much in public causes ; and then they sat down, and I sat down, and the curtain went up.

Even I, not much of a playgoer, could not be interested in that play, much less moved by it. It was intended to be cynical, and was only silly, because everyone was a dummy to whom it was impossible to ascribe human motives. But I could be interested in Sylvia. She had a fairly important part as a peeress, and there was a drawing-room scene into which she entered on her return from some great occasion. She was wearing a tiara and a flowing cloak of crimson velvet. A rainbow of opals shimmered at her neck, and on her feet were gilded shoes. She looked beautiful, and I comforted myself. If you've seen nothing else, you've seen that, I said. Her entrance, and the few flippant words she had to say to her husband about the ball she had just left, ended the act. The curtain fell, and there was dead silence in the theatre. I started a small applauding noise on my own, hoping to break the hoodoo. It sounded like one pair of frightened feet pattering on a cold midnight pavement. A man said: "Excuse me," and brushed my hands to a standstill as he went by to seek, in the bar, fortitude for the last act.

When the final curtain fell there was a little polite and formal applause, a translation into sound of a pat on the head to a dog who has done his best; and in the midst of this came a shrill derisive whistle from the gallery. A few more whistles joined in; but even this dissent was not hearty. It petered out, and the audience petered out, and I went round to the stage door and gave the doorman half a crown with a note to be delivered to Miss Bascombe. For theatrical purposes she called herself Miss. I had her address, and could have called on her there or written to her; but sending a note from the stage door seemed to me the thing a young man-about-town should do.

5

I hoped that she would ask me to come to her dressing-room, but she didn't. The doorman, a shrivelled little fellow with thin hair, peered at me over steel-rimmed spectacles and said: " Miss Bascombe would like you to wait, sir." He didn't offer me a chair, and I mooched about outside his cubby-hole. He disregarded me, giving me the feeling that in his time he had seen too much romance, with little good coming of it all. When Sylvia appeared in about twenty minutes' time he said, without looking up: "This is 'im." Sylvia said: "Thank you, Albert," and Albert said: "S'orl right by me, my dear. Good night."

The theatre was on Shaftesbury Avenue. Sylvia took my arm and said: " My flat's handy. We've only to cross the road."

We crossed half-way, arm-in-arm, and paused on an island, under the brilliant lights, with the after-theatre traffic humming about us. I thought she squeezed my arm a little tighter; or was she simply urging me on? For she said " Now!" and we crossed to the other side. We passed through a door between two shops: one of them an eating-place full of smoke, and the steam of cheap food, and chatter, and cigarettes stubbed out on smudges of gravy. It depressed me. It wasn't Sylvia, or at any rate it wasn't my image of Sylvia. I thought of the flat where I had passed a night long ago: the trees in the strip of garden, the quiet, Sylvia's nightdress lying on a chair. I asked: "Can you sleep with all this row going on?" She said: "I can sleep anywhere. And my rooms are at the back. It's quieter there."

We climbed two flights of dimly lighted stairs. She opened a door and switched on a light. It was a tiny vestibule. " Leave your things there," she said, and I hung up my hat and overcoat and scarf and followed her into the sitting-room. " Now sit down," she said. "I shan't be a moment." She passed through a door which led, I guessed, to her bedroom. I looked about me. It was a small room, but elegant enough. I recognised the deep couch and some of the pictures and bits of furniture. They had been in the other flat. But the place was pokey, with a sense of making do, as though she had come down in the world.

She was back in a few moments. She was wearing a tailor-made grey suit, with the very short skirt fashionable at that time. She sat on the big couch and crossed one of her slim legs over the other. "Now stand up," she said, "and let's have a good look at you."

I did so rather sheepishly. She said: "You're a man! I wouldn't have recognised you. I remember the first night I met you. You were a boy—about fifteen, weren't you? It must be eight or nine years ago. You were rather afraid of drinking a glass of sherry. Are you used to it now?"

"I should love a glass of sherry."

She brought a decanter and two glasses from a cupboard and put them on a table in front of the couch. We sat side by side and I drank to her health. She lit a cigarette and said: "Did you think that play awful?"

"Yes. But I thought you were very beautiful."

She laughed. "It's too late for my beauty or anything else to redeem what's dead and done for. We were told to-night that the show folds up on Saturday."

I said I was sorry, and she assured me: "You shouldn't be. When a thing's finished, cut it out. Still, it's hard luck on some of them. As for me, I'll be able to have a rest in the country. You must come down and see me there."

She told me that she had taken this Shaftesbury Avenue flat because it was handier for most theatres than her old one. "But I must have somewhere to stretch, so I've bought a cottage in Buckinghamshire. I intended it for week-ends, but now it'll have to put up with me till another producer wants me."

We talked desultorily after that: about Janet, about Mr. Chown, about what I was going to do with myself now that I was at liberty to choose. It was friendly, but it wasn't what my imagination had built up. In the long stretches of time between our few meetings I had thought much of her; but now I felt it unlikely that she had thought of me. I was disappointed. Our meeting was being a flop, like the play.

A silence fell between us, and in the midst of it she put her hand to her mouth and yawned. She might as well have thrown a bucket of cold water over me. "You're over-tired," I said.

"I'm afraid so," she admitted. "This play was born dead, and it's exhausting work pretending that a corpse is alive, even for a few weeks."

"You must get to bed," I said, like a nurse. "It was thoughtless of me to intrude on you to-night."

"It's no intrusion at all, darling." I knew the worth of "darling." It meant as much as the kiss she had given me at Penruan when I was a boy. I rose to go, and I wondered whether she would kiss me now. I thought she wouldn't, and she didn't. Nor was any arrangement made about another meeting. I walked back to my miserable little hotel, and my new shoes hurt me all the way. I thought of a phrase Sylvia had used. "When a thing's finished, cut it out." I wondered if she had been handing me a proverb to be pondered.

I had to find somewhere to live, and the quest kept me from brooding. Well, it almost did. But I couldn't help thinking of my dreariness with that girl Jessie Lewis on the night when her soldier came home, and of my dreariness with Sylvia. If I had wanted something to happen I had done precious little to help it on. Was I always to be hopeless and helpless with women, except ones like that nurse who had thrown herself into my arms? And I didn't like having things thrown at me. I could still blush to think how easily that baggage had collared me for her own purposes.

I stayed obstinately in my horrible hotel, and one evening, having nothing better to do, and recalling the episode of the nurse, I wrote a thing that was half fact and half fiction called *An Easy Pick-up*. It saw me through an empty evening, and I had the sense to know how bad it was. I tore it up. But it showed the way the wind was blowing, and I went to bed feeling happier than I had been for some time.

The autumn turned to winter, and in December I found my flat. It was the top floor of a house in a street off Baker Street. A sitting-room, a bedroom, a bathroom and a bit of a kitchen. I had been obeying the Merriman precept of living on income, not capital, but now the rash and reckless George Ledra came along and said: "While you're at it make a job of it." And I did. There were plenty of shops in the streets round Bond Street to tempt the guineas out of my pocket, and I let myself go on furniture, pictures, lighting, carpets, curtains. I hung old Fred Byle's portrait over my Adam fireplace, with a strip light to show it up; and on a bitter mid-December day I sat down for the first time in the completed place. It satisfied me. I had carried in with me a cold meal bought at a shop and I opened a bottle of Liebfraumilch. I ate and drank in the beautiful room, and then sat on the couch with a spot of brandy before me and looked at old Fred's smiling worldly face. There was a carnation in his buttonhole. I held up my glass to him. "Well, Fred, here we are again—Fred Byles and Ledra. The old firm. Here's to us." I drank, and said "Damn it. Let's stay in association. Let's put the old name on the door." And after that I went out and ordered the bronze plate inscribed *Fred Byles and Ledra,* and when it had been made a few days later I screwed it with satisfaction to my white enamelled front door.

For some months I had heard nothing of Bob Meagher, but I sent him a note giving my new address, and on a cold January morning he rang my door-bell. I made a pot of coffee and we sat down to talk. "You know," he asked, "that Merriman has sacked my father?"

I admitted with shame that I didn't. Since leaving Manchester in the autumn I had written to no one there. "Well, it was the first thing the old so-and-so did when he bought you out," Bob said.

I asked what Mr. Meagher was doing now, and he said: "Living with me."

I thought of the tiny house in Coventry. Now that Wendy had produced another child it sounded as though the place would be a tight fit. I said so, and Bob laughed. "You don't think I've stayed there, do you? I left that place long ago."

I should have guessed it. There was an air of competence about him. "I didn't go to Coventry to stay there," he said. "I went to learn my job."

I told him: "Mr. Merriman once called you 'some sort of mechanic in Coventry.'"

"So I was," Bob agreed. "But not the sort of mechanic *he'd* understand. And yet he should have done, you know. He was always yapping about beginning at the bottom."

I refilled his coffee cup. He said: "I've been up there five years, you know. Three were enough to teach me what makes an internal combustion engine tick. For the last two I've been on the management side."

"You've been keeping it all pretty dark."

"Well, there were two reasons for that. One is that I've got a few ideas I wanted to keep under my hat till they ripened; and the other is that I can't waste my time writing to a chap who answers one letter out of ten and then with a postcard."

I accepted the rebuke, and said I was surprised that he'd got into management.

"That was a bit of luck, as it happened," he said, "though I'd have got there somehow without it. I wanted to know both sides. Well, a chap who'd been in tanks with me was a director of our company. I suppose this getting together with the old comrades business will soon wear off, but he did ask me to join him in a drink now and then. Besides, he once saved my life.

We needn't go into that; but perhaps he thought that, having saved it, he ought to do something for it."

"I suppose you had the nerve to put it that way, Bob?"

"Well—I did. Delicately, of course."

Once he'd got a foot on the ladder he began to climb. "One day Mr. Brimble—that's this tank type I'm telling you about—was up against an administrative problem. He said in a casual sort of way, as though he couldn't be bothered with it: 'I think we can safely leave that to Mr. Meagher.' Well, my heart didn't half jump, because the fact was that he was foxed and hoped I'd see a way out for him. I did, and things went on that way. They found all sorts of jobs that could safely be left to Mr. Meagher."

He sounded pleased with himself, and I felt sure he had reason to be. In Manchester he had been all vague speculation, like a gardener who sees a garden in his mind's eye. Now, I thought, some roots have gone down and some young leaves are unfurling.

I asked him what had brought him to London, and he said: "Vulgar ostentation. I want to take you out to lunch and show you my new car."

We talked till half past twelve, and then we went down, and I admired his car, which was standing at my door. It was an Apollo, the latest model of his firm. I got in with him and praised its comfort and style generally, while he pridefully explained details, gadgets, that I didn't understand. "Well, there she is," he said. We'll leave her here till we've eaten. Then I'll give you a run."

He walked me all the way to Stone's Chophouse. "Might as well walk while we can," he said. "It'll soon be a lost art."

We ate Indian curry, which I detested, but it seemed to be the thing to eat in that place, so I ate it. "You know, George," he said, "George Augustus Sala used to eat here, and not so long ago at that. Strange to think of him going out and calling a hansom cab to take him back to the *Daily Telegraph* office. A hansom cab! I'm told there are still a few in the country. Can you believe it?"

He lit a cigar and gave me his vision of London. "Now here we are," he said, "all on the ground floor so to speak. But before you know it, there are going to be so many motor cars and buses and motor-bikes that the ground floor won't hold 'em. The railways have already gone underground. Beneath our feet at this moment, George, they're rushing about north, south, east and west. Well, they've claimed the basement, and I suppose we'll have to let 'em keep it. That means that we'll have to dig deeper and make a sub-basement. And then we'll have to go up, too. There'll be a first floor to begin with, elevated roads weaving about all over this town, and in time

94

over every town. And then they won't be enough. We'll have to build a second floor; and so it will go on with traffic roads going down and down and up and up, till we have a tower of Babel with its roots in hell. That's what a city is going to be like in the future and not the very far distant future at that."

"And what happens when the world's oil supply runs out?"

"That won't change anything. Men have always found the power they needed to push them about the world. Wind on the seas and horses on the land to begin with. And then there was steam and then there was oil; and when oil packs up there'll be something else."

He looked at me with a smile showing through his cigar smoke, as though he hoped he was terrifying me. I said: "I shan't live to see it."

"You won't," he assured me. "But you'll see the beginning of it. Now we'd better get back and pick up the Apollo. Then we'll root out my father."

"I didn't know," I said, as we walked up towards Piccadilly Circus, "that Mr. Meagher was in town."

"Oh, yes. I'm just giving him an outing really, but he thinks he can be helpful."

"In what?"

"You'll see."

As we walked I pondered his picture of the city of the future. "You know, Bob," I said, "it can't be, unless every family in the country owns a car. And I can't see that happening."

"Can't you, George? Then you underestimate the power of suggestion. You first make people feel that if they don't own a car they're poor trash unfit to mix in decent society. Then when every family's got a car you make the wife feel that she's being cruelly ill-treated if she hasn't one of her own to use when her husband's taken his to town. All that's easy, George."

We got into the Apollo, which impressed me as it glided away like skates over ice. Bob was a superb driver. We drew up at a small hotel. "This has to suit the old boy for the moment," he said. "He'll be having a suite in the Savoy soon."

Mr. Meagher came out and shook my hand. "Well," he asked, "how have you been getting on with this madman?"

"So you feel it, too, Mr. Meagher?"

"Never mind what he feels or you feel. Let's get on the Great West Road," Bob said.

There were still, then, on the Great West Road a few relics of the fine agricultural land through which the road had run for centuries: a patch of apple trees, a decaying barn, even a house or two, a plough or two, a horse, a donkey. A pig or two rooted alongside a shaft-tilted cart.

"It's wonderful," I said, "how people stick to the land."

"They won't stick much longer," Bob said. "They'll go the

way the hand-loom weavers went when water began to turn the wheels."

We drove as far as Slough, then turned and drove back again. It was dusk and the lights were going up in the town when we dropped Mr. Meagher at his hotel in Oxford Street, near the Marble Arch. "See you at dinner to-night, Dad," Bob said. "George and I are going to have a little talk." He put the Apollo into the hotel garage and we walked to my rooms. I drew the curtains, switched on the electric fire, and made some tea. Bob looked about him with appreciation. "You've done yourself well," he said. "I suppose you'll soon be looking for a little place in the country too."

"If chaps like you leave me any country to look about in. And if I can find something fairly cheap. I haven't got money to burn."

"Oh, yes, you have," he assured me easily. "My old man was still with Merriman when your deal went through. He nosed out the figure. You'd have done a lot better if you'd sold to someone like Jimmy White."

Jimmy White was one of the fly financiers of that time. He was soon to come to a lamentable end.

"Still," Bob said, "you've got money to burn, and you could have a lot more."

"Tell me how."

"That's exactly what I've come here to do. This afternoon I saw what I think will be just the place for us."

We talked till long after the dinner hour. Bob rang up his father and said: "You eat, Dad. I'm up to the eyes"; and then we went on talking. At any rate, Bob Meagher went on talking. He had seen the piece of land he wanted for his factory. He was going to make, he assured me, the best car, and the best-looking car for the money, to be had in England. "In five years, George," he said earnestly, "I've learned how to make cars and how to sell cars, and I'm not going to continue doing it for the Apollo people. I'm going to do it for myself and for those who've got the sense to come in with me. The market is going to be immense. There are few people who realise how immense. But I tell you that where you see ten cars now you'll be seeing fifty in a few years' time and a hundred a few years after that. And if people don't want 'em— well, there are ways of making them want 'em, and want anything else if it comes to that."

I have lived to see all this come true. What I didn't realise then was that in Bob Meagher I was looking at a man who combined in the highest degree two aptitudes: remarkable engineering ability and insight into human weakness and vanity which could make people see themselves as supermen, gods almost, because they owned a machine which they could very well have done without.

My cautious Merriman instincts fought hard against Bob's persuasions. I protested that it was all moonshine to talk as he was doing when he hadn't even bought a bit of land to start building. He said almost angrily: "I tell you I've seen what I want," as though to want a thing was the same as to have it; and, indeed, that, more or less, was how it was always to be with him.

"Well, George," he said at last, "you're not the only pebble on the beach. I've interested a few people already, and between them they've promised a fair whack. I'm putting the chance in your way because I like you and because my father likes you, and so does Wendy, if it comes to that."

I couldn't help laughing aloud at finding the unsuspected affection of the complete Meagher family thrown into the scales; and this laughter almost caused Bob to walk out. The seasoning of humour had been omitted from his make-up. I calmed him down and promised to look into the matter. It was a cold still midnight when we went down into Baker Street and walked the short distance to the hotel where he was staying.

7

This impetuous visit made me think of Sylvia, and the house at Penruan, by sheer contrast. In the days of my first knowing Bob, when we had tramped about on the Derbyshire moors, I had told him about that ruin and Sylvia's determination to bring it back to life. He had answered shortly: "I could think of something better to do with the money." For me, I was not on either side. Extravagant human attitudes amused and interested me, towards whatever direction they tended.

But thinking now of Sylvia, I was ashamed at the way I had neglected her; and as I thought this, sitting by my fire when I was back in the flat, it seemed odd to me that I should ever be in the position of having a choice whether to neglect or court her. Ever since I had met her so long ago, her idea had been magnetic: it drew me, leaving me no choice at all. As soon as I was free and in London, seeing her had been the first of my intentions; yet now here I was chiding myself for a mere breach of social manners. I told myself that furnishing the flat had obsessed me; and indeed I had given so much thought to finding exactly " it " where everything in my rooms was concerned, that I half persuaded myself that this preoccupation explained everything. But I knew that it didn't. Sylvia, entertaining me for the first time in her flat, and thus creating a moment that I had long dreamed about, had found me without desire.

I switched off my fire and walked into my bedroom, telling myself, proud of my adult understanding: "You were fifteen, awakening to the thought of women, when you first met her. She was twenty-five and very beautiful. And, as it happened, the next morning there was that nude bathing business that fixed her in your mind as nothing else could do. And all the romantic circumstances of that moment. You were bowled over. Any lovely woman could have done it. Still, you'd better see how she's getting on."

As soon as I had had breakfast the next morning I rang her up at her country cottage and asked if it was in order for me to propose myself for lunch. She sounded surprised to hear my voice, and I gave her the long explanation that I had given myself about my work on the flat. "Well, come by all means," she said. "I'll be glad of company." Despite my ruminations of the night before I was rather annoyed. I would have liked her to say that she would be glad to see me, George Ledra, not some vague thing called company. She sounded altogether casual. She told me what train to catch at Baker Street, and said she'd meet me with the car at her station, which was a couple of miles from the cottage.

I was about to set out for Baker Street station at eleven o'clock when Bob Meagher turned up, looking as though he had just come out of a pressure cooker, as, indeed, he metaphorically had. I gave him no time to break into what was obviously to be impassioned speech. "I'm dashing to the station, Bob. I must catch the 11.20."

"Sit down and listen to me," he said.

He was in the lobby inside my front door. I took down my hat and put it on. He removed it from my head and hung it on the hook. He propelled me through the door into the sitting-room and said again: "Sit down."

"Well, at any rate give me time to ring up and make my excuses."

"Very well. Don't be too long."

I rang up the cottage and was answered by a voice not Sylvia's. I asked who it was and was told: "I'm Mrs. Gibbs. I comes in by the day."

I asked if I might speak to Mrs. Bascombe, and Mrs. Gibbs said: "She's gone into Amersham to buy an Aylesbury duckling."

I asked her to give Mrs. Bascombe Mr. Ledra's apologies and say that he was unavoidably detained in town. He would be writing.

"Now," Bob said as soon as the telephone was on its stand, "there's no time to waste."

Nine o'clock had found him at an estate agent's office, and negotiations had begun for buying a site on the Great West Road. "Then I managed to get in half an hour with Lord Packer. He's as good as promised to join the board of directors if the thing gets going. He knows damn all about motor cars but everything about finance, and his name will look well on the prospectus. Now, how much are you putting in, George?"

"I said last night that I'd think it over."

"Damn it, haven't you done your thinking yet?"

"Well, it's not eleven o'clock."

He looked at me in desperation. "Who's your business man? I suppose you've got one?"

I had. The Manchester bank manager who had been chairman of my trustees had put me in touch with a London firm of chartered accountants who now looked after my affairs. "Very well," Bob said. "Come on."

The Apollo was at the door, and I gave Bob the address in Threadneedle Street. "Leaving your money rusting," he snarled. "You need a nanny. Thank God you got to know me."

There was a whirlwind hour in my accountants' office. Mr. Lampson was a prudent man, and sat unmoved as Bob's names and statistics were snowed upon his head. He was not to be rattled. "You want money. We have it," was his attitude. When the tornado had blown itself out, he said: "Thank you, Mr. Meagher. Will you please retire to the waiting-room? I'd like to speak with Mr. Ledra."

When we were alone he rang for coffee and said: "And take a cup to Mr. Meagher in the waiting-room." I liked Lampson. He was putting Mr. Meagher in his place, refusing to be stampeded into a corral. He made clear to me all that was proposed and pointed out that Mr. Meagher undoubtedly had a number of influential people behind him. "But we mustn't play ducks and drakes with your money, Mr. Ledra, till we have a few more facts and figures. Will you leave it in my hands? I wouldn't like Mr. Meagher to rush you."

He gave the impression that an avalanche in full career would have a job rushing *him*, and when he called Bob in again he told him that he thought the proposition worth consideration, and no doubt Mr. Meagher would be able to provide more information on this point and that and the other. Even Bob was somewhat subdued by his judicial coldness. "And you mustn't bother Mr. Ledra further," Mr. Lampson said. "He has agreed to abide by the advice of our firm."

Bob stood me lunch at a City chophouse, and said I was lucky to have a chap like that looking after me. Six weeks later Mr. Lampson advised me to put five thousand pounds at Mr. Meagher's disposal. "I think," his letter said, "we have managed to cover all but quite unforeseeable contingencies. We shall be the better able to keep an eye on your affairs seeing that we have been appointed accountants to the new firm." I smiled. Without raising much dust, old Lampson knew how to pick up something that was under his nose.

8

The letter reached me at a happy moment towards the end of February. One could smell spring in the air. There were a few golden-hearted tulips in crystal on my table as I munched toast and drank coffee. By my plate lay a letter that I took up and read again and again. It was from the editor of a weekly paper notable for its high thinking and low circulation. I had been walking towards Hyde Park Corner and paused to look at Byron's statue. A tortoise-shell cat was on the plinth, looking up at the poet. It yawned in the offensive way cats have when considering things that humans believe worthy of reverence. When I got home I wrote a brief article about contemptuous cats. I called it *Puss and the Poet*. I say I wrote it, but I only began to write it. It took me three days of writing, rewriting and polishing. All for twelve hundred words! And that is how it was to be with me through my writing life. I am no Trollope whose words were whipped into keeping pace with the watch ticking away on the table. I could never create anything. I could only decorate and embroider a thing seen or an idea that my mind played with. I don't think I have ever deceived myself into believing that my work amounted to anything; but as time went on I could count on a disproportionate " write-up " from a few critics whose wits would have been thrown into confusion and despair if they had happened on anything so coarse and earthy as a new Balzac. If I was incapable of contributing a page to the missal, my drawings round the edges, my decoration of a capital letter, sent them into small squeaky raptures.

It was one of those moments one never forgets. The heartening day, blue, and billowed with rounded whiteness, these flowers upon the table, the satisfactory letter from Mr. Lampson, the sense of being in my own place and free to come and go, and this half-opened rosebud of promise that I hoped would presage a whole Chelsea Show of colour and renown, even the humble guinea that was promised me by an accepting editor: all this made it a festal morning and my heart was ready to respond to whatever it might bring.

The telephone bell rang. It was Sylvia.

" Good morning, George. What a wonderful day! "

" It is a wonderful day," I assented.

" Your mouth sounds full of toast."

" My mouth is full of toast," I agreed.

100

"What a lazy life you live. I finished breakfast an hour ago."

"Accept my felicitations. I have the deepest admiration for those who rise with the lark."

"You sound in a merry mood."

"I am in a merry mood."

"Oh, lord, can't you do anything but agree with all I say?"

"Try again, and see."

"Would you agree to give me lunch? I'm just off to catch the train for an hour's shopping. Could we meet somewhere at one o'clock?"

"I should love that. Rule's, in Maiden Lane?"

"Yes. And don't order Aylesbury duckling."

"To order Aylesbury duckling is the one thought festering in my mind."

"I couldn't face it. I had to eat a whole one all to myself not long ago."

"Then you were very greedy. You should have given half to Mrs. Gibbs."

"We'll talk about that when we meet. Till one, then."

I rang up Rule's to make sure of a table and at twelve o'clock I began to loiter towards Maiden Lane. The day was fulfilling its promise. The flower shops in Wigmore Street were running over with daffodils and tulips, mimosa, freesias and all the flowery fun of the springtime fair. They were an admirable foil to the shops of the surgical instrument makers, though even these failed to depress me. Indeed they uplifted me with the thought that it would be a long time before I needed an abdominal belt or an elastic stocking. A pet shop was full of blue Persian kittens, and King Charles spaniel pups, and budgerigars, marmosets and, improbably, a small white kid. I played for a moment with the idea of saying to Sylvia during lunch: "Would you like me to give you a small white kid?" but decided, on the whole, against it. Still, I said to myself, you are getting on. You wouldn't even have dreamed of saying that to the goddess you saw running on the golden beach. You are beginning to see Sylvia as a woman.

Maiden Lane looked as depressing as I had always found it, but smelled of Covent Garden, which excused everything. It was a smell I loved.

She was ten minutes late. I can never describe women's clothes, and I was to discover that Sylvia never bothered about current fashions. She wore what she fancied, and what she fancied that day made her look as though she had left a troika outside, with the ponies pawing the snow. She was all blue-grey fur. Her hat, her coat, her gloves, gave her the look of a vivid animal with a shining healthy pelt.

"How is your moujik?" I asked. "Shall I send him down a gallon of vodka?"

She embraced me. We kissed, and under the fur of the hat her eyes sparkled an inch from mine.

I said: " Sit down, Mrs. Bascombe. I'm quite glad I came."

So there we sat in that room full of old play-bills and prints of jockeys, pugilists and actors, and we drank sherry and nibbled salted almonds, and then we ate dover sole with the usual trimmings and drank a bottle of Barsac, and followed that with Brie. She said she'd like coffee, and with my coffee I drank armagnac.

I said: " I don't know what my poor father would have said had he lived to see his son carrying on like this. Before I left to join Mr. Chown for the first time he warned me off drink and women. And look at me now. He was a teetotaller."

" So far as drink goes," she said, " you must do as you please. As for women, you're quite safe with me. I've just got engaged to be married. I suppose that's why I feel so excited."

So that accounted for it: the glow of the face, the sparkle of the eyes, the feel of a warm animal running over with life. And I had been fool enough to think that taking lunch with George Ledra was the cause of it all.

I said, " I wish you joy, Sylvia."

" Oh, there's no need to *wish* me joy. I have it here."

She put a hand on her breast. It was a slightly overdone gesture, and I thought of Mr. Chown saying to me: " How well these actresses speak their lines!"

But well spoken or ill, that line deeply depressed me. I looked at my watch with that suggestion, so useful, of another pressing engagement, and called for my bill.

In Maiden Lane she stopped a taxi and asked: " Can I give you a lift anywhere, George? I'm going to Bond Street."

I thanked her and said I must dash along to Fleet Street where I was seeing an editor. Her fur paw waved to me through the window as she drove away.

9

It doesn't take long for a car to vanish, whether east or west, out of Maiden Lane. Literally in a few seconds she was gone. The sky was still blue and the small loitering clouds were snowy, and I was warm with wine and brandy, and I was as miserable as hell.

I walked slowly eastwards and told myself not to be a fool. I had long since abandoned the boyish thought that I was in love with Sylvia, and I had never believed that she was in love with me. What I was feeling now, I said, was merely the backwash of a tired wave that I had once pretended was engulfing me, but that for a long time had been clearly ebbing, to lose its shape in the anonymity of the ocean. The ocean was there, and quite a lot of waves were in it, and some day one of them would be my doom; but it was as well to give up pretending that Sylvia and I were any more than a callow boy and a woman advancing towards middle age who had nothing between them.

This damnable habit of mine, of putting my emotions into what I hoped were tolerably well-turned phrases, saw me as far as Chancery Lane. There were some good stationers' shops there, and I had business to do. I was not a man who could give his best by writing with an ordinary pen on ordinary paper. My pearls which were to be cast before kings and queens demanded something in keeping with their own quality. I spent half an hour on the examination of excellent paper, and at last gave my approval to some that was little short of vellum. I ordered half a dozen reams of this in quarto sheets. Since the musical direction of all my work has been *lento*, I still have some of this. There were quill pens, too, with the advantage that they did not need to be sharpened with a pen-knife, but could be fitted with nibs. I bought a handful in various pleasing colours, and a supply of mauve sealing wax. I ordered a seal to be made, G and L pleasantly embraced, and commanded that all this should be sent to my flat. I dawdled home, uplifted by a sense of the stern resolution I had shown in providing the necessary armament for the battle of life.

I picked up an evening paper from a newsboy in Baker Street and re-entered my flat at four o'clock. The bright day was waning. A nip had come back into the air. Better be done with the day at once. I switched on the fire and pulled the curtains and toasted a couple of muffins. As I sipped my tea I turned over the pages of the paper, an amusing enough contrasting prelude to the long evening's reading of Sir Thomas Browne that I promised myself. My eye lighted on a small paragraph at the bottom of a column. " Miss Sylvia Bascombe's engagement is announced to Mr. Clarence Conway. Miss Bascombe, who is 34, is the daughter of Margaret Napier, one of the outstanding actresses of her time. Miss Bascombe and Mr. Conway (aged 19) are also on the stage. They played together in a piece which recently had a short run at the Princess Theatre."

A spiteful little paragraph. I was surprised that my hand was trembling as I put down my tea-cup. I was swept by a flood of emotion: a mad wish to punch the nose of the writer of those insulting lines, and a deep compassion for Sylvia. I longed to be with her, to comfort her. I thought of the eyes that had sparkled over the luncheon table, the look of resurrection that was in her face. And I felt at the same time a hatred for Mr. Clarence Conway. A boy. Aged nineteen. Only four years older than Sylvia's daughter Janet. I had seen him in the play and tried to recall him but could not. A nonentity then. Without for the moment realising it, I was walking about the room, screwing the newspaper's neck. I didn't wash up. I didn't read Sir Thomas Browne. I went straight to bed with my mind seething, and I couldn't sleep.

10

In the morning I thought I had behaved badly to Sylvia. When she told me that she was engaged to be married, I should at least have been civilised enough to offer my felicitations. She would now be thinking me the prince of boors, as unlicked a cub as when I arrived at Penruan to study with Mr. Chown. I decided to put this right, to meet her and speak graciously to her. It was high time I had a country walk. I would take a train to Amersham, ramble to her cottage, casually look in to pass the time of day.

I got into a first-class carriage at Baker Street and found myself the only person in it. The train had just pulled to a start when a man wrenched the door open and flung himself, panting, into the seat opposite mine. When he had recovered his breath a little he said: " That was a close thing! Nearly missed it. Forgive me for butting in like that. Especially as I've got a third-class ticket. I just seized the first door-handle I saw."

I liked the look of him and was amused by his candour.

" I'll hop into a third at the first stop," he said.

" Why bother?" I asked. " Diddle the company for once. I won't give you away. Anyway, you have a first-class look. If an inspector pops in, we'll swap tickets and I'll take the rap. It would be an experience to be up before the beak. Give me something to write about."

" Are you a writer?"

With all the assurance of a man who has sold twelve hundred words, I said: " Yes."

He looked at me with admiration, and I filled my pipe and puffed away as I imagined Carlyle might have done when he wished to annoy the susceptible Ruskin.

" What do you write—novels?"

He lit a cigarette from an expensive-looking case, and I noticed the excellence of his linen, the gold links in his shirt-cuffs.

" No," I said airily. " It may come to that. But on the whole I dislike novels. My line is *belles lettres*. Still, as I say, I may be forced into the depths."

He smiled at me. He was a fair-haired youngster with candid blue eyes. His smile was worth seeing. " You know," he said, " depths may be a good word. I always think of Conrad, for example, as a man in the depths. He's a diver, don't you think?—and brings up a pearl now and then."

We had passed our first stop and he hadn't changed to a third-class carriage. I was annoyed that he had caught me out on my own word, and said: "That's rather a high faluting figure of speech."

He blushed. "Sorry. I suppose I shouldn't talk to a professional like that. But though I couldn't write a line myself, I'm enormously interested in writers. Now look at Henry James. Would you say he had depth?"

I hadn't read enough of Henry James to give an honest answer. I gave a dishonest one. "No," I said.

He brightened at that. "Well, that's one thing we agree about. He ties himself up in knots and gives an *impression* of profundity; but really, you know, he's like those chaps who get tied in ropes and then shoved into a sack to amuse the crowd on a street corner. Everyone knows there's a trick to it and that they could get out inside a minute if they wanted to; but they heave and struggle and utter lamentable noises so as to make it *seem* that something tremendous is going on. A lot of writers are like that."

Well, that's an example of how we talked, and the journey passed with pleasant speed. I found myself more and more liking his combination of modesty and a readiness to stick to his own point of view. But what I was not prepared for was what he said as the train drew into Amersham station. "Well, this is where I get out. Thank you for putting up with me. In case we meet again, my name's Clarence Conway. What's yours?"

"Oddly enough," I said, "it's Amersham. Andrew Amersham."

"What a coincidence," he said, and leapt eagerly to the platform. I saw Sylvia advance no less eagerly to meet him. I kept my hat over my eyes till the train was out of the station, and at the next stop paid excess fare, and spent the day walking madly.

I was unable to decide what I felt about Sylvia. Who has ever been able to "decide" where an obsession is concerned? And looking back on it all, I think obsession is the only word I can use. I was like a satellite obsessed by its sun: now at a farthest point of orbit, now rushing to proximity; but, whether the one or the other, never beyond the pull of attraction. Putting it on a mundane level, one thing I learned that afternoon was that a casual attitude to a woman is easy enough to maintain if you can persuade yourself that it is you who are providing the attraction; but it is another matter when she makes clear that she can do very well without you, and *intends* to do without you so far as her bed is concerned.

It would have been easier if I had been able to dislike Clarence

105

Conway, if he had proved to be what the sneering evening paper had suggested: a juvenile nonentity with the sly skill to attract a rich woman not far from the frustrations of middle age. But it would have been absurd to pretend that he was anything of the sort. He was a nice boy, intelligent and unpretentious, though I couldn't bring myself to believe that he was the man for Sylvia. I should think that he was all this, but there was another side to him that Sylvia was to discover.

I went to sleep that night with my head swirling, and decided in the morning to leave it all behind me for the moment and retreat upon Cornwall. I didn't want to intrude upon Mr. Chown, so I wrote to Jose Gomm and asked if he could keep me a room at the Absolution. He replied in a letter headed, in beautiful script, "Gomm, Antiques, Helston," to say that he was now settled in rooms over his shop, but that he had made the necessary arrangements with his father.

This being settled, I wrote to the editor of *Parnassus*, who was to print my twelve hundred words, and asked him to send the proof to Cornwall. I felt I owed it to him to see that nothing hindered the publishing of a contribution that might turn the tide of fortune for his magazine. I had not been in Cornwall a week when I received a letter from him, returning the manuscript of *Puss and the Poet*. He said that things were not going well with *Parnassus*; and indeed they went so ill that it packed up a few weeks later. I felt that life was at its lowest ebb.

CHAPTER SIX

1

I left London in early March sunshine, ran into mist at St. Austell, and reached the Absolution in a downpour of rain. There was a high wind, too, blowing the tops off the waves as they crashed upon the reefs that were almost at the inn's door. There, in that rain-sodden cleft in the cliffs, howling with elemental voices, I wondered why I ever put up with the caged comfort of my rooms off Baker Street. I could almost forget Sylvia. The hullabaloo lasted for two days. I clambered about in borrowed oilskins, sou'wester and gum-boots in the daytime, and after my evening meal in the small sitting-room I would go into the bar and make a pint of beer see me through the evening. The weather took charge of the conversation. It was of wrecks and hurricanes, of how the *Mohican* was pounded to pieces on the Manacles, and of how here, in this improbable place, John Wesley had once been spending a night with one of his flock when a French barque was driven on to the reef. Old John's host ran and shook the evangelist out of his bed, shouting " A wreck! A wreck! " It was Tiddy who loved to tell that tale. " Just converted, Jack Retallack was," he said, " but a wreck was another matter. He thought old John would want to be there to share in what come along, but old John 'ad other views. 'E was there all right, with 'is 'air and 'is white bands flying, and 'e called down God's own damnation on any man who didn't 'elp them poor souls in distress. Not so much as a yard of timber was pinched that night, and the next day John preached, standin' on ole Mrs. Pydar's garden wall, an' there was a great ingatherin' of souls. Aye, 'e damaged the wreckin' industry beyond count, did old John."

On the third evening Mr. Chown appeared in the bar. Old Gomm seemed to know what was expected of him. He poured a pint of ale into a pewter tankard and brought it across to where Mr. Chown had joined me on a settle by the fire. I saw that the tankard was Mr. Chown's property. His initials were engraved on it. The corner seat of the settle was his, too. I had sat in it the first night I was at the inn, and had been warned off. " That be the Professor's," Gomm said briefly.

The Professor now raised his tankard to the company, took a long swig, and smacked his lips. " Well," he said to me, " you've been here three days and haven't had the courtesy to pay me a call. I hope you forgive me for intruding upon you."

I said I had been more or less imprisoned by the weather and intended to call upon him the next day. " Nevertheless," he said, " you have been seen clambering about the rocks. My spies have been busy."

I said that his spies must be pretty tough birds to come over from Penruan in the weather we had been having; and he agreed that they were. " In my youth women were all dimples and dimity. We were permitted to know from ocular evidence that they had ankles. If these were the termination of calves, that was merely a matter of conjecture from one's knowledge of anatomy. Now I have a pair of hoydens who display their knees, and so conjecture mounts from a new starting-point."

I asked him who the hoydens were, and he said: " My feminine acquaintance is so restricted that you should be able to guess."

" Janet, I suppose, for one."

" Yes, and Medea Hopkins."

He called for his tankard to be refilled, snipped a cigar and lit it. I filled my pipe. " Not that you will address her as Medea when you meet. What do you know about Medea? I mean the original lady of that name."

" Only a few trifles," I said. " She poisoned her children, got

107

rid of a rival by sending her a poisoned robe, and at this moment is married to Achilles in Elysium."

"That is all right so far as it goes," he agreed. "I think it unlikely that Miss Hopkins will do any of these things, so she has wisely chosen to be called Clare."

I asked what Janet was doing in these days, and he said: "She continues to worship at Miss Hopkins's shrine. In the autumn Miss Hopkins is to begin a course of study at the London School of Economics. For myself, I'd rather see her poisoning her young. But that's her affair. It seems to me a poor preparation for entering Elysium as Achilles' bride. Janet, I fear, will follow in the same direction. You shouldn't stuff yourself up like this in a pub night after night. Time enough when you're my age. Do you think, Tiddy, that Mr. Ledra will reach that age?"

"Well, Professor," Tiddy said, considering me with compassion, "there's a flush in his cheek that may be 'ealthy or 'ectic. P'raps we'd better leave the decision to God."

"Yes," Mr. Chown said, getting up and knocking back the last of his beer, "that is usually the wisest thing to do in the long run. Come now, young Ledra, take a breath of air. The moon is up."

It was, indeed. The night was still, and the sea that had been battering the reef for three days did no more than mutter. We walked in silence for a while, and then Mr. Chown asked me what I was doing with myself. I told him of my flat and of my hopes to make something of myself as a writer. I even told him of the little piece that *Parnassus* had accepted.

"You'd better let me see it," he said. "Have you brought it with you?"

I had. It was something I would not willingly have parted with.

"Come and have lunch with us to-morrow and bring it with you. I'll tell the girls to expect you. We're eating up at the house while they're there."

At that moment the house came into view, ahead and away to the right. From this angle, its roof-line was against the opal shimmer of the moonlight on the sea. The air was so clear that the saplings growing from the ruined half of the walls were sharp-cut upon that radiance. One or two of the windows were smudged with dusky light. The place looked beautifully, incurably romantic, and not a whit different from what it had seemed when first I set eyes on it ten years ago.

We stood silently looking at it for a while, and then Mr. Chown sighed. "Poor Sylvia," he said. "Do you know this young man she's going to marry?"

"I read about it in a newspaper. No, I don't know him."

"You should stay with me, you know, when you come to
108

these parts," he said. "If you must drink, we can go over to the pub and drink together."

He wandered on, forlorn in the moonlight, and I realised how lonely he must be. I stood for a long time looking at the moon-shiny ruin, so unchanging, like one of those dreams of frustration in which, try as you will, nothing comes to the conclusion you desire and you wander for ever down a long dark street.

2

I had enjoyed the three stormy days. They had knocked some of the town tameness out of me. But no less I enjoyed this morning. The air was washed and heartening. As I took a dally-ing course towards Penruan the sun was shining and a lark sang a way up his infinite ladder. I avoided the house and made for the narrow valley that led to the seashore. I wanted to sit and look about me on the seat where once I had come upon Janet, escaped from school. But the small shelter had fallen in, and the seat itself was a pile of rotting wood. The woodlice—grammersows they call them down there—were all over it, and as I kicked at one of the planks their jointed armour, cunning as an armadillo's, came into play and they turned into little black impregnable spheres, no bigger than green peas.

I rolled a mackintosh that I was carrying and put it down for a cushion upon the damp moss, and I sat there, companionable with the woodlice, and looked and listened. Nothing had been done. I remembered the first time I had met Jose Gomm and how he expounded his schemes and Sylvia's for the resurrection of the house and the taming of this small valleyed wilderness; but the wilderness was gaining on human intention. Long lianas of old-man's-beard tied up branches into bundles, and already the spears of this year's further advance were breaking green on the brown. Camellias bloomed everywhere, but ground elder and winter heliotrope were thick about their feet, while briars and convolvulus were taking a stranglehold on their limbs. A few tall conifers rose above the undergrowth, the larches were already starred with green buds, and a magnolia, as tall as any I had seen, had its crown clear against the blue, a sight to take the breath away, those hundreds of creamy cups, the sun shining upon them and through them, a splendid affirmation above this lost decrepit paradise.

The tinkle of hidden water was in my ears, and vibrant over that gentle note was the wild echoing cry of the birds. This green damp gulch was full of them. They at any rate would not wish things to be other than they were. There was incessant traffic of wings and voices. The blackbirds' bills were not more golden than their songs, and the lesser fry, the wrens and robins, warbled and twittered, restlessly flitting here and there, penetrated, it seemed, to the marrow of their small brittle bones by the fertile suggestions of spring. Above the tops of the tallest trees rooks made their squabbling clamour, and those harsh discords were one with the music of the moment, an absorbed and undisturbing part of the harmony.

It was all most beautiful, but steeped in unbearable melancholy. I got up and walked quickly to the house, seeking human company.

3

Janet and Clare Hopkins were sitting on the paved terrace whence you could look over the trees of the descending gulch and out to sea. It was a long time since I had seen Janet. She was no longer the wild-eyed flibbertigibbet that I had known. She and Clare Hopkins came forward and shook hands, and I saw that they had in common a gravity that I found attractive and reassuring. I suppose my mind was over-full of the froth of that post-war decade. I had read much of what the papers called the Bright Young Things; and once, returning after midnight to my flat, I had come face-to-face with one of their antic exploits. There were about a dozen of them hoydening round a sedate London square, the girls, wearing baby clothes, nestled in perambulators and sucking gin through the tubes of feeding-bottles; the men adjusting the coverlets of the prams with rather too obviously exploratory hands. They were all howling their heads off in ribald song; and a policeman who intervened had his helmet knocked into the gutter and used as a football. He laid hold of one of the youths, and the girls thereupon scrambled, negligibly dressed, out of their prams and tried to rescue their friends. But one of them fell flat to the ground. I stayed long enough to see her carried on a stretcher to a hospital, hopelessly doped with cocaine; and to see an old gentleman, his sleep disturbed, emerge in pyjamas from one of the houses and discharge a blunderbuss at the starry sky.

The newspapers gave so much emphasis to cocaine-addicts, bottle parties, and the dubious night-clubs that one could well imagine all London to be corrupt, and so the sight of these two girls was reassuring.

"Good morning, Mr. Ledra," Janet said. "Uncle told us you were coming to lunch." She introduced me to Clare, and added: "Sit down here."

I sat between them on the long seat. Janet was sixteen then, and Clare, I supposed, a year or two older. Books were lying on the seat, and as I can never resist peeping at what people are reading I craned my neck and looked at the titles. Near Clare

110

was J. M. Keynes's *Economic Consequences of the Peace,* and Janet had been reading *I'd Rather be a Pagan,* a comparison of Greek life with life in a modern capitalist society, by Mr. Chown. I had read and admired it, and, rightly or wrongly, thought it the sort of book Ruskin might have written had he been living in our time.

Janet said: "I'm sorry, but lunch is off. It's such a gorgeous day that Clare and I decided on an expedition." I told her not to bother about me: I could walk back to the Absolution for lunch.

Clare said: "Perhaps Mr. Ledra would care to come with us?"

She smiled at me, and I liked the warm contralto of her voice.

"I'd love to come," I said, "if you can put up with me."

At that moment Mrs. Tiddy came out through the great front door, looking like a scrawny boiling fowl under the arch of Trajan. "Them samwidges is ready," she announced briefly.

"Oh, Mrs. Tiddy," Janet said, "Mr. Ledra is coming with us. Could you cut a few more?"

"I can and I will," Mrs. Tiddy said, "but if Mr. Ledra's to be Built Up, 'e needs more than samwidges for 'is dinner."

Clare said: "I love the idea of Mr. Ledra becoming a Built-Up Area. Like Ancoats, or Limehouse, or the Gorbals."

"Then we'd have to decentralise him into something like Bourneville or the Hampstead Garden Suburb," Janet suggested.

We went into the house, laughing, and Clare threw Mr. Keynes on to a table as though glad to be done with him for a while. I looked about for signs of change, of advance in the reclamation of Penruan, but things were much the same as before. Janet, guessing my thought, said: "It's the same old white elephant. Now and then Mr. Gomm brings over a thing or two from his shop in Helston, or Mother sends something down from London. But it's all bits and pieces that never seem to add up. Why on earth Mother bothers with it I don't know. She might just as well have bought the Colosseum in Rome and tried to bring it back complete with Christians and lions."

Mr. Chown ambled in and heard her last words. "That, at any rate," he said, "would have been a paying proposition. I wouldn't mind the job of managing a show like that. I know lots and lots of Christians, worthy chairmen of boards of directors and such like, who would serve an even worthier purpose as lion-meat. What do you think, Miss Hopkins?"

"Now, Mr. Chown," she said, "you're not going to draw me out again. You know what I think. You can't go back: whether to Tudor England or to Rome."

"But, dear lady," Mr. Chown protested, "why on earth not? Why do you assume that to go forward is necessarily admirable?

111

There's a lot to be said for going back now and then. Especially when the way forward is obviously to a precipice. Not," he added with a grin, " that I don't think Sylvia's making a fool of herself with this rat-hole."

Mrs. Tiddy plonked a small packet on the table. " More samwidges," she announced, and retreated.

" More samwidges," Mr. Chown said, " means, I presume, that Mr. Ledra has found better companionship than mine."

I apologised, and Janet said: " You can have him when we're gone. We're off to-morrow."

" Bear that in mind, George," Mr. Chown said. " You are just a piece of property. They can have you to-day. I can have you to-morrow. You have no say in the matter. Really, the manners of the young to-day are beyond praying for."

Janet kissed him, and for the moment I saw the witch I used to know.

" No blarney," Mr. Chown said. " I'm just lumber, and you know it."

" Surely you don't need us," Clare said a little maliciously. " You've got Plato."

" There is just the odd chance," Mr. Chown retorted, " that Plato will still be there when Mr. Harold Laski is gone."

He walked out on to the terrace. " Now you've really hurt him," Janet said. " Come along. We'd better be off."

Each put a raincoat, a thermos flask of coffee and sandwiches into a rucksack, took up a walking-stick, and were ready. We got on to the Helston road by eleven o'clock. " I hope you're a good walker, Mr. Ledra," Clare said. " We're going a long way."

" We'd better call him George," Janet suggested, as though naming some hitherto unidentified object, " and he can call us Janet and Clare."

They were good walkers and kept me moving briskly. " Where are we making for, Janet?" I asked.

" Well, first of all, we shall walk into Helston and call on Mr. Gomm. He has a motor car, because that leg of his makes long walks difficult, and he has to get about to sales and things. So he's got this ramshackle second-hand outfit—more of a truck than a car. We're going to the north coast, and there and back in one day is a bit much, so we shall persuade Mr. Gomm to run us to a place called St. Erth, or somewhere about there. Then we shall walk to a hill called Trencrom, then back to where Mr. Gomm left us. He'll be waiting to pick us up again and bring us back to Helston. From there we walk home."

" Put like that, it sounds nothing," I agreed. " But it seems rather to depend on Mr. Gomm."

" Oh, that'll be all right," she assured me airily. " He's rather sweet on Mother, and, besides, she's his best customer."

I said: "This all sounds to me rather immoral," and to my surprise Clare said: "Janet is utterly unscrupulous in getting what she wants. If you don't know *that* about her, you don't know a thing."

"I think you've both bitten off more than you can chew," I assured them. "It's ten miles to Helston, and doing it both ways makes twenty. Then there's the scrambling about at the other end. It looks as though you've let yourselves in for thirty miles."

Janet looked unconcerned. "One can *always* get back from Helston," she said. "I was once brought on the step of a policeman's bicycle."

I remembered the occasion and told Clare about it. "It was at a moment when she was passionately interested in Swinburne."

"Children have these phases," Clare said temperately. "I trust that by now she's got over *that*, at all events."

I wasn't too certain. I asked Janet where she was living now, and she said: "Oh, Mother and I play Box and Cox. When she's in her cottage I'm in her flat in Shaftesbury Avenue, and the other way about. We *do* meet sometimes for a week-end. I don't impose myself on her. I think she likes her liberty. Most children are frightfully inconsiderate to their parents, who, after all, are entitled to lead their own lives."

I asked Clare for news of her mother, and she said: "Oh, Mother's been dead for a year or more. I live with Uncle Bill."

"In case you don't know," Janet explained, "Uncle Bill is Mr. Justice Brighouse."

I had heard of that redoubtable judge, and asked Clare if there were any other relatives. "Well, yes," she said. "There's a father about somewhere, but I don't see him. He and Mother were divorced. I don't think he liked her books, and one thing led to another. Uncle Bill suits me all right. He's Mother's only brother. A bachelor."

"He lives in the gloomiest house on the South Bank," Janet said, "with the gloomiest man and wife to look after him. If he sees you about the place, he gives you a look as if he wonders what you're up before him for, and then scuttles off to some dark and secret den."

"He's all right," Clare said complaisantly. "One must take life as it comes."

She had the imperturbable solidity of a law in mathematics.

It was well past two o'clock when we walked into Helston. Janet and Clare went into Jose's shop, and I stood outside, looking into the window and the room beyond. A few choice objects were arranged with a lot of space around them, and somehow they depressed me. They seemed so much like bits of loot from fallen fortunes. Which is what they were. That Crown Derby tureen, which had once smoked with soup, would never smoke again, but would stand on a pedestal, ornamental and useless; and the ebony-handled silver punch ladles, arranged like crossed swords in front of it, would be polished and admired but never desecrated by being dipped into punch. Everything there seemed a fragment chipped away from a gracious way of living that was sliding to oblivion, and when Jose, beckoning through the window, called me in, I thought that he, too, had a look of quiet desperation.

We shook hands, and he said: "Things are a bit slack at the moment. I'll be able to run you along, as Janet suggests."

He hobbled away to a nearby garage and returned driving a disreputable truck into the back of which he threw some old cushions. Clare and I sat upon them, and Janet sat next to the driver's seat. Jose locked the shop door and we rattled out of town.

The day remained glorious: no wind, not a cloud in the pale blue sky. Jose avoided the main road and we wound through lanes with primroses blooming in the damp ditches and the hedges incandescent with the flowers of sloe. Making the best of what he probably thought a bad job, Jose said: "I should have been coming this way soon, anyhow. There's a widow I want to call on. She was in Helston the other day and said she had a few things I might care to see."

He told us about the widow. Her husband had run a small holding, mostly growing flowers for the spring market. "He was killed in the war," Jose said. "She tries to carry on, but it's hard work and she can't afford to pay for help. Even with a widow's pension she can hardly make ends meet. It's not her own land, either. There's the rent to pay. She belongs to a good family, but they've been on the down and down for generations. The only thing they've managed to keep hold of is some good furniture."

"And now you're kindly relieving them even of that," Janet said.

Jose looked uncomfortable. Clearly there were parts of his job that he didn't like. "I pay good prices," he said defensively. "If a seller doesn't know what a thing's worth, I don't take advantage of his ignorance. And there are plenty who do."

"The world," Clare said with the self-confidence of the young, "is very badly organised," to which Jose answered brusquely: "You're telling me. Do you know how to put it right?"

"It's a matter of simple economics," Clare assured him, "a matter of a more equitable distribution of the national income."

"I know," Jose agreed. "It's just that. You try getting on with it."

"I shall certainly do my best."

"Splendid," Jose said. "That's a good girl. I wish you luck."

A few minutes later he pointed to a cottage lying at the end of a lane: a well-built snug little place, the townsman's dream of rural bliss. "That's it," he said. "But I'll take you another mile or two. Janet tells me you're going to Trencrom. There and back's more than a bit of a walk. You'll wear your feet out."

The girls protested, but he held to the road, and when he put us down we had not far to go. "I'll be here to pick you up in two hours' time," he said. "And then I'll run you through to Penruan. I've got to go there anyway to see my father to-night."

We climbed down. His old truck squealed into a rusty turn, and he was gone.

Clare said: "' Beware of them which devour widows' houses, and for a pretence make long prayers.'"

I was a bit tired of her. "There's all sorts of pretence," I said, "and the most abominable pretence is made by people who think blueprints and blue-books are the cure of human ills. Jose's a friend of mine, and I don't like hearing him talked about as if he were a highway robber."

She was taken aback, and began "But surely . . ."

"Surely nothing," I said. "I've no use for surely this and surely that. The only sure thing is that nothing's sure."

"But that's anarchy."

"I don't give a damn what it is," I said. "It's my opinion, anyhow. And now if you two want to climb this hill, go and climb it. You'll find me here when you get back."

Janet tried to soothe the moment. "What about your sam-widges, George? They're in my rucksack. You'll starve to death."

"Then you can heave my corpse into Jose's truck and take it to a cemetery or a crematorium. I don't care which."

Clare said: "Let's get on. The man's mad."

It was a narrow climbing lane, and a signpost pointed to Trencrom. They moved away, and I sat in the grass, and wondered if I were indeed mad. I was surprised at my own sudden outburst. I suppose it was because I was saddened by Jose's obvious lack of prosperity, and I was saddened by the story of the widow and the light it shed on the crumbling edges of life amid which Jose's traffic was conducted. I couldn't stand, in face of that, the idiotically over-simplified views of pamphlet-fed chits like Miss Hopkins.

I sat there smoking till I was able to laugh at myself a little, then called at a cottage and asked if I could buy a cup of tea. I did better than that: I ate a good meal of cold beef and pickles and cold apple-pie and cream, and, excellently fortified, followed the girls' route up the hill.

There wasn't a soul in sight. I could feel the dynamo of that

115

early spring day throbbing beneath the surface of the land, smell it in the air, hear it in the vibrant cries of the birds. And there was more than that. I was acutely aware of what Wordsworth calls " something far more deeply interfused," a sense, which can speak to you whether in an ancient town or in such a countryside as this, of man's immemorial coming and going. I was aware of the ebb and flow of living and dying in a strange way that was beyond my understanding, but none the less real for that. It was a disturbing place, that crust of soil on a great depth of granite ; and when I came in sight of Trencrom, a bold hill rising up against the sky to my right, I saw the granite itself, sticking up through heather like reefs through a purple sea, tumbled upon it in great weather-worn boulders, and on the topmost point, clear upon the blue sky, I saw the girls, gazing into the overhead infinity where a pair of buzzards now lay negligently on the void as though it were a bed, and now soared through it with power and majesty.

I stayed where I was. I had no wish for company. I gave myself to the day's intimations, sitting in a hedge behind which a ramshackle cottage seemed to be falling apart in a patch of neglected land. As I sat there an old codger came tramping along, looking like a professor playing at boy scouts. His hatless pink skull was fringed with a fuzz of white hair. The neck of his shirt was open. He wore a tweed coat and khaki shorts and hobnailed boots. A blackthorn stick was in his hand and a ruck-sack on his back. He puffed happily at a clay pipe.

He stopped to give me the time o' day, unslung his rucksack, took out an apple and chewed upon it. He sat beside me, and I looked at his hale cheeks and the diamond-blue of his eyes. " I never miss Trencrom," he said. " Nothing else like it in England. Been up?"

I said that I hadn't, that I was new to the district.

" I came down when those girls came up," he said. " You don't want chattering females up there. A place to be alone."

He told me that from the top you could see the sea, on a clear day, to the north of you and to the south. " You look right through from the Hayle estuary to the bay at Penzance. See what that means?"

" Trade route," he said briefly, chucking his apple-core over his shoulder. " Eat plenty of apples," he said, " and your guts won't go far wrong."

He leisurely charged his blackened clay, lit it with a match held in delicate long-fingered hands, and said: " Yes. That's the way they went. You see, they dodged Land's End, which wasn't a pleasant place to come round in the sort of boats they had then. Probably the same sort of curraghs that you see off the Irish west coast to-day."

He stroked his bare rounded knees. " Probably gold," he

116

said. "Some of it would be gold, anyway. They were wonderful
goldsmiths, those old Irish. I've seen some of their things.
Priceless. I'm talking about the days before Christ," he said
calmly. "A hell of a time before Christ, if it comes to that.
Well, these Irish chaps sailed into Hayle or thereabouts, and
then the stuff went overland to the bay at St. Michael's Mount.
Marazion probably. There it went aboard for Brittany. A
quick journey, and all the markets of the Continent, such as they
were, at the other end."

He smoked in silence for a while, then said: "What about
highwaymen, eh? I've often wondered about that. Those
caravans crossing the narrowest neck in Cornwall, eh? Must
have been a temptation. Easier than tin-working. That's what
they did all round about here. Oh, God knows how long ago.
You'd have to go back century beyond century. Neolithic. Up
there on the hill there's a neolithic settlement. Such as it was. I
suppose the so-called huts were nothing more than a few slabs
of granite to keep out the wind. Anyway, my boy," he said,
getting up, pocketing his pipe, and taking another apple from
his rucksack, "here you are, surrounded by pre-history. The isle
is full of noises. Little dark men, chattering in heaven knows
what lingo."

He looked up at the hill, his eyes full of speculation. The
girls were scrambling down. "Well," he said, "here come some
noises I *don't* want to hear. But don't forget your Byron.
Where'er we tread, 'tis haunted, holy ground."

He slung on the rucksack and took a bite of the apple. "The
only good woman ever did to man," he said, "was to teach him
to eat apples. Incomparable for the bowels. Cox's orange
pippins if obtainable. Good day to you."

I stood up and looked at the cottage behind me. Only then
did I notice a small bill pasted on the wall. "For Sale," it said.

4

I didn't want to sponge on Jose, so from the Absolution I rang
up a taximan in Helston and asked him to call for me early
the next morning. At Hayle I picked up the key of the cottage
from a house-agent, who, unlike his tribe, admitted that he was
not selling perfection. "You'll find no amenities," he warned
me.

I wasn't looking for amenities. Last night I had spent an
hour studying a map. The names I came across bewitched me.
Amalebrea, Uny Lelant, Towednack, Praze-an-Beeble. What
sort of people were they who had first mouthed such outlandish
syllables? I thought of my old codger: "Little dark men,

chattering in heaven knows what lingo." The last western inhabitants of land which, once you had crossed the few miles to Brittany, you could cover on foot—given time and patience! —to far Kamchatka.

The taximan drove me to the cottage, and I told him to come back in an hour's time. The large iron key grated in a rusty lock. I pushed the door open for some air to precede me, and then stood back to look at the outside. The place was built of irregular chunks of granite, roofed with slate. The windows were small. There was a pipe that carried rain-water from the roof down into a sump. I stamped on the top of the sump and found that it was covered by a slab of thick slate. A pump stood alongside. I tried the handle and found it was seized up. That would have to be put right. It looked as though it would be my only water supply.

Inside, the house was dark. It had four small rooms. It had no damp courses. Plaster had been smacked on to the inside of the granite blocks, and this plaster had fallen away in places. Every room had a leprous look. In each my feet crunched upon fallen chalk. The stairway was narrow and almost vertical. The two small bedrooms had windows looking south.

The place was altogether deplorable: no sanitation, no gas or electricity, a chancy water supply, a primitive and cumbrous piece of machinery for a cooking-stove. And it was altogether irresistible. I went out into the patch of stony land at the back and pondered its conversion. But pondering soon came to an end. The wreck of an old deck-chair was lying there, and I sat in it and looked about me. There was nothing so conventional as a garden wall to shut out the view. I gazed upon mile after mile of rolling fields and woods and hills, arched over by the cloudless blue sky. Fearless tits and wrens fluttered and pecked almost at my feet, robins sang their small confidential songs, and the blackbirds and thrushes seemed as though they could not cease from singing. All my cautious self took wing and soared out of sight, and the extravagant George Ledra remained carolling loudly with the birds. He was thinking of two people: Jose Gomm and the woman who had given him lunch yesterday: when the tooting of a motor-horn announced the return of the taxi.

I drove into Hayle and told the house-agent that I had decided to buy. He sighed and said: "Ah well, *caveat emptor,* you know"—most unusual conduct, I thought again, for a house-agent. But then everything was unusual that morning. I told the taximan to drive to Helston. I was there just before one o'clock and took Jose to lunch at the Angel.

Jose knew everybody. Having been born and bred in that narrow neck of the peninsula, and being taken hither and thither upon it by his present trade, he was as knowledgeable as

118

an electoral roll. I told him about the cottage, and he said that he knew it and that I was a fool to buy it. He said that if it was the site that pleased me, I should pull the place down and build a nice little bungalow. And he didn't advise even that. " You'll have to boil every drop of water you use. When there's any to boil."

I told him about the cottage where I had eaten lunch the day before. " You mean Joe Carbis's place," he said.

I asked him if Mr. Carbis was a likely sort of person to be entrusted with the key and to keep an eye on the cottage when I wasn't living in it. He said: " Well, you've got to get it into order first, and Joe might come in there."

Joe Carbis, it seemed, was one of those handymen who are fast dying out: builder, carpenter, undertaker and all the rest of it. " He's got a place in Hayle," Jose said. " But why you should want to employ a good man on a bad building beats me. Pull it down."

" Not a stone," I assured him warmly. " The outside will remain exactly as it is, bar two things. I'll want a new front door of decent oak, and every window must be twice its present size."

While I was at it, I elaborated the dream. " That room on the left when you go in will be a kitchen and dining-room in one. The room on the other side of the passage will be my bedroom. The two rooms upstairs will be knocked into one to make a sitting-room-study."

" Cost you a packet," Jose said.

I looked at his thin painfully brushed clothes and felt ashamed. " There's something in it for you, Jose," I said. " It's got to be furnished. You'll have to find the furniture. Don't overdo it. The necessary minimum."

He grinned. " I understand," he said. " An aboriginal peasant's cottage outside, and restrained luxury within."

I had to admit that that was what it came to.

I had a good many talks with Jose about it, and now and then we called Joe Carbis into consultation. We made lists and we drew plans, and when I went back to London a month later I hoped that my investment in Bob Meagher's business would turn out well. I had committed myself to what Jose called a pretty packet.

I spent that summer in Brittany. I hadn't been there before, and I was fascinated by its likeness to Cornwall. I imitated the old codger I had met at Trencrom, bought a rucksack and a pair of shorts, and wandered about getting tanned like old leather. In farmhouses and roadside pubs I now and then came on bits of furniture that would have suited the cottage and that I could have bought; but I thought of Jose and left it all to him. Feelings of guilt and shame returned whenever Jose

119

came to mind. I wondered what right I had to be living as I was: with a handsome flat in London, a cottage being prepared in Cornwall, and myself living in neither but wandering the earth, drinking too much French cider (my equivalent of the codger's apples) and having no care in the world.

At any rate I hoped I hadn't. I had a more or less permanent address at a small hotel in St. Malo, to which I came in from my forays now and then; and there letters reached me from Bob Meagher, reporting progress. There were plans and blueprints, and, towards the end of the summer, a large photograph arrived, showing a web of steel that had arisen on the Great West Road, with a hoarding in front of it labelled Meagher Motor Industries Limited. It looked enormous. For the first time I began to grasp something of the magnitude of Bob's ambitions. In the letter enclosing this photograph he wrote briefly: "This should do for making a start. We shall be in production by this time next year."

There were progress reports from Jose Gomm, too, but they were more sober. Now he had found a nice little table, now a few chairs, and again some attractive hanging lamps. "An old house was gutted near here recently, and Joe Carbis bought some fine oak beams for next to nothing. He says he could rip them into shelves for books in that big room you want for a study. What do you say?"

I said go ahead, put on my rucksack, and started off for another week's perambulation, wondering again about this odd life: Bob Meagher (I hoped) making me a lot of money, and Jose and Joe Carbis cautiously spending a little, keeping things cut to the last penny. I wondered what my austere hard-working father would have thought of it all, and, thinking of him, I thought of Fred Byles whose hedonistic features smiled upon the wall of my London flat. He, at any rate, I felt, would have said: "Go to it, boy. We're young only once," and with this dubious sanction I comforted myself, for it was the sort of advice that we all find irresistible: the advice to please ourselves.

5

I got to know some Breton fishermen, and in October I accepted an invitation to go fishing with them. They said they would be putting in to Penzance. The idea pleased me: to make in reverse the sea journey along which the traffic had flowed in the days of the little dark men to whose village I was bound. From Penzance I took a taxi to Helston and spent an evening with Jose. He had dug up from God knows where a Tudor bed with fantastic hangings. It took up a great deal of the space in his shop, and I slept on it in a sleeping-bag.

In the morning he brought me a cup of tea, and sat on a Regency chair alongside the bed talking while I drank. "I don't know," he said, "whether Sylvia would approve my housing a tramp in that bed. She's half-inclined to buy it. She's had a look at it, and she's coming to see it again in a day or two."

"Oh, so she's in these parts, is she?"

"Yes. She's got a bit of structural work in hand at last. You know that big raw wall to one side of the lounge? Well, that's been stuccoed over, and a doorway made in it. The door at the moment opens into ruin; but now a few masons are there, rebuilding the walls of what will be a large drawing-room. There's not much to see yet. They've done very little but clear out trees and bushes. When that's done, they'll get started on the walls. There's to be a big bedroom over the drawing-room. I hope this bed will go in there."

"Looking a bit ahead, aren't you, Jose?"

"I'm afraid so. But it's something to see a start made after all the talk."

"Where does she get the money from?"

"Her mother was rich, you know—old Chown's sister. Ever read her life?"

"I didn't know one had been written."

"Oh, yes," Jose said, pouring me more tea. "And a very odd life it seems to have been. A sort of *femme fatale*. A lot of men in her life one way and another. But so far as that goes, the book gives more hints than facts. Anyway, the man she was married to couldn't shake clear of her infatuation, though he appears to have had good cause to. He left her a fortune that came to Sylvia."

"I've been told *she* married a rich man, too."

"She did, even richer than Margaret Napier's, I should say. No. There's no lack of money."

He got up and knocked out the pipe he had been smoking. "I'll go and get a bit of breakfast ready. Then we'll run over to Trencrom and see your place. I think you'll like it." He paused by the door and said shyly: "By the way, I'm getting married to-morrow. That widow. You remember? The one I called on about the furniture last March. She's a nice girl."

"Girl! I thought she was a widow."

"Oh, all widows aren't hags, you know. She married young. She's only twenty-six."

I got out of bed and waddled in my bag to the door and shook his hand. "I hope you'll be very happy, Jose."

"Oh, I shall," he said simply. "No argument about that!"

We picked up Joe Carbis in Hayle, and Jose's rattling truck

took us up the hill to Trencrom. I didn't know what to expect. I had left so much to these two, confident that all would be well. It was.

From the outside you wouldn't know that much had happened. Some new slates had been patched into the roof and the walls had been pointed here and there. The patch of land the cottage stood on was still a waste of bramble and thistles. We pushed open the gate and walked round to the front door. That was new: a noble chunk of seasoned oak, with wrought-iron hinges from the forge of a local blacksmith. Jose gave me a big iron key. "Better open it yourself," he said.

The door swung in sweetly without a groan. I walked not into the dark passage I had expected but into one full of light. A long thin window had been taken through the end wall. That and the side walls were whitewashed, multiplying the light. The doors leading to the rooms on either side had been removed. Joe Carbis said briefly that they had been nothing but a mass of worm-holes held together by dust. The new doors, like the front door, were slabs of oak, but thinner, held in place by more elegant hinges. From the ceiling between them a lamp hung down, with an oil-container of bronze and a shade of frosted glass. There was coconut matting on the floor.

I stood for a moment, amazed that a little more light and a slap of whitewash could produce this feeling of clean uncluttered elegance. Jose became impatient and opened the door on the left, leading into what was to be my kitchen-dining-room. "We had to be pretty thorough here," he said. "All the plaster had to come out and a new lot go in. The same with the other rooms."

Here again the window-space was doubled, and this was done by increasing its length, not its height. A sturdy granite mullion stood in the middle, with a wing of the window opening on either hand. But the colour of the room fascinated me more than this. It began with the curtains hanging in front of the windows. I fingered them: leather, soft and pliant as linen. "I'm afraid," Jose said diffidently, "that'll put you back a bit. Old Spanish stuff. If you think I've overstepped, say so. I can sell 'em elsewhere."

I looked at the curtains of rich oxblood red. "Not on your life," I said.

"They gave me the idea for the rest of the room," Jose went on. "I hope you don't find it too dim."

It was dim, but enchantingly so. "I'll tell you what we did," Jose said. "A trade secret. I picked it up from a book about the Boers. I read that they flattened down their earth floors and then smeared liquid cow-dung over them. The book said they used all sorts of colours that could be mixed in with the dung. Well, Joe was more than somewhat doubtful, but we tried it on

122

the cement of the floor, and found that when it was dry you could polish it as if it were wood. So we slapped it on the new plaster of the walls and ceiling as well. And there you are."

There we were. I passed a hand over the walls. They were like silk.

From this now richly sombre room the old piece of infernal machinery known as a Cornish range had been removed. In the rectangular gap where it had stood was a battery of shining oil-cookers. A small oaken refectory table and four leather-seated chairs were in the middle of the room. Against one wall was a dark-oak Welsh dresser whereon a dinner-service was displayed. "That won't cost you much," Jose said. "Just cottage stuff, but rather nice, I thought."

He looked about him with satisfaction, obviously relieved at my pleasure. "An experiment," he said, "but it came off. Of course, you'll use only candles for light. Silver would be best for the candle-sticks, but I leave that to you."

We crossed the passage to the bedroom. Here again the cement floor had been polished in a bizarre Boer fashion, but this time a light blue. The plaster of the walls was distempered yellow, a difficult colour, but Jose had got it right. There were rugs of the same yellow round the bed—a divan with a flowered chintz headboard. The bed was made up. "My wife bought the bedclothes," Joe explained. "We thought you might be tempted to spend a night or two here. It's all aired."

Again the long mullioned window, with curtains of flowered chintz that fell from ceiling to floor. In front of them was a rather lady-like kidney-shaped dressing-table and mirror. There wasn't room for much else except a small chest of drawers. The whole room, in contrast to the other, had a feeling of light and gaiety.

"Well, so far so good, Jose," I said. "Now let's have a look at my study."

The bleak narrow stairway was now lighted by a small circular window, little bigger than a port-hole, that had been punched through the wall. The raw wood of the treads and risers was painted black, and the treads were covered by strips of white rubber. "Not so much chance of breaking your neck," Jose explained. A hand-rope running up the wall opposite the little window helped that, too. I paused at the door. "This had better be good," I said. "It's where I shall work."

"It's not bad," Jose promised.

Remembering the two little dingy rooms which I had commanded to become one, I opened the door.

The light was the first thing that struck me. Each of these rooms had had one small window, looking to the south. I had asked Jose to put windows in the north walls, too, so that I could look out upon Trencrom. And now it was one room with

four long windows, and the walls were grey-green, and upon the
floor was linoleum in large chequers of black and white, like
the floors you see in so many old Dutch pictures. The curtains,
now drawn back, were of black velvet, and a few black beams
fortified the ceiling. It was rather breathtaking. "I'll see you
downstairs," I said to Joe and Jose. I wanted to be alone in my
plain but splendid room. I looked at the empty bookshelves,
gaping like fledgelings for food, at the brass chandelier that
would take ten candles, at the two fireplaces. The fires were
laid, and alongside each was a rush basket full of logs. Except
for a small writing-table and chair, there was no furniture, but
over one of the fireplaces hung a large print of Vermeer's
Music Lesson, a picture which evidently had suggested to Jose
a good deal of what the room should be.

I looked out through one of the northern windows upon the
bulk of Trencrom, gentle under the autumn sunlight. It would
not always be gentle. I thought of the little dark men cowering
there in their stony winter huts, and I felt a fraud. I called to
Jose to come up, and told him so. He said: "Don't be a fool.
Your little dark men did the best they knew. There's no
reason why you shouldn't do the same."

But there seemed no sense in pretending, outside, that this was
a peasant's cottage, while inside it was, in its mild way, palatial.
"Sylvia," I said, "is at any rate trying to turn a ruined
mansion into a mansion in repair. What am I trying to do?"

"*Quién sabe?*" he asked, as though he had just been washed
ashore from the *Absolución.*

"Well, that's what we'll call the place," I said. And the
address I put on the notepaper was "Quién Sabe? Trencrom."

6

I could have stayed there. The bed was aired and furnished. A
visit to Hayle would have provided the food I should need for
a few days. But I got into Jose's truck and we went back to
Helston. We ate lunch there and then I took a taxi to Penruan.
Mr. Chown was not in the lodge. I remembered that he walked
every afternoon. I strolled down to the house to see what the
builders were doing and found that they were still heaving out
roots, taking down such stone as remained standing, and laying
it in orderly piles. Sylvia, wearing a grey tweed skirt and a rust-
coloured pullover, was superintending the work. I had not seen
her since the day when we lunched at Rule's and she had told
me of her engagement to young Clarence Conway.

She kissed me and said: "What on earth have you been
doing to yourself? You look like the lord of the harvest."

The wandering summer in Brittany had turned me golden. So,

too, was she, and I said so. She explained that she had found nothing worth doing in the theatre and had spent the summer at her cottage in the country. "I've been offered parts," she said, "but nothing that I fancied, and I'm one of those lucky people who are well to do, and can pick and choose. Or is that unlucky? Do you think one should just do the job that comes along? It might build into something more solid than I seem to achieve, going on as I do. What do you think?"

We moved away from the men and walked on the terrace, looking out to the tranquil autumn blue of the sea. She put her arm through mine and looked at me inquiringly. I said I didn't know what advice to give her. To me, the theatre was just enchantment. I should hate to know too much about the mechanics behind it. "I should think," I said, "Clarence Conway would be better qualified to speak about such things."

Abruptly she unhooked her arm from mine and walked to the edge of the terrace. She stood there with her back to me, not speaking. I had said the wrong thing. After a moment she moved towards the house. "Come in. I'll give you some tea."

I asked if Mr. Chown would be joining us. "No," she said. "He's in London and will be there for some time. He loathes the place, but his book is coming out at last. He's been working on it for five years."

I followed her into the great hall and admired the plasterwork that Jose had told me about. It seemed to me an extraordinary piece of work: a vast arabesque of fruiting trees and birds and beasts. "There aren't many people in the country who could have done that," she said, "but I managed to find one who could. That's how I've always imagined it. I'm giving the plaster a year to dry. Then it will be painted. It should look like a tapestry. Indeed, it is copied from a tapestry."

She was speaking perfunctorily, not really interested. Her wits were wandering. "I'll go and make the tea," she said. "Mrs. Tiddy's gone."

When she came back and poured out the tea I asked again about Mr. Chown, feeling guilty at not having once written to him throughout my wander-year. "He'll be all right," she said. "Janet is looking after him. They're using the Shaftesbury Avenue flat."

"And Janet? Is she still enamoured of Miss Hopkins?"

"They don't see so much of one another as they used to because Miss Hopkins has become engaged to an archæologist. He wants to marry her at once and take her out to what he calls his dig. It's in some hot sandy place somewhere."

"So she's transferring her attention from the souls of the living to the bones of the dead?"

She refilled my tea-cup and the conversation drifted to a standstill. The afternoon was declining; the great room dusked. It

125

was a moment in which, had the wall been painted, the figures upon it would seem to stir, the leaves to tremble.

I said: "What's the matter, Sylvia?"

She piled the tea-things on to the silver tray, put a hand into a pocket of her sweater, and took out a newspaper clipping. She dropped it on the table, took up the tray, and went without a word.

I sensed that in the cutting was tragic matter. I hardly dared to take it up, but at last did so.

"Mr. Clarence Conway, who arrived in Hollywood a month ago to take the lead in the film *Lions Sometimes Roar*, was married yesterday morning to Adèle Arachon, who is to play opposite him. This is Miss Arachon's fourth marriage. The first was to . . ."

I didn't go on. I dropped the bit of paper on to the table, disgusted by my own feeling of liberation. I didn't turn when I heard the slight sound of Sylvia coming back into the room. She stood just within the door, and presently said: "The man-eating bitch!"

I got up then and went to her and put my arms round her. She cried quietly with her head on my shoulder. I murmured soothing words and patted her back like a parent tranquillising a hurt child. But she was ten years older than I was. I looked at her face and couldn't believe it. Her eyes were luminous with tears, and her skin, because of the open-air summer she had enjoyed, was luminous, too. Luminous gold. The feel of her ripe breasts pressed against me made me hold her tighter. I kept my left arm round her, and with my other hand took out my handkerchief and gently dried her eyes. When that was done, she held her head back, poised on the splendid pillar of her neck, and we looked steadily into one another's faces. I put one hand upon her breast and with the other gently brought her face to mine. We stood like that for a long time, then she gave a sigh which I hoped expressed happiness as well as comfort, and she pushed me aside. She left me standing there and went out of the room.

I wandered out to the terrace. The workmen were gone and the western sky was a smoulder of weaving dusky smoke shot through with sparks of crimson and ochre. Presently I heard her voice: "George!"

I went back into the hall and shot the great bolt.

"George! Come up here."

I had never been off the ground floor of that house, and now I climbed the great stairway up which, on my first night there, I had watched Janet run like a lapwing. I went slowly, and moved into a dark corridor panelled in oak, carpeted in crimson.

"Here, George."

The door was open and I walked in. She was as naked as in

126

the moment when she had seemed a goddess wading out of the
opal sea. The room was almost dark and the sheets were turned
down on a splendid four-poster bed. She moved towards the
bed and said: " Comfort me, darling."

I locked the door and began to undress.

7

There was light in the sky when I woke up. Sylvia was asleep,
her arm under my neck. The light grew and I lay for a long
time looking into her face, which was fulfilled and content. Her
eyelids were blue: I didn't know whether by nature or artifice.
Her lips were a little open, revealing perfect teeth. Her disordered hair opulently strewed the pillow.

I was not surprised by what had happened. I had always
known that it would happen. From the moment when we had
sat in the room downstairs, I then a boy of fifteen, and the
firelight had played in the silken valleys of her clothes and upon
the loveliness of her half-revealed breasts, she had leapt upon
my imagination as Woman ; and my sight of her the next
morning had transformed imagination into concrete knowledge,
a picture photographed upon the mind, that I had never been
able to dismiss. She had blown my puberty to a fever pitch
which had made me an easy victim of that hussy in Manchester.
Since then, I had been chaste.

I lay listening to the small sounds of the awakening morning:
the night's heavy moisture dripping from the trees, a drowsy
twitter of birds, a sigh of water upon sand ; and these heard
sounds mingled with sounds imagined: the soft footsteps of the
day, climbing out of the east. I thought of Baudelaire: *La
douce nuit qui marche*. And this was the gentle morning,
relentlessly following.

I let it all wash over me, lying relaxed, flooded with the peace
that followed the conflict of the night. And it had been conflict. I thought of the nurse and her crude quick satisfaction.
Sylvia had not been like that: not by any means.

I had been watching the light swelling upon the window-pane,
defining the mullions, and now transforming a vague blob of
shape into a white rose, blooming untimely. Behind it, the
grey pearl of the air was slowly suffused with blue. Then
Sylvia's free arm came up out of the bedclothes, golden to the
elbow, white to the shoulder, and her hand gently turned my
head towards her. She knelt up in the bed, the clothes spilling
from her nakedness, as I had watched the morning sea once do,
and looked down into my face. The wave of her beauty, arched
over me, sent a drowning shudder through me ; and then the
wave broke and the conflict began again.

127

The next thing that woke me was the sound of voices, the thud of hammers, the falling of stone. It seemed odd, as I lay listening with closed eyes, that the world was going prosaically on, unaware that miracles were happening. I stretched out my hand to touch Sylvia and encountered only rumpled sheets. She was gone. She was soon back, carrying a tray with buttered toast, coffee and apples. I sat up in bed, and she laid the tray on my knees, pulled the stool from the dressing-table alongside the bed, and shared the meal with me.

We ate looking at one another, our eyes full of the night's knowledge. She had made up carefully, and was wearing the clothes of yesterday—the tweed skirt and rust-coloured sweater. The sudden fulfilment of so long a dreaming left me incapable of surprise. If *that* could happen, anything could happen. If I had been capable of surprise, I would have been surprised that we were so easy with one another. There was no shyness on either side, but there was an underlying excitement. We believed that what had happened would happen again soon.

When the meal was over, she gave me a perfunctory kiss, not wishing to rouse me at that moment. She said: " Mrs. Tiddy will be here soon. I shall just have time to swill these things, and then I shall have to eat the breakfast she will prepare. I'll tell her that I invited you to stay the night, so you'd better go into the room opposite this and knock the bedclothes about a bit. The bathroom's farther down the corridor."

I asked her to bring up the rucksack which contained the few things I had brought with me. " I've put it in your room," she said, and went away with the tray.

I picked up my clothes from the carpet, to which I had thrown them hurriedly the night before, and crossed the corridor. I got into the small single bed and heaved about in it realistically, then took up my shaving tackle and went to the bathroom. Whatever else she intended to do with this house, Sylvia did not intend to reproduce a medieval bathroom. If there was such a thing. I don't know. The room I entered was luxurious and steeped in a warm scented smell, which told me Sylvia had been there before me. I shaved, lay soaking in hot water for ten minutes, and then went to scatter a few convincing evidences of occupation about *my* bedroom: a couple of books on the dressing-table, a sweater on a chair, a fistful of small change on the mantelpiece.

When I went down, Sylvia was finishing breakfast in the small dining-room, where John Collier's portrait of her mother, Margaret Napier, hung above the fireplace. Mrs. Tiddy was hovering about in the room. "You're the last one we expected to see," she said.

"Oh, you'll be seeing a good deal of me from now on."

She looked from me to Sylvia and from Sylvia to me. "I shouldn't be surprised," she said, and went out—well, meaningfully.

I sat down and took another cup of coffee and nibbled some toast. "What did La Tiddy mean by her exit line?" I asked.

Sylvia smiled. "Well, you don't live in these rustic parts so long as she's done without realising that the worst you suspect is probably charitable."

9

She brought her new car round to the front door—a cream-coloured two-seater Bentley. She had told Mrs. Tiddy that we should eat out. "Mr. Ledra will not be staying here to-night," she added. She told me to pack my rucksack, and I did so, full of misery. I put it into the boot and climbed in alongside her. "Where are we going to?" I asked.

"Wherever you like."

In the passionate overthrow of all my normal thoughts and preoccupations last night I had forgotten my cottage at Trencrom. She knew nothing about the long patient work that had been going on there through the summer, for I had told Jose to mention it to no one. It was about half past twelve, and I said: "Let's eat in Helston and then go to the north coast."

We did that, the lovely car purring through the lovely autumn afternoon. Sloes and blackberries were dewy in the hedge-rows, and on the telegraph wires swallows were restless, agitated with premonitions of the year's end. I said: "Why did you tell Mrs. Tiddy that I should not be at Penruan to-night?"

My voice was flat. She said: "Because I meant it. We must be sensible, darling. Penruan is definitely not London."

"Well, what are we to do?"

She would not fall into my glum mood. "I have no doubt," she said, "that that will be revealed to us."

No; she would not be glum, but presently she began to look grave. She stopped the car on a lonely stretch of road and turned to me. "I think I know what's worrying you," she said. "You are asking yourself whether last night was a reaction after that news about Clarence Conway. Well, it was. Of course it was. Up to a point." She put a hand on mine and went on: "But I hope you don't believe, darling, that I'm in the *habit* of reacting in that way to life's disappointments."

I mumbled that of course I didn't.

"Very well, then. Why do you think it happened?"

" You really mean that I *meant* something? I myself?"

" George, it's for you to find the answer to that."

She was asking me if I loved her. Suddenly—it was shocking to me to discover—I didn't know the answer. I knew only that through all those years I had desired her. Shame overwhelmed me. Was I doing anything more than nag for a repetition of a devastating and triumphant experience with a skilful woman?

I had intended to take her to my cottage and to make love to her there. My mind suddenly shocked into a doubt, the idea seemed distasteful. We went no farther than Hayle. We walked on the sands of Carbis Bay, and she talked to me, reluctantly, but as if she thought it was something I should understand, about Clarence Conway. " It was a mistake," she said. " Almost from the beginning I knew that. He began to borrow money from me. Well, he called it borrowing. I hated to refuse it, and at the same time I hated to give it, because it made me wonder whether I meant anything more to him than a money-box. He was always most careful to give me I.O.U.s. Somehow that made it all the more distasteful. Fancy I.O.U.s between people who love! I always burned them."

Altogether, I gathered, the news from Hollywood had been both a shock and a relief, a vortex of feeling that I had helped her to sort out.

When we got back to Helston I took my rucksack from the boot and said I'd find a room in a hotel for the night. " In the morning I really must get back to town and start some work to make up for this loafing summer."

She seemed surprised. " I shall be going back myself in a day or two by road. Couldn't you wait till then?"

" I really must get organised." It sounded lame, even to me.

" Then I'll give you a ring when I'm back. All right?"

" I'd love that."

Her head was leaning out of the car. She was expecting me to kiss her. I kissed her, and noticed what I had not seen before. There were the tiniest wrinkles at the corners of her eyes. I walked into the hotel thinking of the swallows on the telegraph wires.

When I had eaten a solitary dinner I strolled across the road to Jose's shop. There was a hand-written notice on the door. " Closed till Friday, 9 a.m." This was Wednesday. Only then I remembered Jose's wedding. He had given himself a sadly brief honeymoon. I felt conscience-stricken, self-regarding and miserable. I went back to the hotel, wrote a few lines wishing Jose joy, and enclosed a cheque, asking him to buy himself a wedding present. Then I went to bed, feeling no happier.

CHAPTER SEVEN

1

The excuse I had given Sylvia—that I had work to do—was only
an excuse; but, all the same, when I entered my flat in the
late afternoon of the next day, I found that I did want to work.
I ate at a restaurant in Baker Street, and went back through a
nippy air, well content to be alone. I drew my curtains, switched
on my electric fire, and sat down to sort out an idea or two. I
read through the notebook that I had carried with me in
Brittany and Cornwall. It was satisfactorily full of suggestions,
like an artist's sketch-book. Hardly a sound reached me from
my back-water of a street. I began to write one of my little
pieces. That is what they are called by the critics who don't
like them. Mr. Ledra's Little Pieces. Mr. Ledra's confetti.

I wrote about the old codger I had met at Trencrom. I
finished it the next day, and though I felt that there was still a
lot to be done to it, I decided to show it to Mr. Chown. I
remembered that he was staying with Janet in the Shaftesbury
Avenue flat. I was never easy when thinking about him. I had
been sent to him to be turned into a Greek scholar, and I had
made nothing that he would have considered to be headway. It
wasn't my fault that my father's death had ended our association,
but I knew and he knew that, even if there had not been that
ending, I was not the sort of stuff he could do much with. It was
because of this that I did not want him to think that I was a
hopeless fool. He might despise my Greek, but I hoped my
English would please him.

He himself answered the telephone when I rang up the flat.
He had often expressed himself forcibly to me on the subject of
telephones—"those damned pieces of copper wire that permit
fools to rush in on the meditations of angels"—and I suppose
it was because of this that he spoke crossly. "George Ledra?
Should I know you?"

"I was a pupil of yours once, sir, at Penruan. You remember?"

"Oh, *that* Ledra! Well, what is it?"

I talked him round, and he agreed to eat luncheon with me—
"provided," he said, "it's at Simpson's in the Strand where they
know how to cook mutton. You'd better let me choose the
wine."

I agreed that he might have the privilege, and he chose well,
and accompanied me afterwards to my flat, mellow in a taxi-

131

cab. "This damn' great Babylonian pandemonium," he grumbled. "Have you looked about you? They're tearing down the few things that a civilised gentleman would care to look at, and putting up God knows what. Ant hills. Towers of Babel."

I settled him in a comfortable chair and gave him a cigar to soothe his passage through my manuscript. He hadn't read far when he began to laugh. "Good God!" he said. "It's old Bagley. Gwynn Bagley. He was a fellow of St. Dominic's in my time. Anthropology. That was his line."

He expressed no opinion about my little piece. He went on about Mr. Bagley. "He was known as Jimmy Bones, and his rooms as the boneyard. He was a perfect damn' nuisance at college meetings. I liked him. He was a character, and there aren't many characters now, in the universities or anywhere else. Machine-made. Turned out on a lathe. That's the sort of chaps we get now, and we'll get more of 'em."

He lolled in his chair and looked at the portrait of Fred Byles. "Now that looks like a character," he said. "Who is he?"

"I don't know much about him. My father knew him slightly, and my grandfather very well. I keep him there just because I like the look of him. I've been told he ended in gaol."

"I'm not surprised. A lot of good men have done that."

He stayed till four o'clock, and I offered him tea.

"No. I'm leaving this stinkhole to-morrow. I must get back and chuck my things into a bag. All except my tails. I've promised to take Janet out to-night to some sink of iniquity."

"Are tails worn?"

"Why not? I've had mine for twenty years, and I certainly don't intend to buy one of these monkey-jackets that boys wear nowadays."

I said that with me it was the other way about. I hadn't tails, and couldn't imagine myself in them.

"Well, if you like to come with us, put on your monkey-jacket. Possibly Janet won't mind my inviting you. Do you dance?"

"Reasonably well."

"Try, George, to do things very well indeed. Don't smatter. I dance excellently—the waltz, the polka, the lancers—the whole lot of 'em. But I don't want to get too tired. You'll be a useful second string for Janet. Be at the flat at about nine."

When he was gone I fell asleep, my mind bemused by the thought of Mr. Chown vigorously dancing the polka, in tails, on a modern dance floor.

I took a taxi to Shaftesbury Avenue. Janet opened the door—a Janet new to me. I had known the posing capricious witch; and the awkward tomboy who used to run away from school; and Miss Hopkins's pupil, wearing the gauche togs appropriate to a belief that life was real, life was earnest. The little entrance hall of the flat only just held the two of us. It seemed to be full of the rustle of her golden silk, the exhalation of her perfume, the dancing of her eyes. The cut of the dress exposed her breasts, firm and white. She was almost as tall as I was. She took my hand and said: "Hallo, darling." It was no more than a catchword. In those days, you were darling or Aubrey or Richard long before you were Mr. Smith or Mr. Jones, even if it were ever remembered that you were one of those prosaic fellows.

She drew me into the sitting-room of the flat. "Uncle's nearly ready," she said. And in a whisper: "I'm so glad you came."

"He'd have given you a thoroughly good time. He'd have hurled you through the lancers till you were bruised from head to foot."

"You've saved my life," she said. "Have a drink."

She was utterly self-possessed. She had reached the moment when a girl becomes a woman.

She gave me a very dry sherry, and held a match to my cigarette, laughing into my eyes.

"How is Medea Hopkins?" I asked with a hint of mockery, as though inquiring in the Rue de la Paix of someone known long ago in Petticoat Lane.

"Perhaps you've heard that she's engaged to an archæologist?"

"Yes. Your mother told me.

"Poor Mother! Why does she drag out her life in that dreadful ruin?"

"You thought it romantic once. You used to lie awake listening to the voices of drowned sailors. Or so you said."

"What a little fool I was! Well, about Medea, or Clare as she now calls herself. She's become a perfect bore. Thank God she's getting married next week. I couldn't have borne any more confidences about the perfections of Roland. They'll spend their honeymoon in Petra or Carthage or somewhere."

"Are you jealous of Roland? Or do you resent him because he's deprived Britain of a promising recruit to the ranks of our economists?"

She blushed a little. "You're talking for effect."

"Why else should anyone talk?"

She sipped her sherry. "At all events," she said, "I decided against taking up economics. I've been working like mad at shorthand and typing. I want to be a secretary—to someone interesting, of course."

"Yes. That goes without saying. When you're ready let me know, and I'll look around among the Prime Ministers, Poet Laureates and outstanding film actors of my acquaintance."

Suddenly she laughed and clapped her hands, a girl again. "Oh, it's so good to talk nonsense to someone. D'you know, Uncle's rather dull? Is that a terrible thing to say? He's so good, but so dull."

Mr. Chown came in from the bedroom. "I'm neither good nor dull," he said. "Good, indeed! There were times when I would gladly have strangled my father. But my hands were too small and his neck was too thick. As for dull! Do I look dull, George?"

"No, sir," I said. "You coruscate."

He looked equipped to dance Sir Roger de Coverley at Dingley Dell, but over his arm was a cloak which he now threw upon his shoulders, imparting to himself an air of convivial brigandage, a resemblance to those types Lautrec liked to draw at the Moulin Rouge.

He helped himself to sherry and announced: "It is twenty years since I last danced. I was then fifty, and this suit was a bit easy. To-night there is a definite equatorial constriction. I think I had better not dance over much with you, Janet."

"Please don't worry to do so," she begged him. "You will be quite happy if you turn me and George loose to romp like colts in a field."

"That sounds to me rather dissolute, my dear. The moral prop of Medea Hopkins has been removed too suddenly and completely. Romp, indeed! Even your mother would disapprove of that," he said, as though Sylvia's moral character were notoriously half-way to dissolution. "Have you ever danced with Sylvia, George?"

No, I had never *danced* with Sylvia. I suppose it was only fancy, but I thought he was considering me with curious speculation. I was looking at Janet, dewy as a flower before sunrise in April; and I was thinking of Sylvia, her face leaning from her car window outside the Helston hotel: a face on which I had seen, with something of shock, the first signs of fading bloom: and I knew that it was with Janet, not Sylvia, that I wanted to dance. Mr. Chown continued to look disturbingly at me. Then he filled my sherry glass and cried with a clutch at modernity, at being in league with my youth and Janet's: "Well, one for the road! Then we must be off."

He had told me at my flat that afternoon that he had promised to take Janet to some sink of iniquity. We found ourselves at one of the tables edging the dance floor of the Savoy. He took up the huge bill of fare that looked like a history of human gluttony, and said: "I think you are both too young to know your way through this fabulous labyrinth. You had better leave it to me." The waiter was French, and in that language he and Mr. Chown conducted what sounded like a furious verbal battle, which at last Janet cut short by saying to the waiter: "Do you speak English?"

He agreed that he did. "Then listen. I don't want any soup. I'll have cold breast of chicken with a simple green salad. Then I'll have fruit salad, and that will be all."

I admired her coolness, and said meekly: "That will do for me, too."

Mr. Chown looked at us in dismay, as Napoleon might have looked at a general who had suggested cutting out the conference and getting on with the battle.

"You can't dance if you're gorged," Janet said.

"Well, if it's to be one or the other," Mr. Chown assured her, "I know where my duty lies." And he and the waiter fell to it once more.

I was not much of a dancer, and neither was Janet, but we threw ourselves into the tide, hoping it would bear us along somehow, and had reached that rather idiotic moment when the band stopped and we stood in the middle of the floor, clapping till it started again. A voice hailed me, and, turning, I confronted Bob Meagher, who took my hand and said: "You know Wendy, I think?"

I should not have recognised this lady as the efficient Miss Merriman of Messrs. Fred Byles and Ledra. She was, as they say, dripping with diamonds, or perhaps they were not diamonds. At any rate, she wore a lot of stuff that twinkled and sparkled: at her ears, round her neck, upon her arms and wrists. She was a little stouter, and she looked handsome and happy. I introduced her and Bob to Janet, and Bob said: "Look, George, Wendy and I have been watching you two. You'd better take some lessons from experts, or you'll get nowhere."

The band began to play again. Bob took hold of Janet and Wendy entrusted herself to me. She chattered. She chattered of old days and her runaway marriage, and of the wonders of Bob and of her two children and of the house they had at Hatch End. And all the time that she was chattering she was subtly and unobtrusively taking command of the dance steps and leading me in the way I should go. Out of the corner of my eye I could see that Bob was indoctrinating Janet, and I teased Wendy about the skill with which he had snatched up a pretty girl. Wendy wasn't vulnerable. "It's just that Bob hates to see anything badly done," she said. "I agreed with him that it was about time you and Miss Bascombe were taken in hand."

When the dance ended, I introduced them to Mr. Chown, who was forcing his way through the carcase of some spiced recondite fowl. He got up and bowed to Wendy and invited them to sit at our table, which they did, having finished their own meal.

I danced only once more with Janet that night, for Bob and Wendy insisted on regarding us as cubs to be licked into shape. At midnight Mr. Chown expressed his disappointment at there having been not a single polka or minuet, in which, he said, he had been hoping to partner Janet. As it was, we had now better go home.

Bob said: "I have a car here, sir. Allow me to drive you."

We dropped them at their door in Shaftesbury Avenue, and I told Bob not to bother about me: I'd find a taxi.

"Get back into the car," he said. "You're coming home with us. I rang up from the Savoy to tell 'em to have a room ready."

"I decline," I said, "to appear in the streets of Hatch End to-morrow morning still wearing evening clothes."

"What do you take me for?" Bob demanded. "D'you think I'd forget a thing like that? You won't appear in the streets. You'll step straight into this car and be driven to your flat before we go on to see the works."

D'you think I'd forget a thing like that? That was Bob Meagher. He did not forget things, and disliked the suggestion that he might do so. Standing there in the chilly midnight street, I felt very young and small.

"Do as Bob says," Wendy advised me. "He just wants to show off his house."

He got into the driving seat, and she sat alongside him. I had the whole comfortable back of the car to myself, and fell asleep. I didn't wake till the stopping of the car waked me, and then I got out to face a lighted welcoming porch. It was a moonless night and there was not much more than that to be seen. I helped Wendy down, and Bob drove off to the garage. From a small entrance hall Wendy took me into a comfortable sitting-room where an electric fire was burning. "Now," she said, "I'm straight off to bed. I'm fagged out. I'll tell them to send in some coffee. That's what Bob likes when he sits up jawing all night, and I know that that's what he'll want to do to-night."

She gave me a cheek-brushing conventional kiss and hurried away.

I threw off my overcoat and sank into a downy chair by the fire. Presently the coffee things were wheeled in on a trolley by a man who appeared to be about thirty years old. There was a flex attached to the bottom of the chromium stand on which the milk and coffee pots stood. He plugged it into a gadget in the skirting-board. All very efficient. He took up my overcoat and draped it neatly over his arm, and carried it away.

Bob came in. "That was Brookes," he explained to me. "One of my Tank Corps chaps. I found him just married and also absolutely broke. Pretty well starving. He and his wife look after us. Worth their weight in gold."

"I hope you weigh them every pay-day."

He gave me a very cold look. It was saying again: "D'you think that I'd forget a thing like that?" And I learned in time that the Brookeses had nothing to worry about.

"Fill your pipe, George," Bob invited, and filled his own. "We haven't had an all-night session since I used to haunt your digs in Withington soon after I was demobbed."

I didn't say that an all-night session was the last thing I wanted to begin at that moment. I obediently filled my pipe and he poured two mugs of almost black coffee. "You're a lazy devil, you know," he said. "All through last summer I bombarded you with stuff about what we're doing, and as far as I can see I might as well have been throwing pebbles into the Atlantic to form a causeway to America. Well, now you'd better learn something."

I learned very little, but I had the sense to know that he didn't expect me to. I was only one of the men who had lent him money. He wanted to talk, and I was a handy audience. The one thing I did learn was to respect a dedication I did not understand. It was four o'clock in the morning when he said: "Well, that's how things stand at the moment. As I told you in one of my letters, we expect to be in full production by the middle of next summer. Full production, that is, within the limits of our building. How things go from that point will determine the extent of new building. We've got the land for it. To-morrow—or rather later on to-day," he amended with a grin—"you shall have a look at it for yourself."

He got up, knocked out his pipe, and yawned. "Breakfast at eight," he said. "I'll show you to your room."

By daylight I was able to see that Bob had a nice little suburban place: a brand-new house standing in about an acre of land planted with brand-new trees. In fifty years' time it would either begin to look a place that grew there or be brushed aside by London's stampede in that direction. It was a page on which all the writing had yet to be done, and I had an idea that Bob would not do it. He would be elsewhere.

Wendy was not up, or up and tending children somewhere. We had breakfasted, and I was wandering, evening clothes on me, under the pale sky of a russet autumn, looking at the young trees—their trunks no more than thumb-thick—silver birch, rowan, larch, whitebeam—and Bob came out of the garage, as familiarly as a dog out of its accustomed kennel, and joined me on the grass. Spotless grass, unsullied by the fall of leaves, for there was nothing much in the way of leaf to fall, and so the grass was prim and suburban, immaculately dark green and light green from the alternate pressures of yesterday's mower. It needed only the net to go up and the boys and girls of the local tennis club to come out, chattering and swinging rackets. I thought of Trencrom, and Trencrom made me think of Sylvia and of her half-ruined house beside the ageless sea.

"It'll do for the moment," Bob said. "It has its points. The children run round naked on this grass, and I must say they look pretty good on it. Like to see 'em before we go?"

"No," I said.

"All right. I'll run you to your place and you can change and come and see the works. Did I tell you Jocelyn had a sister?"

"Jocelyn?"

"My son, you dense oaf."

"Oh, yes. You did tell me."

The car was waiting on the staid road outside the front gate. We got in. "Well, then. He has a sister—Viola."

"Did you name her after the flower or the musical instrument?"

He looked sideways at me with displeasure. "You take nothing seriously," he said.

He rather oppressed me. His life was so cut-and-dried. His works; his house that would do for the moment; his Wendy, dripping with diamond-like adornments; his Jocelyn and Viola. I was prepared to bet that the education of both was already insured.

"This," he said, "is a graph of production."

We had walked along a corridor. The rooms on either hand, Bob explained, would be occupied by what he called the executives. A door at the end of the corridor, labelled Managing Director, was to be his own scene of operations. It was bigger than any of the other rooms. "Prestige demands that," Bob told me. "In a show of this sort, prestige and size are closely related. They always have been. Think of the captain's cabin looking out from the stern of an Elizabethan warship."

There was a vast desk in the middle of the room. I looked at it with admiration. It was the only thing I had understood in the whole of that fatiguing morning: a lovely Chippendale desk of mahogany, with a red leather top and a chair upholstered in red leather to match. Everything in the deeply carpeted room had this touch of magnificence. There was nothing that I should have thought of as coming under the heading "commercial appointments." Nothing except what he called the graph of production, hanging on a wall. I did know enough about graphs to understand that they recorded achievement or lack of achievement. But the line on this graph was already filled in. It sloped, satisfyingly, from the bottom left-hand corner to the right-hand top.

I had not found much to say about the amazing things that Bob had shown me, but now I ventured: "I suppose this represents the production that is hoped for?"

He walked to one of the windows, which were hung with expensive curtains, and I joined him there and looked down, realising how cunningly this window was placed to command a view of everything that we had spent the morning going through piecemeal. We could see even the company's playing field, already turfed, and edged with stripling Lombardy poplars that looked like a wall of defensive spears. I could feel that everything which was merely under my eye was in his mind, a series of links, each leading to the next, and all adding up to the final word Production.

"That graph," he said, "is there to make clear to every member of the executive staff what I expect to be done because I know it *can* be done. If it is not done . . ." He left it unsaid.

"That's all very well," I agreed, "but it only takes us halfway. Production is one thing. Selling the product is another."

There was a grim look on his face, and I was glad that I was not one of the gentlemen from the executive corridor making this suggestion in the Managing Director's room. "I think," he said, "that if that situation threatens to arise I shall know how to deal with it."

He looked at his watch. It was one minute before half past twelve. Precisely at half past a trickle of workmen began towards one of the canteens. These were men engaged in the still unfinished work of getting the place ready. Bob put away his watch, satisfied of punctuality. "There are three canteens," he explained. "Two are out there—one for workmen and one for foremen. The executives' canteen is here, inside. My meals, when I want them, will be served in this room."

Prestige again. "A different sort of crockery and cutlery in each canteen, Bob?" I suggested mischievously.

"But naturally" he said, without a blink "Now, if you're ready, I'll run you to town. I've booked a table at the Café Royal."

5

I got back to my flat at about half past three. The telephone bell was ringing. "I just wanted to let you know that Uncle got away all right this morning," Janet said.

"What's so remarkable about that? One generally does get away if there's a train to be caught."

"Yes, I suppose one does, but I thought you'd like to know."

"Well—thank you for allaying my anxieties."

"You sound surly. I'm sorry if I've butted in at a bad moment. Are you busy or something?"

"I was about to begin an essay on that curiously flat serenity that broods over a wealthy suburb on an autumn morning," I lied. "Do you know what I mean? Not a worm out of place in the earth. The sun smiling rather than shining. Each bird waiting its turn to maintain the thin melodic trickle. . . ."

"You're talking for effect, as you were doing last night," she broke in. "But, seriously, do you write?"

"Yes, now and then I do. Very beautifully."

"How exciting! I had no idea you were a writer."

How should she? How should anybody? Not even Sylvia knew that I occasionally sullied a virgin sheet.

"We know very little about one another," I said. "Medea Hopkins came between us. I feel I owe it to your mother to keep an eye on you, seeing that Medea is no longer your guardian angel."

"Oh—Mother!"

"It is now twenty minutes to four. Taxi-cabs are continually passing your front door. Hop into one and you will be here in time for tea."

"I don't even know your address."

I gave it to her. "I'll be right along," she said.

That is the nonsensical way it started.

I decided that I had better make an impression, so I laid some sheets of paper upon my blotting-pad and wrote a title: "*Mist and Mellow Frightfulness.*"

I began: "Last night the stockbroker homeward plodded his weary way from the station on the Metropolitan line. He had embarked upon the five-fifteen from Baker Street, uplifted by a sense of satisfaction at a comely balance between the goings-on of bears and bulls. As he plodded, he noted the barbered lawns of friends and neighbours. It was but a decade ago that bulls had bellowed on the pastures now tamed to tennis courts; and there, at Tanner's Corner, had been a pond in which the great beasts plashed their cloven hoofs. Now it was a swimming-pool, tiled in blue, in which the lady friends of Solomon Solomons, descending like suave arrows from the diving-board, squealed and splashed. As for bears, their bones had been found, to testify to a barbaric age, happily done with.

"The stockbroker's brief-case swung rhythmically from his chubby hand as his chubby eye peered from well-nourished creases upon these evidences of man's restless, eternal, and on the whole successful march from anarchy to order. He thought of Kathleen, even now preparing the pre-prandial drinks, and . . ."

The door-bell rang. "Will you pay the taximan," Janet asked. "I haven't a bean."

I went down and paid the taximan. When I returned she was bent over the writing-table. I picked up the solitary sheet and put it into a drawer.

"What beautiful handwriting you have," she said.

"I have been receiving certificates and medals for it since the age of six," I erroneously informed her. "But that is not something that will impress an editor."

"Let me sit here," she said, "and look at all your lovely things while you make the tea. I thought you'd have it ready."

It was a bad moment to ask anybody to tea. I had been away all the summer and had laid in nothing but a few necessaries. I apologised as I carried in a pot of tea and some biscuits. "Would you rather I took you out?" I asked.

"No, no," she said. "This is lovely. You have a lovely place, and I've never been in a writer's flat before."

We sat by the electric fire, with the things on a low table between us. She had thrown off a light coat. She crossed her legs, and I noticed that they were very beautiful. Her face was beautiful, too, especially her eyes. They were darker than I had remembered, and the lashes were long. She was curiously poised. She looked a woman, but now and then her speech was childish.

She said: "Uncle tells me you have just come from Penruan. Did you see anything of Mother when you were down there?"

I found it distasteful to talk about Sylvia. "She was kind enough to put me up for a night. It was only a flying visit. I went mainly to see a cottage I've bought on the North Coast."

"How was Mother? I'm worrying about her. I mean about that horrid little man she got engaged to. Did you know about

141

that? Did you know he'd thrown her over? He *was* a horrid little man. He used to come down to the cottage, and he tried to make me once."

She said it unhesitatingly, without a blush. She was a woman all right.

"I did know that she was engaged," I said. "But I've been out of touch—away in Brittany for most of the year. What have you been doing?"

"I told you. I've been learning shorthand and typewriting. I want to be a secretary. Do you need a secretary?"

"No. I write few letters, and I like to write them with my own hand. As for the rest of my writing, a week's work could be dealt with by an hour's typing. I'd better send it to some typewriting bureau. That will be cheaper."

"Do you know of anyone who wants a good secretary?"

"Are you a good secretary?"

I saw that she was taking this thing seriously. She said: "I can't say. I'm a good shorthand typist. I can take dictation up to a hundred and forty words a minute, and what's more I can read what I have taken. Mother bought me a typewriter and I work hard on it for hours every day at the flat. I can type at a really good speed, accurately, and I've been studying the lay-out of letters. I know a lot about the English language. Unusual words wouldn't flummox me."

"I don't think business men use many unusual words. You'd have to get used to words like *in re yours* and *the codification of the aforementioned statistics*. Can you write *the codification of the aforementioned statistics* in shorthand?"

"Yes."

I handed her a pencil and a scrap of paper, and examined what she wrote. "Excellent," I said, not knowing a word of any shorthand system. I refilled her cup.

"I'm not a fool," she unnecessarily informed me, "and I know that shorthand and typing are only the tools. Being a good secretary needs more than that."

"What does it need?"

"Well, understanding one's employer and what helps him and what worries him, and keeping the worries away from him as far as possible."

"I feel," I said, "a deep shame at entertaining so intelligent a young woman on tea—badly made—and biscuits—a bit soggy."

"There you go again—talking for effect, and not very well. I suppose that would be the worst of becoming secretary to an author."

"You would be lucky if it were the worst."

"I can take care of myself," she assured me calmly. "I learned the facts of life when I was a schoolgirl."

She lit a cigarette, and I lit my pipe. I said: "I really am

142

sorry to have given you such an abominable tea. May I take you out somewhere to dinner?"

"I should love that. Shall we go where we can dance? I was ashamed of myself at the Savoy last night. If we're to dance at all we should learn to do it properly."

"All right. But not at the Savoy. I can't afford it."

"Neither could old Chowny. That dinner skinned him. He borrowed his fare to Cornwall from me. That's why I couldn't pay the taximan."

She got up, laughing, and I helped her into her coat. "I'll call for you at eight," I said.

6

We found a place in Charlotte Street where the food wasn't too expensive, and the dance floor and band were excellent. There was not the sense of so many eyes on us as there had been at the Savoy, and we were easier with one another, and danced a little better. We enjoyed the evening and said that we must do it again.

"Often, please," Janet said, as I wished her good-bye in Shaftesbury Avenue at midnight.

I was ready for bed, but as I was opening the front door a young man who was pacing up and down restlessly approached me and said: "Are you George Ledra?"

"Yes," I admitted. "I'm George Ledra at 12.30 a.m., hell-bent for by-byes. See you in the morning."

"Please," he said. "I shall be enormously busy all day to-morrow. Seeing printers and so forth."

I still had to make effective contact with printer's ink. The word printers settled it. "Come in," I said.

I sat him by the fire and produced sherry and the soggy biscuits. He was hatless and wearing a heavy overcoat that almost engulfed him. He threw it upon the floor and sat down with his feet enveloped in it. Baggy flannel trousers, a scarlet pullover and a green tweed coat with frayed cuffs. His shoes looked none too good.

"Dodge," he introduced himself. "Hubert Dodge."

"The only Dodge I know is the man I bought my biscuits from this morning. Not very good ones."

Dodge's Stores proliferated all over London and the provinces.

"My father," he explained to my astonishment. The owner of Dodge's Stores must be something near a millionaire, and Hubert looked as though all he stood up in could be bought for twopence. He was a strange creature: thin, dark, with enormous wondering eyes, heavily lashed. My mind filed him as the Startled Fawn.

"You remember Anthony?" he asked.

I puzzled my head and could not remember Anthony.

"Anthony Chambers, I mean. He'd have made a go of it if he'd had a bit more money to tide him over while winning a public."

I remembered that Anthony Chambers was the editor of a magazine that had sunk, bearing George Ledra's little piece to the bottom.

"I knew Anthony up at Balliol. He was in his last year when I was a freshman. He was running a little university magazine called *Advance*. I helped him, and when he went down I took it over. My father didn't like that. It was a bit to the Left."

I asked: "To what, Mr. Dodge, do I owe the honour of this visit?"

"Oh, I'm sorry. You want to be off to bed. I forget things like that. I hardly ever sleep. I don't think these are days when men should sleep—do you?"

"Well, in reason I'm wedded to my pillow-slip."

I gave him more sherry.

"This is the point," he said. "I'm starting a magazine. So I looked up Anthony. Though he didn't make a go of his own thing, he has experience. He knows about paper-buying and printers and so forth."

"What is Anthony doing now?"

"He's thinking of going into films. He feels he'd make a good producer."

Hubert's stag-eyes dimmed. Even he, I imagined, had heard of many men sharing Anthony's feelings, and meanwhile "standing in" with shabby suits and doomed faces.

"Well," he said with a sigh, "Anthony gave me your name and address. He liked what you wrote. Said it had quality."

"That was kind of him," I said sincerely.

"I'm calling this thing *Now*. It'll be mainly political. I hope you won't mind that? Rather Left."

"I'm afraid that anything I write will redden no dawn."

He was becoming more and more knotted. His long fingers were twined into a cat's cradle, and his legs were plaited.

"Please," he said, "don't make the mistake of thinking that political minds are nothing else. I aim at political minds that comprehend all sides of life. There must be an admirable essay, and the cleverest crossword in the world, and sparkling criticism of books and plays and music, and a smashing cartoon. Oh, don't think of us as a horrid little red rag."

I got up, impressed by his odd personality, and he disentangled his limbs' convolutions and said: "Well, thank you for putting up with me. I *had* to wait till you got home. I hate starting on a job and not going through."

"We've settled nothing," I said.

144

"No, we can't at this stage, can we? Send me a lot of your essays. I must read them for myself. I could have gone to other people, but I want *new* people. I want people to make the magazine and the magazine to make the people."

He started for the door. "Your overcoat, Hubert," I reminded him.

"Oh, yes. What a fool I am. Thank you, George."

The Christian names sounded like a compact. He gave me the full force of his smile. It would have melted granite.

"How's it for money?" I asked.

"Oh, that's all right. Father has guaranteed any losses for five years. He hates the idea, but he'll keep his word. I think I have Mother to thank for that."

"You haven't by any chance engaged a secretary yet?"

"Oh, lord! That's another thing. I should, shouldn't I?"

"Don't be in a hurry. I may be able to help you there."

We shook hands. "It's rather late," I said. "You'll have difficulty in finding a taxi."

"Oh, that's all right. I shall walk."

"Have you far to go?"

"No. I'm still living with Father. Portman Square."

"Good God!"

Portman Square. He looked as if it might have been a flat over a grocer's shop in Pimlico.

When Hubert said that he had his mother to thank for his father's financial help he was speaking the truth. He had her to thank for more than that. When I met her I saw that, for one thing, he had to thank her for those enormous onyx eyes. They were her own eyes all over again. She was a Polish Jewess. Her father was a lawyer, a highly-educated man who couldn't keep his fingers out of political pies. Exactly what the trouble was that made him fly from Poland I never knew; but he did, and brought his daughter with him. She was seventeen and had been training to be a professional pianist. Her father died of tuberculosis soon after arriving in England, and she was left without a penny and with only a smattering of the English language.

J. Wilson Dodge, as Hubert's father loved to sign himself, was then on the up and up. He had been born in Bermondsey, where his parents owned a small grocer's shop. They were dead, and J. Wilson Dodge was thirty years old and the owner of six grocer's shops, when he met Hannah. It was a sentimental and romantic meeting. I can imagine what Hannah looked like then: the long oval ivory face with the black hair framing it and the eyes bigger than ever from hunger. Her father had been dead for a week. She had no job, no home, no friends. Nor did she know how to set about getting any of these things. It was a cold winter night. She was standing where Villiers Street joins the Strand, shivering in the wind that blew down to the river. Dodge at that time had rooms in Villiers Street. He was on his way home from the second house of a music-hall. I can picture his warm overcoat, his red, cheerful, rather insensitive face. It was no night for dallying. He was brushing round the corner when he heard the foreign-sounding piteous voice. "You can give me some pennies, please?"

Once a year Hubert used to entertain the staff of *Now* at his father's house in Portman Square. J. Wilson Dodge was never present, but Hannah always was. We would feed on the choicest delicacies while Hubert, who seemed to need food as little as sleep, hovered among us looking like an outcast who had been brought in from the street and did not dare to join the lordly revellers. When we had eaten, we would go into the music-room and Hannah would play to us. Always Chopin, at his most heart-rending and nostalgic. Save for a flicker of fire and the light of the tall standard lamp falling upon her, the room would be in darkness. Always on these occasions I would feel that I could look for ever at that still magnolia face rising out of the dress of ivory velvet, at the fingers as long as Hubert's, at the eyes as huge as his. And I could imagine those eyes hungry, literally and physically hungry, and that face chiselled down by starvation to an even finer line than that which now gravely defined its beauty. It is the face of the Mother bending over the Child in a picture I have of the flight into Egypt. And, looking at Hubert looking at her, his fingers writhing with emotion, I tried to imagine J. Wilson Dodge, warm in his frieze overcoat, chuckling over the broad music-hall quips and innuendoes, coming suddenly upon *that*. It was not a thing a man was likely to forget, and he never did forget it. He could refuse her nothing, not even her wishes for their only child, whom he would have liked to see sharing at any rate a little of his own hard commercial predilection.

He took her to his rooms and told his landlady to feed her and put her to bed, and a month later he married her. Now, in the Portman Square house, he had his own rooms. I was in them only once and found them to be stark and practical. "This is *me*," he said. "The rest of the place is *her*."

And obviously it was so. The furniture and the fabrics, the Manets and the Renoirs, the grand piano and the atmosphere that absorbed all these things and gave them significance— that was Hannah. And pervading the beauty and serenity amid which she lived was the crying sadness that wrung my heart

146

whenever, on those annual occasions, I listened to her playing the piano, as though she were assessing and expressing the transience of even the loveliest things that men can do.

The oddest thing about my meeting with Hubert was that I forgot Janet. She was not a woman easy to forget. Perhaps forget is the wrong word. Anyway, she retired to some back room of my mind and I settled down to do what Hubert required of me. "Send me a lot of your essays," he had said. Well, that was impossible. If I wrote, and polished to my satisfaction, twelve hundred words a week, that was as much as I could normally do. But now, excited by the impact of Hubert's personality, I resolved to do twice as much and let him have two essays in a week's time. I browsed through my overflowing note-books, found two subjects, and astonished myself by finishing the job in time.

I had put the polish on the first of them when Hubert rang up. He asked: "Do you know Cutler's Alley?"

I did not. "It's off Pall Mall," he said. "Runs through to King Street. You can't miss it. Could you come round this afternoon? Number Twenty-three. I've got a long lease on the place. Come and tell me what you think of it."

I found Cutler's Alley. It was so narrow that, standing in the middle, you could almost touch a wall on either hand. Tradition lingered. A surprising number of the shops still sold cutlery. There were a few newsagents', a few tobacconists', a shop that sold nothing but gloves, socks and expensive silk ties, and a cosy-looking pub called The Grindstone. A slit of sky allowed a little light to fall into the lane. It was mid-afternoon, but the electric bulbs glowed in all the shops.

The number Twenty-three was on a black door between a tobacconist's and The Grindstone. I rang the bell, pushed the door, and faced a flight of uncarpeted stairs. A light burned at the top, revealing Hubert, who opened the door in which the flight ended. I ran up and stepped into a narrow passage with a door at either side. Hubert's bony fingers crushed mine. "Come in," he said. "You're the first person to see the offices of *Now*."

"This is my room," he said, opening the door on the left. "And this is as far as we've got with furnishing."

A long oak refectory table stood in the middle of the room, with a blotting-pad, inkstand and pen-tray upon it. A ream of quarto writing-paper. A chair to sit in. That was all. I had brought my finished essay with me, and I laid it on the blotting-pad. "There," I said, "is *Now's* first contribution."

"No," he said. "I worked last night on the editorial—what shall we call it?—pronunciamento?—for the first issue. I think it will do." He put my little piece into an envelope, wrote "Ledra" on it, and said: "I'll read it this evening and let you know what I think. Mother'd better have a look at it, too. I'd like her to see anything edging on *belles lettres*."

I hadn't met Hannah then, and was rather surprised.

"Have a look at the rest," he said.

The rest was a room much like his own on the other side of the passage. A stair led to another floor, and here again were two rooms. They had dormer windows. In one of them he said: "I suppose this will have to be the secretary's room. Have you done anything about that?"

"I'm afraid I haven't yet."

"Well, bring her along some afternoon. Can she make tea?"

"I suppose so."

"Very few people can," he said. "And I drink a lot of tea. I see there's a gas-ring where she can boil water."

He looked about, pondering. "I think it will do," he said. "Don't you? So many offices are just full of show. Quite unnecessary. And most of the stuff for *Now* won't be written here. We needn't be cluttered up with a lot of staff. Yes. It'll have to do."

He wrung his hands as though in despair. "Well, you'd better go," he said. "I've just got time to run round and see some second-hand furniture that may be useful."

I invited him to join me at tea. "No, no. Editors can't afford time for tea, unless it's pushed in a cup under their noses. Only essayists can give themselves to such orgies."

I left him, not overwhelmed with belief in the future of *Now*. But it had a future, as we shall see.

9

I walked round to Shaftesbury Avenue and found Janet at home. She let me in and returned immediately to the typewriter at which she had been sitting. I glanced over her shoulder and read: "Well, then, wot we waiting for? The money's there, ain't it? Ain't it in the 'ands of the Dook of Westminster an' blokes like that? Well, then, why don't the toilin' millions step in an' take it? They created 'is welf, didn't they . . .?"

"Did they?" I asked.

"I don't know."

"Then I'm ashamed of you. A disciple of Medea Hopkins should know the answer to a simple question like that. What is all this, anyway?"

"Shorthand practice. Hyde Park Corner. I go all over the place. I take down the sermons in churches."

"H'm. You seem earnest to succeed. Would you like to be secretary to a Hyde Park Corner orator?"

"I wouldn't mind. Some of them are much more fun than the parsons, and talk more sense."

"It's time someone was looking after you. You'd better come out and let me give you some tea."

She put on her hat and coat and said: "Mother'll be here soon to look after me." She handed me a letter. "Go on. Read it. Nothing private."

"Darling,—I was pleased to hear from Uncle that you are well. But he says you are working far too hard on this secretarial business. Are you really serious about it? I see many difficulties, and I can't say I like the idea of your plunging in among a lot of strangers. Goodness knows what sort of set you may find yourself among. We must have a good talk about it when I join you next Monday. There's so much that I could protect you from. . . ."

"Have you come to that bit about protect you from?"

"I'm just reading it."

"What does she take me for? She can't have been any older than I am when she married."

"Perhaps she thinks being married protects you from."

I went on reading: "I've been offered a part in *No Mean City*, that new play by Gerald Frost, and I've decided to accept. There'll be the usual doddering about in the provinces after rehearsals, and then I hope—as usual!—that we'll settle down to a long steady run in London. Don't do anything irrevocable, will you, until you see me? The men have done pretty well on the new walls here, and I hope you'll like the way things are going when you see them. Till Monday then, darling. Mummy."

"I was thinking," I said as we sat in a rather dingy tea-shop, "of suggesting something irrevocable. No. Don't look alarmed."

I told her about Hubert Dodge and *Now*.

"It would be wonderful!" she said. "Being an editor's secretary would be *something*. I've been horribly afraid of landing up in some enormous place where they have what they call a typists' 'pool,' and all the poor fish swim sluggishly round till a bell buzzes and a voice says: 'To Room 49.' I couldn't stand that. This thing at *Now* would be *personal*, wouldn't it? I *must* find a personal job."

I told her that *Now* was a leap in the dark for Hubert, and that it would be a leap in the dark for her, too. I didn't want to raise extravagant hopes, and played it down. "These new weeklies bob up now and then, but it's a devil of a job to grab a public and keep it. Most of 'em peter out."

"But you say Mr. Dodge's father has masses of money."

"Yes. And people with masses of money are always the hardest to squeeze a penny out of. Hubert says he's guaranteed for five years. Well, it may be a different story when the money begins to dribble down the drain."

But Janet was not to be discouraged. Her eyes were alight. "I *know*," she said, "that this is going to be my thing. When can I see Mr. Dodge?"

"Let's dance again to-night, and I'll take you round to him in the morning."

And that is what we did. Hubert was *distrait*, making up what he called a dummy. He talked of nothing else, except to say to me: "Oh, your bit's all right. Mother loves it." And to Janet: "Oh, yes, there's you. All right. You'd better be here at ten to-morrow morning. That all right?"

Janet said dutifully: "Yes, sir."

He smiled, took hold of a lock of his black hair with inky fingers, and twiddled it to and fro. "Sir!" he said. "That's good. Makes me feel like an editor. Take her away, George."

CHAPTER EIGHT

1

Mr. Chown's book was dedicated to "The Memory of F., who made my Sister happy." I bought a copy, read it, and enjoyed it insofar as a man like me could enjoy a book like that. It was full of allusions that went over my head; and, though it had a success among scholars, it had no other. Not that Mr. Chown would want any other. He was suspicious of writing that gained popular applause. He didn't even know that this last book from his pen pleased those few readers whom he set out to please. He died on publication day, and his obituary notices in the newspapers were obviously nothing but a recapitulation of the few facts about himself that he allowed to appear in *Who's Who*.

He died suddenly, just as autumn was verging on winter, in the bar parlour of the Absolution. Jose was visiting his father at the time. Mr. Chown had wandered along to the pub, taking with him a couple of bottles of claret. That men should take their own drinks to the Absolution was something that Jose's father didn't approve of; but Mr. Chown did it now and then and was tolerated as both an old client and a character. He said to Jose that these bottles were the last of something special that had better be drunk while the drinking was good. "Let's down 'em, my boy, before I'm called upon to verify whether one does indeed, elsewhere, down nectar."

"There was something odd about him," Jose told me. "It was angina, you know, and the doctor said it was pretty certain that he'd had attacks before and told nothing to anyone."

He had drinks served to his old cronies, sat quietly for a few moments, and then died in a spasm of agony. He was carried into the parlour behind the bar and laid on the sofa. Jose drove his battered truck into Helston and returned with a doctor, who found nothing to do except formally write the death certificate. The customers had dispersed, and Jose's father had reverently closed the pub.

In one of Mr. Chown's pockets was found a note concerning his burial. He wished this to be at sea, "with no ceremony whatsoever, Pagan or Christian."

Sylvia and I went down to Cornwall for the committal to the sea. She had to take a few days off from the rehearsals of *No Mean City*. Janet did not come with us. She and I had quarrelled the night before, and I think that was the reason, though she produced another. We went in Sylvia's car, and, at the end of the tiring day, bumped over the rough road to the Absolution where we were to stay for the night. It had been a dreary journey, mist-soaked for the last miles; and I lay sleepless in my small room, listening to the rising wind and a menacing boom of waves on the reef.

Jose had amused me, years before, by the tale of how, when a youth, he had made a coffin that would have pleased Chippendale. He had made Mr. Chown's. When I came down in the morning I saw it lying on the cold stone slabs of the passage, just inside the front door. Jose had regarded the making of the coffin as a pious duty. I am sure it was excellent work, but I couldn't bear to look at it. I hurried into the parlour where Mr. Gomm had a massive breakfast awaiting me and Sylvia. Neither of us did more than nibble at toast and drink lots of coffee. "You'd better fill up," Mr. Gomm warned us. "It's going to be a rough old job out there."

Old Tiddy came in, wearing seaboots and oilskins that shone with rain. "Aye," he confirmed, "the pair of you'd better wrap up." Drips from his sou'wester fell into his coffee cup as he took a warming drink. The motor-boat in which the coffin would be taken out to sea belonged to him. "Now my advice to you, midear," he said to Sylvia, "is to give it up. You stay ashore, midear. Mr. Ledra an' the rest of us can 'eave 'im over without your 'elp. 'Ark at that now."

Rain hit the window like thrown pebbles and the wind's note rose higher. "No job for soft women, this ain't," Tiddy said, filling his pipe. Sylvia said nothing, but looked at him almost with hatred.

"Put these on," Mr. Gomm said, and brought in oilskins and a sou'wester from the back-kitchen. Sylvia did as she was told,

151

and I tied the hat beneath her chin. She wouldn't put on Wellingtons, but I did.

"Well, it'll get no better an' they're waitin' outside," Tiddy said, "so we might as well go."

Three fishermen were cowering in the porch. They came into the passage and they and Jose hoisted the coffin on to their shoulders. Tiddy went in front of the bearers and Sylvia and I followed behind. The sky was a scurrying grey, and the incoming waves were whitening on the reefs. The feet of generations had worn a path to a spot where a shoulder of rock rose up and made a patch of comparative quiet. Here three men were holding the motor-boat as steady as they could. She was rising and falling on the swell. The engine was ticking away in neutral, and the stink of petrol made the boat an offensive intrusion into the clean though savage weather.

Tiddy got down and gave Sylvia a hand into the boat. He put her on the stern seat alongside the tiller. Then Jose got in, and he and Tiddy stood up in the plunging craft to take one end of the coffin from the other men. It was a ticklish operation. The coffin was stowed under two of the thwarts to which ropes were ready lashed. These were passed under and around the coffin and made fast with expert knots. "Can't 'ave that plungin' about, as it would in a sea like this," Tiddy explained. "We'll ship enough, you'll see, midear, without that takin' us off an even keel. There's lead in there, you know, as well as Mr. Chown, so's 'e can go to the bottom expeditious."

The rain was bucketing down. In our oilskins we gleamed like seals. Tiddy sat by Sylvia and Jose sat near the engine-casing, his hand on the gear-lever. The other men sat on the thwarts, with their legs arranged on either side of the coffin. There didn't seem much room for me. I got forward, and knelt looking out over the bows.

"Put 'er slow astern, Jose midear," Tiddy commanded; and we backed away from our bit of rocky shelter. "Ahead now." Her bows swung out as Tiddy turned her a little to starboard. "Now slow ahead," he shouted, and we were out, facing into the incoming tumult of the sea.

"Give 'er a bit of speed, Jose."

I marvelled at what we were doing. It seemed to me madness as I clung with both hands to the gunwale. To my untutored eye there was nothing ahead but a chaos of rocks, now visible, now submerged by a chaos of hissing sea.

Tiddy shouted above the wind: "Keep your head well down, Mr. Ledra. I want to see what I'm at."

I sank down till only my eyes and my forehead were above the bows. The water swooshed whitely down off the rocks ahead, and Tiddy shouted: "There! Now you can see 'em. See those

152

two points, Mr. Ledra, standing up like goal-posts? Well, we got to steer between them two, and then we're out of it."

I saw the two rocks for a moment, and then the sea obliterated them again. I looked back over my shoulder and saw Sylvia at Tiddy's side, white-faced and tense, and Tiddy himself competent-looking and concentrated as I had never seen him before. Even as I looked his face relaxed, and he shouted: " A bit more speed, Jose."

We were outside the reefs. Crests from the waves were hurling themselves aboard with spiteful energy. A douche hit my face and ran down my neck and dribbled upon my spine and navel. The sky flowed over us like a funeral march, and the wind was an incoherent lamentation. Water was beginning to wash about in the boat, swirling round the coffin and seeping through the bottom-boards into the bilge.

" Won't 'urt to start that old pump," Tiddy said; and one of the mutes sitting on the coffin reached and jerked the pump-handle up and down. " 'Ow far d'you reckon to go?" he asked.

" Another arf mile'll do it," Tiddy assured him. " We'll be able to give Mr. Chown thirty fathoms."

So on we went, rushing down the glassy slopes and climbing the hills into the white toppling drench that by now had my teeth chattering with cold and my eyes smarting with salt.

Suddenly Tiddy shouted: " This'll do. Now listen, all of you. Don't nobody move 'and or foot till he's told. Keep your weight even in the boat. We got to put Mr. Chown over, not all go in with 'im. You three amidships there, undo them knots. We're goin' to heave Mr. Chown over the port side. Understand that? The port side. Now wait for yer orders. Keep 'er movin', Jose."

When the knots were untied, Tiddy threw a tin of yellow grease into the middle of the boat. " Get 'old of that, Mr. Ledra," he said, " and while them chaps keeps Mr. Chown steady you smear that good and thick all along the gunwale amidships on the port side."

I crawled amidships, got hold of the tin, and did as I was ordered, digging my fingers into the grease and spreading it half an inch thick.

" Now swing Mr. Chown round," Tiddy ordered, " pointing towards that there grease. Now, heave him up and rest him on the gunwale."

This was done. " Remember, he's 'eavy," Tiddy warned us, " to say nothing of the lead in that there coffin. So you chaps slide him up gradual, and when 'e's arf-way remember there's going to be a good ole weight on the port side. Two of you can do the pushin'. That grease'll make 'im go easy. The other one of you, and Mr. Ledra, and you Jose, move over to starboard when Mr. Chown's poised proper. Understand?"

The two men began to push, and as the boat fell over to port three of us moved our weight to starboard. Then Tiddy shouted excitedly: "In the name of the Father and of the Son and of the 'Oly Ghost, let 'im go."

Thirty fathoms. A hundred and eighty feet. It was a good deep grave.

"Back amidships," Tiddy was shouting; and as I went I looked aft and saw Sylvia blinding her eyes with her hands, though there was nothing to see of Mr. Chown's descent. The water was chaos above him, and the sky was chaos above the water, and between the two the wind kept up its disconsolate crying. I wondered whether Tiddy's words of committal had constituted Christian burial and violated Mr. Chown's wish; but it seemed not to matter much one way or the other.

2

There was an air almost of festivity at the Absolution. Mrs. Tiddy had prepared a hot meal; but Sylvia and I, when we had changed out of our drenched clothes, were in no mood to celebrate. She took nothing but a couple of eggs beaten up in hot milk and brandy, and then apologised to the company. She said she must leave at once. "Are you staying, or would you like to come with me?" she asked.

I said I would come. It was just after midday, with the rain still pouring down, when we set out. Neither the experience that we had just endured nor the weather we were driving through could be expected to produce cheerfulness; but I was burdened by a feeling that something even more than these was lying on Sylvia's heart. I tried several times to lighten the moment, but she did not respond. I gave it up. We left Plymouth behind us, and the weather cleared. She lowered a window and let some air into the stuffy car. Somerset was still in the fag-end of autumn, and I tried again. The pale sunlight lying like gold on a hill of bracken. How lovely it was, I said unnecessarily.

She said, not looking at me: "What's going on between you and Janet?"

I had thought that this would come. But it came so suddenly, so unexpectedly, that I was taken off guard.

"Me and Janet?" I stammered. "Why, what makes you think . . ."

"When I came back from Cornwall for these rehearsals," she said, "I thought there was some reason to expect that you would be glad to see me."

I would have been a fool if I had not understood what she
154

was talking about. "But I *was* glad to see you. Surely I've never given you any reason to think otherwise?"

"You have cheapened me," she said bitterly. "I should feel cheaper still if I had to explain what I mean by that. You are not so dense that you can't see what I'm getting at."

I could see what she was getting at. Off and on since boyhood I had longed for the realisation of a dream. I had longed that the superb woman whom I had seen so intimately so long ago might lie even more intimately in my arms. The dream had come true; and I had no doubt that Sylvia was willing to recreate the moment, that she had returned to London expecting to do so. And I had shown no eagerness to accept what she had to give. What was even worse, I had found plenty of time to give to Janet, though I had found none for her.

We were nearing Taunton. She said: "Though we met so rarely, I was fond of you. I sometimes wondered whether I was in love with you. When you left Manchester and came to live in London, I thought: Now he'll have plenty of time. We'll see a good deal of one another. We shall find out how we stand. But you hardly came near me. There was a day—do you remember?—when you rang up and proposed yourself for lunch, and then, when I was out, you rang up again and cancelled it. I couldn't believe, after that, that you cared much one way or another. And that was when Clarence Conway came along."

She said no more for a long time, and I, too, was tongue-tied, guilty and miserable. Presently, she said: "Well, we did come together at last. I'm afraid I misunderstood your feelings, but at all events I know now that I didn't mistake my own."

I longed to be able to say: "But you didn't misunderstand. I love you, Sylvia."

I couldn't, nor could I bear to remain in her company, feeling humiliated as I did. I said: "Do you mind if I leave you now? I shall stay here for the night and come on to-morrow by train."

I got out and took my suitcase from the boot. She allowed herself a little spite, and, by God, I thought, she's entitled to it. "I'll let Janet know you'll be back," she said.

3

I booked at a hotel and went up to my room, feeling exhausted. Mr. Chown's death and then that crazy and terrifying hour in Tiddy's motor launch, and then Sylvia's sad reproach, left me as weary as a wrung-out dish-rag. I lay upon the bed and fell into a deep sleep. The sound of the dinner-gong woke me. I soused my face in cold water and went down, feeling a little better. When I had eaten I strolled into the lounge where a fire was burning, and from among the magazines on the table I picked up, unexpectedly, the latest issue of *Now*. I turned at once to the column signed Megaera. The last line read: "Miss J. H. Brown-Smith has started well. A little attention to writing, structure and character should raise her to the depths of her profession."

I had been in the *Now* office talking to Hubert Dodge when Janet came in with some letters she had typed. Hubert had induced a few publishers to send books for review, and from among these he took up a novel and gave it to her. "If it would amuse you," he said, "have a go at writing five hundred words about this."

Janet and I had arranged to meet that night at the place in Charlotte Street where we danced. She was not there. I waited for half an hour beyond our meeting time and then took a taxi to Shaftesbury Avenue, knowing that Sylvia would be occupied elsewhere with rehearsals. Janet was reading the book that Hubert had given her, and I said lightly that it must be enthralling to make her forget our appointment.

She said coolly: "Oh, I didn't forget. You were there when Mr. Dodge gave me this, and I thought you'd realise that I would want to get on with it."

"You take reviewing a little more seriously than is usual," I said.

She laughed. "Who wouldn't take this seriously? Listen." She read an appalling passage. "I'm enjoying this," she said. "I think I can do something with it. I never dreamed that Mr. Dodge might give me this sort of work."

I said crossly: "Oh, the review books are dished out to any dog's-body."

She was on a couch, with her legs bunched up under her, and she was wearing a pair of enormous tortoise-shell spectacles that I am sure were unnecessary. She glared at me through them and said: "I think you misunderstand Mr. Dodge. I'm sure that's not his standpoint for *anything* that appears in *Now*. And even if it were, I should try to make him see differently."

I was annoyed. I said: "I like to see little girls full of ambition. But to be serious for a moment, are we dancing to-night?"

"No," she said. "If what I write is a wash-out, I don't suppose any more reviewing will come my way. In that case, we shall see."

I wanted to kiss her good-night, but the spectacles would have made it feel like kissing a chartered accountant. I went home crossly.

I was at the office in Cutler's Alley a few days later, and

Hubert introduced me to a youngish man with the splendid name of J. V. Alcott-Lucas. Happily, he was spoken of and to as J.V. He looked like someone who had come to stay, for he shared Hubert's room and had a desk there. He was a barrister, and he had become tired of sitting in his chambers waiting for the client's knock. In a year, I gathered, he had been junior in one case and had twice picked up jobs as poor man's counsel. He had filled in his time with writing, and, hearing about *Now*, had turned up in the office to show Hubert an article signed Levite, exposing some legal absurdities. They liked one another, and Hubert took him home to dinner. Over the meal J.V. Alcott-Lucas and J. Wilson Dodge got on well together, and it was J. Wilson Dodge who pointed out with common sense that a barrister could be a useful member of a journal's staff. " Keep you out of mischief," he said to Hubert. J.V. himself liked the idea, and there he was, both contributor and legal eye. Levite's articles became famous, and so, in a lighter vein, did Megaera's.

When I first met him, he and Hubert were discussing what Janet had written. Hubert was surprised and enchanted. Janet pulled no punches, and, as she had not written a review before in her life, she was free of the dreary clichés of the profession. She never in all her time as a reviewer so much as discovered " perhaps the most promising young novelist I have come across this month." She refused to put in nice jammy phrases that publishers could quote over the reviewer's name, so giving that poor soul an eminence he could not otherwise aspire to. Her method was sheer cock-shy, knocking over the Aunt Sally with the cheeky abandon of a disrespectful *gamine*. Her work smelled of naphtha flares. It was J.V. who suggested the pen-name Megaera. " One of the Furies, you know." They decided to hold up the snippet she had written until she could amplify it with a few more reviews. So the first of her celebrated and dreaded columns was launched. She gloried in being loathed and spoke of herself as " the blind Fury with the abhorred sneers."

Sitting there in the Taunton hotel, I remembered how I had gone home smarting when she had dismissed me from the Shaftesbury Avenue flat. I couldn't take her seriously: the little *poseuse* I had first met in Cornwall, obviously, as I thought now, oppressed by her mother's reputation, small though that was, and trying, in reaction, to assert herself against it; the runaway schoolgirl, still at the same trick. She didn't seem to me solid till she showed an unexpected resolution in fitting herself to be a secretary. That suited me, because a secretary might expect to have evenings off. But now, it seemed, she had her own ideas about how her evenings should be spent, and these didn't include me. I went to bed telling myself not to be a fool. A chit like Janet was hardly likely to write anything worth

157

reading. Hubert would regretfully put her stuff into the waste-paper basket, and she would then see where she belonged.

I was heartened the next morning by receiving a letter on notepaper headed " The Parthenon Press." I had never heard of the Parthenon Press, but it seemed that its proprietor, Mr. Nigel Wendron, wished to make my acquaintance. I rang up the telephone number that was on the notepaper, and Mr. Wendron asked me to meet him over lunch at Scott's. I found him to be a youngish, fair-haired, blue-eyed man, rather anxious-looking, as he well might be, for I learned as we ate that he had just bought the assets of a bankrupt publishing house and was trying to put it on its feet under a new name. The assets included a few titles that he hoped would keep him afloat till he got going, but he must, he said, find some new authors. To my surprise, he regarded me as one. *Now* had appeared only twice, and he had read my two little bits, which appeared to enchant him. The Parthenon Press, he said, must be rather special. So long as it paid its way and kept him in bread-and-butter, he wasn't after the big splashy successes. He wanted a reputation for the small excellent thing. " I suppose I'm a miniaturist," he said quaintly, chewing at his Dover sole. " I want my Hilliards and Cosways." He said my little things reminded him of Logan Pearsall Smith, a writer of whom I had never heard, but I took it for a compliment. He thought, he said, refilling my glass with Chablis, that out of the fifty or so articles I would write in a year for *Now,* the best might be selected to make a charming annual book for connoisseurs.

You may not believe it, but I am a modest man. I had never thought of my stuff as ambrosia for connoisseurs to browse upon, but Mr. Wendron said he had no doubt that, if I went on as I had begun, that is how it would turn out to be. Armagnac with our coffee made me see this as not impossible, and we parted on the happiest terms. " Of course," he said, " there can be no question of a contract till the material's there, but I'd like to rope you in for my stable, if that's possible." Feeling like Pegasus, I said I'd love to be roped into the Parthenon, and went down and waved him good-bye as he stepped into the taxi that his imperious gesture with a rolled umbrella halted at the kerb.

It was a good thing that this happened on the day after Janet had snubbed me. As I say, I am a modest man, but I don't like to go about feeling modest all the time, and Janet had made me feel more modest than I cared to be. When I got back to my flat, I stayed there for the rest of the day, looking at a space in my book-shelves and imagining a finely printed Parthenon volume appearing there each year. I couldn't live on it. My pay from *Now* was little more than a token, though Hubert said that that would be seen to when the paper established itself. It did, and he kept his word; but, even so, that and the income from the books which Nigel Wendron in time published would hardly have kept the most amiable new-born wolf-cub from my door. However, I hadn't to worry about that. I smoked, and pleasantly planned my life. My stuff could be written as well in Cornwall as in London. May to October could be spent at Trencrom and the winters here in the flat. Fortunately, the winter was before me. It would give me time to see more of Janet, to let her understand that she mustn't mistake my modesty for fatuity. I decided to see her in the morning.

During the evening while these thoughts were chasing themselves through my mind Janet was writing her first review. By the time I reached Cutler's Alley in the morning she had, trembling, handed it to Hubert. Hubert had shown it to Alcott-Lucas, and Janet had been summoned, still trembling, to the joint presence. Hubert, I imagine, was ready to overwhelm her with praise, but Alcott-Lucas was a more cautious type. He did the talking and said the review was the sort of thing they wanted when it was called for. He added with a smile: "Mr. Dodge and I feel that it's called for more often than is generally understood."

Janet could take a point as quickly as the next girl, and she knew that she had written what was wanted. They said nothing to her about a weekly article, but gave her two more novels and asked her to have a go at them.

That was the position when I arrived in Cutler's Alley just before lunch time. Janet's office was on the floor above that occupied by Hubert and J.V. I went straight up there, knocked, and peeped in. I didn't know what sort of a moment I was intruding on. As I see it now, I am sure that Janet had caught at any rate a glimpse of what was before her. She had rightly interpreted Alcott-Lucas's hint and understood the meaning of Hubert's obvious approbation. You may say that what followed from that moment didn't amount to much. To be a novel-reviewer feared for the accuracy with which wounding darts were thrown—"Miss Schyne's heroine is born stone-dead, yet the story of the burial needs 368 pages"—this sort of thing may not amount to much, but it meant so much to Janet that when I opened the door she was sitting at her desk with a look of stunned exaltation on her face. I think she was seeing herself at last as a person, not as Sylvia's troublesome daughter.

That room has a skylight, and the midday sun of the early winter day fell through it upon her face. She had just celebrated her seventeenth birthday. She looked very beautiful and older than her years. You would have taken her for twenty.

I said like an uncle: "I've come to forgive you and to take you to lunch."

"Forgive me?"

"Yes. For wearing those dreadful spectacles the other night. I wanted to kiss you good-night, but . . ."

"George, you needn't think it always necessary to talk like this. Don't treat me as a child."

"Well, where shall we eat? Have you ever been to Prunier's? It's only a step."

"I can't go anywhere to-day—not to a dallying-place, anyway. I'll just go out somewhere for a sandwich."

I was nettled. "Don't you *like* coming out with me?"

"I really can't afford the time. You know what Mr. Dodge's writing is like, and there's old Foster's too. The man who does the political commentary. They've got to be disentangled and typed before the printers will look at them. There are letters to do, too."

"Janet, aren't you beginning to take yourself too seriously?"

I didn't know that I was shattering a dreaming mood. What she wanted was to be alone. "Oh, for God's sake," she said, suddenly angry, "do you think I have nothing better to do than dance or eat, or this or that, whenever *you* want me to?"

I had come with a pleasant picture in my mind of George Ledra, leisurely feeding, imparting to his companion the important news that the Parthenon Press was interested in him, and watching the dawn of respect in that companion's face. The scornful accent on *you* was more than I could bear. I was about to answer angrily when Hubert came in. "Oh, I beg your pardon," he said, as though the place were mine, not his. "I just wanted to give Miss Bascombe this to copy." He was carrying some papers. "Have you heard that she's done us a nice little review? We've asked her to try one or two more."

I grunted and went, without giving Janet another word.

I was seeing little of Sylvia. The rehearsals were strenuous, and I was content to believe that they would leave her too exhausted to welcome my attentions. Sometimes, sitting alone in my room, under the sardonic observation of Fred Byles, I would recall the vigorous night I had spent with her at Penruan, and my wandering fancy would recreate the moment with Janet in Sylvia's place. The hypocrite in me would say that, for Sylvia, that night had been an aberration, an uncontrollable reaction against the hurt of young Conway's villainy, an assertion of her worthwhileness to a man. In a more balanced mood she would see this, realise how much more fitting it was that my devotion should be engaged by someone younger.

After Janet had dismissed me, I saw neither of them for a week. Then Janet rang me up and calmly proposed herself for lunch. She sounded gay, as well she might be. What had happened was that, in the meanwhile, she had written two more reviews and Hubert had arranged for her to do the lighter sort of novels every week. She was to get a small addition to her pay as secretary. She had come not for the pleasure of my company but to glory and drink deep of my admiration.

This small turn in her fortunes affected her looks. I was proud to be seen with her. Her eyes sparkled. She told me of the barbed method which Hubert and J.V. liked so much, and I said: "I had always imagined public executioners to be poor hang-dog-looking devils. Now I see that the motto of the fellow who cut off King Charles's head was Service with a Smile."

"They're such fools," she said. "Readers should be told the truth about them."

"Ah, you're fulfilling a mission! I imagined for a moment that you were feeding your sadistic hunger. And what if Miss Schyne is really some poor hard-driven Mrs. Smith, toiling day and night over a typewriter to keep a son at Eton—a son destined to be some day the most enlightened Lord Chancellor since Eldon? Do you realise that your frivolity may be harmful to the public interest?"

I could see that she hated the word frivolity. Her little fists clenched, whitening the knuckles on the light blue tablecloth. She looked adorable.

"You're talking for effect again," she said. "It's one of your many weaknesses."

"I glory in talking for effect, and my talk seems to have been effective. You come here, like a man from a knacker's yard, his hands dripping after a day's callous labour, and you expect me to see you as St. George, rescuing the poor public from foul-smelling dragons. I feel certain that Miss Schyne smells very nice, and that she has a second son at Harrow destined, forty years on, to let light into all sorts of dark corners. You alone stand between her and the fulfilment of that beneficent dream. I shall order twelve copies of her book."

She sulked like a child, and held her open hand over her wine-glass when I made to fill it.

"So much for the public weal," I went on, "which owes more than you suspect to the humble toil of dedicated widows. Then we come to authors themselves, people with sensitive egos. One drop from your poison pen could drive them on a cold winter night along the Embankment, looking wild-eyed upon the dark water, the promise of oblivion. A splash. One more unfortunate gone to her doom. And her murderer, who has never written a creative word, lolls in luxury in her mother's flat, toying with a de Reszke cigarette."

"That's one thing I sha'n't be doing," she said unexpectedly. "This bit of extra money means that I'll be able to have a flat of my own. A room, anyway."

That, as much as her small success, was what had made her eyes shine. She was about to cut the umbilical cord, run away for the last time, stay away. I was too dense then to see this. I was too fond of my own highfalutin' garrulity. I said: "I'm glad I'm not a novelist in danger of falling into your hands. I'm merely an essayist, but one already watched by influential eyes."

I went on to tell her about Nigel Wendron and the Parthenon Press. She listened more attentively than I deserved. So attentively that I tried to tone down the impression of belittling her own work. "Don't take me too seriously," I said. "I do congratulate you, and I think Hubert is lucky to have you."

She was spooning at an ice like a child. "I don't know *how* to take you," she said. "I don't know when you're talking nonsense and when you're not."

"Never mind. So long as you know when the Miss Schynes are talking nonsense. That's what matters."

She brightened, and I noticed a small stain of ink near the nail of her right index finger. It brought her before my imagination. Sylvia at a rehearsal. She alone in the flat, working away towards what she hoped would be some little measure of fame. I felt tender towards her.

"You can be sure of one thing," I said. "I hope we're very good friends."

"Of course we are. We always have been."

"Never mind always. I mean now. And I mean friends rather specially. Can't you ever take a night off nowadays? I shall have to lodge a complaint with Hubert."

"Oh, you mustn't worry *him*. He's marvellous. He works his fingers to the bone."

"But need *you*? Couldn't we dance to-night?"

"Well . . ." She was still dubious. "All right, then. Call for me at nine."

She got up. "Now I must be off. I'm up to the eyes."

They were sparkling eyes again. She watched me count notes into the waiter's tray. "Oh, George," she said. "What a lot of money! I hardly earn that in a week. You make me feel like a kept woman."

"At any rate, don't let me keep you now. Back to your wage slavery."

She gave me a token kiss and went.

I called for her at nine. The night had turned cold and wet, and I told my taximan to wait. I was eager to seize her, whisk her down, hold her hand (I hoped) on the way to our dance place. She was not ready. She was wearing her office clothes, sitting at her typewriter, her face hidden behind the horrid great spectacles. The door had been on the latch, and I had walked straight in, with no more than a perfunctory knock.

She looked up, startled. "Oh, heavens! Is it nine already?"

I felt deflated. "It is, and I have a taxi waiting. I'd better go down and tell the man to go."

When I got back, the spectacles were off her nose, the cover was on the typewriter, and she was standing beside it, yawning. "What a day it's been! One thing after another. I was late back from lunch, and Mr. Dodge, who'd lunched off a sandwich in the office, didn't take kindly to that. Then there was a lot of stuff to type about the libel case." She sat down. "Would you be a darling, and make me a cup of tea? You'll find everything in the little kitchen-place. I didn't get in till seven, and I've eaten nothing. I loathe preparing my own food."

I glumly did as she asked. As she sipped the tea I said: "What's this about a libel case?"

"Nothing, I hope. Mr. Dodge thinks it'll blow over. That's the advantage of having a barrister on the staff. It was old Foster, the man who does the parliamentary commentary. He writes like a wasp buzzing."

"He's not the only one."

"Oh, God!" she said. "We're not going to have Mr. Ledra all over again on the ethics of reviewing? I couldn't stand it. I tell you I'm tired."

"Too tired to keep your appointments."

"I'm very tired indeed, but I shall keep my appointment. I shall be a bit late. What of that? As soon as I've drunk this tea I shall change. After all, your dancing isn't something my soul has been yearning for all day."

"And as for the ethics of reviewing . . ."

She rose quickly to her feet and took up a book. "If you start that again, I'll throw this at your head."

I started again. The book hit me over the right eye.

"Now I feel better," she said. "I'll go and change."

The telephone buzzed. "You can deal with that while I'm changing." She went into the bedroom, and came back a quarter of an hour later, looking enchanting: carefully made-up and wearing the dress I liked—a golden tissue. I was just putting down the telephone after a long conversation with Jose Gomm, who had rung from the Absolution to tell Sylvia of her uncle's death.

I said: "That was Jose Gomm. Mr. Chown has died suddenly."

It would be pleasing to record that in the presence of death all our animosity vanished. It didn't. My head ached from the blow with the book and from the sudden shock of this news. Janet was very quiet in her own world of thought and feeling. I knew that I had nothing to do with what was happening there. We stood like strangers by chance in the same room.

I said: "I'd better find Sylvia. Where are these rehearsals taking place?"

She told me, and I went there in a taxi-cab. The weather had worsened. The tyres hissed, throwing out spray like the bows of

163

a catamaran. The windows steamed, and the taxi stank. I told the man to wait, and offered to take Sylvia home. She was deeply upset, but dry-eyed. She said: " Don't bother about me, George. We're nearly done for the night. I may as well get through with it."

I kissed her, and she accepted the kiss almost greedily, as though it were comforting.

" If you'd like me to come with you to Penruan, I will."

" Yes. I'd like that. How did you hear the news?"

" I happened to be at your flat."

And, going to her flat later, she would see Janet, like me, in evening clothes. And that is why I found myself lonely in a Taunton hotel, pondering her sudden question: " What's going on between you and Janet?"

CHAPTER NINE

1

I am not good at making swift dramatic decisions, taking bulls by horns, and so forth. Life had drifted me along to where I then was. The only decision I had made for myself was to leave the cotton trade, and even this was in a sense made for me, because it was the work of my father and of his father and of Fred Byles that provided me with the easy way out. And now, in this matter of Sylvia and Janet, I decided to do nothing, to see neither of them, and let the affair work itself to what end it would. I told myself that my writing was the important thing, as though that weekly brevity, that over-polished bit of nothing much, provided an excuse for my existence.

So I lay low, writing in the mornings, walking in the afternoons, and reading at night. I posted my stuff to *Now,* avoiding the office. There was one lunch with Nigel Wendron of the Parthenon Press, who buttered me up satisfactorily and was able to assure me that, thanks to the energy of his partner Leadbitter, a man with much experience of publishing, the firm was getting through its teething troubles. " The old firm was hopelessly over-staffed," he said, " and not by very intelligent people at that. Leadbitter has been sacking right, left and centre."

Smoking one of Wendron's cigars, I didn't think of those not very intelligent chaps going home to tell their wives that they were out on their ears. The firm was being made safe for Parthenians like George Ledra. That was what mattered.

Another irruption into my solitude came on December the

twenty-fourth. I was writing when the door-bell buzzed, and there was Bob Meagher. He crashed in like a cyclone and said: " If it's coffee-time I'll join you."

It was coffee-time. I had got into the habit, when I brewed my breakfast coffee, of making enough for mid-mornings, too, and putting this into a thermos flask, so that there need be no interruption of my commerce with the Muse. It was an old womanish habit, and I was tending to fall into that sort of thing. Fortunately, there was enough for two cups. I put together my precious sheets of near-parchment, carefully wiped the nib of my pen, and cleared a space on the table.

" Doing your *Now* stuff?" Bob asked.

I had no idea that he was aware of the existence of *Now*, let alone my " stuff." I said so.

" The worst of chaps like you, George," he assured me, " is that you've got parochial minds. You've been a damn' sight too coddled all through your life. A pity you were born just too late for the Army or Navy. That might have helped. Why should you be surprised because I read *Now*? I try to keep in touch with everything that's going, the Press included. Whoever is running that paper has got his head screwed on right. The article on the money market is worth the price if there were nothing else. Then there's Megaera, whoever that may be. I don't read novels, but the way Megaera boots the novelists round is always good for a laugh. The only stuff I haven't read since the first number is yours. No guts in it. Still, I suppose there are a few maiden aunts among the readers."

I thanked him for his thoughtfulness in calling to give me this information.

" What I called for is to ask you to come and spend Christmas with us. Wendy's idea, not mine."

The very name Wendy made me wince. It also made me think of her father. " Does she get any news of Mr. Merriman?" I asked.

" Yes, and pretty bad news at that. Cotton's going to hell. You got out of that just in time, my boy."

I thought of Mr. Merriman " at the top of the tree " that he had always been so anxious to climb, and the tree shaking, down to the very roots.

" Well, come on. Get your hat and coat."

" I haven't said I'm coming yet."

" Of course you're coming. Just bring a toothbrush and pyjamas. We sha'n't be having any ceremony."

" All right. I'll wash up these cups."

" Oh, wash 'em up when you get back. Come on."

So I went, and had a very merry Christmas. Wearing a paper hat which I detested, I played snakes and ladders with Wendy, and ping-pong with Bob, and helped old Mr. Meagher with his crossword puzzle. I allowed Master Jocelyn Meagher, wearing an Indian outfit, to hit me over the head with a tomahawk, and I ate too much and drank too much, and went back thankfully two days later to wash up the coffee cups, glad of the small sedative occupation.

Sylvia's new play increased her reputation. I didn't wish now, as I had done when a boy, to collect and worship the critics' notices, but I did read what they had to say. Without much dissent, they found that the play was good and that her work in it was good, too. I went to see it myself, and agreed with them, but this time I didn't send a note to Sylvia's dressing-room, nor did I write to congratulate her. I hadn't seen her since we parted in Taunton. Her question—" What's going on between you and Janet?"—was unanswered, and I didn't want to answer it. They were both, I hoped, happy and well occupied. As for me, I had work to do. It helped me to feel that my existence had some justification and that the lazy self-indulgent tempo of my days was the best fitted for an artist of my sort. During my stay with him at Christmas, Bob Meagher kindly told me that to be an outside contributor to *Now* was the worst possible thing for me. " You should be on the staff," he said, " if not of *Now*, then of something else. You should *belong* to something. I shudder to think what will happen to you when you have even more money than you have now—which of course you will have when we get really going on the Great West Road. You're nothing but a damned ghost, writing about what you see through windows. It's time something *happene*d to you, George."

" Perhaps you'll go bust," I suggested, " and my money will go down the drain."

He looked shocked at this heresy, didn't deign to answer it.

So I passed through the remainder of that winter, a lotus-eater in the land where it is always afternoon, and when April came I ran by accident into Janet. I overtook her as I was turning out of St. James's Street into Pall Mall. I hadn't seen her since she threw a book at me five months before. It was three o'clock in the afternoon, and I reminded her that when she had last taken lunch with me Hubert had been annoyed because she was late back at the office. I hoped she wasn't making a habit of the thing.

" Oh, that was a long time ago," she said. " I'm afraid you're out of touch, George. I'm not the office typist now."

We had walked as far as the Athenæum, and as if to em-phasize her independence she crossed the road towards the steps leading down into the Mall. " Let's take a turn," she said.

It was a beautiful day. We sat on a seat in warm sunshine. " I suppose you do read *Now* as well as write for it?" she asked, and when I nodded she went on: " Well, then, you know Cassius."

Cassius was the paper's theatre critic. "You don't tell me you're Cassius as well as Megaera!" I said, surprised.

"That is what I am telling you," she said with satisfaction. "Hubert"—she had always called him Mr. Dodge till now—"is all for what he calls a fresh approach, having things done by people who haven't got corroded with all the old prejudices and clichés of a job. Though Mother's an actress, I've seen very few plays, and Hubert thought that was a good reason for my writing about them. So now I'm Cassius, and I do a few other odd things about the office, and there's a new typist."

Across a blue distance the Whitehall silhouette was insubstantial in the spring light. It was a day for miracles, and what she had told me seemed miraculous enough. I said sincerely: "You're doing it well." She was pleased. "But you haven't Cassius's lean and hungry look."

Indeed she hadn't. She had the look that comes with success, not self-satisfied but eager and confident. She was well-dressed. Her gloves, her shoes, her hand-bag—everything which women, I believe, call accessories—was right. I felt glad in her own obvious gladness.

"I was terribly afraid," she confessed. "You see, there was Mother, and *her* mother. I seemed in a way to belong so closely to the theatre that it would have been terrible if I'd made a mess of it. And then Ibsen, Strindberg—all the people critics drag in. I knew nothing about any of them. Believe it or not, I've never seen or read a play by Shaw! I told myself to forget all that. What you've got to write about, I said, is what this thing is doing to *you*, and never mind the ancestry of play-writing or acting or anything else. Just write of the moment and of what you are seeing and feeling in it." She added modestly: "It seems to come off."

I felt humble in her presence. She had seemed to me so flibbertigibbet that I was amazed at the suddenness of her transformation. As if reading my thoughts, she said: "I suppose you can't be Chowny's great-niece and Margaret Napier's granddaughter for nothing."

"And Sylvia Bascombe's daughter," I said.

She didn't answer that.

"Are you still living with Sylvia?" I asked. "The last time I saw you, you were talking about finding a flat of your own."

She said that she had a little place and detested it. "You know *Now* can't pay well. It's going ahead, and it will pay better in time. Hubert's always apologising. But at the moment it's glory without cash. Or very little."

I asked her as delicately as I could whether Sylvia, who was a rich woman, made her an allowance. "It's there if I want it, but I'd rather be on my own feet," she said fiercely.

The idea came into my head suddenly. I said: "You know,

Janet, that I have a place in Cornwall. I shall be going down there next month, and I don't suppose I'll be back till October. If you'd like to move into my flat, it's yours. I'd like to have someone keeping it warm."

"That's very, very sweet of you, darling. But I don't think I ought to."

"I should be proud to house an infant prodigy."

She got up and smiled. "You'd find me a weighty infant," she said, "if you got me round your neck."

We looked at one another under the burgeoning green of a tree. Then she kissed me suddenly and walked back towards the steps. She called over her shoulder: "I'll think about it and let you know. And thank you so much for introducing me to Hubert."

2

When I left for Cornwall in May I posted to her the key of the flat. A few days later she wrote to say that she had moved in. "I'm afraid Mother is annoyed. One would imagine from her attitude that you were still here, that we were sinfully sharing the flat. However, I see little of her now. The office keeps me pretty busy all day, and in the evening she's at the theatre. That's one advantage of having an actress for a mother. It lessens the chances of collision. And the General Strike is giving us plenty of collisions without that one. Hubert is all for the strikers, and Alcott-Lucas is, in a wobbly sort of not-quite-convinced fashion, on the other side. He's not driving a bus or a railway engine or anything of that sort. A pity. It would keep him out of the office. As it is, he's here, and he and Hubert argue all day long. The last word is Hubert's, of course, so far as the policy of *Now* goes, and that supports the men. For the first time in my life, I've met Hubert's father, the formidable J. Wilson Dodge. He was here in the office, making it pretty clear that his money is behind *Now,* and that he objects to its being spent on supporting a movement that he dislikes and obviously fears. Hubert was firm, told him that he couldn't allow Dodge money to have one pennyworth of influence upon *Now* policy; but when the old man was gone he was shaky. We walked home together. As you know, Portman Square isn't far from this flat. He said: 'Thank God Mother's at home. Come in and meet her.' And so I did. Mr. Dodge didn't appear. She is a wonderful woman, Hubert's mother. They didn't say a word about the strike or anything of that sort. We had a small simple meal, and then went into her music-room where she played for us. I've been brought up, as you know, in shocking ignorance, and so I can't tell you what she played, but it was

168

beautiful, and she was beautiful, and she did what I am sure she was trying to do: she was calming Hubert's mind and being one with him."

I was reading the letter in my study, looking out at the bleak foreboding summit of Trencrom, and thinking that we were having quite a lot about Hubert. Then she spared me a line. "It really is terribly kind of you to let me use this place. It's much quieter at nights than my old room, and I sleep better. And then you have all the mod.-con. that makes living so much easier. And I *love* the old gentleman whose portrait looks down on me so knowingly from the wall as though speculating without much charity on the position of a girl in a bachelor's flat. Well, *au revoir* and all love. I'm told there's a chance that the strike will be called off to-night."

It was. The letter was dated May 12, 1926. I put it down, feeling rather flat. She seemed to be doing nothing but fling Hubert at my head, as once she had flung a book. I strolled out into the small rocky waste patch that served for a garden behind the house and was about to sit down in order to enjoy the wide prospect of hill and sky when an infernal racket announced the arrival of Jose Gomm. He had a genius for finding old trucks that could neither start nor finish without an accompaniment that sounded like the collapse of a structure built out of a hundred tin trays. I went round the house. He was coming through the front gate, carrying a red leather box, which looked like a small version of a Cabinet Minister's dispatch box. He handed it to me, and I admired its colour and high polish. On the lid the letters H.C. were stamped in faded gold. "Hector Chown," Jose said. "Here's the key." He produced it from his pocket.

"What's in it?"

"I don't know. Mr. Chown's affairs, such as they were, were looked after by a lawyer in Helston. Not long before he died the old boy handed him this, and said it was to be given to George Ledra six months after his death. I suppose it's some sort of keepsake he wants you to have. The lawyer chap, knowing I was coming this way to-day, asked me to deliver it." He took a paper from his pocket. "This is a form of receipt for you to sign."

I signed it with my fountain-pen and gave it to Jose. Then I took the box upstairs and put it on my study table. "I'll see what's in it later," I said. "Let's go and eat in Hayle."

We did, and that night, the weather having turned coldish, I lit a fire in my study, filled my pipe, and sat down to examine Mr. Chown's legacy.

There was a letter addressed to me. There was a bundle of quarto sheets written upon in Mr. Chown's clear and beautiful hand. There was a packet of newspaper cuttings, and another packet containing letters in various hands.

The letter addressed to me was dated a month or so before Mr. Chown's death. It said:

"Dear George: It seems years ago now since, looking for a cigar, I came upon your small reliquary containing some newspaper cuttings about my niece Sylvia and a bracelet that had belonged to her mother, my sister Margaret. I don't suppose anyone will think it worth while to write a life of Sylvia, but there are several lives of Margaret, and some day perhaps you will read them. There are three things they all mention: that she was the granddaughter of a baronet of ancient vintage; that she lived when little more than a child with Arthur Craven; and—but this is more hinted than said—that she was the woman who brought Fred Byles to ruin.

"I was only once in your London flat, and there over the mantelpiece was Fred, just as I had known him: cheeky, almost cocky, self-confident and full of lovingkindness. Lovingkindness is the thing I most remember about Fred. I don't think I have known a better man.

"It was seeing Fred's picture there that persuaded me to tell you what I knew about him. It seemed to me that he was likely to be a legend in your family and that you might grow up with a false idea of him. He might, by the time he reached your ears, have degenerated into a common crook. It was your family's association with Fred that caused me to have you here in the first place. Perhaps your father told you that, long before you came to Cornwall, he and I had some correspondence. The name Ledra struck me at once, because I had known that Fred's firm was Byles and Ledra; and then one day your father must have had a slack moment in the office, and he wrote to me on the office paper. There it was: Fred Byles and Ledra. Like a ghost out of a past that I was beginning to forget.

"So when he asked me to coach you two things happened: I wanted to look on a face that would give me a human link with a happy time in my life; and the blood, or the bile, or whatever it is that stirs in pedagogues, stirred in me, and the idea of once more doing something towards creating a living soul took hold of me. About that side of the matter, the less said the better. I was not disappointed, because long experience had taught me that a man with the instincts of a true scholar is as rare as a March swallow; so I settled down to doing little more than enjoy your company. Thank you for it, George. It came to me at a time when I was beginning to feel old enough to be Homer's grandfather. You and the Witch were like those maidens who, if we are to believe the Scriptures, were put into the ageing David's bed. They couldn't work the trick, but they did their best. A sad time comes when the best isn't good enough. We do what we can with a protégé or two, a pub parlour, and, thank God, the past. I have been occupying myself with the past, with the story of my sister Margaret and Fred Byles. You will find it in this red box. It belongs to a time when I was translating the odes which may or may not have been written by Anacreon, who, a flowery writer tells us, 'sang in graceful strains the praises of the Muses, of wine, and of love.' Margaret said I must have something beautiful to keep my manuscript in. This box is what she gave me.

" Well, by the time you read this you will have done me the last service of helping to 'commit,' I am sure someone will say, ' his body to the deep.' Thank you for that. *Ave atque vale.* Hector Chown."

It didn't take me long to read this, but it took me long to think about it. It explained a good deal: a feeling I had had that, though I knew myself to be a failure scholastically, the sort of person in whom Mr. Chown can hardly have been expected to take much interest, yet there was an interest, at times almost an affection, which I found it hard to understand. It explained winter moments when, by the fire in his study, he would fall to musing, his eyes upon me as though I were in some way concerned with whatever it was that occupied his mind, and I would have a sense of having been a starting-point from which he had wandered into a far region of experience and reminiscence. But like an epicure with a choice feast before him, I took my time. To-morrow would be soon enough for going on to discover what Mr. Chown had to say about Margaret Napier.

4

Margaret Napier (I read when I sat down to it the next night) was twenty when she left Arthur Craven. She had lived with him for four years. I was a few years older than she was and had just got my first academic job: lecturer in Greek at St. Michael's, Oxford. I saw a good deal of Arthur Craven. He was a noble old skeleton whose bones were just concealed by a thin covering of parchment. He always wore a black skullcap. His burning eyes, and the black eyebrows contrasting with the white beard, seemed to demand a genuflexion. I liked him. He was dedicated. In his way, as I in mine, he was a searcher for beauty. I could only discover and try to exalt the beauty that

171

others had made immortal. He was a creator. But he was humble and gentle—perhaps too much so, for he was over-fastidious, at times almost womanish. There is a lot of woman in any creative artist. There was too much of it in Arthur.

He was wealthy. Those were days when ironmasters and wool and cotton merchants had houses with wide wall spaces. From the Royal Academy they would order lengths of canvas as their wives ordered dress lengths. Craven's pictures were among the most coveted, and his sculpture was prized by the municipal overlords of public gardens. My sister Margaret, as a dryad, naiad or innominate nymph-in-general, is now on many a civic plinth, presiding over the ordered seasonal march from daffodils to dahlias. He worked her hard as a model. In his paintings, she is everything from Andromeda to the young widow of a cornet of horse shot at the battle of Naseby. Her power as an actress was as great as her patience on a model's throne.

There was and still is, in memoirs, a great deal of chat about them. Inevitably, she was taken for his mistress, and the talk became the more vivid as her own career developed. By the time she was twenty she was already considered outstanding. She was never his mistress. The worldlings find it hard to believe in a relationship which they cannot understand, but those two were able to give to one another, and to receive from one another, both a human friendship and a profound inspiration. Margaret left him because the development of her own powers made it impossible to go on dividing her being. I myself advised her to make the break: he was taking too much out of her. They continued to meet from time to time, but the greater a friendship is the more completely it ends when end it must. All my life's experience has taught me that a broken friendship can never be mended. The infrequent meetings petered out; and that episode in Margaret's life was over.

I want you to have a true picture of her, George. I am not writing about a saint, but about a passionate woman. I think she would have become Craven's mistress had he wanted her; but he wanted only an image of youth and beauty. That is what he worshipped in her, with his own youth long flown; but to her, awakening to maturity as a woman, the stress of the relationship could have been something else. I suspect Craven to have been impotent.

But I want to leave speculation alone and tell you the facts as I know them. I have mentioned in my letter to you that writers about Margaret always recall that she was a baronet's granddaughter. They don't mention the baronet's son—my father and Margaret's. I have told you that he was a violent man who knocked me and my mother about. It was not till after his death that I learned another thing about the burden my

172

mother had to bear. He was outrageously unfaithful. And reading eighteenth-century memoirs in which that side of my family often figures, I found that the Chowns, men and women alike, had a monstrous record for their fornications and adulteries. Margaret inherited this tendency, and my own life has been nothing to write home about.

Neither so far as Margaret is concerned nor so far as I am concerned do I owe you or anyone else an accounting under that head. I am dealing here with her, and I shall say only that she had many lovers and that, whatever she may have been seeking in them, she never found it. Her life was as tragic as her art, and it was in tragedy that she excelled. Though she died young, we shall not, I think, soon see a greater actress of Shakespeare's tragic women. Look again at that picture by John Collier that you have seen so often. I have persuaded Sylvia to let me have it here in my own room, because, with little time before me, I wish to draw nearer to that beautiful exalted sister whose image reminds me of my youth, as, once, her living flesh reminded Arthur Craven of his. Look at it. That is not Ophelia as commonly conceived: a foolish little virgin wronged by a melancholy prince. That is a woman who has probably been in the prince's bed, and is about to die overwhelmed by a realisation of his tragedy, as well as her own. That is how she always played it, and tore people's hearts to bits.

I think that when she married at twenty-five she did it, as much as for anything, in an effort to straighten out her disordered life. She married a nonentity named Ronald Coast. He was a rich man, about forty years old. The family had been for generations getting richer and richer on the coal and iron of South Wales, assisted by the heir always marrying someone as rich as himself. Ronald Coast was the first to break away from this tradition. He had political ambitions, but lacked the brains to realise them, and he married where no money was. His father had recently died. His mother was outraged and did not attend the wedding or even meet Margaret. I gave away the bride, and I remember that Henry Irving, who looked like an archangel masquerading as a man-about-town, was one of those who signed the book in the vestry.

Coast had been elected as Liberal member for the constituency surrounding Swynton, a mansion in Dorsetshire which had been bought by his father, but he made no mark whatever on the life of his times. There was a house in Belgrave Square for the sessions of the Commons; and when Parliament was up he would go down to Dorset where Swynton was famous as a place of political entertaining. Gladstone himself was there occasionally, and it was a home-from-home for all the young pushing men in the party. Disraeli once said that if God had wished to come down again to earth, he would be undecided between Sinai and Swynton, and in his confusion would probably compromise on Hughenden.

But please don't think, George, that Margaret became involved with these people. Coast was such a fool that he had expected her to do so. Nothing had been said about the matter, but when the House rose in the autumn following the marriage he took it for granted that she would throw up what she was doing and go down to Dorset to be the gracious hostess of the grouse-shooting Liberals. (There was excellent shooting round about Swynton.) And what was she doing? Merely playing Lady Macbeth! She was staggered by the man's idiocy. " I'm very bad at pouring out tea," she said. " Couldn't your mother do the job?" And Mrs. Coast did so. She jumped in like a shot, and ever thereafter was the hostess at Swynton.

I didn't see much of Coast, but I did manage a talk with him during this crisis. I tried to make him see what her acting meant to Margaret. I must have failed, for he said: " But the play could go on. Surely anyone can act?"

Disaster for Margaret was inevitable with such a man as Coast. Oddly enough, she was, unlike me, proud of her ancestry. The Chowns had never *done* anything, but they had *been* something. They had flair and panache. The men had been friends of kings, and the women had been kings' mistresses ; though by my day the family had fizzled out into nothing more than Lords Lieutenant, High Sheriffs, and such other totem-poles. Margaret knew more than I did about the Chowns in their hey-day, which was in the seventeenth and eighteenth centuries, and this touched off a quarrel with Coast when he returned from that first sojourn at Swynton after their marriage. She was bored in the Belgrave Square house and, saying nothing to him, took a flat in St. James's Street. When he discovered this on his return, he was enraged. He talked about her duty to think of the dignity of his family, and of how this was tarnished when his wife lived in what he called conditions more than dubious. I never learned the ins and outs of that row, but Margaret on her high horse could be formidable. I imagine that was the first time Coast had ever been talked to *de haut en bas*. She was never prideful about her own achievements, but could be icy with fools who talked of the stage in general as though it were peopled with riff-raff. And that was what Coast did. She told him coldly what she thought of the human conditions in his iron-works and collieries, and offered to organise a matinée for the relief of his victims. She could say the most deadly things with an air of sweet reasonableness, while Coast could never control his temper. She won that bout. She returned to Belgrave Square—" now that I'm not just one of the dust-sheets "—but Coast agreed to her taking a flat whenever he was long away and, what's more, he agreed to pay the rent.

He was infatuated with her. After that quarrel he was ready to be her lap-dog. He had come back from Swynton where he had been lording it among people eating and drinking and shooting heartily at his expense, feeling no end of a great man; and she venomously pricked the balloon and showed him his just proportions. She even suggested that politics was such a long way round to do a normal decent thing. Wouldn't it be quicker if Swynton were used as a convalescent home for some of his asthmatic and tubercular workmen and women? "How jolly it would be to see them tucking into grouse and salmon."

I can imagine, George, the relish with which she would quietly make a reasonable proposal like that. No man not infatuated with her would have put up with her for a month. But Coast managed to maintain some sort of *modus vivendi* for five years. It was all ups and downs. When he came back from a stay at Swynton under Mama's vigilant eye things were prickly and difficult. He wanted to be the great man, the influential politician, but Margaret would never have it. He had to accept life on her terms. There wasn't enough in the man to make him over-ride her. Her beauty kept him in subjection, and when he was subject she was charming. But he never knew when the charm would break. He once tried to persuade her to go down and talk in a constituency being fought by one of his friends. She said: "Yes, if we can make a fair exchange. I'll go down and talk if you'll play Bottom for a week." He'd never heard of Bottom and was disgusted. There was bound to be a break sooner or later, and it came when Margaret met Fred Byles. But before we talk about that I'll step ahead and say that there never was a *formal* break. He didn't divorce her, and he lived for ten years after Fred was sent to Dartmoor. Then, to her surprise, and everyone else's, it was found that he had left her a whack of shares in Coast, Pennington and Camelford, the combine in which the old firm of Coast was the greatest influence. His mother contested the will and lost her case. She was then a crazy old thing of ninety. Margaret, knowing her own mania for spending, formed a trust for the benefit of Sylvia. Sylvia would like to get hold of the capital and blue it all in recreating Penruan, but she can have only the interest, and that makes her rich enough, without what she got from Bascombe. Unlike this surviving academic male of the family, the women have known the way to riches, as expertly as their ancestors in which are called, I believe, the days of yore.

Well, now for a new act. The curtain goes up on Fred Byles. It was in the year 1890 that I met him. Margaret was then thirty, and Fred, I suppose, about fifty. It was the Long vacation, and, knowing that things were tense between Margaret and her husband, I stayed in London to be near her. She was living in her flat in St. James's Street; Coast was at Swynton;

and London was pretty empty. All the best people were away, shooting things. Margaret was without a job at the moment, and that always made her restless. I stayed at my club and took her out every day. I was fond of rowing then, and sometimes we went down to Maidenhead and on to the river; or we would dine at the Star and Garter at Richmond; or, even, she would take a busman's holiday and we would go to a play. Anything to keep her occupied. I sensed her dreadful restlessness, and I feared a relapse into the ways she had followed during the five years before she met Coast. I was more than half convinced that once, already, during her marriage, she had had a brief affair. It wasn't my business, but I would rather it didn't happen.

On that September day in 1890 we were walking in the Park. It was a lovely mild afternoon and I was proud to be walking with Margaret in the glorious hey-day of her beauty: all pale-blue flounces with a pink hat and a pink parasol. We sat down to watch the people driving by. There were not many, for, as I say, the moors and country houses had absorbed the élite, and this made all the more remarkable the outfit that came towards us. I don't know what you technically call those contraptions that are pulled by trotting horses: not a horse trotting in the normal way, but in that stylised fashion which involves bringing the knee up till it almost touches the chin and folding the leg backwards from the knee down. That is the sort of horse that was coming towards us—a nice chestnut—and sitting up straight as a pole in the contraption behind it was a man wearing a grey topper, a grey frock-coat and trousers, and with yellow gloves holding the reins. There was a white carnation at his button-hole, and he looked what we called then a regular old dog. Well, you *know* what he looked like, George. His portrait is over the mantelpiece in your flat.

With his gingerish side-whiskers and moustache, he looked so completely a caricature of an ageing roué that I could feel Margaret shaking with suppressed giggles beside me. I dug my elbow into her ribs as a command to behave herself, but Fred looked too good to be true, and she couldn't resist waving an ironic hand as he drew level. He raised his topper, stopped the horse, and leaned towards us. He ignored me, but looked steadily at Margaret for a moment or two, and then said: " Margaret Napier, isn't it?"

I didn't want to be involved with a stranger, so I got up, and Margaret rose with me. I said: " Miss Napier is my sister. We're just moving on," and took her arm. But Margaret resisted my attempt to lead her away. "Yes," she said, " I'm Margaret Napier. How did you know?"

" I've seen you in every part you've played." He paused, looking at her hardily, twirled his moustache like a villain of melodrama, and added: " But you've never looked so lovely as
176

now, when you're playing no part at all." He paused again, then said: "My name's Fred Byles. I come from Manchester. I'm in cotton."

I said: "I congratulate you, sir. Now we really must be going."

But Fred was not to be put off. He said: "I know you're not in a play at the moment, Miss Napier, so, if you're free to-night, I'd feel it a great honour if I were allowed to entertain you to dinner. You and your brother, of course. I owe you a lot."

When he said that, I was aware of sincerity. He was clearly admiring her as a woman, but I was sure he honoured her as an artist. And he looked more than twenty years older than Margaret which, in fact, he was. A change from brotherly company might amuse her. I asked: "Would you like that?"

"Yes," she said.

We met him at the Café Royal at eight o'clock.

George, I sha'n't try to give you Margaret's love story in detail. For one thing I don't know the details. I shared that dinner with them at the Café Royal, and that was all. Between that and going back to Oxford I didn't see her again. But the dinner remains clearly in my mind. Fred chose the food and the wines, and he chose exquisitely. He was an old hand here. The *maître d'hôtel* and all the waiters knew him. His remark "I'm in cotton" recurred in my memory without conviction. This was his *milieu*. He was dressed up to the nines—full fig. He talked a lot about actresses and horses, and I discovered that he was a member of a reasonably reputable club in St. James's Street where I knew that the card-playing was pretty heavy. If I had found that one of Arthur's more flamboyant knights—say Lancelot—was also a stock-jobber I could not have been more surprised by the man's duality. Whatever he might be in Manchester—and I could not imagine him there—here in London he was not a Manchester cotton man up for a spree: he was a metropolitan who knew his way about. From Margaret I had learned enough about actresses to feel that, where they were concerned, his stories were true. He talked of nights out with George Augustus Sala. You've probably never heard of Sala. That famous old rake-hell journalist was then approaching the end of a classically disreputable career.

From what he said that night, and from what was afterwards established, I can give you a general picture of Fred's London life. He had a small house in St. John's Wood, looked after by one man-servant. When he wanted horses—and he adored the creatures—he hired them, whether for riding or for driving. He loved to cut a figure in the Park. Apart from breakfast, he ate all his meals in expensive restaurants, and more often than not had an actress to share them. Some of the actresses from time to time shared the house in St. John's Wood. He gambled heavily at his club and suffered the consequences of being an indifferent player. He had faultless taste in plays and in acting. He knew English dramatic literature right through from the mysteries and miracles by way of Shakespeare to the Restoration. "After that," he said, "there's nothing bar a few flukes like Goldsmith and Sheridan." He talked about women. "The art of a great lover," he said, "lies at the precarious point between roughness and tenderness. Romeo is a sentimental adolescent and Petruchio a swaggering cad. The great lover is Othello."

I'm not asking you, George, to accept these æsthetic views of your grandfather's business partner! I'm telling you how Fred talked that night at the Café Royal. But, of course, there *is* the question of the business partner. I wish I had met someone who knew him in Manchester. He was a flaunting wide-open sunflower of a man, and I can't imagine what sunshine he would find there. Normally, it was only his week-ends that he spent in town. The train service between London and Manchester is good. He always travelled down after the office had closed on a Friday, and took the train back early on Monday morning. But his summer holiday was always spent in London, and it so chanced that that September day when Margaret and I met him in the Park was the first day of three weeks' freedom from cotton. Perhaps otherwise things would have turned out differently. Three weeks during which Coast and his sporty fellow-Liberals were popping away at the birds round about Swynton. To a man like Fred and a woman like Margaret it was heaven-sent. Cotton or no cotton, Fred Byles was the sort of eighteenth-century man on whom Chown women had lavished themselves: men who exemplified that juncture of roughness and tenderness that Fred spoke of: connoisseurs, builders of great houses and gardens, collectors of works of art; and at the same time ruthless hunters after all sorts of carnal satisfactions.

Two days after Margaret met Fred Byles I knew that there was no point in my remaining in London. I went back betimes to Oxford, and left it to the Fates.

Three weeks later she wrote to ask if I could come up to London. I did. She met the train at Paddington and did something she had never done before. She threw her arms round my neck, hugged me as though she would never let me go, and kissed me again and again. She didn't speak, and it seemed touch and go whether she would laugh or cry. At last she smiled. I don't suppose, George, you've yet encountered the moment when everything is in a woman's smile? I'm an unprepossessing old reptile, but I've known it once or twice. Margaret's smile told me all I wanted to know. I couldn't miss its significance: the radiance of a few seconds in which the body and the spirit are one, in a satisfaction that is absolute.

She said: "Let's go to the Park." We went in a hansom cab, and we sat on the seat where we had been sitting when Fred like some new planet swam into our ken; and for a long time we said nothing, but I knew that she was living again that moment, seeing the absurdly stylised trotting of the horse and the ribbons in Fred's hands and the hardy, almost impudent, appraisal in his eyes.

She put a hand on mine and said: "At last I know what love is."

I looked down at her hand and saw the bangle on her wrist—the bangle, George, that you picked up on the sand at Penruan and put into your reliquary, not knowing what a relic it was. When you were gone and I found it in the cigar-box I was battered by wave upon wave of reminiscence. I was back on that park seat, and the October day was tender, and that fragile hand was lying in my lap—the hand that I had seen blood-stained as she wrung it in a horror of dread and a black tumult of ambition. She was a great Lady Macbeth. But it was small and frail and beautiful—a curled pink shell. She saw that I was looking at the bangle, and twisted it on her wrist. "Fred bought it for me in Paris," she said.

I despair of making you understand all that was in her speaking of his name. Not much of a name. Fred. But I wish to God I had ever been able to give or to receive the love that was in her speaking it. My love for her was the nearest I ever came to it.

I asked: "What are you going to do?"

She was not interested in what she was going to do. I might as well have asked a rock rolling downhill what it was going to do. She would talk only of Paris. She had not been there before, and I could well imagine that in the autumn light it was beautiful. They dined out, went to picture galleries and theatres, visited the dress shops. She asked: "Do you know what the French mean by a *salon particulier* in a restaurant?"

She was smiling in mischievous reminiscence. "I'm not a monk," I explained.

Whatever she had been going to say about *salons particuliers* she left unsaid. But I could guess. I had divined in one evening enough about Fred to assume that they would be part of his *milieu*.

She switched from the subject and held up her hand with the bangle shining on her wrist. "This is by Fabergé," she said.

I told her that I had never heard of Fabergé, and she said: "Neither had I. But Fred says he's very special. He works mostly for royalty."

"Then I suppose Fred had to pay a royal price?"

"Yes," she admitted. "I didn't want him to buy it, but you know what he is."

"I'm afraid you have the advantage of me there, my dear."

The silence held for a time, and we watched a few thin leaves falling and touching the grass with the ghost of a sigh, as though glad that their task, whatever it had been, was ended.

"I'm not well up in shooting," I said, "but I suppose it's about due to finish."

She took the reference. "I don't know," she said, "except that somehow I must go on seeing Fred." She added, with a flippancy quite out of character: "Perhaps the House will have some all-night sessions."

I took her hand and asked: "Is there anything I can do? Can you suggest anything at all?"

Her face became grave. "I'm afraid not," she said. "I don't know where I am. I'm full of light, and yet I'm moving into the dark."

"You're quite sure of Fred?"

"Ah! If only you knew him as I do!"

I never did, and I don't know what it is in a man that can work in a woman the miracle of obsession. But here it was, and I had to accept it. Fred Byles's side of the matter was easier to understand. Women and the theatre were his life. And here these two flowed together in a great tragic actress whom he could worship both for her body and her art.

She said: "Hathersage is putting on *Antony and Cleopatra*. He wants me for Cleopatra."

At that my heart lifted. She had never played Cleopatra, and I could imagine how the passionate excitement of studying such a part would absorb all that was in her. If anything could put Fred Byles into the background, this was it.

She got up and said: "I've turned it down. At the moment, I must be free."

I didn't argue with her, but my heart went cold. Give up Cleopatra for Fred Byles! My God! What did she take him for? An archangel?

I wish, George, that I could be telling you this face to face, instead of writing it. I should like to see your reactions. I can, for example, imagine you asking me: "Why wasn't there a divorce and a marriage?" As for a divorce, there was Coast's point of view to be considered. Divorce then was not what it is now. You may have heard of the case of Parnell and Kitty O'Shea. That would have been all right if it had been possible to keep it quiet. When it came into the open, all hell was loose. Divorce could wreck a career then, even for the "innocent party," and this was especially so in the case of a politician. People were credulous. Politicians were knights in armour, waging war on the evil dragons that threatened the lesser breeds. We've learned a bit of sense, I hope, but that's how it was. Coast was nothing much in the political world, but he thought he was, and there was a chance that, if the Salisbury government went and Gladstone came back, some piffling government post might be offered him. He would no more have accepted the blazing publicity of divorce than dance a fandango on the floor of the House. Remember, this is 1890. It was in November of this year that divorce sent Parnell into the wilderness.

It is odd to think of such political considerations affecting the career of my sister, but there it was; and, even if Coast had divorced her, there could have been no marriage, for Fred Byles was married already. She was in what seemed to me the most desperate coil, but it didn't for a moment mitigate her happiness. She loved Fred and Fred adored her, and that was all that mattered. I learned later that in Paris he had told her of his marriage. It was not till long afterwards that I knew about it.

Fred's marriage was all of a piece with his happy-go-lucky and disordered life. He was a Cheshire man and in his younger days was a member of a hunt there. He cast his eyes on some of the ladies of the hunt, especially on one who was the daughter of a titled family. To put the thing briefly, Fred, who could use any opportunity, chose a hunt ball to snatch a moment from dancing, take the lady outside, and put her in the family way. Her people insisted on a quiet wedding, and then told the lady that they had done with her. By the time Fred met my sister Margaret, he had a son of nineteen, just gone up to Oxford. The boy had no brains and won no scholarship. Fred was paying every penny. He seemed to love spending money, even on a thing like that! The marriage was a disaster. The lady soon had plenty of reason for seeking divorce, but she didn't like the word, and knew her quixotic Fred. They separated, and she signed a legal document binding himself to pay her more than she would have got as alimony. As a gesture, a flourish, a bit of Bylesian bravado, he added the promise to see to the boy's education up to and including the university.

I expect your head is aching now at the financial mess Fred had got himself into. But he himself never knew a headache. He was a member of clubs in both Manchester and London, he had a house in each town, he couldn't resist horses, actresses or other well-disposed women. He was in the hands of money-lenders, and his heavy playing at his club sank him deeper into the pit from which he hoped the playing would extricate him. His trip to Paris, and the Fabergé bangle, were financed by a money-lender. Withal, he was the happiest and most generous man I have ever met. I don't intend to write about my sister's love affair. I know nothing about it, except that, on our few occasions of meeting during the next six months, she was in a blaze of love. I had not realised how exalted a woman in love

181

could be. At times it frightened me. In March she told me she was expecting a child—and that was Sylvia. In April Fred was arrested.

You will find in this box all the newspaper cuttings concerned with the trial, though I don't see much point in your wading through them. Please yourself. The only thing I wish to emphasize is that the evidence showed that Fred had been helping himself to the firm's money for long before he met Margaret. At first they were small sums and they were replaced. Then they became larger and were replaced in part. I can see how his mind was working. It was the firm's money and he was part of the firm. What was wrong with a temporary loan? So it went, and the loans became more and more difficult to replace, and the lenders were pressing. A rising clerk in the office spotted what was going on. He didn't mention it to your grandfather, but, in an innocent-seeming but I think malicious way, to the firm's accountant. Then nothing could stop the machine from rolling to its conclusion.

Margaret's name was not mentioned at the trial. I attended the court with her every day, and shall never forget poor Fred's utter bewilderment. It was just that—no sense of sin—a small boy who finds that taking a tart from the pantry now and then is considered wicked beyond belief by his elders and betters. When he was sentenced, he bowed civilly to the judge, then turned to where Margaret and I were sitting behind the lawyers. His radiant sunflower smile bloomed upon us. He went below, and that was that. I'm told he was a model prisoner. They gave him light work in the prison library, but he died before his sentence was up.

There was an old dame named Wharncliffe who kept the grocery shop in the Yorkshire village where Margaret and I were born. She was kind to us. She knew about our home conditions, and the parlour behind the shop was our frequent refuge. She was an old maid and she adored Margaret, who kept in touch with her. Miss Wharncliffe, in the days of Margaret's early fame, spent a week in London at my expense. One night I did her proud, took a box at the theatre and trotted her along to see Margaret act. She couldn't make much of it, but the occasion bowled her over. The theatre was something then—men in boiled shirts, women bejewelled. They called for Margaret, and when she stood alone on the stage, looking small and sad and exhausted, and that galaxy rose to her, and the wave of its enthusiasm surged over her, old Wharncliffe sat with tears streaming down her face, sobbing " Oh, Maggie! Oh, Maggie!" No one else would have dared to call her that. I took her round to Margaret's dressing-room, and Margaret embraced her and said: "Well, Wharny, I did it just for you to-night." And all she still could say was: " Oh, Maggie!"

Forgive me, George. How I go on about Margaret! But you should have known her!

When we left the court on the day of Fred's sentence we went to her flat. There were no tears, but she was dead. She said: "I've written to Wharny telling her all about it and asking if I may stay with her till my child is born. She says it will be all right."

Wharny was eighty then, and still running the grocery shop. The news lightened my heaviness. No arrangement could have been better.

Margaret said: "I shall travel to-morrow. Will you see my husband and tell him about all this and ask him what he thinks should be done?"

I saw her off, and wrote a letter to Coast asking for an interview. When he knew that Margaret was expecting a child he said that he "approved of her prudence" in going to Yorkshire. I was amazed by his calmness. I had expected to be involved in a stormy scene, but there he sat in his cosy library, smoking a cigar, wearing a purple velvet smoking jacket, and discussing the matter with the coolness of a Foreign Secretary settling a small frontier dispute in a remote colony. He didn't know who the father was, and he didn't ask. Yes, he said, he knew that Margaret had been playing the fool, and he trusted that this would bring her to her senses.

"Do you mean," I asked, "that you want to have her back?"

"Of course I want to have her back. People know that I'm married, and expect to see my wife in my house. Occasionally, anyway," he added a little bitterly.

And that, no doubt, was it. He was worried about what people expected. Appearances must be maintained at all costs.

"My mother," he said, as though he were a boy of ten, "disapproved of my marriage. Well, I don't want more disapproval than I can help, from her or anybody else."

He knocked the ash from his cigar into an ash-tray, and I noticed that his hand was trembling. Through that chink I perceived the desolation of his landscape. The statesmanlike calm was a thin lick of paint on a suffering human being. He was by a good deal my elder, but I got up and put a hand on his shoulder. I said nothing, but looked down at him, and his little pursy mouth quivered and he stopped being a statesman.

He said: "Margaret has done me a great wrong."

I agreed with him and said so.

He stubbed out the cigar and said: "I've been a great fool, I know. I've always tried to make her understand my way of life, and I've never tried to understand her. But she *has* wronged me. She has."

I said nothing, and after a moment he went on: "Well, there

183

it is. We're in a pretty mess, and how are we to get out of it without scandal? That's the question."

I said: "You told me just now that you want Margaret back. Do you mean that you want *her,* or simply that you want to avoid scandal?"

"Of course I want her. Why on earth do you think I married her? And of course I want to avoid scandal. What good would that do to her any more than to me?" He added with the only touch of humour I ever heard from him: "What would Mrs. Kendal say?"

Mrs. Kendal was the shining example of domestic fidelity in the theatre at that time.

A secretary knocked and entered. "You're due at a Committee of the House, sir, in ten minutes."

Coast got up and, to my surprise, shook my hand. "I rely on you," he said. "Do what you can."

I left the house with a feeling that the rather dumb brute had more affection for Margaret than he had ever been able to make known to her, even though he was incapable of love as she understood it.

Miss Wharncliffe proved to be a wiser bird than I expected. There were people in our village who still remembered Margaret and whose tongues would have wagged had she borne a child at Wharny's instead of in her own home. So she booked rooms at a remote village on the north-east coast, telling the landlady that her granddaughter who was expecting a child would be with her for a long holiday before returning to London for the birth. They stayed there for the whole summer, and then, alas! they had miscalculated the date and the child got born. I was up there once or twice in the guise of husband, and now that I shall soon be beyond the reach of justice I confess that a bogus birth certificate was made out, in which I appear as Thomas Robinson, carpenter, of Hornsey.

This was the end of Margaret's romantic life. In the biographies, no one has dared to say plainly that Sylvia is illegitimate, but it has been hinted at, and one writer went so far—and so far astray—as to suggest that she was the daughter of a prince who was living so notoriously in defiance of his father's and mother's principles that any conceivable bastard was fathered upon him. I tell you the truth because, when I saw Fred's portrait in your room, I guessed you had some liking for him.

Margaret gave up her flat, returned to Coast's house, and developed a good deal of affection for him, as well she might, for, having said he wanted her back, he acted as though he meant it. There was no word of reproach and no reproachful conduct. She even went so far as to go down, when her work in

184

the theatre permitted, to his place in Dorsetshire. His mother, on such occasions, was not among those present.

Sylvia grew up as Miss Coast. Coast had a great affection for her, and so long as he lived she believed herself to be his daughter. The only sensation Coast ever caused in the House was to die there—the rousing climax to a dull speech on foreign affairs by Lansdowne.

Well, that's about all of it, George. Margaret made a lot of money in the theatre and Coast left her very rich. She returned to the flat she had occupied in Fred's time and lived an exemplary and rather dull life there. Dull except when she was acting. She was superb to the end. She died in 1911. Sylvia was by then already on the stage and married to Bascombe. I have lived long enough to see him dead, too, and Sylvia, consequently, still further enriched. The women of my family are unlucky in love—my mother, my sister, my niece—but Margaret and Sylvia at least grew rich out of it, which my poor mother never did. And I have not known how to make a penny more than my job brought me.

How all these things rushed back upon me when I saw poor Fred's picture hanging in your room! It was then that I decided to tell you the whole story. I wonder whether, one of these days, Fred's picture and John Collier's picture of Margaret will hang side by side? If beyond the grave, earthy or watery, we are aware of what happens on this odd unsatisfactory planet—a state of things I find it difficult to believe in—then the conjunction of Fred and Margaret would certainly cause me to apply for a day off from whatever angelic occupation may have been allotted to me in order to do a bit of private, as distinct from cosmic, jubilation. And even if, as seems likely, I am unaware of it, raise a glass, should those two come together, to one who loved them both.

5

Here Mr. Chown's manuscript ended. There were still the newspaper cuttings and the letters. The cuttings didn't interest me. I knew the story in general, and that was enough for me. I would never make one of those historians who think a week's research worth while if it has told them how much Queen Elizabeth paid for her shoe-laces. The letters were more interesting. They all belonged to the time after Fred's death. They had pathos. It was moving to read the girlish trivia which "your loving and obedient daughter Sylvia Coast" addressed, from a school in the South of England, to "my adorable Mummy," who was Margaret Napier. Margaret's own letters

were full of the things which, I guessed, she thought the child
would like to hear: what clothes she had worn at a party, what
flowers were in a bouquet that had been presented to her, how a
kitten named Blacky Boy was getting on, and how well a canary
that had been ill during Sylvia's holidays, now was. In one
letter Sylvia said: "Adorable Mummy didn't write to me last
week, and this is the first time she has not comforted the
sorrows and tribberlations I endure in this place. But Daddy
was here at the week-end, and he said that you are working
hard on a new play, and that I must not worry you. He said
he gave a dinner and that you wore blue silk and were lovely.
He said: 'Do you love me?', and I said 'Of course I love you,'
and he said 'That's all right then.' Give my love to Blacky Boy.
I love him and Daddy and you. I can't think of anyone else, or
of anything else to say, so close with love."

Then Coast died. "Darling Mummy,—When we were going
in to breakfast Miss Pack came and said would I go to her
room and have breakfast with her. I did, and she told me that
Daddy is dead. Oh, Mummy, now you have no one but me. I
love you and will try to be a good girl, but I have cried in Miss
Pack's room all day because I loved Daddy too. I hated him
when he shooted at pheasants at Swynton and I cried and he
said I'd understand some day that men had to shoot pheasants.
And now I'm sorry I hated him, because generally I loved him,
as I do now. Will you let me . . ."

The rest of this letter was missing, and there was only one
other—from Sylvia to Mr. Chown. It was of a much later date.
It belonged to the time when Margaret Napier was dead and
Sylvia, absurdly young for such a step, was married to Bascombe.

"Dear Chowny,—It was lovely to be able to get away and
join you at the gorgeous Encaenia ceremony at Oxford. You
and all your friends dressed up in your doctors' gowns—oh,
what a gorgeous lot you were, and what a poor unplumaged
hen you made me feel! And then at lunch to seat me next to
the Professor of Anthropology! I felt all the time that he was
trying to 'place' my bones—neolithic? paleolithic? However,
he very beautifully handed me a flower when it was over, and
he hadn't talked to me too 'learned.' Indeed, I was surprised
at his knowledge of the fluffier plays now on in London.

"It was sweet of you to take me on the river in the evening.
The perfect setting for making such a revelation. And, of course,
it is about the revelation that I'm writing. I don't know whether
to blast you or thank you. Here am I (I may as well now tell
you) with an infant stirring in me, and this is the moment you
choose to tell me that I am a poor little bastard! Well, on the
whole, I'd better opt for thanking you. If you hadn't told me, I
suppose sooner or later someone else would have done so less
186

kindly, and I must say that in that book about Mother there are hints and innuendoes that made me think. Still, if one half of my parentage has to go, I'd rather keep the Chown half than the Coast. It had always seemed queer to me that after Mr. Coast died Mother and I never came in sight of a Coast again, but sailed on together as though all the Coasts in the world had faded on the horizon.

"I hope that some day, since you have half lifted the curtain, you'll be willing to tell me *all* that lies behind it. I think I'm entitled to know who my father was. Don't you agree? I knew Mother well enough to be certain it's no one I need feel ashamed of. So think it over, and in the meantime, believe me to be, dear Chowny, ever your loving Sylvia."

At the bottom of this Mr. Chown had written in pencil: "I never did tell her, George. Would it have been kind to let her know that her father died a convict? I can't say. Perhaps you can."

6

When I had read all this straight through, I spent another hour browsing upon it here and there. It was then midnight—a midnight of full moon. Through my window I could see the flanks of Trencrom, a checker of light and shade under the serene shining. I went out, crossed the path, and began to climb. It's not much of a hill, Trencrom ; but it's profoundly evocative. Even if one had not read the guesses of the archæologists, it would be impossible to walk upon it without feeling that it was holy ground ; holy with the aspirations and despairs of unnumbered generations, from the little dark men whose homes had been not much more than rabbit-burrows among these rocks to my own sophisticated contemporaries, who had reached the point of egoist eminence from which they could look back and ponder, and deduce, and speculate upon human life and conduct through all those years, and still be as baffled, as far from the answers, as the creatures whose bones were beneath my foot.

I sat on the topmost rocks, and listened to the night, its silence deepened by the calling of the owls who hovered down there over my cottage, shining white as a skull, and over the fields about it where little scurrying creatures would hear that calling and stand transfixed, knowing it was death's voice, and I looked out on a milky shining opalescence over the land and over the sea on which the coracles had floated, bringing from Ireland a store of gold and saints. And suddenly I remembered those words that had crossed my mind—holy ground—and I recalled that they had been spoken to me by that apple-chewing

187

old codger who paused by the cottage on the day when I first saw it and was sitting by the wall, watching Janet and Medea Hopkins climbing the hill. I had later told Mr. Chown about him, and Mr. Chown, who would laugh no more, had laughed and said that he was certainly that old Billy Bones who had been one of his colleagues at Oxford. Billy Bones undoubtedly would be professor of anthropology, and ten to one it was he, arrayed in academic glory, who had sat next to Sylvia, then feeling Janet stirring within her, at the Encaenia luncheon, and had shown a knowledge of fluffy plays, and charmingly handed her a flower. No doubt, I thought with a smile, he had concealed from her his belief that the only good woman had done to man was to teach him to eat apples.

And so here, where I had thought to wash my mind for a while of the whole matter, forgetting the present and the recent past in the backward stretch of time's immensity, they were about me again: Sylvia; and Janet, alive though not yet born; and Mr. Chown. Sylvia, I was sure, would be wearing the bangle that Fred Byles had given to Margaret Napier. And so they, too, came crowding into my reverie; and Fred brought with him my father, and the grandfather I had never known, and Mr. Merriman, now, I had heard, ruined in the cotton slump. It seemed as though this inconsiderable hump of land called Trencrom were a magic mountain, with the power to abolish the incidents of time and to make time itself a palpable force, an ever-rolling stream that bears all its sons away.

7

It was a disgracefully lazy summer; but then, given half a chance, I am a disgracefully lazy person. I have always disliked Bob Meagher's up-and-doing philosophy. I didn't want to "belong" to things, to be for ever buzzing about, proposing, seconding, moving amendments and asking that the motion be now put. It was through no virtue of my own that I was able to abstain from these activities. The work of others had given me the means. But even had I been under the compulsion of earning a living, I think I should have been better pleased with a job that gave me small pay and large leisure than with one the other way about. It seemed to me that half the intelligence and freedom of the world was already being choked by the fog arising from committees, conventions, conferences and convocations, parochial, national and international, that kept everybody's nerves exacerbated, and that there would be a better chance of tranquillity if all those people, dashing about in all those aeroplanes, to all those countries, saw less of one another's ugly

188

faces. Now we can't catch a fish or grow a tomato or take an egg from under a hen without a committee to tell us how to do it.

Well, I for one wasn't having any part of all that, and I don't regret or apologise for this way of life.

It was an easy summer. I spent my days in the sea and in the sun; and this was more pleasant than it is now; for we hadn't yet reached the time when the "oppressed masses," whom everyone was out to help with laws, rules, regulations and injunctions, madly broke their bonds each summer, and, with the help of hire-purchase and Bob Meagher's products, surged like beauty-devouring locusts into even this remote corner, clamorously demanding that all they had fled from— radio and cinemas and concert parties and the Late Night Final —should be provided to make Arcadia endurable. You can hear, even to this day, a great sigh of relief burst from the breast of Trencrom when, in late summer, that tide turns again home.

Sometimes I went down to Penruan to see Jose. His father had died and he had taken over the Absolution, which was a free house, untied to a brewery company. He found time to scout around the country after goods for his Helston shop, which was now managed by the attractive widow he had married, and the best of these things he always reserved till Sylvia, to whom he was regularly writing, decided whether she wanted them or not. Moreover, he was still her clerk of the works, receiving her orders about the restoration and seeing that these were carried out.

One afternoon, when the pub was shut, we went over there together. Mr. Chown's lodge had been let to an artist and his young wife who paid a peppercorn rent on condition that they kept an eye on the house. We called on them before going farther, and Jose introduced us. "Mr. and Mrs. Redmayne. George Ledra."

Harry Redmayne was one of the dungarees and pullover type of artist, a youngster with fair tousled hair and incipient beard. Some of his pictures were leaning against the wall in the big room that had been Mr. Chown's study. He, clearly, had heard of Picasso. Elsa Redmayne was a girl in her early twenties. She had just come down from Newnham and had the yearning face of a Rosetti model. She was clothed, too, in the flowing flowery silks that the ladies of that time had liked to wear. When Jose said: "George Ledra," she yearned towards me and held out a long white hand, and said, awe-struck: "Not *the* George Ledra?"

I said that, so far as I knew, there was no other bearer of that rather odd name. "George Ledra of *Now*?" she persisted.

I saw that, among much high-brow periodical literature scattered upon a trestle table, were copies of *Now*, and I admitted my identity. Her blue eyes swam with rapture, and all she could utter was an incredulous " Oh!"

After a moment she recovered and asked: " When you have seen the house, would you honour us by taking tea here?"

I consented with the democratic magnanimity of a king who breaks a sight-seeing tour to take tea in a miner's cottage.

" When I was a child, I once saw Rupert Brooke," she said, " but I never thought . . ."

Jose took me by the arm and led me out. " Too much of that would be bad for you," he said.

This was an August day. Sea and sky were a burning blue, and the gold of ragwort blazed in the field between the lodge and the house. As we drew near, the sound of lazily chipping hammers fell through the hot silence. I remembered that there had been a sagging wire fence between the field and the mansion. Now there was a splendid balustrade of granite that looked as though it had been there for ever. It was mottled with lichens, and between it and the wall of the house was a fine stone pavement. I halted, laying my hand admiringly on the sun-warmed granite. Jose sat on the capping, for his leg was none too good after our walk. " Very nice," he said. " I found it at a place that had been burned out and abandoned. Got it for next to nothing beyond the cost of bringing it here and putting it up."

" I suppose next to nothing was a few hundred pounds to Sylvia?"

" Well," he said with a grin, " I found it irresistible."

" You seem to get more fun out of this place than Sylvia does."

" I shouldn't be surprised," he admitted. " I sometimes wonder whether she'll ever live in it. I've found a few good masons. Come and have a look at 'em."

We went towards the sound of the chipping hammers, and there the men were, shaping quoins and keystones and mullions. They were taking it easy. They had rigged an awning to keep off the sun's blaze, three old men, looking at the stone, and feeling it, and tapping it, pausing now and then to light a pipe or take a swig of cold tea from a can. I said: " There is nothing better for a man than that he should eat and drink and make his soul enjoy good in his labour."

Jose smiled, and quoted from the same wry source: " And I hated all my labour wherein I laboured under the sun: seeing that I must leave it unto the man that shall be after me. And who knoweth whether he shall be a wise man or a fool!"

He looked affectionately at the old men and said: " They're about the last of 'em in these parts. The fools that follow after know nothing beyond slapping one concrete block on top of another."

I remembered this part of the house as I had seen it when a boy: the walls half gone, the roof gone altogether, ferns and saplings in every cranny, trees sprouting from the floor. Now, though much remained to be done, the herbage was cleared, what stone remained was straightened and strengthened, and the great mullioned oriel window that would be the chief feature here was beginning to take shape. Jose said: " The room was panelled, you know. I have a pretty good idea how it looked. I'm making the panelling myself in such spare time as I have, and that isn't much. I've managed to get hold of some good wood."

" Poor Sylvia! " I said. " When this lot's finished she won't have a penny left to bless herself with."

" The panelling at least won't be in the bill," he said. " That's my contribution to a job worth doing."

" I think you're in love with the place more than she is, Jose."

" Well, there's that, too."

Too . . . I wondered what else there was. I wondered what his feeling had been for Sylvia herself.

I left him with the masons and went into the occupied part of the house. I wanted to have another look at Margaret Napier. There she was, wearing the bangle that Fred Byles had given her and that my profane hands had held without understanding. I looked at her with new eyes, eyes opened by Mr. Chown's narrative, and in her eyes I seemed to see all the world's sorrow. I glanced at the date of the painting: it was the year after Fred had died in Dartmoor.

Jose appeared in the doorway. " Come on," he teased me. " You mustn't keep your public waiting."

My public at all events had prepared a grand spread. I decided that when the Parthenon Press published my first collection of essays I would send her a signed copy. She served us as reverently as Hebe, though I'm afraid neither of us looked outstanding as a god. Jose drove me to Helston, where he had to close the shop and pick up his wife: and from there I took a taxi home to Trencrom. After my evening meal I sat down to write to Sylvia.

8

" *My Dear Sylvia,*—It is a long time since I have seen you or written to you. I don't even know whether your play is still running, for down here I enjoy the luxury of not reading newspapers and I have no radio. This afternoon I went to see Jose Gomm, and together we inspected the work at Penruan. The balustraded terrace is very lovely, and the great new room arising to balance the old one is obviously going to be lovely, too. Jose has discovered three old gnomes who seem to do nothing but sit about, tapping away at stone, yet a miracle is in process of being born out of their labours. For the first time, I believed this afternoon in what you have all along believed in: that Penruan can live again.

When I got back from this afternoon's visit I found a letter awaiting me from Bob Meagher. I think I have spoken to you once or twice about Bob; and Janet, too, may have mentioned him. She had the pleasure of dancing with him at the Savoy when Mr. Chown took her and me along there to dinner. Bob is an impulsive person, and his letter was impulsive. It was to tell me that I may expect to see him to-morrow. Not ' May I come?' Just ' I shall come,' and, what's more he intends to stay for a day or two. I suppose I am to sleep on the floor. There is only one bed.

I shall welcome him after my fashion. And when am I to welcome you? I should like you to see this place, my hut in the wilderness, and I am sure that you want to see what is happening at Penruan. Is there any hope of your play coming to an end? Or is it blasphemous to use the word hope in such a connection? I suppose I shall leave here early in October. For one thing, Nigel Wendron of the Parthenon Press wants to see me not later than that for a talk about a little book by me that he hopes to publish for Christmas. That's cutting it fine, but we've already made most of the decisions about it.

Let me know, dear Sylvia, how things are with you and whether you may be expected. When we last saw one another in Somerset you asked what was going on between me and Janet. The answer is: Nothing. *With love, George.*"

9

Bob Meagher arrived at about six o'clock in a dust-stained slim two-seater, the first of the Meagher models. They were all named, appropriately enough, after wild beasts, killers. This one was the Meagher Lion. The Panther, Puma, Leopard, Tiger, and many other carnivores were to follow. Bob was to prove one of the people most ardently concerned with deaths on the roads. When, in the years to come, this question arose after every Christmas orgy and Bank Holiday *battue*, he was always one of the first to be consulted by Authority about remedies. He was full of ideas: wider roads, fly-overs, tunnels, and all the rest of it. He would never accept my simple-minded view that it was an elementary matter of mathematics: cars kill and maim, therefore the more the cars the more the deaths and

192

maimings. Therefore the solution is to ask everyone who wishes to own a car to show cause why he should possess a lethal weapon. So long as men have legs for covering short distances and public transport for longer journeys, such cause would be difficult to produce. Bob dismisses this as reactionary sentimentality, and adds brutally: " You're doing well out of the death-roll, anyway." Which is true enough.

But that night he had other things on his mind. I happened to be at the gate when his car came cautiously bumping over what passed with us for a road. He looked more hot and cross than his long journey accounted for, and his first words, as he stepped out and banged the door, were: " A bloody nice place to drag me to, I must say."

I pointed out that I hadn't dragged him anywhere, but he passed over this and asked: " Where do I leave the car?"

" Where it is," I told him happily. " Unless you care to come along with me to see a chap named Carbis. He's got a shed you could back it into. It's the best part of a mile down the road."

He wouldn't do that. " The point about a car is that it takes you from door to door," he dogmatised.

Between the road and my garden wall was a strip of rough grass. " That'll have to do," he said, got behind the wheel and backed her in.

I hoped he would take some notice of Trencrom. Not that Trencrom would much care whether he did or not ; but I was disappointed when he brushed an eye over it as casually as though it were a municipal rubbish dump. I pushed open the garden gate, led him to the back of the house, and invited him to sit down upon the seat that dominated the immense view of fields and hills. The evening shadows were beautiful—long, and full of the exciting colours that shadows hold within their grey, and the cumulus clouds were still, like anchored galleons.

He didn't sit down. He said: " Let's go in and have a drink."

We went up the narrow stairs to my large study. It had been a hot day, and the room was gratefully cool. He sat down at once in a comfortable chair and thrust his long legs out in front of him. He looked exhausted, and I had a feeling that the exhaustion was caused by more than his journey across so many shires.

I opened the cabinet where I kept drinks, and he said: " Whisky, if you've got it."

" Help yourself," I said, and put the bottle and a syphon of soda on the table by his chair. I was still hoping for some comment on this hermitage which the Irish saints who sailed over here in their coracles might have thought a little overdone, but there wasn't a word. He poured in a lot of whisky, splashed a little soda on to it, and took a deep drink. Then he sat hold-

ing the glass in his hand, looking straight in front of him. I
asked: "What's the matter, Bob?"

"Nothing," he said.

I poured myself a drink, more water than whisky, and said
"Good health!"

He didn't answer. I carried my drink to the window and
stood looking up at the hill. I said: "There'll be a full moon
about eleven o'clock. The view'll be marvellous from the top.
Would you like to climb up, Bob?"

He finished his whisky, and said in a more human voice:
"George, don't try to amuse me. Leave me alone. What I
should like is to go and eat somewhere and then get to bed
early. That do you?"

We ate at a place I sometimes used in Hayle, and when we
were back at the cottage I showed him the bedroom. "I hate to
turn you out," he said.

"You needn't worry about that. I do a lot of vagabonding."

My spare bed was a wooden frame on to which I had tacked
a criss cross of wide webbing. I took it into the garden, got into
my sleeping-bag and was soon asleep. I was worried about Bob,
and perhaps that is why my sleep was invaded by a dream in
which he was making deep dips into the money-bags of Meagher
Motors. Fred Byles of all people caught him at it and denounced him, as some clerk had denounced Fred.

10

I awoke to a world of birdsong and misty light. The moment
was gratefully cool, but this mist would soon clear and we
should have another scorching day. I looked through the
window of the downstairs bedroom and saw that Bob had disappeared. I went into the kitchen and got breakfast ready, and
while I was doing that he came in. He didn't look so strained
as he had done last night, but he looked sad. "I've been having
a walk," he explained briefly.

We ate, and I tried chaffing him. "How is the Great West
Road standing up to your absence, Bob? I've always thought
of Meagher Motors as something that would collapse without
you."

He said dogmatically: "There's something wrong with a
business that has an indispensable boss. The first thing a boss
should do is find the men who can make him dispensable. Then
he should occasionally have one in on the carpet and blow him
to bits. And he should keep the whole lot guessing who is top
favourite."

I apologised for introducing the topic. "I expect you've come away to forget all that."

"No. It's not that. And it's not something I can deal with by forgetting. I've got to settle it, one way or the other."

He spoke in a voice that didn't invite prying. "I'd be glad if you'd take me about a bit," he said. "I haven't been in Cornwall before."

"I think you'd enjoy a run down to Penruan on the south coast. It's the place where I spent a few years before my father died and I went back to Manchester to study my trade under Mr. Merriman."

"A pity Mr. Merriman hadn't the sense to know when to get out of the trade," he said.

"I suppose he saw himself as the captain nobly going down with the sinking ship."

"A captain who lives melodramas is a fool," Bob assured me firmly. "He should have the intelligence to keep an eye open for accessible rafts. Well, I'll go and give the car a look over."

That would keep him happy, I hoped. I made his bed, washed up the breakfast things, and we set out in time to eat luncheon in Helston. I told him about Penruan as we ate. "It belongs to Mrs. Bascombe, the actress. I expect you remember her daughter Janet? You danced with her at the Savoy one night."

He had forgotten that, and he had never heard of Sylvia Bascombe.

I asked him how Wendy was, and he said briefly: "As usual."

And how were Jocelyn and Viola? Jocelyn would be going to a prep. school in a few months' time, and Viola was learning to ride a pony. I gave it up. I found myself against something hard and impenetrable.

We reached Penruan at about three o'clock. A few miles before getting there, I saw Harry Redmayne out upon the moor, with his easel set up and a small rugged tor in the distance the obvious motif of his painting. And so it was no surprise, when we reached the lodge, to find that it was Elsa, bare-headed, floating in a cloud of silks, who opened the creaking gate which sounded as though its hinges hadn't been oiled since that far-off night when Tiddy dumped me there and drove off into the darkness.

She greeted me respectfully, and I introduced Bob and asked if I might show him over the house. "We're not supposed to show *any*body over the house, Mr. Ledra. Actually, our job is to see that nobody *does* go there. But, of course, you're rather special."

I grinned at that, and she blushed. "I mean," she hastened to add, "Mr. Gomm has told us how you lived here and what a friend you still are of Mrs. Bascombe. So I suppose it will be all right."

She went back into the lodge to bring the immense iron key of the front door.

"Your friend Mrs. Bascombe has a pretty taste in door-keepers," Bob said.

"That chap we saw painting on the moor is her husband," I explained.

"All right. I'll remember."

But he didn't seem displeased when she said that she thought she ought to go with us. "I'm glad though that showing people round isn't really my job. It would interfere with my writing."

"Oh, you're a writer, too?" I asked.

"Well, not in your sense," she said modestly, "not creative. I'm trying to do a book on Medieval drama. A thesis for a doctorate."

She looked so young and simple. "Oh, dear," I said. "I could never bring myself to call you Doctor Redmayne."

"Well, I don't expect you'll have the chance. I shall probably fail. My name's Elsa."

"Much better than Doctor," Bob approved.

Elsa took her time. She showed us parts of the house I had never seen. Though I had known Penruan for so long, it was the lodge, not the house, that I had lived in. The big entrance hall and the dining-room: I hadn't seen much more than that. And Sylvia's bedroom, I remembered, with both a blush and a tremor of desire. Most of the rooms Elsa was showing us hadn't been furnished or even decorated. I became bored and said I'd go and see how the masons were getting on. I left them and had descended the staircase when, feeling in my pocket for my pipe, I found it was not there. I remembered, then, that I had left it on the window-sill in one of the unfurnished rooms. I went back for it, and was passing the room in which I had left Bob and Elsa when I heard her say sharply: "No!" and Bob's voice answered: "But, Elsa . . ."

That was all. I was out of the house like a shot. It was about a quarter of an hour later that I came upon them again. They were looking up at the main entrance, with the words carved in the stone: *Rien sinon pour Dieu.* "That's the motto of the Polzeaths, the people who built the place," Elsa was explaining like a travel agency guide; and Bob said: "Well, thanks, Mrs. Redmayne. It's been most interesting."

I asked him if he'd care to see the new bit of work in progress. "No," he said sharply. "Let's get back."

That night, when we had eaten, I did at last persuade him to climb Trencrom. I liked to be up there at some time or other every day. I had even slept on the summit. The place fascinated me as deeply as the Mont Sainte Victoire fascinated Cezanne. We sat with our backs against a stone still warm from the day's sunshine and smoked our pipes. I said: "Bob, how long have you known Elsa?"

I imagine that he had been anxious ever since his arrival to find the relief of getting the thing off his chest. But he was not a man who found it easy to unveil himself. However, now that I had drawn the cork the stream flowed. He didn't even ask how I knew that he and Elsa had met before.

The step-mother whom Wendy had never met, Mr. Merriman's second wife, had died, and on top of that Mr. Merriman found himself a victim of the cotton slump. Bereaved and virtually penniless, he had written to Wendy. She showed the letter to Bob, who said curtly: "Answer if you like, but don't drag me into anything. I don't want to meet him. He made my father's life pretty miserable and he thought I was worth as much consideration as a dish-cloth. If you've forgotten that he tried to prevent our marriage, I haven't."

Wendy answered: "And how do you think our marriage has turned out?"

Bob was flabbergasted. He could not conceive that marriage with him could be anything but perfect. But as the story poured forth I began to see Wendy's point of view. He didn't take her to dance at the Savoy any more. For one thing, the birth of Viola had been difficult, and Wendy was physically not what she had been. She tired quickly. For another thing, the Savoy was not so handy. They had left their neat suburban villa and were farther out in the country where Bob had bought a Queen Anne house to befit his growing status. There were some acres of land and a gardener and a gardener's assistant, and that quiet deft factotum Brookes, whom I remembered meeting, was promoted to butler, with his wife as housekeeper. And there were a parlour-maid and a cook.

I began to see the new set-up, the business magnate-cum-country gentleman, and Viola learning to ride a pony, and Wendy, in whose praise boring ream upon ream used to reach me from Coventry, having nothing to do, and no resource that would help her to make her own life, and becoming dull, afflicted with the greyness of the un-useful, the unwanted. I have no doubt she was provided with masses of clothes and jewels. These, too, belonged to status.

Without knowing what had brought it about, seeing before his eyes only the fact, obvious to himself, that he had given Wendy everything a woman could desire, Bob became conscious that his own satisfactions had diminished. His new home, he told himself, was in any case too far out on those many occasions when the affairs of Meagher Motors were arduous or he had to dress for his growing number of dinners in town. So he took a service flat in Mayfair, and that, of course, would relieve the tension on Wendy no end.

It was at one of these business dinners that Bob met Elsa. She was Elsa Comby then. Her father was a City merchant—"Not much of a one," Bob said—and Elsa was on vacation from Newnham. It was a dinner to which womenfolk were invited, and Mr. Comby, a widower, had brought Elsa along. Bob found her placed next to him at dinner, and that was the beginning of it. After dinner they danced. She was a naïve creature and Bob was so courteous, and apparently so far removed in age from anything but parental status, that she confided her simple story. She was already engaged to Redmayne and didn't dare to tell her father who had a wealthy suitor in view. In short, she was in the position that Wendy had been in at Manchester, and she proposed to solve it in the way that Wendy had done, with a runaway marriage.

Bob didn't tell me what means he found to pursue her, but he did pursue her hard and fast until a letter from the Penruan lodge told him that she was living there, married to Redmayne.

But that happened some time farther on, and it was while the affair was bubbling in Bob's blood that Wendy showed him the letter from Mr. Merriman.

"How do you think our marriage has turned out?"

I can imagine his alert mind instantly throwing up defences, even while guilt was stirring beneath the conscious level of his thought. Between them they bedevilled him: the conviction that Wendy had nothing to complain about and the subtler knowledge that she had everything—or at any rate would have if he could make Elsa see his point of view. He shifted the burden of these complex emotions on to the ground of a challenge.

"Even assuming," he said, "which is something I don't grant, that there's anything wrong with our marriage, would your father's presence here make things any better?"

It was strange, sitting there upon that remote rock in the cold unpassioned moonlight, to be transported to the passionate scene in that house I had never visited. It was passionate only beneath the surface. It seems that tempers were guarded, and Bob did not know whether Wendy's question sprang from some guess at what his town flat might imply or whether the letter from Mr. Merriman had flicked a vague dissatisfaction with her empty life to the surface of her consciousness.

Like a mechanic faced with some engine fault he asked: "What can I do to make you feel more satisfied with things?"

An impossible question. What woman would abandon her right to be understood by saying "You must do this and that and the other thing," as though instructing a child in elementary manners?

Wendy fell back on to the question of her father's letter.

"You realise, don't you," she said, "that neither of us has seen him since we married?"

"That is how we both wanted it to be."

"It's not how I want it to be now. I'm not suggesting that we should ask him to come here and live with us. Far from it. Even though," she added sadly, "that might be a change from having no company all day but Viola and her pony. But I see nothing against asking him here on a visit."

Bob switched his ground. "What's wrong with Viola and her pony? Naturally a child wants an interest. The pony is Viola's. You should make an effort to enter into other people's lives."

"I'm not so good as you are," she said, "at entering into other people's lives."

That, once more, made him wonder what she knew. He felt on dangerous ground and got up. "Well," he said, "have it your own way. Ask him here for a visit if you like. I must be off."

When he was at the wheel of his car, ready to start for town, Wendy came out and said: "I shall not ask him. If he is to be asked, you must do the asking."

Viola rode up on her pony, and Bob drove very slowly as far as the entrance gates so that she might trot alongside. Even this agreeable piece of customary ritual did not soothe him, and, once outside the gates, he opened the throttle wide.

Mr. Merriman did not come to stay. Bob did not see Elsa again. They had a lunch engagement for that day, and she did not keep it. He heard nothing from her till a letter reached him from Penruan Lodge, clearly intended to give him his quietus. But, with the incurable optimism of his kind, Bob said to me, as we went down towards my cottage: "I thought the very fact of her giving me her address might mean something."

"I imagine, Bob, that it means she's an exceptionally unsophisticated girl who thinks, quite rightly, that her marriage should protect her from wolves. Women do have these odd notions, you know."

"What do you recommend me to do?"

"*Me* recommend something to *you*? Come, Bob, you haven't sunk so low as that. But since you ask, I should say, 'Go back to Wendy. Sell more and more motor cars, and live happily ever after.'"

That night, in the garden, I got down again in my sleeping-bag. When I awoke Bob was gone.

CHAPTER TEN

1

Janet took the use of my flat more coolly than I liked. Indeed, she took me altogether coolly. Not more than half a dozen letters from her reached me during that summer, and these became slimmer and slimmer, mere notes saying I am very well, thank you. How are you? At the beginning of October I wrote to let her know that I should have to turn her out in a week's time; and when I reached London late in the afternoon of a beautiful autumn day she had vanished. The key of the flat was tied by a boot-lace to the door-knob, and on the sitting-room mantelpiece was a note from her, thanking me for the use of the place and adding that she had now found a comfortable flat near the office and would be moving in there when she got back from her holiday. "Sorry I'm not at home to welcome you. As the youngest member of the staff, I've had to wait till the others finished their holidays. It was only yesterday that Hubert told me to clear out for a fortnight. I'm leaving this morning for a place in the Highlands. All thanks. Janet."

It seemed a bit cool to me; but I forgot my annoyance the next day when, over lunch, Nigel Wendron handed me the page proofs of my book. I took them back to the flat and spent an hour lolling on a couch, looking at the title page and flicking over the pages. Especially looking at the title page: *Traveller's Joy* by George Ledra. There is something very odd about that moment, something both satisfying and disturbing, when, for the first time, one's private name becomes public property. What would happen? Would I be keel-hauled by the critics or publicly crowned like a bard at an eisteddfod? As it turned out, nothing much happened one way or the other. It took me a long time to build up such gossamer reputation as I have.

By tea-time I had finished with my narcissism and was starting the serious business of reading the proofs when the telephone rang. It was Hubert Dodge. Janet had told him, he said, that I was back. How was I? I said that I was well. And how was he? And how was Janet?

"Oh, she's gone up to my father's place in Sutherland. He's got a cottage up there and rents a bit of shooting. He goes up every year."

"I can't imagine Janet clumping in brogues across the heather and bringing down two capercailzie with a left-right."

200

"Neither can I. I think she loathes that sort of thing as much as I do."

"Well, what's she doing? Shooting poisoned arrows at herds of lady novelists?"

"She is just keeping my mother company. Mother loves the Highlands and loathes the shooting. She went off this morning. Quite suddenly last night she asked Janet to go with her." He paused a moment, then added: "Janet happened to be dining with us. She looks in most nights. Mother's taken quite a fancy to her. By the way, your contract with *Now* ends in December. Do you want to renew it?"

"Do you want me to?"

"Yes. I'm very pleased with your stuff, and so is Mother."

"What about Father?"

Hubert was no man for jokes. "Oh, he leaves all that to me," he said solemnly. "But one thing I can tell you, he's pleased with us on the whole. We're slowly gaining ground. If we go on as we are, there's a chance that we'll break even next year."

"Well, if you think I'm adding a mite to that good work, renew the contract for a year."

"I'll do that. Good-bye."

I was pleased that the contract was renewed, but not so pleased to find that Janet was on such close terms with Hubert's family.

2

Hubert wrote to me a few days later, confirming the renewal of the contract and adding: "I have just heard from Mother. She has an idea of giving a party to the *Now* people when she gets back to town. She suggests November 5th. Would you care to come, and bring someone along?—not necessarily connected with the paper."

Thus, almost casually, was born the great series of *Now* parties. Those who didn't like the paper thought there was something significant about that anarchic day November 5th.

I decided to ask Sylvia if she would care to come with me. It was almost a year since I had seen her, and I hadn't much reason for supposing that she would want to see me again. However, London was lonely. I never suffered from a feeling of loneliness in my isolated cottage under Trencrom. Aloneness, yes; but that is another matter. It is only amid thousands that I can feel lonely. I was ignorant about music and didn't go to concerts. I read for hours and hours, and spent hours and hours in the National Gallery and the Tate and at the Wallace Collection, and in looking at the art dealers' windows in the
201

Bond Street region. It was in Bond Street that I saw a superb piece of Orrefors glass. Embodied in the fabric of the vase was a sailor sinking through an upflowing fountain of oceanic bubbles, and down below a mermaid with open arms was waiting to receive him. I bought it, wincing at the price, and hoping that Sylvia would accept it. I remembered that her embraces could be warmer than any that a mermaid would find it possible to bestow in the circumstances depicted.

I was walking home with this treasure when, in Orchard Street, I saw a figure that looked familiar. I was on the side where Selfridge's shop stands, and the man was window-gazing on the other side. I saw only his back, but I was certain it was Mr. Merriman. I had no wish to meet him. Indeed, I had a strong aversion, a wish *not* to meet him. I was on the point of escaping into Selfridge's when he swung round and looked across the road. I half-heartedly raised my hand in a gesture of recognition, and he returned this with a more emphatic salute and began to cross towards me. There was nothing to do but to wait for him.

I think I have told you that he always wore spats. He was wearing them now, and somehow they contributed to the horror of his appearance. To most people, I suppose, he would not have looked horrible: he would have looked merely shabby and moth-eaten. But, to me, this clinging to a fragment of his old respectability had a touch of horror. His clothes had always been old-fashioned because he liked it that way. Now they were not merely old-fashioned: they were disreputable, and clearly that was because he had nothing else to wear. His old frock-coat had stains on the satin of the lapels; his silk hat was a caricature; the spats were dirty. His eyes, which had always been protuberant, were now blood-shot, too; and as my body put out a hand to take a hand of his, my spirit recoiled and shivered. He was, as they say, all present and correct; but each bit of him was soiled and debased, adding up, somehow, not to a caricature but to, at last, a true portrait of the man as I had, even when a boy, imagined him to be.

He raised his silk hat an inch or two and said: " Good morning, Mr. Ledra."

"Good morning, Mr. Merriman. How nice to see you. I didn't know you were in London."

" Oh, yes," he said. " I work here now. I like to come West for my morning constitutional, but I mustn't dally. We open at two."

"Who are we?"

" My firm, I mean. I've gone into the cinematograph business."

Even to an innocent like me, there was something fishy about this answer. I looked at my watch. Just on noon. Frank curiosity took hold of me, and I said: "You've time, I hope, to come and take a bite with me?"

"I shall be delighted to do that, Mr. Ledra."

We walked on into Baker Street and I took him to a restaurant I sometimes used there. He ate hungrily, but had little to say, and I couldn't think of the right questions to put to him. At one o'clock he said: "Well, duty calls. I've cut it rather fine."

I apologised for having delayed him and said: "Let me call you a taxi."

"That would be uncommonly civil of you, Mr. Ledra," he said. "I shall need some time to change into my business suit."

I gave the taximan ten shillings and took care not to overhear the address Mr. Merriman whispered. I went back to the flat thinking: "The poor devil's pretty well starving," and all day long I couldn't read or write for thinking of him.

3

Mr. Merriman's business suit was a commissionaire's uniform. I discovered this the next day. As I was washing up my breakfast crockery Bob Meagher came on to the telephone. "Good morning, George."

"Good morning, Bob. Where are you telephoning from so bright and early?"

"Early! I'm telephoning from my office. I've been here an hour." There was reproach in his voice.

I waited for him to develop whatever was in his mind, and presently he said: "Could you take lunch with me to-day—here, in the office. Sorry I can't come into town. Too busy."

I said that I'd be glad to come. "Good. A chauffeur'll pick you up at 12.30."

And at 12.30 precisely, answering the ring on my bell, I confronted the chauffeur, a grave middle-aged man dressed in a navy blue uniform that looked as though it had been cut in Savile Row. We went down, and at the kerb was a superb car, very different from the two-seater in which Bob had driven himself to Trencrom. The inside shone with polished wood and leather and silver. A thick fur rug was folded on the seat. The chauffeur opened the door deferentially, but I said: "D'you mind if I sit up forward with you?"

He graciously permitted this, but I felt like a passenger in a ship who had refused to occupy a specially prepared first-class cabin and insisted on joining the captain upon the bridge. It was not the right thing to do, but it gave me an opportunity to question him. I discovered that he was "Mr. Meagher's personal chauffeur." This car was reserved for Mr. Meagher. There were other cars for the use of heads of departments, but not of this quality. "Though we hope, sir, to be turning out something equally impressive before long, and then of course we shall use our own product." Yes: Mr. Meagher did as a rule drive himself, " but you will understand, sir, that there are occasions when that would hardly be *comme il faut.*"

I didn't know whether or not to commit the sacrilege of tipping the captain, but I chanced it, unobtrusively slipping a ten-shilling note into a receptacle on the dashboard. Thus I would not be *seen* to be tipping him, and a grave inclination of the head showed that he appreciated this social delicacy.

The car stopped with an equal delicacy: not a ghost of a jolt or jerk. It was as though it had been halted by a kiss upon a foam-rubber cushion.

A uniformed man was there to open the door; and the captain said: " A guest for the Managing Director," touched his cap, and purred away to whatever celestial harbour housed his caravel.

The doorman conducted me across an echoing tessellated pavement and handed me over to another man, not uniformed, repeating the sesame: " A guest for the Managing Director." This being preceded me to a lift containing a seat of polished red leather which suggested that the journey would be infinite and that repose would be needed on the way. My conductor murmured: " The Managing Director's floor," and off we went, again without a jolt, as though riding on a cumulus cloud upborne by favourable currents. I was not aware of stopping, but the bronze doors noiselessly unfolded, and my conductor walked before me down a long corridor of polished wood, deeply carpeted.

I had been here before, but then work was in progress and things were rather rough and ready. Now a deep silence, an emanation of holy awe, brooded upon this luxurious tunnel. I noted the names upon the glass panels of doors as we walked along, and one of them was " Mr. G. H. B. Meagher." On the door which closed the vista there was no name, only a proud designation: The Managing Director.

Here at last, like a shriven soul closing its skyward journey, I breathed a sigh of relief. I couldn't believe that at the end of all this I was to meet only Bob Meagher. But I was not yet to meet anyone. To the left there was a door labelled: Secretary. It was upon this that my conductor tapped, and murmured, when the door was opened: " A guest for the Managing Director."

The girl asked: " Are you Mr. Ledra?"

I said that I was, but I was troubled lest I be asked to produce an identity card to prove it. However, the girl accepted me at my face value, whatever that may have been, and said: "Come in, sir, please." I entered the room and found two other girls tapping away at silent typewriters. My girl explained: "The secretary is with the Managing Director. She will not be long."

She indeed came in at that moment, a motherly-looking old soul, wearing spectacles, rather untidy. My girl explained who I was, but further parley was cut short by Bob's voice bellowing: "If that's you out there, George, come on in."

I went in and collapsed upon a chair. Bob looked at an electric clock upon the wall. "Good," he said. "One o'clock precisely."

A beautiful Chippendale table to seat a dozen people, an object that Jose Gomm would have loved and wished to acquire for Penruan, stood at one side of the room, surrounded by its appropriate chairs. A battery of bell-pushes, each a different colour, edged Bob's desk. He pressed one, and, as though a signal had been awaited, the main door of the room—not the one leading to the secretary's office—opened silently to admit a rubber-wheeled trolley, pushed by a boy in black trousers and a white jacket. Behind him came a man in black trousers and a white jacket. While they were laying cutlery and crockery upon the table Bob opened a cabinet. "What will you drink, George?" he asked.

I looked upon several shelves of ambiguous bottles: recondite, abstruse, esoteric and mysterious; and with pathetic fatuity opted for gin and tonic. The table was laid, and the high priest's acolyte went into the passage and wheeled in a bucket containing the débris of an iceberg. Plunged neck-down within it was a bottle of champagne, its stern afloat like a foundered ship's.

Standing at the window, sipping my gin, I saw that the Lombardy poplars, which I had last seen young and hardly taller than cricket stumps, had shot up in mathematical row upon row, defining paths, edging the sportsground, and having an air of internment more severe than if they had been granite walls. Between them, hordes of workers were scurrying to various buildings, which I knew to be canteens, as industriously as creatures treading the mazes of a scientist's intelligence testing set-up.

Bob said: "Menus."

The white-coated man handed him four printed cards. He read them carefully, initialled each, and handed them back. "All right," he said. "We'll look after ourselves." And when the priest and acolyte were gone he said to me: "I like to know what the people are eating. It's a small detail that shouldn't be neglected." He swallowed the remains of a complicated cocktail that he had mixed for himself. "Well, sit down, George."

I felt debased by the thought that I had of late had the temerity to entertain this Being in my hovel at Trencrom. But I fought against this feeling, for I knew pretty well what Bob was up to. He was giving me the whole works—the sort of show that would be put on to impress some top-notch visitor from the Continent—in order to assert himself in my eyes. He had always suspected a certain levity in my view of his doings, and here he was, saying: " Well, it's not all that long since we tramped the moors round Manchester and talked of these things, and here you are. This is what has come of it." And I am sure it was with the same object that, half-way through the meal, he rang a bell and said to the messenger who answered it: " Give Mr. Veering my apologies, but say I'd like to see him here at once. You'll find him in the managers' canteen." And when Mr. Veering, a man twice his age, came in, he said: " Oh, Veering, I'm terribly sorry to drag you away from your grub, but I forgot to ask you whether that tangle with United Alloys is cleared up."

When Mr. Veering had assured him that the tangle was cleared up and had returned to his grub, Bob had the air of saying: " You see. Veering is one of the top men here, but if I want him he has to come, no matter what he's doing."

Before this, he had lifted the cover of a silver tureen and released a fragrance. " Nice stuff, this," he said, holding the shining cover admiringly. " You remember the Eagle that was sold up a few months ago?"

The Eagle was a City chophouse of great antiquity.

" I had a lot of their plate bought in."

The soup was delicious, and so was the chicken which lay in its dish ready carved, and so were the vegetables and the Charlotte Russe and the cheese. I should have preferred to drink something other than champagne, never a wine that enchanted me, but Bob enjoyed displaying expertise in the removal of the cork. The coffee was excellent. He produced a box of Corona cigars, and we relaxed in leather chairs.

" Drambuie?" he asked. I surrendered.

It was two o'clock, as a hooter announced ; and sitting there watching the blue-grey lazy smoke and savouring the Drambuie, I gave my bemused mind over to cynical cogitation upon the hurry in which Bob's life was supposedly lived. It made me think of a contrast: Mr. Merriman taking me out in Manchester to an exiguous war-time lunch, fidgeting through it, and announcing far sooner than he needed to do: " Well, I must be back at the office."

I said: " I ran into Mr. Merriman the other day."

" Ah! Now Merriman is just what I wanted to talk about."

Wendy, I gathered, the girl Mr. Merriman had named under the inspiration of the Elf of Kirriemuir, had had her way. She had invited her father to luncheon. The handy Mr. Brookes, that member of Bob's old tank-crew who was now turned butler, was versatile enough to drive a car at need; and, as Wendy had never driven anything more demanding than the treadle of a sewing-machine, which she did quite a lot in the Coventry days, it was Brookes who drove her car when she needed it. Dormers, Bob's Queen Anne house in Surrey, was a good three miles from Dorking railway station, Mr. Merriman's destination; and when Wendy arrived there the passengers were already disembarked from the train. So that, instead of receiving her father's salutation in the comparative privacy of the station—private, at all events, from the eyes of Brookes—it was as she stepped from the car that he came towards her, glorious in the light blue with scarlet trimmings and with, upon his cap and lapels, the emblazoned information, *Majestic*.

Even Wendy, I imagine, guilt-stricken though she was at the thought that she had been neglecting a parent in need, must have felt that she would prefer a frayed and tattered seediness to the opulent, the impeccable, splendour that threw light-blue arms around her and pulled her head down upon one of the Majestic shoulders. At last Mr. Merriman released her with the simple words, that could have been lifted from a George R. Sims melodrama: " My daughter! I am come to this!"

" In front of Brookes!" Bob said.

" And what did Brookes do? Hand in his resignation?"

" He naturally did what he is paid to do. He opened the door and they got in."

Savouring in my mind this remarkable scene outside Dorking station, I was aware both of its comedy and its pathos. The comedy moved me most, not the less because I had a new sense of Mr. Merriman: I saw him as an artful dodger who realised the financial advantage that might lie in the threat of creating impossible situations.

" It was last Saturday," Bob said. " Viola was not at school. They met her as they were coming up the drive."

Viola, as usual, was as inseparably attached to a horse as a hump is to a camel. She rode alongside the car, and sat proudly aloft as her mother and the grandfather she had never met got out on to the gravel. She does not seem to have liked what she saw. " She had him weighed up," Bob said proudly. " She said: ' Mother, I promised Clarice that I *might* ride over and take lunch with her. I think I will.' And off she went."

At luncheon Brookes reverted to his function as butler, and with his acquired impassive gravity of that dwindling race waited upon his mistress and her father at luncheon.

" I know damned little about what happened after that," Bob said. " I suppose they prowled round the house and gardens, but whatever they were up to, I know what that man came for;

simply to make me a laughing-stock with my staff and neighbours in the hope of putting a screw on me. If the old fool wanted to come at all, couldn't he have hired a decent suit? If he had done that, I could have overlooked the whole thing. As it is, I have forbidden Wendy ever to have him in the place again."

It was clear to me that the whole affair had planted in Bob a deep feeling of humiliation, and that this was, in part at any rate, the reason for my ostentatious entertainment that day. He was dishing it up, both to impress me and to salve his own hurt. What was worse even than this was that the affair should have come at the moment when his relations with Wendy were, in any case, bad enough. That phrase "I have forbidden Wendy . . ." had a chill ring in my ears. The verb to forbid, as I saw it, had no place in the vocabulary of marriage, and Wendy was a woman not without spirit. She had had the guts to defy her father where Bob was concerned, and she might easily decide to reverse the process.

However, I am not much given to offering advice. Especially in a case like this where it would be laughed at. I crushed the fag-end of my cigar into a Royal Copenhagen ash-tray, and heaved my surfeited bulk out of the chair. At that moment the door leading to the secretary's room opened and she said: " Sir Francis is here, sir."

" Very well," Bob said. We shook hands and I went out.

4

Sitting in my room that night, I looked at the Orrefors glass which I had taken from its wrappings and put on the mantelpiece beneath Fred Byles's portrait. Fred would not have liked to be in the sailor's unpromising situation, but the mermaid would have pleased him. She had a number of points of obvious attraction. I had bought her for Sylvia, but liked her so much that I was almost inclined to keep her for myself. She made me think of Sylvia, as I had seen her, on a far-off autumn morning, providing the mellow fruitfulness to match that season of mist: as I had seen her before her complete emergence declared that she was no mermaid but a woman who set my heart pounding. I thought, too, of Mr. Chown, wavering downwards through the ocean, not as this sailor was, his astonished face surmounted by a flat coquettish cap a-flutter with ribbons, but darkly bound in oak and weighted with lead. Mr. Chown, who had known old Fred, Sylvia's father, and was the brother of Margaret Napier.

So my musing went, and carried me to the moment when we returned from that sea-burial to the Absolution and Sylvia and I had set off for London and parted at Taunton. I had not seen her since, and that was all but twelve months ago. I had

208

written to her once, just before Bob Meagher had come down to Trencrom, and she had not answered.

It was eleven o'clock. I went to the telephone and rang up the flat in Shaftesbury Avenue. Sylvia had just come in from the theatre. "Not the George Ledra I once knew?" she asked when I had announced myself.

"The very same."

"I thought you were dead."

"I have been, more or less—dead to the world down in Cornwall."

"I shall be there myself to-morrow, and I want a good night's sleep."

I thought she would hang up on that, but the line seemed alive, and I said after a moment: "I was going to suggest a meeting. If you're leaving to-morrow, could it be to-night?"

"Is it something important?"

"It's always important to meet you."

She gave what is called a hollow laugh, and said: "Very well."

With this discouraging permission, I went into Baker Street and found a taxi.

She looked very pale. She had cleaned off the theatre make-up and hadn't put on any other. We shook hands without enthusiasm, and she said: "I've been in this play now for the best part of a year, and it looks like going on. I'm beginning to walk through my part like a zombie, so I've begged a bit of a holiday. I'm allowed to leave it to an understudy for a fortnight. I shall go down and see how Penruan is getting on."

She was wearing a housecoat that looked as though it had been made from the material of an old Chinese garment. The thick ivory silk was emblazoned with peacocks' feathers and little sneering apes. It crackled as she walked to a table where she had set out drinks and cocktail biscuits. I asked for a little whisky and a lot of soda water. She gave herself the same and sat on the couch at my side. "I owe you an apology," she said.

I drank to her good health and asked: "Whatever for?"

"For what I said to you at Taunton. You must forgive me. You can go about with Janet or anyone else you like. I don't see what right I have to question your doings. But I was in a dreadful state that day. The ghastly weather had terrified me, and the ghastly smelling motor-boat that made me feel sick, and dear Chowny being pushed over the side. . . ."

I took her hand and said: "Don't call it all back. And don't think you have to apologise to me for anything."

I had hastily packed the Orrefors vase and now stripped off the tissue-paper. "I've brought you a present. I hope you'll like it. It makes me think of the you I first saw."

I held up the wrist that was never separated from the bracelet that Fred Byles had bought in Paris for Margaret Napier. "I mean the morning when I found this on the beach. It had slipped from your wrist."

She looked at me in surprise and speculation for a moment, then saw the point. "You mean you saw me and Janet . . .?"

"Yes."

She laughed immoderately. "Well; you must have thought us a pair of brazen hussies."

"I thought you were the loveliest things I had ever seen."

The perplexed look returned to her face. "But it was Chowny who sent it back to me—long after it was lost."

I told her about the reliquary, and how Mr. Chown had come accidentally upon it. "Well, I was glad to have it back," she said. "It belonged to my mother. It was given to her by my father—whoever he may have been."

"Haven't you ever tried to find out?"

"No. I thought the secret might pop up some day, but I never worried much about it one way or another. You see, I was brought up as though I were the daughter of Mr. Coast, the M.P. my mother married. It was only after he and Mother were dead that Chowny told me I was illegitimate. He knew who my father was, but wouldn't tell me. He said that perhaps some day he would. Well, it can never happen now."

She took the vase into her hands and turned it this way and that. "It's beautiful," she said. "Thank you."

There was a small table near the couch, and she put the vase upon it and looked at it as she sat at my side. "Yes," she said again, "it's a lovely thing," and she temperately kissed her thanks upon my cheek.

I wondered if I loved her, ever could love her, ever could, in my selfishness, love anybody. She put an arm round my shoulder, and we sat there leaning lightly upon one another and I thought of the first night I met her. I was a boy of fifteen and she was twenty-five, and she had given me just such a casual kiss as, in thanks, she had given me now. It had set me aflame, and now it did nothing. I remembered that I had been to bed with her, and even that did nothing. And yet, with it all, I was happy to be there, silent in her company. I looked sideways at her face. It had a scrubbed defenceless look: such as I am, here I am. She was thirty-five and I was a man. Would she ever be anything more to me than the rosy Venus who walked out of the waves in the dawn of that day, and in my dawn? Not so much a woman as a symbol of Woman? She was no longer such a symbol.

Her face looked lonely, and there were crinkles about her eyes. For me, I felt lonely, too. The noise of the nocturnal traffic came up to the room: motor-horns blared, and there was an undertone of swishing tyres, of footsteps, voices. It was a forlorn moment. For the first time in my life I had a premonition of age. With our bodies touching, we were far apart. And yet the distance between us was aching with desire for something that would destroy it. I felt this, and sensed that she was feeling it, too.

As if knowing what was in my mind, she said: "We meet and part, meet and part. Nothing ever grows between us."

I said inadequately: "I'll write to you at Penruan. And you must write to me. You never answered the last letter I sent you."

"No. I was annoyed with you. You said there was nothing between you and Janet, and I didn't believe it. I agree that it was not my business to ask you anything about it, and I shall never ask such a question again. But seeing that I did ask, I didn't like that flat denial. And even though I shouldn't have asked, there *was* some reason why I should have done so."

I knew what she meant. She had shared her bed with me.

"I admit," I said, "that I had been seeing Janet whenever I could. We were going out to dance that night when news came of Mr. Chown's death."

"I knew that. And then there was that dreadful burial at sea. I intended to say nothing. But by the time we reached Taunton my mind was in shreds. I'm sorry."

She got up, the stiff silk crackling about her. "I'll write," she said.

We embraced then warmly and she kissed me on the mouth. "Don't deceive me," she said. "I think I can stand any sort of truth. But don't deceive me."

5

During the fortnight Sylvia spent at Penruan I received several letters from her and from Janet. I answered Sylvia's at length, Janet's briefly. It was a long time since Sylvia had seen Penruan, and she was delighted with the progress. "I met an old man in the garden—if you can call that neglected valley a garden. He must be all of seventy. He had no right to be there, but I can't be strict about the 'private property' that so many people hold to be sacred, and anyway the old man—Tom Collins —seemed so much a part of the place that he was no more an intruder than one of the trees. 'Knowed it in his youth,' he told me, and was severe about the condition it was in now. 'Bad enough then, but this be damnation turrible.' He left these parts when young to 'better himself' he said, and has knocked about by land and sea for more than half a century. 'Buried three wives I 'ave,' he told me, 'one in Rangoon, one in Rio and one in Fremantle. So I thought it was time I got back 'ome before

I landed in more trouble. No good to me they wasn't, not one of 'em, an' the last was damnation turrible. I gave the first of 'em a praaper old set up with a damn' great marble angel on top playin' an 'arp like mad, and the second one an 'eadstone, an' as for the last I gave 'er turf, an' grudged 'er the daisies that'll grow in it. Aye, damnation turrible she were.'

"So here he is, a neat little blue-eyed man, looking sailorly, with a double-breasted blue coat and a peaked cap, and he was smoking thick twist that he cut up in his palm. The smoke smelled damnation turrible. 'Reckon I got another twenty years to go,' he said, ' an' just enough to keep me in thick twist and a pint a day at the Absolution, which is where I drank my first pint of all. I was fifteen then an' courtin' a girl named Mitchell. That pint gave me such ideas that she landed me a smack in the kisser that sent me reelin'. An' that's why I left 'ome in the first place.' I had a feeling that that, roughly, is why he has left a good many places in his time.

"Well, as you see, George, we had quite a session, and only at the end of it did I tell him that Penruan and these gardens were mine, and I asked him if he'd like to have a go at making them less damnation turrible. The old thing was delighted, and said that he could find an odd jobber now and then to help. He's worth having if only as a genius of the place, and at any rate he can hardly make things worse. I've arranged with Jose Gomm to pay him and any odd jobbers he finds, and to give him a pint now and then. I hope this won't cause him to look upon the local girls as once he did upon Miss Mitchell. He seems *capable de tout*. Miss Mitchell, I gathered, is still living in one of those geranium-covered cottages near the Absolution, virgin as on the day she sloshed her man. 'And for me,' says this turrible old fellow, ' it were a great deliverance. I don't like wives as live too long.'

"So there we are. Indoors and out, things are moving, and I'm already feeling refreshed and ready to return to the horrid old play. My love. Sylvia."

When she was back, we settled down in a friendly routine. Every day, unless there were some reason against it, we took lunch together, she paying the bill one day, I the next. On Saturday nights I would call for her at the theatre and she would drive me down to her cottage beyond Amersham. It was a small but charming place, isolated, for to reach it one had to trundle along a little-used lane, and there it was in a field at the end, not more than a labourer's cottage that had been touched up a bit. On the ground floor there was only a kitchen and a large raftered room that served all purposes. We ate in it, and in the evenings sat in it and talked by candleshine in front of the fire. There was electric light, but we preferred the candles after a day spent mostly in walking about the countryside.

Upstairs, there were two pokey bedrooms and a bathroom. We didn't share a bedroom. All through that winter of 1926-27 we were virtuous friends. In the morning I would hear a tap on my door and Sylvia's voice saying: " Finished with bathroom," and I would take my turn. Then I would go down and help her to get breakfast ready. Often, in the evenings, we would read to one another, usually some old standard novel, and at midnight we would have a last drink, kiss, and say good-night. On Monday morning, the woman who " did for " Sylvia, and who never appeared on Sunday, would turn up with an appraising look on her face. We were both amused by her tactful acceptance of a situation that did not exist.

Sometimes, on Sunday evenings, we just sat by the fire, musing or desultorily talking. I told her about Bob Meagher and Wendy, my years in Manchester, my sad life under Mr. Merriman. On her side, she had not much to tell. She had been unhappy with Bascombe, but had little to say about it. On the whole, what struck me was her friendlessness. In the theatre she had only acquaintances. " It is true," she said, " now that Chowny is dead, that the only person I know really well is Janet. And I know little enough about *her* nowadays. And now, of course, there's you."

I was glad that now there was me. I had never known a woman well. I had missed being mothered. This unpassionate domesticity with Sylvia was something that, a month or two ago, I could not have imagined. It was immensely to my liking. It ended in March. We were walking the turf spread over Chiltern chalk in the pleasant sunshine of early spring when she said: " There's bad news, darling. Our wretched play is going to America."

We had half expected it. The play was the most popularly successful that she had ever appeared in. There had been whispers of American interest, and now here it was. " We run for another month, and then we're off. Not all of us. One or two parts will be taken by Americans. But I'm to go."

6

The company sailed from Southampton in late May, and I went down and saw Sylvia off. I hadn't been in Southampton before, and as I like wandering about, haphazard, in towns new to me I spent the night in a hotel and after breakfast went out to make the acquaintance of Southampton. At about noon I saw, to my surprise, walking the pavement in front of me, that tarnished version of Mr. Merriman whom I had taken to lunch in Baker Street. My instinct was to halt, to let him shamble away out of

213

sight, but there was a compunction, a twinge of pity; and, as well, Mr. Merriman had known Fred Byles in whom, since I had read Mr. Chown's memoir, my interest, always sharp, had quickened. So I followed the more than ever deplorable spats, the greening frock-coat, the silk hat that looked as though made of cat-skin stroked the wrong way. Something in a shop window caught my eye and for a moment I stopped to look, and in that moment Mr. Merriman disappeared. There were no side turnings in sight; the shops were not of a sort I could imagine him wanting to enter. But there was a pub. I dismissed the idea: Mr. Merriman was almost fanatically anti-smoke and anti-drink. Doubtfully I pushed open the pub's swing-door, and there, sitting on a tall stool at the mahogany bar, he was. I stood behind him and said: "What'll you have, Mr. Merriman?"

He swung round violently on the stool as though taken red-handed in crime, saw me, and said: "You! Well, blast my soul!"

Such words in his mouth were as startling as the thought of liquor gurgling down his gullet. They convinced me that something was wrong. I put an arm through his and drew him towards the door. "Let's go and find something to eat," I said. He came with the shamed reluctance of a child caught in naughtiness. He shambled along at my side, and presently said: "I work my way up to the top of the tree, and then the bloody tree collapses."

That, beyond all things, was a thing he would never compre-hend and accept. The Lancashire cotton trade, the idol of his monolithic devotion, had collapsed, as so much was then collapsing, and had let him down. That was the core of his tragedy: his betrayal by what he had believed to be good and everlasting. It's not so much associating with the devil, but backing the wrong god that must always end in tragedy.

All very well, I said to myself, to sit here virtuously thinking philosophic thoughts, explaining (as you believe) Mr. Merri-man's tragedy. What are you going to *do* about it? Do you pass by on the other side, like Bob Meagher? Is Mr. Merriman a man to you, or a victim of ineluctable forces, to be left to the devices of the economists who, no doubt, will include his case in the better world they promise us?

I was sitting up in bed. A chambermaid had laid upon my knees the tray with morning tea and biscuits; and if Mr. Merri-man had been standing there beyond the brass knobs at the foot of the bed he could not have been more disturbingly pre-sent in my consciousness. And what was giving my mind its itch was this thought: You sold out to him. You walked out of Byles and Ledra with all he had, and all his wife had. If you had stayed in, you would be more or less where he is.

Yesterday, after we had eaten, I took him to the station and saw him on to the London train. At the booking-office I swopped the return half of his third-class ticket for a first; and the very idiocy of this gesture—this pink pill for an afflicted elephant—was now among the thoughts that made me squirm. There was no reason why I should not have travelled back with him; but I couldn't face it. I had had enough of him at lunch.

He had let himself go, abandoned the façade behind which he had sheltered when last we met. He was a cinema commissionaire and made no bones about it. He had tried for all sorts of other jobs but there was always a snag: he was too old, or ex-servicemen were preferred, or this, or that. At first he talked big: he had been the managing director of a cotton firm, a man with a life-long commercial experience, but he soon learned that the less said about that the better. Successful men are not anxious to associate with failures, even though failure was inescapable. He had had one bit of luck: he had owned a house, and that was not involved in the firm's failure. A house had an inflated value at that time. Living on this nest-egg, now brought to the table, he wandered about Lancashire, answered advertisements, and was humiliated to find that what he considered his enormous economic value got him nowhere in the world into which, an anachronism, he had survived.

He spent a day in Bolton at a moment when his search had become automatic and he did not expect results. It was a winter day—one of those days when all the Ds are on parade: dull, depressing, dreary, dank and dark, enough to plunge anyone into the dumps and doldrums. Dereliction and disaster damped his thoughts, and in the small hotel where he spent the night—little more than a pub—he was shivery with the onset of influenza. He ate, then went into the writing-room to answer yet another advertisement, and there he met a friendly commercial traveller who said: "What you want, chum, is a bloody good brandy and lemon."

He tried it, and it did him good, so he went on trying it till brandy became too expensive for his dwindling purse. Now he was on beer, and he had developed, understandably, a taste for pub bars where friendly chat and badinage took the edge off his loneliness. Here, too, he acquired the diction that had startled me. If he was no longer one of the bosses, at least he could be one of the boys. He had no inner resources: he had to belong: and he soon acquired the language of his new tribe.

That, more or less, is where Mr. Merriman found himself at the time of our encounter in Southampton. His search had brought him at last to London, and all that London had to offer was a Whitechapel cinema. "Looked at one way," he said, "it was bloody good. It did give me a chance to save my best suit for when something more appropriate comes along."

So the spark was not extinguished. At least, he would not

admit that it was. He didn't mention his call on Wendy, and it was not a point I felt I could raise. But, to my surprise, he said he had seen Bob Meagher, whom he described briefly with a noun and an adjective that need not be recorded. It was soon after his startling appearance at Dormers, and I could imagine that Brookes the butler had told Bob about the drama of that occasion. Miss Viola, too, may well have left her father in no doubt concerning the reason for her sudden decision to run off and take lunch with her friend. "I had left my address with Wendy," Mr. Merriman said, "and I suppose she passed it on to that so-and-so, thinking he might do something for me."

What Bob did was to invite his father-in-law to call upon him at the office on the Great West Road. "I thought this was something at last, and I put on my best suit."

It was something indeed. No car was sent to fetch Mr. Merriman, and there was no invitation to lunch. Apart from that, Bob gave him the whole works, as he had given them to me.

"I went by bus, and when I saw the size of the place I was ruddy well staggered. 'This is it,' I thought. 'That young sod has seen his duty at last.' When I showed the letter he'd written to me I was received like royalty and passed from hand to hand: down corridors, up in lifts—you can't imagine it, Mr. Ledra."

Thus Mr. Merriman reached the secretary's office, and on the way he saw, as I think he was intended to see, the name of Bob's father painted on an important door. When the secretary opened the door of the Holy of Holies and announced: "Mr. Merriman to see you, sir," Bob's voice shouted: "I'll send for him when I'm ready," and said Mr. Merriman, "there I sat for three bloody quarters of an hour of my valuable time before a bell buzzed and I was shown in."

Inside five minutes he had been shown out again.

Bob was standing, looking out of a window, and he spoke with his back to his visitor. "Mr. Merriman, you may remember that you tried to kick my father out of Byles and Ledra. You may remember that you tried, quite successfully, to kick me and your daughter out of your life. Nevertheless, you seem to think that you have the right to call in fancy dress at my home whenever you feel like it. Well, now that you've seen that home, I thought you might like to see this, too. Between them, they should add up to quite an education. But don't let me see you in either of them again."

"Then," said Mr. Merriman, "he turned round but didn't look at me. He pressed a button on his desk and then went and looked out of the window again. I was shown out the way I had come in."

As I sat in bed in the Southampton hotel, sipping tea and

nibbling biscuits, a part of me was saying: "Well, you asked for it." And another part of me, a much larger and deeper part, was loathing Bob Meagher and thinking of his clever act as about the dirtiest trick I had ever heard of. And I thought of Mr. Merriman, at this moment waking up in his one-roomed Whitechapel lodging, the commissionaire's uniform hanging behind the door, ready to be put on, to serve through another day of ignominy. For the quest that had brought Mr. Merriman to Southampton had failed like all the others.

7

Mr. Merriman had left his address with me, and curiosity took me to Whitechapel. I couldn't get the man out of my mind. I was plagued by contradictory feelings. I wanted to do something for him, but I didn't want him about me. I felt as one might feel about an old abandoned dog who deserved a bit of comfort so long as this was not provided on one's own fireside mat.

I went in mid-afternoon when he would be on duty at the cinema. The whole of that part of London was new to me, and infinitely depressing. June was come, and it was a hot day in which the narrow streets simmered, their miasma unfanned by so much as a rustle of wind. A notice in a fish-and-chips shop window said: " Frying to-night "; and the very words filled my nostrils with the nausea of fat bubbling under its emanation of blue smoke. This shop, and a corner pub, and a shop of versatile scope, bearing in its window the words: "Do not ask for credit. To refuse might offend " seemed to make the social amenities of the region. It was haggard, hopeless, inhospitable, and the sky above it was blue and beautiful. This was the street in which Mr. Merriman lived. I passed through it quickly, trying to look as though my being there had a purpose ; and I thought of Mr. Merriman's little " villa " in the Manchester suburbs where, of a Sunday afternoon long ago, I would genteelly take a cup of tea with him and Wendy, looking through the muslin-curtained window at his chrysanthemums and dahlias. The good old days, when he was still climbing to the top of the tree.

In the doorway of the house where Mr. Merriman had his room a grey wrinkled woman was sitting on a wooden kitchen chair, darning a sock. I wished her good afternoon as I went by, and she looked at me, blear-eyed and expressionless, and said: " It is an' all. An afternoon like this is something to be thankful for."

The sunshine, turned on beneficently free, warming her thin bones—something to be thankful for.

217

I said, rather angrily, and annoyed that I had been trapped into conversation at all: "I don't see much to be thankful for round here."

The old eyes, grey like opaque pearls, turned up towards me, and she said: "Well, things is better with me than they were. Got a good lodger now. Things was bad before he come, but now I can just manage."

I moved on, pondering the oddities, the degrees, of human existence. Mr. Merriman's disaster was her salvation, and there she was, peering with half-blind eyes at her task of gratitude: darning his socks.

I wanted no more that afternoon, but more was to come. I turned the corner into another street and collided with Bob Meagher. We both recoiled sharply, each astonished to see the other there. What Mr. Merriman had told me about his Tantalus visit to Bob's office, and this glimpse of the circumstances in which he was now living, suddenly acted on me like a chemical combination that produces an explosion. My mind flared into anger. I roughly pushed Bob away, and crossed to the other side of the street. I walked swiftly, almost ran, and came to a point where this second street joined a main road, jangling with traffic. There I understood the meaning of seeing red. I felt what was like a blood-flash cross my brain, for, parked smugly out of the way of the traffic, just within the quiet of this by-street, was the shining motor car that had wafted me to my luncheon on the Great West Road. A hatred of myself, of Bob Meagher, of Mr. Merriman, fused in a tumult of chaotic feeling, and as Bob overtook me, laid a hand on my arm, and asked: "What's all this about?" I shook him clear, rushed into the road, and leapt on to a tramcar that was just moving off. I jumped down as we were passing a taxi-rank, hired a car, and went home.

8

About an hour later Bob Meagher rang me up. "I'm staying in town to-night," he said. "May I come and see you?"

"Please yourself; but if you come, make it after nine o'clock." I should have dined by then: I didn't feel like being his host. The day was still hot when he arrived, wearing a suit of corn-coloured tussore silk and a Panama hat. Without invitation, he sat down and threw one leg over the other. I noticed for the first time how small his feet were. The toe of one of his shoes, which I was sure had been made specially for him in Jermyn Street, was jigging and twitching. That's what called my attention to his feet, and I was always to watch for it when I wanted to know his mood. His face gave nothing away.

"Did you enjoy your gloat?" I asked.

"Yes. What a hell of a place to live in."

I said: "Hell's territories are fairly extensive and can look pleasant enough."

"Keep that sort of stuff for your books. What took you down there?"

"I wanted to see for myself where Mr. Merriman lived."

"Why?"

"What's this—the Old Bailey?"

He switched his ground. "Look, George, I didn't like it when you pushed me aside and bolted as if I were something poisonous. What's it all about? I haven't got so many friends as all that, nor, I imagine, have you."

"I wasn't feeling especially friendly this afternoon. I thought that sort of thing went out with Hieronymus Bosch."

"I don't know what you're talking about. Try to remember that I'm a garage hand."

"Bosch liked to paint pictures of damned souls writhing in unimaginable hells. Well, that's fair enough. But I don't like the smug grins on the faces of his lookers-on. They make me want to spew. And so did you this afternoon."

"You still haven't told me why you were there."

"And you still don't realise that you have no right to ask. Would you like some coffee?"

"No, thank you. But I'll smoke if I may."

"Do."

We lit our pipes and sat there at a deadlock. The toe of his shoe continued to twitch. It was as symptomatic as the tip of a cat's tail. I watched it, fascinated. It always pleased me to have discovered some new peculiarity in a person I thought I knew well.

"Well, Bob," I said at last, "if you have anything to say, let's start from this. I intend to tell you nothing about Mr. Merriman. Not that I know much about him, anyway, except that you humiliated him by tricking him into seeing your splendour, and then treated yourself to a pleasant afternoon gloating upon his squalor. Both these things disgust me. Now let's go on from there."

At that, he began to pour out his *apologia,* and, like most of such outpourings, it amounted to nothing but a self-defence, with no attempt to see any point of view but his own. Mr. Merriman had certainly tried to stop his marriage to Wendy. But that was a common enough thing to happen and it needn't involve life-long bitterness. Mr. Merriman had underestimated Bob's capacity—call it, if you like, genius in his own line. But what had there been to make him aware of it? I had not been aware of it myself. Mr. Merriman had been harsh with old Meagher, who was as good a man as himself; but professional

219

jealousy was not such an unusual thing as all that. Mr. Merriman, down and out, had tried to insert himself into the happy sphere of Bob's prosperity. Well, who wouldn't? He had done it in a stupid clownish way that might make Bob look ridiculous, but wasn't he well-founded enough to be able to brush that off like a cobweb?

My mind registered all these objections as he talked, but I said nothing. I knew that there was nothing to say because, primarily, the reason for Bob's disturbance of spirit had nothing to do with any of this. These were the blinkers he was putting on his own eyes to hide the stark fact that his association with Wendy was proving unsatisfactory, and that this had begun before Mr. Merriman swam back into the picture. Mr. Merriman was proving a godsend, because he was providing the excuse that would conceal the reason, and Bob, sucking at a cold gurgling pipe, was using him for all he was worth.

I waited till the spate eased before slipping in my test question. I had put a decanter on the table and we were both sipping our whisky when I said: "D'you remember those Redmayne people—the artist and his wife who live in the Penruan lodge?"

Bob was raising the glass to his lips, and the sudden stop, the holding of the glass suspended for a moment, provided the symptoms I had been looking for.

"Yes," he said, and carried the glass to his lips.

"I see," I said, "that Redmayne's having a London exhibition. It's opening next week at the Lafayette Gallery."

9

The Lafayette Gallery is now well known, but then it was little more than a small shop window in a Mayfair back street. Elsa Redmayne had written to me about her husband's exhibition—a simple-minded letter in which she assumed that a man who wrote weekly in *Now* would be in touch with all that was doing in every sort of artistic direction. She said that she and her husband had no money for advertising, and neither had the gallery, and she asked my advice about publicity. All I could do was tell her that, as the gallery would get its commission on sales, it was Lafayette's responsibility to have notices printed and sent to those newspapers which were accustomed to writing about art shows. I sent her a list of them, and she wrote in reply that she was too diffident to tell Mr. Quayne his business. Was there anything I could do?

I felt diffident, too: not about seeing the owner of Lafayette, but about having anything to do with Elsa Redmayne. It seemed to me an explosive point where Bob Meagher was concerned, and I wanted to keep clear of it. However, she was rather pathetically appealing, and in the course of the afternoon walk I looked in at the Lafayette Gallery. A young man with startling blue eyes and a rough-and-tumble of curling brown hair and a bushranger sort of checked shirt and flannel bags and list slippers said that he was Peter Quayne and that he was running the show.

I liked him. He was smoking a meerschaum pipe. The smoke ascended from the head of a most mammalian nude negress, big enough almost to be the figure-head of a small ship. He had one room over the shop for living quarters. He hadn't much in the way of stock, but what he had was charmingly displayed. There were a few very fine things of the English water-colour school. I bought a picture of Windsor by Paul Sandby, and that set me back a bit, and let me see that Mr. Quayne knew the value of his own goods. He knew his job in other directions, too. On a table was a small pile of printed invitations to the Redmayne show. " For the newspapers," he explained, " and for the connoisseurs."

" How do you get to know the connoisseurs?"

" I've got a pal in Kent's. He pinched some names from their list." Kent's was an important gallery.

I decided that Peter Quayne knew his way about and that it would not be long before the negress gave way to a Corona and the wild-west costume to what the invitations call " morning dress." I have lived to see it so. Lafayette of Brook Street now means something, and whenever I go in there Peter welcomes me as the first man to have bought a picture from him.

The printed cards gave me a chance to slip in a word about the Redmayne exhibition, though I said nothing about knowing the Redmaynes. Quayne seemed anxious to dissociate himself from the show. " It's not one I should have put on myself," he explained. " But Redmayne wanted to hire the gallery for a week, and I'm not so flush that I could refuse the offer. He brought a few of his things to show me. Too derivative. He's got nothing of his own. Still, that's only my opinion. He may stumble on something of his own some day."

He clenched his pipe in his teeth as he talked, and this caused the negress to send out red sparks that alighted within the open-necked shirt. " Damn the woman," he said, flapping at his chest with open palm. " She's always doing that. Well, I'm putting up the shutters. Like to join me in a cup of tea?"

In the room over the shop we sat on a couch that, he explained, was also his bed. A Chippendale table and chairs were the only other furniture. He put the kettle on a gas-ring and produced a tin of biscuits, and we exchanged reminiscences as young men will. His father was the curator of a municipal gallery in the provinces. "He tried to keep me out of this racket," Peter said, recharging his lethal Ethiopian. "A curator is sure of bread and butter, and the old man wanted me to be sure of mine. However, when I finished at our local university and still insisted on running what he calls a picture shop, he was very decent about it. He gave me a whole year to trot round Europe at his expense. So I do know what a picture ought to look like. Though," he added with a laugh that produced another volcanic eruption, "there seems a growing difference of opinion about that. Another thing I did while I was abroad," he said, "was attend any art sales that were going. That was pretty valuable experience, too."

It was a good day. We yarned till dinner time, and then I took him out to eat, and after that we went back to my flat and continued the yarn till midnight. "Send along anyone you can to this Redmayne show," he said on leaving. "He's got a nice little wife, and I shouldn't like to think that she was starving."

10

When Bob Meagher was gone after our rather brusque showdown, I wondered whether I should hear from him again. It would not have surprised me if he had cut me off as dramatically as he had cut off Mr. Merriman. It was unexpected, therefore, to receive, a few days later, an invitation to dine at Dormers and spend the night. "You'll be able to meet Jocelyn and Viola," Bob wrote, but this repelled rather than allured me. "Jocelyn has been in the school san. with mumps and is home to recuperate. Viola, of course, is always with us."

Bob himself drove me down on a Saturday night; I stayed throughout Sunday, and was driven back on Monday morning. Jocelyn had shown me his collection of butterflies and his stamp album, and I had occasional glimpses of a horse bearing Viola hither and thither. I admired Dormers, its gardens and ponds and the wide arm of woodland thrown about it in a protective half-circle. It was all very beautiful, a typical setting for serene English domestic life within what is called now, I think, the higher income brackets. And this, I am sure, is what Bob intended to show me. He was aware that I believed his life with Wendy to be at the point of disruption; aware, too, that my guess was right. But he was not yet ready to admit this. He was not the sort of man who can walk out of a woman's life, leave her and her children, and feel no pang of pain, no shame at abandoned responsibility. His mind must have been in chaos, knowing what he was about to do, yet clinging still to the pretence that he was not about to do it.

222

So I was there to witness the felicity of the Meagher household, to feel, Bob hoped, that no man would destroy so lovely a domestic setting unless the unbearable conduct of others pushed him to do it against all his own best intentions.

The moment I most vividly remember of that week-end is the Sunday afternoon. Viola had ridden away to take tea somewhere, and Jocelyn was busy with a dam which he was building in the hope of turning a thread of stream into a bathing pool. A telephone call had come for Bob during lunch, and he said: "I'm afraid I'll have to shut myself up for an hour. That call meant work. I'll have to get some figures ready to take with me to the office to-morrow."

After the meal he went to the room he called his den; and Wendy wandered into the garden. I sat in the drawing-room, glad to be alone for a moment, and then strolled out into the pleasant spring sunshine. Dormers was at its best. The beech trees were in young green feather, and on the lawns pools of daffodils, unregulated, haphazard here and there, charmed the sight. Beyond the lawns was a long range of greenhouses that I had not entered, and I walked towards them. I was about to enter the first, and almost retreated. Wendy was there, sitting on a white-painted iron chair, doing nothing, and, taken off guard, looking like death.

She saw me, and got up. "Come in, George," she said, and she put an arm through mine and we walked along an avenue of shelves bright with little pots of scillas and snowdrops, chionodoxa and miniature daffodils. It was a lovely greenhouse, and at the end of it there was a circular pond in the floor, in which, when their time came, lilies would bloom. A few sluggish carp moved through the water. We sat on a half-circular seat and looked down into the pool. The gulping of a carp made quite a sound, and from without came the babble of rooks, quarrelling about living-space in the ample trees.

Wendy had become far too stout, and she had never had much sense of dress, and I suspect that of late she had been letting herself go: this Wendy concerning whose graces and virtues Bob had kept me posted in his long letters from Coventry. She said: "I sha'n't mind leaving all this."

I contrived a look of astonishment. "But, Wendy, why should you? You've hardly settled in."

She brushed aside my pretended innocence, and said: "Father wrote to me about the way my husband called him to the office and then insulted him."

Not Bob. My husband. There were Arctic wastes in the word.

"And even that," she said, "is only incidental. If this business about Father hadn't blown up, it would have been all the same. He was looking for a handle, and Father has given him one. I know he behaved like a fool, coming out here dressed as he was, but he was always a stupid man."

I was glad that she had made this switch away from Bob, and kept to the new track. "Oh, I don't agree with that, Wendy. My father had great faith in him."

"Then your father was wrong about him," she said calmly. "He was always stupid. Old Mr. Meagher knew more about running Byles and Ledra than he could ever have learned. If he hadn't sacked Mr. Meagher, he might at least have hung on till better times. Still, he is my father, and my husband should have shown him some consideration."

Then she was back to her main point. "Still, as I say that's all a side-show. Who is it, George?"

I could have told her about Elsa Redmayne, but I didn't. I knew in my bones that Elsa Redmayne had no more to do with Bob's wish to leave Wendy than Mr. Merriman had. She, too, was a side-show. It was after he had set up his flat in London that Bob met Elsa. The main point, to me, was the setting up of the flat. It was a symbol of separation, of Bob's desire to see as little of Wendy as possible. When or why that desire overcame him I did not know. But there it was. For whatever reason, Wendy was beginning to grate on him. As I read him, he was, for all his hard factual success, a romantic. He had *panache,* and he loved *panache.* The one romantic gesture of Wendy's life had been the headlong flight to share poverty with Bob in the Midlands. That accounted for his torrential letters to me. But one grand gesture couldn't hold a man like Bob Meagher for life. She had lost her figure, she had lost enthusiasm and zest, she had become dowdy and dull. He would have loved to see her riding a horse with Viola, or driving one of his own speedy cars, or looking a queen when she went to Jocelyn's school at half-term.

Just as, when Bob had poured out to me his animus against Mr. Merriman, some corner of my mind answered all his points, so now, watching a tit flying to and from a nest that she was building in a corner of the greenhouse, I found myself answering Wendy's case against Bob. I knew it would be senseless to say: "There's a young married woman named Elsa Redmayne," because I knew that that rather silly little mouse was merely the first thing to attract Bob's attention when he began to hunt. It would need something different from that to take him and hold him. So I said to Wendy: "So far as I know, there's no one at all."

She made to get up from the chair, and was so clumsy in her movement that I put a hand under her elbow. When she was up, she leaned for a moment heavily against me. I remembered with a pang the night when I had run into her and Bob at the Savoy, and she had taken my dancing in hand.

I said hypocritically: " Be patient, my dear. I dare say you'll find that you've been worrying about nothing at all. Let's go and see how Jocelyn's getting on with his dam."

She made the only " crack " I ever heard from her—a sad one at that: " He *doesn't* get on with his dam. He's much happier on his own."

We walked out into the sunshine. Bob came across the lawn from the house. He said: " What about a walk?"

" I'm feeling a bit done up," Wendy answered. " I'll go in and lie down till tea-time."

Bob and I walked alone. " I do loathe sluggish habits," he said. He waved his hand comprehensively round his domain. " All this, and spring sunshine. Lying down!"

11

Peter Quayne did his best for Harry Redmayne, and so did I. A few days before the show opened I asked Peter and Janet to take lunch with me, and Janet promised to speak to Hubert Dodge and see that *Now* sent a critic along. I chaffed her. " I suppose you have Hubert in your pocket?" And to Quayne I said: " It isn't every little upstart who goes holidaying in Scotland with her boss's mother."

To my surprise, Janet's face flamed rather than blushed. She was furiously angry, but said nothing. I had the sense to drop the subject and go right back to the Redmaynes. " They live in the lodge at your mother's place."

Peter said that some of the pictures were landscapes of those parts. " Then I'd like to come and have a look at them myself," Janet said. " I don't like lots of pictures smothering me, but I do want just one for my flat. Perhaps this will be it."

After luncheon I went back with Peter to the gallery, and helped him to shift everything from the ground floor up to his bed sitter. " I want Redmayne to have this room to himself," he said. " Give him a fair chance."

He picked up Redmayne's largest picture and leaned it against a wall. It was a Cornish landscape with a studied gaunt angularity. " I'll put this one by itself on an easel in the window. With a nice arty bit of tat hanging round it. You know? It might draw a few people in."

" It'll look better," I said, " with a red tab in the corner. I'll buy it, and perhaps I'll give it to Janet for her flat."

He thanked me and smiled. " Trying to make your peace?"

" Well . . . yes."

" You certainly seemed to put your foot into something at lunch. I admired her restraint. She was dying to whip the skin off your back."

I said judicially: "Not long ago she would have done just that. She is a girl who is improving."

I wrote a cheque for the Redmayne picture, and walked home thinking of Janet. She was indeed improving. She was still an imp, but she was no longer a child. The imp was to remain with her always, but not as her whole self, which once it had seemed to be. It was the slave of her intelligence, and she kept it, mostly, on a chain. Physically, she had reached an early maturity. She was lovely to look at.

I wondered where I had gone wrong in my remark about Hubert Dodge. I learned in time from Alcott-Lucas. Everybody in the *Now* office had taken note of Mrs. Dodge's affection for Janet, and also of a real, but not yet aggressive, tendency on Janet's part to—"well," Alcott-Lucas said, measuring his words in his legal way, "not to trade on it. That would be putting it rather over-emphatically. How does one give words to a nuance? I just can't express how we all felt that she felt that, if something should bring it to the touch, some—well, some *imponderable* might, after all, have weight and bring the scales down on her side."

I said: "Thank you, Henry James. You've put it in a coconut shell."

"Really," he said, his egg-shaped bald head and sharp bleak features looking, somehow, the portrait of cold blind justice, "we were tempted to believe—or, at any rate, to admit that such a belief was not fantastic, even though we couldn't entertain it—that Janet may conceivably have extended the mother's undoubted affection for her into some emotion that embraced Hubert, too. Am I putting this clearly, dear boy? I don't want to misrepresent anything or anybody."

I said that I thought I could translate it adequately for my own rough and ready purposes.

We had lunched at his club, and were now in the smoking-room. He ordered brandy for us both, and it came in balloon glasses. He embraced his with both hands, swung it gently round and round, sniffed, sipped, sighed with carnal satisfaction, and lit a cigar. The blue smoke spiralled from his pursed lips, substantial as his thought.

"It came to a head," he said. "No one admires more than I do a lucid dexterity, but there are moments when a veil, an innuendo, floating between what is intended to be understood and what is, in fact, said, makes a necessary difference between impunity and—and——"

"Finding oneself in jug," I offered.

"Well, yes. I have heard it put so. Is the brandy to your satisfaction, dear boy? Good. Then to conclude. Something that Janet had written about a novel caused me to raise, at our weekly convocation, this question of wrapping the necessary

226

flannel round one of her brickbats. She defended her position, and I, as the header-off of our tender craft from dangerous latitudes, had to insist. She was—well, a little upset. She appealed to Hubert, who was sitting next to her. She put her hand—is it too much to say, affectionately?—on his arm. Do you know Hubert well, dear boy?"

My commerce with *Now* had tended to be more and more by post. Rare, indeed, was a look into the office. No, I said, I couldn't claim to know him well.

Alcott-Lucas tapped cigar-ash into a tray and sipped his brandy. "You are not unaware, I trust," he said, "that there are men who do not rush out of their way to invite the affections of women? Hubert, under pretence of needing some papers, crossed the room, picked up odds and ends at random, and sat down again at the other end of the table. He said: 'J.V., we accept your view of the matter. Now, what's the next thing?' So, simply, it was over. Well, dear boy, we breathe again."

12

Bob Meagher rang me up and asked: "When is this Redmayne show opening?"

"It's open. But don't worry. If you want a Redmayne picture, you'll find plenty unsold."

"You'd better take me there," he said imperiously. "I'm not used to those places."

"You only have to walk in. After all, they're shops, like any other. I know they try to engender a holy atmosphere, but that's part of the sales technique."

"You'd better take me," he insisted, and we fixed a time for meeting later in the day.

Well, it's his look-out, I thought. If he expects to find Elsa Redmayne there he's going to be sucked in. Elsa had arranged to come so that she could take turns at the show with her husband; but she had fallen ill, and Redmayne was doing a melancholy mooch round the shop all day long, to Peter Quayne's disquiet.

I sensed Bob's disappointment as soon as we were inside the door. He knew nothing about pictures and didn't pretend to know. He talked politely enough to Redmayne whom he had met when I took him over from Trencrom to Penruan. To keep up the pretence that he had come to see the paintings, he went so far as to choose one haphazardly and write a cheque for it. Then he was anxious to be off. It was tea-time, and there was a tea-shop across the street. Peter Quayne said: "Your young friend Janet has been in, George. I believe she's taking tea over the road."

I wanted to tell her about the picture I had bought and ask if she would accept it. Bob came with me. We joined Janet at a quiet table in an alcove, and I introduced them. " Not that you need introduction," I said. " You've met before."

I reminded them of the night when Wendy had tried to improve my dancing and Bob had danced with Janet. Janet had forgotten it. Bob recalled it only vaguely. " I seem to remember something about it. We took you home, didn't we, George?" And, turning to Janet: " But I only remember you, Miss Bascombe, as a little girl. That's how I thought of you, anyway."

She was a little girl no longer. She was a beautiful young woman, *soignée* and self-possessed. I think the rebuff from Hubert Dodge, of which Alcott-Lucas had told me, had gone deep. Hitherto, she had had her own way with everybody: with her beloved Chowny, with her mother, with her school teachers, whom she tolerated only until she wanted to walk out on them. Then, at the *Now* office, her wounding talent had given her a special place from the beginning, strengthened by Mrs. Dodge's affection. Reducing Alcott-Lucas's ponderosity to my own common level, I could believe that she thought herself free to do more or less as she pleased. Now she had heard the crack of that cold logician's whip. The lesson added something to her. But not yet enough, because, to carry the matter to the conclusion that was not reached for some time, I must tell what happened. She saw Hubert privately and persuaded him to over-rule Alcott-Lucas. " Miss Hartshorn's novel, like all the rest of her work, makes me think of an old tigress too feeble to find her own meal: preying on bits of the corpses left by nobler hunters." This was printed; Alcott-Lucas resigned; an action was brought; and, reasonably enough, the words were interpreted as charging Miss Hartshorn with plagiarism. She was awarded heavy damages, and old J. Wilson Dodge, who paid them, insisted that Janet be sacked and Alcott-Lucas reinstated. And that is what happened. To my surprise, Alcott-Lucas showed a more tender side than I thought him to possess. He personally intervened with Wilson Dodge and persuaded him to have Janet back on the paper. There was the proviso that Alcott-Lucas was to read every word she wrote and to have final power concerning it. Janet accepted this. She had at last learned something she badly needed to know, and she boasted to me long afterwards that, though her articles were as sharp as ever, Alcott-Lucas had never altered a word. By then, it wouldn't have mattered so much to her because her affair with Bob Meagher was obviously heading for marriage. " To think," Bob said to me, " that that Redmayne chit might have been at the exhibition! Ten to one, I'd never have met Janet."

I recalled the long letters from Coventry during the neo-Wendy age, and headed him off.

13

Sylvia wrote to me from America every week, and every week I wrote to her. Towards the end of May, when I was thinking of going down to Trencrom for the summer, a letter from her said: " We're packing up here quite soon now. As I've told you, our play hasn't hit the Americans as it hit the people at home, and it's dying a natural death. The death rattle is due at any minute."

I was glad to know that she was coming back. Not enraptured, not even excited, just glad. I looked up at the picture of Fred Byles, and pondered the headlong coming together of him and Sylvia's mother—a coming together of which Sylvia herself was the consequence. I was incapable of such tempests. I thought of the long sequence of our relationship. There was her emergence into the dawn, but the memory of that was beginning to wear thin. Any boy would have been moved as I was by the moment. Nothing significant had followed it. Almost all our meetings had been unplanned, casual, and not especially emotional. We had once gone to bed together ; but, as if to cancel that, we had spent a couple of months sleeping each night in adjoining bedrooms and meeting at breakfast like well-behaved visitors to the same hotel. Our kisses were casual.

I couldn't imagine myself borrowing money and blueing every last cent of it on a Paris spree with Sylvia. I couldn't imagine myself doing anything desperate about her. But I could imagine—indeed, I knew in my bones—that if this gladness at her homecoming had not been real, then I should have been desolate beyond words to tell.

14

I was sitting down to write and tell Sylvia how glad I was that she was coming home when the door-bell rang. I found Mr. Merriman standing on the mat looking goggle-eyed at the plate attached to the door: Fred Byles and Ledra. I had forgotten the moment of nonsense in which I had had the thing engraved and put there. "What the hell," said Mr. Merriman, whose four-ale-bar diction was still capable of startling me, " is that there for?"

I had no idea why he had come, and hoped he would soon

229

go, but I could hardly do other than lead him into my sitting-room. I pointed to Fred's picture and said: "That's Byles and I am Ledra. That's all it means."

He was wearing all the ruins of his posh clothes. He removed the ruffled hat and laid it on the table. He gazed open-mouthed at the picture. I had an odd feeling that the encounter surprised Fred as much as it did Mr. Merriman. They seemed to look at one another not only with amazement but with hostility.

"It's a small world," Mr. Merriman said at last with customary insight. "I never thought to see *him* again."

"Well, there he is. Will you have sherry or whisky?"

"I don't take anything so early in the morning as a rule," he said righteously, "but this being a special occasion, make it whisky."

"Forgive me if I join you only in coffee," I said, and brought in the thermos flask that I had prepared at breakfast-time.

"Your very good health, Mr. Ledra," he said, adding only a little water to his drink.

"And yours, Mr. Merriman. This being a special occasion, will you disclose the speciality?"

"I can disclose it briefly," he said. "I am a ruined man."

He seemed to me to have been ruined for so long that this did not strike me as special.

"I am here," he added, as though this were a climax moment in a Victorian melodrama, "to throw myself upon your mercy and your charity."

The cuffs of his greenish frock-coat were whiskered. The uppers of one buttoned-up boot were coming away from the sole. "I am," he said, "out on my ear. The Majestic is one cinema of a chain. The proprietors have seen their patriotic duty, and only ex-servicemen are to be employed. There's more flags than one, Mr. Ledra. There's the flag of British commerce, and you and I helped to keep it flying. I appeal to you as an old comrade-in-arms."

George R. Sims couldn't have written better lines for him. I said: "A fat lot I did, Mr. Merriman, to keep any flag flying. I wasn't worth tuppence a week to the firm."

"You rendered service according to your capacity, which I admit was not outstanding," he assured me pompously.

I pitied him, but I also loathed him. I always had done. Nevertheless, I was in his debt. He was one of those trustees who had guarded my affairs when I was a minor, and guarded them scrupulously, to my advantage.

"What do you want?" I asked brutally.

"Want?" he cried. "I want recognition of all my years of service rendered to British commerce. But that's something I'll never get. I am a suppliant, Mr. Ledra. That's all I am, a mere suppliant, begging a crust."

He assumed a humble and hang-dog look which didn't help. It made me dislike him the more.

We sat in silence for a moment, and I pushed the biscuit-barrel towards him. He dipped biscuits into the whisky and munched them. I could have said: "Why don't you ask your daughter to help you?" but I dared not do that. Poor Wendy was on a sufficiently sticky wicket without my sending down a few extra fast ones.

He broke the silence at last. "There it is, Mr. Ledra. I'm in your hands."

We both rose. I gave him a fiver. "I'll see what I can do," I said. "If anything turns up, I'll let you know."

15

I had gone a few days before this to see Richard Cobden's statue in Camden Town. God knows why. I do the oddest things. In a mean street of the region I saw a notice swinging from a bracket: "Tobacco, cigarettes, newspapers." Being short of my brand of tobacco, I made for the place, hoping they might stock it. They didn't. They seemed to stock very little except the more lethal kinds of tobacco and flyblown cigarette packets and the sort of newspaper whose pictures are dedicated to fair love's ripening breast. The ting of the door-bell brought a small man shuffling down the stairs which appeared to lead to living quarters above. His woebegone eyes peered at me through spectacles, as though reproaching me for having interrupted him in some desperate work—such as committing suicide. I bought a few packets of cigarettes that I would never smoke myself or have the nerve to give away, and noticed, as I was going out, an announcement stuck to the glass of the door: "This flourishing business for sale as a going concern." It looked as though it were indeed going and would soon be gone.

All this came to my mind as I sat there, after Mr. Merriman was gone, contemplating the sardonic face of Fred Byles. Fred said to me: "I know what you're thinking about, but don't be a bloody fool."

I took no notice of him, and continued to examine the idea that had come to me. I was afflicted by a sense of sin where Mr. Merriman was concerned. Little though I liked him, he had done me service and he had worked hard for my father. He had bought Byles and Ledra from me, and that was the hardest thing of all to bear. I was in clover. He was, as he had put it, out on his ear. I decided to buy the tobacconist's shop in Camden Town and give it to him. It seemed a measly return for what he had done for me, but it was something. He was a

231

good business man, and, if his recent experiences hadn't utterly undermined him, he should have no difficulty in learning how to run that small shop and at any rate make bread and butter out of it.

I felt very righteous, but not righteous enough to bother my head with the technical business of buying the place. I rang up Mr. Lampson, my business man in the City, and arranged to see him that afternoon. I gave him the whole story of myself and Mr. Merriman and my scheme for his salvation ; and I should not have been surprised if Mr. Lampson had clapped me on the shoulder, tears in his eyes, and told me I was one of the best.

He took off his large horn-rimmed spectacles and rubbed his wise-looking tired eyes. " Well, yes," he said dubiously. " From what you say, it sounds as though no one could make it worse than it is. Possibly there's a living in such a place, and possibly there isn't. What if the thing flopped? You'd have poured your money down the drain."

I must have looked deflated. " It's worth looking into," he said, " but I think we should proceed on different lines. I'll get someone to make a few inquiries, and then, if we decide to proceed, we'll buy the place in your name. I don't see the point of handing the whole thing over to Mr. Merriman. Put him in as manager, but don't burden yourself with promising him a salary. After all, he'd have rent-free living-room, though you should charge him a pepper-corn rent for that, so as to establish your rights ; and then he could take a percentage of the profits. Make that as high as you like, but insist on something—say five per cent for yourself, again to establish your rights. Of course, you'll want proper book-keeping. We'll look after the audit, so that there'll be no chance of his doing you down. If he'll take it on those terms, there's a great advantage : it will put him on his toes. The more he makes the more he'll keep. If, as I say, the thing should flop, at any rate you'll be able to sell the shop for what it's worth, and so all will not be lost."

I felt like a knight, ready *cap à pie* for rescuing a damsel in distress, advised by some wise old Arthurian courtier on the pros and cons : the cost of horse and lances, for example, balanced against the possibility of the maiden being a wealthy heiress.

However, there it was. No good having a Mr. Lampson if you didn't use him. He did, indeed, clap his hand on my shoulder as we both rose, but not in whole-hearted commendation. " Remember," he said, " we're always here to advise you. I'll let you know how things turn out."

I didn't expect gratitude from Mr. Merriman, but I got it all the same. I am quite sure that, had our positions been reversed, he would have done nothing for me; and, knowing this, he was surprised into gratitude. I didn't expect, either, that he would take hold of the opportunity I put in his way. But he did, he made a success of it. The down-at-heel and sordid place was transformed. It avoided both the old filthiness and that anti-septic brightness of a hospital ward that shops go in for now. It became what Mr. Merriman himself called chummy: a word that nauseated me, though it did express what he was trying to do. I kept away from him. I didn't visit the shop either as a customer or a friend; but occasionally he wrote, sending me a " progress report." These didn't need even to be read: I posted them on to Mr. Lampson. My attitude to Mr. Merriman was ambivalent. Seeing him stricken by the roadside, I had poured oil and wine into his wounds, but I was eager then to cross to the other side again and leave him to the business of healing or not, as the case might turn out.

It was about a year after Mr. Merriman had moved into this shop in Malpas Street, Camden Town, that I received a letter in his copperplate handwriting. I detest copperplate handwriting, with its mechanic precision that rubs all individuality out of a script, just as I detest the discourteous scrawls whose meaning must be guessed or left undivined. I detested even more the phrase that invited me " to meet Mrs. Meagher and I " at tea next Sunday. On the whole, I seem to have been in a fairly detesting mood.

I wanted to turn the thing down, but I hadn't seen Mr. Merriman since he took over the shop; and, after all, Mrs. Meagher was Wendy. I wondered what she was up to in Camden Town. So at four o'clock on that Sunday afternoon I stood before the attractive door with its bright brass knocker and rapped an announcement of my presence. Mr. Merriman himself opened the door. My first arresting eyeful of him showed me the Merriman I once knew. Save for the bruise-coloured bags under the eyes, and a flabbier hang and tremble of the jowls, this could have been the Merriman who called upon me in Fallowfield when my father was dying. The frock-coat with a flower at the lapel, the splendid trousers, the spats: all was there, and I am sure it was all there because he wanted to say: Merriman is himself again. He is not a man that fortune can knock down.

The door was painted olive-green. It had a pleasing fanlight. The passage behind it was cream-washed and stair-rods gleamed on crimson carpet that climbed to the next floor.

"Come in, George," he said familiarly. "Wendy is tittivating herself. You know what women are."

His smile invited me to share his knowledge of feminine frivolity. He preceded me into the room behind the shop. So perfectly was he recreating the atmosphere of these far-off widowed Sunday afternoons in his small house at Altrincham that I should not have been surprised to look through a window at a back garden dizened with whatever flowers might be seasonably abloom. But Camden Town uttered its ban, and illusion faltered. Not so much, though, that I was not almost expecting a young unwithered Wendy to enter and preside at the teapot. Wendy came in, stout, greying, dressed in unsuitable mauve, and said: "Good afternoon, George. Everything's ready. I'll carry in right away."

I said she must allow me to do that, and followed her into the kitchen. It was as spotless as everything else, and, what is more, it was modernised. I began to wonder. Mr. Merriman was making the shop pay its way; but it seemed to me that his profits would hardly cover what had been spent here. I said casually to Wendy: "This place looks as efficient as a ship's engine-room. And they're not fitted up for nothing."

"Far from it," she said. "But I'm here so much that I wanted the place to be decent."

She took scones warm from the oven and put them on a plate. "After all," she said, "I may be here for good before long."

The floor was covered with cork lino, comfortable to the feet. The pots and pans shone in orderly rows on shelves. It was, in its small way, a dream of a kitchen. But, situated here in a Camden Town back street, it could hardly be, I thought, the dream that had dazzled Wendy rushing from Manchester to Coventry on a day now long ago. I considered her with pity: the down-turn of the lips, the eyes that looked as though they had lost the knack of smiling. I took up the tray and carried it towards the sitting-room. Just before we got there, she turned and said: "I'm glad, you know. I've had just that little bit too much."

The bit too much was Janet.

When Sylvia came home from America we greeted one another with quiet happiness. I went down to Southampton to meet her, and looked after her as I would have looked after an elder sister. I didn't want her to suffer the fatigue of travelling straight to London, so I had booked two bedrooms in a Southampton hotel. I took care of her luggage, and did all else that the occasion demanded. When we reached London the next day, I went on with her to the cottage near Amersham and saw her settled in. Now that she wasn't playing in London, I met her only at week-ends, and we spent these as we had done before her going to New York. Throughout the weekdays I was restless without her and the week-ends brought us both the mellow content that suited our mood at that time.

In the late autumn Hubert Dodge's mother gave the annual party to members of the *Now* staff and their friends. Sylvia went with me. There was a splendid buffet, a splendid floor for dancing, and for the first time in my life I danced with Sylvia. The restful months she had been spending in the country, unworried by the cares of her profession, had given her a serenity which was the mood most serviceable to her beauty. Some women shine the more brightly through excitement and some through anger; but, however it may once have been with her, Sylvia now, in the moment of her first autumnal premonitions, had a beauty that moved me deeply. She was dancing with her head on my shoulder and I kissed her neck. I said: " I love you, darling," and she answered simply: " I know."

What more she would have said I can't say, for at that moment she lifted her head from my shoulder and her expression changed. She was looking across the room, surprised.

It was Janet.

These parties were informal, people drifting in and out as they pleased. Janet had come very late: close on midnight. Bob Meagher was with her.

We left the floor and sat on chairs at the side and watched them dance. There were people in dinner jackets and people in lounge suits, and even one or two *avant garde* types in corduroy bags, tweed coats and open-necked tie-less shirts. Janet was wearing peacock-blue silk, and Bob, alone among the men, wore tails, white tie, and a gardenia at his lapel. As they danced, he took it from his buttonhole and pushed the stem through the coils of her dark hair.

Sylvia asked: " Who is he?"

" Bob Meagher. Inevitably Sir Robert Meagher soon. Possibly Lord Meagher, or whatever fancy title he may give himself, in the long run."

"He's very handsome," she said.

He was. Sedentary though his days were, there was something in Bob's make-up that repelled fat. Tall, dark and alert, he was the handsome stranger of any witch's forecast.

Sylvia said: "He looks like Money."

"His looks don't lie," I assured her.

"How do you think Janet looks?"

"Very well," I answered temperately, shirking what was the fact: that she looked lost, hopelessly beleaguered and beguiled, ripe to his hand.

Sylvia said: "She tells me nothing."

I wondered what there was to tell, if anything. A stupid proviso. Obviously something. But what?

3

In whatever way it may have come about, Wendy had got wind of Elsa Redmayne. I could have guessed that from the atmosphere in the greenhouse at Dormers when I stayed there for a week-end. She herself told me later how she had got wind of Janet, too. Soon after her father took possession of the shop in Camden Town she came to see how he was getting on. Her North Country domestic sense was grieved by what she found. She told Mr. Merriman that she would spend the whole of the next week-end with him, deciding what needed to be done to make the pig-sty habitable by humans. Bob had never kept her short of money, once money began to flow his way; and I suppose she got a satisfaction out of spending Bob's cash on the rehabilitation of Bob's victim. For so she considered her father to be. Coventry was far behind, when Merriman was the ogre and Bob was St. George. Her emotions had swung full circle.

So there she was in Camden Town, with money for immediate needs and a note-book for making a plan of her sanitary campaign. She was there early on a Saturday morning, having let Bob know that she might be back on Monday and might not. They parted on bad terms for she had told him what she intended to do, and he raved at her folly the more as it stirred in him a sense of guilt because his own treatment of Mr. Merriman had been brutal.

"You seem to forget Coventry and all that that word means," he said with the hypocrisy of a man in love, for he knew by now that Janet was something other than Elsa Redmayne, and that he was prepared to forget far more than Coventry to secure what he wanted.

236

A most absurd incident, that only Wendy could have contrived, blew the situation sky-high. She spent the morning fussing and grumbling about the Camden Town house, and after lunch went up to inspect the bedroom where she was to spend the night. It was Mr. Merriman's, and he had exiguously furnished it on a few pounds I had given him. He said he would sleep on the floor " anywhere." One thing he naturally had not provided was a woman's night-clothes. Opening the suitcase she had brought, Wendy found that in the passion and excitement of her departure from Dormers she had forgotten to bring her own. Mr. Merriman thoughtlessly suggested that she could sleep either naked between the sheets or, clothed, upon them. Either course seemed shocking to her sense of provincial propriety. It was Saturday afternoon and the shops were shut, so she could not go out and buy what she needed. The whole day's proceedings had overwrought her and she quarrelled with her father. He, pompously insensitive, reminded her that all her troubles sprang from flying in his face years ago and preferring an upstart swine to the security of a respectable home. Poor Wendy must have hated Bob, her father, and all the world; and, her nerves shredded, she said she'd go back to Dormers and come to Camden Town next week, properly provided for a stay.

There was no Brookes to meet her at Dorking. She took a taxi-cab and reached Dormers in time to find Bob and Janet sitting down to dinner.

Usually, dinner at Dormers was a simple enough matter; but just as, when I had taken lunch with him on the Great West Road, Bob had unrolled the whole continent in which he now had mastery, so, for a special guest, he liked Dormers to show itself off in all its potentialities of luxury. Wendy unceremoniously entered the dining-room straight upon her arrival, tired and rather disarrayed, not bothering even to go upstairs to tittivate herself. She just walked in, threw her dowdy hat on to one chair, sat down on another, and said to Brookes: " Just bring me a plate of soup and some toast. Then I'll get to bed. I'm very tired."

Amid the napery and crystal and silver, the well-arranged flowers, the glow of a table-lamp which placed as it were a private pool of gentle light amid the sombre outskirts of the room, she must have been to Bob as accusing a presence as any ghost conjured up by Shakespeare to make a comment on human sin or a disquieting prediction concerning its consequences. She was outside the pool of light, so that he and Janet must have had the uneasy feeling of being upon a stage, observed with irony, amusement, or contempt by a spectator in the stalls.

Bob was inadequate to that moment, and I don't know who could have mastered it. The dinner had so completely the air of prearrangement, of attention to ceremonial detail, that there

237

was no explaining it away. He said: "You know Janet Bascombe, Wendy. Do you remember? We met her and George Ledra at the Savoy. We all danced together."

Wendy didn't answer that, but when Brookes came in with a tray, bringing her toast and soup, she said: "I'll go straight up to my room, Brookes. Have it sent up there."

Telling me of the affair, Wendy said: "I remembered that I was there only because I'd forgotten my night things. I wondered whether that girl had remembered hers. Not, of course, that they would be so necessary in her case. However, the evening broke up for them. I hadn't been long in my room when I heard the car starting. My husband was taking her to the station. I heard him drive back, and soon he was turning the handle of the bedroom door. But I'd locked it, and it stayed locked. I don't know where he slept. I stayed in bed till he'd gone in the morning."

That was the end of the shining adventure which began with the flight to Coventry. When she returned to the tobacconist's shop she did not leave it again. Mr. Merriman regarded this as in some sense a personal triumph, a smack in the eye for Bob Meagher. But it was Wendy, turned cold-blooded and efficient, who decided what was to be done. Years afterwards, she made me her confessor and we talked of those days. She and her father had by then bought a small, almost ruined, Georgian house overlooking the Pool of London, and had made it quite agreeably livable. We sat on a charming balcony as an autumn dusk was settling on the Pool and the sky towards Westminster was flushed purple. Ships were beginning to move east on the full tide. "I like it here," Wendy said. "We could have gone into the country, but this is more like Manchester."

It seemed to me to be remarkably unlike Manchester, but it was the sense of urgent congested living that, I suppose, pleased her. She had had enough of houses like Dormers. Mr. Merriman was taking a holiday—in the Trossachs of all places!—and I had dined with Wendy at a candle-lit table. Perhaps it was this that threw her mind back to Janet Bascombe and Bob dining so cosily together. "My arrival must have been a bomb to those two," she said. "But I felt like a damp squib."

She went back to Camden Town the next day, and did a day's hearty charing. "It made me feel better," she said. "I was doing *something*, at any rate, and after the life I'd been leading that was a nice change. In the evening I went to see Sir Robert."

There was a sneer in the words. Bob's knighthood had recently been announced.

"I rang up his flat from a call-box and found he was in. He didn't want to see me, but I insisted, and I went. We had it all out that night."

She poured coffee, and I lit my pipe, and watched the lighters sliding by, dark on the dusk.

"I blackmailed him," she said. "Or perhaps that's putting it a bit too strongly. I asked him if he wanted a divorce, and he said that he did, and gave me a whole catalogue of the insufficiencies that made me no good as his wife. I told him that I had no intention of discussing my insufficiencies or his. I had come to talk business."

She said that he had not, and never would have, any legal reason for divorcing her; so the only thing to be discussed was the conditions on which she would divorce him. "I told him he could arrange the thing as he liked. He could be discovered with the usual slut in the usual hotel bedroom, or he could be discovered in bed at Dormers with Janet Bascombe. 'Have it your own way,' I said, 'I sha'n't worry.'"

She told him she had no intention of bringing up his children. "I don't like Viola, and as for Jocelyn, he wouldn't thank me if he had to swap Dormers for a tobacco shop in Camden Town."

Bob had given her a certain amount of stock in Meagher Motors and she said she felt entitled to keep that, but wouldn't accept another penny. She discussed the whole matter so efficiently, and gained each point so cleverly as it came along that Bob must almost have wished he'd made her a director of his company. He may have wished it the more ardently as he watched the unfolding of the Merriman story in the years that followed. They made a success of their shop, and then told me to find a new managing tenant as they were buying a shop of their own. They concentrated on little broken-down businesses, not all tobacconists', put them in order, installed managers, and then moved on to the next. They were now in clover, doing little but stroll round inspecting their concerns and cracking the whip where necessary. Mr. Merriman had shed his profanity. He was his old Manchester self, with the added virtue of taking a glass of wine now and then.

"My sight's not so good as it was," Wendy said as we sat on the river balcony that night. "Go and get me my glasses, George. I left them on the mantelpiece."

I went back into the room and saw a picture postcard of stags and heather propped up near the spectacle-case. I shamelessly read Mr. Merriman's inscription. "My heart's in the Hielands a-chasing the deer. (R. Burns.) Love, Dad."

However, that was a long time ahead, and here we were, Sylvia and I, at the *Now* party in 1929. Janet was twenty. I had always thought her a beautiful child, and now she was a beautiful woman. It was not the static beauty of the dumb female animals whose pictures recurred in the society magazines: it was a beauty full of fire and flashes, changeable as her moods. That night she was lit up. She didn't see me and Sylvia: she was seeing no one but Bob Meagher. Even when the dance took them swirling past the place where Sylvia and I were sitting, still she did not see us; but Bob did, and he waved a hand to me as they went by. When the dance ended, I went over to them and said to Janet: " Your mother's here."

She turned to where Sylvia was sitting and smiled towards her, but didn't seem to want to do more than that. She wanted to do nothing but dance with Bob. Then something unexpected happened. Hubert's father, the formidable J. Wilson Dodge, came into the room. It was not his custom to attend these affairs, and he had not come now for the joy of meeting what he doubtless thought the odd types that Hubert gathered about him. He was looking for Hubert, having some matter to discuss with him. Hubert was not in the room ; he was no dancer ; but Wilson Dodge's eye fell upon Bob. He went up to him and shook his hand. " Good God, Meagher," he said. " I didn't know that you patronised this sort of thing."

His contempt for this sort of thing was obvious, and he took it for granted that Bob would welcome nothing so heartily as an opportunity to escape. He put an arm through Bob's and sought to lead him from the room, saying, " Let's go to my den," but Bob resisted till Janet said: " You go, Bob, but don't be too long."

Wilson Dodge, who had not realised that they were together, gave her an unfriendly look and bore Bob away.

Janet sat with me and Sylvia, and Sylvia said: " You gave him permission to go as though he were your property. Tell me something about him, darling."

Janet answered, almost harshly: " We are to be married. That is, as soon as certain difficulties can be dealt with."

" I wish you had told me earlier. It's rather a blow to learn so suddenly that an Adonis like that is to be one's son-in-law, especially as he looks about my own age. Well, I hope the difficulties are not serious."

" It depends on whether you consider a wife and two children to be serious."

She flushed, and her voice sounded hostile. I saw J.V. Alcott-

Lucas on the other side of the room and took the opportunity to escape. "Excuse me," I said to Sylvia. "I'll be back in a moment. I expect you two will have a lot to discuss."

"I don't see that, in an affair of this sort, discussion . . ."

I left her to end her speech in Sylvia's ears alone, and went over to Alcott-Lucas. "There's drink in the next room," he said pertinently, looking as though he had authenticated this fact before announcing it. "I must say that Hubert has mastered the laws of hospitality."

His eye-glass, fortunately attached to a black silk cord, dropped from his eye. He fumbled for it, but could not find it, and said solemnly: "Tell me, dear boy, did I see J. Wilson Dodge—I will not say gracing but momentarily imposing upon the company the—er, what would you say?—the—well, did I?"

"He looked in," I said.

"Admirable, concise," Alcott-Lucas said. "You have the gift of speech. Your very good health, dear boy. Why did he—if I may borrow your clean-cut concision—look—well—in?"

"I think he was looking for Hubert."

"Now you hedge, dear boy. *You think*. Do you *assert*, with the Book in your right hand, that he was not—well, let us not use the odious word snooping—yet what else, what other definition, presents itself?"

"Calm yourself, Alcott-Lucas," I said. "He wasn't looking round to see who was tight."

"Then perhaps one more beaker—eh?" he suggested.

He served his purpose, kept me occupied while Sylvia talked to Janet. When I went back to the dance floor Bob Meagher was returning from his session with Mr. Dodge, and I saw Janet get up and go towards him eagerly, as though glad of the chance to end a talk that she had not much liked. She was evidently all set for more dancing when Hubert appeared for the first time that evening. He was wearing a white sweater that had seen cleaner days, flannel bags and carpet slippers. His eyes, peering through a fringe of hair, looked worried ; but then they always did, as though he were hoping to be untrue some report he had heard of the world betterment. He said to the bandsmen: "You can break it up for half an hour. Go and give yourselves a drink." To the rest of us he said: "Will you come along now, please. Mother's going to play."

It was the moment when Mrs. Dodge intended to plumb the depths of remembering Poland.

Hubert went out, and Bob said to Janet: "Is this obligatory?"

"Afraid so, darling," she said, "but you can shut your eyes and give yourself to dreams of internal combustion. There'll be more dancing later."

They moved away, following a thin reluctant taggle making for the music-room. Sylvia and I were alone and I said: "I
241

don't suppose there'll be a count of heads, so let us absent ourselves from the felicity of Chopin's Dead March."

She went up to get her things, and I waited for her, pacing
like a chessman on the black and white marble squares of the
entrance hall. J. Wilson Dodge came down the stairs, wearing
a brown woollen muffler and a felt hat, and for some reason or
other carrying a small Gladstone bag. He paused for a moment,
and said: " Is Alcott-Lucas tight?"

" I think so, sir."

" Good!" he said, slapping me on the shoulder. " I'm not
afraid of many men, but Alcott-Lucas's icy brain always terrifies
me. Glad to see a chink in the armour. Well, good night." And
off he went, looking rather like a burglar clocking on for the
night's work. He suddenly made me think of Mr. Merriman—
birds of a feather, but this one was the downier bird.

There was an enormous chandelier lighting the stairs, and as
Sylvia came down—gold slippers, a golden wrap—I *saw* her,
for the first time in many a day. We had become, I thought, too
accustomed, too familiar, meeting in nothing but diurnal plati-
tude. One should see a woman now and then dressed like this,
coming down a staircase like this. It is a great moment when
a woman comes down a noble staircase if she knows how to do
it. It demands poise, a perfection of movement. She came
slowly, beautifully, inevitably. I would have kissed her, but a
footman was standing in the hall. I said to him: " Will you
look out and see if a taxi's handy?"

" I will *ring* for one, sir," he said reproachfully ; and in two
minutes the taxi was at the door. I gave the address of my
flat. We could have walked it in ten minutes, but Sylvia was
not dressed for walking, and a gentle rain was a-blur in the
November midnight.

5

When I awoke in the morning I looked at the sumptuous cloth-
of-gold thrown hastily upon a chair in the bedroom, and at the
golden slippers which, comically, were ranged side by side upon
my dressing-table. She had not been in my flat before, and I
looked at these signs that she had now entered with a happy
impetuous vengeance. We had stood off and on with one
another for so long that I felt again, as I lay there in the grey
reluctant London dawn, a tremble of surprise like the tremble
that had taken us both the night before. We had no sooner
shut the door behind us than we were in one another's arms,
she, as obviously as myself, overcome by desire. We stood
kissing to exhaustion, and then, without a word, she threw off
her clothes as impetuously as if they were rags and went into

242

the bedroom, dragging them behind her in one hand. When I followed, there they were, thrown anyhow, and she was taking off one shoe—her only, inadequate clothing—and placing it carefully beside the one which stood already on the dressing-table.

I looked at her, sleeping soundly, the lips slightly parted upon her white teeth, her face suffused as though with lingering sensations of ecstasy. One long white arm lay out of the bed, the lightly-clenched hand brushing the floor. I eased myself out on to the carpet, took up the arm, kissed the hollow of her elbow, and put the arm back under the warm bedclothes. She smiled, but did not awaken.

When I had bathed and shaved I prepared breakfast and wheeled it on a trolley into the bedroom. She was sitting up in the single bed, laughing. "And what amuses my lady?" I demanded.

"I was wondering how on earth we fitted into this."

I poured the coffee and said: "You'd better write to Jose Gomm. He seems to be able to get anything you want. Ask him to get hold of the Great Bed of Ware, for, from now on, we shall certainly need wider accommodation. Though I must say," I added, "that last night proved that love will find a way, be the bed wide or narrow."

"Jose would think we intended to get married."

"Well, don't we?"

I looked at her sitting up naked in the bed. She was thirty-eight. Her body was beautiful, her breasts as firm as on the misty morning when I picked up her bracelet from the Penruan sands. It was on her wrist now, her only clothing.

"Don't we?" I repeated, knowing with a sudden overwhelming certitude what I wanted the answer to be.

She looked at the bracelet, turning it round and round as though it were a talisman that might supply the answer. Her head was bent over it, and the flow of hair down her spine broadened out on the pillow.

"I'm too old for you," she said.

"I didn't think so last night."

"Oh, that——" she said, almost wearily. And then, seeing that the words had hurt me: "I'm sorry, darling. That was very beautiful. But there's more than that, you know."

I said: "Don't talk to me as if I were a child. I know as well as you do that there's more than that. I'm asking you to share my life, not only my bed. Do you want to?"

She said incongruously: "Give me some coffee."

I did, and as she sipped it, her forehead still creased as if with anxious thought, I said: "If you really want to know, I'm asking you to marry me so that I may have the honour of being Bob Meagher's step-father-in-law."

Her laughter spluttered into the coffee cup. "Well, if that's
243

what you want, it would be cruel to stand in your way. We'd better seal the bargain. Take away these cups and get back into bed."

We spent the dreary November day in bed; and then we shared a bath and dressed and went out to an early dinner. She had nothing with her but the splendid clothes she had worn for the dance, so I put on a dinner jacket to match the glory. A year's-long barrier was down between us, and we chattered endlessly, liberated. I told her of how, on my first day in London as a man-on-his-own, I had bought ready-made evening clothes to visit the theatre where she was playing and found myself assisting at a flop. She had forgotten that night, and I had forgotten things that she remembered. We were back in the flat by nine o'clock, and sat contentedly side by side, holding hands and speaking little, wrapped in a sense of security and quiet happiness. Old Fred Byles smiled down upon us, and I reflected that if I was to be Bob's father-in-law, Fred was to be mine. "Who is he?" Sylvia asked; but this was not yet the moment for telling her. "He's long been dead," I said. "His name was Fred Byles, and he was a partner with my grandfather in founding the firm I got my money from."

"He looks a proper old rascal to me," she said. "A spark if ever there was one."

"Well, between ourselves," I admitted, "he had a reputation that way."

Towards midnight she drew nearer to me on the couch, put her arms round me and began to kiss me. Her caresses became more and more unmistakable. "Oh, that——" I said, as she at last got up and went into the bedroom.

6

In the last week of December in that year 1929 we were married in a registry office. We had told no one of our intention to do so, and, after spending the night at my flat, we set out for Penruan the next morning. We went in Sylvia's car which, while not in the class of Bob Meagher's state chariot, was comfortable and reliable. We took it easy and stayed for a night at Exeter. The next morning as we were taking breakfast Sylvia said: "I've done this journey a good many times, but I've always gone through Okehampton and dodged Dartmoor. Let's have a change and go over the moor to-day."

We started at about ten o'clock, and we had just left Moretonhampstead behind us when the weather began to thicken. The wide sweeps and prospects of the moor contracted. The swirls of fog, with no wind to drive or disperse them, loitered about in the air and on the land, coalescing here and there into larger agglomerations through which Sylvia drove at a crawl. Now and then groups of the ponies that live and breed on the moor galloped by, half-seen, their long tails streaming, wild and beautiful.

The weather worsened. Where we had been driving through patches of fog into long clear stretches of road, we were now moving through gloom that opened only here and there into a brief corridor of light. Sylvia switched on headlamps and taillights, and presently drew off the road on to a patch of wayside grass. She said: "Let's wait here for a bit and see if things get any better." She switched off the lights, and in the sudden silence when the motor died we moved closer to one another. We had been living together for a fortnight; we had been married for a day; we were still in the mood when, unless something active occupied our attention, we instinctively went into one another's arms. There, with the brownish mist wavering eerily about our close secure shell, as though we were in a submarine beneath a muddy sea, we did so now. I had discovered how insatiably passionate Sylvia was once her barriers were down. She liked to make love in odd circumstances, and our circumstances, odd enough at that moment, excited her. But suddenly her excitement died. Her eyes looked frightened; and then I, too, saw the face that was pressed to the car window.

Whatever that face may have been, it would have been natural enough for me to see it as horrid and menacing. I remembered some talk I had heard in the breakfast-room of our hotel in Exeter: talk of an escaped convict who was said to have got away in the direction of Plymouth. Well, this was not the way to Plymouth; I had no doubt that this was the convict all the same. But I did not see him as horrid and menacing. The sight of him filled my heart with pity. He was no older than myself, and white and thin, with a red streak down his face that could have come from a scramble through thorns. Wherever he had got it from, he was wearing a shabby suit that was not a convict's rig. He looked hungry and desperately frightened.

For a moment we stared at one another through the window glass; then I opened the door and stepped out on to the turf. Only then I saw that in his hanging-down hand he held a heavy thorn club. I shut the car door behind me, and half my mind was thinking of this perilous moment and half of Fred Byles. Fred Byles, too, had been a convict on Dartmoor. What would I have done if I had found him trying to escape?

I said absurdly: "Good morning. What can I do for you?"

He stared at me and did not answer.

"What do you want?" I asked.

His grip tightened on his cudgel. "I want 'er," he said.

Even this did not surprise or disgust me. How long he had

245

been behind bars I could not know, but, for however long it may have been, he had been without a woman. Again Fred Byles recurred to my mind: passionate, parted with a brutal finality from Margaret Napier whom I could well imagine to have been as ardent as I was now finding Sylvia, the fruit of that ardour.

I looked compassionately at the young man. His face was hungry for more than food. How long he had been exciting himself by watching us I could not say. He did not look the sort of man who would be content to remain a *voyeur*.

I saw a shudder pass through him and his hand tighten on the cudgel. Shut in with him behind those dun curtains, I felt at last an access of fear. Since leaving Moretonhampstead we had not seen a soul. That was not a road much used in the dead of winter.

At that moment Sylvia opened the car door and began to step out. Her long legs, clothed in silk, were exposed to above the knees, and again a shudder of desire convulsed the young man's face. " Out of my way!" he said to me in a strangled voice, and his tongue passed horribly over his lips. I said to Sylvia: " Get back into the car." As she was doing so, he rushed suddenly upon me, the club raised. " I'll beat yer brains out," he said. " You've 'ad your turn. Now . . . off."

I knew murder in a man's eyes when I saw it. I was unused to any sort of combat, and had been trained neither to box or wrestle. I obeyed the instinct of an animal and raised my right foot. Before he could use the club that he now swung over his head I drove my foot, flat-soled, into his stomach with the weight of primitive ferocity behind it. He went down, moaning, clutching his stomach with both hands.

I got back into the car, and Sylvia and I had not a word to say to one another. She drove slowly on, her hand shaking on the wheel. I think we can hardly have covered more than three miles in the next crawling hour, and then we were through the worst of the fog. Soon the Two Bridges Hotel came upon our sight, an unexpected haven. Sylvia gladly agreed that it would be unwise for her to drive any more that day. So there we stayed, and after dinner an evening paper came up from Plymouth. A paragraph said that the escaped convict had been found in a Plymouth lodging-house; and in the stop press column a few lines dealt with a vagabond named Trevenna, concerning whom the police had received many complaints from molested women. He had been picked up on the moor that afternoon.

We passed through Princeton the next morning, and there it was, a solid block of masonry, a solid block of historic misery, Dartmoor Prison, where we had housed the captives of our wars: Frenchmen, Americans: and men like Fred Byles. The

246

leaden sky weighed down on it; and I looked at the bangle on Sylvia's arm, and thought of Fred placing it on the arm of Mr. Chown's sister Margaret. In Paris, during that last mad flare-up of his romantic life. Then, swiftly, this. I had often thought of it. Now I realised it, and shuddered through every bone and sinew. My God! What a cage for that gay old bird! What a cage for Sylvia's father! No wonder he died there.

7

We were anxious to be home at Penruan, and so we left the Two Bridges early and were soon over the Tamar, into Cornwall. A night's sleep had calmed Sylvia's abraded nerves. She drove steadily, and presently made her only comment on the horrid happening of the day before. " I don't think," she said, " I shall ever take that road into Cornwall again. And thank you, darling."

It seemed strange to receive thanks for the murderous mule-kick into the stomach of that poor mentally deranged wretch. I felt horrible about it, degraded, but what else had there been to do? And, too, I pondered, as we went smoothly on under happier skies, I should now be the more reluctant to reveal to her what Mr. Chown had left me to reveal or not, as I chose. Dartmoor would have for her a double darkness of association; she had seen the prison, and she had felt the dread of that would-be violator.

But these thoughts cleared away. She began to talk of Penruan. " Thank goodness," she said, " I've paid for the work there as it went on. The place is now as good as finished. If it hadn't been, it would have had to stay more or less a ruin."

I was amazed. I couldn't believe what those words implied and I chaffed her about them. " But, darling, when news of our wedding leaks out, everyone will know that I married you merely because you are very rich. Jose Gomm told me that years ago, and even Mr. Chown overcame his reticence once to talk of money. He left me in no doubt that you could buy up the Woolworth heiress. Don't tell me that I sha'n't have the pleasure of sponging upon you."

We had halted for lunch at the Red Lion in Truro, and she told me what had happened.

"When I was playing in America," she said, " I ran across that horrid little man Conway. Do you remember him?"

I did indeed. I told her how I had run across him accidentally when travelling on the Metropolitan line with the idea of calling upon her at her cottage, and how I had watched her meet him at Amersham station. " I didn't know who he was till

247

that moment," I told her, "and oddly enough I thought him charming and intelligent."

"He was all that," she said. "He could turn on the charm like a headlight. And he didn't lack intelligence. But he was a bad hat all the same. He'd relieved me of a lot of money before he went to America on that film job."

I remembered the film job, and the girl he had met and married. It hadn't lasted long; there had been two other Reno weddings since then.

"I met him one night outside the theatre in New York. He was hanging round, obviously on the watch for me. I was fool enough to ask him to take supper with me at a restaurant. 'What!' he said. 'In these clothes? The price of a new suit would be more useful.' I took him to a shabbier place than I had first suggested, and I did give him the price of a new suit. That's how it began. I found he was notorious. People warned me off him as a well-known public nuisance. But I felt sorry for him. He looked such a poor little shop-soiled runt. The charm could be still called up when he wanted it, but I never knew whether I should meet the charmer or a most offensive little boozer. I told him at last that I'd had enough. I didn't mind giving him money, but I did object to every last cent being boozed away. Then he became really offensive. He made a great scene in a restaurant and started shouting about the things he'd be able to tell some columnist. 'All your goings on,' he said, though I had no idea what he was raving about. That was the last time I saw him. I suppose I must have been looking distressed, because a man who was dining alone walked across and whispered something to the restaurant manager, and in no time at all Master Clarence found himself being quietly hurled into the street."

It was odd, sitting there in a sedate hotel in a sedate country town and listening to this echo of emotionally violent life in a great capital so far away. I took her hand as we waited for coffee in a quiet lounge off the dining-room.

"I hope," I said, "that your deliverer wasn't a wolf merely chasing another wolf off from appetising prey."

"He was all right," she said, "except that he's the reason why I've lost so much money."

He was a lawyer named Chester Allen. He asked Sylvia to join him at his table, and she did so. Chester said he'd seen her play—had liked it so well that he'd seen it three times—and he had recognised her as she came in with Clarence Conway. "I hope I did the right thing," he said apologetically. "I guess that bum was becoming a bit insufferable."

She told him all that she thought he needed to know about Conway: and he said: "I've met him before, you know. It was over a spot of blackmail. He was threatening a girl who, alas,

248

had been foolish enough to be blackmailable. She came to me about it, and I personally saw Mr. Conway and explained one or two points of law to him. I'm sure he recognised me to-night, because this wasn't so long ago. So I think you needn't let the thing worry you any more."

They often met after that. Chester was fond of taking ladies out to dine—"but only as Galahad or King Arthur might have done. He loved to talk of plays and books and paintings and the state of Europe. Especially the state of Europe. He'd done the rounds—London, Paris, Vienna, Rome, Venice—and he admitted that Europe had points. But he was sorry for anyone who didn't use it just as a holiday place. It was all built on thin ice, and the ice was due to crack any minute. Give him the United States every time. The States could stand anything that came along. Economically and commercially, the States were built on rock."

Our coffee came, and Sylvia lit a cigarette and slowly exhaled the smoke. "See, darling?" she asked.

But even yet I didn't see. But I saw soon enough. Chester Allen was an honest well-meaning man who gave the wrong advice, and Sylvia was innocent enough to take it. Chester pictured the satisfaction she would feel when her money was transferred to New York and the European stock markets were tottering. She gave him authority to act for her, and he acted. And here we were in a Truro hotel, and the time was the last month of 1929. "There's not much left," Sylvia said, "of what I transferred to America, and every day things get worse." And 1930 was about to dawn, revealing the worst yet.

I thought it no part of my business to inquire into her money affairs, and said: "I've got enough for two, darling. You won't have to sell your car."

She laughed. "I'm not exactly ruined," she said. "I had at any rate the prudence to draw the line at transferring only half of what I had. Jose Gomm and Chowny were right, you know. I had more money than was healthy for me. I'm glad I spent some of it on Penruan while the going was good."

8

Tom Collins, that ancient mariner whom Sylvia had left in charge of the Penruan gardens, presented himself on New Year's morning like a corporal with a half-platoon reporting for duty. There were five of them in a line on the gravel, with Collins standing a yard to the front. He had said that he would be there at ten o'clock, and here he was. As Sylvia and I stepped through the front door I almost expected to hear him

249

shout "Shun!" and it would have been amusing indeed to see the five behind him try to obey. While Collins himself was natty in a blue suit and a peaked sailor's cap, the others were as slouching and unkempt a gang as you could have assembled anywhere between Land's End and the Tamar. Not a man of them looked under seventy, and they were knotted like old briar roots. Collins said: "These are the boys, Mrs. Bascombe." The boys grinned at us, and in a spirit of courtesy we grinned back at them and wished them a happy New Year.

"The boys 'ave done the job," Collins announced, and Sylvia, prepared for this moment, gave them a pound each and told them to get away to the Absolution. Tom Collins remained, and said he'd like to show us what he and the boys had done. We had already seen something of it. The great fields between the lodge and the house, the field through which Janet and I had stumbled on the night when I first met her and Sylvia and Mr. Chown, the field I remembered as tangled with burdock and thistles and ragwort, was now, if not a lawn, at any rate a smooth green expanse which could be scythed. A cow was grazing, and here and there a newly-planted tree was settling down. "Mine, Mrs. Bascombe," Tom explained, referring to the cow. "She keeps the place neat an' she's as 'armless as a child an' I drives 'er to 'er shed every night."

The shed was behind the cottage that Mr. and Mrs. Tiddy had occupied. Now they had both uttered the death rattle, and Tom was installed in the cottage.

Sylvia, I could see, had a tenderness for this old rascal. She said she didn't mind his using the field, and she explained that she was no longer Mrs. Bascombe. Tom Collins shook me by the hand and congratulated me. His hand was small like the rest of him, but it heaved on mine as though my fingers were anchor flukes being wrenched out of an exceptionally sticky bottom.

Now, on this New Year's morning of 1930, he set off down the valley that I remembered as a wilderness of briars and old-man's-beard and every other thing that could climb and twist, bind and strangle. It would never be conquered. It would always put up a fight. But for the moment Collins and the boys had it in check like a small Roman outpost among barbarians. Rotting limbs and fallen rubbish had been hauled away and burned. There were vistas down which you could look, and, what pleased me most, the bed of the tiny stream had been cleaned so that the water flowed clean and singing, with, here and there, a small dam that banked it up and so permitted it to tumble in toy cascades. From the path alongside the stream boulders and tree-roots had been wrenched. You could walk in comfort from one end of the little valley to the other. Half-way down, where there had been a tottering shelter—the one near which, years ago, I had met Janet fled from school—there was a seat with a shingle-roof above it, and you could sit there and listen to the fall of one of the cascades and look at the land rising opposite, lit already here and there with the white and pink and crimson flowers of camellias.

And there we sat, Sylvia between me and Tom Collins, and he cut black twist into his palm and filled his pipe and lit it. He looked around complacently, clearly pleased with his achievement. " It were a devil to do," he said.

" I can well believe it," Sylvia said. " You and the boys have done a good job, Tom. I hope you'll stay on and keep it as it is now. I shouldn't think you'll want five of the boys any more, but take a couple on now and then."

" Aye, that suits me," he said. " An' what about that ole lodge? Them funny things you've got there now tell me they're goin'. If I settled in there I could keep a better eye on the cow. An' that'll save me the rent of the old cottage where I am now."

He had it all worked out, and that's how it was in the years to come. The Redmaynes had told us that they were tired of their isolation, and when they packed up a few weeks later Tom Collins moved in. A collection of ship-models moved in with him ; and, where Mr. Chown had meditated on the Greeks, Tom no doubt meditated on other Odysseys and other Helens.

That morning, he left us sitting there on the seat. It was a fine day, warm and sunny. There was a stir of birds, an occasional pipe of song. The lovely flowers bloomed and the water whispered its way down to the sea. I held Sylvia's hand and thanked God for Fred Byles and Margaret Napier and their sinful commerce in Paris.

CHAPTER TWELVE

1

Sylvia was forty-one when Paul was born. We had not expected children, and Paul had the distinction of having a sister, or at any rate a half-sister, Janet, twenty-four years older than himself. A lot happened in that year. Old Mr. Meagher died, Bob and Janet were married, and Mr. Merriman and Wendy bought the third of their small businesses and went to live at their house overlooking the Pool of London.

It was news of this move that led Mr. Meagher to talk to me about days that were long before my remembering. He was living with a housekeeper at a small place not far from the works on the Great West Road. I had met Bob in town, and he said that the old man had been away from the office for a few weeks, not very well. It would be gracious if I looked in to relieve his boredom. I did so, and found him shockingly changed from the man I knew in Manchester and whom I had seen only once or twice since Meagher Motors was founded. He was sitting, wrapped in shawls, in an easy-chair, complaining of the cold, though a bright fire burned and I found the room stuffy. The place smelled of sickness. A glass and a few bottles stood on a chair at his side. He had grown a beard, and that and his hair were white. His nose was thin and blue, mottled with broken veins, and the hands, that lay on his lap with a pathetic look of being tools laid down for good, were ridged with purple. Propped up on the mantelpiece were three photographs in silver frames. There was Bob in Tank Corps uniform, and that rather shook me because it was so unlike the Bob I now knew. Seeing him so often, I had not noted the changes in him as they modified his face. This was the face of a handsome youth just moving into manhood, touched with laughter, intelligent and frank. Bob was still handsome, but now there was no hint of laughter and there was more than a hint of hardness that could deepen to brutality.

There was a photograph of my father and one of Fred Byles. I had not seen a photograph of him before, and had sometimes wondered whether the painting that hung in my flat was indeed Fred as he had been or a perhaps not very competent painter's glorification of what was before him. But this was Fred all right: the same jaunty face, the same impudent smile twitching the lips, creasing the eyelids. He was in riding clothes. I got up to peer more closely, and Mr. Meagher said: "That's how he used to come to the office. He would go straight into his room and get into a town outfit for going on 'Change."

Yes: my father had told me that.

I said: "No photograph of Mr. Merriman?"

I turned towards him as I spoke, and to my surprise his sick, tired old face suddenly lit with animosity. "That swine!" he shot out.

Well, there was reason for that, I thought. Mr. Merriman, in charge of the office after my father's death, had not treated him well. To me, he had always been kindly and helpful and I had thought him as competent in the business as Mr. Merriman himself. But he had been, as Mr. Merriman would have said, kept in his place, and his place had been adjudged to be a pretty small one. However, I was a little surprised at the vehemence of those two words.

"Well," I said, "he looked after my affairs all right, and I'm glad he's out of the mess that he found himself in when the firm went bust."

I told him then of Mr. Merriman's increasing prosperity. He

252

had heard nothing of it, and seemed unpleased to hear of it now. But he permitted himself to say feebly, leaning forward and spreading his hands to the fire as though ice were in their bones: "I'm glad for Wendy's sake. She was a good girl, and Bob's a fool. But him . . ."

No more came. His face convulsed, and I feared that, bent forward as he was, he would pitch into the fire. I took hold of him gently, eased him back into his chair, and touched a bell-push alongside the chimney-piece. To my relief, it brought the housekeeper. She took in the situation. "His drops," she said, and measured a few from a bottle into a glass. His head was back, his mouth open, and she poured the drops between his lips. "That'll bring him round," she said, "and the nurse'll be here soon. You'd better go now, sir. He ought not to talk so much."

Walking away from the house through the bleak weather, I wished he had talked more. I felt oddly shaken, as though I had been on the verge of a discovery. I made up my mind to visit him again and gently lead him to the point where he had left off. But he had left off for good. He died in his sleep that night.

2

This was in January, and in June Bob and Janet were married. I had expected it to be a quiet affair, but Janet, to my surprise, wanted the whole bag of tricks. The wedding took place in the Chapel of the Savoy, and it was my business to give away the bride who had so unexpectedly become my step-daughter. Ever since the engagement, Bob had been showering money upon her. He had shifted her out of her flat near the *Now* office, where she continued to work, and installed her in a set of rooms on a first floor in Piccadilly. He furnished them splendidly, intending after the marriage to make them his London home as well as hers. I had called upon her there once, about a month before the wedding, and enjoyed the lovely view across the Green Park. She had the company of a personal maid who lived in, and of a cook-housekeeper who came daily. The rooms were spacious, the furnishings splendid. She gave me tea at a pie-frill table in the window, so that we might enjoy the contrast: the Piccadilly traffic, a flowing foreground to the great expanse of trees and grass.

I twitted her about her splendour. "It's Peter Quayne," she said. "You remember him?"

Yes, I remembered the day when I had taken Bob along to Harry Redmayne's poor little exhibition at Quayne's shop, and we had crossed the road to take tea, and there Bob met Janet.

253

"You wouldn't think, would you," she asked demurely, "that Bob was a sentimental man?"

Wouldn't I? You should have read his Coventry letters about Wendy Merriman, I thought. And to her I said: "Sentimental? Bob? I should have thought him as sentimental as a carburettor."

"But he is, you know. As often as he could, he would arrange for us to take tea together in that little shop."

"One of these days he'll buy the place and put a plaque on the façade: 'Here Robert Meagher met his doom.'"

I don't think she liked the gibe, because the rebel in her was comatose. Bob could do no wrong. But she let it go.

"Well, Peter Quayne was sometimes drinking tea there, and Bob took a fancy to him. When it came to furnishing and decorating this place he turned the job over to Peter. Of course, by then Peter was branching out—doing all sorts of things besides pictures."

Yes, I had watched Peter's progress. I thought of Jose Gomm. Peter was doing what Jose would have liked to do; but one man gets shot in the leg and has no money, and another is luckier. That's how it goes.

"I suppose Bob helped Peter when he was launching out?"

"Oh, yes. And now Peter's paid back every bean."

I looked about me. Peter Quayne had certainly done a job. The rose-pink carpet, the rose-pink walls with discreet touches of gold, the pictures not so modern that they would startle Bob, but all the same not what Bob would have bought for himself, the delicious furniture and china. We were drinking out of Rockingham cups.

"I suppose when you're married you'll be saying good-bye to *Now*?"

"Oh, no. I'm still there, and I shall stay there."

"Not content with scalping literary widows who work hard to raise their hungry broods, you take the bread out of some needy woman's mouth."

"Yes," she agreed. "I don't see why all this should make me stop working. Bob likes the idea of my *being* something, and, for that matter, so do I. It's not as though we intended to have children. We don't."

"You'll have Jocelyn and Viola."

"Oh, they're both at school. And after that there'll be the university, and then I suppose there'll be the job of earning their daily bread. So it doesn't look as though I'll have anything but holidays to cope with."

She was twenty-four. I smiled to think how confidently she had arranged the unpredictable vista of her life. I kissed her and wished her happy hunting. "See you on the day," I said. "Mind you're properly dressed."

254

"It's all laid on with a clothes-hire firm," I assured her.
"Even down to the gardenia."

Peter Quayne was Bob's best man. There he was, standing
beside the bridegroom at the altar as I came in to a burst of
flowers and organ-music with Janet on my arm. I had taken a
taxi to the Piccadilly flat, and was more than competently
arrayed, feeling an awful fool from grey topper down to
lavender spats, the spats especially. They made me think of
Mr. Merriman, and Mr. Merriman made me think of Wendy,
who was the last person I should have been thinking of at that
moment. I paid the taxi off, for Bob Meagher had told me
that transport from Piccadilly to the church would be provided.
A lift took me to the first-floor rooms, and there I found Janet's
maid fussing over some finishing touches or other. Janet seemed
all right as she was. I thought of the bare-legged ragamuffin
who had opened the door of Mr. Chown's lodge to me on a
blustery night when I was fifteen. I looked at the tall girl with
ivory silk flowing down her body to lavender shoes, at the
coronet of orange-blossom, the samite translucent veil. Long
lavender gloves hid her arms, and in her hands was a bouquet
of cream roses.

I am a fool, I know. But I couldn't speak for the tears that
rose to my eyes at the sight of that beauty. I bowed, and I took
her hand, and kissed it through the glove. I stood up and
looked at her. We were of equal height. "Am I all right?" she
asked. I nodded, for still I could not speak.

The maid had moved to the window, and now announced excitedly: "They're here!"

I did not know who "they" could be. I had expected that
the transport which Bob had promised would be some such state
chariot as he had sent to take me to my memorable luncheon
now long ago. Janet followed the maid to the window, and I
joined them there.

"That's not for us!" I cried, aghast.

"It is," Janet said simply, as though accustomed to even the
most vulgar and ostentatious of miracles.

It was the sort of coach the Lord Mayor rides in when remembering the ancientry of his office: sparkling glass, gilded scrolls
and knobs and bosses, two white horses, a wigged coachman in
front, silk-stockinged, and a footman just jumping down from
the back. It was a sight, a magnet, a sensation. The flow of
walkers along the pavement stopped and congealed into a staring
mass. A few bobbies appeared as unaccountably as if they had
dropped from a police station in the sky. I trembled at the

thought of going down and getting into the caravel glittering in the sunshine of the June morning.

"Where on earth did Bob get this from?" I demanded. "Buckingham Palace?"

"I shouldn't be surprised. Let's go."

"What do I do? Shower ducats on the lieges?"

"You just get in and take me to church."

It was as simple as that. The policemen parted the crowds, making a line of pavement to the coach door. The footman picked up the hem of Janet's flowing veil, reverently put it upon her knee, banged the door and leapt to his seat. I saw a few press photographers shooting away, and guessed that Bob had arranged for them to be there. "Motor magnate's bride goes to church behind horses," the headlines said that night. Even on his wedding day, Bob could remember Barnum.

Bob and Janet, Sylvia and I, shook hands with the guests at the reception in the Savoy Hotel, and my inconvenient memory recalled the night when Wendy had been there also, wearing overmuch of not very good jewellery, and she had danced with me and Bob with Janet. But there was too great a noise for me to think much of that or anything else. Hordes of Bob's business friends were there, and all the *Now* people, and there was a lot of drinking and a making of fatuous speeches such occasions engender. Bob and Janet soon disappeared to dress for their journey. No glass coach this time. They stepped into one of Meaghers Motors' most elaborate productions which was drawn up at the Embankment entrance of the hotel, and we waved and shouted as they drove away. No one knew where they were going to. Bob told me later that they just shot round the block, came into the hotel again at the Strand entrance, and went to bed.

4

Sylvia looked very beautiful in a fluff of blue tulle and a white hat. She also looked rather tired. "Let's get straight away home," I said.

When we said "home" now we meant the cottage beyond Amersham. We rarely used my flat. It was a convenience if we wanted to sleep in town. My books and the other tools of my tenuous profession had been taken away. Behind the cottage was an old barn that had been neglected all through Sylvia's time there, and for long before that. We had spent a lot of money on it. A covered passage of brick now connected it with the cottage. A great open fireplace was built at one end, and windows were let through on the side which permitted us to look at the land sloping up to the beeches that crowned the chalk

256

hill. The walls were whitewashed. It would be possible, when the time came, to put in a ceiling, and over that could be a bedroom and a big playroom for Paul.

We lived simply. A woman came in daily, and now that Paul was there a nurse was engaged to look after him. The two bedrooms, in which Sylvia and I once slept decorously apart, were all we needed. The nurse and Paul used one, Sylvia and I the other. It was difficult to say why we bothered with anything else, but I sentimentally clung to my place at Trencrom and Sylvia to Penruan. That was a long-cherished dream. She had made it come true; and, like so many dreams, it seemed to have little point when realised. But there it was, connected with too much of the past for her to throw it lightly away.

As we drove home on the day of Janet's wedding, she said: "Paul is three months old. If Janet has a child in nine months' time, which isn't unlikely, it will be a strange thought that my son is only a year older than my grandson."

"It is indeed a strange thought," I agreed, "but like so many thoughts, strange or otherwise, there it is and there's nothing you can do about it."

"What do you think of this wedding? You know Bob better than I do. What are the chances of their being happy?"

"I don't know. Nine times in ten the people coming away from a wedding, as we are doing now, don't see how anything could go wrong. Perhaps two out of the ten couples achieve what is called happiness, though happiness is something I wouldn't like to have to define."

"And what happens to the other eight couples?"

"Two come a hopeless cropper," I dogmatised, "and six get along, compelled by circumstances to hang together, but feeling that somewhere there's been a catch in it."

"I've never met Bob's first wife. What is she like?"

"Oh, people are like this at one time, and like that at another, and all along they're different things to different eyes. That's why you can't make predictions about weddings. Wendy was, to me, an intelligent girl when I first knew her. To Bob, she was a bird of paradise. Now he sees her as a dowdy hen, her father sees her as the comfort of his declining years, and I see her as a bit of a bore."

"How do you see me?"

"As the mother of an entrancing child who fortunately bears a strong resemblance to his father."

"You don't think I'm too old for you?"

"I have not yet detected any signs of senility."

"But when you're seventy, I'll be eighty."

"You are a reliable mathematician. When I'm a hundred you'll be a hundred and ten. I promise that when that moment comes we'll talk this matter over seriously. Perhaps I'll put you into a home for decayed actresses, so that I shall be free to swing a gay leg. Till then, we'll assume that other things count more than a slight disparity in age, and we shall be able to watch Bob and Janet. Their disparity is greater than ours."

"Where are you going to send Paul to school?"

"Naturally to St. Paul's. I want the boy to feel at home."

She began to laugh. "I do love you when you talk nonsense," she said.

"Then your love will have plenty to feed on. I'm not capable of talking much else. Perhaps I should have gone to the London School of Economics with that girl Medea Hopkins."

"My first husband never talked nonsense," she said.

I looked at her sideways, surprised. She had never before mentioned Mr. Bascombe.

"I don't want to hear about your first husband," I said. "I want to know nothing disparaging about the ghost of Bob Meagher's father-in-law."

But nonsense would not put her off now. "I don't know," she said, "how I came to marry him. He did nothing but read *The Financial Times,* ring up his stockbroker and play golf."

"Three harmless preoccupations of many a respected English gentleman," I assured her. "Men have been knighted for less."

"One day he was so glum because he'd been defeated in a golf championship final that I couldn't help laughing at his childishness. I found him in the garden snapping a club across his knee. I told him not to act like a baby. He glared at me, then hit me across the head with the broken end of the club and punched me in the face. I had a black eye."

I put my hand on hers lying on the wheel and stopped her. "Please don't go on. If you had to tell me that, all right; but don't go on. I can reconstruct the beast from this one bone."

We were approaching a roadside tea-garden. "I want to kiss you," she said. "Let's go in here."

There was no one else in the tea-garden. Tea was brought to us in an arbour where we were secluded, and as soon as we were alone she threw her arms round me. I took off my grey topper and laid it on the table, and said: "Kiss me with circumspection. Remember, I'm wearing lavender spats, and gentlemen in lavender spats don't give way to indecorum."

She began to laugh again. "I feel disgustingly passionate," she said, "for a mother just come from her daughter's wedding."

"It is wrong," I agreed, "for daughters to put ideas into their mothers' heads, but it's drawing on towards Paul's bath-time, and it's my turn to bath him to-night. We'd better be going."

"These people will be surprised. We've eaten nothing."

"I'm trying to save them from an even more shattering surprise. Come along."

At home I changed into easy clothes, put a towel round my waist, and had the pleasure of soaping and ducking Paul, with Sylvia and the nurse standing by uttering cries of unnecessary warning and advice. I gave him a final swoosh through the length of the bath and he grinned at me and gurgled. "You see," I said. "He recognises a master-hand."

I dried him tenderly and dabbed powder on him where I thought powder should be, and handed him to the nurse. Sylvia and I stood looking at the mite, smiling at us out of blue eyes. "*You*," I said to her, "have a daughter. *We* have a son."

She had changed out of the wedding finery, and we went arm-in-arm up the swell of land and sat down under the beech trees. It was a glorious evening of full summer, the intense heat mitigated, and air saturated with a scent of hay new-cut. We hadn't a word to say to one another, and we didn't want to kiss. We were content just to be there in the summer night, looking down on the little house where our son was sleeping.

5

Bob Meagher rang us up the next morning. "Where are you speaking from?" I asked.

"The Savoy Hotel."

"I thought that by now you'd be in Antibes, or one of those damn'-fool places."

"No," Bob said. "I'm just sitting here at a window, looking at Old Father Thames rolling along, down to the mighty sea. Janet is combing her hair."

This was gay chat for Bob.

"It's very pretty hair," I said. "I've seen it streaming down to her buttocks."

There was an explosive noise. "Don't reach for your gun," I told him. "It was a long time ago. She'd be about seven or eight, I think. She'd been bathing. It was down at Penruan."

"Oh. Well, I suppose that's all right."

"Of course it's all right. I'm the child's step-father. I rather suspect that you're my son-in-law, but I'm not sure of that. If you are, I'll see that you treat me with proper respect."

"Don't talk rubbish," Bob said. He tired of nonsense quicker than I did. "You get on with your shaving and let me have a word with Sylvia."

"Let me tell you that I was shaved and at my desk at six a.m. As for Mrs. Ledra—yes, you may speak to her."

Sylvia took the receiver. "Yes. Of course you may. . . . Yes. . . . As long as you like. May I speak to Janet?" She talked to Janet; and when that was over she said to me: "Bob wants permission to spend the honeymoon at Penruan. Apparently they'd made no plans at all, and Penruan was a sudden idea of Janet's this morning."

"A nice idea to have," I said, "and nice to have a mother who can gratify it. How long are they staying?"

"It depends on the telephone."

"But there is no telephone. Telephone indeed! What would the Polzeaths have said? *Rien sinon pour Dieu*. I can't imagine them wanting to ring up the Almighty. Can you?"

"No. But Bob wants to be able to ring up his office. He's willing to pay for putting the telephone in. Their first idea was to spend a fortnight down there. That would have taken them to the middle of July. But with a telephone they could stretch it to cover at any rate part of the children's holiday. Even with that, Bob says he'd have to dash up to town now and then. And he wonders if you and I could go down for a fortnight or so when Jocelyn and Viola are there."

"I always thought Bob had a kind heart. But that he should go so far as to allow you to spend a fortnight in your own house —well, I must say that touches me."

"It will be pure joy," she assured me. "Chowny was always chaffing me about wasting my substance on making a museum. Now it will be a family house, a home. And that's what it ought to be."

Bob Meagher got things moving quickly. Within a week there was a telephone at Penruan, and Janet celebrated this by ringing us up at Barn Cottage. "I'm writing you a long letter," she told Sylvia, "to let you know how we're all getting on." When the letter came, it said:

"Darling Mother,—It was wonderful making the journey by road instead of by rail as in the old days. Not that the roads were up to much according to Bob's standards, but he says it will only be a matter of time before common sense is applied to that. I don't know whether you've ever met Brookes, who was with Bob in the Tank Corps and has been with him ever since. I think Daddy has met him if I may call George Ledra so."

"She certainly may not, the horrid little chit," I said. "Daddy, indeed!"

"Be quiet," Sylvia said, and went on reading: "Well, as you don't keep any staff at Penruan, we sent Brookes and his wife a day or two ahead to get things in order. Fortunately Brookes drives a car very well, and he'll be able to nip in and out of Helston in no time to buy food and whatever else may be necessary. I remember making that journey on the step of a policeman's bicycle, with my arms round his blue waist. I was thrilled."

"She would be, the saucy little hussy."

"Be quiet, darling, or I'll stop reading."

"Well, Mummy," the letter went on, "Bob thought that as there was plenty of room in the car, his secretary, Miss Bell, might go along with the Brookeses. She's a dear spectacled thing, old enough to be Bob's mother, devoted to him and wonderfully competent."

"Let's add this up," I said, "and see where we are so far. Brookes, wife and dear old spectacled thing, plus Bob and Janet make five. When the holiday comes, Jocelyn and Viola, with or without horse—and I expect she'll want to ride from Dormers to Penruan—will make seven. You and Paul and I, Daddy, will bring the total to ten. Presumably, we shall be permitted to take Paul's nurse. Eleven."

"Penruan can take eleven and seem empty," Sylvia said.

"I recall that Janet used to bring school friends. Perhaps Viola will bring a team of equestriennes. We shall need grooms."

"We shall manage," she assured me equably. "And now we're coming to the end of the letter."

"I must say that Brookes and his wife did a wonderful job, and we've been immensely comfortable here. The only snag is the cars. Bob does loathe seeing cars parked all night in the open, and, as you know, there's no garage. You used to leave your car lying about anywhere, and the thought of that makes Bob wince. I expect he'll want a good talk with you about this situation when you come, presumably adding your car to our two."

Sylvia read steadily on to the affectionate valediction: "Bob joins me in love to you and Daddy."

I ground my teeth. "What we shall have to do," I said, "is put up a large flickering neon sign near Chowny's old lodge: "Hotel Splendide.""

She flipped my face affectionately with the letter. "Don't worry, Daddy," she said. "It'll come out all right in the end."

6

Tom Collins and the boys had been working like beavers. When I was a youngster seeking a bathing-place on my first morning at Penruan I had made a wide detour in order to reach the sands where I found the bangle. Now the beavers had eaten a way through the timber at the bottom of our little valley and made a usable road, so that one could go in comfort from the house to the water. "That wily old salt won't be happy till he's turned this place into a Lido and ruined you with the wages bill," I warned Sylvia.

She was not perturbed. "All his ideas are good ones," she said. "Look at the stable."

The stable arose like a mushroom. Viola did not ride to Penruan on a horse, but as soon as she arrived she demanded, as of inalienable right, to know where she could hire one. Bob fixed her up with a riding school at Helston. Brookes motored her in every morning after breakfast and brought her back in time for luncheon.

"Waste o' time that be," Tom Collins declared. "Let the maiden hire a pony for the 'ole 'oliday. I'd soon run 'er up a stable in my little ole field."

No one was left in any doubt that the little ole field now belonged to Tom. But Sylvia paid the wages of the boys and the cost of the timber when the stable went up. Brookes was commanded to drive Tom and a few of the boys to the timber-yard. There was no reason why the boys should go except for the ride. They looked like hilarious but rather apprehensive gnomes as they set out, but they found a pub where they dulled their fears, and came home singing. The timber had been chosen, and Tom had commanded that it be in his little old field the next day. Hammers, saws, planes, chisels and hundred-weights of nails came back with the boys on that first journey. There is an old English tradition that if a house can be built and roofed between dusk and dawn the builder has a right to live in it. The stable didn't go up quite so quickly as that. It took two days, manger and all, with Viola superintending down to the last detail. "I'll look after the dung, m'dear," Tom assured her. "That'll help the vegetables in the corner of my little ole field." With no one's permission, the turf had been removed from the "corner" which made a sizeable vegetable garden, fenced in. Whenever Tom presented one of his carefully written labour bills, you would find two items at the end: "Plus vegetables supplied to the house," and "plus time, labour and materials in raising same." He was more than an old man of the sea. He was an old octopus, with tentacles twisting in all directions round Sylvia's neck.

But she didn't mind. She had an affection for the blue-eyed rascal, and said that if he had shot an albatross he wouldn't have written a poem about it. He would have sent in a bill! "To destroying albatross" and "Plus time, labour and material in destroying same." And he'd have taken care, she said, to shoot with the captain's cross-bow, not his own.

The holiday passed happily enough. Most of us wore any old clothes. Only Bob dressed as though a stylish outfitter had dolled him up for a holiday in some smart Riviera resort. Yet he was the one who spent hours every day indoors. The telephone was in a room that Sylvia called "Bob's office," and there, in a blue blazer and white flannel trousers, with a wisp of batik silk knotted carelessly round his neck, he would immure himself with Miss Bell and a typewriter. The morning began with a long talk on the telephone to London, and once during the holiday he commanded two heads of departments to motor down for a conference. Another time, he returned the compliment by spending two days in London. Janet alone was enchanted by these activities of a prince of industry. It was she who, when she heard that two "chiefs" were coming to Cornwall, motored to Helston and returned with a store of assorted wines. "You know, Daddy," she said, aware how the word infuriated me, "when Bob's here you should keep some sort of a cellar. Not that he drinks much himself, but he likes to be a good host when he entertains."

"I see your point," I agreed. "Send the bill to Sylvia. To wines from Helston, £35 10s. To time, labour and materials in procuring same, £5."

"I think," she said to Sylvia, "Daddy's enchanting when he gets annoyed. We must really do some more of it."

Bob's absorption in affairs left a lot of time on her hands, and she spent most of it with Sylvia. They would disappear down the path that the boys had cut and laze for hours in the sun, in and out of the sea. They both looked wondrously fit and attractive, and they drew closer together in sympathy and understanding than I had ever known them.

Viola was engaged with her own equestrian affairs. She had told Tom Collins that the field was excellent for jumping practice, and he, with an eye to his monthly bill, had readily agreed. So now there was a circular course with bars on uprights, and furze hedges, and all the other paraphernalia that she demanded. What with that, and riding the pony about the country, she was a self-centred young person who made no demands on the time of the rest of us.

This left me with Jocelyn, who was fourteen years old; and thinking of those fourteen years gave me a sense of time's passing. This boy, I reminded myself, Wendy's son, Mr. Merriman's grandson, is only a year younger than you were when first you knocked on Mr. Chown's door. And Janet, who answered the knock, is just a year younger than Sylvia was then.

I had seen Sylvia and Janet vanish towards the beach, and Viola in jodhpurs, slapping her leg with a crop, making towards the field, and I was imagining the stammer of the typewriter as Bob and Miss Bell proceeded with their mission of littering the roads with more and more corpses and maimed citizens, when Jocelyn strolled out of the house and joined me on the terrace. Till this holiday, I had not seen him since the day when he was building a dam in the garden at Dormers—the day when I talked with Wendy in the greenhouse and knew that the bonfire which had blazed at Coventry was now a smoulder, a thin smoking, fed by damp domestic rubbish.

He sat down on the granite balustrade, a rather pale boy, brown-haired, brown-eyed, too serious, I thought, for his years. He was wearing an open-necked shirt, khaki shorts and rubber shoes.

"It's a bit of a job," he said unexpectedly, " getting used to these new relationships. What are you—if anything—my uncle?"

"I've never thought that out," I said. " I don't see that I'm a relative at all. I'm just married to your mother's mother. So far as I can see, that makes me a sort of unofficial grandfather. For convenience, you'd better call me Uncle George. Or just George, if you like."

He swung his thin legs and said: "You talk about my mother's mother. But would you call a step-mother a mother? I can't, you know. I've tried, and it sounds silly—not real."

As usual, I tried to dodge the issue. " What about a walk?" I suggested.

"No thank you," he said. " I don't much like walking." And then relentlessly back to his theme. " You see, for a time, when one came home for holidays, there was no mother at all. That was odd enough, especially as Father hasn't much time for us children. Well, it's not so bad for Viola. He's potty about her. Now there comes the time when there's this Janet, and I'm told to call *her* Mother. Well, I just can't, and that's that."

"I don't think she'd mind if you called her Janet," I suggested.

"I don't think that would do," he said gravely. " Of course I know chaps who have step-mothers. They come to school at half-term and the chaps call them Winnie or Madge. It sounds frightfully bogus to me. A mother's a mother when all's said and done, and you don't call your mother Winnie, do you? —not if you're in your right mind. A mother's a mother, and a pal is a pal."

"Couldn't a mother be both?"

"Well, yes, in a way she could," he said judicially: " but a *step*-mother couldn't."

It was no good. I couldn't steer him past the block in his mind.

"And look at Viola," he said ; and for the first time a smile attractively transformed his face. " Not that she's much to look at, though she's not a bad kid. But look at her now."

"What's wrong with her?"

"Well, all this horse business. I can't understand anyone who wants to ride horses and play cricket and get their shins hacked in rugger scrums. That's what makes school a minor hell. However, to come back to this horse business. It was

264

always a bit excessive, but, as I say, she's not a bad kid and one could overlook it. But now she's plumb crazy. It's horse all day. She's never in the house except to scoff a bit of grub and go to sleep. The only surprise to me is that she doesn't share the horse's oats and sleep in the stable. Well, what's she up to?"

I didn't answer, and he answered for himself. " She's just keeping out of the way of this Janet."

At that moment Janet and Sylvia, huddled in bathing wraps, came from the beach. Janet shouted gaily: " Hallo, Jocelyn! We've just come up for our mid-morning coffee. We'll have it here on the terrace. Wait for us. You too, Daddy."

Jocelyn said: " Oh, but I love walking. Uncle George and I are just off." He slipped down from the balustrade, took my arm, and hauled me down, too. " Come on, Uncle George," he said. " It's not good to mooch about all the morning."

As soon as we were out of earshot of the terrace I said: " Damn your eyes, Jocelyn. I wanted that coffee."

For the first time this seemed to establish something between us. He laughed. " The way you said that reminds me of Bill Crake. Bill's always saying ' Damn your eyes, Joss.' I think you'd better call me Joss, seeing that circumstances have united our destinies. Jocelyn is just the sort of idiocy parents *would* think of."

" Who is Bill Crake?"

" Oh, his father's a corn-merchant. Makes millions, I expect, out of adulterating the people's food. We call Bill the corn-crake."

" He's at school with you?"

" Yes, thank God. There's no one else there, among either teachers or taught, who could be honestly included in *homo sapiens*. As for the Boss—that's what we call the headmaster— Bill and I are agreed that he has some way to go before he qualifies as one of the primate apes."

" I should think," I said, " that you and Bill Crake are universally beloved."

We sat down in the heather and looked out to the blue sea. He said: " You were a pretty crafty old bird, marrying the Sylvia woman, seeing that it let you in on this. Quite a place, isn't it?"

I agreed that it was. " I like the house, too. It would be better, of course, if the Bell woman were not there. And the Janet woman, too, if it comes to that. I could have the old codger to myself now and then."

He pondered this for a while, chewing a stem of heather, then said: " I was all set to spend this holiday with Bill Crake. His old man has a house in the South of France. Then this Janet says that if I joined them here instead, that would be a good

265

chance for us all to get to know one another. Well, I ask you, George, what sort of psychology is that?"

I hadn't an answer, and he said: "One thing I like about you is that you don't shine in conversation. You're restful."

"You have conversation enough without my assistance," I assured him.

"That's what Bill Crake says: 'Damn your eyes, Joss. Stop nattering and let a man think.'"

"Does the corncrake think?"

"Not much. He's a man of action. He wants to be a soldier. A pro, I mean, not one of these week-end chaps. But his old man wants him to go in on the corn racket. If this notion persists in the old man's noodle, Bill plans to run away from home when he's finished with our alleged place of learning."

"And what do you plan to do, Joss?"

"I don't know, George. I'm not an outstandingly decisive character. For the moment, seeing that the old codger has taken this irrevocable step, I shall just dree my weird and see how the cat jumps. But there are times when I think of making a huge fortune out of writing murder mystery stories. I suppose that's one of the few jobs where one doesn't have to have practical experience. Or does one?"

7

When Sylvia said that Penruan would absorb our gang and still look empty, she was speaking the truth, and this was especially so when we met for dinner. Most of our meals were eaten in the dining-room ; but in the evening we gathered in the vast hall, with the doors open upon the fading light. I should never forget my first impression of the room: its big oblong table, the chandelier lit with candles, the fire burning in the grate and the brick wall hiding the ruined half of the house. There I had dined with Sylvia and the enigmatic Mr. Chown, and Janet, a wayward child, had flickered up and down the great stairway, moaning her poetic nonsense about the moon and drowning sailors. It would always be there: half a fantasy that my own chaos of spirit had created, half something that had happened. What happens and what the backward-turning imagination creates as having happened are often different things.

Now the room was more imposing, but without fantasy. In place of the brick wall was the new, stuccoed thing that Sylvia had said would look like tapestry, and did. The candles in the chandelier had given place to gold-shaded electric light, and electric light gleamed in sconces over the fireplace, now without flame. We had drawn up our chairs, I remembered, to the

266

flames that were full of salty colours, green and blue and orange, and Sylvia had kissed a boy good night.

The room absorbed us all, swallowed us up. I sat at one end of the table with Janet on my right and Miss Bell on my left. At the other end Sylvia sat with Bob on her right and Viola on her left. In between, where there was room for three or four more on either side, Joss was isolated, looking across to our timid nurse. It was the nurse, Miss Collum, who began the break-up of the party. She rose and asked: " May I go, please? I think I'd better see that Paul's all right."

" Go by all means," Sylvia said, " if you wish. But the boy sleeps like a log. If you'd like to stay for coffee, do."

But Miss Collum went. It wasn't Paul she was worrying about. This was her reading-time, and she would snug down in the bedroom till lights out. She had a profound addiction to books about life in a girls' school, portraying the career of one Mollie. I had seen the pile on her dressing-table: *Mollie at Marchester, Mollie in the Fifth, Mollie's Rebellion, Captain Mollie, Mollie's Miracle*. I had thumbed one of them through and found the dialogue enchanting. " Oh, golly," cried Mollie, " why frowst in bed on such a lovely night? Look—I have a clothes-line that we can tie to the head of the bed and slither down into the orchard." Mollie was full of these mad pranks, and with glad release Miss Collum now went to join the revels in the moonlit orchard.

Miss Bell followed, saying something about " clearing up those few things "; and Bob said: " I don't think you children need coffee, do you?"

Viola didn't. " I'll just go and have a last look at Bonny," she said, but Joss didn't follow her. He said gravely to Bob: " I think I'll join you for once. One must learn sooner or later to hold one's coffee like a gentleman and I may as well begin."

" All right. Coffee for five then on the terrace, Brookes."

Bob lit a cigar and I lit a pipe. The night was very quiet. No one spoke for a time, then Janet said to Jocelyn: " And what have you been doing with yourself all day, darling?"

" D'you know," Joss said thoughtfully, " I think we'd better drop the ' darling ' from the word go. Suppose you came to school for half-term and accidentally called me that. It would ruin my career. Now, as to what I've been doing, I've been moping around thinking of old Corncrake in France."

" But this is a very lovely place to be in," Janet said.

" Too much feminine company," he assured her. " You see, Crake's father is a widower. So there'd have just been the three of us, and we could easily have dropped the old man and got around on our own."

Bob said: " I'm afraid, Jocelyn, you'll have to make do with
267

us. All of us put together may not add up to Crake Junior, but we're doing our best."

"I concede that, sir," Joss said. "You all get full marks there."

Sylvia asked: "Why don't you come and swim with us, Jocelyn?"

"Would you very much mind," he asked, "calling me Joss? George here and I agreed that Jocelyn is rather pompous."

"I prefer Joss myself," Sylvia said. "What about the swimming?" and Janet joined in the invitation. "It would give us a chance to get to know one another better," she said.

Joss took a sip of coffee, put down his cup with deliberation, and asked: "Need we?"

There was a moment of stunned silence. Then Bob, throwing away his cigar, began to start to his feet, looking as though a torrent were about to burst from him. Sylvia, who was sitting next to him, put a hand on his arm, and he subsided.

Through the dusk came Viola, looking an absurd little thing in the jodhpurs she wore from morning to night, the velvet cap, and the pig-tail at her neck. She must herself have been feeling very lonely, and she walked into our silence whose menace she could not help feeling. She looked from one to another of our angry or confused or shocked faces, and then she began to cry. Janet got up and put an arm round her shoulders, but she broke free and ran to Bob, got on to his knee and flung her arms round his neck, her small body shaken by uncontrollable sobbing.

Janet went into the house, keeping her face averted to hide her own tears, and Sylvia went after her. I said quietly to Jocelyn: "You'd better come with me," and we walked away, leaving Bob alone on the terrace, kissing the back of Viola's neck and mumbling endearments.

8

Joss and I walked for a mile or so without speaking, then he sat down on a boulder and said: "This place will be as good as any, George. Fire away." He looked steadily out at the moon-lit water, and waited. I asked: "Why did you say that, Joss?"

"I don't know. It just came."

"But you intended something to come, didn't you? You didn't join us at coffee only for the pleasure of our company."

"Good man," he said. "You have an analytical mind."

I barked at him sharply: "Stop that! Clever-boy talk won't take any rises out of me, you know. I don't like smart alecks."

He didn't answer, and I let the silence go on for a bit, and then said: "Well, what's it all about? I take it your friend Crake didn't ask you to go to France with him?"

"No."

"That's just a story to give you an excuse for being unpleasant to everyone?"

"Yes."

"Well, then. Tell me about it."

There was no need for him to tell me; but I thought it a good idea to let him talk.

"I haven't hidden anything from you, George," he said. "I told you this afternoon. First there was no mother, and then there was Janet."

"I knew your mother well," I said. "I remember her marrying your father. They were pretty hard up in those days. I didn't see much of her after they were married. How did you get on with her?"

He considered this carefully, and then said: "So, so. I was used to her. She fussed more than I liked, and she was a bit dim, but I was used to her."

I have never swallowed the dogma of the psycho-analysts: that all boys love their mothers and hate their fathers, and that with girls it is the other way round. I believed that Joss was speaking the simple truth. He had found Wendy dim, but he was used to her.

I asked him: "How did you get on with your father?"

He hesitated; his glib pseudo-adult speech was deserting him. Then: "I'm a bit afraid of him, but on the whole I like him."

"Why should you be afraid of him?"

"Well, he's always so *right*."

"But that's nonsense, Joss. All you mean is that you respect his opinions."

"Yes; but he's so short about my own."

"I shouldn't worry about that. It would be better if he were a patient man, but he's not. I know that all too well. You can't expect him to be perfect."

"At all events, he's not dim."

"You don't seem to like dim people."

"I certainly don't."

"Perhaps your father doesn't, either."

He saw where that was heading; and I didn't like what I was doing. I was sorry for Wendy. But that was over and done with. It seemed to me a matter of common sense to try and make the best of the situation that now existed. I said frankly: "You know, Joss, some men *do* get tired of their wives; and sometimes wives die and men marry again and children find themselves with step-mothers in that way. It's very hard to expect the children to look at it from any point of view except their own. They've been used to one woman, and now there's

269

another. That can be very upsetting. But there *is* the father's point of view."

"I see that," he agreed rather sadly.

"Tell me, Joss. If you could choose, would you rather be living with your mother without your father, or living with your father without your mother?"

It was a dreadful question to put to a boy, but my short knowledge of Joss made me think that he had something of Bob's ruthless mind. He hesitated for a moment, then said: "Father's more exciting."

I sighed with relief and got up. "It's time we were in bed," I said, and we walked in silence back to the house.

9

Sylvia was standing in the bay of our bedroom window, looking out at the full flood of moonlight on the water. I came up behind her and held her, enjoying the feel of her body through her nightdress. "Well?" she asked. "How did the lion-taming go?"

"Not bad for a first effort. I'm only an amateur."

"I wonder whether Paul will be like Joss?"

"Why should he be?"

"I mean when I'm dead and gone and you're married to a young beautiful blonde."

"I don't like blondes; and anyway I intend to be like those dogs one reads about but never meets. I shall lie on your grave, refuse all food, turn up mournful eyes, and die. Paul will then go to a state orphanage, avoid the perils of a public school and university, and be a credit to his country."

"It sounds as though we ought to take immediate action for Paul's good."

"Yes, but let's go to bed first. We may discover some reason for wishing to remain alive."

We discovered a good reason, and then sat up in the moon-lighted bed. Leaning back on the pillows we could still see the shining path on the waters. The night was at peace, and we were at peace. It was difficult to believe in such a day as that on which we had been out there together, bucketing in a stinking motor-boat, dropping old Hector Chown into his chosen grave. Our heads lay one against the other; we enclosed one another with our arms.

"How did Janet take that little toad's remark?" I asked.

"Janet's got a lot to learn," she said, "and that toad's remark was the beginning of the first lesson. She's had her way with everybody: with her school-teachers, with me, and for that matter with you. She could twist old Chowny round her finger."

I agreed. "In the *Now* office she wanted to be taken as the talented little girl who couldn't do wrong."

"I'm afraid she thought she could walk into Bob's life and that Bob's children would think her a remarkably pleasant change from a dull mamma."

"And so she is, but the children have yet to discover it."

"The most extraordinary thing happened," Sylvia said. "When you had walked that little heathen away to begin your missionary efforts Viola was sobbing in Bob's arms. I don't know why. She hadn't heard what Joss said or seen Bob's horror at the words. But I think the air must have been charged with something horrible. I've got a theory, you know. We've all thought of Viola as someone self-sufficient, having a whale of a time with that horse, and free of commitment to any of us."

I agreed that that was how I had thought of her.

"Well, I believe we've all been wrong. She's a lonely little creature who thinks none of us has any use for her. She sees you and me all over one another and both of us all over Paul. She sees Bob and Janet in their undisguised love; and as for Joss, he's an egocentric little type. So she's been keeping clear of all of us, consoling herself with that dumb brute. Last night her thin bubble burst."

"What was the extraordinary thing that happened?"

"Janet wept in my arms."

Sylvia said that when I had gone away with Joss she and Janet were in the hall. Bob carried Viola in. She was clinging to him, her body racked with almost hysterical crying. Janet laid a hand on her head and said soothingly: "What is it, darling?"

Viola shook her head in unmistakable repudiation and nestled closer to Bob, who carried her upstairs. "And then," Sylvia said, "there it was: Janet's head on my shoulder, and she shaken with sobs as violent as the child's. I felt that I should carry her to bed, but she's a bit heavy for me; so there we stood, with me muttering darlings as Bob was doing to his daughter. It was the first time in my life that Janet had done that to me. I enjoyed it."

"You are a connoisseur of sensations."

"We all seem to have been doing things for the first time. How did you get on as a Dutch uncle?"

I gave her a rough sketch, and she approved. "What now?" she asked.

"I think that Joss has seen the light. At any rate a candle-gleam. We'd better go to sleep. To-morrow may be Waterloo."

"I hope some Blucher will turn up in time."

Blucher was there before the battle started. He took the form of Jose Gomm. While everyone else was asleep Sylvia and I walked down the path that Tom Collins's boys had made. We wore nothing but dressing-gowns and list slippers. The day was still sleepy-eyed as we dropped these and waded into the water that was smoking with milky vapour. We swam, and we ran on the beach, and while we were drying ourselves I said: " Mind that bangle. I don't want to have to rescue it a second time."

She looked at me inquiringly. " I picked it up the first morning I was here," I said. " I had come out early to bathe. You and Janet were before me."

" I remember now. You told me about that long ago, and I had the modesty to forget it."

She blushed. I was amused that, looking back through all those years, she could blush because of that far-off happening.

" It was a moment of exquisite pleasure," I said.

" You horrid little boy."

" It fixed you in my mind as nothing else could have done. You probably owe to that moment the marital bliss you now enjoy."

Her face became grave. " I tremble to think," she said, " how different you find me."

" I don't know whether you are thinking. You certainly are not trembling. And you would be lovely to me if you were trembling like a jelly."

" You adorn your compliments with beautifully poetic images," she said, and laughed.

We kissed, and dried ourselves, and went back along the valley.

On the terrace we found Jose Gomm. He was obviously hurt by not having been forewarned of our coming.

" Quite a crowd of you here, I'm told."

" Yes," I said. " You remember Sylvia's daughter Janet?"

" Indeed I do. I knew her before you did."

An edge of reproach in the voice.

" Well, Janet's married. To the motor-car chap—Bob Meagher. She has two step-children. That makes up the bunch, except for the retinue—assorted ladies-in-waiting, seneschals and varlets."

" Well," Jose said, " don't stand about in this cold morning air. You'd better go and dress. May I stay to breakfast?"

When we came back his stick was tap-tapping on the flag-stones. He was wearing ancient blue tweeds, and, with his tall thinness and Spanish face, he looked distinguished.

"Put you in the proper rig, Jose," I said, "and I can imagine you out there commanding a galleon, bearing down to meet Drake."

He gazed out on the water, now diamond-flashing in the sunlight. "You know," he said, "it was just here that they sighted England. The Lizard was the first land they saw."

"Who was that, sir?" asked Joss, coming up to join us.

"The Spaniards, my boy, sailing their Armada against that heretic witch Queen Elizabeth. There was a house here then, not looking much different from the house behind you. It was new, as so much of this house is new. Can you imagine it, my boy? The people at the windows, looking out and seeing *that*. They'd known for a long time that it was coming, and there it was, and a wonderful sight it must have been. All that canvas."

"I'll bet it didn't help 'em to enjoy their breakfast," Joss said.

Sylvia introduced Jose to Joss, and then Janet came out, fresh and beautiful in primrose linen. She didn't look as though last night's crisis had caused her to lose any sleep. Joss, too, as though that bad indelible moment, irrecoverable now that it had played its part in our small personal history, had never been, ran up to her and said: "Oh, Mother, this is Mr. Gomm. He knows all about the Spanish Armada. It sailed right past here—out there on the water."

He was so excited by his discovery of the actuality of what, till now, he had known only as "history" that he was bursting to share his knowledge. I anxiously watched Janet, who, for all her debonair appearance, must have been still smarting under the moment that Joss's volatile mind had already dismissed. I feared that she might use his approach, his almost unconsciously blurted "Mother" to reciprocate too heavily and too significantly; but she was admirable. She merely half brushed Joss's shoulder with an arm laid for a moment lightly round it, then came up and shook Jose's hand.

"You're incredibly handsome, Jose," she said.

He smiled at her. He had always been affectionately amused by her childish follies. "I'm told," he said, "that you're settling down into staid wifehood."

"Yes," Janet said. "I have a wonderful husband. He does everything for me. He's even provided me with a ready-made family."

Joss, who had sidled up and was gazing admiringly into Jose's lean face, said: "Yes. Me and Viola."

"Oh, there's a Viola, too, is there?"

"Yes, but she's just a kid and likes riding horses."

"Don't you?"

"No. They're so tall."

"What do you like to do?"

"I'd like to sail right out on the water where the Armada went by."

"Well, that's easy enough," Jose said. "I've got a sailing boat, and we could go as soon as we've had breakfast. We could make a day of it—land somewhere and have a picnic. What about you, Sylvia?"

"No. That water has other associations for me besides the Armada."

"Well," Jose urged. "You, Janet? Would you care to come? The sea's as flat as a pond."

Janet looked at Joss, pondering. "I don't want to butt in," she said.

"Oh, nonsense," Jose assured her. "We'll want someone to do the household work—make the picnic fire and all that sort of thing. Don't you think she'd be useful, Joss?"

To my consternation, Joss looked at me, and there was a question in his eyes. I nodded. "Yes," he said. "Do come. Mr. Gomm and I will find lots for you to do. You can take our orders."

"Gladly," Janet said.

Jose punched Joss in the ribs. "Anyone who calls me Mr. Gomm gets thrown overboard. Jose to you."

Joss grinned. "O.K., Cap'n," he said.

11

Breakfast was haphazard at Penruan. You drifted along when you liked. When the four of us went in from the terrace Bob was there with Viola. Joss allowed himself the proud duty of introducing Jose to Bob. "He knows all about the Spanish Armada, and he's going to sail us right over the place where the Armada went."

"Us?" Bob asked.

"The invitation includes me," Janet explained.

He couldn't mistake her look of gratification. Some traces of worry cleared from his own face, and he said: "That's very kind of you, Mr. Gomm. It'll be all right, I suppose?" He had a landsman's distrust of the sea.

Jose reassured him. "We'll embark from outside my pub," he said, "which is a mile or two along the coast. It's a horrible bit of coast, but I've known it since I could crawl, and I know when it's naughty and when it isn't. I promise to return your wife and child safe and sound."

Janet gave Brookes orders about sandwiches and so forth; and an hour later Bob drove the three of them along the bumpy road to the Absolution. As we waved them off Viola shouted:

"Be back soon, Daddy." Then she turned to me and Sylvia and said: "Daddy's going to spend a whole day with me."

I think she had been wondering how, in order to achieve this paradisal day, they would be able to get rid of Janet. Now that the problem had solved itself she looked happier.

"That will be lovely for you," Sylvia said. "What are you going to do?"

"Daddy won't tell me. He says it's going to be a mystery day."

She began to wander towards the stable, and we went with her. She seemed surprised and asked: "Do you like coming with me?"

"Of course we do, you silly little goose," Sylvia said. "We wouldn't come if we didn't. Do you mind?"

Viola said: "Of course I don't, you silly little goose," and looked up, as if startled by her own daring, wondering if she had gone too far.

Sylvia laughed outright, and I said: "How you geese cackle at one another. Can't you give a man a moment's peace?"

"*I* can't," Viola said. "I'm so happy."

"That's only because you'll soon be getting rid of the pair of us," I twitted her.

"Oh, no!" she promised earnestly. "I'll come back and love the two of you."

"You women always come back," I said. "I remember Janet coming back. I was staying down here then with Janet's old grand-uncle, and one day Janet popped up. We thought she was at school hundreds of miles away, and there she was looking a dreadful ragamuffin. She'd run away from school."

"Not Janet! She'd never do a thing like that!"

"Don't you believe it, goose. She was a proper little devil. She'd come from Helston on a policeman's bicycle step."

"Not Janet!" she repeated.

I continued a human build-up of Janet, trying to create some four-dimensional objective thing that the child could look at in place of the subjective creature of her own mind. "Just three cackling geese, that's what you are—you and Sylvia and Janet."

I left it at that, and we went on to the stable where Viola groomed the horse and gave him feed and water. "There," she said, when it was done. "Now he should be all right till I come back from my mystery day. A change won't hurt me."

"And when you're back it won't be a mystery any more," Sylvia said. "You'll know all about it."

"Yes. But it'll be something lovely. I'm sure of that."

"Well, that's how things are. We've got to find out about them, and they often turn out to be lovelier than we expect."

We walked back to the house and overtook Tom Collins

trudging to the kitchen with a basket of vegetables. "There'll only be the staff in to lunch," Sylvia told him.

"What am I to do then," he demanded, "when the men come to start on them ole garages? They're due this morning."

This was news to us, and we told him so. "Mr. Meagher know all about it," he said. "He drawed the plans. I've got 'em in my little ole place. Room for three cars. That'll take a bit off my ole field."

Sylvia looked annoyed, and at that moment Bob drove up, back from the Absolution. She asked him what it was about. He was all sweet reason. "But, Mamma, we agreed in principle that garages were necessary."

"Don't call me Mamma," she said. "If I were your Mamma I'd put you across my knee and take a slipper to you. What do you think this place is—the Great West Road?"

"But we agreed in principle. I was merely relieving you of detail. After all, I'm paying for the garages."

"Who says so? "

"I do."

"You can't order buildings to spring up here just because you're paying for them."

"Do you, in principle, want the garages?"

"If you say 'in principle' again I'll——"

"Do you—in principle?"

"Yes, I suppose I do."

"Very well, then. Collins, you have the plans. When the chaps arrive they can get on with the foundations. Hop in, Viola."

She hopped in, and they were off on a mystery tour.

Sylvia stood there, half-amused, half-outraged. "You see," I said, "how master-minds trample towards their objectives."

"Well, I *do* want the damn' garages," she admitted.

"You may safely entrust your daughter to that man's care, Mamma. She'll never starve. Now, what are we going to do with our own lovely day?"

"I think," she said, "it's time you showed me this white elephant you have at Trencrom."

I had never taken her there. It had been my own place, not to be shared even with Sylvia.

"When I bought it," I told her now, "I had no idea that some day I'd be marrying the owner of this much more monstrous white elephant. I had in mind a retreat for a literary recluse, far from the distractions of women, and that sort of thing."

"That sort of thing? I suppose you mean Paul?"

"Well," I said vaguely, "I had a sort of hermitage in mind. A quiet cell. And here I am, landed in a medieval monstrosity."

"You're all doing your best to be kind and understanding

276

with me this morning—you and Bob and Collins. Well, I'd better let Brookes know that we shan't be in to lunch."

She was surprised by my little house. I had told her it was a peasant's cottage, and so it was outside, squatting there, whitewashed, in its patch of rough untended land, looking out on a wide prospect of fields and wooded hills. But what Jose, Carbis and I had done inside was another matter. She was not only surprised but amused—or so she said—shocked by my vandalism. "At Penruan," she said, "I've done nothing but reconstruct what once was there."

"Nonsense," I said. "Did the Polzeaths have a private electric plant, and modern sanitation, and bathrooms and a telephone? And," I added to rile her, "garages?"

She defended herself. "Those are all things they *would* have had if they had stayed with their house. But no peasant on earth would have turned his cottage into what you have here." She ran her fingers over the wood of my writing table. "But still, it's very nice," she conceded, and gave me a kiss.

"It will do," I said. "When we're tired of splendour we can leave Master Paul and all the accessories of your pretentious Versailles and come here to live like peasants not too near the poverty line. It will be our Petit Trianon."

It was pleasant to walk about the little house, and to talk nonsense, and to lounge in deck-chairs among the gold of the ragwort in the unkempt garden. We motored to Hayle for lunch, and then came back and dozed in the sunshine. I did more than doze: I fell fast asleep. I was awakened by a loud voice shouting: "Can we get a cup of tea here?"

Well, it was one of the things to expect if you lived in what looked like a cottage on a Cornish road. I had done it myself often enough. Sylvia still slept. I stumbled, sleepy-eyed, to my feet and found myself confronting the last man I expected to see in that part of the country. It was Mr. Merriman, but not such a Mr. Merriman as I had seen till now. His pudgy face was inflamed by undigested sunshine, and he was not wearing spats. They were the first things I looked for: I had never before seen him without them. He was wearing flannel bags and heavy, nailed, brown brogues, a thin tussore coat and a white shirt open at the neck. His trousers were held up by a belt that remorselessly divided his stomach into two halves that bulged below and above this equator. A Panama hat completed his disguise.

"Well, Mr. Ledra!" he said, and with equal invention I said: "Well, Mr. Merriman!"

"Wendy's outside," he said.

Sylvia slept on. I steered him away towards the front of the house, and there, sitting on the roadside grass, was Wendy: she, too, surprisingly apparitional. She wore a very short grey flannel skirt, a dark blue blouse, no stockings. Her fat brown legs finished off in white rubber-soled shoes. A rucksack lay beside her. She sprawled to her feet, and Mr. Merriman introduced us as though we had never met before. "My daughter Wendy. Mr. George Ledra."

Mr. George Ledra, my chaotic mind was thinking, who is married to Sylvia Bascombe, mother of Janet, now married to your late husband, Bob Meagher.

I expressed great pleasure at this unforeseen meeting and congratulated them on their looks of rude health.

"We're taking a bit of holiday," Mr. Merriman explained. "Time was, as you know, Mr. Ledra, when I couldn't afford such luxuries. There were your father's affairs, and then there were yours, and then there was my Great Misfortune. But nowadays life's a bit more cheerful, what with Wendy back and one thing and another. We decided to take a holiday. Staying in Hayle and doing a lot of walking."

I apologised for not being able to provide them with tea. This was just a little hide-out of mine, I explained, and I'd only looked in for the day. Otherwise, I'd have had food in the house. I suggested that they should try Mrs. Carbis's cottage, just down the road, and I was asking providence to get them moving in that direction before Sylvia woke up. She woke up and came calling: "Darling! Where are you?"

There had been all that upset at Penruan last night: Viola crying her heart out on Bob's shoulder, Janet on Sylvia's, and Joss morose and defiant. They wanted their mother. Well, here she was, but Sylvia didn't know it; and Wendy didn't know that Sylvia was the mother of the girl who was now Bob's wife. And for that matter, Mr. Merriman did not know, so far as I was aware, that I myself was married. There was nothing else for it: I introduced them with the simplest formula. "This is my wife. This is Mr. Merriman and his daughter Wendy."

I couldn't remember whether I had ever mentioned Mr. Merriman to Sylvia, and I did not know whether Janet had ever told her mother that the woman she was supplanting was named Wendy, and had once been named Merriman. I dithered in the dark, hoping for the best. I had to throw some light on my relationship with this parboiled holiday-maker, and said: "Mr. Merriman was once in cotton. He managed my father's firm and was one of my trustees after my father's death." And while I was saying this I was thinking: "He was there from boyhood. He was there in the days of Fred Byles who spent the firm's money on Margaret Napier and, in Paris, bought her the bangle that I see on your arm."

Sylvia was gracious. She looked warm and a little tousled from sleep, and very beautiful. With the coming of Paul her looks had taken on a tranquillity that made her seem as young as when I first knew her.

278

She shook hands with Mr. Merriman and Wendy and said: "Then you and my husband are *very* old friends."

"And they were hoping that we could give them tea," I said.

"Well, that's not difficult. I want tea myself."

I recalled the cryptic letters Dean Swift used to write to a lady-love—letters in which the word coffee always meant a lot more than it said. "I am longing to take coffee with you." And so now when Sylvia said: "I want to take tea myself," I thought "And oh, how I want to take tea with you! We've never taken tea together in this little house, and you look warm and welcoming."

But it was not to be. She said: "We'll drive into Hayle, and you shall take tea with us there."

The reiteration of the expression maddened and excited me, especially when I recalled how she had wanted to take tea in an arbour when we were going home from Janet's wedding; but all this was brushed aside, and, with Mr. Merriman sitting alongside Sylvia, and Wendy sharing the back seat with me, we drove into Hayle.

There was a house with a garden that looked upon the water, and tea-tables were set out there. At the end of the garden Michaelmas daisies and dahlias of Burgundy red were blooming. While Mr. Merriman and Sylvia were gorging on Cornish cream and strawberry jam and splits, Wendy, who had so often sat with me at Sunday afternoon tea in the days before Coventry, and had looked with me through the window at just such flowers as these blooming in her father's strip of garden, took my arm and said: "I believe those Michaelmas daisies are some of the new Ballards. Come and see."

We wandered along the border, out of ear-shot, and she said, pretending all the time to an interest in the flowers: "So that's Bob's new mother-in-law?"

"Yes," I said. "How do you know?"

"Well, Bob took care to have a splash in the papers, didn't he? That absurd glass coach that you drove to the church in with the bride! Don't you remember what it said underneath? 'The bride, accompanied by Mr. George Ledra, husband of the bride's mother.'"

The blue sky, and the silky sea, and the hum of the last industrious bees ravaging the flowers over which we bent our heads. I waited for something scathing, something harsh or bitter, to tear it all apart. But Wendy said simply: "I congratulate you, George. Is her daughter as beautiful as she is?"

"I'm afraid so."

She sighed. "I was afraid so, too. Well, there it is. But I want you to know this. I'm not broken-hearted."

"I'm sure you're not."

"Well, it wasn't so sure as all that, you know. But I never

279

really took to a posh life. I'm settling down well enough with Father." She peered shortsightedly as a pair of red admirals alighted on the flowers. "But I do miss the children. However, I never tried to keep them. Bob can give them more than I could."

"Does Mr. Merriman know who it is that's tucking into the buns with him now?"

"Oh, yes. And you can see how fascinated he is. But, between you and me, he's only too glad to have me back."

"Then," I murmured, as pompously as a whisper allowed, "all is for the best in the best of all possible worlds."

I straightened up from this preposterous gazing at the flowers and for the first time looked her full in the face, saw the brimming of the unshed tears, and went back to the table, leaving her there to recover her composure before joining us.

CHAPTER THIRTEEN

1

Sylvia never went back to the stage. Our life developed a gentle routine, mostly rural. Neither of us was ambitious. It was about a year after our return from entertaining Bob and Janet at Penruan that a letter came offering her a part in a new play, and she turned it down. "You see, darling," she said, "not quite the best woman's part. Just a safe second-rate role that no one could go far wrong in."

I had never urged her to give up the theatre, but I had always hoped that she would. However, I dutifully admonished her to be sure she wasn't taking a step she would regret. "It may not be the best woman's part. But what about playing it so well that you'd steal the show?"

She smiled and shook her head. "The way to play a secondary part well is to play it in a secondary fashion. Leading ladies don't take kindly to over-brilliant seconds."

We were taking breakfast at Barn Cottage. I refilled her coffee cup. She looked a little down in the mouth, as though dismayed by her own assessment of her worth. The picture of Margaret Napier that had been for so long at Penruan was now hung here, over the mantelpiece. Sylvia looked at it and said: "That's the cause of all the trouble. I don't suppose I should have dreamed of the stage if it hadn't been for her. And she's too much to live up to."

She fiddled with the letter, reading it again, and presently said: "I loathe being second-rate, and I've always been too well-off and self-indulgent to put in the real hard work necessary to make me anything else. At any rate, that's the way I've always explained the situation to myself. I don't think I want to go on bluffing. I'm second-rate—well, just because I'm not first-rate."

She posted her letter of refusal, and it was a rather sad day. Nothing more was said of the matter, and I think her depression was due not so much to giving up a profession which, anyway, she had not practised for a long time as to facing the reality that she had now accepted.

As for me, I had never been ambitious. I had my small unimportant niche and was satisfied with it. Of their sort, my bits and pieces were, in my view, better than most, and I sometimes hoped that one or two of them might eventually find continuing life in some worthwhile anthology. Financially, even with the yearly volumes that Nigel Wendron published, they hardly kept me in hair-cuts.

We settled, then, into a routine. From Sunday to Thursday we were at Barn Cottage. After breakfast on Friday we motored to town, visited friends, saw a show or danced together, spent the night at the flat and on Saturday evening motored back home to avoid the horror of the Metropolitan Sunday.

Our routine broke in 1934. Occasionally, during our visits to town, we asked Janet to take lunch with us. She was continuing to work for *Now*. She and Bob reversed our own pattern of life. They spent most of the week in their Piccadilly apartment and the week-end at Dormers. We had once, on a Friday night, been asked to take dinner with them in Piccadilly. "Our usual thing, you know," Janet said. She had rung me up at the Barn.

"What is so usual about it?" I asked.

"I mean we have a few friends in every Friday."

"Quite informal?"

"Well, perhaps a dinner jacket."

"All right," I promised, "a dinner jacket and lady to match."

"We look forward to seeing you." Just a shade of condescension in that. "Eight for eight-thirty."

It was about twenty past eight when we arrived—the last of the party. A footman—believe it or not—I had thought the breed extinct—a footman with silk stockings and all the other appurtenances of that fantastic brood took my hat and coat, and Janet's maid led Sylvia away to a bedroom. When Sylvia returned she put her mouth to my ear and whispered "Hired for the occasion," nodding towards His Resplendency who threw open the door and announced: "Mr. and Mrs. George Ladders."

There were ten people in the room and Janet swam out from

among them and embraced us one after the other. " So glad you could come, darlings," she said.

She was wearing—if one can wear nothing—what I see the fashion columns call the deepest-plunging neck-line. Her dress was of cream silk, with a crimson rose at the point where the two lines of the plunging V met. She looked radiant, self-possessed, and, I thought, a trifle smug.

"Eh, lass," I said, remembering Lancashire, " this is a bit of a surprise laike. What's goin' on 'ere?"

Her look told me that frivolity was unwelcome. She took an arm of each of us and said: "I think you know most of the people here."

I knew her and Bob and Alcott-Lucas and Hubert Dodge and Peter Quayne. I took a drink and attached myself to Peter, who was accompanied by a striking but over-painted red-head, wearing, inevitably, emerald-green velvet. She held a Siamese cat by a scarlet lead. She was Jane Lancaster. A show of her pictures in Peter's new gallery was at that moment being much talked about, vociferously damned or breathlessly praised. A nude woman suckling a little horned imp at each of three breasts and meanwhile smoking a cigarette in a long jewelled jade holder was a masterpiece or a disgusting perversion according, mainly, to the age of the critic. It was entitled Paternity. Peter left us together and went to speak to Sylvia. A passing waiter presented a tray of drinks. Miss Lancaster selected one and handed it to me. " Vodka," she said huskily. " It's a drink the Russians use."

I thanked her for this information. From the identical cigarette-holder of her famous picture she tapped ash on to the carpet and left me. Her cat looked back at me with withering contempt.

I crossed the room, attracted by the woman Alcott-Lucas was talking to. She was the tallest thing there, male or female. She must have been six foot two or three and as thin as a bean-pole. She was webbed in a film of black that looked as insubstantial as smoke. A vast flower made of purple velvet was on her breast and another right on the crown of her head. Her face was bony and incredibly aristocratic. Her eyes were dead, but gave an impression of having once been vividly alive. It looked as though for her only make-up she used flour, rubbed in hard anywhere. Alcott-Lucas introduced her as Lady Millie Cottingley. Even I knew that the head of the Cottingley family was a duke and that not one of them had a penny, except perhaps Lady Millie herself, who ran an expensive dress shop in Bond Street. As a child she had been painted by Whistler. I knew the picture: a little girl in blue, wistfully lovely. I knew something, too, of Lady Millie's story, for she had shamelessly sold it recently as a serial to a newspaper: the story of youth and middle age when this extinct volcano had been active, attracting and shattering. It was said that there was no one living who had ruined so many marriages. She herself had never married.

"Will you take Lady Millie in?" Janet asked. People were moving towards the dining-room. To take Lady Millie in would be, I thought, some job; but I kept the flippant notion to myself.

Peter Quayne, who was sitting with Sylvia opposite me, was looking about him with satisfaction, as well he might. I had no doubt that this room had cost Bob a pretty penny, and that most of it was in Peter's pocket. It was all Georgian except the pictures. The most ancient picture was by Sickert. It already looked a bit old-fashioned, surrounded by a coruscation of flaming modernity.

Bob sat at the head of the table with Jane Lancaster, whose cat was sniffing without obvious approval at a plate of chopped chicken on the floor beside her chair. At the other end of the table Janet's companion was a man who had been introduced to me as Sir Harry Jones. Or so I thought. But he spelled himself jjones. Fair enough. If you could have ffoulkses why not jjoneses? Or for that matter bbyles or lledras? He was a stiff, stoutish, middle-aged person with a clipped brown moustache. In deference perhaps to his small additional j he wore a monocle. I had heard about him. He was a man who bought property, turned it into something else, and then sold it or rented it. He had bought a duke's town house in one of the squares and turned it into a towering building with offices at the bottom and flats at the top. It looked like a filing-cabinet. And he did all the other things that would naturally go with a man who would do that. He had reached the stage where he was giving away a lot of money. Oxford University had benefited and rewarded him with an LL.D. The sort of man, I thought sourly, that Bob would want to know. He was a dumb sort of brute. Janet was trying to entertain him, but he had little to say and his attention was taken up with Jane Lancaster at the other end of the table. His monocle seemed to be trying to send her heliograph messages. Her jewelled cigarette-holder, fuming at her lips between each course, flashed no response. Lady Millie was regarding him with cynical interest. She kicked my ankle under the table and whispered: "jjones may be a w-wolf, but believe me that's no l-lamb."

Hubert, who was on Lady Millie's right, said: "No, indeed. She's the mistress of one of these Russian princes who escaped being taxi-drivers in Paris. There are a few, you know, who got away with the boodle."

Lady Millie sighed, and looked at Miss Lancaster with sparkless eyes. "Lucky child," she said. "To have it all before her!
283

But I'm not sure about that cat. I used a cheetah. I must try and find time for a word with the girl. What are her origins? Has she any blood?"

Hubert had to admit that she had none. Her father, he said, was a tram-driver in Salford.

Again Lady Millie sighed. "A pity. Blood does help. Not," she conceded magnanimously, "that it's everything."

Sylvia, on the other side of the table, was having heavy weather with Alcott-Lucas. There was a new wine with each course, and his family motto was not *Retro me, Satanas*. The talons of Henry James were deep in his flesh, and his sentences convolved themselves through commas, semi-colons, colons, dashes and brackets to some vision of a far-off full-stop, which he would triumphantly reach and ask: "You see what I—well, shall we say, to put it plainly, mean?"

"Well, roughly, yes," Sylvia would concede, looking anguished.

Peter Quayne came to her rescue. He began to talk about the fun he had had in furnishing these apartments, where he had found this, how he had persuaded Bob to buy that: and Alcott-Lucas settled happily down, dreamy-eyed, toying with a glass and making only one more contribution to Sylvia's entertainment. He touched her arm, looked at her fixedly, and said: "Sempiternal. That's the word. The *mot*, as one might say, *juste*? You see what I mean?"

"Thank you," Sylvia said. "It's the only word," and she turned again to Peter.

The ladies left us and we settled down to port. At any rate, Bob and Sir Harry jjones did, and Bob, I noticed, had drunk virtually nothing during the meal. Peter, Hubert and I declined the port but took Armagnac; and Alcott-Lucas asked to be excused. Would Bob give his apologies to the ladies and have a taxi called for him? I went down with him, and watched the cab depart into the hiss and seethe of Piccadilly. An odd creature. His pen wrote with the terse directness of Swift, but his tongue was another matter.

2

Well, those were the sort of parties Bob and Janet gave on Friday nights. Sylvia and I were not invited to many of them, and whenever we decently could we turned down such invitations as came. I remember a Friday later in that autumn. We had bathed Paul and Miss Collum had taken him off to bed. We ate our early evening meal and then walked through the corridor to the barn. It was a shade on the cold side, and I put

284

a match to the fire—always a heartening event, the first fire of the autumn. I sat down to correct proofs that I had received that morning from Nigel Wendron and Sylvia read a novel. When I had done all I had intended to do that night I put down my work, and she put down her novel and looked across at me and smiled. " Better than Piccadilly? " she asked.

" Much better. Better than a theatre dressing-room? "

She hesitated for a moment. " Yes. On the whole I think yes."

" No regrets? "

She got out of her chair and came and sat on the couch along-side me. " Of course there are regrets," she said. " You can't spend as many years on a job as I did on that one and not feel an itch now and then to be back at it. It's a question, I suppose, of *on the whole*. And on the whole, I'm glad I chose as I did."

I made up the fire, and came back and put an arm round her. Her head went down on my shoulder.

" So am I glad," I told her. " But you do know, don't you, that, if ever you change your mind, you mustn't think of me."

" I shan't change it. There are actresses, you know, who can go on to their dying day, just moving from Juliet to Cleopatra and Portia, and on to Lady Macbeth. There are others who can't. Their last days are a hag-ridden search for something, anything, to put a scrap of lard on to a crust. I don't want that."

I suppose the thought of those actresses who can go on and on was stirring in her mind, for she said, half to herself: " I wish I knew more about my mother."

" There are books on the subject," I reminded her.

" I know. I've read them all. I'd like to write one myself. I'd like to find out *everything* and put it down. Not necessarily for publication."

" I should hope not. If you intrude into my territory I'll start rehearsing Hamlet." I felt a twinge of alarm, and wanted to head her off.

She said: " I remember her red leather box. She used to put all sorts of things into it. When I was a girl I tried one day to open it, but it was locked. I'm sure that if it still exists and I could get hold of it I'd have all I want."

I thought of the day when I sat in my room at Trencrom and opened the red leather box. I had later brought it to London, and it was now in the bank. She would have to be told, I said to myself. She would have to be told sooner or later. She would have to learn who her father was and where he had died.

I said: " If you want the red leather box you can have it. Mr. Chown left it to me, and I have it in the bank."

She rose in amazement, and stood looking down at me, her back to the fire. " How long have you had it? "

"Ever since Chowny died."

"And you've read what's in it?"

"Every word. Most of it's by Chowny himself."

"Why didn't you tell me?"

"You'll know that when you read it. Chowny said I must please myself whether I showed it to you at all."

She paced to and fro, torn between excitement and displeasure at my withholding the secret.

I said: "Mr. Chown loved your mother very much. He naturally didn't want to make her secrets known to everybody."

"But to me—her daughter . . .!"

"You know that Margaret Napier's life was what is kindly called erratic?"

"I know that I'm illegitimate, if that's what you mean."

"Do you want to know who your father was?"

"Who doesn't? Though I must say that at this distance of time the matter seems academic."

"Do you remember how we motored across Dartmoor during our honeymoon, and what happened?"

She shuddered. "I shall remember that brute to my dying day. But what on earth has that . . .?"

I interrupted. "I kicked him. I thought he had escaped from Dartmoor, and it happens that Dartmoor means something horrible in my mind. I've often regretted that kick. But there it was—instinctive—a kick at Dartmoor. At all the abomination your father was compelled to live with. If it had been a warder or the prison governor himself, I think I'd have kicked all the same."

She looked at me, utterly unable to understand.

"Your father," I said, "was a convict at Dartmoor. He died there."

She sank down beside me with a strange little cry. She said nothing. I kept my arms round her, and I think I comforted her. We sat like that before the dying fire for half an hour and then went down the corridor to bed. I went into town the next day, and in the evening left her alone in the barn with the red box. She called me at about ten o'clock. For a time she said nothing about what she had been reading. We had our evening drink and I lit my pipe. "Well, now," she said, patting the couch. I sat down at her side and could feel that the tension of the night before was gone out of her. She said: "I like my father. What a flashy old fool he was! Can't you see him, that day he first met Mother in the park, driving his stylish trotter? Tell me all you know about him."

"I can tell you only what other people have told me. I never met him. Don't forget, he wasn't even my father's partner. He was my grandfather's. All I know is what my father told me *his* father told him."

286

"Well, even that. Tell me."

I dredged my memory for every last crumb. She was insatiable. Everything about him amused her. Even his name.

"Byles! What a name! If Mother had married him I'd have been Sylvia Byles. How would you like to be married to Sylvia Byles? I feel she would be splenetic."

"Well, if it comes to that, you *are* Sylvia Byles, apart from a few formalities of registration. And I can't say that it changes my feeling that you are wonderful. Oddly enough, I've often had a sneaking satisfaction at being married to old Fred's daughter. I've looked at his picture often enough and thought: 'Well, you old rascal! So you're my father-in-law.'"

"We must have his picture here," she said. "We must hang him up alongside Mother."

I said that I should like to do that.

"D'you know what I feel about him? He was as innocent as a lamb."

This seemed to me to be going a bit too far. "After all, he was tried, he had no defence, and he was found guilty. I shudder at the thought of his going to Dartmoor, but the law is strict about commercial probity."

"I don't care a damn what the law is strict about," she said. "I can feel Fred in my bones."

"So you should. I suppose he's there."

"And I *know* the sort of man he was. He was a child, and what he wanted he took. He didn't ask whose it was."

"Life can't be lived like that."

"Can't it? What about you? That morning when you spied on me and Janet——"

"I didn't spy. You just happened to be there. Fortunately."

"When you spied on me and Janet," she went on relentlessly, "you saw my bracelet on the beach and you wanted it. So you picked it up and kept it. It's the sort of thing a child would do."

"Fred was no child."

"That's all you know about him. I should say he was. He was a silly innocent, in the old meaning of those words."

"You should have played Portia at the Old Bailey. A Daniel come to judgment. You'd soon have found out how much ice is cut by sentimental notions."

But I couldn't deflect her. Fred had found an advocate. I had dreaded the moment when, if ever, I revealed to her the secret of her parentage. But so far from being shocked or even depressed she was exhilarated, and I remembered that her mother was a Chown, though she had called herself Napier, and the Chown women, so far as I had read about them, had delighted in scintillating scallywags.

She twisted the bangle on her wrist. "And to think," she

said, "that it was Fred's gift to my mother that you found and treasured as a memento of me! Tell me all about that."

"You know all about that."

"But tell me."

"I was a young innocent," I teased her, "who'd never had anything to do with women before, and you were indiscreet enough to kiss me. What more is there to say?"

"Quite a lot. I could have had you up at the Old Bailey, charged with stealing a valuable Fabergé jewel."

"Why didn't you?"

"Well, I knew nothing about it till I read Chowny's screed. At the time he told me some cock-and-bull story. Did you love me—even then?"

"We're an old married couple," I told her, "with a son and heir, a daughter who entertains Siamese cats in Piccadilly, and a son-in-law who is a master industrialist. It is high time we forgot the sentimentalities of our youth and went to bed."

"What a good idea," she said.

3

In the spring of 1935 I rang up the Piccadilly apartment and asked if I might speak to Mrs. Meagher. I recognised Brookes's voice as he replied pompously: Her ladyship is not at home. Who is speaking, please?"

"O.K., Brookes," I said, "you can come off it. It's only her ladyship's step-father. I've read the morning papers, too."

He spoke more humanly. "Oh, it's you, sir. Her ladyship's gone to the *Now* office, as per usual."

I rang up *Now* and spoke to her. "Congratulations, Janet, from me and your mother."

"Thank you, George. How is Mother?"

"She's here, a yard from me, dandling your minute brother upon her knee, and looking like a madonna in rude health. Thank you for having such a mother."

"Not at all. I'm always glad to do what I can."

"Are you going to carry on with your job at *Now*?"

"Why not?"

"I just wondered."

"Of course I shall carry on. Haven't you noticed? Fleet Street is full of Debrett-spawn."

"How is Bob feeling about all this?"

"Well, I hope he's a bit calmer now. He was furious when he left home this morning. It was that awful Merriman person. He had the nerve to ring up and offer congratulations."

I put down the receiver and told Sylvia of Mr. Merriman's

telephone call. She didn't know much about Mr. Merriman, except that Janet had supplanted his daughter and that we had once met him and Wendy at Hayle.

"Why should Bob be so angry as all that?" she asked. "I suppose the poor man meant well."

I said that I doubted it, and told her all that I knew about Mr. Merriman. "He loathed Bob, and did all that he could to prevent Wendy from marrying him." I told her, too, on the other side, that Mr. Merriman had been a good steward so far as I was concerned, and I spoke of the twinges of conscience I sometimes felt because he had bought the business from me, thus enriching me and, in the short run, beggaring himself. "That's why I set him up in the tobacconist's shop in Camden Town."

"You've never told me anything about that."

"No; that's George Ledra all over: doing good by stealth. On the judgment day you'll be surprised when my record is read to the assembled host; and there I'll be, modestly, with down-turned eyes, scraping a toe on the golden pavement. It may all help to get *you* in."

"Is Mr. Merriman still in Camden Town?"

It happened that a few months ago I had made a call there, to see how he and Wendy were faring. I found a manager running the shop, which looked smart compared with what I had once known it to be; and he told me where I should find Mr. Merriman. I took a taxi there—it was at Notting Hill Gate—and to my surprise found an ironmonger's shop, with Mr. Merriman behind the counter. Wendy came down from the rooms over the shop and joined us. Mr. Merriman was full of confidence, and explained the scheme he had formed of moving from one small business to another, establishing it, and then moving on: a scheme which, as I have already said, he carried through with pertinacity and success. Wendy insisted on my going upstairs and taking tea. Her father remained to look after the shop. She was all gratitude to me and admiration for her father who had, she explained, registered a private company, Merriman Enterprises, with him and her as directors. She proudly showed me the printed notepaper with her name on it, and the typewriter on which she dealt with correspondence. I kept her glued to this subject, fearing a return to the more personal note that had embarrassed me in the tea-garden at Hayle: but I needn't have worried. She didn't mention Bob and the children then or on any later occasion. There was just one side-reference when I was wishing them good-bye and good luck. "It's so good," she said, "to be useful again to someone—to be *doing* something."

I now told Sylvia of all this, and she kissed me and said: "So long as nothing worse than this comes up out of your hidden life

I shan't complain. I feel sorry for that girl. I thought they were a pathetic-looking pair when we met them at Trencrom. You should ask them out here to tea some day."

"Darling! They'd bore you to tears."

"You used to go to tea with them in Manchester."

"Well——"

"Well, why not return their hospitality?"

"I know very well why the sly old dog used to ask me to tea. He thought I'd be a useful husband for Wendy. That's one reason why he was hopping mad when she bunked to Coventry with Bob."

"Darling—to please me," she wheedled.

"I don't see much pleasure in it, for you or anybody else."

"He knew Fred Byles."

"Good lord! He was only a junior clerk about the office in those days."

"But he may remember *something*."

"Oh, you've got Fred Byles on the brain. Very well, then. We'll have to ruin a Sunday afternoon, I suppose "

4

Sir Robert and Lady Meagher did not spare time from their important lives to visit me and Sylvia at the Barn until the summer of that year. We didn't mind. We were content with one another—quite scandalously and anti-socially so we learned from Janet when at last they did look us up. Jocelyn and Viola would both soon be home for the long summer holiday, and Bob had rung up to suggest they should spend it with us. "God knows when I last had a holiday," he said, "and there's a chance now to combine one with business. I want to be away for a couple of months, giving the markets a look over in South America. I've had a word with J. Wilson Dodge, and he says he can arrange for Janet to take time off to come with me."

"And since when has Mr. Wilson Dodge been editor of *Now*?"

Bob laughed easily. "He's not editor, but as you very well know the paper still isn't paying its way, and Dodge controls the money-strings. He'll manage it all right."

"And since when has he been interested in whether Janet has a holiday or not?"

"He doesn't give two hoots for Janet, but he wants to oblige me."

"You moneyed boys hang together, eh?"

"That's about it."

So there it was, and would we look after the children during the holidays and see them back to school when it was over?

290

We agreed to do this, and Sylvia and I felt that the long-delayed visit to the Barn was at last arranged in order that they might look us over and decide whether we and our environment were up to scratch for so important a commission.

They must have felt reassured, especially when we said that for part of the time we would take the children down to Penruan.

"Send Jocelyn out a lot with that Jose Gomm chap," Bob said. "Toughen him up a bit. The young beggar seems to live with his nose stuck in a book."

"I suppose," I teased him, "that we can rely on Viola living with her behind stuck to a horse?"

"Girls don't matter so much," Bob said. "They get married, and you can count on me to see that she gets married to the right person."

Well, I thought, that was Mr. Merriman's idea, too; but Wendy had a different idea, and we know what came of that. But I said nothing of this to Bob, who really was becoming a bit too God Almighty and omniscient for me.

We weren't very well set up for entertaining at the Barn, so we motored them out to a hotel for lunch, and then we came back and climbed the hill behind the cottage and sat in the welcome shade of the beeches. It was a sweltering day, a-drone with high summer. I don't know how it started, but Janet got on to the theme of Hitler and Mussolini. Sylvia and I agreed that they were a couple of outsize warts, and then Bob, who had been lying full-length on the grass, suddenly sat up, looking angry. He said to Janet: "I read quite enough of that sort of thing in your rag, without having it buzzing about me when I'm looking for an hour or two of quiet."

Janet let the matter drop. "Very well," she said. "I know you admire the pair of them, but we've agreed to differ. So let's say no more about it."

Bob's anger subsided. He patted her hand and said: "That's a good girl." Then he lay back again with a handkerchief over his face. Sylvia and I exchanged glances over his recumbent body. We didn't need to put it into words, but we were saying to one another that we had witnessed something very dangerous indeed.

They wanted to be back in time for dinner at Dormers, where J. Wilson Dodge was joining them and staying for the night. They agreed to entrust the children to us, and when the women were out of the room Bob said to me confidentially: "It won't hurt Janet to have a good stretch away from her poisonous friends."

It was two years since we had seen Joss and Viola—two years at a changeful time of life. Joss was sixteen and Viola fourteen, and we thought them both improved. Used as we were to our two-year-old Paul, we found them almost adult. They were both at Sherborne, where there is a girls' school and a boys' school, and we arranged with them to travel on their own to Gwinear Road, near which station long ago Tiddy had met me with his pony-trap and driven me through the wartime dark to Penruan. There we would meet them with the car. We had decided not to spend any part of the holiday at the Barn, and we travelled down to Cornwall a week ahead of the children. We had hoped that Bob would lend us Brookes and his wife, but he decided that they needed a holiday. They were to go to the South of France at Bob's expense for a fortnight, and then be back at Dormers to look after a wealthy American business man who wanted a *pied à terre* in the English countryside while making a long holiday-cum-business visit like Bob's own visit to South America. " You can't neglect the opportunity to do a good turn to a man as rich as that," Bob said frankly.

When I told Sylvia of this she laughed. "Well," she said, "I'm afraid I never did much about Janet's future, and I shan't blame Bob for leaving no stone unturned to make it happy and glorious. As for us, we'll have to try and rustle up some village crones. I'll write to Jose about it."

"We'll be able to park Paul on Miss Collum and more or less look after Viola and Joss ourselves."

"I hope they'll need no looking after. They're old enough now to look after themselves."

And so it turned out to be. We met them at Gwinear Road, and as I lugged Joss's suitcase down from the rack he said: "Please allow me to do that, sir." Every inch the well-mannered public school boy. Long grey flannel bags, and the school blazer, tie and cap. He shook hands gravely. As I insisted on holding to the suitcase, he took Viola's; and, looking at Viola, I thought: "I hope that Sylvia and I have a daughter." We never did.

I wondered where she got her looks from—this daughter of Bob and Wendy, this granddaughter of Mr. Merriman and of old Mr. Meagher. None of them accounted for her. She was not a beauty, but there was about her something of style, of grave quality, that I found moving in one so young. She put up her face for Sylvia to kiss and said: "Thank you for inviting us." Her voice had the beauty that her face lacked.

As we drove to Penruan I told them of the first time that I

had come that way, behind a pony, in the pitch dark. "I suppose you'd prefer to do it *on* a pony," I said to Viola. "Would you like us to hire one for the holidays?"

"It's very kind of you to think of that," she said. "But no, thank you. I don't ride any more."

"Oh, dear!" I chaffed her. "I thought you were a proper Amazon who would go on riding bigger and bigger horses all through life."

"Oh, no," she explained, as though I were the child, and she the adult. "You can't count on what you'll do all through life. All sorts of things can come along to make you change, and sometimes you change without even knowing why. That's how it was this time. I just didn't want to ride any more."

"It's all piano now, sir," Joss said from the back seat; and Viola confirmed this. "I do spend a lot of time playing," she said. "But I'm afraid I made rather a late start to be really good."

"Bless my soul! How old are you?"

"Fourteen."

"Well, there's a life before you."

"Yes, but look at all the wasted years behind me."

She sighed with such comic gravity that I had to laugh.

"Mozart was touring Europe when he was six," she said.

"How do you know?"

"Well, naturally, I read the lives of the composers."

"He was buried in a pauper's grave," I told her.

Then she said something that did make me sit up. "No. It was a king's grave. And how many sumptuous graves contain paupers."

Joss said: "She'll go on if you encourage her, sir."

But I didn't want to. What on earth, I was thinking, have Bob and Wendy managed to create between them?

6

The next morning I rang up Jose and said that Joss and I would be coming over to see him. Joss had shed his school clothes and was wearing nothing but khaki shorts and rubber shoes. "It's very good of you to put up with us, sir," he said as we dawdled through the hot morning. I told him that any further remarks addressed to sir would be ignored. He was shy of calling me George, so we compromised on Uncle George, and Sylvia became Aunt Sylvia. That was as good as anything, for it would have been difficult to establish what, in fact, our relationship to the children was, if there was any relationship at all.

Bob had rung up that morning from Dormers to tell the

children that he and Janet were just about to leave for Southampton and to wish them a happy holiday. "He's taking the
car," Joss said now. "I asked him if he couldn't hire a car in
South America, and he said not a car like the Meagher Panther.
It would be an advertisement for the firm."

It sounded as though he didn't think much of the idea, but it
wasn't my business to probe. After a moment he said: "A bit
ostentatious, I thought. Still, people have always been like that,
haven't they? I suppose the chap dashing about behind a four-
in-hand thought himself a cut above the man in a Victoria, who
thought himself superior to the tradesman in his trap. Isn't it
odd how people *must* have something to swank about? Something that isn't *themselves*?"

"It may *be* themselves," I told him. "Or at any rate an
image of what they want themselves to be."

"Well, I don't want to be a Meagher Panther," he said, and
we left it at that.

Jose was looking well, contained, calm, in a way that few
people in London seemed to be. We sat on a bench outside the
Absolution and he gave me a beer and Joss a glass of lemonade.
We looked out at the calm sea, saying nothing for a time. And
that was an agreeable change, too. People who always want to
talk, and expect me to talk, bore me intolerably. We watched
the lazy moving water, blue and white and purple, and the gulls
loafing upon the air, and a couple of gannets, far out, quartering
the sky with incredible speed before dropping like projectiles
that disappeared in the upthrown fountains of their impact.
The vicious reefs showed their backs, reminders of other times,
other manners.

I asked Jose about his Helston antiques shop.

"It survives," he said. "That's about all you can say for it.
The Missus looks after it, and I run the pub. I'm at your
service, Joss, in closing hours."

So we came to the object of the visit, and Joss and Jose
made their plans. Jose inquired about Viola, and I said: "I
don't suppose you know anyone who could lend her a grand
piano?"

Jose grinned, and said to Joss: "George is always trying to
catch me out. Now he wants a bit of linenfold panelling, now a
Georgian wine-cooler, and so forth. He always hopes I won't
be able to find it, but I always do. Don't I, George?"

"You haven't done badly so far," I assured him.

"Well, I can put you on to the best grand piano in Cornwall,"
he said.

He was in no hurry. He renewed our drinks, and we lit our
pipes and smoked for a while, and then he said: "Ever heard
of Eliza Hartman?"

Even I, utterly uneducated in music, had done that.

" She lives not far from here—I mean literally from this spot. I could throw a stone now into her front garden. Sometimes I go along there and play the fiddle."

Well, that was another thing I hadn't known about. " I nearly drive her mad," Jose said. " But I suppose I'm better than nothing."

Eliza Hartman was a concert pianist, never of the first class, " but so good," Jose said, " that you always wondered why. But there it was: she could clear all the obstacles except the last one. However, she managed to live by it, and the critics took her seriously."

She was nearly sixty years old, and, despite the increasing infestation of the roads by motor cars, continued to go about on a bicycle. She was knocked down by a car in Kensington High Street and bones in her right wrist were broken. That was the end of her concert career. " She still plays," Jose said, " but only to herself—and to me. There she goes—look."

The village was nothing but a street tucked into the concave hillside, and out of one of the geranium-covered cottages, a few doors down from the Absolution, came a rather dumpy, not impressive-looking woman: squat and dark and carelessly dressed in black. She saw us, and waved, and then took the path that climbed the hill behind the village.

" Regular as clockwork," Jose said. " She's off on the morning constitutional."

Like Mr. Chown, Miss Hartman had discovered the village long ago ; and now, since her old career was broken, she made the break a clean one, and came to settle here. " You know what those cottages are," Jose said, " just two up and two down. She had to knock the whole ground floor into one room to get her grand piano in. She sleeps up above and eats next door with old Mother Penhaligon. She won't cook. Sometimes she looks in at the Absolution and has a glass of beer with the boys and damns their climate for what it does to her piano-wires. She has a tuner in every week from Helston."

I told him about Viola. " There's no piano at Penruan," I said.

" I know. And hardly a book since Mr. Chown went below. The place is barbarous."

But I knew he was proud of it, as he had reason to be, and I asked him to come over and take luncheon with us some day. He promised to do so, and to bring Miss Hartman with him. Then he and Joss got down to more serious matters, and I walked away and left them to arrange what their programme should be, wind, weather and circumstances permitting.

Thus, almost casually, I fixed the pattern of the holiday. A lucky fluke drew Viola and Miss Hartman together. The old girl had written a few pieces for the pianoforte, and Viola's music-teacher at school had used them in the course of her lessons. I don't suppose they amounted to much, but I do know how the heart of a young would-be writer flutters on meeting someone established and recognised. Often he outgrows this phase of worship, but it is a salutary and important phase all the same. God help youth without heroes. So it was that Viola flew to Miss Hartman like a chip of iron to a magnet; and the old girl, lonely and perhaps a little bitter, loved the child and was pleased with the adulation. She was not rich, but she was well enough off to be self-supporting, and she scorned the delicately hinted idea of payment. I was amused to see how, even in non-musical matters, Viola followed Miss Hartman's example. Morning was the time for exercise, and so she dutifully swam and walked. After lunch she walked over to the village and was back in time for dinner. Then she went off to her bedroom and read the books that Eliza Hartman had lent her. Thus Sylvia and I saw little of her, but were content, for the child lived in a cloud of excited happiness. This happiness overflowed into her relationships with us, but we knew that we were merely recipients of emotions nourished when she was not with us.

7

Remembering Jose's remarks that all Miss Hartman's doings were timed by clockwork, I walked over to the village one morning and was strolling along the little street when her door opened and she came hatless over the threshold. She was always hatless, exposing an uncared-for mop of iron-grey hair. Her eyes were black, and could sparkle when she was excited. We stood talking for a moment, and then I said: "Well, I mustn't hold you up."

As I hoped she would, she said: "Oh, rules are not all that sacred. Come in and have a look at my place."

Even now that two rooms were one it wasn't a big place. There was a Steinway grand, and one wall was shelved all over to take a library of gramophone records. A gramophone with a great flowering lily of a horn stood on a table. She had put in a new open fireplace built of granite. It was like a bit of Stonehenge: three monoliths, one, to serve as a mantelpiece, lying on top of the other, upright, two. On this were a few signed photographs of musicians, including, I noticed, Paderewski. The walls were distempered a pale pleasant green, and there were no pictures. There was a fine carpet, and a roomy couch stood in front of the great fireplace. I thought it a good livable room.

" Sit down," she said. " I'll make you some coffee. It's the only thing I can cook."

We sat side by side on the couch, watching the brown seethe of the coffee in the glass bowl of the machine.

" I'm glad to have this chance to thank you," she said. She filled my cup.

" Whatever for?"

" For your books. Fill your pipe, if you'd like to. I'll join you."

She expertly fingered tobacco into a pipe and lit it. We smoked and sipped companionably. But I felt uncomfortable. So, apparently, did she, for she said after a moment: " I wanted to thank you when you gave me lunch the other day, but I couldn't bring myself to do it."

" Well, don't bother now. But thank you for what you said."

" My eyes are not what they used to be," she said. " When that damned motor car knocked me down it not only broke my wrist but gave me an awful smack in the head. My sight has been odd ever since, but thank God I know my way about a keyboard without it. But I've been advised not to do much reading. However, your things are so short. I treat myself to one most nights before going to sleep. Some of 'em I've read again and again. They're like little blessed madrigals."

I blushed, and managed a few more words of thanks.

She refilled the coffee cups, and said: " Really, it's because of you that I took Viola on."

" Please don't ever let her think that. The child needs loving for the sake of her own bright eyes."

" You needn't have said that. I'm not completely daft."

I asked her whether it was permitted to inquire about Viola's talent or lack of it.

She blew out a thin reed of smoke, considering. " She could come to something," she said. " Whether she will, of course, is another matter. At the moment she's all woolly enthusiasm. It's a necessary stage. Discipline is something else."

" I suppose you're thinking of what's going to happen when this holiday is over?"

" Yes, I am. Of course, she ought not to go back to a school where music is just incidental. By the time her schooling is over she'd probably be playing *Annie Laurie* faultlessly."

" Unfortunately I'm not her father."

" I know all about her father," she said with a wry grin. " It was a damned Meagher car that knocked me over. I ought to let the child stew in the parental juice."

She got up. " Well, I'd better take what's left of my walk."

We parted outside the door. She put a hand on my arm and said: " If you have any influence at all with Viola's father, get him to have the child prepared for the College of Music. It could be worthwhile."

On the beach Tom Collins was preparing to go aboard Jose's cutter with Joss. Tom was an expert in the art of justifying his existence. There was his little ole vegetable garden, full of stuff that prospered without much need of oversight. There had been the garages at which he fussed about, doing nothing but give unnecessary orders to men who knew their jobs. There had been Viola's pony, which she had fed and groomed herself; and there was his little ole cow that Sylvia had learned to milk, and often did. All of it added up to little enough, but Tom Collins could feign a harassed overworked existence better than the next man; and now he had seized the chance to fasten himself to Joss and spend hours loafing about on the radiant summer sea and picnicking on the beaches. " Don't 'e worry about me, midear," he would say to Sylvia. " I'll fit it all in some'ow, if it kills me. Just you milk that little old cow if I'm not back. I'll see to the rest."

She encouraged him, and so did I, because he was good for Joss. Jose couldn't often get away, and Tom knew, and loved to impart, a range of sailing lore beyond Jose's reach. He had spent a life in sailing ships, and he was a martinet. Joss one day had spliced two ends of rope together, practising what Tom had taught him, and the old boy took the ends and pulled the whole thing apart. " A fine old splice that be," he said contemptuously. " If you 'anged a mutineer to the yard-arm with a rope spliced like that, down 'e'd come and break his danged leg. You can't treat a man like that. 'E'd go limpin' all 'is life."

And what's more, he had voyaged, he had seen the world. He enlarged Joss's horizon, though I sometimes prayed that heaven would seal his lips concerning the more recondite phases of his time ashore.

Well, there they were, stowing the grub-basket into the forepeak, Joss, as usual, wearing little more than a fig-leaf, Tom neat in navy blue with a white sheathing to his peaked cap. The cutter had no auxiliary engine, and going out through the reefs was a tricky job at the best of times. The mains'l ran up, and I was glad to see that it was Tom who took the tiller, for that part of the voyage at all events. Away out over the spot where, in different weather from this, we had dumped old Chowny, I saw the jib and foresail shake free, and off they went: another day, I hoped, that Joss would relive for many a month to come.

I turned into the Absolution, had a drink with Jose, and strolled home to lunch, well content.

On the warm stones of the terrace a mattress was laid, with a bit of cover over it to ward off the worst of the heat while Paul slept. So far, anxiously though I watched for them, I had not discerned in him any talents save this talent for sleep. In that, he was profoundly accomplished. Every morning and every afternoon he would flop down on the mattress and pass into oblivion, and at six, when he was put to bed, he would make a real go of it, sleeping till seven the next morning.

I had met Viola coming home from her determined morning exercise, a wet bathing-dress and damp towel slung over her shoulder, and we paused together, looking down at the child. He was just awaking. His blue eyes opened. His rosy fists rubbed them, and, bathed in innocence as though he had just come into the world, he smiled and looked at the day. "Light!" he announced, and struggled to his feet, a stark-naked two-year-old thing of fat creases, dimples, pink rotundities. He could stagger about, fall, grin, heave himself up, stagger and fall again. All wonderful in my eyes.

Viola picked him up and kissed him and handed him to Miss Collum, who was coming out of the house. Viola and I lingered on the terrace, looking at the white sails of Jose's cutter trying to trap a little wind. I asked her: "Had a good morning?"

"Oh, lovely, lovely! I feel as though the sun will never stop shining."

"Any schemes for this afternoon?" I teased her.

But she was too serious to take things teasingly. "Why, Uncle George, you *know* what I shall be doing."

I was so full of joy for her and for Joss, for myself and all of us, that I kissed her. She looked surprised, and asked: "Are you pleased with me?"

I wished the world could stay like that.

Summer.

Noon.

Happiness.

There was a time when you watched people sail west, and you didn't know when you would hear from them again. It might be a week or more before they could even beat past the Lizard. Now an aeroplane hops them over the Atlantic in a day; they scribble an air-mail letter, and you are in touch again more quickly than if, a century ago, they had taken the road to Dover.

Bob and Janet hadn't flown, but they had gone in a swift steamer; they had written air-mail letters, and here they were delivered by a slummocky girl who wore a sailor's peaked cap to give an official air to her otherwise unconvincing self. She handed them to us through the car window just as we were about to set off. "From furrin parts," she said.

But nothing was furrin now. We were all too ghastly familiar, piled on top of one another, jostling one another, growsing and snarling at one another, trying to push one another off the merry-go-round that whizzed ever more quickly. Less and less time to stand and stare, whether at the stars or the daisies.

The writing showed that mine was from Bob, Sylvia's from Janet. "We'll read them when we get there," Sylvia said.

We were going to Trencrom. The holiday, thanks to Jose, Tom Collins and Miss Hartman, was leaving us a lot of time to be together. And delightful though we found the children, we liked best these times when we could do as we pleased: talk or be silent, make love or just lie on the ground and look at the clouds and grab and fondle a handful of grass or heather, feeling the wonder of these tender or tough earth-created simplicities. We were rapturously in love. I hadn't to bother even about my little weekly piece for *Now*. I always kept a small store to see me through such times as these.

We stopped in Helston to visit Jose's shop, for we liked to buy something there now and again, and this time we were seeking a gift for Miss Hartman. Furniture was out of the question: her house was too small: but we found a gorgeously barbaric necklace of semi-precious stones, with, for pendant, a rough cabochon emerald. Then we went on to Trencrom. We had brought tea in thermos flasks and a few meringues, and, leaving the house unvisited, we toiled with these, under the pitiless sun, up the rugged hill beneath whose stones the little dark men kept their centuries of sleep. On the top not a breath of wind was stirring and the heat filled the air with a thin gauze of opal. The northern sea shimmered and lost itself in a near horizon. The more distant southern sea, where now Joss would be sailing, was invisible.

We ate our slender meal, blessedly alone. That was not so long ago, but a little time is enough to let many djinns out of bottles, and to-day even our dark beloved hill would give you no privacy on such a day as this. We lay there listening to the hum of bees among the heather, and the calling of gulls in the air, and we watched the buzzards, which are ever thereabouts, glorying in the height and space of their splendid liberty. At last Sylvia said: "We'd better read these letters. Do you feel like me about letters, darling? I'm always a bit reluctant to open them."

"Take your courage in both hands. Read me Janet's, and I'll read you Bob's."

She read aloud: "Darling Mother,—I am enceinte."

She put the letter down, convulsed with laughter. "Well, talk about coming to the point! I wonder how a mid-Victorian girl would have put it?"

"Dearest Mama," I suggested. "I hesitate to broach a matter which you may think indelicate, but there are signs that God is about to bless my union with Sir Marmaduke."

Sylvia read on: "At first I thought it was sea-sickness, because, as you know, I'm not used to travelling; but now there's no doubt about it. I consulted an English doctor out here, and he confirms my fears. I say fears, because Bob and I didn't want children, and thought we'd taken every precaution. But still, I expect you know how it is sometimes."

She paused again. "She seems to have a low opinion of me," she said.

The letter went on. "Bob is none too pleased. Anybody would think I'd produced these symptoms automatically, just to annoy him. And he is annoyed. He'd been looking forward to a wonderful romantic holiday, and of course a child in the womb doesn't contribute to that. However, there it is. I thought I'd better let you know at once. As for the rest, anyone who wants South America can have it. I was looking for something wonderful, and I'm not finding it. The poverty of the poor is appalling, and the riches of the rich are offensive. Not that I've seen much of the place yet, but if I have reason to change my mind I shall be surprised. Aren't these air-mail letter-sheets wonderful? You just have room for so much—no frills. Especially with a large handwriting like mine. I'll let you know how things go. Love to you and Daddy. Janet."

Sylvia folded the letter and slipped it into her hand-bag. "I move," she said, "that the matter is outside the scope of the committee, and that we proceed to the next business."

I opened Bob's letter.

"Dear George,—After no more than a day or two, one can already say that this is a splendid place. The Ambassador received us most hospitably, and is aware of the importance of trade links, which he's all out to strengthen. He is arranging a little dinner for me and Janet to meet some people who may be useful and their wives. So the ball has started rolling, and I have no doubt it will gather momentum as we move from place to place. I'm confining myself to the Argentine and Brazil. That will be giving me plenty to go on with. His Excellency, I was glad to notice, uses the latest model Meagher, and I was proud to see the car flashing through the streets with the British flag on the bonnet. Such things count. Well, this is just to set your

301

mind at rest, and Sylvia's—to let you know that we are safely arrived and that things are not unpromising. Ever, Bob."

"Has he written in vain," I asked Sylvia, "or is your tortured mind at rest now that you know Bob is on the spot and on the make?"

"He doesn't seem much interested in my embryo grandchild," she said.

"From what Janet writes," I told her, "that is a thought that lies too deep for tears, let alone an air-mail letter. And, after all, first things first. Vive la commerce anglaise! Viva el comercio! Prosperity is one thing: posterity another."

"You take it lightly."

I picked up the tea-basket and helped her to her feet. We set off downhill. "Not at all," I assured her. "I'm one of those clowns who laugh with tears in their eyes. Poor Janet."

CHAPTER FOURTEEN

1

In the spring of the next year, 1936, Sylvia and I went down to Penruan to see Viola who was living with Miss Hartman. Paul was old enough to be left, and Miss Collum was delighted to have him to herself. I had asked Bob to come with us, but he had to be in Coventry. He had not seen the town since he and Wendy left it so long ago, and to go back now, the great industrialist, the spokesman for the boss class, was something he could not resist. Coventry is a fairly central place and he had summoned distributors and salesmen of Meagher products from a wide area. He was to be host at a great banquet, and he was to speak. I remember the speech. It was widely reported in the Press. "Abroad, what do we see? The dictators strut. Well, let them strut. But don't allow their strutting to make us shiver in our shoes. On every hand we hear talk of what we should do to oppose them. Why oppose them? Let them oppose themselves, which they do by the increase of their own hot air. That, in itself, will soon be enough to burst those bubbles. To their insanity what need we oppose except British sanity? And what is greater sanity in the long run, what more beneficial, more contributory to the food cupboards and the bank-books of all sorts and conditions of people, than a steadily growing trade, both at home and abroad? Don't let the antics of these gentlemen overseas worry you. All this marching and shouting and saluting may be their way of trying to get ahead. It's not likely to collide with the British way, which is work, work, work. I am proud of you all, but I want to be prouder. I am proud of what we have made between us, but believe me it's only an infant. We must feed it with our faith and our enthusiasm and make it grow. Above all, don't follow the bad current fashion of thinking that we have a mission to interfere in Europe. Europe to us is a market, nothing more . . ." and on and on.

Mr. Chamberlain, a few days later, spoke of "the exemplary sanity" of Sir Robert Meagher ; and Alcott-Lucas in *Now* wrote an article headed: "Burying his head in a motor-bonnet." There was a row about that. Sylvia and I, happening to be in town, rang up Janet and asked her to take lunch with us. She came along looking none the worse for the miscarriage that had destroyed her child, but she was clearly worried about something. We knew that Bob had become increasingly intimate with J. Wilson Dodge, and we now discovered that, despite Hubert's continued hope that the paper would financially break even, it was in fact tending downwards. The circulation was steadily rising, but it was not a paper that attracted advertising. Money was flowing out of Mr. Wilson Dodge's pocket, and he had persuaded Bob to join him in trying to keep the thing afloat. Bob had the bright thought of taking a full page to advertise the latest model Meagher car, but Hubert had the old-fashioned idea that editorial responsibility extended even to the supervision of advertising. He declined to print the advertisement, though he knew that Sir Robert had joined his father in standing between him and his paper's ruin. That was bad enough, and Janet confessed that life in the Piccadilly apartment was sultry. Bob tried to persuade Janet to give up working for *Now,* and Janet, looking round the splendid room and thinking of Dormers in the background, asked: "What am I to do if I give it up?"

Bob was staggered. "Do? Isn't being my wife something that gives you enough scope?"

Janet knew that the answer was "no." At the *Now* office she was a person in her own right. Being Lady Meagher, with a maid to dress her, a cook to cook for her, a chauffeur to drive her car, and a husband to provide her with everything but children, was not her idea of living at all. I'm sure she didn't put it that way, but she left Bob in no doubt that being on the staff of *Now* was something that mattered to her.

"Anybody'd think," Bob said, "that you agreed with what the blasted rag stands for."

Janet was determined to keep calm, and at the same time she wanted to clear up this matter once for all. "You know, darling," she said, "that what I write never comes within miles of the paper's politics. I'm just on the frilly side, like George

Ledra; but still, I do, on the whole, feel sympathy with Hubert's ideas. Most sensible people nowadays do."

"*I* don't. And what am I? A jackass?"

"If you're so annoyed with the paper, why on earth did you put money into it?"

"If you think that's an unanswerable poser, you're mistaken. Wilson Dodge is in it because his wife is crazy about this boy Hubert, and she keeps badgering her husband to help the thing. I'm in it because Wilson Dodge proposed it to me, and he's the sort of man one wants to be on the right side of. His firm has seventy-seven branches. He recently scrapped all his old delivery vans and replaced them with Meaghers. And his firm will soon be bigger still. He's about to pull off a merger with Town and Country Cafés. They have shops everywhere. Does all this sound too mercenary for you? I call it sensible give and take."

Janet looked troubled, toying with her food, eating next to nothing. "It was so much like South America," she said. "All the time out there, it was running after the men one must keep on the right side of. We dined with them, we went to the opera and the theatre with them, we danced with them and their wives and daughters. We literally never saw a soul for the sake of his bright blue eyes."

She produced a copy of that morning's *Now*. It contained the *Burying his Head in a Motor-bonnet* article. "This of course," she said, "has put the tin hat on it."

Sylvia and I skipped through the article, and we could see that it was indeed a pebble from David's sling, smack between Goliath's eyes.

Janet declined a sweet, asked for black coffee, and lit a cigarette. "There's been all hell loose in the office this morning," she said.

She and Alcott-Lucas had been in Hubert's room when Sir Robert Meagher came storming in. Hubert and Alcott-Lucas had occasionally attended the Friday night dinners in Piccadilly, and Bob absurdly called this to their minds. "You two," he said, "who have eaten at my table—to stab me in the back!"

Alcott-Lucas put up his eye-glass and stared at him. "I never stab a man in the belly," he said.

"If you think this is an occasion for feeble quips . . ." Bob began, when Hubert intervened. "Sit down, Sir Robert," he invited, "and you," to Alcott-Lucas, "please leave us."

Alcott-Lucas went, and Bob remained standing, the current edition of *Now* strangled in his fist.

"I can quite understand why you are annoyed, Sir Robert," Hubert said equably, "and, as editor of the paper, responsible for all that appears in it, I must face your wrath."

The wrath overflowed as Bob stormed up and down the room,

and the gist of it was that only a man lost to all sense of honour would write in that way about a person who was helping to pay for the very paper on which the offence was printed, and that Alcott-Lucas must go.

When the storm had subsided a little Hubert said: "I am afraid, Sir Robert, you were mistaken if you thought that lending money to the paper gave you any say in editorial policy. We thought your speech showed that you completely misunderstood the dangers that exist in Europe, and we said so. We should go on saying so as pungently as possible if occasion arose. But if it has to be said again, it won't be said by Alcott-Lucas."

"I hope you've sacked him."

"No. We shall all miss him, but he has resigned in order to travel in Europe and see for himself what is happening. He hopes to write a book about it. It's time a few eyes were opened."

Bob discharged another broadside, but Hubert, having said all that he had to say, just sat, patiently waiting for the end. This refusal to be drawn, to reply by so much as a word, at first irritated and finally disconcerted Bob, who stammered, stopped, then said: "I might as well be talking to a stone wall."

"Yes, Sir Robert."

And that was that.

"Well, for the moment, that is that," Janet said. "But I'm afraid it's not the end of the story."

2

We had found Viola in an odd mood. She was happy to be with Miss Hartman but despondent about her own achievement. "It is to be expected," Miss Hartman assured her. "Any sort of artist does not walk on the flat. There are times when he wants to blow his brains out, and times when the Hallelujah Chorus is inadequate to express his joy. At the moment Viola is a little depressed."

Still, here she was, and that in itself was something of a triumph for me and Sylvia. At the end of the long summer holiday the year before, we had taken the children back to their schools. A month later Bob and Janet returned from South America. We went out to Dormers for the week-end to hear their news. I was strolling with Bob in the woods behind the house on the Sunday afternoon and he thanked me for looking after the pair and inquired about their behaviour. I told him about Miss Hartman. He had never heard of her, but this was not surprising for he had never heard of Mozart. I explained who she was and what had happened between her and Viola.

" Did you know," I asked him, " that, for her age, Viola is rather better than most as a pianist?"

" No," he said, as though the matter could not possibly be a concern of his.

" What do her school reports say about it?"

" Heaven knows. I never read the things. All I ask of the place is that she should learn something there of poise and manners. She seems to be doing that."

" Miss Hartman thinks it would be a good idea if she left school now and concentrated on music. When she's reached a certain standard she might be admitted to the Royal College of Music in London."

" Who's running Viola's life—me or Miss Hartman?"

" Quite what do you mean by running a life?"

We were sitting on a fallen log, with late October sunshine falling upon us. Dormers lay below, the light turning the stone golden, and here and there upon this gold flamed the last leaves of Virginia creeper.

Bob knocked out his pipe and looked at the indisputable evidence of his own success. James Gibbs designed this house. Capability Brown laid out the landscape. The passing of two centuries had done the rest.

" Running a life?" Bob asked. " I ought to know. I've run my own, haven't I?"

He was grey. Struggle had chiselled his features which were thin and handsome and hard.

I said: " You have every right to be proud, Bob. When we used to ramble the moors, just after you were de-mobbed, I for one never thought your obsession would lead to this. But you were running your *own* life, weren't you? You were just following your nose. Happily nothing much got in the way."

" Don't you believe it," he said. " A good deal got in the way, but I knew what to do about it."

" I'm talking about running someone else's life. Viola's, in fact. She wants to follow her nose, too."

He gave an impatient gesture. " I know what's good for the child," he said. " Strumming on a piano! What on earth can come of that?"

" I'm afraid I can't answer. Perhaps nothing. All I'm asking you is to make an act of faith on the strength of Miss Hartman's advice. She's a woman who knows what she's talking about."

" What's it done for her? A cottage without a bathroom or W.C. next door to a country pub. That's not exactly what I want for Viola."

" Isn't the question what Viola wants for herself? Supposing your father had said that pushing off to Coventry to work as a mechanic at a bench wasn't what he wanted for you?"

" I think he knew me, George. He had more sense than to get in my way. No. Leave Viola to me. Let's go and join the girls at tea."

During the week-end " the girls " backed me in badgering Bob. Sylvia had briefed Janet, who was all in favour of the Hartman project. But it was no good. Sir Robert was a rock, unshakable by our puny spray.

It was Janet who settled the matter. At least I am pretty sure it was though she would never admit it. All I know is that a letter to her from Viola, which Janet showed me, was all woe. Bob had written a good manly letter, telling the child that he had heard of the idea of her going to study with Miss Hartman and that he was sure she would, when she was a little older, see how unsensible that would be. Meanwhile, she must be a good girl and learn all that her school could teach her, and so on and so on.

Following this letter, Viola unburdened her heart to Janet. Reading between the lines, I could see what had happened. During the holiday, she had been walking on air. Now she had landed with a bump on hard earth. The consequence was a dreadful feeling of frustration. The letter alarmed me with its note of hysteria. The next week Viola ran away from school, and I know in my bones that Janet, herself an accomplished escapologist, advised her to do it. It had been her own way of solving all problems. But Viola was not so accomplished and was recaptured, wet through and shivering with cold, after spending a rainy night under a hedge a few miles from the school. Sir Robert was summoned. An attempt was made to patch up the situation, and Viola remained at school till the term ended. But throughout that term what had been a docile scholar became a creature now all lassitude, and now a focus of trouble. Bob was beaten, and Janet's joy thereat cannot have sweetened their relationship.

3

Back at the Barn, I rang up Meagher Motors and asked if I might speak to Sir Robert. I was put through to that dear old soul Miss Bell, who was a dragon in the path of either telephonic or personal approach to her boss. She was usually kind to me, though there were times when I could hear her scales rattling and smell the sulphur of her breath. This was one of the kind days, and I was put through at once to the room which I could so well remember: the room where Bob had gorgeously overfed me, where he had talked to Wendy's father with his back turned, and whence he could survey the comings and goings along the many roadways of his kingdom. With all this in mind, it was almost banal to ask: "Could you and Janet lunch with us at the Barn next Sunday? We've been seeing a bit of Viola and could give you the news."

"I don't know about Janet," he said. "You could get her at her office at this time of day. As for me, I can't make it. I've got a golfing engagement."

He had recently taken to golf and employed a pro to watch his every stroke. I didn't take the business as seriously as he did, and said: "Can't you get out of it?"

"No. I'm playing with Wilson Dodge in the morning, and in the afternoon he and I are partners in a foursome against jjones and Baldrick."

I saw how it was: all big shots. There was no point in persisting. "All right then. I'll ring Janet. Viola sends her love."

"That's sweet of her," he said, not meaning it. He had not forgiven Viola for preferring Steinways to stallions.

I rang up Janet. "Yes, darling. Delighted," she said. "But ring off now, there's a good boy. There's a flap on here."

I put down the receiver, feeling forlorn, outside the current of great events. "Janet will come, but not Bob," I told Sylvia. "He has a golfing engagement."

"I'm not sorry," she said. "He's like a bear with a sore head nowadays, what with Viola and Janet."

Janet had done nothing to conceal her pleasure at what had happened to Viola. Nor did she relent in the matter of *Now*. She thought that Alcott-Lucas's article was called for: "though I wish," she said, "that it hadn't been you, Bob, who got it in the neck."

"You need have no regrets on my behalf," he told her. "D'you think I care twopence what a wretched Grub Street hack thinks or says?"

"Yes, I do," she told him frankly. "You would like to be altogether above criticism. And it does happen, you know, that Alcott-Lucas is not a hack. He took a double first at Oxford, he's profoundly acquainted with foreign affairs, and he writes almost as keenly as Swift."

"I don't know who Swift is," Bob accurately replied, "and I don't care. But I do know something about what makes the stability of this country, and that it's workers, not scribblers."

Then Janet said an utterly unforgivable thing. "I wish you'd be honest with yourself, Bob. You know as well as I do that you don't care a damn about the workers. All you care about is making more and more cars and trucks, and consequently more money."

"Then," she said to me and Sylvia, "he went up like a rocket. Wasn't his place on the Great West Road a model, and so recognised throughout the country? Weren't his wages good, and wasn't his pension scheme generous? Didn't he provide playing-fields and give holidays with pay? I waited till he came down again, and then I said: 'You know very well that all these things are *demanded* by working people nowadays and that if you don't give them they'll go to someone who does.'"

Sylvia and I looked at one another gravely. "I do wish, darling," Sylvia said, "that you wouldn't quarrel with your husband."

Janet laughed. "You and old Chowny should have brought me up better," she said. "A child should be seen and not heard. The pair of you encouraged me to say what I thought and do as I liked. Isn't that so, George? Wasn't I a little horror when you first met me?"

I agreed that she was. "Very well, then," she said, as though that settled everything.

4

At luncheon on the Sunday Janet turned up with Peter Quayne. It was a long time since I had seen Peter. He looked prosperous, and I had noticed that of late he was using a whole page of *Country Life* almost every week to advertise his shop and what was in it. And what was in it was becoming increasingly important. I noted the light grey flannel suit, the maize-coloured silk tie, the brown suède shoes. He was a good-looking man and seemed younger than he was. He was about my own age, which then was thirty-five. I remembered that the first time we met, when I went to see him about the Redmayne exhibition, he had talked of his father, curator of a northern municipal art gallery. The old man was now retired and was helping Peter in his business. They lived together in a flat over the shop. I knew that Peter and Janet were acquainted. They could hardly help being, seeing that he was responsible for "creating" the Piccadilly apartment and was often at Janet's Friday night dinners. I wondered how well she knew him outside these professional contracts, and whether she used Bob's golfing appointments to serve her own amorous ends, especially now that she and Bob had reached one of those thorny patches that newly married people think will never come their way. But they come all the same. She and Bob had been married now for three years.

These thoughts were passing through my mind as we drank sherry in the big barn.

"I hope you don't mind my bringing Peter," Janet said.

"We're delighted to see him," Sylvia assured her. "As you know, we don't go in much for cooking here. We shall be
309

taking you out to a hotel, so there's no question of stretching the joint."

"We had arranged to go down to Brighton," Janet said. "But when you asked me here, we decided to wash that out because there's so much to tell you."

Well, that answered part of my question, I thought; but then I was left guessing again when Janet said: "Bob was coming with us. But then this golf business cropped up and he begged off."

It all sounded innocent enough, and I wondered how true it was. I was looking at Peter and Peter was looking at Janet. It was a look full of admiration. Admiration for what? The skill with which she had skated round a tricky corner?

"When I rang you up at the office," I said to Janet, "you said there was a flap on. Nothing serious, I hope?"

She put down her sherry glass, and shook her head when I made to refill it. "Couldn't be worse," she said. "When we got to the office that morning, Bob and Mr. Wilson Dodge were waiting, so to speak, on the doorstep. Hubert and I happened to arrive together, and I think we both guessed what this was all about. These two had the hang-dog look of bailiffs come to sequestrate a property. Of course, we asked them in heartily, as though they were bankers come to congratulate us on being at last out of the red. But they weren't playing. They took chairs and remained dumb and grim."

I knew Bob in that mood. It wasn't a comfortable one to face.

"They said," Janet went on, "that what they had to say must be said to the whole editorial staff. Of course, the staff in question chose that morning to be universally late. I tried to bridge the gap by offering cigars. We keep a few for special occasions. Like two black crows doing a simultaneous act, they croaked a refusal."

"Don't spin it out like a clever little girl," I said. "Come to the point."

"I'm only trying to conceal my broken heart," she said. "We're sunk."

Mr. Wilson Dodge and Sir Robert Meagher had made it clear that they had done with financing *Now*. Family considerations alone, they said, had permitted them for so long to keep alive a paper which so far as its political side went, was all that they disliked.

"We could have put up with a lot in the general way, but this direct attack on Sir Robert, this biting of the hand that feeds you," said Mr. Wilson Dodge, coining a phrase, "seemed to us on the one hand base ingratitude and on the other just damned silly."

As though this remark were a prearranged signal, they both

rose and made for the door. "As from now," said Mr. Dodge, as they passed through it, "you can expect not one brass farthing from either of us."

"Then, of course," said Janet, "there arose the flap into which you intruded. We talked and talked and there were a thousand suggestions, but we all knew that none of them meant a thing. *Now* is as good as dead."

It died that year with the last issue of July. Janet presided over its death-throes. On the day of the "flap" Hubert promised to make a last appeal to his father and Janet to her husband. If only one of them would stay in, the paper might struggle along till another financier was found. Or, even, Hubert's cherished dream might come true—the dream that he was telling all financiers to go to hell and that his paper was paying its way. The only effect, as one might have guessed, was to damage still further the personal relationship of the four people concerned. Mr. Dodge and Bob Meagher just could not understand what a paper like *Now* was trying to do, and, when Hubert and Janet argued the matter, they did nothing but force into the open hitherto undisclosed gulfs of disagreement. In Janet's case this was made worse by her having been on Viola's side in the matter of the piano. It was the winning side, and Bob wasn't going to have her on the winning side again. As for Hubert, he put it to his father that he didn't expect him to approve of *Now,* but he did ask him to accept that the world would always be full of conflicting views and that, in a healthy state, these were freely allowed to engage one another. Mr. Dodge replied firmly that he had no objection to this provided that each side paid for its own ammunition.

Hubert bought a palliasse and put it down on the office floor. He slept there and didn't go home again. He had always been a highly strung youth, and the obvious approach of the end of his dreams affected him deeply. I looked into the office only once during those last weeks and found him looking crumpled and unkempt. He was beginning to grow a beard. He and I were alone in his room and I could have wept for him. "Look, George," he said. "We've been obliged to cut down this week. Do you mind very much if we leave your thing out? Technically you're entitled to ask for the pay, but if that could be postponed. . . ."

"Print it if you want to, and never mind the pay. Damn the pay, and damn your eyes for suggesting that I'd bother about it."

"You're a good man, George," he said, which I doubted. "But it's not only a question of pay. It's the price of paper. Not that pay doesn't matter. I've had to sack two men this week, and that was pretty heartbreaking. I'm finding out how many good people there are in the world. Those two men

311

refused the money they were entitled to in place of notice. And Janet has been working for nothing for a long time. All the same, I feel as though I'm wading through a morass—sinking."

He was like a child caught up in a difficult adult situation. "I wish Alcott-Lucas were here," he said. "He could have helped me. He's a funny old devil, but he's got horse sense, and that, I fear, is what I lack. I'm beginning to think I was never cut out for journalism. I'm going to do something practical for once."

He lit a cigarette with shaking fingers, and after a moment went on: "I hear often from Alcott-Lucas, but I don't need what he tells me to realise that there's going to be a proper showdown in Spain. And something's got to be done about it. Is the Hitler and Mussolini trick going to work for a third time? If it does, then we might as well throw up the sponge. Civilised Europe will be done for."

I looked at the puny body and at the eyes gone fanatical. "You're not thinking of fighting, are you?"

"Why not? What about Byron?"

"Oh, damn Byron. He was fifty per cent showman, trying to convince people that even a poet with a gammy leg could be a man."

"Suppose it was like that? Wasn't it worth trying?"

"Come out and have something to eat and drink."

"No, thank you. I'm handing over to Janet, and there's a lot to be explained."

"She's going to edit the paper?"

"Yes. She's got a lot of practical common sense."

I hovered, reluctant somehow to leave him. He took my hand and said: "Thank you, George, for all you've done. Don't worry about me, there's a good chap. Alcott-Lucas will look after me. He's going to Spain, too."

But Alcott-Lucas couldn't look after himself, much less Hubert. In the issue of *Now* which Janet had to announce was the last, she recorded their deaths in Barcelona in an air-raid carried out by the side they had gone to support.

5

Sylvia and I had attended most of the annual parties given for the *Now* staff and their friends, but we hadn't got to know Hubert's mother. She was far too elusive a person to be known from a few casual contacts. However, there was an acquaintanceship that justified, we felt, a visit of condolence. We were told when we called at the house that Mrs. Dodge was at the *Now* office, and went on there. I could pretend that I wanted

312

to pick up some of my unpublished essays which I knew were lying about, and this would make our call, we hoped, less painful than a formal visit. It was a broiling midsummer day, and the alley in which the office stood was still and stuffy. It seemed so little time since I had first called there to find that boy, alight with a missionary fervour, pushing out the frail barque that he believed to contain redemptive cargo. The newspapers had printed pictures of Barcelona after the raid: a chaos of smashed buildings, smashed bodies. That was where the voyage had so quickly ended.

We climbed the echoing wooden stairs slowly, trying to defer, if only by seconds, the moment we dreaded. To our delight, Janet was in the reception room out of which the editorial room opened. There was no apparent reason for our delight. She looked ghastly, all in. But she was a buffer. Even here in this small outer room there was already that feeling of dust and desolation that settles so soon upon a place whose purpose is ended. Janet was tying papers into small bundles. "These," she said, indicating one of them, " are the unpaid bills."

We talked in whispers. Mrs. Dodge, she told us, had appeared unexpectedly. She had never before been in the office and had come, she said, to see where Hubert had worked. "It is something I must remember," she said.

"She's in there now," Janet said. "I couldn't bear being with her, so I'm fussing about here till she's gone. You remember I went for a holiday with her once to Scotland? Well, she's been on about that, recalling all that we did, and she says she wants me to go and live with her in Portman Square. She's quite forgotten that I'm married."

We knocked at the door and went in. Janet said: "You remember my mother and her husband, don't you, Mrs. Dodge? They've come to see you."

"How kind of them," she said. "Please sit down."

She was herself seated in Hubert's chair. She had always worn black, so it was no surprise to see her wearing it now. The little room was stuffy and littered, and she sat among it all imperially. "What can I do for you?" she asked. "I'm afraid you can't have the editor's personal attention. He was killed in Barcelona, you know."

We didn't know what to do. There would clearly be no formal condolences. I stammered some nonsense about having come to discuss an article I had written, and Janet took up this line and said: "You'd better leave that for the moment. We'll talk about it later."

"Thank you," I said formally. "I'll do that." And we turned to go when Mrs. Dodge said: "Now that you're here don't hurry away. Tell me about my son's death in Barcelona. Do

313

you think it was worth while? Do you think it has served any purpose?"

Out of a depth of banality, but not knowing what else to say, I answered that all lives dedicated to great causes, even though they seemed to be thrown away, must avail in the end.

She considered me almost quizzically, and said in the coolest possible voice: " That's the sort of nonsense I used to hear when I was a girl in Poland. It is nonsense, you know. Waste is just waste. Well, you'd better go after all. You have nothing to say to me."

And indeed I hadn't. I went, sweating with confusion, and Sylvia and Janet followed. When the door was closed Janet said: " Just leave her to me. I'll get her home somehow, and then we'd better meet for lunch somewhere."

But we didn't meet for lunch because at that moment we heard a shot and rushed back into Hubert's room to find his mother dead. She had carried a small pearl-handled revolver in her reticule. The pretty-looking toy was still in her right hand and in the left was a letter addressed " To Almighty God." It was read at the inquest, and, though it was cool and logical, the coroner said that its wild blasphemy showed her mind to be deranged. A verdict was returned accordingly.

6

When, a few days later, Sylvia and I did meet Janet at lunch, she told us that she had said to Bob: " Well, that's two deaths at your door."

This was hardly fair, but it showed the dangerous point to which their relationship had drifted. " I didn't want to discuss Hubert with him," Janet said. " All I wanted was for him to clear up the financial mess. Otherwise, we shan't wind the thing up, as they say. We shall be dragged through the bankruptcy court. For Hubert's sake, I shouldn't like that. It would be a rather dingy end."

" Don't forget," Bob said, " that I'm one of the principal creditors. I shan't press you for what you owe me, and I'm sure Wilson Dodge won't press you either. Whatever the other odds and ends may be, they can't add up to so much."

" I know," she said. " It's not much, and that's why I thought you wouldn't mind paying it."

Bob was in a bad mood. Hubert, goodness knows, was not a public figure, but the manner of his death and Alcott-Lucas's, and the well-known fact that *Now* was staggering along under difficulty, caught the attention of some Fleet Street writer who took the trouble to make a few inquiries. He discovered that

Sir Robert Meagher and Mr. J. Wilson Dodge had been the chief financial backers of the paper and that their support had been withdrawn immediately before Hubert left for Spain. Without saying so, he left it to be inferred that this withdrawal had been the cause of Hubert's going. So Bob was writhing under a double grievance: it had been revealed that he had supported a paper he wouldn't have touched with a barge-pole, and, by implication, he was accused of an inhumanity that had sent Hubert to his death. Certainly Janet tackled him at a bad moment, and when she put into plain words what the writer had cautiously hinted, she was optimistic indeed to expect him to be pliable.

They were taking breakfast in Piccadilly, and on the wall was a picture by Picasso. It wasn't an outrageous Picasso. It was a pleasant enough example of his blue period. When Janet said that only a small sum was needed to keep *Now* out of the bankruptcy court, Bob said curtly: "Once and for all I want you to understand that I have said my last word on this subject, that I shall not find another penny, and that I deeply regret your ever having had anything to do with the damned rag."

Brookes put his head round the door and said: "The car is waiting, Sir Robert."

Bob dabbed his lips with a napkin, got up, and saw the Picasso.

"What is that damned thing?"

"It's a picture by Picasso."

"What's it doing here?"

"It's been here for three days and you haven't noticed it."

"I should call that a tribute to any picture," Bob sneered. "Who told you to buy it?"

"I haven't bought it. Peter Quayne suggested hanging it so that you could live with it for a time and decide whether you wanted it."

"Well, I've now lived with it for a time and I don't want it. Do you and Peter Quayne think I'm made of money and that I'll buy everything you care to stick under my nose?"

"It's an investment. Doesn't that interest you?"

"If you said that to hurt me, you have succeeded. Try not to hurt me too much."

He was wearing a tussore suit. Brookes handed him a Panama hat. Janet, standing at the window, saw the luxurious gleam of the waiting car, the dark blue uniform and kid gloves of the waiting chauffeur. She said as Bob left the room: "Don't work too hard, darling. Just try to make ends meet."

It was not a comfortable lunch as she told us of these things. We were at Rule's in Maiden Lane, eating Dover sole and drinking Chablis. Janet pushed back her plate and said: "It's too hot to eat—even something as light as this."

Despite her make-up, she was looking careworn. A wash, I was sure, would reveal a pale face to match the sadness in her eyes. Sylvia said: "You're beginning to learn something about the facts of life, darling."

I wanted to edge the conversation away, if I could, from Hubert and the obduracy of Bob and Mr. Dodge. So I took up Sylvia's remark. "It always amuses me when earnest people throw their weight behind novels that, as they say, teach young people the facts of life. All that those books do, as a rule, is express in disgusting language what the youngsters already know very well indeed. I should take a lot of convincing that the most prim Victorian miss didn't know from the impulses of her own body what the facts of life were. The Victorian novelists just took this for granted."

Janet laid a hand on my arm. "That's very sweetly put, George," she said. "You must write a letter to *The Times* about it. If it will help, I'll follow up with one saying that I can't remember the time when I didn't know the facts of life. But in the meantime, it's not what we're talking about. Order me a soufflé, will you? I can't look even this charming fish in the face."

She said to Sylvia: "How right you are. Bob and I have been married for three years. At the beginning, he would have given me anything. He'd have bought that Picasso, for example, like a shot, even if he loathed it. And he'd have cleaned up *Now's* financial mess without batting an eyelid. Already we've reached this point where everything I want to do—about the paper, about Viola, about Picasso—brings us on the edge of a quarrel."

She toyed with her soufflé and sipped iced coffee. "Do you know, the other day he said: 'Why don't you take up golf? It would keep your mind off all these things.' Now, in the name of plain common sense, why should a husband want to keep a wife's mind off the things that she lives for?"

"He takes a Miltonic view," I suggested. "'He for God only, she for God through him.'"

"Oh, he's for God only all right," she agreed. "But there are Gods and Gods."

"The trouble with you," Sylvia said, "is that of all your facts of life, Chowny is the chief."

Janet said simply: "I think you're right. 'Being dead, yet speaketh.'"

She finished her coffee, and for the first time smiled. It was so beautiful a smile, so full of tender reminiscence, that it touched my heart. "Fancy being married to Chowny!" she said.

We all sat silent for a moment, contemplating the incredible proposition. "No good," Sylvia said. "He was married to

Pallas Athene and would have been at sea with a mortal wench. You'd better face the hard fact that you're married to Bob Meagher."

We tried then to look the facts in the face. Bob was adamant, and Mr. Dodge out of the question. His wife and son being so brutally dead, it would be indecent even to think of approaching him. "That leaves you," Janet said.

"Yes," Sylvia agreed, "that leaves me."

"And me," I said.

"Oh no," Janet exclaimed. "It's angelic of you to offer, but——"

"Be quiet, girl," I said, "when your father-in-law is speaking. I said ' and me.' Get out the figures and let me and Sylvia have them. We're both disgustingly and undeservedly rich. I feel I owe something to Hubert."

I was remembering the first night he called on me, so young and beautiful and eager, and how his enthusiasm had channelled my own dilettante efforts into something considered and systematic.

Janet was close to tears. "It will be a wonderful memorial to him," she said, "to bury his life's work without any raw ends. Well, I'd better go and tell Peter to collect his Picasso."

She picked up her hand-bag and gloves and hurried away, leaving me and Sylvia looking at one another in something like dismay. "Curiouser and curiouser," Sylvia said after a moment. "And one is so damned helpless. Well, let's get home to Paul."

It was not until the next morning that Sylvia returned to this matter. We were eating breakfast out of doors, as we liked to do in the summer, and she was so obviously not with me that I ate in silence and left her to her thoughts. She said presently: "What I mean is, why couldn't she have rung him up?"

"Who? The fishmonger?"

"Don't be stupid. You know very well what I'm talking about."

"You over-estimate my mental agility."

"Why should Janet have to go to see Peter Quayne about the picture? Why couldn't she have rung him up and said: ' Sorry. You must come and take this picture away'?"

"Well, she's out of work and at a loose end. Perhaps she wanted a walk."

She looked at me pityingly. "If you choose to believe that. . . ."

The subject petered out. She put the breakfast things on to a tray and carried them into the house. I went to my desk in the barn and settled down to work. "Thank goodness," I thought, "the end of *Now* at least makes no difference to me." Whether or not the bits of my little annual book had appeared elsewhere, Nigel Wendron still wanted the little annual book.

It was otherwise with Janet. She was out of work and I pictured her alone in the *Now* offices which had always been dim and had become dreary with dust and memory. There she would have to stay for a time, tying up ends, meting out a neat death to so many dreams.

When Sylvia came in with my eleven o'clock coffee, as she liked to do, I said: "I've got Janet rather on my mind. I shall go up to town this afternoon and see how things are with her. Perhaps I can help."

She kissed the back of my neck as she bent over me to put down the coffee. "Sorry about my wicked daughter, darling," she said. "Do I lay too many burdens on you?"

"Your wicked daughter is a woman much to my liking. I should hate her to be some predictable miss, running through life on tramlines."

"You married into an odd bunch, I'm afraid. My mother and Chowny and your Manchester tragi-comedian Fred Byles. We've all had a hand in Janet, and your poor innocent little self gets involved in our nonsense."

I was not at all pleased to be called a poor little innocent. A man likes to feel that he can be a bit of a lad at need, and I said ungraciously: "Well, let me get on with my work. I've got a wife and child to keep."

She laughed at the idea of my work keeping a wife and child. A couple of rabbits in a hutch might just have managed to survive on what I earned. She ruffled my hair and left me.

7

The door of the *Now* office was locked. I rattled the handle, lifted the flap of the letter-box, and shouted through "It's George," thinking Janet might be within, secured against intrusion. But no one was there. I was walking down the dark stairway when Mr. Merriman appeared at the bottom, Wendy at his side. The encounter astonished us all three. Mr. Merriman was the first to recover, and he advanced up the stairs, beaming with bonhomie. He shook my hand and said: "Well met, George. This is a great moment for Merriman Enterprises. I'm glad you're here to share it. Wendy and I don't forget that it was you who set me on my way when things were pretty black."

To my surprise, he took a key from his pocket and opened the door of the *Now* office. "The agent," he said, "told me that the place wasn't vacated yet, but that the tenant had no objection to my taking a look round. All her stuff is locked up. Come on in, George."

318

Still baffled about what this portended, I went into the familiar room. "My word!" Wendy cried characteristically, "some cleaning's needed here. Did you ever see a room in such a state?"

Now that we were off the dark stairway I could see Mr. Merriman more clearly, and it was the Manchester Merriman risen from the dust that had clouded his recent years. He looked well, buoyant, and he was wearing new spats. There was a carnation at the lapel of his dark coat. He removed his silk hat and put it on a table, from which Wendy instantly removed it. She took a newspaper from a chair, opened it at a clean page, and then reverently laid the hat upon it. She, too, was looking well, though dowdy.

I slowly gathered the story. Since I had last seen them in the ironmonger's shop in Notting Hill they had, as Mr. Merriman put it, gone ahead. He spoke of one or two lucky speculations. "Not that I approve of speculation, George. Investment is my motto. But it's a poor soul who never rejoices in doing now and then something he doesn't approve of. My infidelity to my own basic principles," he said pompously, "bore fruit, and now I'm faithful again. Just a deal on the side with the devil."

He was in good self-satisfied form, and explained that they had just bought the house overlooking London Pool of which I have already written. "Home is one thing," he said, "the office another, and we hope that henceforth never the twain shall meet."

Putting it briefly, Merriman Enterprises were on the look-out for an office in central London, and he and Wendy had come to see this one. "We don't want the upstairs part of the premises," he said. "The agent tells me he already has a bite for that. The entrance lobby and this room will do us very well."

I was praying that Janet would not arrive. Lady Meagher suddenly and unexpectedly face to face with Mrs. Meagher would create a situation I didn't want to be involved in. My prayer was answered. They pottered about for half an hour, discussing where this and that should go, and it gave me a sick feeling. It was like being in a house recently occupied by some loved person now dead, and watching a new tenant callously deranging a warm familiar shrine.

They invited me to come out and join them at tea. I made my excuses and walked with them as far as where the alley entered Pall Mall. I saw Janet coming down from the direction of St. James's Street, and went back into the alley and waited for her there. She looked lonely and agitated. I couldn't bear the thought of her being up there in the death-house, slaving away by herself, and I didn't want to go back there to keep her company. I took her arm and said: "What you need is a nice hot cup of tea with Uncle George." She said nothing, but came with unaccustomed docility. I didn't tell her about Mr. Merriman and Wendy. I said only that I had seen a new tenant looking over the place, and advised her to mop up quickly and have done with it.

"Yes," she said. "That is what I intend to do. All the papers I need are bundled. I have only to go in and pick them up. I can work on them at home." She sipped her tea thoughtfully and added: "Bob can hardly object to *that*."

"Why should he?"

"Well, we were a bit uncomfortable at breakfast this morning."

It seems that he had suddenly looked up from his newspaper and said: "I have decided after all to clean up the mess you've got yourself into."

It sounded so ungracious that she didn't answer. She didn't tell him that Sylvia and I had already promised to look after the mess. He waited for a moment, then asked: "Now that this thing has come to an end, what do you propose to do?"

"That's something I'd been thinking about," she said to me. "Indeed, I'd taken some steps. D'you know Betty Newnham?"

I didn't, and she explained that Lady Betty Newnham was a daughter of the Earl of Llangenny—"one of those hard-up earls whose daughters have to earn a living. Betty's a nice creature. She's been once or twice to our Friday night dinners. She edits a monthly magazine called *Housecraft*. There's a chance of her giving me a job on the staff."

Janet told Bob this, and he said: "I don't want you to take this job or any job. Indeed, I make it a condition of paying the *Now* debts that you shall at last realise that your place is here —in your home and mine."

"So I get nothing unless I pay the price?"

Bob said sententiously: "Life's like that."

"I agree. I've always found it so. And whatever may be the price of being free to use such brains as I have, I'm ready to pay it. Here is this place: servants to do everything. I'm not expected to poke my nose into the kitchen, though I am graciously permitted to decide what shall be cooked there. Not that I care tuppence what I eat and drink, as you know very well. I'm not expected to take up a duster or even turn down my own bed. Your children are at school, and I'm not allowed to have any. You don't want a wife. All you want is an odalisque, and that's a job I don't like."

Bob said: "We appear to be quarrelling."

"If it's quarrelling for a wife to tell her husband that she wants something more than sitting on her Paquined behind in a luxury home, then we're quarrelling. If we were poor, if there was something for me to stay at home and look after, I'd stay at home. And that's not just part of an argument. It's a fact.
320

I'd enjoy doing it, and I *could* do it very well. But I'm not prepared to mooch round here like those chaps in the National Gallery who have nothing to do except see that no one pinches the pictures."

Bob said masterfully: "I have spoken my last word. I don't think you're likely to find the money anywhere else."

"You're glad that *Now* is dead, aren't you? It never occurred to you, I suppose, that I was happy there—that I liked Hubert and Alcott-Lucas and that I liked what the paper was trying to do. That has meant nothing to you. You're glad that it's necessary to pay the undertaker, and you can't do even that without conditions."

She couldn't move him. He merely said: "Well, you know what the conditions are."

Only then she said: "The money has already been found."

That shook him, and he tried hard to discover who had promised to pay. She wouldn't tell him. She never did; neither did I or Sylvia. Rather deflated, he went down and was driven off to the Great West Road. "So you see," Janet said, "as I told you, we were a bit uncomfortable at breakfast."

I walked back with her then to the office, and she gathered the papers that she had prepared to take home. I waited for her at the bottom of the stairway, and presently she came, the wooden steps echoing forlornly under her feet. "Well, that's that," she said.

She tried to smile, but she was saying good-bye to too much for the smile to be successful.

8

A week or two later Sylvia and I were surprised to receive a letter from Wendy asking us to take dinner with her and her father at their new house. It was written on rather classy notepaper, with the address embossed in Gothic letters at the top. "We're not asking anyone else," Wendy said. "But Father had the idea of christening this new and we hope permanent home, and it seemed to both of us that you were the people to ask. After all, George, it was you who set Father's feet on a happier path when it looked as though the blows of fate had finally overwhelmed him."

I had never seen it in that light, and I was surprised to find Wendy putting it so flower-fully, for her conversation was bleak and practical. But I have noticed that it is often this way with people unaccustomed to writing. A pen after all was once literally a plume, a thing taken from a bird's wing, and so these scribes do their best to be air-borne. Our correspondent signed herself "Wendy Merriman," and that, too, gave us something to think about: a formal renunciation of Bob Meagher, an alliance with Papa.

The happier path on to which I had put Mr. Merriman seemed to have provided him with a bit of money to spend. We found, when we arrived at the house, that it had had what Wendy called a real going-over. "You know what that means, George, having been born in Manchester. We get used to muck up there and have to learn how to deal with it. Would you believe, Mrs. Ledra, we have to wash our curtains every week!"

Wendy herself had opened the front door to us, and pointed out with pride the nice old wrought-iron lantern that hung above it, and, at the side, the socket into which a link-boy might thrust his burning brand. It was pleasant to think of Mr. Merriman, accompanied by a small Lucifer, and with cambric frothing his wrists, strolling home from a rout in the early hours. Instead of taking us upstairs, Wendy took us down. "I want you to have a look at t'basement," she said, with a slight lapse into her native idiom. "We're rather proud of it."

The front room of the basement looked out upon area steps, but, sunk though it was, the room was airy, painted white and carpeted in coco-nut matting. A few framed railway posters brightened the walls and a couple of wicker-chairs were at the fireside. A half-blind-looking crone got up from one of them, and Wendy said: "You sit down and rest your bones, Mrs. Midgley." There were two single beds in the room.

"Well," Wendy said, "that's the staff's bed-sitter. We won't go into the kitchen because Mrs. Rowlands will be busy with the dinner."

We went out and were climbing the stairs when I said: "Mrs. Midgley puzzles me, Wendy. I'm sure I've seen her somewhere before."

"You can't have. You're mixing her up with someone else. She's an old thing who used to live in the East End, and Father lodged with her when he was a commissionaire in a cinema. Doubtless," she said, falling back almost into her epistolary style, "you recall that regrettable phase of his life. Well, when he left to go to the tobacconist's in Camden Town, she would have starved if he hadn't done something about it. No other lodger would go to her because she was too blind to be of much use, and she had nothing to live on except an old age pension. Well," she said proudly, "Father just managed to pay her rent, and when we took this place he brought her here. An old horse out to grass, you might say, Mrs. Ledra. She can't do much more than scrub the steps, but fortunately she gets on well enough with Mrs. Rowlands. They both like Ludo."

Never say die, I thought, when it comes to human beings.

Who would have believed Mr. Merriman capable of so kindly an action? Certainly not I.

"It was a very nice thing for your father to do," I said.

"Well, I suppose it was fellow-feeling. When you're half-starved yourself, it seems easier to be a Christian."

She took us everywhere, even into the bedrooms. Everything was fresh and pleasant without being elaborate. She had not called in a Peter Quayne. She told us with pride of this bit of furniture and that. "I found this in a junk-shop in Shoreditch. Had to embroider a new seat for it myself. Rather nice—don't you think?" It was. A pleasing Georgian arm-chair.

The pictures were not what I would have chosen. They were reproductions, mostly of those holy consumptive youths and goitrous ladies that the Pre-Raphaelites loved.

It was almost with awe that Wendy paused outside a door. And a beautiful door it was, panelled mahogany shining like a new chestnut, with the original Georgian furnishing in brass. "This," she said, "is the dining-room."

Mr. Merriman was standing with his back to us, looking through a fine bow window at the traffic of the river. I think he had thought out the pose, like Napoleon. Or could it have been like Bob Meagher, looking down at his kingdom? He turned and shook hands with us effusively and, still holding on to us, drew us to the window. "Come," he said. "Behold my domain."

He was as proud as if it were literally his. The evening light was beautiful upon the water and upon ships, cranes, ware-houses and wherries. "The Romans," Mr. Merriman said, "looked at that."

Well, at the waterway. It was hardly likely that they had looked at much else of this that lay before our eyes. "It was the natural route," said Mr. Merriman, "for conquerors striving to be at the heart of things. The Normans built the White Tower."

And here was Mr. Merriman at the heart of things. If he wanted to consider himself one of the conquerors I had no objection. But I didn't want the history lesson to go on. So I handed to him a little parcel that I had been carrying all this time. "Sylvia and I would like you and Miss Merriman "—I remembered the signature on her letter—" to accept this house-warming present."

He took the parcel and bowed to Sylvia like a shop-walker seeing a valued customer off the premises. He cut the string with a pearl-handled pocket-knife. We had been rather extra-vagant and had bought him a small head of a child in bronze by Epstein. He turned it in his large hands which looked as though they would be apt with a pick and shovel, and gave a little exclamation of pleasure, which may have been simulated. "It shall have the place of honour," he declared, and placed it on the marble mantelpiece between two china vases that were nothing to write home about. "It reminds me," he said, "of Wendy when she was a child. Did I ever tell you, George, that I named Wendy after a girl in a play by Sir James Barrie? You may have heard of it. It was called *Peter Pan*."

"Yes. You have told me that."

"I'm sure Sir James would have seen the likeness. Well, we have come through some dark clouds into sunnier weather, and this will help me to live again in a climate I once knew."

His great paw patted Mr. Epstein's girl on the head, as though she were a good dog, and he said: "Well, to my duties as mine host."

On a good pie-frill table in the bow of the window were two glasses, a decanter of sherry, an open silver box of cigarettes, an ash-tray and a box of matches.

"Help yourself," he invited largely. "Wendy and I do not indulge. We are both strictly T.T. There was a time when I lapsed, but I'm back on the Straight and Narrow, or, as they say to-day, the water-wagon."

"Mrs. Midgley was responsible for that," Wendy said. "Father couldn't both drink and pay her rent, so he paid her rent."

She seemed proud of this, and there was no reason why she shouldn't be.

We took sherry and wished them good health and happiness in their new home.

The door opened, and a stout body entered, whom I took to be Mrs. Rowlands, who had been busy in the kitchen and who liked a game of Ludo with Mrs. Midgley. "We're ready," she announced. "You come and bring the veges. I'll bring the joint."

Sylvia asked if she could give a hand, but Mr. Merriman said: "No, no. Between them, Wendy and the Staff will manage very well."

It was a dinner I had eaten hundreds of times in Manchester when Mrs. Burnett was housekeeping for my father. No preliminaries. Straight on to the joint, which was roast beef, and with it, roast potatoes, cabbage and Yorkshire pudding. All very well cooked and, as Mr. Merriman assured us, Eminently Edible. "I detest French kickshaws," he said in a voice which condemned the frivolity of the entire Gallic race, though he didn't know what a French kickshaw was, for he had never crossed the Channel. "The French," he told us, "say that the English have a hundred religions and one sauce. Well, that's how it should be, and perhaps," he added, straying a little towards *non sequitur,* "it may explain the outcome of the Battle of Waterloo."

We all waited while he devoured a second helping of roast

beef, as though it were roast Frenchman, and then we predictably moved on to apple dumplings and Stilton cheese. Coffee followed, and it was horrible: the only horrible thing about the meal. Sylvia and I drank sparingly of a red wine. " I get it from the corner shop," Mr. Merriman told us. " The man there says it's *vin ordinaire,* which means ordinary wine. I hope it is to your taste."

We assured him that it was exquisite, a wine to be savoured, not gulped down in large quantities. " It has," I said, " a *je ne sais quoi,* which means a heaven knows what."

The ladies retired after Mrs. Rowlands had cleared the table. Mr. Merriman and I sat on, but not over our port. I was glad of that anyway—a detestable liverish wine that I abhor. We drew easy-chairs to the window and sat looking out upon the darkling river. The sky was a flush of evening colour and lights began to bloom on the shore and on the ships. I asked if I might smoke my pipe, and he said: " By all means, dear boy. You are in Liberty Hall."

I congratulated him on the excellent recovery he had made from his sad days after the bursting of the cotton boom, and he said: " Yes, George, I think I may fairly say that I am out of the doldrums and sailing with a fair wind. To a man who had managed the affairs of Fred Byles and Ledra running a tobacconist's shop was not difficult. Indeed, it was such child's play that I asked myself the simple question: Why not let someone run it for me? From there it was an inevitable step—though it was Wendy's idea—to build up other little shops in the same way. There are now eight of them, and I'm in negotiation about two more. In that way, as Wendy wisely points out, all our eggs, if I may so put it, are not in one basket. Though she has her ambitions and may yet persuade me to share them."

I smoked in silence, confident that he needed no prodding to develop his scheme. " She sees me as a Tycoon," he said with a laugh that didn't dismiss the idea as absurd. " As I say, George, we now have eight shops and will soon have ten. When we have a dozen, it is Wendy's idea to sail into more ambitious channels."

Wendy and Sylvia came in at that moment. The river was now dark and a half-moon hung in the sky. Sylvia made the conventional if deserved comments on the beauty of the place the Merrimans had chosen to live in, and Mr. Merriman said, looking fondly at his daughter: " Only the best is good enough for Wendy. My dear, I was telling George about your schemes for our future."

Wendy didn't mind talking, and she talked confidently, like one who knew the ropes. My mind went back to a Sunday afternoon when she and I had sat in the greenhouse at Dormers, watching the carp. I remembered her neglected appearance, her mental and spiritual confusion in the knowledge that Bob was finished with her and that his saying so was only a matter of time. Now, although she would attract no eye in a crowd, she had regained the confidence that had been sucked out of her by Bob's failure to use her capacities. She was too stout for her years; she still didn't know how to dress; and the thick-lensed spectacles that she had taken to wearing obscured the eyes that had been her one good feature. But she was a woman, esteemed as a woman loves to be, and she had something to do. I don't know whether she ever pined for the children whose pining for her had been so soon dispelled. If so, she gave no sign of it.

"When we've got twelve shops," she said, "we can take a risk on four of them. It leaves us a good margin of security. Then with the proceeds of the four small shops we can buy one big shop. I've been going into it, and I know that the income from one sizeable shop in a good neighbourhood is far greater than from four small ones in back streets. When the one big shop is definitely established we can sell four more small ones. . . ."

"And so on," I put in with a smile, "till you buy up Harrods."

"Well, perhaps not that," she conceded, "but it might be possible to reach a position where the shops we then owned—they would all have to be the same *sort* of shop, of course—would attract the attention of some really big firm who wanted to buy them. If we agreed to a merger, there would be no reason why Father shouldn't have a seat on the board."

Mr. Merriman's chest was swelling with the wind of this dream. "Now, now, Wendy," he said not too severely. "I've warned you about counting chickens." But there was no doubt from the look of him that he would not be surprised if asked to-morrow to be a director of something like Debenhams.

"I don't suppose it can be done in under ten years," Wendy said placidly; and I was aware of a pig-headed dour resolution in the woman that was prepared to hang on longer than that, and move forward inch by inch.

As we were driving home, Sylvia said: "Bob was not very intelligent in letting a woman like that run to seed."

"She's not my idea of domestic bliss."

"Neither does Janet appear to be Bob's at the moment. What *does* he want?"

"A peerage to be going on with, I should say. I could do with something more accessible. Can you guess what?"

"Yes. But don't excite the driver."

CHAPTER FIFTEEN

1

Late that summer of 1936 Sir Harry jjones invited a party, including Sir Robert and Lady Meagher, to join him on his yacht for a Mediterranean cruise. Jane Lancaster, who was now attracting attention with pictures in which everyone walked on hands instead of feet, was one of the ladies. Bob accepted the invitation, but Janet asked to be excused. She had taken a job on the paper that Lady Betty Newnham edited and said that she still had everything to learn. She would take no holiday that year. Bob, who had not wanted her to take that job or any other, believed this to be a way of dodging the party, and said so. Janet didn't answer this directly but asked: "What happens about Viola's holiday?"

"I'm surprised," Bob said, "that Viola's concerns should any longer be expected to be mine. It wasn't my wish that she should spend her time loafing about in Cornwall."

Janet let that go. They had had words enough about it already, and she had the sense to see that, though Bob professed to have no further interest in Viola, he might easily, in a moment of exasperation, step in after all and ruin a work that had been well begun. She said: "I really do want to stay on, Bob. Betty Newnham took a risk in employing me, and I don't want to let her down. There's still everything to learn. This is a very different paper from *Now* and I'm all at sea."

"Well," he conceded, "you must please yourself. But it wouldn't hurt you to meet some new people."

"But, Bob, I know almost everyone who's going on this jaunt. And, honestly, so far as some of them go, I don't want to deepen the acquaintance."

"You don't go on a cruise of this sort for the sake of people's blue eyes. You go because they're the sort of people that you're expected to be about with."

"We left it at that," Janet said to me and Sylvia. "I felt rather sick, because he really meant what he said. I suppose the next thing will be that he'll buy a yacht himself and expect me to be a gracious hostess to a pack of Midases and floozies. Everybody knows that the Lancaster girl is Harry jjones's wench."

"Well," I said, "he hasn't a wife. Perhaps he intends to marry her."

327

"He's just as likely," she said, "to go into a monastery and take vows of poverty, chastity and obedience."

She stayed in London; Bob motored down through France to join the yacht; and Sylvia and I took Paul and Miss Collum to Penruan, where Viola and Jocelyn joined us. Miss Hartman had gone off to the Continent, to tag along to one concert after another. "We shall get postcards from her with views of Salzburg, Bayreuth and all those places," Viola said. There was a touch of affectionate mockery in her voice. I was glad to hear it, because I dislike heroes and heroines. It is excellent for youngsters to have them, but the sooner they grow out of them, or at any rate put a tinge of scepticism into the relationship, the better so far as I am concerned. The way Viola said "Salzburg, Bayreuth and all those places" suggested a reaction against an overdose of indoctrination.

She was a beautiful child, grave for her fifteen years; but you couldn't diagnose the beauty and say that it was her eyes or her mouth, her complexion or her voice. It was the elusive totality of her: youth, and vitality, and a dedication that harmonised her qualities. One felt that she was a person. She was much more balanced than Janet had been at her age. When we arrived we found her walking on the terrace, wearing a light grey skirt and a tan sweater. She kissed us, but didn't kiss Joss, whom we had picked up at school and brought along with us, and that, I think, was because Joss so evidently didn't want to be kissed. He was seventeen, with a deepening voice. Another year at school and he would be off to Oxford. He said casually, as though they had never been parted: "Hallo, Vi," lugged his trunk out of the boot of the car, and carried it into the house. She watched him go with twinkling eyes that seemed to weigh up, and be amused by, his aloof masculinity.

Paul was asleep in a cradle wedged into the back of the car. Viola lifted him out tenderly. "I'll carry him up," she said. "I know where he'll be sleeping."

She went, followed by Miss Collum, who was inclined to cluck at being deprived of her rights as a pack-horse. I looked at Sylvia. "Well, here we are again. *In loco parentis.*"

"And very odd it is," she said, "to think of the parents. Bob on a barge full of rather tatty Cleopatras, and that Wendy girl dreaming by the Thames of a commercial empire. They seem oceans apart; but really, you know, they're of the same blood and bone. Janet will never make Bob the wife that a bit of common sense could have made of—well, I hate the daft name, but I must say it—of Wendy."

328

Viola went every morning to perform the operation which Joss
called having a bash at Miss Hartman's piano. In the afternoons
she sometimes came with me and Sylvia in our cavortings about
the county—to a beach or to the moors. Sometimes she walked
or swam alone; and now and then she went sailing with Joss
and Jose. So far as Joss went, sailing with Jose *was* the holiday.
Sylvia and I didn't amount to much as mariners, and so the
holiday, while it gave us contact with Joss, didn't do much to
deepen our acquaintance with him. He had become so keen a
sailor that Jose changed the name of his boat. That is said to be
an unlucky thing to do, but I have never heard of any ill
consequences following such a change. Anyway, the little cutter
was now the *Joss and Jose,* and Joss loved nothing better than
to drink a half pint of ale manfully with the old men who
gathered in Jose's bar, and then to get aboard and sail all day.
Jose, who had never had an addiction to Mammon, was at any
time ready to leave the pub in charge of his pot-boy.

There was a day when we saw Joss go off after breakfast
wearing as usual nothing but bathing-slips. Viola walked with
him as far as the village and Miss Hartman's piano; and Sylvia
and I carried Paul in a laundry basket down through the valley
to the beach. Not a soul seemed ever to come there. Cornish
beaches were like that in those days. It is a fact that, except
Sylvia and Janet, I had not seen anyone upon that beach since
I first stumbled down it through a dewy autumn morning when
I was as old as Viola was now. It was a golden arc, lying
between two arms of rock, and the sun was flooding it with
light and colour. With scent, too; for the heat released the
smell of the thyme that grew upon the hills, and this drifted
down to mingle with the damp smell of seaweed piled in the
cleft to which the sand ran up. The tide was rising, but there
was no wind behind it. The water slipped up the beach languid
and listless, as though its journey across the Atlantic had fagged
it out.

We had carried Paul with nothing but a blanket over him, and
we took this away and poured him out to run upon the sand.
The sturdy toddler ran down to the end of the tired sea and
when a wave, after its recession, rose again and fell in a wide
lacy fan, he would get behind it and with his wooden spade try
to sweep it higher up the sand: a Canute in reverse. We took
off our clothes and lay in the sun, lazy and content, watching
the child and the gulls screaming over him, and the infinity of
water stretching away from that finite speck who was trying
to hasten its immutable processes. Sylvia and I were often so

much in tune that we divined one another's movements of thought; and she said now: "He'll learn in time that it can't be done. There's a lot that you have to wait for, and even so you often don't get it."

I could never be alone with her in such moments as this, and even in more prosaic moments, without tenderness flooding me; and, looking down at the breasts that were as proud as when I had first seen them, and at the lovely flowing lines of her body, I marvelled that men were ever harsh with women. "What is it," I asked, "that you have failed to get?"

"Oh, I've been a lucky one. I was thinking of other people, especially of Janet," she said, "and for that matter of the Wendy girl, too. What is Janet going to do? It's all nonsense for a woman, or for a man, come to that, to talk about a 'career,' as though that could ever in itself be enough to live for. Careers are a curse. Working for a living is one thing, and has to be done; but when men and women begin to talk about careers they cease to be human. Look at Bob. All he wanted Janet to do was decorate his damned career."

"Well, we'd better go and decorate this damned Atlantic Ocean," I said, not wanting this mood at this time. "Let's swim."

I took her hands and pulled her to her feet, and we ran down the sand, past the child still indefatigably challenging the impossible, and threw ourselves into the opal water. We hadn't intended to swim and she had brought no bathing-cap. Her hair came loose and streamed on the water. "You look like a mermaid," I said.

"Nonsense. If you don't know by now that where a mermaid begins to be a fish I'm not a bit fishy, you never will."

Paul had for a change pursued a retreating wave. And then an on-coming one knocked him over and rolled him up the beach. He began to howl, and we swam in, scooped him up, and ran him up the sand. The blanket he had been wrapped in had to do as a towel for all three of us. We dressed and walked home. "You know," she said, "I feel so mad about Bob that I sometimes wish Peter Quayne would teach him what a fool he is."

3

Viola was on the terrace, and, seeing Paul naked, for we hadn't wrapped him in the damp blanket, she took him in her arms and said: "Should you do that? Won't he catch cold?"

"Not in this sun," Sylvia assured her;; but she seemed unconvinced and with a gentle solicitude carried the child into the house. Watching her go, her face bent over the face of the naked babe, I thought she looked immemorial woman, and her indefinable beauty moved me deeply.

That afternoon we left Paul in Miss Collum's care and motored to Trencrom, which Viola had not seen. I wondered more and more why I had spent so much money on the place, for I hardly ever went near it nowadays. When I was amusing myself with its creation I had not thought that I should live in Penruan. "Perhaps," I said to Viola who sat with me in the back seat, "you won't have another chance to see the place. I feel inclined to sell it."

Sylvia half-turned her head to say: "You'll do nothing of the sort. It's a lovely little place, and, anyhow, who would buy it? As it was, you might have got rid of it, but now you've made it a costly thing, and who would buy a costly thing that hasn't even a water-supply? Besides, some day we may have to sell Penruan, and then your place would be nice to fall back on."

The idea of Penruan being sold appalled me. What I had done at Trencrom was a pinprick compared with the money, tears and toil that had been lavished on the great house. I said to Viola: "You never saw Penruan as I first knew it. I was then as old as you are now. I've watched the slow working of a miracle."

"It is very beautiful," Viola said. "When I was last here with Father I didn't notice it much. I think I notice things more now."

Well, that was how it should be. "It was sudden," Viola said. "It didn't *grow* on me as they say. It was on a day last winter. Miss Hartman and I had walked that way and the evening was coming on. It was a wild evening and there were splashes of stormy colour in the sky, and Penruan was standing with that for a background. I suddenly saw how beautiful it was."

She was a quiet child. This was the first time she had ever said to me anything that one might call a confidence. I felt proud. I knew what was happening to her. I recalled a day of long ago. In the winter before my father had sent me to Mr. Chown I had gone for a country walk with a school friend, a reserved boy who rarely opened his mouth. We walked towards Knutsford. In the leaden-dull of the afternoon, still, and with a frosty threat in the air, we came to a mere and stood looking at the broken reeds draggling the water's edge. It was so quiet that you could have heard a gnat's wings, but not even a gnat was stirring. Suddenly my friend said: "The sedge has withered from the lake, and no bird sings."

It seems incredible to us in middle age that there was a time when we had not heard a great poem, read a great novel, seen a great play or picture, or listened to a master's music. I had

331

not read that poem of Keats, and my young friend now spoke it from beginning to end. It was one of those moments that shift the foundations of one's personal life. Something out of eternity had come through into time; and, by that much, life could never be the same again. Of course, I didn't think or say anything of that kind. We walked on, and drank tea at a wayside cottage, and came out to find the snow beginning to fall, and with hunched powdered shoulders marched down to Knutsford station and took a train to Manchester. But there it was. I had been on the road to Damascus.

Thinking these things as the car idled through the torrid afternoon I knew, and was glad, that Viola, too, had been along that eye-opening road. It was a road not without dangers, for new-born souls are delicately susceptible.

I had written to Mrs. Carbis, who kept an eye on the cottage for me, to say that we were at Penruan and might come over to Trencrom, and she had seen that there was water in the place and fuel for the spirit stove and a few things to eat. I proposed a climb to the top of the hill, but Sylvia said it was too hot for mountaineering and that she would stay down and have tea ready by the time we returned. So Viola and I climbed the hill alone. I recall a girl brown as a nut, with lively eyes, wearing a rather full skirt made of some flowing material patterned in a confusion of rich batik colours. She wore sandals and no stockings, and a floppy hat was bound about with the same material that made the skirt. I talked to her of the dark aboriginal men and told her the legends of the Irish saints providentially arriving in these parts, borne over the seas sometimes on leaves, sometimes on millstones miraculously unsinkable. She smiled and said: " All things are possible."

" Well, at all events," I said, " however they did it, they got here and they kept at least a glim going in a pretty dark time."

" We can do no more than what lies in us. That is what Miss Hartman is always telling me."

The light mocking smile that had been in her eyes when she spoke of Miss Hartman's postcards from Salzburg and Bayreuth was there again. I guessed that Miss Hartman was a bit of a preacher, and that the child was not sorry to be for a moment off the chain. She must have guessed what I was thinking, for she added swiftly: " Mind you, Miss Hartman is good for me. Discipline hurts no one."

The last four words sounded like a " quote " from Miss Hartman again, so I let the matter lie, and we stood on the top of the hill where a sea-breeze caught us and flattened the clothes upon her body, showing me her budding maturity. She stood with one hand, going up in a lovely arc, holding on her hat. " Yes," I thought. " She is beautiful."

Rather shy of the moment, she said almost abruptly, without

looking at me: "I'd like to thank you and Aunt Sylvia for what you've done. It's meant a lot—almost everything. Music is so much more than itself. Do you see that?"

I said that I did. "Very well, then. Thank you."

It was a moment she had obviously struggled hard to meet and have done with. Now that it was over, she turned to me gaily. "Race you down the hill," she said, and we ran pell-mell towards our waiting tea.

About a week after this the letter came from Janet. "Dear Mummy,—I hope you and George are enjoying life a bit more than I am. I wouldn't wish 'my enemy's dog, though he had bit me' to be in London in this grilling heat. To stick to the post of duty, learning one's job, is all very well, but I was more than a little glad to get out into the country last week-end with Peter. Pray dispel the evil suspicions which, I am sure, rise in your mind at sight of his name. It was old Mr. Quayne's idea. I don't think you've met him. I was asked to take dinner with him and Peter, and he prettily informed me that I was looking like death, and ought to get out of town more. Well, I've certainly been working over-hard, and wondering what Bob is up to, and so on. All I know is that the jjones yacht touched at Ragusa and that Bob sent me a picture postcard therefrom with the assurance on the back that it is a 'pretty place.' A man of insight, you see. When Peter took up his father's tale and suggested running down to Oxford and getting on the river I had been reduced by the pair of them to feeling that if I didn't do just that I could hardly survive another week; so we went and lazed under willows and smelled Rupert Brooke's 'unforgettable, unforgotten river smell,' which is just the same on the Isis as on the Cam, though I don't imagine Rupert would have admitted that."

We had finished breakfast on the terrace, and Sylvia was reading the letter aloud as we sat there at the littered table. "She's a long time," I intervened, "coming to whatever she's coming to."

"Aren't we all?" Sylvia asked philosophically; and went on reading.

"Well, I did feel the better for that day, and the sight of Peter poling away with charming mastery and insouciance didn't diminish my pleasure."

"Now she's approaching her theme," I said. "Hold your hat on."

Sylvia looked at me disapprovingly. "And the bit about Peter would have rejoiced the heart of Ouida," I told her. "I suppose it's the way they write on *Hearth and Home*. I can see the large coloured illustration."

"Betty Newnham had been away for a bit of holiday herself," Janet's letter continued, "and when she got back she took up the tale the Quaynes had been telling me. I was overdoing it, and so forth. Well, the upshot of it was that she almost ordered me to get out of the office for a week, and that is why you'll be seeing me next week-end. Do you think Peter could have that bedroom with the lovely view down towards the Lizard . . .?"

"I admire," I said, "the charming mastery and insouciance with which she makes this transition to Peter's coming."

Sylvia asked gravely: "Well, what do you think of it?"

"Is that the lot?"

"There's a bit more."

"Finish it. She may throw light on whether Peter is to have the apricot or pale blue blankets."

"Of course," Janet went on, "you won't mind Peter, will you? Penruan has always been a bit of a Liberty Hall."

"A good pull-up for libertines?" I suggested. "It's a long time since I enjoyed a letter so much as this."

"I'm not enjoying it a bit," Sylvia said. "Of course we'll be glad to see her and Peter. But the thing worries me."

I wasn't enjoying it either ; but I didn't see why I should do Bob's weeping over spilt milk. No doubt Ragusa was a pretty place, but there were moments when it was unwise to leave a wife in order to make that discovery.

The letter tailed off with an explanation of how easy it would be for old Mr. Quayne to look after the gallery, "and Peter really does need a holiday as much as I do," and so forth. "Ever lovingly, Janet."

Viola, who liked to take her breakfast with Paul and Miss Collum, came out wearing pale green linen. She stood in the old stone porch, the early light upon her, looking cool and fresh, as lovely as the morning.

"Look," she said. "There they go!"

Out to sea we could see the *Joss and Jose* spanking along under all sail. Joss had snatched a breakfast in the kitchen and dashed away for an early start. He and Jose were going to make a day of it, sail to Falmouth, sleep aboard, and sail back in the morning.

"How he loves it," Viola said.

She stepped out on to the terrace and Sylvia, moved as I was by her youth and innocence, kissed her. There was a postcard for the child—sure enough from Bayreuth. "Work hard on the Nacht Musik," it said monitorially.

"Are you going to work hard on the Nacht Musik?" Sylvia asked her.

"Oh, not to-day," she said, holding her arms out to the sea and sky. "To-day I shall just wait."

We didn't ask what she was waiting for. Her exalted mood disturbed us.

334

Peter drove Janet to Penruan by night. A long motor journey is
often made by night in these days in order to avoid the Gehenna
of day-time roads. But then, though the traffic on the roads was
increasing, it had not become so bad as all that, and I think they
came by night because it was a romantic thing to do. There
was a full moon. It took them longer than they had bargained
for, and they didn't reach Penruan till ten in the morning. They
had breakfasted on the road, and both were so tired that Sylvia
suggested they should get to their beds and sleep till lunch time.
They did so, Peter in the lovely room looking towards the
Lizard. Joss, who preferred Jose's company to our own, was off
for the day, not sailing this time, but going with Jose on a
jaunt to see furniture that might be worth buying here and
there in the country. Viola had been to Miss Hartman's cottage
to do her morning's work, and she returned just before one
o'clock. There was no sign of movement from above, and
Sylvia said: " I'll go up and have a peep. If they're sleeping I
won't disturb them."

She came back and reported that they were both dead to the
world, so we ate lunch without them, and at two o'clock Viola
went off to take her dutiful afternoon exercise. At about half
past two Peter came down alone. We told him that Janet was
still sleeping, and he said: " Let her have her sleep out. She's
exhausted. I don't mean by the journey. She's been looking
dreadful for a long time. I'm not surprised."

We gave him a sandwich and a glass of beer as a stay-bit. He
ate and drank and filled his pipe. " She's had a shaking-up, you
know," he said. " *Now* meant a lot to her, and so did the people
working on it. The way Hubert and Alcott-Lucas and Hubert's
mother died knocked her endways, which, of course, is why she
rushed into this new job. That's been pretty grilling, too,
because really, you know, it's not up her street at all. I suppose
the way Sir Robert pushed off didn't help."

He was self-possessed and matter-of-fact, and I tried to angle
him into a more committed attitude. So I thanked him for
giving Janet such a pleasant day at Oxford. " She wrote to us,
and seems to have enjoyed it immensely."

" I think she did," he said. " I was pleased about that and so
was my father. The old man was getting quite worried about
her. He hasn't seen much of her, but he liked what he saw. He's
very fond of her. But there. He's one of those old dogs who
can never resist a pretty girl."

"While you, I take it, are securely armoured?" I chaffed him.
" Oh, I wouldn't say that. I'm rather fond of the company of

women: that is, if they're intelligent. That Lancaster piece took to haunting me, you know, and nearly drove me round the bend. She's got the brains of a newt. Janet's another matter. I'm sorry about this upset with Sir Robert. I'm sure it's nothing but nerves caused by these recent disasters. I'm hoping this holiday will put her in good shape and that she'll be as good as new by the time he gets back."

He had shuffled down in bedroom slippers, and said: "Wait here, George, till I get some shoes on. We'll take a walk if you'd like to."

Sylvia and I looked at one another. "A pretty piece of cross-examination," she said.

"Well, what do you make of it all?"

"It's what Janet's going to make of it that worries me."

"Should it worry you? Shouldn't you be glad?"

"Oh, it's a mess," she said. "When an illusion goes, what happens in the vacuum?"

She went into the house, passing Peter who was coming out. He and I set off to walk down the valley to the sea. The spring-time glory of camellias and mimosa, azaleas and rhododendrons was over, and the larches' fresh emerald was changed for a green that was almost black. The day was hot and the song-birds were silent, but all the same that valley could not help being a lovely place. We walked without speaking to where the mouth of the gulch widened, and there was the burning gold of the sand and the blue of the sea poised almost without motion between the fall and the flow of the tide.

There wasn't a sail or a funnel on the water, not a human being in sight. Utter silence held the afternoon, silence through which the heat poured almost visibly down. We stood there as though the rays of light had skewered us to the sand, listening to this most moving nothingness, and out of the quiet came suddenly a voice, singing. It came from away on our left. There, about ten yards from the cliff, was an upright slab of rock, a wall high enough to hide anyone who was on the sand behind it.

"Theoretically," I said to Peter, "this is a private beach, so private that Sylvia and I are rather immodest when we use it for bathing. We just throw off our togs and go in. I suppose this songster is some more reticent bather, drying and dressing."

The singing continued, not very good as singing goes, but light and pleasant. It was a girl's voice, and she was singing, "Drink to me only with thine eyes."

"If I were a plutocrat with a private beach," Peter said, "I would employ bevies of girls to sing as I dallied on the sand and swam in the water. Girls with voices like this one. Beautifully unprofessional. A hundred miles from Covent Garden. Just ' singing of summer in full-throated ease.' "

We were about a hundred yards from the concealing slab of rock. The little song was sung to the end. "But might I of Jove's nectar sup, I would not change for thine."

There was silence again, and then Peter began to sing the same song. It has a lovely tune for harmonising, and I could not resist joining a bass to his full and free baritone. We finished, and looked smiling towards the rock, as though inviting whoever might be there to take note of how singing should be done. Viola's face peeped over the top, hair streaming. I knew that footholds were there. Seeing me, she climbed higher, waved her hand which clutched her bathing-dress, and then gave an agile leap that landed her on the sand. Her feet and legs were bare, and she was wearing a dress of lovely peacock-blue, which the wind of her jump sent billowing airily to her waist.

I whispered to Peter: "Janet's step-daughter. Bob Meagher's child."

She came with a swift easy stride towards us, her face, innocent of make-up, rosy from towelling. She was rather tall for her age. As she came she wrestled with her hair, twirling it up hastily into some sort of order on her head and fastening it with a bit of dark blue ribbon. And how lovely that gesture is, I was thinking, when a woman raises both hands unconsciously to the crown of her head.

She curtsied, and said: "I thought I had the world to myself."

I introduced her to Peter, and she said: "Now please excuse me. I must go and get my things. I've been gathering beautiful shells. And I must put on some more clothes. When I heard people about I just threw on this dress."

Yes. Her jump from the rock had made that clear.

"Join us at tea," I said. "We'll be strolling back. I expect Janet will be up by now."

Peter and I started off towards the house. He was as quiet as the afternoon which, following the irruption on the sand, had settled down in brooding heat.

"How old is she?" he asked suddenly.

"Who?"

"Why, Viola, of course."

"I'm not quite sure. Fifteen or thereabouts. She's studying music—the piano's her instrument."

He looked behind him, and said: "Ah! She's overtaking us. We'd better wait."

We waited till she came up, and went on to find Sylvia and Janet already taking their tea on the terrace.

There were eight of us to dinner that night, and Sylvia was in a mood of grandeur. Usually we ate in the little dining-room where I had first seen the John Collier portrait of Margaret Napier, but when the spirit moved her Sylvia would have the meal served in the great hall. I had first seen it with one wall of harsh make-shift brick; but now Sylvia's dream had long since come true, and the brick had been modelled upon with stucco, and the stucco had been painted I do not know by whom, but so airily that it seemed to be a tapestry, and a white unicorn with a medieval lady embracing it was the centre of a scene full of hounds and huntsmen and flowering trees. It was frankly based on a tapestry I had seen pictured elsewhere, and was none the less lovely for that. It stole the eye from all else in the room, though all else was beauty: the fireplace, the immense table at which I had sat feeling lonely with Mr. Chown and Sylvia long ago, the candelabra which Jose had rescued from a doomed mansion, and that was lit that night to hang above us with prisms flashing.

It was rather hard on us men, because the women dressed up and we had no clothes to match theirs. When Peter and I and Viola joined the tea-party Joss and Jose were there. Viola kissed Janet, throwing her arms about her warmly. She had not forgotten that Janet had been on her side in the dispute with Bob about staying down here with Miss Hartman. Janet said: "Oh, darling, what have you been up to? Your hair is like a crow's nest."

Peter said: "No, no. It looks more like a dryad's top-knot," and I, seeing Viola look a little crestfallen at what she took to be a rebuke, said: "I remember strolling one afternoon down the valley and finding an appalling little creature, about as old as Viola is now, looking like something the cat had brought in. However, it was human. It had just run away from school and had come in from Helston on the back of a policeman's bicycle."

Joss saw the point of my story. He began to laugh. "I'll bet that was Janet," he said. "That's one up on you, Janet. Viola does at least look human."

To my surprise, Janet did not take it well. She had just risen from a long sleep, given herself a thorough grooming, and was *soignée* to the finger-tips. She didn't like being reminded of that horrid little girl, and she didn't like it that three of the men present had spoken on Viola's side. Her face flushed, and she was obviously about to make a sharp comment when Sylvia chipped in. "Darling," she said to me, "we're going to have a dinner party to-night. Jose, who neglects his pub shamefully and will end in the bankruptcy court, has agreed to come. It's so long since we had a celebration."

"What are we going to celebrate?" I asked.

"Don't ask silly questions. A celebration doesn't need to have a reason. One feels like celebrating and one celebrates."

Viola said: "It's a lovely idea, Aunt Sylvia, but I've never been at a grown-up dinner party. I'm too young."

She was sitting near Peter, who impulsively put a hand on her arm and said: "Oh, but it would be nothing without you," and Jose backed this up. "I'll tell you what," he said. "Let's have dinner here and then all pack into the cars and go along to Miss Hartman's place. We'll finish the evening with music. You shall play to us."

A confusion of pros and cons at once arose. Joss said: "Count me out. I can't stand being played to. And besides, Jose, there's a lot to do aboard if the boat's to be fit to sail to-morrow. You can dump me and pick me up when the strumming's over."

Janet asked coldly: "Have we Miss Hartman's permission to invade her house?" and Viola protested most sharply of all. "Oh, no, no! I couldn't. Really I couldn't. I'm not fit for it yet. Really I'm not. You'd all feel embarrassed and I should feel ashamed."

Jose said: "As for Miss Hartman, Lady Meagher, the old trout wouldn't mind. I know her well enough to assure you of that. And Miss Viola's playing—well, I've heard it. I'm living almost next door. And I for one have never felt embarrassed by it."

I think that formal "Lady Meagher," putting her outside the close circle of friendliness, grated on Janet, and she clearly disliked the concentration of attention on Viola. When Peter said: "I should love it. Will you play for us?" and Viola said: "Very well," Janet went into the house. "I'd better fall in with the majority then," she said, trying to make it light.

Everybody drifted away except me and Sylvia. "Rather rash, don't you think, this celebration?" I asked. "Have we enough food in the house?"

"Of course we have. Jose's the only one who wouldn't be feeding here anyway, and I think we can get over that. A few fancy trimmings—that's all that was missing, and I've rung up that nice hotel in Helston. They'll send them over last thing, and they've rustled up a waiter, too. Don't you think I'm wonderful?"

"Yes. And what's more to the point, Peter Quayne thinks Viola is wonderful."

I told what had happened during the afternoon. "I often wondered," I said, "what was going on between Peter and

339

Janet. Well, I feel pretty sure that he's happy in her company, very sympathetic and helpful now that she's passing through a bad patch, and that that's all you can say about it."

"But, Viola! She's nothing but a child. And he's—what is he?"

"Just about Janet's age, I should guess. Twenty-seven or eight. And Viola's about the age I was when I first came down here."

"What's that got to do with it?"

"I fell in love with you."

"Yes, but has Viola fallen in love with him? You say he's taken with her. Well, he may be. She's an attractive child. If you like I'll be rudely biological and say that no one can miss the fact that she's ripe for her years."

"I don't know whether she's in love with him or not. This whole conversation is absurd. They met this afternoon. They've been in one another's company for an hour or two, and here we are, speculating like two old hags at a débutantes' party. All I can say is that Mr. Ledra's sensitive antennæ caught a vibration, and I'm warning you."

It was a successful dinner. I put on a lounge suit, which was as far as I could advance towards grandeur, and went down to find Peter similarly dressed. There was a table with drinks and he was suggesting this and that to Miss Collum, who was refusing all and looking rather alarmed at his overtures. She was an odd creature with an air of distinction that nothing in her character justified, except her devotion to Paul. She had dressed for the occasion in an outrageous purple confection and looked like a young aristocrat embarked for the guillotine and wearing her most abominable clothes so that her best should not be soiled when the knife fell. As Peter and I drank our sherry she contented herself with chewing an olive, and managed to give an air of social bravado to the simple operation.

Janet came down next, dressed to the nines, as she used to be for the Friday nights in Piccadilly. Peter was attentive to her, gave her a cigarette and the iced Dubonnet she asked for, but he was watching the great stairway, and I knew he was waiting for Viola. There the four of us stood, Miss Collum venturing upon a second olive with the look of making a night of it. I was aware of a feeling of strain and uneasiness, and to ease the situation began to talk of my first night in that room and of how Janet had come down from bed and sat on Mr. Chown's knee and demanded to be allowed to drink wine. "Yes," she said. "I remember that well. I remember how horrible I thought the wine was and how I pretended all the same to like it. 'Just like life,' as they say. You have to pretend to like it, however bitter it tastes."

It was a little speech so uncalled for and out of character that
340

I looked at her in surprise, and was glad when Miss Collum, rousing herself to her social duty of keeping a conversation going, asked pleasantly: "Would you really say that, Lady Meagher? Isn't life fundamentally sound and decent?" With a swish of silk, as though Miss Collum did not exist, Janet turned towards the stair and said: "Our hostess is forgetting her duty to be here to receive her guests."

And here the hostess was, coming down with Viola. It was obvious to me that Sylvia had been at work on the child. Viola was wearing the peacock-blue dress that she had worn during the afternoon, but her thin bare legs were now clothed in silk and she was wearing pretty blue slippers. Her hair had been brushed and brushed till it shone, and some confection had been added to it, some knack out of Sylvia's theatrical knowledge, that seemed to add a halo. Sylvia herself was regal. I was proud of her. She looked, in dusky silk, a queen bringing with her a loved princess. Janet gave one look at her mother and at her husband's child, and turned away. In that second her eye caught mine, and I saw again the runaway child I had met by the ruined seat in the valley, a child with no firm anchorage, all at sixes and sevens. Unobtrusively I took her hand and gave it a little squeeze. She looked at me in surprise, then read all that I had tried to say of sympathy and reassurance. She whispered: "Thank you, George," and the hired waiter came in and announced (what was untrue): "Dinner is served, Madam."

We sat down and dinner soon was served. Sylvia and I were at the head of the table and Viola and Peter faced us from the other end. On our right, Miss Collum had Jose for a companion, and on our left were Janet and Joss. They were a strangely-assorted pair, for Joss was at an age and in a state of mind when he wished to show contempt for what he no doubt would have called elegant flim-flam. It is true that he had not turned up wearing the khaki shorts that were usual with him. As a concession to "company" he had put on a pair of flannel bags blotched with paint and tar and a roughly-knitted seaman's pullover of greasy-looking white wool. His voice was breaking and he would soon need to shave. His finger-nails were unashamedly filthy. He and Jose had been the last to arrive. They came in a down-at-heel truck belonging to Jose, who had never, within my knowledge, had any other sort of motor conveyance. When one of them died under him and had to go to the scrap-heap, he had an infallible flair for finding its twin, with another year or so of rattling and asthmatic life before it. That night he and Joss hauled out of the back of the truck a bulky-looking object draped in sacking and carried it into the hall. "I thought you might like to have a look at this," he said to Sylvia. In that place it looked as incongruous as Joss looked sitting next to Janet, or as Mr. Merriman must have looked when making his memorable call *en commissionaire* at Dormers. "It's something rather nice that Joss and I came on this afternoon," Jose explained.

"Put it in the most remote corner you can find," Sylvia instructed him. "We'll have it unveiled after dinner."

Jose, though he was not consciously running to seed, or rather hurling himself to seed as Joss was doing, was rarely a figure that would have earned a commendatory leading article from *The Tailor and Cutter*. But that night he had at least dressed as well as he could. He was newly shaved and wore a double-breasted suit of dark grey with a spotless white shirt and the reticent tie of his Oxford college. He had even allowed himself a touch of ostentation. His cuff-links were made from jewelled buttons that he had cut from a Georgian waistcoat. "Reputably reported," he informed us, "to have been a gift from Beau Brummel to the Prince Regent. Or would that make them disreputable?"

I envied his looks. He was taller and thinner than any other man there and he had a dark southern skin and dark blue eyes. He was enjoying himself. This was the first time he had been present at a social gathering in this room that he had done so much to create, and he rejoiced in the approval of Peter Quayne whose knowledge of antiquities was almost, though not, at that time, quite as great as his own. He knew of Peter's growing reputation and referred to an article that Peter had written in *The Connoisseur*.

Peter, like the rest of us, didn't dislike hearing his work praised. The wine was good and we were all in an outgoing mood, even Miss Collum, who was making do with a thimbleful of gin fighting a losing alcoholic battle with a tumblerful of tonic water. "You see what it is to be famous," Peter bantered Viola. "One of these days people will be talking to you in this way."

It was clear to anyone who cared to look that Viola was delighted with Peter's company and that she loved what Jose had to say about him. She was drinking water, to the contempt of Joss, who swigged beer with what he hoped was a robust maritime gusto. Janet, at his side, was very quiet. She had tried once or twice to make him talk, but it had fallen flat. She looked like Queen Elizabeth being kind to an unresponsive deck-hand back from circumnavigating the world with Drake. She tried Oxford, to which Joss would be going in a year's time, but Oxford was something to which he wasn't looking forward with enthusiasm. "Fancy having no boats except those ridiculous shells that eight men sweat in on the river," he said.

She said to Peter: "What do you think, Peter? Joss is

contemptuous of the river at Oxford. We've found it agreeable enough, haven't we?"

Peter, who was at that moment talking aside to Viola, looked up, on finding himself addressed, as though he had just noticed Janet's presence in the room. "Sorry, Janet," he said. "You were saying . . .?"

"I don't think Joss has ever seen the river at Oxford. He thinks it's going to be terribly dull, and I'm trying to disillusion him. It can be exhilarating, don't you think?"

Peter was clearly wondering what to do about this leading question when Miss Collum saved his bacon. "If I may intervene," she said, "I have certainly found it so myself."

All eyes turned upon her. An occasional mouse-like twitter to Jose was all she had thus far contributed to our entertainment. "I didn't know you had been at Oxford, Miss Collum," Sylvia said.

"Oh, not as an undergraduate, I assure you. I am speaking of one solitary occasion. After a Commemoration ball. I jumped into the river from Folly Bridge."

A deep silence fell. That the even tenor of Miss Collum's amble along the cool sequestered vale of life had been thus dramatically punctuated was like news of unguessed licence behind conventual walls.

"Perhaps I shouldn't go on," she said, but our released tongues unanimously demanded to know All. She sipped the dregs of her gin and tonic water, and thus fortified, continued. "An uncle of mine was a tutor of Brasenose and I was spending a few days with him and his wife. I was but sixteen."

"A notoriously dangerous age, Miss Collum," Jose assured her.

"For me," she said, "it was all but fatal. I could not swim, and I was wearing very little."

A hush descended again, in the middle of which Jose breathed: "Ah—h!" Miss Collum blushed, drank again as deeply as she could from the depleted dregs, and said: "Perhaps I should not have mentioned that detail. Pardon me. But it is so vivid in my own mind."

Gazing before her and speaking like a medium in a trance, she said: "There was a young man named Widdershins. Hilary Widdershins. Of Merton, I think. Or it may have been Lincoln or Exeter. I am sure it was not Jesus. He called to take tea with my uncle and his wife. It was a few days before the Commemoration Ball. He asked me if I had ever been to a Commemoration ball and I said no, for indeed I had been strictly brought up. Technically, at that time I was a Plymouth Brother. My conversion had taken place a month before, and my baptism in the preceding week. So that," she said with a giggle, "I knew what total immersion meant."

Jose had discreetly replenished and fortified her glass. She now looked at it, seemed surprised to find it a widow's cruse, and was emboldened to continue. "The long and the short of it was," she said with bravado, "that I was persuaded to attend what I knew to be a sinful gathering. But it was enjoyable, very enjoyable indeed. My aunt had furnished me with some clothes of her own. I was a big girl for my age, though innocent." She looked round the table. "Am I being a bore?"

There were cries to her to go on, even a little applause. "I could not dance," she said, "but that was no great disadvantage, for Mr. Widdershins was strong and pulled and pushed me round the floor, and when we weren't doing that we sat at little tables and ate lovely food and he provided me with what he assured me were fruit drinks. It was a very hot night and they made me feel as though the marquee was swaying. Well, we needn't go into all that. I suppose it was the excitement of my first dance and those clothes that my aunt lent me. They were negligible. Most improper, I thought, for a tutor's wife. Somehow they increased my sense of sin, for till then I had never worn anything but flannel next the skin. I still think it is best." She looked in turn to Sylvia, Janet, Viola. "Don't you agree?"

"Well, yes," Sylvia said guardedly. "In reason and in season."

"Be that as it may," Miss Collum said, "it was well after midnight when Mr. Widdershins took me outside the marquee. He put his arm round my waist and laid his face against mine. I said sharply: 'Mr. Widdershins!' thinking that would deter him, but it did not."

"It rarely does," Jose assured her.

"I should have thought," she said, "that, coming from the lips of an innocent girl, it would have been enough. And he knowing, as I had thought it my duty to tell him, that I had been converted only the month before! But did even that deter him? No. The next instant his hand was in my bosom. That is the sort of clothes they were."

She looked, almost accusingly, at Sylvia and Janet. Viola was irreproachable.

"Well," she said, "I ran. I didn't know Oxford well. I just ran and ran at random, and I found myself on Folly Bridge with Mr. Widdershins in hot pursuit. Often, even now, the sound of feet running through the midnight haunts my dreams. I was by then exhausted. I leant there, trembling. As he drew near I climbed upon the parapet. I shouted: 'If you touch me, Mr. Widdershins, I shall jump.' He touched my leg, and I jumped."

Fortunately, Mr. Widdershins jumped, too, and was a good swimmer. "He shoved me on to my back," said Miss Collum,

" and seized me by the hair. I said: ' Mr. Widdershins, I'll have you sent down for this, but he gave a heartless laugh and said he was Hamlet come to rescue Ophelia from her watery bier. And he just went on swimming. He must have towed me for half a mile, and I lay on my back and looked up at the stars and listened to him singing an improper song at the top of his voice. Confidentially," she said, lowering her tones, " I rather enjoyed it. If you are destined to have only one adventure in Oxford, I suppose it may as well be memorable."

It seems that they at last found an empty punt into which Mr. Widdershins heaved her. There was a rug in the punt and he wrapped her up in that and poled her to Magdalen Bridge, which was not far from her uncle's house. He carried her through the dawn to the house and explained that they had been taking a walk along the river bank when she had slipped and fallen in and that he had had to jump in to rescue her. She was put to bed with hot-water bottles and woke up none the worse. " How much worse I might have been," she said darkly, " I leave you to guess. However, I thought it best to let them accept Mr. Widdershin's explanation as the true one. And to think that that man took Holy Orders! He is now a High Anglican curate at a church in Houndsditch. I often pray for him."

We all felt that Mr. Widdershins was indeed a man to be remembered, and that Miss Collum had made the party. There was a shuffling back of chairs, and Jose said to Joss: " So you see, my boy, you must not underrate the Isis. Now, let's show Sylvia what we found for her."

Miss Collum said she had better go up and see that Paul was all right. The rest of us crowded round the sacked object in the corner of the room. When it was unveiled we saw that it was a cabinet in rose-wood, furnished with long drawers that had exceptionally fine brass handles. Jose pulled out the drawers one by one. They ran like silk. Sylvia passed her hand over the lovely wood. " We thought you might like to have the first offer," Jose said.

" It's beautiful," Sylvia agreed, " and it's kind of you, Jose, to let me see it. But I don't see that I have any *use* for it. What is it intended to be used for, anyway?"

Jose, too, stroked the wood. He said reverently: " It belonged to Sir Christopher Wren."

Peter Quayne opened his eyes at that and joined the wood-strokers. " Good lord," he said. " Wren! That's something. Are you sure of it?"

" I've had my eye on it," Jose assured him, " literally for years. Yes. It must be three years ago that the old girl who owned it asked me if I would be interested in something that had belonged to Wren. I pretended, as one always does, that there

345

was nothing very remarkable about that, but allowed myself to be dragged to a back bedroom, and there was this. There was a bit of tenth-rate embroidered cloth on top and a Victorian mirror standing on that. It was being used as a dressing-table. I was thrilled. I could see at once that whether it had belonged to Wren or not, it *could* have done. The period was all right. Naturally, I rather pooh-poo'd the thing and asked what made her believe so fantastic a story. She told me, and it rang true. I've been able to check it. Since then, whenever passing that way, I've asked her whether she was ready to sell her relic of Sir Christopher—always, of course, with a grin of disbelief, and always with a dread that I might find it gone."

"You people are inhuman," Sylvia said. "What were you trying to do? Wear the old girl down to parting with it for thirty shillings?"

Jose didn't answer that. He said: "A month ago she told me that she was packing up. They'd been well off, those Pellews, but it was the old story—a slow decline of fortune. There were two sons. One went to America, and the other stayed behind, farming with his own hands the few acres left out of what had been quite an estate. Well, he died, and the boy in America, who had done pretty well for himself, had invited old Mrs. Pellew to come and live with him. And there she was, winding up her affairs, as they say. This cabinet hadn't been long with the Pellews. She had taken it with her when she married. It had belonged to her father, who was an architect. And that's what it is, as you see—a cabinet for holding an architect's plans." He paused, pulling the drawers out one by one. "Who knows?" he said. "Sir Christopher may have kept in these drawers the plans for St. Paul's."

We stood, silent and enthralled, looking at the cabinet. At last Peter Quayne said: "What do you want for it?"

"What—for you to take it up to London and flog it to some American millionaire? If it came to that, I could dispose of it through Sotheby or Christie. I'm still giving Sylvia the first offer."

"I don't want it," Sylvia said decisively. "I'm not an architect."

"Neither am I," said Peter. "And I don't want to sell it. I want to give it away."

He looked at Viola and smiled. "It would be a lovely thing," he said, "to keep music sheets in. Would you accept it, if Jose will sell it to me?"

Despite the smile, he brought out the words with difficulty, and a silence followed them. Everybody in the room, except Joss, was aware that this was not a common moment. It was one of those moments when the present and the future rush together and collide. The silence stretched out till Joss said: "Look.

Will you count me out of this music Viola's supposed to be giving you? I expect you've heard of that bore called Holiday Tasks. There are a few books I'm supposed to read, and if you don't mind I'll get to my room. Thanks for the slap-up dinner, Auntie Sylvia."

He went, and at the same moment the hired waiter put his head round the door and asked: "May I clear away now, Madam?"

We couldn't take up the point where we had left off. Sylvia threw open the door on to the terrace and said: "It's full moon. Let's sit outside for a while. I'll go and get a cloak. I'd better bring something down for you, too, Viola."

Jose and Peter went out, and Viola followed them. Janet and I were left alone in the hall. I waited till the man from Helston had gone towards the kitchen with a loaded tray, and said: "You'd better get a cloak, too, my dear. It's all right out there for us men, but, as Miss Collum suggested, you ladies are lightly clad."

"Lightly clad!" she said. "I feel naked. I feel exposed and thrown out."

I put an arm round her and kissed her. "Are you in love with Peter?"

"I don't know whether I am or not," she said. "But I do see that at this moment it would be to him merely an academic question."

"Wear your cloak," I said.

She murmured:

> *Why didst thou promise such a beauteous day,*
> *And make me travel forth without my cloak?*

and added: "Yes. I suppose it's the only thing to do."

"I'm afraid it is. After all, Peter didn't promise you any sort of day, did he? Don't let yourself down."

"Play up, play up, and play the game," she mocked me. "Laugh with tears in my eyes. You're a well-intentioned old fool, George."

She kissed me, and went slowly upstairs, and came down with her cloak.

I thought it likely that she would not wish to come with the rest of us to Miss Hartman's cottage. Perhaps she didn't, but she came nevertheless. She got into Jose's rattle-bones with Peter, and Viola and I were driven by Sylvia, who, I remembered, had married when little, if any, older than Viola was now. Sylvia asked: "How do you feel, darling? Are you up to playing?"

Viola said: "I feel as Miss Collum did. I'd like to jump into a river. Still, I promised to play, and I shall do my best."

347

I don't remember what she played or how she played. I should have been a bad judge of that, anyway. All I remember is a standard lamp shining down on the piano and on the child's fair head and consecrated face, and Peter sitting in the shadows with his elbows on his knees and his head in his hands, and Janet never once looking at Viola but all the time at Peter. I remember that when the music was over she kissed Viola and said: "Thank you. That was very beautiful," but whether she meant what she said or was speaking from under her cloak I don't know. At all events, I heard the tones of renunciation, and they made me feel both sad and content. I hoped Bob would come home in a good mood.

We said good-bye to Jose and all got into Sylvia's car. Peter sat with her in front, I in the back seat with Janet on one side of me and Viola on the other. I put an arm round the waist of each, praying that the loving kindness I felt for both of them would not be ineffectual.

When we were back and they had all gone to their rooms, I took a drink out on to the terrace where I could be with myself for a few minutes and calm my raddled nerves by a sight of the moon-flooded sea. To my surprise, Joss was there, sound asleep in a deck-chair. I woke him gently and sat down by his side. He yawned and said: "William Makepeace Thackeray's *Vanity Fair*. James Thomson's *City of Dreadful Night*. Can you tell me any good reason, George, why I should bore myself with either?"

"I could," I said, "but this seems to me an inappropriate moment for doing so. There are lots of things, you know, Joss, that we don't want to do, but all the same there's a point in doing them."

He was young and perplexed. He seemed much younger than Viola.

"A long time ago," I said, "you told me that you wanted to write murder stories. How do you feel about that now?"

"I was talking bosh. I don't want to have anything to do with books—writing 'em or reading 'em. And I loathe the thought of going up to Oxford. You didn't go, did you?"

"No, but I wish I had."

"It seems a rule in life, doesn't it, to wish for what we can't have and to grouse about what we've got."

Life had so pampered me that I found his young perplexities difficult to reason with. He got up and said: "Well, I'd better be off to bed. There's always a good sleep."

I watched him go, and felt that I had failed him, and presently followed him up the stairs. I passed the room with what Janet had called the lovely view of the Lizard, and hoped that Peter was having happy dreams there. I passed Paul's room and heard the child faintly whimpering and the soothing
348

whispers of Miss Collum. I passed Janet's room and hoped that, if nothing else, the profundity of her frustration had lulled her to sleep.

Sylvia was sitting on the edge of the bed. "Where on earth have you been, darling?" she asked. "I seem to have been waiting for you for ages."

Well, that, at any rate, was good to know. When we fell asleep the dawn was at the window.

CHAPTER SIXTEEN

1

When that holiday was over Sylvia and I saw Joss back to school and went with gladness home to our barn. Peter and Janet had gone back to London some time before, and we left Viola with the returned Miss Hartman. The question of the cabinet that may have been Sir Christopher Wren's was settled satisfactorily. Sylvia and I went into conference about it. We didn't like the idea of Peter's giving so expensive a present to a child he had just met and whose feelings were in an adolescent turmoil that might settle down, once Peter was gone, into forgetfulness of him. The whole business seemed to us too sudden, almost bizarre, for outright encouragement. The only thing certain was that, whatever Janet's feelings for Peter had been —and they could well have been only a reaction against Bob's thoughtlessness—they were now without hope.

Peter so clearly wished Viola to have the cabinet, and she so wished to have it, that we decided to make it a communal gift. The essential significance would have gone out of it for both of them, but we saw no way of avoiding that. I had a word with Peter, and he reluctantly but sensibly saw what we were getting at. I had a word with Jose, too. He was amused by the pother but said that, since the gift was to be communal, he'd come in by sacrificing what would have been his profit. Even so, the price was steep. Sylvia, Peter and I produced about a third each, and Joss and Miss Collum, who got wind of what was going on, said they wanted to put their bit into the pool. With a fine ignorance of what such things cost, Joss handed me half a crown and Miss Collum five shillings. We let them believe that this took a weight off our minds, and we had a tea-party on Viola's sixteenth birthday and handed over the cabinet. And so, as we were rolling home together through a day of autumn tenderness we felt that even Bob would not be able to find fault with us. I was altogether in one of my best moods.

For one thing, I had suddenly conceived the idea of a play, complete in all its details. I was panting to be at work on it, and work I did, very hard, throughout the next month. When it was finished I was myself surprised by its originality. Sylvia wanted to give it a look over with a player's eye, but I wouldn't allow that. She should see it in its beauty on the first night—a play that Margaret Napier would have been proud to appear in. I still have it in a drawer of my desk, together with several other plays, finished or half done, and two and a half novels. These poor rejected brutes are necessary silent monitors, telling me to remember that I am an embroiderer, and nothing else. I have to comfort myself with the knowledge that Mr. Ledra's little pieces have faithful if few admirers and that there are several ladies whose night-tables would be incomplete without those opium pillicules.

Nigel Wendron of the Parthenon Press has recently acknowledged this somnolent effect by issuing a score of them in what he calls the Ledra Bedside Book.

We had hardly been back a week when Bob rang up rather peremptorily: "When are you two coming to give me a report on my children?"

We waited on him in the splendour of his Piccadilly rooms. He was looking, as the newspapers say of princes, bronzed and well, and Janet seemed tranquil and easy. We asked Bob how he had enjoyed his cruise, and he said: "Well enough, but I'm not sorry to be back, and not sorry, either, that Janet has given up this nonsense of going out to work."

That was the first we had heard of it. Janet said: "I have decided to become a dutiful home-loving girl."

"About time, too, you silly little gadabout," Bob said. But there was affection in his tone. He said: "If you want to know how you really feel about a good wife, go for a cruise with a cargo of daft bitches."

Brookes, now reaching maturity as a senatorial butler, was serving the dinner. I said to Bob: "Pas devant les domestiques," to which Brookes answered: "I approve of Sir Robert's sentiments, sir," and handed me the potatoes.

"That Lancaster woman," Bob said, "is as hot as the electric chair, but she does know something about music."

It seems that Miss Lancaster occasionally spared time from her more serious avocations to entertain the company on a grand piano in the saloon. "Always, mind you," said Bob, "with a bottle on a table alongside her. It's one of her little ways to take her drink straight from the bottle."

One night she had played, and Bob, with no interest, but merely not to seem altogether uninterested, asked: "Who's that by?" and she said: "Eliza Hartman."

The name seemed familiar, and at last it registered, as heaven
350

knows it should, for it had been bandied about enough when
we were fighting Viola's battle. He said to Miss Lancaster:
"Will that be the one who had to give up concerts because of
an accident?" and she said: "There is only one Eliza Hartman. That accident was a dreadful loss to music. I never
missed hearing her when she was in London. She's not much of
a composer, but I like that bit I've just played. As a player she
was splendid."

Of course, Bob couldn't resist saying that he had succeeded
in inducing Miss Hartman to take his daughter as a pupil.
"Your daughter is lucky," she said, reached for the bottle, and
knocked hell out of a Chopin Polonaise. "It sounded as
though it was supposed to be guns," Bob said. "It nearly blew
the ship apart."

2

A week after this I said to Bob: "Now that you've settled down
and got a grip of Meagher Motors again you ought to see Joss
and Viola."

"What d'you mean—got my grip again? D'you think I can
ever afford to lose my grip? There are such things as long-
distance telephones. Anyway, the Christmas holidays will be
here soon and I'll see the children then."

I told him that a holiday presented a formal and inescapable
obligation. A surprise visit was another thing. I was especially
anxious about Joss. I hadn't forgotten the talk I had with him
that night when we had all come back from hearing Viola play.
He had lost a mother, who may not have been an ideal mother
but was at any rate a focus to his home life; and Janet was not
the sort of woman a boy would take to as a mother-substitute.
During her recent visit to Penruan, obsessed as she was with
Peter Quayne, she had hardly spoken to Joss. Viola was more
happily situated. She had her grail.

I said nothing of this to Bob: I merely urged him to give
them an unexpected treat. Fortunately, Janet's decision to stay
at home had put him in a good humour. He agreed to spend a
few days in the West Country and asked me to go with him.
We travelled in the most luxurious of cars, chauffeured by the
ambassadorial driver who had called for me, I remembered, on
the day when Bob gave me lunch on the Great West Road.
That made me think of the invitation Bob had given to Mr.
Merriman to visit him there in order to humiliate him, and I
said: "I've seen old Merriman once or twice lately."

I was not surprised that the mention of Mr. Merriman's name
did not please him. But I was surprised that it seemed to upset
351

him deeply. He said nothing, and during the few days we were away I saw no newspapers—a pleasure I increasingly tended to give myself. But when I was back Sylvia handed me one of the cheaper rags to which she was addicted, and said: "This will amuse you." A big headline cried: "Corner-Shop Man fights Motor Magnate." I had noticed here and there about town the growth of Meagher Motor Showrooms. The most palatial was in Piccadilly, not far from Bob's apartment, but smaller ones were all over the place. This newspaper story concerned a small shop in Kensington. Meagher Motors had bought a shop on either side of it and awaited the moment when the lease of the middle shop should fall in, so that that might be bought, too. One might have expected them to buy the fag-end of the lease, but the occupier of the shop would not sell. He had always disliked motor cars, and his loathing of them was deepened when his Yorkshire terrier, named oddly enough Nero, was killed by one. He declared that Nero's death had hastened the death of his wife, and this put hatred into his attitude to Meagher Motors who continued to press him to sell the five-years' lease that was still to run.

It chanced that he was acquainted with Mr. Merriman, to whom he told the story. According to the newspaper, whose investigation seemed to have been thorough, he said to Mr. Merriman: "I don't want to stay in the damned place now that my wife and poor old Nero are gone, but I'll be damned if I let the place go to Meagher Murderers, Ltd."

It is not difficult to imagine how Mr. Merriman's ears pricked up at the name of Meagher, and he forthwith offered to buy the remainder of the lease. He did so. He was the Corner-Shop Man of the headline. Meagher Motors were now badgering him as they had badgered his predecessor, but, as the paper said, "the Little Man is standing firm against the blandishments of Big Business."

It made a nice heart-touching story, illustrated with photographs of Mr. Merriman, white carnation, spats and all, of the village Hampton who had sold him the lease, and of Nero, looking like a small chewed-off piece of hearthrug. If there had been nothing to the story but the death of Nero, that would have been good for a thousand tears. As the writer said: "The simplest emotions of the human heart may well prove strong enough to resist all the blandishments of clinking coin."

We were allowed to have Joss for an afternoon, and when we had bloated him with luncheon in our hotel Bob proposed a run to the Dorset coast. Joss said: "Couldn't we go for a good long walk, sir? I could take you to some grand places round here. I'm rather anti-motor, you know. Take ships. My friend Jose Gomm has a motor in his boat, and sometimes we use it if we run into a flat calm. Then, when the wind comes again and we stop the damn' thing and the sails fill—well, it's a different world. A better one."

Bob looked at his son as though he had encountered some strange new animal. " I don't think," he said, " a world without motors would be very attractive to me. If Columbus had had motors in his boat he'd have got to America a bit quicker."

" But he never got there at all, sir."

" Of course he did."

" No, sir. He got to some outlying islands and thought they belonged to India. That's how the people came to be called Indians. It's possible that the Vikings *did* get to America hundreds of years before Columbus was heard of. And they had no motors. The whole world was laid out on the map before motors were dreamed of."

Bob looked at his offspring with wonder. " You see, sir," Joss persisted, " discovery was a tough job. It needed tough men. Motoring makes men soft. They'll soon be forgetting even how to use their legs."

" Well, if you wish it, let's use ours," Bob said. " Come on."

I wanted them to be alone together, and said: " I'm going to be soft. May I have the use of the car this afternoon, Bob?"

I got the ambassador to drive me to some of the lovely houses I knew to be in those parts: little homely Tintinhull and lordly Montacute and a few others; and then we went on to Dorchester and I stood in front of Max Gate and bared my head, thinking of Thomas Hardy and all that my mind and spirit owed to him. The ambassador got out and stood beside me. " Do you read Hardy, sir?" he asked. I assured him that I indeed did, and he said: " One of the Immortals, sir."

Strange how a few words can shift the ground on which men stand. We looked at one another, then held out our hands and shook without a word: and when we moved on I sat beside him in the front and we talked about books and about his family, especially about his daughter who had just come down from Oxford and was to marry a man in the Foreign Office. Up on the Downs he let the car dawdle, and said: " Far from the madding crowd. A trite expression, sir, but on this occasion appropriate, I think."

" Do you and Sir Robert ever talk books?" I asked.

" Oh, no. Sir Robert encourages nothing personal, except with Brookes, an old comrade-in-arms, sir. I hope you will not mention my daughter to him."

Bob had returned Joss to school by the time I got back, and over a drink in the hotel lounge he said: " That was a good afternoon. The young devil disagrees with everything I say. But we did talk as man to man, and that's the first time it's happened. He's got quite a headpiece."

We set off for Cornwall early the next day, and were a few

miles from Penruan when, in mid-afternoon, we saw Miss Hartman and Viola striding along the road. We slowed and drew up alongside them. They were an odd-looking pair: the child angelically bloomed with youth and love, the old woman grizzled, gruff and leathery. Both were bare-headed and both wore shoes that looked fit for kicking chunks out of Everest. Bob got out and Viola kissed him and cried: "Daddy! Whatever are *you* doing here?"

"Why shouldn't I be here to see my daughter?" Bob demanded gallantly. "And this lady, I presume, is Miss Hartman?"

Miss Hartman looked at him without enthusiasm. She knew all about the reluctance he had shown when Viola's music was discussed. However, Bob was being the courtier. "How can I thank you, Miss Hartman," he asked, "for agreeing to take charge of Viola? How is she progressing?"

"Considering," said Miss Hartman, "that she was brought up in a home where a motor-horn was the only musical instrument, and that she literally never laid fingers to a piano key till she went to school, she is progressing reasonably well."

"Get in," Bob said. "We'll drive you home."

"Indeed you won't, sir," Miss Hartman assured him. "These afternoon hours are sacred to physical exercise. I must look after Viola's body as well as her soul."

Even this Bob took well enough. "All right," he said. "Till later." And off he went.

During the few days we spent at Penruan I kept out of the way, and Miss Hartman saw to it that Bob kept out of the way of Viola's work. From nine to eleven in the morning Miss Hartman played and talked to Viola about what she was playing and about how she was playing it. From eleven to one Viola played, and then she played again from seven till ten. In the afternoon Bob was permitted to take his daughter for a walk; and one day, when they were gone, I put myself in Miss Hartman's path and she hustled me along through the mild autumn weather. I wanted to talk to her about Viola, and suggested that we should sit down while we did so, but she said: "I can walk and talk at the same time, thank God." And she certainly could. I asked her if it were true that Viola had never touched a piano till she went to school, and she said: "Yes. The child was brought up barbarously. She should have been dumped on to a piano-stool as soon as she could toddle. If that had been done, she might have been at the Royal Academy of Music now. As it is, it'll take me two years to make her fit to have a shot at a scholarship."

I told her that I knew nothing about the training of musicians, and asked her what this scholarship amounted to.

"Oh, it's a hell of a thing," she said robustly. "It's the

354

Associated Board scholarship I'm talking about. Dreadfully competitive. It's not only for pianists, you know. People compete on all sorts of instruments, and there are only six scholarships to go round among the lot of them. The winners are pushed into the Royal Academy of Music or the Royal College. They don't, as a rule, have any choice in the matter."

"And you think Viola has a chance?"

"Chance? Well, roughly the same chance that a thoroughbred has to beat a dray-horse over a hundred yards."

I reminded her that the other competitors were hardly likely to be dray-horses.

She swiped at the heather with her stick and gave her deep chuckle. "She's a cert," she said. "If only these wretched men would leave her alone."

"What wretched men?"

"Any wretched men. What a curse you all are."

I apologised for the existence of my sex. "We didn't do too badly till you women started offering us apples and other consolations."

"It's this father of hers that I'm worrying about at the moment, and this man Peter Quayne who was snooping round while I was away. I can't say much to Sir Robert because he's paying me handsomely; but I've written to Mr. Quayne and told him to suspend his correspondence during the next two or three years."

"And what does he say to that?"

"I don't know what he *says*. He just goes on writing."

"You can't bring up a musician in a vacuum," I argued, "any more than you can a writer or a painter. I've listened to pianists who have struck me as perfect to the last touch, but perfect as a corpse is when an American beautician has prepared him for burial."

"Don't you argue with me," she said fiercely. "There's enough life and death in this village and on these moors and in that sea to create a Beethoven. You just tell this Peter Quayne to lay off. I'm not bothering at the moment about troubled depths. I'm trying to create something crystal clear. And now walk with me if you want to, but don't talk. It disturbs the rhythm of my breathing."

I asked Bob how he got on with Viola, and he said: "She's a woman, you know. I've been so used to seeing her in school clothes that I've always thought of her as a child. But she's a woman, and with a devil of a will of her own. I asked her if she'd play to me, and she refused point blank. I told her about a chap I'd known during the war. We had a piano in the mess, and you only had to ask him and he'd sit down and rattle out anything you wanted. An absolute pro he was. She didn't seem interested. She said perhaps she'd play me something in two or three years' time."

We had motored over to Helston to eat a meal in the Angel, and were taking coffee and brandy in the lounge. "Another thing," he said. "She's been giving me my orders."

"They grow up, Bob," I consoled him. "I think Viola's growing up pretty satisfactorily. What are the orders?"

"She and Miss Hartman are coming up to town for a month in the winter, so that they can go to first-class concerts. Well, that's all right. We can just squeeze 'em both in at Piccadilly. 'Only to eat and sleep,' she said. 'I'll be practising all day.' I asked her why she couldn't make a holiday of it, and she said hearing the concerts would be holiday enough, but she'd have to work all the same. Does this sound a bit rough?"

I said that it did. "Well, then, I'm putting it badly. It was all done very nicely. She's a charmer, George; she made me feel that I had to do everything she wanted."

"And what does she want?"

"I'm to find an empty room and put a grand piano into it. I said we could have a piano put into the big room in Piccadilly; but no, she must have a room to herself. So, of course, I agreed, and said the room would be there with a piano in it when they arrived. But that wasn't right, either. Miss Hartman must choose the piano."

He looked at me with a quizzical yet proud grin on his face, and I knew that Viola's fight was won, so far as he was concerned, now and for ever. "She's a remarkable child," I said. "You should be proud of her, Bob."

"I thought she might like to ride a bit in the Row, and I asked if I should arrange about a horse. She said: 'Oh, damn horses, Daddy.' I don't know where she gets her language from."

"I think Miss Hartman could tell you."

3

I was so tickled by the newspaper story of the Little Man facing the might of Meagher Motors that when I got back to town I wrote to Mr. Merriman formally inviting him and Wendy to lunch. He replied with a letter full of sentimental warmth. It contained, I remember, the phrase "the dear dead days beyond recall." My kindness, he said, was such as he would expect from one who had set his feet upon a rock when o'er his head clouds were lowering and he was floundering in a bog of financial incertitude. I'm afraid he never forgot that, insofar as I had any profession at all, I was a writer, to be written to

356

accordingly. He couldn't, he said, accept the kindness of myself and my dear lady, for he was at what might prove the cross-roads of his existence. All his powers were engaged, and might well be so for some time.

"I fear," I said to Sylvia, "that the *Evening Sun* has written his part and he's made up his mind to play it. We must let him simmer for a bit. He says here that when an auspicious moment presents itself he will snatch the golden opportunity to renew an acquaintance which he prizes beyond rubies."

"He's a soapy Sam," she said. "I hope Bob squashes him."

"You have a prejudice against him. I've noticed it more than once."

"Well, you don't love him, do you?"

"Not exactly. But remember that I set his feet upon a rock. I'm naturally interested in his career."

"I don't trust him, and one of these days I'm going to find out the truth about him."

I knew that she was up to the eyes in an investigation of her mother's affair with Fred Byles. She was for ever studying the books about Margaret Napier and the long document that Mr. Chown had written. Mr. Chown had said that a young clerk had called the auditor's attention to irregularities in the books of Fred Byles and Ledra. That fact alone prejudiced her, for she was sure that the young clerk was Merriman.

She now said: "D'you remember telling me that just before Bob's father died you called upon him and mentioned Mr. Merriman's name? What was it that he said then?"

The moment came back to me: the old man worn to a shadow, wrapped in shawls, sitting by the fire in an over-heated little room. I couldn't recall much, except that the ancient had said venomously "That swine!" when I spoke of Mr. Merriman.

"Well, there you are!" Sylvia exclaimed. She refilled my coffee cup. "Isn't that enough?"

"Enough for what?"

"Enough to condemn him," she said unreasonably.

"I'm afraid that in a court of law it wouldn't be enough to condemn anyone of anything. What do you mean—condemn him?"

"You forget at times," she said, "that Fred Byles was my father. I'm quite sure he was not the sort of man who would defraud his partner. I want to clear his name."

"Are you suggesting that the young Merriman stole the money and covered up by giving himself an air of innocence—calling the auditor's attention so as to turn it away from himself?"

"Why should Mr. Meagher speak of him as he did? He obviously knew something."

357

"But, darling," I urged her, "you mustn't jump to a conclusion from no evidence at all. Of course Mr. Meagher knew something. He knew that there they had been—boys together in that office—and it looks as though they never liked one another. And Mr. Merriman got on, as they say. He became the top dog, and from what I saw of the pair of them when I was in the office I know that he treated old Meagher badly. Bob's father knew as much about cotton as Mr. Merriman did, but he was never allowed a shred of influence or authority. The top dog was determined to stay on top, and he lost no chance of humiliating his rival. So there it was—a lifelong feud, and if that's not enough to account for a few bitter words on a deathbed I don't know what is. And if you want to add a bit more to the account, remember that Mr. Merriman tried to stop Bob from marrying Wendy. That's another thing that would hurt old Meagher and make him bitter."

I thought it was a good lawyer-like speech. She got up and said: "I'll get to the bottom of it yet."

"Then you mustn't be surprised if you find something disagreeable at the bottom."

She turned at the door. "Are you suggesting that I shall find that my father was a thief?"

She didn't wait for an answer, but went out angry with me for the first time in her life.

4

In January of 1937 Mr. Merriman wrote to say that he would like to accept our invitation. The fight with Sir Robert was won. A photograph in the *Evening Sun* showed the Kensington shop with a notice pasted on the window: "These premises will be developed by Merriman Enterprises." The *Sun* said: "Jack the Giant-Killer wins." However, that was not the end of the fight. The shops that stood on either side of Mr. Merriman's were of no use to Meagher Motors now. The leases were again for sale, and, working through agents instructed to resell to him as soon as they secured them, Mr. Merriman got hold of both. The dream that Wendy had outlined to me and Sylvia began to take form and substance. It was there in Kensington that the first of the sizeable Merriman shops appeared.

But it was only the first bout that was ended when Mr. Merriman and Wendy called on us in January. I warned Sylvia to watch her step. Mr. Merriman was not yet a convicted criminal, I said, and there was such a thing as an action for defamation. "I'll be as nice as pie," she promised, and added: "But I'll get him yet."

It was a beautiful winter day. The sun had risen a red undazzling disc that you could look in the face; the air was crisp and vital; and the birds that I loved best, the ones that stayed with us the whole year through, not those tourists that came with fine weather like summer visitors to Margate, were busy in the hedges greyed by light frost. Mr. Merriman arrived at about half past twelve, looking reasonably uncriminal. He came in the first motor car he had owned—not a Meagher product, you may be sure—a Rover, with Wendy rather timorously at the wheel. From spats to silk hat it was the complete and immemorial Merriman, with the addition of a magnificent overcoat, collared in astrakhan. His bulging eyes had the benevolent look that the successful can afford. He looked not unlike an ageing ham actor just back from the pay-off after a profitable tour. His fur-gloved paw raised the hat when Sylvia and I greeted him in the porch. I congratulated him on the car, as I felt he expected me to do, and he said: "I owe it to you, my dear George—that and everything."

"Well, come in and warm yourselves up," Sylvia said, calmly and perfectly the hostess welcoming cherished friends.

In the hall Mr. Merriman divested himself of his outer integument, as he put it. He dropped his gloves into his hat, stood the hat on a table, hung his coat on a hook, and rubbed his hands together. "A delicious love-nest," he assured us.

Startled, Sylvia took Wendy upstairs, where she, too, might divest herself of her outer integument, while I led Mr. Merriman through the corridor to the barn. Up above us we could hear the rushing of Paul's impetuous feet. We had recently completed a playing-place up there, and while we were at it we had put a fireplace in the east end of the great room, so that on a nipping day like this its warmth might flow to meet the warmth of the old fireplace on the west. Mr. Merriman paused with head cocked up, listening, and said: "Happy, happy days of childhood. I never knew them, George. From the beginning, I had to Fight My Way Up. Quite a romance. Some day I must tell you all about it. It would make a grand novel. Not, perhaps, that I would read even that one. My life has been too earnest for triviality. I have probably in the whole course of my life read fewer novels than any one novelist writes."

This thought gave him a virtuous look, the becoming look of a Jack the Giant-Killer.

Sylvia and Wendy came in, and Sylvia and I drank sherry alone. Mr. Merriman condescended to eat a salted nut or two— "to keep you company," he said. He looked towards Wendy. "Now, my dear, I think this would be an appropriate moment for making your presentation."

Wendy was carrying a small parcel. "It's just a little thing we thought you might like for the house," she said. "You were kind enough to bring a present to us, so here's one from us to you."

Sylvia snipped the string, unwrapped the paper, and said—the sweet liar: "Oh, it's lovely." She kissed Wendy, while Mr. Merriman beamed. It was St. George and the dragon in bronze: a St. George whose thrust had been so vigorous that the spear, entering the dragon's mouth between serried teeth which reminded me of the reefs near the Absolution pub, came out at the other end of him strong and clear.

I lifted it on to the mantelpiece, between a Ming horse and a Royal Copenhagen stoneware elephant by Knud Kyhn. "Delightful!" I said. "That is where it must stay."

"You see the symbolism?" Mr. Merriman asked anxiously.

Sylvia and I looked at it and racked our brains for the symbolism.

"You are too modest to see it," Mr. Merriman said. "Saint George. That is you, George. You are slaying by your generosity the dread dragon that had me in its grip during the time of my Depression."

I took his hand. "You are too kind," I said. I kissed Wendy. "How can I thank you?" I asked.

It was a difficult moment, and Sylvia and I were relieved when the front door-bell pealed. But we were not relieved for long. I went to the door and on the mat were Viola and Miss Hartman. Viola kissed me impulsively. "Isn't it a lovely day?" she cried. "I thought we'd give you a surprise."

She looked beautiful. Her face shone from walking in the sane frosty air. Her eyes glowed. She was wearing a little fur hat and a long shaggy coat. "We've come at a great pace all the way from Amersham station."

Miss Hartman looked at her with benevolent approval. "I've given her a day off," she said. "She has earned it."

I didn't want the child to rush into an impossible situation. I said: "Now if you'd like to run away, my dear, you may do so. Please yourself. But we have visitors you may not wish to meet. Your mother and your grandfather."

She was a bit taken aback, but obviously not shocked. She asked: "Would they want to see me? That's the thing."

I had come to have great faith in Wendy's common sense. It was she, not her father, who was steering Merriman Enterprises so successfully. She had completely accepted the fact of her separation from Bob, and I was pretty sure she could be trusted with this situation.

Viola said: "It will be almost like meeting a stranger. I hardly remember how she looks."

I gave them chairs in the hall and went through to the barn. "You've been pow-wowing a long time," Sylvia said. "Who is it?"

I said to Wendy: "It's Viola and a Miss Hartman who's teaching her to play the piano. Sylvia and I had no idea they'd be calling. Do you mind meeting them?"

Sylvia seemed more agitated by the situation than Wendy. She said: "Oh, lord! What will Bob think?"

Wendy looked pained rather than agitated. "Have you told Viola that I'm here?"

"Yes."

"And does she mind meeting me?"

"Not a bit."

"Well, then, that's all right. The children are their father's affair, not mine. That was understood between us. But if one of them accidentally comes my way I can hardly be expected to ring my leper-bell and cross the street."

Leper-bell sounded hurt and bitter, but I knew it was directed at Bob, not at Viola.

Sylvia went out to bring the visitors in. I gave Wendy a small reassuring squeeze, and she smiled at me and said: "All right, Saint George." Mr. Merriman, looking rather at sea, was steadying himself with further inroads on the peanuts. Viola had not seen him since his historic visit to Dormers, wearing the gauds of a commissionaire.

Miss Hartman and Viola had shed their coats and hats. Viola came in slim and shining. She walked straight to Wendy, but neither made to kiss the other. They shook hands, and Viola asked: "How are you, Mother?"

She seemed more self-possessed than anyone else in the room, and Miss Hartman whispered to me proudly: "I have been teaching her to face an audience. It is necessary."

Viola shook hands with her grandfather, who cried boisterously: "Lovely to see you again, my dear. You look delightful —a credit to us all."

She gave him the necessary politeness of a smile and then coolly surveyed the room. "Oh, Uncle George," she cried, "what a place to practise in!"

"It's all yours," I said. "I'll have it sent on."

"No, honestly, the place Daddy got for us is as cold as death. We had to wangle three electric fires out of him before we could do any work. Otherwise, my fingers would have frozen on the keys."

Miss Hartman patted her on the head. "They have unfrozen very nicely." And to the rest of us: "She makes great progress. My hopes begin to bloom."

But I wasn't going to have Viola in the middle of the stage at that moment, whether as a pianist or anything else. I offered her and Miss Hartman sherry, which they both took, and I steered them to general conversation in which Wendy could join. Mr. Merriman couldn't. He could do nothing but stare at his granddaughter and offer her peanuts. "As though she were a rather attractive marmoset at the Zoo," Sylvia said to me later.

To the company she said, as they stood chattering by the fire: "I hope you've all got very poor appetites. Lunch has been prepared for six, and here we are—eight. Miss Collum and Paul will be joining us. We're trying to teach Paul table manners. Unlike Viola, he does not make great progress. I'll go and see to things."

Paul made the meal easy. I was glad to let him have the stage centre that I had denied to Viola. He took a great fancy to Wendy, who sat next to him, and transferred to her plate large dollops of whatever was placed on his. "Eat, Wendy. Eat, woman," he commanded; and, transferring his attention for a moment to Miss Collum, who sat at his other side, he seized her plate and poured its contents into Wendy's, commanding again "Eat, woman."

"You see what I mean?" Sylvia said.

"He is a generous boy," Mr. Merriman pronounced, and Paul, to earn the praise, passed him a potato, by fist route, across the table. "Man, eat," he said.

Viola chided him. "Paul, you ought to be smacked."

"Paul *is* smacked—hard," he assured her. "On the bottom," and looked Miss Collum challengingly in the eye.

Miss Collum appeared to be upset. Corporal punishment was forbidden in our house, and she did not miss the glance that Sylvia shot at me. I said: "Miss Collum, you may remove the accused from the dock, take him back to his cell, and deal with him according to his deserts. In the formation of his manners, give him all aid short of war."

When they were gone, Mr. Merriman said: "As I remarked, George, he is a generous boy, but generosity is not enough to fit him to adorn a Lord Mayor's banquet."

"Nevertheless," I said, "I should like to be present on such an occasion. It will be something to see him bestow turtle soup upon the Archbishop of Canterbury's lap."

I was aware of using persiflage to prolong our present security. So long as we had Paul's masterly handling of a meal as a matter of contemplation we were fairly safe, but I dreaded what looked to me like the eternal stretches of the afternoon. I suggested that we return to the barn and take our coffee there, but Viola saved the situation. "Will you excuse us, Uncle George? We came out to walk, and I think we ought to be going."

Miss Hartman approved, and they went, with formal politeness, to Mr. Merriman and Wendy. At the door Viola said: "Did I behave well, Uncle George?"

"Perfectly, my dear."

"I didn't dislike her," she said; and Miss Hartman approved this, too. "I should think not. A sensible woman if ever I saw one."

She was sensible enough not to stay too long. We talked of this and that till three o'clock, not once mentioning Viola, and then she said, getting up: "Well, that was delightful, and we love your house. Thank you for letting us see it. Now we must be off."

Mr. Merriman shook hands and said: "Thank you, George. Remember that life-story when you've nothing better to do."

I said that I would, and wished him success in his Kensington shop. "Drapery," Wendy said. "That's what it's to be. We're going to Wake Up Harrods. Aren't we, Father?"

"We'll have a go," Mr. Merriman promised.

He got into the astrakhan-collared overcoat that at a stroke turned him into a merchant-prince. Clearly he didn't want to remain a giant-killer. He wanted to be a giant who'd take a bit of killing.

5

The next day Sylvia and I went to town. Nigel Wendron of the Parthenon Press had invited me to take luncheon to celebrate the publication of my tenth book. This was not because the book caused any excitement in the literary world but because Nigel liked giving luncheon parties. I remember that he gave one for a novelist who, though rather repulsive to look at, was a notoriously successful seducer. Nigel had asked one of the ladies what she saw in the little toad, and she replied ecstatically: "It's his smell. He smells like honey." The invitations went out "to meet England's best-smelling novelist." Nigel was famous for the invention of nonsensical reasons for assembling a party, and I wondered what monstrous lure he had devised for the present occasion. But the victim was never let into the secret. He had asked me to bring two ladies, and I had invited Janet to join me and Sylvia. There were a dozen more or less famous or notorious people present, including a man who had been acquitted of murder, and had then made money out of a Sunday newspaper by writing the story of his life. It ended with an explanation of how he had committed the murder that he could not now be charged with. I wondered how this dove-tailed with a party ostensibly in my honour, but to leave such a paradox hanging in the air was one of Nigel's ways. He made a speech about the vulgarity of the modern Press and compared it with the reticent perfections of Mr. Ledra, but this hardly seemed to cover the case. Not that that would worry him. He had had another party.

The thing is that after the party we found Bob in the lounge of the hotel. He was waiting for Janet, and that was something new. It seems that at breakfast she had mentioned a film that was being shown at the Curzon Street Cinema—one of those films that one would be drummed out of the P.E.N. Club for not having seen. Bob said nothing at the time, but here he was to take her along. They invited us to have tea with them at five o'clock when the film would be over. It was a raw inhospitable day, and when they were gone we discussed what to do with the intervening time. I suggested the National Gallery; but Sylvia said: "Let's go to the flat." I sensed what she wanted, so we went to my flat behind Baker Street, switched on the bedroom fire, and put ourselves happily to bed. When I awoke she was still asleep, and seeing her lying there in naked beauty I was tempted to let Bob and Janet go hang and to prolong this uncovenanted moment, for Sylvia had the ageless accomplishment of Ninon de l'Enclos. She opened her eyes and smiled at me and said: "Thank you, darling." It was one of her charming habits to thank me on waking, as though I had been a benefactor. She kissed me and got out of bed and began to dress. As I lay watching her she turned and swept all the bedclothes on to the floor. "Get up," she said. "You have an appointment with your stepson-in-law." We could never get over the oddity of the relationships in our family. "It's all so complicated," I said, pulling a shirt over my head, "that anyone could persuade me that Viola is my grandmother."

Viola and Miss Hartman were there when we got to Piccadilly. Fresh from my encounter with Sylvia, I was sensitive to the look of love, and the child obviously was in the seventh heaven. "Sir Robert will be in at any moment," Miss Hartman said. "We have his permission to take tea with Mr. Quayne and his father. We are about to leave."

They went at once, Viola in a flutter of impatient good-byes.

"So Bob knows about this," I said.

Sylvia said: "I am quite idiotically happy, darling. There is something new in the feeling of this place. Something new and good."

We stood at the window, my arm around her, my left hand on her breast, and I could feel her trembling with unabated desire. Certainly for me it was a most precious and holy moment. We watched the lights coming on in the streets and shops, and the dusk folding dark wings upon St. James's Park, and she spoke an old fear. "To see young and beautiful creatures in love makes me feel withered."

Bob and Janet came in. "Sorry to keep you waiting," Bob cried, "but the air smelled so good we walked all the way from Curzon Street."

"Not all the way?" I chipped him; but he was impervious to

364

irony. "Every blessed yard," he boasted heartily. "Didn't we, Janet?"

Janet kissed Sylvia as though she hadn't seen her for a long time. "Every blessed yard," she agreed. "Your son-in-law is becoming quite an athlete, Mother."

She was looking happy, and she hadn't looked happy since Hubert died.

Brookes carried in a tray with the tea things, drew the curtains and switched on the lights. "The office rang up an hour ago, Sir Robert, sounding urgent. I said you were out, and they asked if I could get in touch with you. I took the liberty of saying I didn't know where you were."

"But you did." For a flash Bob looked annoyed, and I imagined him thinking of a moment of importance that had been snatched from him. The film stopping. A message on the screen. "The presence of Sir Robert Meagher is urgently required at . . ."

"All right, Brookes. Let them use their own noddles now and then."

"But, Bob," Janet said as she poured the tea, "that's just what you've never allowed them to do. They're scared stiff of you."

"Oh, well, they can go on being so. But I don't see why they should expect me to have to approve all they do as though they were office-boys. Seriously," he said, addressing us all now, "it's taken me a long time to learn an elementary lesson. When you give a man responsibility you must let him exercise it. Otherwise you kill his initiative. It's been idiotic to expect these men to follow me round like a lot of kids hanging on to my coat-tails."

Janet handed him his tea and smiled at him. "Well, you certainly took time off in a good cause to-day. I find even the best film or play dreary if I see it alone. Did you enjoy it?"

"No," he said frankly. "But perhaps that was my fault, not the film's. And I certainly liked taking an afternoon off with you. It made me feel quite daring. And I wish Brookes would use discretion in putting butter on muffins."

"It's not Brookes's job to put the butter on. And, anyway, that's what you need—a good deal more butter on your stodgy muffins."

"Now you're being enigmatic," he charged her, but clearly enjoying the banter; and Sylvia and I enjoyed it, too. We exchanged glances. This was something new. "Has Janet told you about her new job?" Bob asked us. She hadn't, and he explained that one of the best Sunday papers had engaged her to review novels week by week. "A job she can do at home," Bob said. "Not like all that messing about in the *Now* office."

A flash of pain passed over Janet's face; and Bob saw it. He reached across the table and took her hand. "Sorry," he said. "I know I promised not to mention that again. Shall I tell you something I really believe? I know I was often furious with him and said disagreeable things about him, but in my heart I thought Hubert Dodge a very great man. Sometimes he made me feel pretty cheap."

There was a moment's silence. Bob was uncomfortable. It hadn't been easy for him to say that, and we all felt its sincerity. It was Sylvia, not Janet, who answered. "Thank you, Bob. But don't feel too cheap too often. Because you're not, you know."

Things went happily from then on. We stayed rather late. We had come by train, our rather disreputable car being in a garage for overhaul. Bob magnificently insisted on sending us all the way to the Barn in one of his gilded chariots. I had a moment alone with him, and mentioned Viola and her tea-meeting with Peter and his father. "Miss Hartman says you approve, Bob. I'm glad of that."

Bob said: "Between you and me, George, Peter Quayne was becoming a damned sight too fond of Janet. Thank God that's done with."

6

It was not till the late summer of that year, 1937, that Mr. Merriman and Wendy opened the Kensington shop—the first thing they had turned into something more than a hole-and-corner enterprise. They asked me and Sylvia to be present, but I was glad to have a valid "previous engagement" as an excuse for not going. Bob might have thought it too pointed if I had blessed the enterprise of his opponent with my presence. As it happened, my "previous engagement" was with Bob himself. I forget what it was that he wanted to discuss with me but I remember him saying: "You've got just about enough commercial and financial *nous* to understand what old Merriman's up to. Beyond that, you're a babe in the wood of this wicked world."

I said, rather piqued: "He got those two leases you had bought. He was clever enough for that."

Bob smiled. "George, George," he said, "how you underestimate me! D'you think he'd have got 'em if I hadn't wanted him to? Since he'd got the middle shop they were no good to me, and seeing that I had to sell them, I saw to it that no one but Merriman got them. How's that for turning the other cheek?"

I was surprised, but it would have been too bad to suggest that I had thought him incapable of generosity. "Bob," I said, "you are becoming a nice, mellow, middle-aged Samaritan."

He said: "I felt I owed it to Wendy."

Now here was quaking ground indeed. I could not recall that he had mentioned Wendy's name since leaving her, and I thought it best to pass right over that remark. However, I could not restrain myself from asking: "Did you know that Viola met Wendy at my house?"

He nodded. "She told me about it. She's a frank child. If she had met Wendy and *not* told me, I should have been disturbed. Wendy can be trusted." He switched the subject. "You haven't put your nose into my place since that day long ago when you came and had lunch with me. Then we didn't get any further than my office. I'd like to take you round the place and show you what we're up to."

I accepted this invitation, and he said he'd send a car out to the Barn to fetch me. He had this habit of throwing cars around as casually as another man would throw away a match after lighting a cigarette.

"Send that beautiful ambassador who drove us down into the West Country," I said, not seriously. "He fascinates me. He worships Thomas Hardy."

"Who is Hardy?" Bob asked.

I explained, and he said: "Oh, just another of his writing people. Yes; I know all about that, though he doesn't think so. I pay him twice what I ought to because he's a bit of a character."

Mellower and mellower, I thought; and wondered how Janet had done it. I asked her frankly. She said: "Oh, it's all because I realised what a fool I was being. Seeing Peter with Viola knocked me endways and made me think. So I started courting Bob."

"Courting?"

"Yes, courting. You should know. I'm my mother's daughter. And there was her mother before that. It's born in any woman with a dash of the Chown in her."

I blushed and she laughed, and slapped me lightly in the face. Then she kissed me. "Really, George," she said, "you *are* a babe."

7

At the Meagher works it was the same routine as on my earlier visit. I was expected and was passed from hand to hand as though I were an exceptionally precious ambassador awaited by an exceptionally expectant monarch. All this until I was in Bob's presence. Then the atmosphere was different. He was not out this time to impress me. A simple lunch was served. He drank water and I lager beer. I said: "What about the canteen menus, Bob? I thought they were shown to you for approval?"

"They used to be, but all that can now be left to the person concerned."

There were no liqueurs and cigars. There was not even coffee. I lit my pipe and we went to the window that gave a view of the whole lay-out. "It looks bigger than I remember," I said.

"It *is* bigger than you remember. You should come and see us more often, George. When we started here I took care that there should be room for expansion. We've pretty well used it all up now. I'm looking for a new site. There's a place at Newbury that we shall probably buy—twenty acres with some buildings that won't need too much alteration."

"That building away on the left—I don't think I've seen that before."

"That's where we make gears."

"But every car must have gears. Surely you've always had to make them?"

"Oh, no. We used to buy them. We used to buy a lot of things. But we're pretty well self-contained now. There was a firm in Middlesborough. That's where most of our gears came from. Excellent people, but the depression hit 'em. I heard they were feeling the draught and went up and had a look. I made them an offer, and their terms were pretty steep. Then I had to come and argue it out with my board. They were against it almost to a man. It meant borrowing money, and they didn't like that. I talked 'em over, and the thing's been a success, but I made a whopping mistake."

It was the first time I had heard Bob admit to making a mistake.

"I had all that mass of machinery dismantled and brought down here and had that building put up to house it. I wanted everything under my hand, so to speak. I should have left it where it was and used local labour. Centralisation's a fool's game with the world in its present state. Or do you think the world's a nice cosy place, George?"

"What are you afraid of—another war?"

"Just that," he said gravely. "We still buy a certain amount of stuff from Germany. I go over there now and then, and I don't like what I see."

I felt a chill in the room. It suddenly seemed to me a more realistic room, a room with more significance than it had had when I was here in the early days and we had gloried and drunk deep.

Bob broke the silence. "Well, there it is. If I made a mistake I learned a lesson, too. When you buy out a highly specialised firm like that, buy the brains as well as the materials. I soon discovered who was the brains up there in Middlesborough, and now he's here in charge of our own gear-making."

"Newbury is part of the decentralisation scheme?"

"Yes."

"What are you going to make there?"

"More gears."

"But can't you make all that your motors want here?"

"Yes. But we hope, you know, to make more and more motors; and in the meantime we can sell the gears that aren't needed for our own products. There's an endless market if the stuff is good, and I've yet to see better gears than we are now turning out. And then there's the war to think of. I learned something about tanks in the last war, you know. And there'll be gears needed for everything else. You can almost say the war will be run on gears—in tanks and ships and submarines and aeroplanes and God knows what before the thing's ended."

"A modern gun," I assured him, "will make short work of the most excellent of your gears."

He answered with the only " proverb " I ever heard from his lips. " Gears, like men, should be made to work on the mistaken assumption that they are immortal."

We looked down at the men streaming out of the canteens and hurrying to the buildings sprawled among the tall poplars that now were fine heaven-pointing trees. " Don't forget," Bob said, " that a few months ago the Government decided to spend during the next five years about one thousand four hundred million pounds on armaments. They're rather optimistic in thinking that they're going to be allowed five years. I'm budgeting for something quicker. Look at this."

He went to a drawer, took out a roll of plans, and spread them on the table. They covered the whole works. Air-raid shelters, underground workshops, fire precautions. " The Parliamentary Labour Party Executive," he said grimly, " have expressed a general determination to oppose the Government's policy. I, on the other hand, am going to take the tip. I'm laying in all the material necessary to make these works as safe as anything can be in the circumstances. And I sha'n't wait for war to come. I think I shall smell it some way off, and then these places will become hard facts, and all the people employed here will be warned accordingly and drilled in what will be expected of them."

He rolled up the plans, put them away, and locked the drawer. " Now come and have a look round."

For the first time in my life I walked round the works for which, in the beginning, I was in a small way responsible. Bob talked enthusiastically of this and that wonder, and was almost poetic about the beauty and efficiency of the gear-making department. In any circumstances it would have meant little to me, and that day I followed him in a daze. There had been so much that I wanted to talk to him about—especially Joss and

Viola; but Joss and Viola had shrunk to the proportions of ants whose little hill was on the route of ruthless trampling feet. I had been working on the mistaken assumption that they were immortal.

The man whom Bob had called the brains of the gear-making department was Mark Erskine. I was introduced to him that day at the works and took a fancy to him. He was a gruff middle-aged Northerner, rather stout, with nothing much to attract you in his face except the eyes that were both kindly and intelligent. Bob left us together. "Excuse me, George," he said. "I must go now. You'll find the car waiting when you want it. Show him something about gears, Mark."

Erskine and I strolled round and he tried to lighten my darkness. A foreman came up to him and they talked about something that was over my head. "One moment, Harry," Erskine said. "I've got a drawing here that will make it clear." He opened his coat to reveal a poacher's pocket stuffed with papers of one sort and another. He pulled them out and some fell to the ground. I picked them up. He spotted his drawing among them, took it from me, and left me holding the rest. Among them was a miniature score of Beethoven's Sonata in C Sharp Minor. When the foreman was gone I handed him the score and he took it with a grin. "This is another sort of mechanics," he said. "I'm trying to get to the bottom of it."

"What are you doing to-night?" I asked.

"Nothing in particular. I'm a lone lorn bachelor. When there isn't a concert to go to I stay at home and read scores or Shakespeare's plays."

"You don't dream about gears?"

"No," he said. "Gears come natural. I don't have to work on 'em. I think I must have been conceived by the meshing of two gears in a gear-box."

He pleased me more and more. "Have dinner with me and my wife at the Café Royal," I invited, and he gladly accepted.

I rang up Sylvia and explained what had happened. "I'll stay here in town," I said, "and meet you at the Café Royal at eight. Bob's ambassador will come to bring you."

Then I went to the flat behind Baker Street. Eliza Hartman and Viola were living there now. The time was come, Miss Hartman had decided, when Viola should be in London, hearing all the music she could. The cottage in Cornwall was shut up, and Bob continued to rent the large room and the grand piano for practice. Indeed, he had now accepted the situation so thoroughly that he had bought the piano. There had been some argument about Viola living away from Piccadilly, but Janet had settled that. She understood what was involved better than Bob ever would. "The child must soak and stew in music and, for the time being, nothing but music," she said, "and Miss Hartman will see to that all the better if she's left to herself."

Bob grumbled. "And all I do is pay the rent of the room, pay Miss Hartman, buy a piano, and never see my child."

"One of these days," Janet promised him, "you'll see a child to be proud of. Meantime, leave her alone."

So there those two were, living in my flat, practising every morning in the rented room, taking their afternoon exercise in the parks instead of on the moors, and practising again at night if there wasn't some special concert to attend. It was an intensive hot-house life, and where Peter Quayne came into it I don't know. As Janet kept Bob at bay, so, I imagine, Eliza Hartman kept Peter. He was allowed to take tea with them, I believe, once a week; for the rest, he, too, had to wait for the finished product.

When I got to the flat I rang the bell, for I had sacrificed my keys. Miss Hartman came to the door and looked as though she doubted the wisdom of letting me in. However, she did so, with the whispered command: "Speak quietly. We have taken our exercise, and now Viola is resting. I think she is asleep."

I crawled guiltily into my own room and noted the marks of alien occupation: Miss Hartman's framed and signed photographs of musicians, a photograph of Peter Quayne, plaster busts of Mozart and Schubert. Music scores littered the table.

Miss Hartman opened the bedroom door and peeped in. "She sleeps," she announced. "Now I must give you some good news. I will not bore you with the details of Associated Board examinations, but there are such things, and if you gain a distinction you can try for an Associated Board scholarship. This is highly prized. Well, we have been secret and furtive. We have said nothing to Sir Robert, but we have now done all that is necessary before trying for the scholarship. We wished to say nothing till that, too, is won. As it will be," she promised confidently.

It was, indeed, good news. "But why," I asked, "have you broken your vow of silence for my benefit?"

She seemed perplexed by the question; then said: "Because it is all more than I can bear to keep to myself. You will understand. You, too, are an artist."

I shouldn't have known how to answer that embarrassing remark, but the door opened and Viola peeped in. She was holding a dressing-gown round her and was heavy with sleep. She yawned, and looked a tired child. It was impossible to believe in that defenceless moment that she was anything but a child—just at the age of beginning to be a little ashamed of an old worn-out toy bear. She came in and gave me a warm kiss. I noticed how sensuous her mouth could be—not like some of the pursed-up bits of dry leather that sometimes ceremonially chilled me—and I thought how lucky Peter Quayne was. She said: " Oh, Uncle George! I was dreaming about you, and here you are."

I said that I was flattered to have been in her dreams and hoped they were happy ones.

" No," she said. " They were altogether terrifying. I dreamt that I was sitting for an Associated Board scholarship, and you were the whole Board rolled into one, and you looked grim and disapproving at everything I did."

So now it's in her sleep as well, I thought; and wondered if Miss Hartman was driving her too hard. The sooner that scholarship examination was over the better.

" I won't have you dreaming about me in that degrading way," I said. " Next time you dream about me it must be as a Father Christmas with reindeer drawing a sledge piled high with laurel wreaths, to be placed on your head one above the other till they reach the stars."

At this fond silly thought she clapped her hands like a child ; and it was most moving to watch her and to realise that she *was* a child, and yet, if Miss Hartman was to be believed, an artist.

Miss Hartman said: " Do not excite yourself, my dear. Go and dress." Obediently she went. It was clear that, in all things, Miss Hartman's was the voice from Sinai.

While she was away and Miss Hartman was preparing tea I said: " If you were a man I'd accuse you of playing Svengali."

" Svengali my foot," she said, brusquely, not ceasing her clatter. " I'm a rotten old bean-pole who will last, I hope, long enough for her to climb and reach the sunlight, where she will bloom. Then you can throw me on the bonfire."

When the child had returned and we were having tea I asked if Viola was practising that night, and Miss Hartman said: " But certainly."

I reminded her that some of us had been permitted to hear her play at the cottage in Cornwall, and asked if Sylvia and I and a friend who would be dining with us might hear her that night.

" Ah, that other time, that was different," Miss Hartman said. " Then Viola was not a pianist."

I knew that she was as cagey about the child as a race-horse trainer would be about a filly of exceptional promise who must not be spied on during trial gallops.

" I do not like that she should play in public yet," she said. " She will soon be at the Royal Academy of Music, and then, perhaps a year after that, perhaps even more, she shall make her début at the Wigmore Hall. Then you shall hear her."

The old girl's eyes shone. She seemed to have no doubt of the glory that was then to be revealed. "I think," she said, "that she should be permitted to marry Mr. Quayne just before her début. That is the time to play—when you know fully what love is. I never did, and so I was never what Viola shall be."

This was too much for Viola. She blushed, covered in confusion, and cried: "Oh, Miss Hartman! Please!"

Eliza grinned at her and said: "You see now what a bad character I am. I am prepared to use all means to make you what you can be."

I was as disturbed as Viola, for, listening to Miss Hartman calmly arranging the future, I thought of my afternoon session with Bob. I thought of the plans unrolled on the desk: underground shelters, air-raid precautions, fire-fighting points. How was a début at the Wigmore Hall going to fit into all that? I thought of Janet at Penruan sadly reciting:

> Why didst thou promise such a beauteous day,
> And make me travel forth without my cloak?

Was that to happen to Viola, too?

I think it was as much to cover the moment of confusion as for any other reason that Viola said sharply: "I *wish* Uncle George and Aunt Sylvia to hear me play. They will forgive all my faults."

Miss Hartman looked surprised, quite taken aback; and I guessed that never before had Viola withstood her. She said: "It shall be as you wish," but she said it so sadly, so much as though she were hurt, that Viola knelt at her feet and pleaded: "You forgive me? I do wish it so dearly."

Miss Hartman raised her up and said, over-dramatically but clearly meaning it: "Between us two, I am the one to kneel. Soon we part. When you are in the Royal College I have done with you. I go back to Cornwall. We have been happy. So let us be happy to the end. You shall play to your uncle and aunt if you wish."

And play she did. It was nine o'clock when Sylvia and I with Mark Erskine reached the room she used for practice. Miss Hartman was just unlocking the door and we all went in together. When the lights were switched on we found ourselves in a bleak square chamber with three bare bulbs hanging from the ceiling. The only furniture was a piano, a shaded standard lamp beside it, and a few hard wooden chairs. The dark walls had no pictures and the planks of the floor no covering. There were a few electric heaters which Miss Hartman switched on, and we waited till the room had warmed up. Viola, on entering, had gone to a chair in a far corner and sat down, taking no notice of any of us and massaging her fingers. She was shrouded in a thick dark cloak. When the room was warm she said: "I

373

am ready." We took our places on the wooden chairs. Miss Hartman switched on the standard lamp shaded in golden silk and switched off the other lights. She opened the piano and fixed the prop of the lid, then smiled towards Viola. The child got up, dropped the cloak on to her chair and was seen to be wearing a long dress of the same golden silk as shaded the lamp. Somehow she looked taller than I thought her to be. When Miss Hartman had joined us on the chairs she walked slowly to the piano and sat down, her hands lying open on her knees, her eyes looking quietly in front of her as though she were communing with something we could not see. She had brought no music scores. She said: "Beethoven's Sonata in C Sharp Minor," and began to play.

I am not a critic. I am merely an appreciator. I cannot bear books which tell you, of a picture or a poem, that a colour here or a stress there balances this or that somewhere else. To me, it is like cutting out a thrush's tongue to find the secret of this exultation. I could as soon "explain" a poem as I could explain my religion, such as it is. There is nothing the arts can do to me except knock me endways or leave me cold. When I feel a creeping of the spine and an exaltation that starts my tears I know that I am in thrall to an artist and that analysis of these effects means nothing to me—nothing at all. Carry me on "the viewless wings of poesy" or leave me alone. I only know that that night the child was blurred to my sight by the strange mingling of joy and sorrow that it is the privilege of art to call forth. Great art is in the most literal sense an enchantment. And I sat enchanted. She herself was something other than I till then had known her to be. She could never again be the same to me. She was an artist.

When she had finished none of us stirred. There was not a sound except a great sigh from Mark Erskine. Viola was sitting back, her hands, palms downwards, again on her knees, her eyes fixed ahead. She said: "Chopin's Dead March."

It was a piece of music that I almost dreaded because of the way it could tear me to bits. To me, it never suggests death as the ending of a life that is done with, but death-in-life, the ineluctable sorrow that goes through all our days, the grey sister of Joy. I wondered what Viola would make of that. It seemed to me immensely mature, and I found myself trembling with apprehension. I had heard Mark Hambourg play it and remembered my desolation. Viola's playing of it moved me, but not as I had been moved then. Still, it moved me; and Erskine whispered: "She'll do that magnificently some day."

She didn't pause for long after that, but turned to us with a child's smile and said: "A little gay thing of Dohnányi—one of the Humoreskes," and she rippled through it, lifting our tension, leaving us smiling.

374

That was the end of it. Miss Hartman switched on the harsh lights, closed the piano, and wrapped the cloak round Viola. " Not yet the Wigmore Hall," she said, " but you have done well enough."

What is there to say on these occasions? I am always at a loss. I know that we fussed her, and that Erskine was shy and reverential, and that Viola said to me: " What if my dream had been true, Uncle George, and you had been the whole Board listening to me? What would you have done?"

" I should have put the first laurel wreath on your head," I said, kissing her forehead.

Miss Hartman said: " That is enough now. You must go to bed, Viola."

We stood in the cold street, and she locked the door with a great key, like a wardress incarcerating the piano. I called a taxi and put them into it, and we three stood there till it was out of sight. Sylvia said: " I can hardly believe it's true. Bob and that Wendy girl!"

Erskine said: " The wind bloweth where it listeth," and walked off down the street.

9

By the autumn of 1938 Viola had won her Royal College of Music scholarship; Miss Hartman was back in Cornwall; and Joss, who was due to go up to Oxford when the Michaelmas Term opened, was spending a few days with me and Sylvia at the Barn in Buckinghamshire. He was a restless and unhappy boy. We had radio in the house now. Joss and I were walking one afternoon in the beech woods, golden with autumn, when he suddenly burst forth: " So he thinks so, does he, the damned old fool?"

I didn't need to ask what he was talking about. The night before this, we had listened to Mr. Neville Chamberlain promising us Peace in Our Time.

Joss swiped with a stick at the fallen leaves and said: " Look at it, George. Does it make sense? Here is this bloody wolf Hitler chasing our sledge, and Chamberlain thinks he can buy him off by throwing out someone else's baby. He and Daladier hand over three and a half million Czechs and 10,800 square miles of their territory without a ' by-your-leave ' to the Czechs themselves. Just because the wolf has been baying a bit more noisily than usual. Isn't it common sense to suppose that wolves who can land a meal like that just by yapping will go on yapping for more?"

I wished I was a politician, an economist, a reader of *The*

New Statesman—anyone who knew all the answers to all the questions. But I was none of these things. I was simply a perplexed and puzzled man, deeply disturbed, terrified indeed, by the way in which a few " high-ups " could trample to pieces all the dreams and schemes of humble men and women. I remembered the young soldiers marching through the streets of Manchester when I was a schoolboy and how I had hoped that that war would last long enough for me to join them. I had no such wishes now.

" You'll be in it, you know, when it comes," Joss said. " What are you? Not forty?"

I was thirty-seven.

" There'll be no volunteers this time," he promised me. " It'll be a conscript army from the word go."

He seemed almost to relish the prospect. If men are to be fools, let all share the consequences of the folly. It didn't sound to me as though he was talking nonsense. The trenches had been dug in Hyde Park. The pigs' snouts had been handed round.

" I promise you one thing," he said. " I won't be in it. I've had it out with my father and he knows where I stand. He says I can please myself : go up to Oxford in a month or two or join him at once in the works. He'll find me a job that will make me indispensable when the call-up comes. What d'you think of that, eh? Damn Oxford, I say. I never have wanted to go there. As for the other option—well, I ask you, can you see me watching all the men I knew being shovelled into the fire while I indispensably sit at a ledger totting up the old man's war earnings?"

No, I couldn't see that. I asked him : " What are you going to do?"

" When I've finished my stay with you, I shall go down and do a bit of sailing with Jose. That's a sane occupation. It'll give me time to think things over."

Bob Meagher, who had been rather hurt when Viola abandoned horses for pianos, was now not only reconciled but proud. We had Mark Erskine to thank for that, which is what I had intended when I took him to hear Viola play. To Bob, people like me and Sylvia and Janet were all very well in their way, but it was not a way that wholly commended itself to him. Writing and acting and all that sort of thing had nothing to do with the real work of the world. Erskine was another matter. That a man who believed gears to be important also believed music to be important at first surprised and then impressed Bob, and he began, Erskine told me, to be a bit of a bore, rarely failing to find a loophole through which to drag his wonderchild into a conversation. Viola was now living with him and Janet, and she could do no wrong.

But this was not so with Jocelyn. Here was the first-born, the heir to the industrial empire that Bob had created, and Joss showed not the slightest understanding of the privileges that his birth bestowed upon him. What was worse, he had no aptitude or bent in any other direction that Bob could commend. During these few days that Joss spent with me and Sylvia he was more than usually difficult because of a row with Bob. Janet told me about it. They were at dinner in Piccadilly: Bob and Janet, Joss and Viola. " Viola was rather full of herself," Janet said. " She was on top of the world after winning her scholarship, and, naturally enough, when Miss Hartman was gone, she slacked a bit. She had been keyed up too tight, I suppose. Any-way, she came under a professor who one day expressed surprise that she was a scholarship student. He seemed to have pulled no punches. He'd heard of the Hartman régime, and sym-pathised with Viola at being without her nanny. Viola came home in tears and went straight to bed."

However, the lecture had its effect, and a week later she was lit up with glory. It was simply because the old boy had patted her on the head and said: " I begin to have a dim understanding at last, Miss Meagher, of why the examiners awarded you a scholarship. It is up to you now to go on and enlighten me further."

They were all four at dinner when Viola told this story. Bob had invited Joss that morning to spend the day with him on the Great West Road, and Joss had foolishly made disparaging remarks about the road, and how it had doubtless once been worth visiting when it ran through some of the finest fruit-growing country in England, but now, he said, it should be rechristened Via Abhorrenda ; and when Bob asked what that might mean Joss said: " A road to be abhorred, leading to the Slough of Despond."

Bob said, tolerantly enough: " Well, if it offends you, you needn't look at it. You'll be in the car."

" I'm afraid," Joss said, " that is one of the things I should dislike about it. Before we know where we are, we shall all be in ruddy cars, rushing God knows where, and oblivious of the stinking chaos we are rushing through."

Bob refused to be beaten. " Ah, well," he said, " in a month or so you'll be in Oxford. Perhaps that'll please you better."

" If I have to go to a university at all," Joss said, " I wish it could be Cambridge."

" Why Cambridge?"

" Well, it's not an appanage of a car factory."

Bob said no more, and Joss spent the day walking somewhere in the Home Counties. Then, when they all four met at dinner, Viola bubbled over about the appreciation her professor had shown. " Well, my dear," Bob said, " that is only to be expected.

You know what you want to do, and you put all you have into doing it."

Joss couldn't stay away from fire. "Meaning," he said, "not like some."

Bob said quietly: "I allowed you a certain rope in your conversation this morning, Joss. I'd be obliged if you wouldn't start it all over again. When are you going to grow up?"

"What is there to grow up to? You know as well as I do that there's going to be a war."

"Leave the war out of it. When are you going to grow up?"

"You're dodging my question."

"I'm dodging nothing. I grew up to a war myself, you know. And I agree with you that it's pretty certain we shall have another. I've told you more than once what you can do about that. We can find valuable work for you."

"Are you offering me a funk-hole?"

It was then that Bob suddenly stood up, hurled his napkin to the table and accidentally knocked over a bottle of Burgundy. The wine spread like blood on the cloth. "Oh, damn you, Joss! What *can* I do with you? What can I do?" Bob shouted.

Brookes, who was in attendance, began to fuss over the cloth, and Bob said: "Leave it alone and get out. Get out, all of you."

He sat down again, his head in his hands, his elbows in the seeping red.

They all left him there. Viola was crying; Joss was horrified by the consequence of his own conduct. In self-disgust he went banging out of the house. Soon Janet went back and put her arm round Bob's shoulder, which was shaking with sobs. "I feel such a failure," he said. "Such a failure. And with Joss of all people. I'd do anything in the world for him."

She persuaded him to go up to bed.

10

This was the Joss we had on our hands at the Barn. He was loathing himself, loathing the world he lived in, thinking of his father, half in admiration and half with the contempt which he found necessary to qualify this admiration that he did not wish to concede. His detestation of the increasingly mechanical world was genuine. It was a pity that Bob was the epitome of that world, with no discernable attributes, such as Mark Erskine's, beyond what that world required. These, had they existed, might have furnished a ground for meeting.

Joss's presence about the house disturbed me and Sylvia. It was not that he said or did anything outrageous: it was simply

378

that his presence exuded desolation. We were aware that he was in agony, and any attempt to get him to open up, however cautious and tentative it might be, sent him, emotionally, scurrying away from us like a startled hare. Even normal courtesies made him wince. "For God's sake don't *fuss* about me." What was perhaps worst of all was that a sister younger than himself was receiving a lot of attention and admiration. One evening he was reading the newspaper and it contained an interview with a famous headmaster who had just retired. The interviewer asked: "What lessons have you learned from your years as a teacher?" The headmaster replied: "Well, for one thing, I've learned to keep a cautious eye on the scholarship type. He's our most dangerous material. Precocious scholars tend to crack up. They rarely last."

Joss read this to us and made no comment, but there was no doubt that the words pleased him, though to me they seemed no more than one of those generalisations that I distrust. I could have produced plenty of cases on the other side; but I had reached the stage where I was afraid to oppose anything he supported, for it seemed only to deepen his resolute unreason. There'll be time enough for a good talk with him, I thought, when his attitude has softened a bit; but the time never came. Before going to bed that night he said: "If it's all the same to you, I'll push on towards old Jose in the morning." I am sure that Sylvia shared my guilty sense of relief at being given this chance to wash our hands of him, but we said nothing about it.

In the morning I motored him to Paddington to catch the Riviera Express, and thought of the day so long ago, in the midst of a war, when I, younger than Joss, was for the first time catching this train myself, heading for Cornwall and all that had flowed therefrom. We were a bit early at the station, and when we had made claim to a seat by dumping Joss's meagre belongings upon it, we strolled up and down the platform among the chattering outward-bound passengers, and those antique memories were churning in my mind, when Joss unexpectedly said: "Of all the stuff I ever learned in the English classes, nothing much sticks except a few words from Wordsworth."

"Well," I said hopefully, "that's something. He turned up some pretty dreary earth, but by God when he struck a nugget it shone."

Joss quoted: "'The heavy and the weary weight of all this unintelligible world.' Those are the words I remember."

"Yes, Joss. But he's talking about moments when 'the heavy and the weary weight of all this unintelligible world is lightened.'"

"I know," Joss said. "But it's just those words that stick. How does the weight become lightened, Uncle George?"

He looked as though he didn't expect an answer; and any answer I could have given him was beyond the space allowed us. The porters began running along the train, banging doors, shouting: "Take your seats, please."

Joss leaned out of the window. "I do loathe the sound of banging doors," he said.

The whistle blew, the green flag was waved, and the engine gave its deep preliminary cough. Inch by inch, foot by foot, yard by yard, the train drew out, and I watched till its tail was all I could see. And all I could hear, though the sound had long ceased, was the banging of doors.

11

A week later Janet rang up and said: "Bob's in a bit of a state about Joss. We haven't heard a word from him since he went down to Jose's place—not even to say that he arrived."

I had to tell her that we, too, were without news.

"You know Jose better than I do," Janet said. "Ring him up, there's a darling, and then ring back here. I want to put Bob out of his misery."

I rang up the Absolution with the certain knowledge in my heart that any answer I might get would contain no comfort for Bob. Jose said: "But his visit here was cancelled. Didn't you know that? I had a letter from him the day he was due to arrive. Full of apologies. He said he had lots of things to see to before going up to Oxford and begged the whole thing off."

That was the news I had to give to Janet to pass on to Bob. Nothing was ever heard of Joss again. Bob got the railway people busy with inquiries, and at Plymouth a booking-office clerk was found who remembered a youth showing a ticket for Gwinear Road and asking if he could break his journey and go on later. The clerk said he could, and he described the young man, who undoubtedly was Joss. He did not see him return to the station.

There the trail ended. Joss passed out of our lives through a door leading into the town that was so soon to be pounded to dust. Now it has risen to new life, but for Joss there was to be no new life—none at any rate of which so much as a whisper came through to us. The doors had finally banged upon him.

CHAPTER SEVENTEEN

1

In January of 1939 it was pretty clear that inquiries had come to a dead end, and that there would be no more news of Joss unless he himself cared to break silence. That is, if he were still alive. We were not certain even of that. On an afternoon of bitter cold I was coming away from my agent's office after settling something that was to have an effect on several lives. I had written a short story—an unusual thing for me to do, but I did it now and then. Whatever effect Mr. Ledra's little pieces had on others, they never wholly satisfied Mr. Ledra himself. The wish to do something more creative never left me, but it was not fulfilled except in these infrequent short stories. They were not so short as all that. Six of them made up a volume which Nigel Wendron had published a year ago. Henry Fitch, one of the few men producing films worth looking at, chanced to read it and saw possibilities in one of the stories. It was called *The Child on the Tower*.

I rarely took Paul to London, but I did so that day. He was six years old and he wanted to see the Zoo. We saw the Zoo, and then I took him with me to my agent's office where I was to meet Henry Fitch. When I got there, Fitch and my agent had already been at it for an hour, and I had nothing to do but agree to the financial terms they had arranged. To me, they seemed almost indecently lavish. It would take me years to earn as much with my little pieces.

While we talked Paul sat in an arm-chair, looking at the fire. My agent's office is in an eighteenth-century house that has not been much altered. The open fireplace with its marble surround is still there, and the leather arm-chair in which Paul sat with his legs folded beneath him had a look of venerable domesticity. The boy was lost in some thought of his own, inaccessible to adult comprehension. Fitch was considering him through large horn-rimmed spectacles. He seemed, indeed, more interested in Paul than in me. I, after all, was only the author. My job had been finished when I had written the story that some script-writer would chew into the shape of a film.

When all had been settled, Fitch said: " You have a place in Cornwall, haven't you?"

" My wife has."

" She was an actress, wasn't she?"

381

"Yes. But she hasn't done anything for years. Her mother was Margaret Napier."

"Yes, I know. Could I have a look at this Cornish place? Nigel Wendron was talking to me about it. I thought it might be good for some of our shots."

I said it could be done, and we agreed to settle the times later. Then I walked out into the street—Essex Street. I took Paul's hand and we went up towards the Strand. I chanced to look back, and Fitch, wrapped in a great fur coat and looking like an amiable bear, was watching us intently. He waved and shambled down towards the Embankment.

Where Essex Street joins the Strand I stood with Paul waiting for a taxi to take us to Baker Street station. One ground to a standstill, not, I saw, because of my signal but by order from a passenger already within. It was Bob Meagher. "Get in," he said, "and come back to Piccadilly with me."

I was glad to get out of the freezing wind, but found Bob's face as glacial as the weather. I had not seen him smile since Joss disappeared. His hair was greying, and lines of age were deepening on his forehead and round his mouth. Yet he was at a peak to which, though he had never talked about it, I knew he had long aspired. He had received Society's seal of approval and admiration. The New Year's Honours List named him a Baron. I was travelling with Lord Meagher of Levenshulme. That was the Manchester suburb in which he had been born.

From Piccadilly I rang up Sylvia to explain the delay and Bob handed Paul over to Brookes. He took me to a small room he used when he wanted to be alone, and tea was brought in. I said nothing about my own happy reason for being in town. Bob's face made it seem trivial; and I guessed that he had brought me here to say something that mattered to him. He said that he had been to a meeting in the City and instead of returning to the Great West Road had looked in at Piccadilly in case some news had come. "Of course it hasn't," he said. "I can tell that from Brookes's face."

He drank his tea and lit his pipe and twiddled it in his mouth, puffing erratically. "There are two things," he said suddenly. "About Janet. And about Wendy."

I waited for him to go on, and he had some difficulty. At last he broke out suddenly: "I keep in touch with the police, of course, and they talk smoothly. But I know they don't expect to get any farther. Well, I must have a son. And Janet won't do anything about it. You must ask Sylvia to talk to her."

I was amazed, and completely floored. "But, Bob, surely . . ."

"Surely nothing," he said. "It's her duty as a wife. You speak to Sylvia and get her to make Janet see reason."

There was nothing I could say to that, so I asked: "And what do you mean about Wendy?"

"Well, Joss was her son as well as mine. She ought to know what's happened. You see something of her now and then. I'd like you to tell her."

That would be disagreeable, but not impossible. I said I would do it. We sat in silence for a long time; then he said: "It was a pretty bloody meeting in the City this afternoon. A lot of us discussing what to do if and when. You know. Well, I must ring up the office. Don't forget to let Sylvia know what I have said."

For the first time since achieving his magnificence he forgot to order a car for me. I took Paul down into Piccadilly and we found a taxi which took us to Baker Street station.

2

Sylvia and I decided to go into town to see Janet the next day. The weather remained cold but a wintry sun was shining on a little snow that had fallen during the night. It looked as though this better weather would last. I was hardly out of bed when the telephone rang. It was Henry Fitch. "Would it be all right," he asked, "if I came out and spent an hour or two at your place?"

I explained that I should be leaving for town as soon as I had had breakfast.

"Will Paul be at home? It's him I want to see, not you," Fitch said, putting the author firmly in his place.

I said that Paul would be at home. "Good," he said briskly, and rang off.

I briefed Miss Collum, and arranged with our daily woman to prepare an extra lunch in case Mr. Fitch stayed that long, and at ten o'clock Sylvia and I were getting into the car when an impressive Meagher wagon drove up. Fitch was driving, and alongside him sat what gipsy fortune-tellers call a handsome stranger. The wagon was no sooner still on the gravel than the back doors opened and two more men climbed out. I looked within and saw that the wagon was stuffed with photographic apparatus. There were cables coiled on the floor as though the callers were from the Zoo with a gift of pythons.

Fitch shook hands with me and I introduced him to Sylvia. I explained forlornly that I had ordered an extra lunch for one, and he said: "There are pubs about, aren't there?"

The handsome stranger paced the gravel, looking indifferent to all of us. Fitch said: "Come and be introduced, John. This is John Cavendish. We want to take a few pictures of him and Paul. See how they react to one another. Where is the boy?"

"If I know him," Sylvia said, "he's having porridge combed out of his beard."

Cavendish smiled. It was a smile to win anybody's heart. Ah, I thought, he's to be the lover. I could already see him dressed up as a dandy Cavalier.

It was a simple tale that I had written—of an only child, lonely in a great house, the father away fighting on Cromwell's side, the mother courted by the Cavalier who, after a battle, had arrived by night, wounded. The oldest story in the world. Anything it might have depended on the relationship of the boy and the Cavalier: the boy whose father had been harsh and grim; the laughing Cavalier who made life gay and exciting and for ever delayed his return to his own army. From the tower of the old house the boy one day saw his mother and her lover embracing in a walled garden. And then he watched and watched, torn between his love for the man and what he felt to be his duty. There was a morning when news came that a Roundhead force was approaching; and the boy was sent to the tower so that he might, from that place which overlooked the whole countryside, give warning in time for the Cavalier to conceal himself in what had once been a priest's hide-out. He gave his warning and then went out to meet the Cromwellians and led them straight to the priest's hole. It was his father who dragged the man out; and the boy struck and struck at his father before collapsing, a heap of misery on the floor. The father with his boot pushed the boy back roughly into the hole and banged the door upon him, to stand face to face with his wife.

These things sound absurd in synopsis. It depends on what you make of them. I think I made something, and Fitch, happily, was not one of those half-wits who twist even a tragic tale to a happy ending.

Sylvia went into the house and brought Paul out. He remembered Fitch and shook hands with him gravely, and Fitch introduced him to John Cavendish. They walked away together over the gravel, and Fitch went to talk to the men at the back of the wagon. Sylvia and I got into our car and she drove off. " One thing after another," she said. " That's Paul—easy enough; but what on earth am I to say to Janet?"

3

I don't know what she said, for I left her to it. My job was with Wendy. I rang up the Kensington shop and was lucky enough to find her there. When I suggested lunch she said: " All right. But don't make it anything posh. You come here at one o'clock. I know a place."

I went a little early so as to have a look at the latest Merriman enterprise. I was impressed. It was not pretentious and it was not very large, but it was attractive, it had a lot of customers, and the staff was efficient and courteous. I found Wendy in a small room at the back of the first floor. She was making entries in a ledger and looked round to say: "Sit down. I shan't be a moment."

She finished her job, took off her spectacles, and slewed herself round in the swivel-chair. "Do you ever think of the old firm, George—Fred Byles and Ledra?"

"I'm afraid I don't," I confessed. "My father and your father both tried to make it holy to me; but there it is: my mind never clicked to that sort of thing."

"When we started this place," she said, "my father told me the story of how Fred Byles raided the till. He told it as a warning. 'Look after the accounts yourself,' he said. 'If Mr. Ledra had given only half an eye there would have been no trouble.'"

I said: "I know Fred Byles was sent to Dartmoor, but there are those who doubt whether he should have been."

She got up and put on her coat and hat. "It's an old story," she said. "If you want the facts you should have a word with Father. Well, it can't happen here. Now let's go."

In the street I said: "So you dislike eating in posh restaurants?"

"Yes. It's an absurd waste of money. Of course, there are times when business demands it, but normally I keep away from those places. When I'm in them I can't help calculating what the meal has really cost and comparing it with the bill. I feel swindled, and that's bad for the digestion."

She took me to a Lyons tea-shop. "Order what you like," she said lavishly. "I'll have my usual."

Her usual was a pot of tea, a roll and butter and cheese. I plunged into fish and chips, and followed this with a fruit pie and coffee.

When we were settled down to this banquet she said: "Well, what is it? Business or pleasure?"

"I'm afraid it's neither. It's about Joss. You haven't seen him for years, have you?"

"I haven't seen him since Bob threw me out," she said, not bitterly but as a matter of fact. "I told Bob that their upbringing could be his affair. That's how he wanted it. I kept my word."

It was nothing to do with the matter in hand, but I couldn't help asking: "Did Bob look after you financially?"

"He wanted to. He mentioned a sum that would have kept me in clover. But I told him I was capable of looking after myself. There were two reasons for that. I didn't feel like being pensioned off as though I were a servant that he could now do without. And I didn't want to give him the chance to ease his conscience, which I suppose is what he was after. Vindictive, but there it is. Well, what about Joss?"

I told her, and she was silent for a long time, crumbling the roll on her plate. Then she asked: "Why should Bob think I would want to know about that?"

An impossible question to answer. I said lamely: "After all, you are Joss's mother."

She called for another cup of tea and lit a cigarette. "I don't want to be a humbug," she said, "and pretend to feelings I haven't got. In the books a mother's heart always yearns after its young. Like that woman in *East Lynne*. D'you remember? *Dead, dead! And never called me Mother!* It's all tosh, you know. So far as I'm concerned, anyway. I was upset at the time, more than I thought I'd be. But take it from me, George, a scab grows over a wound, and in time even the scab drops off. If Joss hadn't vanished and Bob had sent you here to say: 'You may see the children as often as you like,' I shouldn't want to. They've been shaped now, and I've had no hand in the shaping."

I could think of nothing more to say. After a moment she asked: "Does Bob expect you to carry back an answer?"

"He didn't say so, but perhaps he'd like a word."

"Well, just tell him, will you, that all the words that matter have been spoken, and he spoke them. He knocked a hole in my life all right, but I managed to fill it up with other things. I'm enjoying life in a way that sometimes surprises me."

She didn't look hard or vindictive. But she looked resolute, and she looked as though she were telling the truth about herself.

She began then to talk about Joss's disappearance in an impersonal way. She didn't for a moment believe that he was dead, she assured me. Whatever he had done with himself, he'd land up somewhere and make a life of a sort. "All that is the matter with Joss," she said, "is that he refuses to be made in someone else's image. We hear a lot about yes-men, but few people realise how parents bend all their will to make their children yes-men of their own ideas. If Joss is refusing to do that, then it's a matter for rejoicing, not tears."

As I have said, none of us ever did hear of Joss again, but to this day I share Wendy's view that he is alive and kicking somewhere. I like to think that he reached some place where he could start an orchid-farm or a tropical-fish hatchery, or do something equally harmless and amusing in a world so full of harmful and hurtful and government-decorated great men.

I had arranged to meet Sylvia at our flat behind Baker Street. Wendy and I had so dallied that it was three o'clock before I left her and half past when a taxi dropped me at the flat. I let myself in with my key but there was no sign of Sylvia. Then I heard her voice from the bedroom. "I'm in here." I went in, and she was in bed. I bent over and kissed her, and she said: "Comfort me." We slept till six o'clock, and then, while she was taking a bath I rang up Miss Collum and told her we should stay in town for the night. She started to burble about the day's doings at the Barn, but I cut her off and went out into Baker Street. I bought a cold chicken, some salad and fruit and a bottle of hock. By the time I returned Sylvia had laid the table, drawn the curtains, switched on the fire, and a soothing lamp. I felt full of well-being, sorry for people whose lives together went agley, and when I had put down my parcels I embraced and kissed her. She smiled provokingly, and said: "Tiens, M'seiur! Assez, assez!"

We ate, and I washed up the things, and then we sat on the couch by the fire and she told me of her talk with Janet. "I felt quite raddled with sorrow," she said, "till you came in."

I learned that Janet, not surprisingly, was unhappy. Unlike me and Wendy, she believed that Joss had taken his own life. "When I married Bob," she said to Sylvia, "it all seemed so marvellous and easy. How could a brilliant creature like me fail to be more acceptable to the children than a dull dreary woman like their mother? What they really felt about her I never discovered; and I can see now that I never discovered anything about *them*. Viola was always the perfectly polite, well brought up little girl; but warmth?—not a ray. Looking back on it, I can't remember her ever coming to me with a single question, a single confidence. When she discovered at school what music meant, she never told me. D'you remember a night," she asked Sylvia, "when she played for you and George and that man Mark Erskine? When I learned of it I asked her why she hadn't taken me along, too. She said: 'Sorry, Janet. Would you have liked that? I didn't think you'd be interested.' As for Joss, he was always as elusive as an eel. I only had to reach a hand towards him and he'd be somewhere else."

Sylvia said to me: "We talked and talked and got nowhere. Though Bob doesn't know the difference between a National Anthem and a symphony, he's enormously proud of Viola. She is a success. And, according to Janet, success is all that matters to Bob. I don't like the way things are going, darling. If Janet is right, Viola is now the First Lady in Piccadilly. The most absurd incidents become important. It seems that at breakfast the other day Viola said: 'Brookes, the coffee is almost cold.' Janet said: 'Mine seems all right.' And then Bob jumped in. 'If Viola says her coffee is cold, I take it the coffee is cold. See to it, Brookes.' In a sane house that wouldn't matter, but, things being as they are, it matters to Janet."

I asked: "Did you know that Janet at one time had rather adulterous feelings towards Peter Quayne?"

"I didn't know it," she said, "but I was beginning to suspect it. I was glad when Viola stepped in there."

"So was I. But it makes another reason why Janet is now feeling that all the sunshine falls on Viola."

"Janet always longed for importance," Sylvia said, taking a candid look at her child. "But she never has been important, you know. She used to think that the bits and pieces she wrote for *Now* were important, but they weren't. Nor are the things she's writing for the Sunday papers. They're all about other people's work, and she tittle-tattles superciliously about other people's work because she can't create anything for herself. And now she feels that she's not important even in her personal relations. One word from Bob which seems to range him with Viola plunges her into misery. And then came this affair of Joss. She feels that just as she missed what was essential to Viola, so she missed what she might have done for Joss."

We sat in silence for a while, feeling desolate. Sylvia's analysis seemed to me accurate enough.

I poured out some drinks and lit my pipe. "What Bob said to me," I reminded her, "was that you ought to say something to Janet about her giving him a child. Preferably a son, I imagine. He's thinking of the continuance of his ennobled line."

"It wasn't a thing I could start," she told me. "I simply couldn't. But, as it happens, she started it herself."

Janet said to her: "You remember when we came home from that South American jaunt soon after we were married I was expecting a child. I was glad, but Bob wasn't. He already had children. My job was to be a decorative wife. Well, I lost that child, and his grizzling attitude had a lot to do with it. It was after that that I decided to go back to work. If I'd had a child of my own I might have been a better mother to his."

"And I suppose there's something in that," Sylvia said to me. "She was particularly revolted when Bob said she should have had more sense than to allow herself to get caught. Caught! What a word for such an occasion! It stuck in her gullet, and it's still sticking, and one thing Bob can be sure of is that he'll get no child from Janet."

We sat in the silent comfortable room feeling almost guilty that life had given us such accord, such instinctive understanding of each other's needs, such loving kindness.

388

"Well," she said at last, "and how did you get on with the first Mrs. Meagher?"

I told her of our luncheon and our talk. "In a way," I said, "she's Janet in reverse. She really was a humble obedient wife to Bob, and she certainly never dreamed that she had any quality in herself. But necessity discovered quality enough to make a life that satisfies her. In her own small way, she's quite a person."

I told her that Fred Byles had come into our conversation. "And what does your paragon condescend to think of my father?" she asked.

"She thinks," I said lightly, "that Fred did pinch the doings. She said: 'If you really want the facts you should have a word with Father.'"

"One of these days," Sylvia threatened, "I'll take her up on that."

5

In the spring of 1939 Viola, who was then eighteen years old, asked her father's permission to become formally engaged to Peter Quayne. He refused it. She had met very few men, he pointed out, and when she was a concert pianist, which she could expect to be soon, she would meet plenty. Then, she mightn't think of Peter with exclusive devotion. And so on. All very kind and helpful and gentle, as an understanding father should be. A week later, she didn't come home one night, and a few days after that a letter reached him from Peter explaining that he and Viola were married. It was a heavy blow to him, not that he had any objection to Peter, but because the child who had become the shining centre of his life had calmly rejected his authority and advice. However, he had the sense not to make a fuss or allow his hurt to appear. He wrote to say that he would be glad to see them any time in Piccadilly, and that they might use Dormers whenever they cared to go there. They never went there, and the visits to Piccadilly were few.

With Viola no longer the First Lady of Piccadilly, as Sylvia had called her—a dubious title, anyway—we hoped that the tension between Bob and Janet would ease. But it didn't. Despite his façade, Bob was shattered by the unceremonious way in which both his children had stepped out of his life within a few months. It left him and Janet face to face, with nothing between them but a full sense of inadequacy each to meet the other's need. "Of course," Janet said to Sylvia one day, "this is the moment when, in the novels, the desolate pair should fall on one another's necks. I think Bob would rather wring mine. Thank God, he's got more work than ever to look after. As well as that place at Newbury, he's organising something up in Lancashire. It keeps him out of the way."

" And what are you doing, darling?"

" What is there to do? I've chucked that Sunday paper stuff, and there's a houseful of servants. Can you suggest anything?"

" You might come down to Penruan with us. We go next week."

" When I was a child," Janet said, " and anything went wrong, at school or anywhere else, there was always Penruan to run to. It was dangerously easy, wasn't it? And old Chowny there to make me feel I was wonderful. Dear Chowny."

" You won't find it dangerous now," Sylvia assured her. " We shall be working like blacks. That man Henry Fitch won't leave any time for danger."

" You'd be surprised at my capacity for running into danger," Janet said. " Especially at Penruan. I once nearly led a Helston policeman astray. He was quite young and had red hair, and he used trouser-clips when he rode a bicycle. One of them came off and the turn-ups of his trousers got entangled in the chain. When he got down to adjust things I said: ' You can kiss me if you like.' He said: ' Really, miss!' and blushed till his face was as red as his hair."

" You're making it up," Sylvia said.

" Of course I am. But I wanted to say it. Wanting to be illegitimately kissed is a propensity of all Chown women."

" Well, it's a propensity there'll be no time to indulge if you come with us," Sylvia said. " And remember your age."

" I'm only thirty. And what about you?"

" Well, what about me?"

" You're heading for fifty, and one has only to look at you and George . . ."

Sylvia blushed more redly than the policeman. " Really, Janet!" she said.

Janet patted her cheek affectionately. " All right, darling." she said. " I envy you."

6

We set off in lovely April weather: Sylvia and I and Paul and Miss Collum and Janet. Miss Collum was in a heaven of delight. Henry Fitch had twitted her: " See that you deliver him safely, Miss Collum. He's precious, and we count on you."

She was in charge of a film star! Fitch's publicity men had already been at work. There had been pictures of Paul in the papers, alone and with John Cavendish. There had been pictures of Penruan and stories of how Sylvia had resurrected it: " Mrs. Ledra, the wife of the distinguished essayist and daughter of the famous Margaret Napier. The grandson of Margaret Napier, Henry Fitch's boy-star, is here seen with Miss Collum, his governess, walking in the grounds of his father's Berkshire estate." And there was Miss Collum, looking as goofy as they come. Nothing like this had happened to her since she had jumped off Folly Bridge into the chilly Cherwell.

It had been decided that the whole film should be shot at Penruan. Some of the company would stay at Helston, and one or two at Jose's pub. Henry Fitch, John Cavendish and Moira Sherman would live with us at Penruan. Miss Sherman was playing the part of Paul's mother, and the crusty Roundhead father was Vincent Ewing. We offered to put him up, too, but one look at the Absolution made him choose to stay there. These were all the principals. The rag-tag and bobtail of supers were housed here and there. They needed only one qualification—to be able to ride a horse and make a convincing dash towards Penruan in the final moments.

When we arrived, technicians had already been about the place for some time; and a barn a mile or so from the house had been hired and fitted up as a studio where the film could be developed and "rushes" shown. All was ready for work to begin. The old house felt very strange as we settled into it that night. The next day Fitch and Cavendish, with Miss Sherman, came down by road.

7

It was a successful film, and Paul did well. Henry Fitch was patient and understanding. He could make the boy do what he liked. And John Cavendish was a man of good humour and happy disposition. But it is not of him and Paul that I must write, but of him and Janet. As the thing developed Fitch made an interpolation into the script. "We must show," he said, "that this laughing Cavalier is a bit of a light-weight. As I'm beginning to see him, he's not in love with the woman as she is with him. He just wants a hide-out from the war and a good time. That makes her situation the more poignant. We must have a short scene that shows him willing to fall for any pretty face."

The scene he invented was this. The Cavalier comes from the garden into the hall where he expects to find his mistress. She is not there, but a saucy maid-servant is. They exchange a few two-edged words, and then he seizes her and is kissing her as his mistress appears from the dining-room. She sees, and understands, but pretends that she has seen nothing. She comes in as the maid runs up the stairway. It is all over inside half a minute.

Work was done for the day and we were eating a late supper when Fitch mentioned this. He smiled at Janet and asked: "Do you think you could look saucy for half a minute, Lady Meagher?"

I don't know whether Sylvia had noticed anything between Janet and Cavendish before I had but she intervened with almost scared abruptness. "Oh, Janet has never acted in her life. I have, you know."

"I'm sure you'd do it splendidly, Mrs. Ledra," Fitch said. "But Lady Meagher looks the part more." He was too courteous to say: "You're too old."

Janet said: "I wouldn't have time to ruin anything, would I? It's only a flash."

They talked it over. Cavendish said nothing except: "I think your idea is good, Henry. It's the way I feel the part myself."

I watched Janet play the part, give herself gladly to his kisses, and then run like a lapwing up the great stairway as I had seen her run so long ago when, a bewildered boy, I first sat in this room. It took a long time to satisfy that perfectionist Fitch. The scene was photographed again and again. A whole morning went into it.

Janet was gay at lunch; and that evening we all trooped down to the improvised studio to see the "rushes." Cavendish sat in the darkness next to me, and Janet was on his other side. As the lights went up I was aware of his arm unobtrusively disengaging itself from her waist.

We walked back to the house, Janet with me, and John Cavendish with Sylvia. Janet asked: "Well, how did I do?"

"Time will show," I said cryptically.

"And what may that mean?"

"You know as well as I do."

She said no more and seemed lost in her own thoughts as we walked towards the house.

Lord Meagher, back from the work he had to do in Lancashire, rang up that night. I answered the telephone and he asked brusquely: "Is Janet with you?"

The question alarmed me. I hadn't known that Janet had come down to Cornwall without telling her husband where she was. "Yes, Bob. We're doing a film down here. I expect you've read bits about it in the papers. Janet thought it might be amusing to see how these things are done."

I could feel the thunder in the air, tingling along the line. "When I read the papers I look out for something more important than what a pack of play-boys and their hoydens are up to."

His imperial pompousness annoyed me. "Come off it," I said briefly.

It deflated him a little, but not altogether. "It's a bit much, don't you think, to come home and find the place empty."

Empty. Joss gone. Viola gone. Janet gone.

"Not even a message left with Brookes. All he knows is that she packed and said she'd be away for a bit."

I began to feel sympathy for him, as I too easily do for anybody. "Well, she's safe and sound," I assured him, "and having a happy time. Would you like to speak to her?"

"No. Far be it from me to intrude upon her happiness." My sympathy switched to Janet.

"Just tell her," Bob said, "that her husband rang up and suggests that she should have been here when he got back."

"I'll give her that message, if you like, but not in those terms. I don't think they'd be wise in the circumstances."

"What circumstances?"

"Any circumstances. Just take your father-in-law's advice, there's a good boy."

. I didn't see why the Baron Meagher of Levenshulme should come the heavy over me. I waited for his answer and heard only the click of the microphone dropping on to its rest. The faint sound disturbed me. It had finality.

I went back into the hall where people were lingering over their coffee and told Janet that Bob was back. "He sounds pretty well fagged, and was disappointed not to find you at home. I can understand it," I said. "What with Joss and Viola . . ."

I left it in the air, hoping to touch her imagination.

Light drained out of her face. Sylvia said: "I could run you in to Gwinear Road to catch the Riviera Express in the morning."

She was just too quick off the mark. Bad timing, Fitch would have said. Janet asked: "Are you so anxious to get me out of harm's way?"

Moira Sherman, who was a bit of a cat, asked: "Harm? Surely no harm ever comes to this remote province?"

She was looking at Cavendish and Janet with amused eyes. Fitch, whose bear-like benevolence embraced us all, watched her through his heavy glasses, and said: "No province was ever more remote than the Garden of Eden. But harm found its way in."

"How old-fashioned you are, Henry," Moira said. "You read the Bible!"

"Yes," he said. "And in it I find the old-fashioned remark that the world of iniquity is the tongue."

Cavendish said: "I do think railway travel is a bore. If Lady Meagher would like it, I could run her up to town to-morrow and be back the next day. There's nothing for me to do at the moment, is there?"

Fitch looked at him shrewdly. "I was going to tell you all," he said, "that I've changed the schedule. I intended to try some shots at that rush of the Commonwealth horsemen, but it can wait. I'm not happy about the scene where you come-to in the mansion and find Moira nursing you. I want that out of the way. We'll retake to-morrow."

Fitch was the law-giver, and so that was that. Moira Sherman said, "I think there's something to be said for solitary railway travel. One can just sit there and go into a sort of happy coma, dreaming through the day."

Janet looked as though she could have slain her, and Fitch said: "I don't want you to go into a happy coma in front of the camera to-morrow, Moira. It's your bit that worries me. Try and look less like Florence Nightingale in the Crimea. Or, if that's how you really think it should be done, for God's sake carry a lamp."

9

I went with Sylvia when she drove Janet to Gwinear Road in the morning. She looked forlorn, like a child being sent away too early from a party. She didn't say much, but just as the train drew out she said, leaning from the window: "This could be serious, you know."

"What could?" Sylvia asked pointlessly.

Janet merely said: "Don't pretend," and settled in her seat.

We watched the train go, and then I said: "While we're here, let's go on to Trencrom. We haven't seen the place this year."

"I don't know why on earth you bother to keep it."

"And I don't know why you bother to keep Penruan. What we need in Cornwall is a perch, not a palace."

"We certainly are over-housed," she agreed. "The Barn, your flat, Penruan and Trencrom. We're idiotically acquisitive."

We went on talking about it because we had to talk about something in order not to talk about Janet. It was not till we were sitting in the waste patch behind the cottage, with the morning sun blessing us and all the brouhaha of Fitch's world faded away, that Sylvia said: "Well, I suppose it's up to Bob now."

I said: "I think two things. One is that it's too late for Bob to do anything. The other is that once he gets over the stab to his self-esteem he won't think much more about it."

394

This view of the matter startled her. "But Bob thought the world of her!"

I lit my pipe and poured out the coffee that I had brewed when we arrived at the cottage. "You look as though you're going to settle down to a disquisition," she said.

"Yes. George Ledra will now pronounce. I don't think Bob thought the world of her. The greatest mistake he ever made, as he now probably realises, was to get rid of Wendy."

"But she's impossible!"

"Then he should have made her possible. It wouldn't have been difficult with a bit of common sense. But that's a thing he never had. At his own business, he perhaps amounts to genius, but common sense is another matter. He hasn't much capacity, either, for romantic love, which is something different from what looks like a good match. Any capacity he had he burned up on Wendy. Did I ever tell you about that?"

"No."

I told her. The elopement, the long letters about Wendy that harassed my days. "With a man like Bob that sort of thing can't last, but if he'd had a grain of sense it could have been a basis, when strains came, for settling down into a workable and worthwhile life."

She lit a cigarette and said: "I don't see any sign of your romantic love settling down to a sort of humdrum shopkeeping."

"I'm not talking about me. I'm talking about Bob. Men like me don't often come," I told her. "God publishes us only in limited editions."

I waited for her endorsement of this obvious truth, but she let the opportunity pass.

"Wendy could have been the perfect wife for him," I went on, "but delusions of grandeur made him see the worst in her instead of the best. He wanted something that would look a bit better in the coronet he always had in view. Janet certainly filled the bill, but I don't for a moment think that he ever felt about her as he felt about Wendy in the old Coventry days. He didn't want children by her. He wanted something that would adorn a dining-table laid for Important People. Lord Meagher's appropriate consort. Second only to Brookes."

I paused to refill my pipe, and she said: "Continue. I begin to understand how the Athenian youths felt sitting at the feet of Socrates."

"I'm glad to know that you have heard of Athens and Socrates. It surprises me."

"Well, how does the lecture go on?"

"It goes on with Peter Quayne. That is to say with Janet on the look-out for the romantic love that she wasn't finding at home. You know what happened to that. There may have been other hankerings that we don't know about. And now there's John Cavendish. A head-over-heels affair, it seems to be."

"And what's going to happen?"

"I don't know. But I'm ready to bet my last shilling that Bob won't give her her freedom, as they call it. He can't, unless he divorces her, and he's been through that once. I don't see his High and Mightiness announcing that another marriage has gone to pot. It would be admitting some personal lack."

We took lunch in Hayle and spent the day there by the sea, glad to be alone, glad not to have to face John Cavendish and prying Moira. We were back in time to see Miss Collum put our small star to bed, his eyes, at least, starry with the miracles that were raining upon him, too tired even to listen to his instalment of *Winnie the Pooh*. I decided that this should be his last adventure into films until he was old enough to make his own decisions about his own adventures.

After dinner Bob rang up again. It was nine o'clock. "Well," he began brusquely, "did you give my message to Janet?"

"Yes, Bob, I did. She left here this morning on the Riviera Express. It was due into Paddington at about half past four."

"That's odd," he said. "She hasn't turned up here."

To me, it didn't seem odd at all.

10

Sylvia and I were not sorry when it was all over and we were back at the Barn. There is no need to say anything more about the film. It made Paul a lot of money that we could have done without and it strengthened John Cavendish's reputation, which was already considerable. Leave it at that.

The by-products of the affair were another matter. We had come to like Cavendish, and Paul thought Uncle Jack, as he called him, a more important and desirable person than his sedate father. In the autumn of that year Cavendish often turned up at the Barn during the week-ends. He and the boy would pack up a lunch and go off on the customary country pursuits: gathering blackberries and conkers and mushrooms, discovering the holts of badgers and the dreys of squirrels. After one such day, when Paul had been put to bed, John stayed to eat with us, and during the meal he said, as embarrassed as a schoolboy: "I've never dared to mention it before, Mrs. Ledra, but do you know that Janet and I are living together? I don't want to be furtive about it."

"Janet has hinted at it," Sylvia said.

"We're not sharing a flat, but we see all we can of one another. We consider ourselves man and wife," he said earnestly,

396

"as we should be if Lord Meagher would consent. I've been to have a talk with him, but he was abrupt—wouldn't even discuss the matter."

He fiddled with his food for a moment. "It seems so unreasonable of him."

"It may be unreasonable," I told him, "but reason rarely comes into a matter of this sort. What he's guided by now is *amour propre*, and so he'll continue to be till something seems to him more important even than that."

"It's so hopeless," he said forlornly. "I hate to think of people like Moira Sherman tittering in corners."

Sylvia said: "Have patience, John. I'll tell you something about the women of my family. They all make disastrous first marriages and happy second ones. My mother did it, though unfortunately when she met the man she wanted and who could have fulfilled her, she couldn't marry him after all. I did it myself," she said, smiling at me. "You wouldn't think, would you, looking at George, that he was any woman's dreamman? But he happens to be mine. And now the same pattern is repeating itself with Janet. Just wait. It will come right."

Cavendish said, rather percipiently, I thought: "I think Mr. Ledra delightful."

"He's a pudding-head, but he keeps me young and happy."

I courteously passed her the sauce-boat.

We saw him off under an autumn moon, and then stood with our arms round one another, looking back at our little lighted house where our son slept, and at the silent moon-frosted countryside, and the trees tranced on the hill. It was a *heilige nacht*, and her body, warm under my hand, was the most blessed thing in it. I kissed her. "Thank you for what you said, darling."

She answered: "Let's go in."

In the morning, she said at breakfast: "You know what I told John last night—about my mother and her affair. Well, I've been thinking of that lately, and about what the Wendy woman said to you."

I had forgotten.

"When you took lunch with her—when Bob thought you should break the news of Joss's disappearance. You got on to Fred Byles, and she said that Mr. Merriman could be a fount of light in the matter."

"Oh, that! Why worry? It's dead and done with a lifetime ago."

"Not for me it isn't. Could we ask the pair of them out here to dinner?"

I would have preferred to leave it alone; but I said: "All right. I'll arrange it for you."

I went up to town to make a preliminary call on Mr. Merriman; and took the opportunity to look into Peter Quayne's gallery. I thought, as I doddered amiably through the pleasant morning, what a long time ago it was since I first called on a Peter then unknown to me. It had been about publicity for the show to be held by that young man who had lived with his wife at Mr. Chown's old lodge. I couldn't now remember his name, but I remembered that Bob Meagher had been more interested in his wife than he should have been. It was at the exhibition that Bob had met Janet, so it had been an affair of some significance, and yet I couldn't remember even the name of the man. He certainly had made no reputation. I should have known if he had, for I was a constant potterer about the West End galleries and a reader of all that concerned the increasingly strange world of painting and sculpture. Jane Lancaster, who married the man jjones, had vanished too, after her lurid morning shout. I never heard of them, and I never heard of J. Wilson Dodge. People drifted into one's life and then either vanished or dimmed. Old Tom Collins, once the tyrant of Penruan, had dimmed into an old bore kept for charity about the place; and odder still was the case of Jose Gomm's wife. She was on our doorstep, so to speak, but a more elusive woman never lived. One accepted that Jose had a wife and that the woman seen in the shop was Mrs. Gomm, but she made no impact.

This prowling round a shadowy topic was the way in which Mr. Ledra's little pieces shaped themselves in his mind as he pursued his vague *flaneur* existence.

I timed my arrival at the elegant gallery for eleven o'clock, when I might expect to be invited to take coffee, and I was not disappointed. Peter was successful enough now to have a staff —a suave young man and a good-looking knowledgeable girl— as well as help from his father, a being whose venerable appearance gave the place a feeling of integrity that made one reluctant to question the prices. It was a combination that made me feel like a mongrel terrier intruded among the borzois and salukis at Cruft's; but I was not wholly out of countenance, for I was wearing my new light grey double-breasted suit, a light grey felt hat that was almost a sombrero, and a lavender tie. I carried a silver-headed malacca cane in a lavender-gloved hand. Pardon all this, but I thought you'd like to know for once how I looked when I went upon the town. I've kept myself in the shadows too long.

Peter and I went out to a coffee-house. Naturally, we talked about Viola, or at any rate he did and I listened. She was still at the Royal College of Music and they had a flat on Parliament Hill at Hampstead. "The other night," he said, "we were asked to dinner by a man who's in and out of my gallery a lot. He's a chap with bags of money and perfect taste. He has one of those mansions on the Heath. He knew that Viola was a pianist, and after dinner he took us along to the music-room. There were half a dozen other guests, and one of them was Sir Hamilton Harty—do you know?—the chap who conducts the Hallé orchestra. Old d'Andria—that's my wealthy customer—asked Viola to play. When she had finished her first piece—a Schubert thing—d'Andria said: 'That is enough. That is perfection. Let us have nothing more to distract our memory of it.' Hamilton Harty was pleased with her."

"You'd better drink your coffee, Peter. It's getting cold."

He laughed, rather embarrassed. "I'm like that about Viola. I expect people take me for a bit of a bore."

"I'm very happy for you," I told him. "And for Viola, too."

It was good that something was going right in a world that seemed to be going increasingly wrong.

We were silent for a moment; then he said: "We went to see her mother the other day."

I started; I must have looked aghast. "Do you know anything about her mother?" he asked.

"I probably know more about her than Viola does herself. I frequently took tea with her in a Manchester suburban cottage, and admired the dahlias and chrysanthemums—which her father called 'mums,' to my distress—growing in the back garden. That was in the far-off days when I was young, innocent, and destined for the cotton trade. Why, a little enterprise," I said with bravado, "might have made me Viola's father myself."

He didn't look as though this was a prospect that altogether pleased him. I told him the old story of how Bob Meagher came home from the war and swept Wendy off her feet and married her.

"Viola told me," he said, "how she and Miss Hartman once called on you out at your place and found her mother there. 'I think I ought to see her again,' she said. It was as simple as that. I knew there'd been some bother about it, so I went out to the house that Viola's mother and her father have on the river, and asked if a visit would be in order. Miss Merriman, as she calls herself now, said: 'I've promised not to see the children. I bumped into Viola once at Mr. Ledra's house. That was an accident. And if she called on me without an invitation that would be an accident, too. So the last thing I intend to do is to invite the pair of you to take tea here next Sunday at four o'clock.' Pretty cute, I thought."

"Good old Wendy," I said.

"Well, we went. And it was a success in its way. Viola was

399

quite firm about it. She said: 'If I want to see my mother I'm not going to let some stupid arrangement stand in my way. I don't see why Father should legislate for all I'm to do in life.'"

"It would distress Lord Meagher if he knew that she entertained such subversive notions."

"Then I'm afraid he's going to be distressed," Peter said firmly.

"Poor Bob! All sorts of people seem determined to distress him." I was going to add: "Have you heard, for example, about Janet?" but decided that it was not my business to spread the news.

"Of course you know about Janet?" he asked.

"I know a great deal about Janet—more even than about Wendy. What exactly are you referring to?"

"If you don't know what I mean I'd better skip it. After all, it's her affair. By the way, have you noticed those two who help in the gallery?"

"I've noticed that Venus and Adonis mooch about your place. The lady would look well rising from a foam bath."

"The other day I overheard them talking. Miss Wheat— Ceres, I think, rather than Venus—asked: 'What are you going to do, Charlie, when it comes?' Charlie Reynolds said: 'I'm R.N.V.R. I suppose I'll hop into the first ship going.'"

The carpet was deep. The waitresses, wearing neat creole-coloured uniforms and goffered caps, moved silently over it. The coffee cups tinkled and the lighting was discreet. It was a most civilised moment; and it all went as cold as death.

We looked at one another, and we were afraid. Peter said: "We've been swindled, you know, right, left and centre. I remember the last lot, as I suppose you do. All that blah—the war to end war. Life was going to be wonderful, wasn't it?"

I remembered Penruan and Janet sighing for Peter.

Why didst thou promise such a beauteous day,
And make me travel forth without my cloak?

Well, it hadn't been only Janet and a personal anguish. It had been the lot of us. Life was going to be wonderful; and we had been swindled right, left and centre.

I said idiotically: "I expect it will blow over."

"I don't," Peter assured me. "Do you think Sylvia would be able to help me in a personal matter? When it comes, there'll be no Business as Usual for me. People won't want the sort of things that I sell and I might as well shut up shop. Would Sylvia harbour the stuff at Penruan? The place is as big as a warehouse, and safer than most, I should think."

I promised to speak to Sylvia about it, and we parted gravely.

I made my call on Mr. Merriman and he accepted an invitation to bring Wendy to the Barn on the following Sunday. I thought it as well to let him know how Sylvia's mind was working, and said: "My wife is very much interested in Fred Byles. I think she wants to talk to you about him."

"What on earth does she know about Fred Byles?" he asked.

I might as well tell him. He'd have to know about it sooner or later. "Fred is her father."

His prominently oily eyes glared at me in amazement. "Nonsense!" he said. "Fred never had a daughter. I know he had a son—illegitimate."

In for a penny, in for a pound. "So is my wife," I said.

I wondered how he would take that, and he took it by sitting down and roaring with laughter. "Well, I'll be damned," he said. "I never knew he had a daughter. But how like him? He was a one, believe you me, Mr. Ledra."

"I hope," I said, "that anything you have to say about him won't upset my wife."

"Upset her!" he crowed. "I should think not. He was a damned old fool with his horses and gambling and women, but he was one of the best, was old Fred. That's how I see him now at any rate. Mind you," he said, reverting to the gravity that he thought became his status as a successful man of affairs, "I didn't always see it like that. I was brought up, you might say, Calvinistically. Smoke, drink and women were anathema to me, and I assumed it to be a man's first duty to Get On in Life. But the mind broadens, Mr. Ledra. The mind broadens, and I hope that my wide experience of Man during my time of adversity instilled into me an understanding of—of—well, shall we say I learned to take 'em as they come. Except my Lord High and Mighty Meagher of Levenshulme. I don't take him at any price. But perhaps it's not all his fault. There is such a thing as heredity, Mr. Ledra. Like father like son."

"I didn't see much wrong with old Meagher," I protested mildly. "He always seemed to me a decent enough chap."

"A wolf in sheep's clothing!" he said vehemently. "A toad. A viper in the bosom."

The picture was becoming zoologically too complicated. "Well, see you on Sunday."

"I shall come armed *cap à pie,*" he assured me, pronouncing the last word as though it denoted some culinary delicacy.

The day of their visit was lovely. Autumn had not far to go: winter would soon be on us, but that day was poised in beauty. In the morning Sylvia and I climbed up to the beech wood The leaves had thinned out, so that we walked on a rustling carpet and looked up at the pale blue sky through a million holes. There was not much bird-song: the birds seem to know better than we do when there is soon going to be little enough to sing about. We looked down to our cottage and saw Paul pedalling proudly towards the road on his first bicycle and Miss Collum running awkwardly behind. We wanted them out of the way and had wangled an invitation for them to spend the day with some neighbours.

What with the apprehension that was now in every mind and the imminence of Mr. Merriman with such news as he might bring, Sylvia was more excited than I had ever known her. "Do you realise," she said, "that I can remember the Boer War?" and she made it sound as remote as Crecy or Lepanto. "That's more than you can do," she said, as though it gave her a kick to be more deeply acquainted with human idiocy.

"What's that got to do with anything?" I asked.

She watched Paul turn out of the gate that led from the lane and said: "It means that Paul will be all right. If this war comes, it will be the third in my time. Surely that will guarantee that men have learned their lesson. There won't be another."

I would have smiled at such feminine self-protecting logic if I hadn't felt more like crying. "Well, that seems reasonable," I lied. "We'd better be getting down to receive the Merrimans or Merrimen or whatever they are."

"He, at least," she assured me, "will bring me good news, if indeed he knows anything about the matter at all."

"And what, in this case, would you call good news?"

"Why, news that my father was not a villain, that he ought never to have been sent to Dartmoor."

I wanted to prepare her for what I had an idea was coming, and I said: "Oddly enough, I can imagine many a man who is not a villain being, all the same, the sort of man who ends in gaol."

She reverted to an old experience that I hoped she had forgotten. "Fred Byles," she said, "can never have been like that dreadful creature who wanted to rape me on the moor."

I reminded her that we had discovered the man not to be a convict after all.

"No," she said, "but at the time I thought he was, and he's always in my mind as the sort of man who gets sent to Dartmoor."

"We know two things about Fred: that he was sent to Dartmoor and that he was nothing like the man we met. Whatever Mr. Merriman may have to tell us, we have Chowny's record, and that is not of an evil man."

"I know he was not an evil man, but I want it to be proved that he was innocent of what he was charged with."

The argument could have gone on all day. She wanted a perfect man; I saw Fred as a gay spendthrift, a happy-go-lucky taker of no thought for the morrow, until the morrow opened a hole that he fell into. Very much, indeed, like the men who had landed us where we were, except that they did not get sent to Dartmoor.

The Merrimans' car came to a stand just as we reached the

house. Mr. Merriman was not sitting with Wendy, who was at the wheel, but in the back. He was wearing an overcoat with a deep astrakhan collar, and had the look of a Russian Grand Duke being driven by a peasant woman from his estate. He sat there till she had descended and opened the door for him. As he got out she gave me a wink. It told me everything. This dowdy woman in black had him weighed up, as, I imagined, she had a good many things weighed up. She didn't mind joining in his game so long as it kept him happy. After we had eaten our luncheon she said: "Father tells me he has some business matters to discuss. I've got business enough of my own to think about. So excuse me. I'll take a walk and join you later."

We took Mr. Merriman along the corridor to the big barn, and he sat ponderously for a time with a despatch case on his knee, creating that air of suspense which Chancellors of the Exchequer enjoy on Budget Day, as though we didn't know beforehand that they are going to say nothing that will be of comfort to any of us.

"Well, Mrs. Ledra," he began at last, "young George here surprised me the other day by telling me that you are the daughter of a very old friend of mine, Fred Byles. I congratulate you, and if Fred were here I should congratulate him." He had obviously rehearsed this flattering start.

Sylvia said abruptly: "My father was sent to Dartmoor and died there. A court of law found him guilty of robbing the firm he belonged to. Was he guilty? That's what I want to know."

"He was and he wasn't," Mr. Merriman said. "Let me explain that. I lived in abject poverty." He was enjoying himself, but Sylvia said testily: "Need we go into that?"

"Oh, yes. We must go into everything. My mother was a widow who had hardly two pennies to rub together. One of those pennies happened one day to be on the kitchen table. I picked it up and pondered its possibilities. At a neighbouring sweet shop there was a delicacy that had long made my mouth water in prospect. 'Caught him, sweet mouse in trap!' That was the label. A sweet white sugar mouse in a trap constructed of black liquorice strips. Two a penny. I took the penny, scooted to the shop and bought the sweet mouse in trap. And what a trap it was! No sooner consumed than it closed upon my infant mind with something like horror. How was I going to put that penny back? But I was confident that I could. There were horses in those days, Mrs. Ledra, horses everywhere, and an enterprising boy could make many a penny by holding them when the drivers were lamentably quaffing strong drink in the Rising Sun. So to the Rising Sun I betook me, as often before. I would find not one penny but many pennies and gladden my mother's heart. But that day not a horse, not a cart, not a driver. At last I slunk home and confessed. My

403

mother judged me, found me guilty, and sentenced me. 'I'll sweet mouse in trap you, my lad,' she said, and gave me a few of the best across the chops with her work-hardened hands."

He paused ; then said : " And that is the story of Fred Byles. His intentions were honourable. Never was there a man who thought less harm. Never was there a man so fatally doomed to be without the missing penny when the day of reckoning came."

Sylvia thanked him, and said : " It's a nice parable, Mr. Merriman. Are you able to give us details of how the thing happened in Mr. Byles's case? "

Mr. Merriman laughed. " Now that's an odd 'un! That's the first time I've ever heard him called Mr. Byles. When I knew him, no one called him anything but Fred Byles or Old Fred. He was that sort of man, you see."

I interposed. " I remember my father telling me that Fred always arrived at the office on a horse."

" Aye, he did that. He used to change in his room. He'd stick his head round the door of the clerks' room and say : 'Come on you,' and I'd follow on. One day Meagher, who was a bit older than I was, started off after him and he said : 'It's that other young tyke I want.' Meagher didn't like that. 'Go on, bumlicker,' he said. I smacked him in the eye, and we were at daggers drawn ever after. Well, I'd have to pull off Old Fred's riding-boots and take his clothes and hang them up and hand him the things he wore for the day's work. He always ended by putting a flower in his button-hole. Then he'd look at himself in the glass and smack himself on the chest and say : 'How do I look, young feller-me-lad? A pillar of society, eh? ' "

Mr. Merriman allowed himself a moment or two to look back at the days of his youth. Then he said : " Aye, he was a one, was Fred. Kept us lively like. Pay didn't amount to much in those days, and he'd often slip a half-crown into my hand on a Saturday morning. Sometimes it would be only a shilling, and he'd say : 'Sorry, young feller-me-lad. The horses have been a trifle dilatory this week,' and if there was nothing at all he'd be likely to say : 'A horse fell down dead.' Then, of course, there were women."

" Why ' of course'? " Sylvia wanted to know.

" Well, with a man like Fred—full-blooded—joy der viver—you know. . . . Mind you, Mrs. Ledra, I didn't approve of it ; but that was an odd thing about Fred : you always made an exception in his case."

I don't think that anything I ever heard about my never-seen illegitimate father-in-law lighted him up as that careless phrase of Mr. Merriman's did. You always made an exception in his case. " You," unfortunately not including judges and juries.

"I should like to have known him," I said.

"Well, you would and you wouldn't. He did me a bit of no good, but I will say this for him: when he was around there seemed to be gilt on the gingerbread. Not that there was much even of gingerbread in those days."

"How did he do you a bit of no good?"

"Well, if you'll excuse my saying so, there are Byleses and Ledras in the world. It was your grandfather in these days I'm talking about. You're a bit like him yourself, Mr. Ledra. A quiet, grey sort of type. . . ."

"I hadn't thought of that. I'll have to turn it over in my mind, Mr. Merriman."

"Now don't you go and get offended," he said. "I'm trying to put the case as I see it. If Old Fred always wanted me when there was something to be done, your grandfather always wanted Meagher. I never forgot what Meagher had said to me, and he never forgave that smack in the nose that I gave him. We were ambitious lads and we became rivals. Meagher was a better book-keeper than I was. I give him that. I'm talking about years later now, when we were the two most important people on the clerical staff. There was a division between us. He was a Ledra man and I was a Byles man. It was only after your father came to the office, Mr. Ledra—and that was a good time after Fred had been put away—that I began to go ahead and Meagher began to lose ground. Your father took to me. And when he died and I was in charge I took care to keep Meagher where I wanted him. I know you thought I was hard on him, but what you were seeing was only the end of a long story. You didn't know all the chapters."

Sylvia didn't butt in any more. She sat with her eyes fixed on Mr. Merriman, fascinated by a mind exposing its old sores and itches, by this ancient quarrel between two clerks whose consequence, she must already have felt, was in the long run to doom her father.

"There came a day," Mr. Merriman said, "when Meagher was head book-keeper, and Old Fred came into the room that Meagher and I shared. He'd been on holiday somewhere in the south of France, and as usual, I suppose, he'd lost a lot of money. The firm had had some important transactions while he was away, and he wanted to catch up with things. Because catch up he could. He may have been an absentee a bit more than some of us liked, but he could catch up. He was a good business man, a better one than your father, Mr. Ledra, and he may well have thought: 'I bring a lot of money in. Why shouldn't I take a bit out now and then.' He said: 'Come and have lunch with me, Merriman. There's a lot to talk about and Mr. Ledra is away at some damned Methodist conference or other.'

"Meagher and I were both surprised, rather shocked. Neither of the partners had taken an employee out to lunch before. Indeed, Mr. Ledra always brought sandwiches to the office. Meagher said: 'I think, as senior of the staff, I could best help you, sir.' Old Fred, who never got on with him, just glared at him and said: 'Come on, Merriman,' thereby," Mr. Merriman said dramatically, " sealing his doom."

When Mr. Merriman came back, very late, from that lunch, he found Mr. Meagher furious. It had happened that when Fred came in with his lunch invitation there had been a junior clerk in the room who overheard the whole matter and had doubtless carried news of it through the office. Meagher said: "He's made a bad choice," and Merriman asked: "What might that mean?" Meagher didn't answer.

"Fred had often made use of the firm's money," Mr. Merriman said now, "and he couldn't have done that without Meagher's knowledge and consent. It was paid back time after time ; and then it was paid back only in part, and finally, as we know, it was not paid back at all. Would it have been? Well, that's the question. It certainly never dawned on Old Fred's mind that it wouldn't. But what things look like in a mind such as Fred's and what they look like in a court of law are two different matters. And I'm sure in my bones that Meagher encouraged him in his nonsense till the deficit was really something. Then he tipped the wink to the auditors and the game was up. Couldn't he have gone first to old Mr. Ledra? You can bet *he* wouldn't have let the law get its clutches on to Fred. So there it was. That judge drivelling about business morality and honesty being the foundation of Britain's commercial supremacy and all that sort of stuff. Mind you," he said, recalling his own status as a pillar of society, "he was quite right. But not in Fred's case. There he was all wrong."

He fumbled in his brief-case and produced a letter. "This is the only letter Fred ever wrote to me," he said. "It's dated from a hotel in Paris—just before the end."

He handed it to Sylvia and I read it over her shoulder.

"Dear Merriman,—As you see, I'm in Paris, and rather pushed for money. I suppose as a partner I'm entitled to draw on the firm's account, but I've done that rather heavily lately and I must hold my hand. Could you, out of the kindness of your heart, lend me £500? Sincerely, Fred Byles."

Just that. Sylvia knew, and I knew, that this was the time when he was in Paris with Margaret Napier. Sylvia fiddled with the bracelet that I had picked up so long ago on Penruan beach. I knew she was thinking that it was in Paris, at that time, that Fred had bought it.

I asked: "Did you send him the money?"

"That's my business."

"Tell me."

"Yes, I did," he said defiantly. "I liked Fred. I had some trouble in scraping it up. But I did, and I'm glad. I never saw a penny of it again."

Sylvia went over and kissed him with tears in her eyes. He recoiled, amazed. "Dear lady—please!" he said.

"I'm glad my father liked you," she said. "And thank you for making me like my father."

CHAPTER EIGHTEEN

1

Sylvia and I had been up to town and had spent the night in my flat; and thus we had the pleasure of enjoying that dramatic moment when the air-raid siren blew, making its comment on Mr. Chamberlain's speech. We had rung up Janet's flat the night before and asked her to join us at lunch. She came, looking pale and exhausted. We ate almost in silence. We were drinking our coffee when Janet said: "There's a good chance that my child will be born fatherless."

We looked at her dumb with surprise. "I didn't tell you about it before," she said, "because I wasn't certain. Now I am. For the second time in my life I'm in the family way. And this time I'm going to keep the child."

"What do you mean—fatherless?" Sylvia asked, greatly troubled.

"I haven't told John about the child, and I don't intend to. He went off this morning to join the army. Perhaps some day he'll come home on leave, a seasoned warrior, and rejoice when he sees the pledge of our love." She was speaking with deep bitterness. "Perhaps he won't," she added.

And, as is the way with me, my mind went hurtling back to another war and I had stopped in London on my way from Penruan to my father's death-bed. I had called at Sylvia's flat, but she was ill, and I was entertained by a friendly girl. Her name flashed back. Yes—it was Jessie Lewis. I was dumb and nervous, and we ate together and played draughts together, and she was patient with me and bored to death. And suddenly a young soldier was there, a seasoned warrior, as Janet said, clattering in the panoply of the trenches, and they had embraced hungrily, and I no longer existed. I had gone on to Manchester and met that nurse and learned the meaning of woman. A sharp flashlight on the war that didn't end war.

Sylvia pulled Janet on to her knee as though she had been a child, and said: "You silly darling! Of course he'll come back."

But he didn't. The poor boy never got beyond a training camp, where he was killed by the explosion of a hand-grenade that he hadn't thrown quickly enough, and Cynthia was born in the great medieval bed at Penruan, a bed that the Polzeaths had owned. *Rien sinon pour Dieu.*

That was in August of 1940. We had sold the Barn. Sylvia and Miss Collum and Paul were all living in the great house, cluttered with Peter Quayne's furniture and pictures. A token window was maintained in London, where Peter's father remained doggedly looking after the business. Peter was in the Navy, an A.B. in a battleship, and Viola, who had not got as far as her début in the Wigmore Hall, was heaven knows where with some Government-sponsored entertainment party.

So we had all been blown apart, and I remained solitary in my London flat. Not long after the war started Nigel Wendron met me in Fleet Street and, war or no war, bore me off to luncheon. It just chanced to be me. It might have been anyone. Nigel could not resist bearing people off to luncheon. As we were eating he asked light-heartedly: "And what are you doing in the Great War, Daddy?" I confessed that I was doing nothing. "Then you'd better come along with me to the Ministry this afternoon," he said.

He had found a job in the Ministry of Information. Indeed, he was head of one of its minor departments. "With power to choose my staff," he told me proudly. He had two rather dingy rooms in a house not far from my flat: one his own, the other for his staff. "My personnel," he said, getting down easily to the jargon, "must not exceed three. One is the typist. Then there'll be you and Joe. You'll all have to pig in together."

Joe Coine had been a newspaper correspondent and had a wide knowledge of what had been happening in Germany. The typist was a girl, regrettably named Flossie. I suppose she had a surname, but it was never mentioned, as though it were a dark secret. She worked like a beaver, far harder than Nigel or Joe or myself, answering the telephone, running with messages to other departments, typing in triplicate. Everything had to be in triplicate—"Even my staff," said Nigel. "There's no reason for it, but it's a mystic incantation."

Later on in the war, when Mr. Churchill had taken command, Nigel imitated his terse authoritative style. I would receive notes from him. "Pray answer this, within an hour, on half a sheet of notepaper. In triplicate."

Before it was all over, I had turned out thousands upon thousands of words, stories of heroism and endurance and that sort of thing, that were circulated to the papers, or spoken on the radio, and were even used at times as points in ministers' speecnes. Like thousands of other *embusqués,* I gave myself a sense of usefulness—even importance.

2

Life in the flat was inexpressibly lonely and at times frightening. I found myself unable to write anything except what I wrote for Nigel, and I could not read. A telephone call was a welcome break upon my misery, and I was glad one night to hear the voice of Bob Meagher. Could I nip along at once and take dinner with him at the Savoy? It was December, 1941. One could still take dinner at the Savoy. Bob wasn't there when I arrived, and I sat in the lounge waiting for him and thinking of a far-off night when old Chown had taken me and Janet to dinner there, and we had met Bob and Wendy, and not long after that Sylvia and I had bumped and bounced about in a motor-boat, wet to the skin, miserable to the soul, and watched Chowny's weighted coffin slip off the plank and take a header into that bit of sea that had for so long provided a free harbourage for done-with sailormen.

And there Sylvia was now, with a child that was mine, and Janet with a child that was not Bob's, in the great house that had been whole and lovely when the proud Armada sailed by, and that the years had gnawed, gouging out its eyes, rotting its bones, throwing insinuous and destructive suckers into its very marrow. For the most part, I had admired and approved Sylvia's enthusiasm, her resolve to make the house once more a thing of beauty, but there were moments when she seemed to me a futile Canute, throwing up bastions of sand against the envious tumult of the years. One summer, when we were alone there, we sat on the terrace, tranquil in a perfect moment of sunset and evening star. The house was all but finished, in so far as it could be, for she was ever devising new and unexpected embellishments. I asked: "When will it be finished?"

"Probably never," she said. "I began it as a whim. It seemed a shame that such a lovely place should die for want of love. I had money and nothing much to do with it. That's why I began it, and then when the war was over it became a thing with me. I suppose you'd call it a symbol."

She sat there musing in the last lovely light, and presently said: "So much was ruined. And so much, they told us, was going to be built up again. There was the League of Nations. I remember going to a meeting in London and hearing Gilbert Murray and Lord Robert Cecil explaining all that. I came out full of an extraordinary joy. I really did believe that we were heading for an earthly paradise. The house began to belong to these ideas. It was going to mean rebirth out of destruction.

409

I remember bubbling over with enthusiasm as I said so to old Chowny."

She looked out over Chowny's wide grave, so placid now, and said: "Dear Chowny!"

"What did he say?"

"He kissed me—and you know he wasn't much given to kisses. I think he was moved by my excitement, but he looked sad. He said: 'That chap Longfellow was wrong, you know. We can't leave footprints in the sands of time. The tides see to that. Here we have no abiding city.' Then he went shambling off like an old crab."

I took her hand, sensing her need for reassurance because, between that talk with Chowny and the moment when she told me of it, so much had happened that gave point to his words. No one in his senses believed any more in an earthly paradise. She looked at me with a pale smile and said: "Well, I suppose I go on with it now because it's become a habit."

"A very good one," I said to comfort her, but wondering if that were true.

3

Bob said: "Sorry I'm late. I was held up by the Minister."

He had been to see the Minister of Munitions. I didn't ask him what about. One didn't ask such questions of so important a personage as Lord Meagher of Levenshulme.

Sir Harry jjones and his flamboyant wife who had been Jane Lancaster were dining, and Bob steered me to a table a long way from them. "Can't stand that chap," he muttered, "or his flash piece."

"Don't you play golf with him any more?"

"I played golf with him when it paid me to do so," he said. "It doesn't any longer."

It was some time since I had sat at a table with Bob and had a chance to study him. His hair was iron-grey, cut rather short, and his square face had a Napoleonic melancholy power. I shouldn't have cared to try to thwart him. His hands were like hammers, but carefully manicured, and he seemed to have given a lot of attention to making his clothes unobtrusively excellent. Plain gold links fastened the cuffs of his shirt. He was wearing the tie of the Guards Brigade. I ventured, as lightly as I could, to ask: "You in the Guards, Bob?"

"You're not the first to ask me that. I chose this tie because I liked the colours. I didn't know it was a Guards tie. And if I had known I'd have chosen it all the same. If I like a tie, who the devil are the Guards to say I sha'n't wear it?"

This prickliness, this sudden bristling, suggested nerves on edge. He seemed so disinclined to talk that I wondered why he had asked me to come. I put the question to him. "Well, here I am. What is it, Bob? What can I do for you?"

The mocking grin to which he used to treat me when I was a boy flashed briefly across his face. "Do? Why, just be here. The ever dependable, ever faithful George. Why are dog-like men in fiction always called George?"

"I'll turn my department on to it. We're good at that sort of thing."

He said: "For the first time for weeks I had a chance to eat in my own house to-night. I rang up Brookes and told him to see that a meal was ready. When I sat down to it I was suddenly aware of myself, and the table beautifully laid, and Brookes in the shadow. And the table might as well have been in the middle of the Sahara. No Joss, no Viola, no Janet. Not even Wendy."

"So you remembered George, the next best thing."

"I felt like whipping off the cloth and sending everything smashing to the floor. I told Brookes to take it all away. And I rang you up."

We were nearing the end of the meal, and I said: "As your doctor, Bob, I prescribe a change of scene. Let's go to my flat."

He called for his bill, scribbled his name on it, and we went, crawling through the dark streets in a taxi. To my surprise he slipped his arm through mine. I could feel him relaxing. He said: "You've got something, George, that I haven't. I wish I knew what it was."

I left him stretched out in an easy-chair by the electric fire, and went into the kitchen to make coffee. I brought it in with a bottle of cognac, and sat on the rug. We lit our pipes and smoked and drank and were quiet. At last he said: "I know where Viola is, roughly speaking. I get an occasional line from her. Nothing more. Thumping a piano, I suppose, in some blasted Y.M.C.A. canteen. It's not good enough. Throwing herself away."

"You'll have to make the best of that, Bob, and so will she. A good deal is being thrown away, including a lot of lives." I said nothing about John Cavendish's life. I was sure Bob didn't know of Janet's child. I had forgotten Eliza Hartman.

"I had a letter the other day from that Hartman woman who took Viola in hand. I had no idea where she was, but apparently she's back in that cottage near Sylvia's place. Viola's been neglecting her, and she wanted the child's address. It was quite a long letter. What you call chatty, I think."

I knew then that it was coming, and I let him take his time. "I hear that Janet's down there with Sylvia."

"Yes. She's been there a long time."

"Miss Hartman says she has a child, a daughter."

From down there on the rug at his feet I looked up at the jut

411

of his jaw clenched too tightly upon his pipe, and at the pain in his eyes.

"Yes, she has, Bob."

"It's not my child. I know when I last saw her, and I can count months up to nine."

"No. It's not your child."

"Then whose is it?"

"I know whose it is, but it's not my business to tell you. That's for Janet, if ever she cares to do so."

"All right. Loyal George. I have my own idea. I merely wondered if you would confirm it. It's Cavendish's child."

Then I admitted it, and added: "Cavendish is dead."

I got up and, leaning on the mantelpiece, looked down at him. His face was grey, and he was obviously worn out. It was not easy for him to face a situation in which gears did not beautifully mesh and carry things smoothly in a predictable direction. He said with difficulty: "If she came home I could shut my mouth about the whole thing."

The whole thing. I wondered whether he had any idea of what the whole thing amounted to. Whether he had ever sensed Viola's innocent part in making Janet feel unwanted. Whether he understood Janet's revulsion from the idea of bearing him a child merely because Joss had vanished, seeing that for so long he had discouraged her having one. The whole thing was something wider than what he was now clearly thinking: that he could magnanimously forgive a slip on the part of a foolish young woman.

"That's very generous of you, Bob," I said.

"When are you going down to Cornwall again?"

"Goodness knows. I see no prospect of it. We're understaffed as it is."

"I think I could wangle it for you and arrange a car. I'd like you to sound Janet out."

I said firmly: "Bob, I won't do it. This is something between you and Janet. I'm not in it. It's not so long ago that you sent me haring off to tell Wendy about Joss. Why don't you deal with these things for yourself?"

He said surprisingly: "Well, so far as Wendy is concerned, I wouldn't mind seeing her again. She was always a comfort. Whatever else she may have been, she was a comfort."

I said, meaning it: "Now you're talking sense. Wendy was always a comfortable woman, and she's become, in her own small way, a remarkable woman, too."

Despite the catastrophe that surrounded him, he couldn't help smiling at that. "Well, if you call running a few shops remarkable . . ."

"I call it remarkable to fulfil one's potentialities. Without your help, she's done that, and you've done no more."

The point of view seemed to surprise him. He said, getting up to go: "Well, there's something in that, George. Thank you for having me round. We ought to see more of one another."

"Nothing would please me better," I said. "I'm as lonely as you are. So is everybody, come to that."

"Mr. Ledra's philosophical gem of the week," he chaffed me, and went off on foot towards Piccadilly.

4

I have never in my life been involved in anything spectacular. Even when my flat was destroyed, it was, so to speak, in a quiet way. There had been nights of tremendous raids when buildings round about were blown to bits or became burning fiery furnaces in which the most sanctified of Hebrew children wouldn't have stood a dog's chance; but I managed to cower through with a roof over my head. Then there came a quieter time. I remember the night at the Ministry's sub-sub-department office when Flossie and I were working very late and she said, bringing me a cup of tea which she brewed with passionate persistence: "Thank God these quiet nights go on. There's been nothing but that one bang. Some Hun shedding the last of his load, I suppose, on the way home from another job."

Possibly that is what he was doing, and who was I to complain? Everyone was doing it. I left the office at midnight and walked home under a bright moon to find there was no home. The situation seemed well in hand. Firemen and so forth were doing whatever had to be done, and I saw no point in hanging about. It was all too clear that my few goods and chattels were dust and/or ashes, so I walked to Piccadilly and rang the bell of Bob's apartments. After a long time Brookes appeared, shorn of glory. He was wearing a horrible dressing-gown and carpet slippers, and shone the light of a shaded torch upon my face. "Oh, it's you, is it, sir? You're late," he said.

You're late! What an odd thing to say! "Well," I assured him, "better late than never, which I might well have been if I'd been spending the evening in my flat. Could you oblige me with a drink and a doormat or something to sleep on?"

"Oh, come, sir!" he said. "We shall surpass such modest expectations."

I followed him up the stairs. "So you've lost your little home, sir," he said disparagingly, as though he would have thought better of me if I'd lived in the Albert Hall. "Well, I suppose our turn will come in time."

"Don't count on it, Brookes. It is not everybody who is favoured by being involved in history's more destructive moments."

He put me into the heavily curtained dining-room, switched on the lights and the fire, and said: " Make yourself comfortable. His lordship is in the North of England. We expect him in the morning."

He went away, and was soon back with whisky and excellent sandwiches. " When you are ready, sir, up the stairs, and the door on the left. That's the visitors' bedroom. It's always prepared. And now, if you'll excuse me, I'll try and catch up on my beauty sleep."

" Yes. Do that, Brookes. Never despair. Good night."

I suppose I was more shaken than I allowed to appear. After all, I was attached to the place lived in for so long both as a bachelor and as Sylvia's husband. I thought of the things that had happened there: Bob coming to urge me to lend him money; young Hubert Dodge waiting to catch me when I returned home one night and insisting on coming up to talk in his excited boyish way about the paper he was founding; Sylvia lying on the bed, shutting her blue eyes and opening her white arms. I sat in a deep chair and closed my eyes, and to my surprise found tears forcing their way through the lids. I was too tired to climb the flight of stairs, and in the morning Brookes found me there and gently woke me, saying: " While you are with us, why not enjoy our facilities?"

5

" Flats cost the earth nowadays, even if you can find one," Bob said. " You'd better stay here. The place is big enough for a family, and," he added bitterly, " there isn't a family."

I had gone in the morning light to see if I could recover a collar-stud or two, but there was nothing—literally nothing but rubble. I had to cadge a day off from Nigel Wendron to wander about the town buying the bare necessaries: another suit, an overcoat, shoes, a dressing-gown, slippers and pyjamas, shirts, a toilet set. With these few things, I moved into the Piccadilly house. It was surprising how little one needed when it came to the pinch. Well, I had often complained to Sylvia that we were over-housed. Now we had got rid of the Barn and a bomb had got rid of the flat. That left Penruan and the Trencrom cottage. I rang up Sylvia and told her about it. " What we shall have to do," I said, " is sell Penruan, find another flat here one of these days, and make do with that and the cottage."

She said: " I don't care if we have to make do with a coalhole, so long as we're there together."

She was trying to sound flippant, but her voice trembled. " Are you all right? You're sure you're all right? You weren't

414

there when it happened? You're not hiding something?" The questions shot after one another.

"If I'd been there when it happened I wouldn't be ringing you up from London. It would be a very long distance call indeed, and you'd be hearing a background music of harps."

"Harps?"

"Yes, harps, Mrs. Ledra. What would you expect—a clanging of fire-irons? I can tell you there are quarters in which I am appreciated."

"Was the place insured?"

"You have a bad habit of dragging my thoughts from the sublime to the ridiculous. You must try and get out of it. How is Paul?"

"Quite devilish."

"Good. Evidently every inch a Ledra. How is Janet?"

"At the moment she's here at my side, suckling her child and crooning to it."

"Give her my compliments, and tell her I approve of breast-feeding. What is she crooning?"

"*Hush thee, my baby.* Do you know it?"

"Yes. *Sleep while you may, for strife comes with manhood and waking with day.*"

I'm a bit of a fool. My eyes fill easily; and they filled now, and I couldn't trust my voice to go on. *Strife comes with manhood.* Poor Janet! She should know. I could see her sitting there. I hoped she was not too unhappy.

"Is Janet happy?"

"Oddly enough, yes. Happier than she's been for a long time."

"Kiss her for me."

"I will."

"And kiss the minute Cynthia."

"Yes, when her lips are disengaged."

"I love you."

"Nonsense. An old woman like me. I'll bet you're having a high time with that Flossie."

"How did you know? I was trying to keep that from you. We're planning to fly together to Bolivia as soon as this lot's over."

"Why Bolivia?"

"Because she adores parakeets."

"Look, darling, fooling apart, are you sure you're all right?"

"As sure as usual. I sometimes have doubts."

"Well, give Bob my thanks for having you."

Then something crackled and suddenly we were cut off. I felt extraordinarily happy.

415

I don't want to sound too high and mighty, but I think I was good for Bob. Not that we saw over-much of one another. Sometimes he would be away for days on end, and there were few evenings when Nigel Wendron didn't keep us at it like slaves. But we did occasionally eat dinner together in Piccadilly and sit down afterwards for a session of reminiscent talk. I don't know quite how we got on to it, but we did one evening get on to the topic of Fred Byles. I asked Bob if he'd ever heard of the man, and he said: "I ran into the name accidentally when I was a youngster. I'd called at the office to see if Father was ready to come home, and without knocking butted into the room he shared with old Merriman. I knew they'd grown up there together since office-boy days, but by the time I'm talking about they were big noises. There'd been a bit of a feud between them, and Merriman was just coming out on top. Well, they were shutting down for the day and throwing nasty remarks about, and the name Byles was all mixed up in it. On my way home I asked my father who this Byles was, and he said: 'He was the partner of Mr. Ledra's father and he was sent to gaol. But that's something *you* needn't worry your head about. It was a long time ago.' Did you know, George, this Fred Byles had been to gaol?"

"Yes. What's more, he died there."

"Well, you know what kids are. The idea of a partner in a firm like that being hauled off to quod fascinated me, and I nagged the old man about it. He said quite crossly—which was unusual for him—' Oh, for God's sake shut up about it. It's played old Harry between me and Merriman for years, and I don't want you butting into it.' I think he felt that I was hurt by his rough attitude, because we were on better terms than most fathers and sons; and he stopped under a lamp-post. I remember it very well. It was a proper Manchester winter evening, with a bit of rain mizzling down; and, looking at me in the light of the lamp, he said: 'I'm sorry I spoke to you like that, Bob. But I was terribly worried. This Byles affair always worries me because I don't know whether I did right or wrong. But I'll never admit to Merriman that I did wrong. Mr. Byles was using money that didn't belong to him. I thought it my duty to stop that, and I did stop it. But now I'm not so sure that I should have done it. When Mr. Byles died in gaol I felt terrible, as if I'd killed him. But I thought *at the time* that I was doing right. You understand that, don't you?' I said that I did; and the old man said: 'Don't mention it again, there's a

good boy. It's bad enough to have Merriman always dragging
it up. Now that he's my boss he can make life pretty
unpleasant.' "

I had thought at one time that Mr. Merriman was the culprit,
and Mr. Merriman's own story had made me think of Mr.
Meagher as the culprit. But they were all mixed up in it: Fred,
Merriman and Meagher; and whether any one of them was a
culprit baffled me to say. We all do horrible things of one sort
and another; but the law doesn't concern itself with some of
them and it does with others. For a long time it didn't concern
itself with slave-owners, and women in coal-pits, and boys and
girls in wool and cotton mills. To Old Fred all these would
have seemed crimes. One thing the law was always hot about
was property, so that you could go to the gallows for stealing
a rabbit. But though an individual mustn't steal, the State
has taken the job over, so that, through death duties, it switches
the very blankets off a dead man's bed. I had long since given
up thinking about the thing and was prepared to take Fred as I
found him, and I found him pretty good.

"When I came back from the war," Bob said, "things had
got worse between Merriman and my father. The old man often
talked of throwing up his job, but he had no other resources. I
began to loathe Merriman, and that gave an extra kick to
running away with his daughter, and later to insulting him
most grossly in my office."

He looked to-night more like the old Bob who used to spin
his dreams in my Manchester rooms after the first war. He was
wearing carpet slippers that Brookes disapproved of and puffing
a foul briar. "Lately," he said, "I'm getting a bit like my old
man. I'm not so sure that all I've done is right. I'd wash out
that scene with Merriman in the office if I could. There are even
moments when I wonder whether I gave Wendy a square deal.
We were very happy, you know, at first."

I couldn't help getting it in. "I know, Bob. You used to
write to me."

"So I did. And I damn' well meant it—every word of it.
Well, I'm for bed."

7

Soon after this Viola unexpectedly rang up. Bob was away, and
Brookes asked if I'd like to speak to her. She sounded gay.
"I'm staying with Mother," she said.

Well, that was a bit of a shock, and I wondered how Bob
would take it.

"When did you arrive?"

"Last night. We've been all over the country, and I don't think we shall be allowed much rest. There's talk of a tour overseas now."

"When shall I tell your father to expect you?" I asked cautiously.

"As soon as it's convenient to him. I know he's up to the eyes, and I didn't want to butt in. How are you, Uncle George? I didn't expect to find you in Piccadilly."

"Oh, that's a long story, my dear. I'll tell you all about it when you come here. And I do think you ought to come here. I know your father expects to be dining at home to-morrow night. Could you come and join us?"

"I'd love to."

"Good. Bring your mother along."

"Would that be in order?" She sounded surprised, a bit alarmed.

"You must have realised by now," I said, "that Uncle George is an anarchist. I'm all against order. Bring her along."

"I'll try," she promised.

Well, I thought, when she had rung off, for good or ill, you've done it, Ledra. I was shaken by my own action, and funked being there to see what came of it. In the morning I wrote a note to await Bob, telling him that Viola had rung up and that she would be seeing him that night. "I should like to have been with you, but there's an exceptionally heavy day in front of me, and I'll be tied by the leg till very late."

I was done with the office fairly early and took Flossie out for a glass of deplorable beer and a sandwich, and asked her what she'd like to do now. "Go to the Windmill Theatre," she said. "I've heard a lot about it, but I want to see for myself what goes on there."

"My dear Flossie, people don't go there to see what goes on, but what comes off. And you can see that any night when you go to bed."

But she was resolved. "I'm so tired of making tea and typing. I want to explore the underworld."

"You'll do that when you're dead. Can't you wait till then?"

"You are a funny one, Mr. Ledra," she said, which is what that nurse had called me in Manchester. I didn't seem to grow up.

I got to Piccadilly at about eleven o'clock, hoping that Bob's visitors were gone, and ready to receive the blast of his wrath. Brookes said: "They're in the drawing-room, sir."

I crept in almost on all fours. If I had had a tail it would have been between my legs, and my eyes must have had that craven and conciliatory look with which dogs convey a sense of their sins. I looked at the three, relaxed and clearly harmonious, and suddenly I had a sense of being one too many. Rarely had a

418

feeling made me happier. I said: "Sorry to butt in, Bob. I just came to say good night. I'm exhausted and for bed. Hallo, Wendy. Hallo, Viola. You're looking well, my dear. Spare me time for a talk while you're in town. Well, good night, all." And I went, pursued by this happy thought that they were glad to see the back of me. I ran into Brookes, who asked, "Can I get you anything to drink, sir?" He never failed to ask me that, as though I were a case, rare in medical annals, of perpetual and quenchless thirst. "Brandy, with hot water and lemon," I said. "Bring it to my bedroom."

I sipped it, sitting happily relaxed, as though an order for reprieve had arrived just as I was setting out for the gallows.

8

"A pity you could not join us at dinner last night," Bob said. "Something happened which I'm sure would have tickled your sense of humour. I notice that it reacts readily to trifles."

"Yes. I laughed my head off over that ridiculous little episode of my home being flattened. What was last night's jot or tittle?"

I wasn't feeling happy. My euphoria had evaporated. I was thinking that Flossie would, any moment now, be telling Nigel that I had taken her to the Windmill. And Brookes had failed to find some marmalade that he had promised.

Bob said: "Wendy brought her knitting."

I failed to explode into mirth, and he looked hurt.

"She produced it from a bag after dinner," he said, as though that made it any funnier.

I spread a little nauseous margarine on my toast and asked: "What did you expect her to produce it from—a bus?"

"I've never seen her knit before," he said, sounding deflated.

"Well, now you have. You see how experience broadens as life goes on."

"What's the matter with you?"

"Brookes has not produced the marmalade that he promised."

"I'm sorry, sir," Brookes said. "My man let me down."

Brookes had a number of mysterious "men" who, at a price, mitigated the rigours of our existence. "I hoped you would overlook such a trifle, sir."

"Whether a thing is a trifle or not depends on the state of the liver and the time of day. Both are inauspicious."

"Don't be a cantankerous old devil," Bob said. I'm afraid I had annoyed him, and he went off in a huff. He had been longing to unravel that knitting, thread by thread. I rang up Mr. Merriman's house and Viola's voice answered. "Is that the Honourable Viola Meagher?" I asked.

She said vulgarly: "Chuck it, Uncle George. Are you going to ask me to lunch?"

"Yes. Do you know where the Ivy is?"

"Of course I do."

"Quite the little woman of the world, aren't you? Very well. The Ivy at one o'clock."

I had over-estimated my danger. Nothing remarkable happened at the office. Flossie didn't even mention our outing. I placidly churned out one of my little pieces that was to go on the air to America, and at one o'clock found a prompt Viola waiting for me at the Ivy. She was looking well and beautiful, and I am always happy in the company of a beautiful girl, especially if she is not one of the woolly-minded half-wits that most beautiful girls are. So my liverish symptoms cleared up, and I asked gaily: "Well, how did the great adventure go last night? Your father tells me that your mother produced her knitting, which is a bad habit women had during the French Revolution. Did any heads fall?"

Viola said: "I think it was a bit of a shock to him at first."

"Well, it would be to anyone. What was it—a pair of magenta bed-socks for Mr. Merriman?"

"Don't be a fool. I wonder how Aunt Sylvia has put up with you all these years. I'm not talking about the knitting. I'm talking about the shock of seeing Mother there."

It would be a shock. Bob hadn't seen Wendy since the divorce, and now she turned up with the girl from whom, it had been agreed, she should keep away. Viola described the scene well. Brookes was knocked off his usual calm perch, but managed to say with a bow: "Good evening, Madam." Then he diplomatically retreated as Bob came bustling out into the hall, shouting: "That you, Viola?"

He came to an abrupt stop, looking wide-eyed at the pair of them. Viola kissed him and said: "Well, darling, how are you? I'm staying with Mother and Grandfather Merriman, and I persuaded her to come along."

Bob rallied splendidly, and said: "I hope you didn't need too much persuading, Wendy." He shook hands with her. "It's pretty lonely here. I welcome a bit of company."

"And he didn't ask then, or at any time," Viola said, "how it came about that I was staying with Mother instead of with him."

"And how did it come about?"

"It was Peter's idea."

My selfish interest in Viola's story had caused me to forget Peter. I asked for news of him, and learned that he was at King Alfred, the training place for naval officers.

"Peter's got a wonderful insight into human beings," she assured me earnestly, all at once the adoring child again. "He's
420

quite certain that Janet will never go back to Father." She asked shyly: "Did you know that Janet was once very much interested in Peter? And that was after she was married to Father."

I said that Sylvia and I had half suspected it.

"Well," Viola said, "that made it pretty obvious that she and Father had drifted miles apart."

She sat crumbling her bread. The marriage ring on her finger looked odd on so young a child.

"You know," she said, "Peter is very fond of Father. And after he'd met Wendy he was fond of her, too. He said to me: 'What fools those two were to part. They're bits of the same stuff.' He called on Father several times during leaves, and found him dreadfully lonely, and then he cooked up this scheme of my staying with Mother and taking her along to Piccadilly."

"I thought it was all my doing."

"Well, you and Peter have been thinking along the same lines. Tell me, do you see any chance that Janet and Father will make it up?"

There was now less chance than ever. There was the small living Cynthia and there was the ghost of John Cavendish. Clearly Viola knew nothing of that, and I didn't tell her. I only said that I thought the chances of patching up that marriage were pretty poor.

She looked at her watch and jumped up. "I must be off or I'll miss my train. I'm going down to see Peter."

There was so much that I hadn't asked her and that I wanted to ask her, but Peter, quite rightly, outweighed me and my curiosity. I found her a taxi and saw her off. There was a lot I should have to tell Sylvia at the week-end when I was due for a few days' leave from Nigel's tyranny.

CHAPTER NINETEEN

1

Bob used to speak of our *ménage à trois*. Not that it was properly speaking a ménage, because Wendy did not live there. She dropped in now and then, but more and more often. I think Bob was surprised at first to find how intelligent she was. She had matured beyond what he had thought possible. With Janet, he had often been at a loss because she didn't take or pretend to take any interest in his business affairs; and, on his side, all that had interested her—books and pictures, theatres and music

—meant nothing at all. I had seen them together only on social occasions when the company kept things moving. When they were alone, I imagine, there must have been long spells of *ennui*, a sense that they lived in different worlds, a growing realisation that physical attraction—though I would be the last to under-estimate that—was not enough. Janet had tried to make it enough. I remember her telling me once that she had been " courting " him ; and she had now and then shanghaied him into her own territory. She took him off occasionally to a film or a theatre, and though, I suppose, he tried to see what these things meant to her, he did not succeed.

Wendy knew no more than he did about the sustaining power of the immaterial. They were both what they would have called down to earth people ; and on that plane they found content-ment in one another's company. Bob's work often took him away for days on end, but now he got into the habit of letting her know when he would be at home, and she never failed to look in for dinner and a talk, bringing her horn-rimmed spec-tacles and knitting with her. It was all surprising enough, but I did not expect it to develop into the miraculous. However, it did. I came home one night rather late to find Mr. Merriman of the company. He came often thereafter. Reconciliation and forgiveness all round were in the air. Bob was happier when the old man was not there, but, if Wendy wanted him there, he was prepared to put up with it.

When I consider the disasters that the war heaped upon some, I think myself fortunate that few people I knew were killed—if I can be said to have really known young Cavendish. There was also Mr. Merriman. Wendy had come alone to dinner, and it had been the usual humdrum evening with gossip about old days in Manchester and Coventry. It was rather boring for me ; but I knew it was excellent for Bob. It enabled him, as nothing else could, to empty his mind for a while of affairs that were heavy and obsessive. Outside the narrow but deep and powerful groove of his mechanical genius, he was a bourgeois who liked his feet on the hob. He had tried the other things and found they gave him nothing. He was ready now to take what Wendy could give.

At about eleven o'clock Wendy got up to go, and I said I would see her home and then walk back. I had a macabre liking for walking in the blacked-out London streets, more stark and stripped and disturbing than anything I had seen at the Windmill with Flossie.

I felt a great warmth of friendliness towards Wendy who had come through so much, fortified in her homely quality, unpre-tentious as good bread, and I held her hand as the taxi trundled through the ruinous dark. She talked of her father, and said how glad she was that he and Bob, if not friends, were at any rate able to meet without rancour. "I'm especially glad," she said, "because Father hasn't long to live. Please don't say a word about it, but the doctors have found cancer, and they tell me privately that he can't escape a time of great pain."

I was shocked, but there is nothing worth saying in a moment like that. I could only press her hand comfortingly. "I wish he could be spared that," she said. "Death is nothing much, but I wish he could be spared the pain."

I asked her if Mr. Merriman knew of the doctors' verdict. "No," she said. "They are going to tell him to-morrow."

But they never told him. It had been a quiet night, nothing but an occasional bang here and there, but one of those bangs was the end of Mr. Merriman. He had come out of his house to take a breather and look at the quiet river when a bomb—quite a small one, we were comfortingly assured—hit the pavement fifty yards from where he stood. A splinter pierced his brain, and he did not suffer.

A few people were still gathered when we got out of the taxi. Mr. Merriman had been carried into his house and a doctor called—one of the doctors who had recently given Wendy such sad news. "It's the best way out," he said. "It's the way I should have liked myself if I'd been in your father's boots."

I looked at Mr. Merriman, lying on the dining-room carpet. The hole in his temple seemed so small a doorway for death. His face looked surprised. To my boyhood he had been formidable and rather terrifying; later he had been absurd. Now he was nothing but an old man, white-haired, dead.

Wendy was calm, though I could feel how deeply she was affected. I asked if I should stay, and she said: "No. You go back. Bob will wonder where on earth you are. Don't disturb him with any of this. Tell him in the morning."

2

I went with Wendy to the crematorium and detested the slow inevitable doors that closed as the coffin slid in. I detested the thought of the swift consuming heat; but I detested also the thought of slow corruption. Death is nothing much, Wendy had said; but that is easier to say than to believe. I don't care whether it's the death of a king or of a cat run over in a back street: that the flame of life should be put out is as mysterious to me as that it should be begotten.

When next Bob, Wendy and I were together, he said to her: "What are you going to do now?"

"What is there to do," she asked, "except go on as I have been going?"

"To begin with," Bob told her, "you should get out of that house by the river. The river is far too useful a pathway for German aeroplanes."

"Father and I discovered all about that when Dockland burned. We stayed there then, and I shall stay there now. It's a nice house."

"I know it's a nice house, but only a damned fool would stay in a house that's liable to go up any minute."

"Don't call me a damned fool," she said sharply. "You became too fond of doing it in the past. Come to that, only a damned fool would stay anywhere in London."

"People have to earn their bread, war or no war," Bob told her.

"I know that as well as you do. I'm one of those people."

"You needn't be. You could live here."

We both looked at him in surprise. "That's not a practical idea, Bob," I said. "Wendy has a reputation to think of."

Now she turned on me. "Nonsense," she said. "If I wanted to live here, it would take more than gossiping tongues to stop me. Bob's idea is something else. It seems to be that there's no need for me to earn my bread. I've tried that. I tried it at Dormers, and it was death. I'm not made for sitting on my behind with servants waiting on me, and me trying to come to life again when Bob brings in a few of his posh friends. I've been through it, and I became morbid and dull and dreary. When I was thrown out and forced to sink or swim I found that I could swim well enough. I liked it, and I shall go on doing it."

"I don't see why you should drag up those old times," Bob said.

"I drag them up because I don't forget them and I don't intend that you should either. One plateful of that was enough for me. Do you remember, George, the day you came and talked to me in the greenhouse at Dormers?"

Over her thick glasses, she looked up from her knitting. I remembered the day very well, and said so.

"When you were gone," Wendy told me, "I wondered what on earth you had thought of me. You'd known me in the office in Manchester—nothing much, I dare say, but at all events alive. And there I was—as near dead as makes no difference. Everything else was going fine: Viola with her horses, and Joss —well, I don't know about Joss. I sometimes wondered."

Joss's name brought Bob to his feet, furious. "Leave Joss out of it," he shouted. "What sort of inhuman wretch are you trying to make me out to be?"

She said quietly: "Sit and calm yourself. That's another thing you were always doing—trying to shout me down if I

424

expressed an idea of my own. There'll be no more of that if I come to live here."

I said: "I think I'd better get up to my room."

"Stay where you are, George," she said. "When Bob left me —and remember it was not I that left him for all his faults— there was a lot of stuff in fine legal writing about what I should do and shouldn't do. I wasn't to see the children and so forth. Well, we needn't have any legal writing now. Word of mouth will have to do. Put briefly, it's this. If I come and live here, it will be as a human being with a right to hold any opinions I like and to express them when I like."

"But you can't come and live here. Bob's married to Janet."

"He can stay married to Janet," she said briefly. "I certainly don't want him to marry me. I know there have been cases of men divorcing a second wife and then marrying the first one again. But I wouldn't marry Bob again for all the gold in Ophir."

She smiled as she said it. A long silence followed.

"Well," she said after a time. "I think that clears the air, and now we can talk of more comfortable things. I've enjoyed coming here to spend evenings with Bob—enjoyed it very much. I have no other friends—none whatever. Have you enjoyed my coming, Bob?"

"Yes."

To my surprise, he was looking at her with admiration. I had heard that in his office his occasional rages were feared; they sometimes left well-nerved men trembling like rabbits before a stoat. It must be rarely that anyone stood up to him like this. And he admired it.

"Now we know where we are then," Wendy said. "I'll come if you want me, and people can say what they like. I'll come as your friend, and as nothing else."

Bob blushed.

"And I'll go out to my job from here just as I've always gone to it from my house on the river. I like earning my own living, and I shall go on doing it. I can assure you of one thing: you'll never have to show me out as you once showed my father out of your office. I'll go without showing any time it suits me."

Bob blushed again. "You remember everything against me."

"Yes," Wendy said as her final word. "But there are still things left, Bob, that needn't be said. Let's hope they're enough to carry us along. That's for you to decide."

425

More and more Americans were appearing in England, but I was surprised to find one as far west as Penruan. I had gone down for a few days' leave; and after lunch Janet and I strolled along the path through the valley towards the beach. I had first known it as a thread of footing through briars and every other sort of vegetable entanglement that had to be stamped down with a boot or beaten down with a stick as one proceeded. Then Tom Collins and his boys had made a clear walkable place of it; but now it was going back to the wild. Old Tom was dead, and his boys could all have been dead too, so far as I knew. Winter streams had shifted the stones that they had laid, so that the going was rugged, and I had to hold the thorns apart here and there for Janet to get through. We came to the place where long ago I had sat on a ruined seat and watched her lying, unkempt and dishevelled, on the ground—a schoolgirl who had run away and, exhausted, was sleeping. The hut that Tom Collins had later built there was in pretty good shape; and when I had hacked away some entanglements we sat down. It was a warm summer day and the place was sleepy and oppressive—like a Douanier Rousseau jungle, Janet said, in which the oddest beasts might appear. But nothing more remarkable appeared than this young American in naval uniform. He gave us the sketch of a salute, and said: " Forgive the intrusion. The lady up at the house has given me permission to come through. I want to see just how steep this little road is."

He was a pleasant young man who looked to be in his thirties, and he sat with us and produced a pack of Chesterfield cigarettes and handed them round. "Quite a place that house is up there," he said. " Medieval, I guess."

I told him that it was, but that a great deal of it was brand-new imitation.

"Sure," he said, " I can see that. I'm an architect back home. I suppose that's why they've given me this road engineering job. The navy's like that."

His blue eyes smiled and he displayed a fine set of teeth. "Well," he said, when we had finished our cigarettes, " I guess I'd better go through to the beach. I expect we'll meet again. The name is Wyke—Alan Wyke—Lieutenant-Commander."

He stood up and saluted. There was a miscellaneous collection of burrs and what not clinging to his coat. Janet plucked some of them off. " Thank you, lady," he said.

"The name is Bascombe—Janet Bascombe. This, oddly enough, is my step-father, George Ledra. The lady up at the house is my mother."

"It sure is a swell place she has there," he said. "It would be quite an idea to take it stone by stone to the States. If I could find a millionaire who was interested." His white teeth flashed again, and he moved off, smacking his way with a small machete.

"He seems to have come prepared," Janet said. "I wonder what he means when he talks about a road engineering job?"

I wasn't there when the bulldozers provided the answer. Nor did I ever see Penruan again after that visit. Perhaps that is why I remember so clearly the little group standing on the gravel to wave me off when the taxi came to take me to the railway station at Gwinear: Sylvia holding Paul by the hand, Janet with Cynthia in her arms, and Miss Collum, who really had no reason now to be with us, except that she had integrated into the family like a poor relation. Some premonition made them look forlorn to me—four of the woman-kind and one sturdy little boy. The last of the garrison, I thought. They might have been a shot from Henry Fitch's film: waving away the Roundhead husband, to clear the decks for the arrival of the handsome Cavalier. Behind them, the sun flooded the placid sea with light, and a ray flashed on one of the stones in the bracelet on Sylvia's uplifted arm. I thought of the morning when I was first there and had found that bracelet on the beach, starting something which was now moving to an end.

The taximan, gruff with the authority of a petrol shortage, said: " 'Op in. We 'aven't got all day." I hopped in and looked my last on a scene that had first met my sight in a blustery winter night during one war, and now, in a blaze of morning sunshine, faded from it during another. No, indeed, I thought, still disturbed by premonition, we 'aven't got all day.

4

I must condense the story of what happened. And, first of all, the lie of the land. Between Penruan and the Absolution pathway goes through a dense wood of hard-bitten conifers. Anything lying in that wood is invisible from the air. It was an obvious place for tanks to lie hidden when the invasion of France was being prepared. And the wooded gully from Penruan to the beach was the obvious way for the tanks to go, when the time came, to the tank-landing craft lying offshore. The path, like the tanks among the trees, would be hidden by lacing boughs. The set-up was perfect for the project. But it was a pity it had to be Penruan.

Soon after I had gone back to town Sylvia was visited by what Janet called " top brass," two admirals, one English and one American. It was a long and friendly conversation. They had not come to ask her to leave Penruan: they had come to tell her. But they did it in a most gallant and gentlemanly way. "It will be a bit of a blow, ma'am, your family having been here through all these centuries, but I guess you'll be seeing the back of us soon enough," the American said.

Sylvia didn't disillusion him. After all, she was a Chown woman, whose family could match the Polzeaths both in ancientry and villainy.

And so Penruan became the headquarters whence similar invasion schemes were co-ordinated over a large strip of the South Cornwall shore. The American Admiral remained in command. A squad moved in and in no time at all the things Sylvia valued were bundled into a few rooms that were ceremonially sealed, and the Admiral's staff took over the rest of the house. Sylvia moved to Trencrom with Paul and Miss Collum. Janet and Cynthia found quarters with Miss Hartman, who was still in her cottage near the Absolution. And on the Admiral's staff was Lieutenant-Commander Alan Wykes.

Jose Gomm wasn't selling much in the way of antiques, or rather his wife wasn't, for she had long been in charge of the Helston shop. The present was too urgent for people to be interested in litter of the past. But the Absolution thrived as never before. It was the only pub within miles of Penruan, and even in the times, which came often, when it had been drunk dry, it became a club to which Americans resorted. The wood where the tanks were to lie was meantime filled with huts in which those Americans lived. All the officers were in the great house, and in the day-time it swarmed with clerks, too. Their work done, off they went to their huts in the woods, and thence to the Absolution, carrying with them, when the beer was finished, supplies of Coco-Cola and other strange liquids. These exiles could get merry even on that, and sometimes rowdy.

The officers did not go to the Absolution. A handful of them made Miss Hartman's cottage their club. The old girl was delighted, and many an evening passed with talk and music. She played to them for hours on end, while the little Cynthia slept above, and Janet served such refreshments as the place afforded. Happily, it afforded more than the English war-time rations. The Americans dumped generous gifts of butter, sugar, tinned meats and all the superfluity of their abundance upon the cottage. And Lieutenant-Commander Wyke provided the shine of his blue eyes and the merry flash of his white teeth.

We in London were for ever having "security" drilled into us. It was a barren week in which Nigel Wendron didn't pronounce a heavy lecture on the matter to his staff of three. And on the wall was a poster urging us to "Be like Dad. Keep

Mum." Not that much ever leaked our way. Down at Penruan, I suppose, the same security lectures were read to the Americans; but I learned from Sylvia later that long before a tank rolled into the wood everyone knew that tanks would roll in there and that they would roll out again towards the Penruan gully. Everybody knew, too—including everybody who should never have known—that the house had more significance than came from accommodating an admiral and his staff, preparing for that one operation. Even Mrs. Carbis, who gave Sylvia a hand at Trencrom, once said casually: " Fancy your house being the headquarters, Mrs. Ledra! " and when Sylvia, who was quite in the dark about it all, asked "Headquarters of what?" Mrs. Carbis backed down. " Oh, don't you know? Well, p'raps I've said too much." Certainly someone said too much to the wrong listener, as we were at last to learn, and pay for.

5

I visited Cornwall only once more before the end, and I did not go to Penruan. I stayed at Trencrom, and I was glad to see that in what had been my big study Sylvia had hung the pictures of her mother and father. They were almost the only things she had brought from the house: Margaret Napier looking distraught by the river; and old Fred Byles, cocky and eupeptic, without, it seemed, a doubt or a care in the world. If you had not lived to see 1914 it was a possible attitude.

" Why these two, of all the stuff you've got there?" I asked.

" Because they're the only two irreplaceable things," she said. " And I've got a morbid feeling that there's going to be a lot of replacing if anybody cares to do it. Certainly it won't be done by me."

We were standing by the window, looking up at the slope of Trencrom, whereupon Miss Collum and Paul could be seen struggling towards the summit.

There were two beds now in my study. Miss Collum and Paul slept up there and Sylvia downstairs in what had been the only bedroom. Life was narrowing.

" I shall stay here for this leave," I said. " I somehow don't want to see Penruan again till we know the best or the worst."

" Janet will be disappointed not to see you. She'll want to talk to you about the possibilities of a divorce from Bob. You met that young American, Wyke, didn't you?"

" Yes. Just a passing word. You don't mean to tell me . . .?"

" I do. Janet is the most Chownish of all women. She was

429

practising on old Chowny as soon as she could stagger. He was under her thumb. There was that boy who was killed in Spain, and there was you——"

"Oh, come!" I interrupted. "Don't let's be nonsensical!"

"Say what you like. I repeat, there was you. And there was Bob and Peter Quayne and that poor man Cavendish. And now there's Alan Wyke. They've motored over here once or twice together. He can wangle petrol. I know the light in a Chown woman's eyes, and I know enough about men to see when they're answering the signal."

"But Bob can't divorce her."

"Why can't he?"

"Because Wendy won't let him."

I had heard it argued in Piccadilly. The *ménage à trois* was working well enough. As the invasion of Normandy drew nearer, the Ministry of Munitions became a more and more hard-driving place, and Bob had less and less opportunity to spend an evening at home. Though Wendy and I were in the dark, he was not, and the knowledge of the imminent fateful moment had him keyed up to a taut and nervous pitch. Having no other resource, he found himself, as never before, in need of the quiet reassurance that flowed from a woman of his own sort. It gave me great pleasure to share those quiet evenings. Bob had two favourite authors, Edgar Wallace and Agatha Christie, and fortunately both were prolific. He would sit there reading one or other of them, looking across occasionally at Wendy, who would be reading a book not differing greatly from his, or knitting with a frown on her rather wrinkled forehead. Sometimes their eyes would meet, and they would exchange a smile full of sad understanding. I could have found it unbearably boring; but somehow I didn't. The sight of those two who should never have parted, and who were meeting again in this atmosphere in which their hands could not quite touch, was to me full of irony and disillusion. They were looking at one another through nothing more substantial than a gauze veil, or something even less tangible than that, but it was, all the same, impenetrable as a granite wall. They might agree to forgive, but Wendy at least would never forget.

There was not much to talk about. Viola was with a concert party in India, and her husband was out of the battle. His ship had been torpedoed, and he had had a frightful moment, swimming in a sea of burning oil. He was picked up by a destroyer, and for a time there was a fear that he would lose his left arm that had been pierced by a shell splinter. The arm had been saved, though it would in future be more decorative than useful. Now he was in an Admiralty office in Bath. So we had no personal anxieties to discuss or batten down, and we avoided the larger issues that were moving to a climax.

When we talked, the talk was very small, and by eleven o'clock we were in our several beds.

One night when Wendy and I were alone, I said to her: " My dear, you look like the competent manageress of a seaside boarding-house. I hope the thought gives you pleasure." I was trying to perk her out of the vacuum in which we existed. Even to annoy her would be something. I did not annoy her. She smiled and said: " Well, except that this is a house and not a boarding-house, and that it is not by the sea, I suppose that's what I am."

Her complacency jolted me. I asked: " Why don't you marry Bob? You know that's what he wants, and you know that, despite all that's happened, you're fond of him."

She said: " Bob destroyed a lot of things in me. I'm still fond enough of him to let him have what's left. But marriage, and all that it implies, is not left. Now, mind your own business, George. I'm fond of you, too, but I don't intend to let you, any more than Bob, overstep the mark."

I knew that there was nothing more to be said, then or ever. I mumbled an apology and went to bed.

And so, when Sylvia spoke to me about Commander Wyke and Janet, I saw nothing in front of Janet but Wendy's blank wall of refusal.

While I was there on that last leave, Wyke drove Janet over to Trencrom in a jeep. There could be no doubt what Janet's feeling for him was, any more than there had been a doubt about her feeling for Hubert Dodge and Peter Quayne, except that now the feeling was returned. During that visit, Wyke said: " Let's go climb that hill, Mr. Ledra," and I went, knowing with no pleasure that he wanted to get me alone to talk about Janet.

So we laboured up the hill, and sat on a slab of stone. It was one of the clear days when you could see the ocean both to north and south. We sat facing south, looking towards Penruan and the wood and the gully off which, in only a short time now, the tank-landing craft would take the cargoes into their cavernous bellies.

Wyke was very restless. He pulled a sprig of heather and twiddled it in his fingers. He said suddenly: " I'm in one hell of a hole, Mr. Ledra." Agitation stopped his speech for a moment; then he got out: " I wish Janet had been frank with me. I could have taken it if she had been frank." He pulled that day's newspaper out of his pocket and asked: " Have you seen this?"

I hadn't. It was a paragraph headed: " Film Star's Fortune for Peer's Wife."

John Cavendish's will had been through the formalities that wills have to go through, and now it was deposited in Somerset

House where anyone could read it and spread its contents abroad. That this was permitted had always seemed to me a barbarous intrusion into privacy; but there it was. I knew that Cavendish had been making some mark and that he had worked in a few very successful films. I had judged him, too, to be a man of careful habits. What the newspaper called his fortune was not immense, but such as it was—about £25,000— it was now bequeathed, the paper shouted, to the wife of Lord Meagher of Levenshulme. "Lady Meagher," the paragraph said slyly, " is now living in Cornwall with her infant daughter."

Wyke's pleasant boyish face was troubled. "I'm afraid," he said, "I've been putting two and two together, as this paper seems to intend that one should."

I, too, wished that Janet had been frank. There was no point now in pretence. "Young Cynthia," I said, "is Cavendish's child."

He lit one of his everlasting Chesterfields and said: "Miss Hartman and everyone down here has supposed it to be Lord Meagher's."

"Naturally. I don't blame Janet for that. It's none of their business."

"But it is mine, Mr. Ledra. I thought it might be possible to persuade Lord Meagher to divorce her. He might have been given the custody of Cynthia, but even if he hadn't it would have been all right by me. But this wouldn't. You don't know my home background, Mr. Ledra." He had thrown his cap into the heather, and was twisting his fair hair with nervous fingers. "Falling in love can be a hell of a thing," he said desperately. "I'm up against everything there is."

He told me about his home life. His father was a Baptist parson in a small township of the Middle West, and he was an only child. The old man was a Fundamentalist who could smell sin a mile off. "He wanted me to be a parson, too. Our first great argument was over the age of Methuselah, which was 969 years, and not a day more or less, because it says so. See Genesis, 5, 27."

He said: "I was twelve at the time, and the old man sentenced me to bread and water. My mother was dead, and Father's sister, as fundamental as he was, saw that the sentence was administered. At the end of a week I went to him and said: 'Father, Methuselah lived to be 969 years old.'"

"Well," I comforted him. "You're a man now, and you can live without lying for God's sake."

"You wouldn't believe," he said, "how that sort of bringing up conditions you. I was twenty-one before I left home, and I'm afraid of him to this day. To begin with, if he got wind of Janet he'd talk about the pomp and vanity of the English peerage, and here am I proposing to marry a peer's wife. And after a divorce at that. It would be no marriage. He'd see Janet as a whore who ought to be wearing a scarlet letter. What's more, she's English, and he loathes the whole damn' tribe of you."

" He couldn't pay us a more delicate compliment."

He sighed, and said: " All the same, if there had been no more than that, I'd have told him to go to the devil, as I've often wanted to do. I could even have put up with Janet's bastard. That's how bad I've got it. But she left me in the dark, and that's another matter."

" She and Cavendish wanted to marry," I told him. " He was a good man. He saw Lord Meagher and tried to persuade him to divorce Janet. But he wouldn't. And I may as well tell you this: I've known Lord Meagher from boyhood, and I know that he would not divorce Janet for your sake any more than he would for the sake of Cavendish. There's a lot behind that that you don't know."

" Damn Lord Meagher," he said desperately. " If Janet would have agreed I'd have taken her and Cynthia to the States and lived with her, marriage or no. But that would have been something that needed confidence all round, and that's what she hasn't given me."

So there we were at a deadlock. I looked at him sadly: yet another who had been promised a beauteous day, and was now shivering in the sleet. I thought of Sylvia, and my happiness was a sort of anguish.

Wyke put on his cap and got up. " Well," he said, " no good tarrying like Moses on the mountain."

" I'm sorry, I'm not God—able to bless you with a revelation."

" Love is revelation enough to be going on with," he said, " for me a revelation of sheer hell."

I knew he'd get over it, but it's no good telling the young that. What was he? About thirty, I guessed. Yes. He'd get over it. Away from this shabby war-stricken country, back in the land flowing with mink and money, he'd get over it all right.

We went down, and Janet was waiting by the gate where the jeep was standing. There were threads of heather sticking to his uniform and she began to pick them off, smiling at him.

" Let it be," he said almost brusquely. " Let's go."

She looked surprised, got in, and off they went. That was the last I saw of either of them. I shall always wish that I had kissed Janet good-bye.

Miss Collum sighed now and then for the splendours of Penruan, but I assured her that it was better for the war effort that she should stay where she was. "You must let the Americans concentrate on their job," I teased her. "Your presence would distract too many minds, and Americans are even more passionate than that young man who caused you to jump off Folly Bridge."

We could have got on very well without her, and the clever boys who study work and motion in industry wouldn't have taken two minutes to discover that she was "redundant." These chaps, I knew, were established in all the far-flung territories of Bob's empire, with the consequence that he was a long way from being the father-figure he had once aspired to be. He was the whipman in the galley, cracking the oarsmen along, and so they were for ever finding new dodges for doing him down. Miss Collum had come to "belong" with us, rather than to us; and this was fortunate when, as things developed, the small Cynthia was added to our little clan.

Meantime, it was a relief to be able to leave Paul with her at Trencrom when Sylvia decided to go back with me to London at the end of that few days' leave. Sylvia had been the boy's school-mistress, teaching him something about discipline, insisting on two hours' work in the morning and two in the afternoon. I was receiving a weekly letter from him, reasonably spelled and composed, and he was able to read the letters I sent in return as well as the works of Beatrix Potter. He could, to some extent of accuracy, add up and subtract, an accomplishment in which his father did not excel. Any complicated problem baffled me. I tried, for example, to work out in what relation Paul stood to Cynthia, but I gave it up. The affairs of Chown women would have got even the College of Heralds into a dizzy mess.

Petrol being as scarce as the elixir of life, we had to travel on the old trusty Riviera Express, which I preferred anyway. On the evening before we set out I rang up Bob to ask if it would be all right for Sylvia to stay in Piccadilly. Brookes answered the telephone and said: "His Lordship is not at home, sir. I'll ask Madam to speak to you."

Madam. H'm.

Wendy said that she hadn't seen Bob for some days and that she knew nothing of his movements. "But of course you must both stay here," she said with a chatelaine's assurance. "I'd love to have Sylvia."

So there Sylvia was in a London she hadn't seen for years.

To have heard and read about it was one thing: to be now seeing it was another. She was tight-lipped at what she saw as we drove from Paddington to Piccadilly; and the next day she chose to wander alone. She went and looked at the hole where my flat had been; she went into the City and wandered among acres of desolation, fantastically grown with buddleia and willow-herb. To look at what the slow erosion of time has done is one thing: a thing not without tranquillity and beauty: to look at this—the bestial assault of men more scientifically civilised than any the world had known—this was something else, something to wring the last dregs of hope out of the heart. She told me that, outside a ruined church, she sat down on a slab that was part of a memorial blasted from a wall, and as she sat she read the only words remaining upon it: " The Peace of God that passeth all understanding." She said: " I didn't know whether to laugh or cry. So I cried, and once I'd started I couldn't stop."

That night Wendy said: " As you know, George, when Bob's here he likes to keep up form. We dine in the dining-room," she explained to Sylvia; " but when he's away I stay here by the fire and eat a sandwich and tell Brookes to go to bed. Let's do that now."

So we did, though Brookes insisted on producing a bottle of hock to wash the sandwiches down. " His Lordship would wish it, with Mrs. Ledra here," he said.

The wine helped, for the sandwiches were of some dreadful ersatz meat that tasted like a slice of a cork mat. Wendy drank tea, and Sylvia and I finished the bottle. The talk turned to Janet, and it can't have been comfortable for Janet's mother. But I could see that she was making generous allowance for Wendy, because, after all, with whatever good cause, it was Janet who had walked out, leaving the door open for Wendy to walk back in.

" If she ever wants to come back to Bob," Wendy said, " and if Bob wants her, I sha'n't stand in the way. Meantime, he seems to want me about the place and I'm fond enough of him to do what I can to give him a bit of domestic comfort."

Sylvia said frankly: " I don't for a moment believe that Janet will want to come back, nor do I think that Bob will want her to. There never were two people less likely to get on with one another. They began to find that out almost as soon as they were married—when they went to South America."

" He wants to divorce her and marry me," Wendy said. " but even if he did divorce her I'd never marry him. I've given him children. One vanished off the earth and the other is more amused by him than anything else, even though he did a lot for her music once he was driven into it. But she knows he had to be driven, and she thinks of him as a kind-hearted barbarian.

Well, I suppose from her point of view he is. Anyway, giving him children wasn't an outstanding success. I don't intend to marry him and give him any more, even if it were now possible. And I want to have the right to go if I feel disposed to."

As I listened to her, speaking as calmly of these intimate matters as if she were giving a public lecture, I was more and more perplexed. One would have guessed from her manner that she didn't care tuppence for Bob, and yet I knew that any such idea was wrong. Maybe you can kill love, but can you kill the memory of a love that has been? It was the memory of the wild days when they had defied Mr. Merriman, defied everybody, and run away with hardly a penny in their pockets, that accounted for this stodgy woman and her stubborn stand. If she kept things as they were she could keep that memory. If she married him again, and again things turned to disaster, there was nothing left. Then she could go if she felt disposed to. Bob wanted more than the old memories. Some corner of romantic feeling made him long to recreate the conditions in which those feelings had had their birth. Heaven knows, I thought, through whose fault so-ever, he has made a mess of his domestic life. The wish to straighten it was understandable enough. But you can't call yesterday back into to-day. There must be a continuous line between the one and the other, or some second-best. It was this second-best that Wendy was offering.

I tried to say something of this to Sylvia as we lay in bed that night. She said: " Leave it alone. All your philosophising won't alter the simple fact that she wants to stay with him and that all the King's horses couldn't drive her into marrying him again. I'm dying for sleep."

7

She stayed for a week, and she told me afterwards that as soon as she was back she tried to go in a hired car to Miss Hartman's place in order to see Janet. I had told her of Alan Wyke's talk with me on Trencrom and she was deeply upset. " Nothing goes right with her," she said. " I've been an even worse parent than Bob Meagher." I had comforted her as best I could, and now she in turn was hurrying to comfort Janet. But she never saw her. Things had happened quickly at Penruan during her week in London. The tanks were in the wood, and off-shore the tank-landing craft were assembling. A great semi-circle of " security " had been drawn round Penruan, with each end of the arc touching the water. An American marine with fixed bayonet stopped her taxi and told her that she could be allowed to go no farther. She saw that on the right hand and on the left there were marines at short intervals, all armed. There was no unguarded way into that arc. She said foolishly: "But the place is mine," and the taxi-driver, who knew her, confirmed this. The marine said: "Sorry, ma'am. You'll be welcome to take it back before long, I hope."

"Anyway," Sylvia said, "I don't want to go to Penruan. I want to go down towards the Absolution inn."

"Sorry, lady. You can't go any farther, not to get to the Absolution inn nor anywhere else."

However, any mystery within that security arc had leaked out of it long ago. German photographic reconnaissance aeroplanes had been keeping an eye on the place; and even as Sylvia set out to return to Trencrom anti-aircraft guns stationed all round the house began their jabbering and spitting. The taxi-man jumped from his seat and gazed up into the sky, and shouted, dancing with excitement: "Got him! That's got one of the sods!" and she saw the aeroplane stall, and spin, and drop, streaming a fiery banner behind it, and hit the sea, just about where Chowny's coffin had hit it long ago.

Sylvia said: "I had a feeling of disaster, and when Paul was in bed I climbed alone to the top of Trencrom. I could hear them long before I could see them; and then searchlights flashed up from the house and from all round it, and there they were, dodging and buzzing all over the sky. I saw some of them limp back the way they had come and some of them fall, but not enough. They were too many, and the bombing began. I could see the explosions in the wood where the tanks were and on the house. Even from so far off as that I could get the scream as they dived. They sounded like furies who loathed the house and were determined to wipe it off the earth. What's that awful word we read in the newspapers? Saturation bombing. Well, that was it all right. Most of the tank-landing ships were sunk, and the tanks in the wood were massacred, and the road down through our valley to the beach was knocked to pieces. I stayed there till everything was quiet again. Everything except the sky. That was red with flames, and I knew that the flames were putting an end to what was left of Penruan."

She told me this later. She climbed down from the hill and rang me up at one in the morning, telling me little except that Penruan was gone. She begged me to come down if I could. I in turn dragged Nigel Wendron out of his bed, and he gave me permission to go. That evening I was at Trencrom.

Janet? No, she said. There was no news of her.

We ate a disconsolate meal. We could not bring ourselves to talk of the fate of Penruan, the possible fate of Janet, and nothing else could be talked of at such a time. So we were silent, haggard with a confusion of hope and fear. And then we heard the sound of a child wailing. We rushed into our little entrance hall, and there, pale and hopeless-looking was Jose Gomm, and the wailing was coming out of the shawled bundle he held in his arms. He managed to say: "Cynthia. She is motherless." Then his voice choked.

Miss Collum had heard the wailing, too. She had come into the hall, and without a word, took the bundle from him and carried it upstairs, rocking it to and fro in her arms and making hushing comfortable sounds.

Out of nowhere came the thought of a telephone call I had made to Sylvia. She had said that Janet was suckling her child and singing *O hush thee, my baby.*

I began to cry.

Jose said: "Sorry. Someone had to bring her. I thought it had better be me. Miss Hartman is still pretty hysterical."

His features were black, his eyebrows singed. "A few of us tried to give a hand with the fire," he explained. "No good. It's finished."

He had brought a flask of whisky in his pocket. "This won't hurt any of us," he said.

Sylvia wouldn't join us. "I must go up and see to the child," she said.

Jose sank into a chair and stretched his leg straight out before him, as I had seen him do when first we met during another war. "Hell—I'm tired," he said. "This leg. It's worse lately and I've been on it all day."

We sat and drank the whisky. Jose said: "It's no good pretending that man is an unteachable animal. Look at bombing. The strides since *my* war have been incredible, and no doubt we shall go on from here."

He raised his glass. "To Homo Sapiens. God damn the meddling ape."

I couldn't join him in that toast, but I could understand his bitterness.

"Poor old Quayne," he said. "I'm afraid all his stuff's gone west."

I tried to get him to the point. "I know you don't fancy the job of talking to Sylvia about Janet. You'd better tell me. I'll pass it on."

He eased his weary leg to a new position and rubbed his tired eyes. He said: "Miss Hartman says that she went out. That's as much as I can get out of the poor old thing. She's almost daft with fright and shock. She went out. That's all. This morning I met that chap Alan Wyke who was always hanging round Miss Hartman's place. He was filthy, with his uniform in shreds. He said: 'Go back. You have no right to be within the security area.' I wanted to laugh, but I didn't because he looked such a wreck. I suppose it was the first taste he and most of 'em had had of that sort of thing. I said:

438

'Come off it. Seeing that all men are created equal, let us equally enjoy this beautiful morning.' I had this flask in my pocket and I gave him a swig. He lit a Chesterfield and said: 'They've given me the god-awful job of searching the security area and identifying the dead. Those men are working over the place with me.' There was a squad of marines combing the ground. It was at that moment that one of them came up and saluted. He asked: 'Do we include the natives, sir?' Believe me, George, he said that. The natives. I was knocked endways. He sounded like a pukka sahib in India in the good old days when an Indian, even if he'd won the V.C., couldn't have it because he was merely a native. I said: 'Speaking on behalf of the natives, I say let's do 'em the favour of counting their corpses.' This marine then said: 'It's a woman, sir.'

"Wyke and I followed him, and there she was, lying in a patch of heather just away from the road—or what was left of it. There was a huge pit just there where the bomb had burst. She was looking all right. That's the odd thing about it, George," he said, his voice at breaking point. "I'd seen it happen in France. Men killed without a scratch. Just the blast of an explosion. Well, there she was in a blue dress, looking as if she were asleep, except that her eyes were wide open and seemed surprised."

I could see the picture: it was how Mr. Merriman had looked —surprised, with open eyes. I suppose it is surprising, when you're walking harmlessly in your own bit of the world, to find death knocking you out.

"It was a lovely morning," Jose said. "The sun was shining on her face and on the blue dress. It was a light blue, a lovely colour."

He took a drink and lit a cigarette with shaking fingers. We could hear footsteps overhead, and the child's wailing went on. Jose said: "It's Jeremiah in reverse, isn't it? *Rachel weeping for her children, and will not be comforted because they are not.* Well, we're improving on the Old Testament and having it both ways."

I let him rest for a while, and then he went on: "Well, as I say, it was a beautiful morning, except for the stink of what had happened and the sight of Penruan—or what was left of it— smoking and steaming into the air, and the wrecked ships littering the sparkle on the sea. There were seagulls flying over. The sun was under their wings and their voices made the place seem incredibly desolate. Do you see what I mean?—Penruan gone, the ships gone, so many men gone. Those birds made you think of when it would be all gone, and good riddance to it. Wyke looked up at them, shading his bloodshot eyes with his hand. He seemed to want to look at anything rather than at Janet. At last he said to the marine: 'Go away and get on with it.' Then he looked at Janet. He kneeled down in the heather and lifted her wrist in his fingers as though he half believed he might feel some life still pulsing there. He didn't drop her hand. He put it down with an incredibly gentle gesture, took off his cap, and looked at her for a long time. At last he turned on me savagely and said: 'Why in hell was she allowed to go out last night?'

"Now, who can answer that, George? I was out myself, and all Miss Hartman babbles is 'She went out.' Why did she go, and who could have stopped her? I said to Wyke: 'Perhaps you know the answer to that better than I do,' and he shouted: 'No! Don't put it on me!' I laid a hand on his shoulder and said: 'I know how it was, son. There's no question of putting anything on anybody except on the whole damn' silly human race. Now you've got your work to do. You'd better get on with it. I'll see to this.' I went back and knocked up a stretcher, and a few of the boys helped me to carry her back. She's lying now in the Absolution."

I thanked him and found him some blankets and put them on the floor. He got down upon them and said: "I'm so damned well all in I could sleep on spikes," and almost at once he was asleep.

8

It was odd and ironical that Peter Quayne, Lieutenant-Commander, R.N.V.R., should be chosen by the Admiralty people at Bath to go to Penruan and make a report on what had happened. Jose had awakened and had a bite of food, and wandered forlornly away on his gammy leg; and Sylvia had gone into Hayle where, Mrs. Carbis said, there was a woman who had a child's cot to sell. Upstairs, Miss Collum was doing whatever had to be done about Cynthia, and Paul and I were mooching in the lane outside the cottage. A naval car, driven by a rather fetching Wren, came along, and there was Peter, looking very different from the man I had known. He had been through a lot before his ship was blown up, and there were a couple of ribbons on his chest. He looked tough, reliable, disillusioned. He told me why he had come, and said: "I thought I'd use the chance to look in on Sylvia and Janet. I didn't expect to find you here."

We sat on the bench behind the cottage, and I told him what I knew. I said: "I'm sorry about your stuff. I don't believe there's a stick left."

"Oh, damn the stuff. One can always start again."

I thought what incredible creatures men were. "One can always start again." Like ants whose colony has been squashed by a boot. You started again, and you were squashed again, and you said again: "One can always start again." I wondered how long it could go on. Would there some day be a final and irreparable squashing?

I told him about Janet, and he seemed to be sorry as one is about a young life senselessly ended, but not more than that. It was a sobering thought: that we could end—any one of us—and even those we had known well would be so entangled with other, and to them more important, concerns that a sigh was as much as we could expect in valediction.

I inquired about Viola, and he said that he heard from her, but never knew where the next letter would be from. She was on the move all over the battle areas, which was more or less all over the world. He seemed to have so much of his own to think about that I didn't bother him with news of Cynthia. It was Paul who said: "We've got a new baby." Peter shook my hand and said: "Congratulations, George. I'll tell Viola in my next letter. Give my love to Sylvia. Say I'm sorry not to have seen her."

We went back to the car, and the spruce little Wren gave him a welcoming smile as though he had been absent for a year and her heart had been breaking all the time. They passed Sylvia without seeing her. She was coming up the lane, lugging the baby's cot.

9

The disaster at Penruan, so final to us, was nothing much in the wide calculations of strategy. There were plenty of other tanks, plenty of other ships to carry them; and they were carried, and the war ended. There was victory in Europe, and at last victory of a sort in Japan. Not of a sort that boded well for future anthills. We were packing up our department when Nigel Wendron drew me mysteriously aside and said: "George, come and eat. I've got good news for you."

Those who hand out the labels, from pinnacled Dukedoms down to the meanest foothills, had recognised his services by making him a C.B.E. "And that's not all," he said. "There's an O.B.E. going for some member of my staff." He looked at me like a king preparing to give the accolade. "I have decided, George," he said, "to recommend you."

He was standing me lunch, and I think he imagined the now-empty bottle to be swaying before my dazzled vision. I managed to recoil with a good act of modest dismay. "No, Nigel. You have overlooked one thing. I am the last living Englishman who has not received this honour. Beg His Majesty to permit me to retain that humble distinction."

"You mean you refuse?"

"I refuse to blight Flossie's life. Her need is greater than mine."

"I shall never understand you, George," he said. "What will Sylvia say when she hears of this?"

"There is little more that she can say. She already regrets that she is not married to a cricketer or a man who can run after a bus quicker than any other in the street. That would entitle her to be her ladyship."

"Then it's Joe or Flossie," he said sadly.

"I'm afraid so, Nigel. Let 'em toss for it. Or, if you want to make your mark in history, why not put up this scheme? Confer it on some poor devil, lying in an unnamed war grave. You could dig him up and bury him in Westminster Abbey and call him the Unknown O.B.E. People love a ceremony. It helps them to forget their sins."

I felt myself getting vicious, and went out quickly, leaving him to gaze after me, perplexed. His mind was a bit unsubtle.

10

You know that we sold the Barn when Sylvia and Paul went down to Cornwall. Now here we were all back in London where we hadn't even a flat. We were staying in a most dreary hotel: myself and Sylvia, Miss Collum, Paul and Cynthia. We had left Chowny under the waves. We had left Janet under the sod of a simple grave in Helston. Ever since that dark and windy night when I first stood in the half-mended great hall at Penruan my links with Cornwall had been growing into a chain. Now, suddenly, I felt the chain snap. I didn't care if I never saw Cornwall again. Sylvia felt the same way. There was still my cottage at Trencrom. Peter Quayne was released from the Navy, and Viola came home—so different a Viola: a woman, not a child any more. She said to me one day: "Peter and I want to take a long holiday together before he starts assembling the bits. Would you lend us your place at Trencrom?"

I said: "I never gave you a wedding present. You can have Trencrom with my blessing."

It was a good way to shed the last shackle.

"But, darling," she said, "I don't know that we can afford to keep it going. It's lovely of you to make the offer, but . . ."

She kissed me, and looked doubtful.

"Don't be silly," I said. "Sting your father. The war has not reduced him to beggary."

"Of course!" she said, brightening. "I hadn't thought of that!"

"Then you'd better start thinking before he gets tired of having a daughter again."

It was arranged.

I had occasionally during the war mitigated my week-end misery by going to Amersham and spending an hour or two with the man who had bought the Barn. He had been in the Consular service, and just before retiring had married a girl in her twenties. What is more, he had been game enough to give her a son. They were ideally happy. It was a charming atmosphere to be in for an hour or two, especially as they had friends in America who kept them supplied with desirable food. I hadn't to feel that I was sponging on their rations. I decided now to go out and see how they were.

I found Mrs. Bentham, whose son had been optimistically christened Jeremy, sitting on a deck-chair in front of the house. She got up and greeted me gladly, but some sparkle had gone out of her and I noticed that she was prematurely greying. She told me that her husband had died a year ago. She made some tea and brought it out, and I inquired about Jeremy. "He's down in Somerset," she said, "at a school moved there for the duration of the war. I suppose they'll soon be back nearer London again."

She sipped her tea and said sadly: "He's so happy at that school, but I don't think I shall be able to keep him there. Things are a bit tight. Herbert had little beyond his pension, and that was never much. I'm afraid I shall have to sell up here and find a job in London. I type pretty well, and I speak French and Italian. I wish you'd bear me in mind if you hear of anything. I know there'll be fierce competition with thousands of girls coming out of the services, and I believe a single room in London costs the earth nowadays. Do you know of anyone who's likely to want this house?"

All of a sudden, nothing seemed more desirable to me than to be back with Sylvia in the Barn again. And with Paul and Miss Collum and the little Cynthia. We could do without a flat in London. We had both come to detest the place, and the less we saw of it the better we would be pleased.

"Apart from necessity," Mrs. Bentham said, "I *want* to work. Now that Herbert is gone there's a hollow I've got to fill up somehow. And there is necessity. Supposing I got five thousand for this place. I couldn't just blue it. I'd have to invest it or I'd soon be as badly off as ever, and I'd be lucky if the investment brought me in five pounds a week. Well—five pounds in these days. . . . You see?"

I begged her to do nothing for the time being, and when I got back to town I discussed it with Sylvia. She was as delighted as I had been myself.

That night I went to Piccadilly to have dinner with Bob and

Wendy. As we ate he said he wanted to thank me for giving the Trencrom place to Viola and Peter. "I'm looking after them till they're on their feet again. Viola has no doubts about being able to earn a living as a concert pianist and Peter— well, you know him. He's an indomitable young devil, and he'll be all right soon enough. And there's another matter I wanted to discuss." He paused, embarrassed. "Thank you, Brookes," he said. "You can leave us now."

"It's about Janet's child," he said, when Brookes was gone. "I don't want to take her off your hands, but I don't see why you should be burdened with the expense of bringing her up."

Janet's child. I wondered what sense of sin he was trying to assuage. He had not wanted a child from her till Joss had disappeared, and then he had wanted a child. The question of a child had bedevilled him. He was trying to buy his absolution.

Wendy said: "You have my child. You have Viola."

He didn't answer; and I knew that whatever domestic peace he was finding with Wendy, he would never forget Janet and the tragedy of her end.

I said: "Young Cynthia is no relative of yours, Bob. But she is Sylvia's granddaughter, and we are well able to look after her. I'm sure Sylvia would want to have full responsibility."

"Very well," he said dully. He looked overworked and grey.

I switched to the question of Mrs. Bentham, explained her circumstances, and asked if he had anything to offer her. "It's not a thing I would know about," he said. "That would be a matter for the personnel department."

"But you could put in a word with them?" I suggested.

"It's not a thing I like doing. They wouldn't be easy if they had the impression that I was personally concerned."

Wendy said: "Well, why not let them be uneasy?"

"Because we want the best people, and you don't get them by inquiring into their sad family circumstances. You get them by inquiring into their ability to do a particular job. And, as I say, that is what the personnel people are paid to do. George is at liberty to ask this lady to send a formal application. She will then receive the usual forms that have to be filled in. That's how the machine works. Once she's in, she will be slotted into the department she is found most apt for, and there she will have the opportunity to take the successive steps."

"You can call them steps if you like," Wendy said. "It sounds to me more like going round in one of those treadmills where pet mice take their exercise."

"Whatever you may call it," Bob told her, "it's how a great interlocking corporation is bound to be conducted."

"It's odd that this matter should have come up to-day," Wendy said. "Because this very afternoon I decided to go in the other direction. I don't run a great interlocking corporation.
444

But, as you know, George, I do own a few scattered shops. This afternoon I went out to see one in a rather remote suburb where I haven't been for some time. There's a chap there who calls himself the manager and one little assistant. And I suddenly realised that they were both afraid of me. They were wondering why I'd come. Was I going to sack them? Was I going to close down the shop? Would they be in the bread-line next week? It made me feel queasy in the stomach. It showed me a sort of power I don't want to have."

Bob interjected: "Someone's got to have it," and I could do nothing but look at the strange spectacle of those two, whom I had known in such different circumstances, confronting one another with their different reactions to human relations.

"I've got no personnel department to look after that sort of thing," Wendy went on with excited and unaccustomed eloquence, "and I don't believe in personnel anyway. I believe in persons and in asking whether they're getting any fun and satisfaction out of what they're doing."

"It would never work," Bob assured her.

"It will work so long as your interlocking corporations don't get so big that they're too big for their boots, too big to know that a man isn't a cog. He's got to know what he's doing and whether it's worth doing anyway."

Bob asked: "And what do you propose to do about it?"

"I propose, as soon as I can, to get rid of all my shops except the last one I bought—the rather big one that we snatched from under the nose of your interlocking corporation, Bob." She grinned at him with friendly malice. "That's where I find myself happiest, and all the people there are happy, too. We're not afraid of one another. There's no employees' committee or any nonsense of that sort. If anything goes wrong we talk it over and try to put it right. We all know what we're doing and why we're doing it. And we believe it's worth doing."

Bob lit his pipe. He was now looking more amused than depressed. "You belong to the Middle Ages," he said.

"No, Bob. That's where you belong. It's your show and all the shows like it that are feudal. Every man in his own niche and knowing nothing about what's going on in the other niches, and with precious little chance of moving out of one niche into another."

"And what do you call your system?"

"We don't call it anything. Sticking a label on it wouldn't make any difference one way or another. It's just something that works and keeps us all happy."

"You didn't think like this at one time."

"No. When Father was alive we thought in our way as you do. We were buying up shops with the proud idea that we were

445

creating a small empire, and we wanted it to grow into a big one. I've changed my mind, that's all. I don't want any sort of empire, big or little. I've seen enough of empires and their ways, and I should have thought you had, too."

Bob continued to smile. " I'm too old to be a convert," he said, " and you can afford these other-worldly ideas because you're living here on the fat of the land."

Wendy's face went crimson, and I thought she was going to fly out. But she said quietly: " I'm here because you need me, whether you realise it or not."

He said simply: " I do. I must put up even with your non-sense."

Before I left, Wendy said: " You send this Mrs. Bentham to see me, George. No. Take me out to see her. That will be more friendly. If I can't find something for her to do, I'll look round for someone who can."

11

To-day, out at Dormers, we read in the papers that the Baron Meagher of Levenshulme has been created a Viscount. I suppose in his way he has earned it. The war has been over for two years, and Bob has been shelling out right and left. He prevented a Gainsborough from going to America and presented it to the National Gallery. He has established what is called the Meagher Foundation for setting up, so far as I can make out, technical schools at Oxford and Cambridge. One of them is to be called the Jocelyn Meagher Memorial College. I hope that Joss, happy somewhere in a field or orchard, will find time to smile at that word *Memorial*. But Bob refuses to admit the possibility that Joss is alive. It would be too humbling to think that the boy had simply walked out in repudiation.

It's a pity that there's no Viscountess Meagher. I should love to see Wendy in a tiara. It would have pleased old Merriman, too. But there it is, and there Wendy is, dowdy as ever, adored by her daughter Viola who visits Piccadilly daily when she is in town. But she is away a good deal on concert tours.

We shall be leaving Dormers to-morrow. The bombing of my flat and of Penruan left us without a stick of furniture, and it hasn't been easy to find what we wanted for the Barn in these post-war days. We didn't want to hurry it, because we know that it will be now our final and only home. It was lucky that the portraits of Margaret Napier and Fred Byles were in the Trencrom cottage when the bombing took place. They will be able to smile at one another now to their hearts' content.

When we leave here, the workmen will be coming in. The place is to be a convalescent home for those Meagher employees who need it. No expense spared. A doctor's house, nurses' quarters, and all the rest of it. Bob hadn't used Dormers for years, and when we were homeless insisted on our staying there. The Piccadilly place is all he has now, and all, he says, that he wants. He has so much that he is being forced back on comparative simplicity in self-defence.

Paul is away at school. There are just the two of us here, with Miss Collum and Cynthia, and a few servants provided and over-paid by Viscount Meagher.

I climbed the hill whence one looks down on the house, and presently Sylvia joined me. We saw Miss Collum leading the small Cynthia into the greenhouse, doubtless to inspect the fat carp that had been sluggishly swimming there on the day when I found Wendy disconsolate, overthrown by a sense of failure and dismay. The clear eager voice of the child came up to us: Janet's child and John Cavendish's. I thought of Janet in her bright impulsive morning, running in the sunlight on the gold beach with Sylvia, who was wearing now the bangle that I then picked up and treasured; and I thought of Janet lying in the heather, wearing a dress of beautiful blue, under the sunlight of another morning which now seemed, so elusive is time, as far off as the first.

Sylvia said: " Cynthia is such a darling. And what a wonderful day! I like to see a child running free, without a cloak."

She couldn't have known how the words pierced me. I took her hand and raised her up. " We'd better go down and pack for our last lap," I said.

Falmouth:
August 13, 1959
February 15, 1961

447